T0365644

ALL THAT GLITTERS
IS NOT GOD

ALL THAT GLITTERS IS NOT GOD

A.K.B. KUMAR

PARTRIDGE
A Penguin Random House Company

To order additional copies of this book, contact
Partridge India
000 800 10062 62
www.partridgepublishing.com/india
orders.india@partridgepublishing.com

DEDICATION

I honestly dedicate this to the fauna and flora killed and cut mercilessly by the human race for their personal pleasure. All these innocent and ignorant categories are losing their lives and no one is there to shed tears.

Besides the martyrs of Army, Navy, Air force and other fighting forces of all the nations—those who laid down their lives for their countries—the dedication of this simple work is also for the Victims of war and terrorism. All those died due to no fault of theirs. Their sprits from the heaven may be shouting the slogan: 'No war and no terrorism on earth' instead of the out dated slogan: 'Anti-war and Anti-terrorism' shouting by men in this hell on earth. Some heartless say: 'Remembering the dead is meaningless' whereas, I doff my hat to those innocents and I wear my heart on my sleeve. Our vision shall be: *There is no war sans arms.* So our oath shall be: *Let's stop producing arms for producing peace. Let's stop purchasing arms for promoting peace. I further dedicate this work to the living who likes these dictums.*

ACKNOWLEDGEMENT

Firstly, I've to acknowledge vote-of-thanks to the Almighty God for providing sound mind and sound body to complete this venture.

Secondly, my sincere acknowledgement to Partridge Publishing Team for throwing light on my manuscript, so that the world wide book lovers could read this fantasy fiction "All that glitters is not God."

Thirdly, I acknowledge my happy home, my Computer companion and of course the nature.

And finally to three of my great friends—Random House, Cambridge and Oxford unabridged dictionaries as they're my only friends while writing; without their clutch and gear of wisdom I couldn't have driven the vehicle of English Language to complete a decade-long-journey to this destination. It was a boon to me having the abundance vocabulary from their treasury of words.

CENTURY 1

0 TO 100 AD

Yes, I was born. Date of my birth: 00-00-0000. I was nameless, parentless and address-less. My basic qualification: Could see, listen, think and speak in *Cosmolish*—a language I could communicate not only with the heavenly bodies, but also with flora and fauna—nature.

I myself accepted an address: Beneath the sky, above the ground, between the horizons and became the first resident of an anonymous habitat.

Sans much search, I could find my mother. I came out from the womb of my mother and was standing on her lap. My mother possesses male and female reproductive organs. But *she* is asexual. Still, she has got innumerable wombs to receive semen from anyone in any form. She can get pregnant even if someone excretes on her body. She is mother not just to me but to all the living things on the earth. Yet she is a virgin. She is neither married nor unmarried. She accommodates everything. Yes, you may wonder who my mother is! She is none other than the so-called Earth. My mother's name is Miss Globe.

My father was *female*. I have never seen *him*. I don't know who and where my father is! My father did never copulate with my mother. Instead of intercourse, my father endured a random-course flight over my mother; instead of sexual ejaculation, it was an act of excretion; instead of semen, what came out was shit and instead of sperm, it was a seed that impregnated my mother and caused my birth. You may be in doubt about the identity of my father, but I categorically state that my *father* is a female bird, who ate a berry of a Banyan tree from somewhere and while flying to somewhere dropped the dung on the ground. It was rainy

1

season and I germinated. This is the statement given my mother about my creator. One may wonder who I am and of what breed I am. I am none but a Banyan shoot, a sapling.

Oh, no! What a damn fool am I to wish to be like a human being! Instead of being the result of an ejection from the genital organ of a male body to the soft and wet reproductive compartment of a female body, I am the product of elimination from an excretory organ of a vagabond female bird to the hard and wet earth. The seed of the Banyan tree in the excreta remained in the womb of Miss Globe like a hermit. Then as the rains came, germination took place. Some gases in the soil assisted the process. The seed-shell was broken; my leg penetrated the ground downwards forming the root; my body emerged above the ground as the shoot: I was born! Of course, it is a very natural phenomenon, but I thank God for giving me the chance to take birth on this earth.

When I surfaced the earth, I could not see anything. It was pitching dark. All I could feel was a gentle breeze that was keeping my body cool.

Suddenly I felt that I was set free, that I was relieved from somewhere and allowed to go somewhere else. But where would I go in darkness? Some minutes ago too I was in darkness. The only difference was that I was under the ground. Now I was above the ground. There I was a molecular form; here I was larger. There my eyes and ears were closed; here they were open. Irrespective of the spatial difference, darkness followed me—as a friend or foe.

I wondered what my future would be. Would darkness and silence be my only colleagues? I waited.

I did not know whether I would live or die. Suddenly I felt I required something to survive, the air around me. I was compelled to inhale and exhale. Yes, I was breathing. After the first breath, I felt relaxed and satisfied. So, I was breathing, without which I felt weak and suffocated. I continued breathing.

I understood that I must continue breathing if I had to live on. But what was the use of living further in the prevailing situation of dark even if I was a crowned prince. Even if I were independent, what would I do to swallow darkness and gulp silence? Then I felt a passion for freedom. Would I attain freedom? If so, freedom for what? To think? To love? I had no answers. *Chheyh* . . . I was greedy to have privileges and perks in the form of freedom. Even before I could gain enough strength to stand on my own feet, my immature brain was having unwanted thoughts. So I stopped thinking and started sleeping.

I did not know how long I slept. I woke up when I felt the heat and light from thousands of torches falling on me. I still felt drowsy. Being a newborn, I could not tolerate the heat and light. Indeed, I was experiencing it for the first time. I could see an empty blue roof above my head. Yes, it was really a blue yard. As time passed, I saw a burning disc appearing in the sky. It was very difficult to look at that disc. The intense heat and light from the disc made me thirsty and weak. I became very weak and felt that very soon I might wither away. So first I cried, and then I shouted at the burning disc, "Who the devil are you? Can't you switch off that light? Can't you put out that fire?"

There was no response. I saw that the disc had changed its position. I waited for some more time. But the disc did not stop showering heat and light on me.

Again I cried, "Cruel creature, where the hell are you going without answering me? I don't like your mischief. At least you dim the light, *yaar*".

The disc did not respond. I had a feeling that somebody was operating it from somewhere else and that the disc was just a reflector. So I tried to swivel my head, but in vain. My shoot-tip was so small that I could neither bow nor turn my head. All I could see was the blue yard over my head and the disc that looked like a floating object in it. But I was surprised to see that the disc had again changed position. Was the disc moving? Why shouldn't I? Or was I moving? No. I could not feel that. I was standing still and erect. The only feeling I had was of the unbearable heat. Definitely, the disc was responsible for that. Then why did the disc not respond? It might not have heard or seen me. Once again I requested the disc not to be so cruel towards me. But staring at me even more cruelly, the disc moved away leaving me alone. Exhausted and drained, I fell asleep. I woke up again as I felt a severe chill from head to foot.

I asked myself, "Where's that burning disc?" I was sweating. Steam came out of my body. Then I began shivering. How clear the visibility was! And now? Now I could not see even an inch ahead of me. Darkness . . . darkness . . . darkness everywhere.

Was it a dream? The disc floated in the sky like an illuminated vessel leaving the harbor for the deep blue sea, leaving me on the jetty like an unberthing party. I prayed it might be real and not a dream when I thought about the pleasure of vision. But immediately I prayed it might not be real but be a dream as I thought of the suffering caused by the heat.

But now it was even more piercing, cold and dark. Who wants these? I cried out: "Hello, who's blinding me? Where on earth am I?"

A harsh voice replied me.

"You, little fool, I am Darkness. I have blinded you as well as the whole place. I saw your hateful face yesterday when you looked at me."

Timidly, I said, "Your face is blank. Why don't you go somewhere else?"

"How dare you say that?" grandiloquently Darkness asked. "It's my place and my time. It is night. Who are you to command me? I am the King here. Understand? You, silly goose."

I replied, "I don't understand anything."

"You will understand my powers soon," said Darkness. "When you were born, I was here. I made the arrangements for your birth. Almost all the physical changes on this earth occur during my time."

"Your Highness Darkness," I said. "Only if and when you go away, I'll be able to see what's happening here."

Darkness said, "You are mistaken. If I go away you won't see what's happening. For most of the wicked and evil events occur in my presence."

"So, you help that, dear King?"

"No, not at all" said Darkness. "I don't help anyone. Someone does it, I witness it."

"But all the acts are performed in my mother's lap. She is the stage and you are a spectator. Isn't it so?"

"Though it's your mother's realm, the regime is mine. Half of the total time of the globe is allocated to me. Without my will and wish, no power on earth could alter the rule of nature. I regulate it", Darkness said challengingly.

I said, "Then who was that chap resembling a blazing disc that moved over my head burning my tender body? Where were you then?"

"Oh, you met him?" Asked His Highness Darkness. "He is His Highness the Sun, the King of the day. He is my reliever. It's time for him to come. I'm leaving. But remember one thing: Do not trust him fully; do not succumb to him. I've no glittering; but Sun glitters! And I warn you, 'all that glitters is not God' OK."

"God!" I amazed, "who's that?"

"Just ask your mother."

Even before His Highness the Sun appeared the whole place was flooded with light. The area brightened up, but I could not see him. All

I could see was the blue yard right above my head like a hemispherical dome.

Then a soft voice called me, "Embryo . . . Embryo . . ."

I kept mum.

Like shaking up a sleeping person, the voice repeatedly called to me, "Master Embryo . . . If you are sleeping, then get up. If you are not sleeping, then answer me."

I replied, "I am awake. I didn't know you had called me. By the by, who are you?"

"You are staring at me and asking me who am I? Well, I'm the Sky."

"I see," said I. "So you are Mr. Sky. I thought you were just a yard. Anyway, I like your color."

"Thanks," said Mr. Sky. "You are green and I'm blue. But sometimes I change my color. Will you hate me then?"

"I shall see later. At the moment I like you very much. Do you like me?"

"I have to."

"Why . . . ?"

"Don't ask me why. Because this sky is very high."

"High?" I asked. "How much high? Are you so high that I can't touch you even when I'll grow up?"

Mr. Sky chuckled. "You *enfant terrible*! I'm so far and so big that no one can ever touch me. I'm infinite. I accommodate all the heavenly bodies. I take care of everything, including you. Nothing else is as big as I am," he said.

"You're so big, but very humble and polite at the same time."

"The big," said Mr. Sky, "always tend towards smallness. Take you for example: You, a tiny child of a tree born yesterday, are craving to touch me. Still you can't bear cold or heat. You want heat when it's cold, cold when it's hot. This is the tendency of all the organisms on earth. Nobody wants sorrow."

Hesitatingly, I retorted, "Why can't you give us only joy? Why are you so particular about providing sorrow?"

"It's not I who give you sorrow or joy. It's God, the creator of this universe."

"Has God got only a stock of sorrow?"

"He has got stocks of both sorrow and joy. But both have to be expended. That's essential for the existence of the universe."

I told Mr. Sky that I did not follow his argument.

"Well," said Mr. Sky, "if it rains throughout a period, there will be flood and all the organisms including you will drown. If it is always summer all of you will be burned to death. So each and every organism on earth has to face ups and downs, hardness and softness, sweetness and bitterness—they have to share agony and ecstasy in life. None has to be blamed for that. Today you may be in the family of haves. Tomorrow you could be in a family of have-nots."

I tried to nod to show that I understood but it was useless.

Mr. Sky, noticing my confusion, continued, "Come on, try to shake your head even if you can't do it. Keep on trying without losing hope, for everything is possible on earth. Why I'm advising you is that you seem to have quite a good span of life ahead on this earth and all the stars point out that you have a good future. So try to do your duty properly, without succumbing to lethargy."

Suddenly I saw that Mr. Sun was moving to greater heights. So, quickly I asked, "Please let me know what lethargy is and what my duties are!"

As I shouted eagerly, there came the answer from His Highness, the Sun.

"First I'll explain my duties."

"Before that, let me know your biodata, Sir."

"Don't call me 'Sir'. Call me Your Highness."

"Oh," said I, "I forgot what His Highness Darkness told me."

"I see . . . ." HH Sun said. "So, you met HH Darkness and he misguided you?"

"No Your Highness. He told me that both of you are Highnesses".

"That Blacky is no Highness. How can two Kings rule the same country at the same time? You little bastard, how do you know all these royal rules?"

"Why do you call me a bastard? I have a father. I resent it." I said.

"I know your parentage. A female father and a female mother. How can lesbianism produce a baby?"

"You are telling me about the human reproductive system. But as per the biology of plants . . ."

"Still you do not know your father. You say your father is a crow. Is it not so?"

"Yes," I said proudly.

"No. Your father is not a crow. I know it. You don't know your father."

"But as per the statements of Mr. Sky, his gentleness is incomparable," I said.

His Highness the Sun replied with concern, "To a certain extent Mr. Sky's statements are correct. Sky is the biggest among our family. Even my habitat is in the field of Mr. Sky. But mind you, he is not big in powers. In power, I'm superior. *Knaa*, you will come to know about it when I explain my duties. Sun continued with a concern, "The prime thing you should bear in mind is that one of my duties is destruction. This destructive quality has two sides—breaking and making. When it harms one, it helps another."

I said that I was unable to comprehend what His Highness was talking about.

Sun said, "Yesterday I heard your cry of distress because my heat and light were hurting you. You felt a burning sensation. But I was helping you to live."

I blinked at King Sun suspiciously.

His Highness said, "The green color, which is essential to your health, is produced by a process called photosynthesis. My light is the force behind that. Then only you can grow. You have gained height of some millimeters. Haven't you?"

I agreed with him.

"You may curse me for emitting the intense heat that weakened you. Until and unless I do my duty properly, to burn myself intensely, there won't be any water-cycle."

"What's that?" I wondered.

"Some days ago the rain came and soaked your mother. Then you germinated. And, have you forgotten the day before yesterday you drank enough water and quenched your thirst and enjoyed a nice bath?"

"Oh, that was your magic . . . ?"

"Not my magic. It's part of my duty without remuneration and you fellows are enjoying the benefits. From time immemorial I perform my duty without fail. My mind says that I have consciously carried out my duty properly, punctually, untiringly, unconditionally and naturally. I'm not exaggerating: Could you please tell me how much power it requires to light up your so-called mother, Miss Globe, to provide you with visibility? How much heat it requires to warm up your mother to eradicate your cold? How many calories are required to energize your mother to feed you? Would you be able to produce these powers yourself? Which captive power plant owned by your mother can compete with me?"

I nodded and kept quiet.

"You are so proud of the fact that you are the pampered son of Miss Globe. Well, a son should be proud of his mother. But don't keep on flattering her so extravagantly. It will only lead her to a complacent life of forgetfulness of her duties. Some plants have got ruined like that. No life is left over there. I warn you that doom shouldn't befall your mother. For countless years, I don't know how many, your mother was also in a very poor and critical condition—not even a single organism was on her. I helped her by providing the life-saving gas and the whole earth rejoiced. You think that your mother is a Miss." Burning more brightly, said the King, "You are mistaken, my dear. She has been wedded to me since time immemorial."

I felt relaxed and said, "So, I am the son of King Sun, the supreme ruler of the Solar System! Shall I call you my father?"

"You are not my son. You remain a bastard, and your mother is a whore."

Shamefacedly, I tried to look down at my mother but my stem was so short that I could not do that. I gathered courage and asked: "Is my mother still your wife? Or did you divorce her?"

"There is no question of divorce," said the King. "She is chained to me. If I have to divorce your mother, first I have to divorce my other eight wives."

"So all together you have nine wives!" I was awe-struck.

King Sun added, "Your mother is my third wife if you count from Mercury to Pluto."

"Do they love you?"

"All of them are at my service. They always dance around me."

"While you are in motion, won't it be very difficult for them to dance?"

"Who told you I'm dancing? I'm stationary as far as you earthlings are concerned."

"But I saw you moving and slowly disappearing."

"It's your mother who moves."

"My mother!"

Angrily King Sun said, "Not only all wives but also their so-called relatives, the satellites, move like dancers in my court."

At night when I met King Darkness, we spoke about the disdainful behavior of King Sun.

King Darkness said, "He'll try to pervert your mind with strange tales. He thinks that he is *the* cosmic handsome and that all the heavenly bodies are attracted to him. But it's false. He doesn't like anything that is colorless. That's why he hates me."

"But you have a color!"

"I'm black. Who counts it as a color? No one recognizes black as a color and everywhere black is neglected and mocked at. There are so many nations and political parties in the world. They all have different colors for their identity. But none accepts my color except death. I'm offered as condolence, not as congratulation. The colorful consider me as colorless and call me names. This disease in society is known as color prejudice."

I told the King of darkness that I could not follow even a word of his narration. He replied that I would learn it gradually. But I was much confused. I closed my eyes to think.

"Please condone me," said King Darkness politely. "Sorry, I shouldn't have opened my heart to you like this, because you are too young to understand my emotions. But on the other hand, this is the right time to inform you about the evils and perils of this world so that when you grow up you'll fight for the rights of the blacks. I'm not injecting any *isms* into you. I'm telling you the universal truth. I help and love all the organisms on this earth more than anyone else. Though I'm black, I have a white heart. There is an invisible inner light in me even though externally I look gloomy. That's why nature has also given me the right to rule this globe."

"But how can two Kings rule one Kingdom? Will the subjects of that Kingdom not be suffocated by dual royalty?" I asked.

"Not at all. Provisions have been made by nature in the mandate that both of us would not rule a region simultaneously. He rules over one half of the globe while I rule over the other. So, none of us is a winner or loser. We are half-time and half-portion Kings."

"Fine. What's the issue then?"

"But King Sun doesn't want to follow the rules of the universe. He always wants to overpower and degrade me. It's nothing but his latent racial prejudice."

I wondered about the racial prejudice prevailing among heavenly bodies. If I were to witness such tugs-of-war even in my infancy, what would happen when I grow up! Poor King Darkness—I love him. His simplicity, his calm and quiet behavior, all made me to respect him. I again thought deeply about color discrimination. I was green. The sky had appreciated my color. But I did not know his sincerity. Green also was glamour-less color, like black.

Now everybody was pampering me and was friendly towards me because I was a good-looking kid. But what would be their attitude towards me when I grew up? Would this disease affect me too? Would I gain some stature in the cosmic society? Would I be able to lead a stately life or would I suffer? The more I pondered the questions about my future, the more answers evaded me further.

I wished I had attained some height and weight instantly. Then only I could bow to see my mother and converse with her. I hoped she could throw some light on the issues that were keeping my mind in darkness.

Now my vision was perpendicular to the sky. The individuals I met and had already got acquainted with were Mr. Sky, King Sun and King Darkness. I knew that my mother was beneath me. I would meet her later. Another individual I saw a few days ago was Mr. Rain. I had missed the chance of getting acquainted with him. I recollected the incident. It had happened all of a sudden, the very next day of my birth. Mr. Rain came and fell on my delicate body. Though I quenched my thirst and had a nice bath, it soaked and choked me so that I could not ask him anything.

Out of all the individuals I had met that far, I had had physical contact only with Mr. Rain. It was a great experience. I really wished Mr. Rain would come again.

Suddenly I heard a hiss: "Hello . . . Hello . . . Do you remember me . . . ?" Blowing cold on my body, some invisible effect moved over me.

Feeling my hairs standing on end, I said, "I don't remember you."

"Why can't you remember me? Once I met you?"

"When!" I did not hide my surprise.

"The day it rained. I was there with Mr. Rain. But you were in the mood of taking bath."

"But I didn't feel your presence that day," I said.

"I preceded Mr. Rain. I saw you. I wanted to be a friend of yours for I love kids very much."

"Then you should have . . . ."

"I'm really sorry, *yaar*. The rain was forcing me to move further. I had no time. As an advance party, I had to move ahead of Mr. Rain. Also, I decided not to disturb you while you were taking a shower."

"By the by," I asked, "What's your name, Mr. Invisible?"

"My name . . . I'm Wind. And what's your name?"

I replied that I had no name.

"OK, kiddy without a name, I have no time. We'll meet later." Saying this, Mr. Wind vanished and I felt hotter. Though Mr. Wind was invisible, I liked him more than anybody else I had met that far. His presence made me happy. I had a feeling that he was clean-hearted comedian. His departure made me very sad.

That evening I felt very uneasy. My body ached; the temperature ran high. It was something like my mother had suffered during delivery. The pain and fever made me shiver from head to foot. It was as if I was being pulled from all the sides. I became unconscious.

Days passed by . . .

I came out of my coma as someone sprinkled water on me. *Ngea!* Light passing showers were everywhere. As the shower passed by I asked about his identity.

"I'm Master Shower, the younger child of Mr. Rain," he answered.

"Please wait, I've to talk to you," I pleaded.

"Not now, brother. I have to reach home before daybreak. My parents have gone far ahead of me."

Bidding 'bye' like a naughty child, Master Shower ran past me. Simultaneously, King Sun removed his veil and stared astonishingly at me. He congratulated me for my maturity. I did not look at him and did not mind him lest I should feel shy of being matured. I felt as though I had adorned myself in winter clothes during summer.

King Sun said sarcastically, *"Arey yaar,* you look handsome! You seem to have undergone an innovative treatment for plant pathology! Look at your hands, legs and chubby cheeks".

Though there was sarcasm in his words, his look was like that of a father appreciating his lean and thin son, who had come on leave from the military and had turned corpulent. I was amazed to see my body with new limbs of branches and leaves. I was proud of my growth. For some time I was enthralled by my own beauty and forgot my space and myself.

King Sun got annoyed. He said, "Aye, don't try to become commander-in-chief the very day you got recruited. If I want I can spoil your career: By converting your beautiful body into carbon. So . . . ."

Panic-stricken, I apologized: "I'm sorry, Your Highness. I forgot myself for a moment."

Without listening to me, King Sun moved away angrily and I felt that the ground beneath my foot was slipping as I considered my own health, the threat by King Sun banished from mind. Unbelievable! What a variation! It is a substitution of a minor by a major. Two tiny leaves with small limbs stretching out to both sides like hands; the aerial shoot acted as my head; the sturdy stem was my body and the bifurcation of stem at the bottom were like two legs. When did this evolution occur? During my coma?

Whom to ask and how to clear my doubts? I did not have the guts to ask King Sun. To Mr. Sky? What happened to Mr. Sky? The blue color had vanished and some white and black patches of smoke-like things were floating instead. *Arey*, I forgot about my mother! Now I was able to bow and turn my trunk here and there. Suddenly, an intense passion to see my mother stirred inside me. How would she look like? Was she beautiful?

With great curiosity, I bent my head and saw her for the first time in my life. With a melodious voice I called her: "*Ma . . . Ma . . .*"

Like a divorcee meeting the spouse, my heart racing, I eagerly waited for her reply. Like a husband anxious about the state of his wife in labor, I waited for her reaction. "Will she accept me as her child? Or neglect and reject?"

Then came her soft answer: "Yes dear, I was longing to hear your call. I was lying flat and you were on my lap. Now you are standing erect and I can see you even from my position. Tell me what you want from me. I am with you and you can give me your agonies and I'll give you all my ecstasies."

Oh! A mother is after all a mother. The invocation itself was like the chanting of a *mantra*. Her glimpse would give you *nirvana*. Talks with her would make you wise. I had known that she was a virgin huntress and patroness of chastity, when I got closer and closer to her.

I told her that I did not need anything except answers to a few questions.

She said, "I know very well that you don't ask any help from anyone unnecessarily, because the moment I gave birth to you, unlike the other organisms that are greedy of bottle-feeding, you were thirsty for freedom. I'm proud of you because you belong to a prestigious family of trees—the Banyan, an elite class. Now take your bow and shoot me with your arrows of questions even if they kill me."

I wanted to launch numerous rockets of questions but did not ignite any. I simply asked her about my birth, growth and health. She explained to me that it was a natural phenomenon. The activities started from the atoms of the seed. Thus the serial progressed towards molecules, cells, tissues, organs, organ systems, and to the organism that is me. And to grow, an individual needs food. The organs such as root, stems and leaves perform different functions for food manufacture—intake of food, digestion and absorption and assimilation of food material. I take raw materials of nutrition and extract energy from the food prepared, through the process of respiration. This energy is spent in the synthesis of growth, a process known as metabolism. Metabolism helps me preserve myself for continuing my race. And as per my mother's opinion, I own very fine tissues with very fine epidermis, cortex, endodermis, xylem and phloem.

As I knew that my mother was not only a person to pamper me but also someone to teach me; the desire to ask more questions grew in me. So I asked her: "How did King Sun, Mr. Rain and Mr. Wind help in my growth?"

She taught me the secret of photosynthesis: The primary mode of my food production required carbon dioxide, water, chlorophyll and sunlight. With the help of sunlight, I changed carbon dioxide from the atmosphere in photosynthesis and chlorophyll in my body could absorb the violet, blue and red components of light from King Sun. During photosynthesis, light energy is converted into chemical energy and stored in the organic molecules like glucose and starch. This energy helped me in respiration.

When Mr. Rain comes and acts on my mother's body she gets wet. My roots drink water from my mother's soaked body like a child sucking milk from the breast. I pass the water on to the leaves via xylem. Along with water I absorb many mineral salts. Then the process of photosynthesis is fulfilled in me.

Whether Mr. Wind moves or not, he is everywhere—as air. You can feel him only when he moves from one place to another over my mother's body. His presence in the atmosphere enables me to absorb oxygen during night and release carbon dioxide; inhale carbon dioxide during the day and release oxygen in proportion. Mr. Wind is an invisible individual, who embraces my mother's body and as and when she feels suffocated, he fans her, controlling her body temperature.

In a nutshell, I was a parasite of nature. My pride melted away as I realized that one could not survive in this world alone. Cooperation, inter-dependence and mutual understanding are as essential as nutrition to life on this habitat. Further, I learned from my mother that I should be grateful to King Sun, Mr. Rain, Mr. Wind, Mr. Sky and so on, but should not feel obliged to them.

The question regarding my father was still pestering my mind. So I asked her about my father. I wanted a clear answer.

She said, "I too don't know who exactly your father is. I have made a mistake. Had I known I would've given birth to a wise child like you, I would have tried to know all about your father."

"*Ma*, I appreciate your love for me. But I can't stand someone calling me a bastard".

"I heard the conversation between you and King Sun. He is such a character. I don't blame you for accusing me of not knowing my husband and his love-making to me even though I was dead asleep when it happened in absolute darkness. I'm fully responsible for answering your question. I'm not evading that responsibility. But you should know one thing: I'm raped and even gang-raped many a time daily. The rapes could be in daylight or in darkness, but I'm the victim. I'm designated as a street-walker by Nature and all use my body as they please.

"How can a whore say exactly who is the father of a child she gives birth to, especially when it is through asexual reproduction? But in your case, I have some hints. When I was busy resisting some wicked play on some other parts of my body, a female *Deserian* duck belonging to a family of migratory birds unknowingly acted as your father without my knowledge."

"*Ma* . . . Please narrate to me the antecedents of my ancestor for I am very anxious to know about my father's origin."

"This is a top secret. Mr. Sky told me about it. He was watching the incident. The birds were on an en masse flight from the eastern desert to the western marshes via this place. They migrate periodically in order to escape the severe cold and to enjoy the warmth of the marshy area. En route they peck at certain berries and fruits for their sustenance although they depend mainly on grains. One day, one of the birds ate a berry of a Banyan tree on its journey. The berry caused indigestion to her. During the course of flight she excreted the seed, and you know the rest of the story. Mr. Sky clearly cautioned me that this fact should be kept confidential. For your life would undergo many changes during the course of history."

I murmured: "So in society, I may be known as a carpetbagger or a gypsy!" But who knows what the future brings forth? I was eager to learn futurology.

Then I told her about the quarrel between Kings Sun, the disc with shinning face, having a halo and the pitch dark colored Darkness sans any aura.

She said, "I know both His Highness Sun and His Highness Darkness from my birth. Sun is a self made God as he glitters by virtue of nature. There are plenty of objects having more glitter in our planetary cosmos. But all that glitters is not God. Unlike King Sun, King Darkness has got lots of merits. He is very polite, simple and nice. You can rely on him. He won't cheat you. If you want to forget the sorrows and miseries of daytime, you should go to the dominion of King Darkness. You will have peace of mind there. Only in that region all the living organisms on me take rest—sleep."

"But I heard all the evil deeds take place by night. Is it true?"

"Not all", said my mother. "Most of them, yes. But it is not the fault of King Darkness. He has no power to resist or to prevent that. He is just a watcher. That is the rule of nature and he won't break that. But most of the essential and beneficial things occur during this time. For example: Your birth".

Then I told her about my meetings with Mr. Rain and Mr. Wind.

From her reply I learnt that some would only help you; some would help and cause trouble for you and still others would only bring trouble for you. You could trust the first and the last because you know their mentality of helping and hurting. You could be attracted or repelled by them as per their characters whereas you never know when the second category would help you or hurt you. A mountain of help would be ramshackle by a stone of trouble. Mr. Wind and Mr. Rain are such characters that you can't believe them. They are companions for most of the time. Like drunkards, they come together, dance pell-mell, sing abusive songs in public places. Mr. Rain has got so many nicknames like Drizzle, Shower, and Downpour etc. As per his behavior Mr. Wind also has got different nicknames like Breeze, Gale, Tempest etc. When they come together like boozers in-law, they are known as Storm, Hurricane and Cyclone. They may smile at you when they appear before you in their real names. But at the same time, they will strangulate you from the back when they approach you in their nicknames. In short, on some occasions, they make you laugh and on others they make you cry.

"It means, *Ma*," said I, "I can believe only you."

In answer, she told me that all the animate and inanimate things were attached to her. Though they could believe her, she loves only those who do good. To others, she was good-for-nothing. By the term good what she meant was: You might lie if it does good to many; you would kill one individual who might kill many; you may burn that which chills; you may chill that which burns; you may destroy that which is harmful! Mother's advice became relevant when I grew up—unless you destroy weeds, how can the seeds grow?

I said, "Does it mean that it is better to eliminate the thing that is going to decay?"

She answered in the negative. Everything will decay one day or the other. It is quite natural that all that is would die: You don't have to eradicate anything. All will perish in its own time.

Though I had no savage intention of eliminating the aged, my question perplexed her a little. So I changed the subject and asked her what gender I was?

She replied that I was lucky to be born a male, for a female had to bear most of the natural and unnatural burdens—more disadvantages than advantages. Take my mother for example: She is the symbol of patience, beauty, kindness, softness, chastity, etc, without which her life will be dull and colorless. Likewise, a woman, though she is synonymous with goodness, is treated as a slave by males. But I was certain that a day of femininity would come when all the females would be like Pandora, Diana, Ceres, Helen, Irene, Lamia, Libitina, Medusa, Victoria, Vesta and they would cut to size the masculine supremacy. A day would come when all the male-gods would have to wear female garments, go to the kitchen and would muse the female. I wondered whether nature would amend the rules of handling of the wonders of menstruation, pregnancy and child-bearing and give those jobs to males.

King Sun was retiring and how beautiful he looked! You could look directly at him without any fear. He was very meek. He had changed his color from yellow to red. He painted different images on the canvas of the sky. I was astounded. From where did he get those cosmic paints and brushes? Was there a cosmic school where he studied this universal form of art? King Sun remained on the screen of the sky like a hero acting the role of a crowned prince throwing the rays of his smile on me. I wished to uproot myself, fly towards him, to hug him, to kiss him, to love him and to marry up with him even if I would melt into nothingness in his embrace. I was jealous that someone else could have been planning the same.

I said, "*Ma*, look at that panoramic designer shirt worn by Mr. Sky! Is King Sun a painter?"

My mother laughed at me, for she might have thought: a writer just writes something for his fancy and the critics flatter him for some other thought, although the writer might not have thought about the reader's interpretation.

"Dear child," mother said to me. "Even at this tender age, I appreciate your interest in literature and imagining things. Writers are the scientists of emotions. They can tickle your mind and heart. But there are branches of science behind the things you behold now. Sun is neither a painter nor an artist. During the course of my rotation on my axis, it is the science of heat and light that you have seen and felt. To know more about them you have to study physics and astronomy."

"But tell me, *Ma*, what are these objects appearing on the body of Mr. Sky? They are shining like prisms!"

"I've to take care of some urgent matter on other parts of my body," said my mother. "You ask me tomorrow."

Crestfallen, I remained in that mood for sometime; at the same time Darkness came to rein.

The whole night I remained fascinated by the vivid-colored objects that appeared in the sky. It seemed that Mr. Darkness had swallowed the entire area obscuring my view of the objects so that I could not communicate with them. So I slept.

While asleep, I had dreams—the objects were playing some games in the vast yard of the sky, and I was one among them. They considered me as their guest and they did not bother how I fouled. I had a feeling that they were inferior to me.

Only when I woke up at daybreak did I feel that it was a folly, merely a dream, and I did not want the dream come true. I did not want to be one among them even if I got a chance, because they possessed pride and superiority complex more than anyone else in the universe.

I was eager to know about them. Were they just products of my hallucination or were they real?

To my surprise, I heard a hullabaloo: "Yeah, you, little child of a tree, yesterday we heard you asking your mother about our identity."

I stared at the sky. They were there but without their usual colorful and designer garments.

The objects said in an alarming voice: "See, Master Tree, we know that some individuals misguided you with their talks. But understand this. Without our mercy you can't live on your mother's lap. You'll be as good as dead if we won't shower our rain of kindness on you. So, don't let all the respect in you flow out. Keep some for us too."

I cleared my doubts. "You may be telling about Mr. Rain. But unless you tell me who in the cosmos you are, how can I respect you?"

"We are known as clouds. The actual parents of Mr. Rain," said the clouds in unison. "The sky is our residential area, far and aloft from you. We have the peculiar quality of changing colors, size and shape as and when we like. We can fly here and there; we can float. If you make us angry we roar and your mother calls it thunder and it's a shock treatment to her. If you make us gloomy, we weep and your mother calls it rain and she takes bath in it. We change even our names to cumulus, cumulostratus, cumulonimbus, etc. We control the climate."

Innocently, I said, "Pardon me; I was not aware of your powerful family. I really adore you all, especially when you don your beautiful garments."

"*Arey* . . . We are the individuals who adorn Mr. Sky. You haven't seen our crown. It has got seven colors. Your mother named it rainbow. She's very ambitious to have it. But we can't give that. It is our halo."

From my mother I understood their family secret—today's clouds may not exist tomorrow. Like dying patients they yearned for everything in the cosmos as early as possible—love, respect, compassion etc. As I learnt more about the clouds I understood that they were the fittest to be called parasites for they needed help from the sun, sky, water and the wind to move, dress and even to exist. Scientifically, they were nothing but a visible mass of water particles or ice formations suspended in the air.

Throughout the day I kept on watching the location, color and changing figures of the clouds. Some were as big as mountains and some others were just patches. Some were agile and some others slow in movement; some resembled black smoke and some others snow.

In the evening all of them appeared clad in their best garments and ornaments and lined up on the horizon as if to witness the retiring ceremony of Sun. As Sun travelled on a route far away from them, the color also travelled far away from them, making them glamour less. My mother said that the clouds were originally glamour less, and it was due to the reflection and refraction of the sunlight that they gained colors to act as prisms.

I could only pity them. I had nothing to contribute to brighten their faces. I knew my benevolence would not solve their problems.

All the clouds disappeared from the sky as though someone swept away the dry leaves from a courtyard. I was still sympathizing with the clouds but in no time the sympathy changed into surprise for I saw a whitish circular fluorescent object in the west. Was it a cloudlet, skulked away from the cloud family that did not want to leave the playground of the sky? This individual stood there smiling at me as if we were erstwhile friends.

Lighting up the sky, it remained there like a neon lamp. The light from it bathed my mother, making her body translucent. Unlike the sun, this was pleasant to the eyes. All this gladdened me, lent pleasure to my eyes.

I bet myself that this individual did not hail from the cloud family. I was sure that clouds had no properties of illumination. On the luminous body I saw some black patches.

King Sun walked off to the west. Was this individual the reliever of King Sun? If so, then would he be a threat to King Darkness? I thought of clearing my doubts from King Darkness rather than asking my sleeping mother.

Reading my desire, Darkness said, in a soft voice, "My dear child-tree, you lack the IQ to distinguish between the cloud and Moon. Where do clouds stand and where does Moon! Clouds are just short-lived creatures. They are mortal, whereas Moon is immortal."

"If Moon is permanent, where was he all these days? I'm seeing him for the first time."

"Moon comes to my region only at times because he is in transit. Nature has permitted the Moon to inspect what's happening on the earth during my regime. I have limited powers when the Moon is present. That's why I'm feeble. You see, Moon is coming closer and closer. If the Moon sees us talking, he will misunderstand that I'm criticizing him. So if you have any more questions, ask him directly."

King Darkness was afraid of Moon. Moon was not such a character to be afraid of. But could you judge someone by the looks? There are things that look pleasant outside but have poison inside, soft outside but rough within, meek outside but harsh inside. This is especially true with feminine things. So, the first question I thought of asking the Moon was about *its* gender. The Moon had moved right above my head.

Boldly I asked, "If you speak, say something about your gender."

"I'm of unisex," said Moon.

The answer pierced my mind like a javelin hit. Swallowing all other questions, I stood stunned. My presumption was true—by look Moon seemed very quiet and melodious but by nature he was quite contrary to it.

Harshly, Moon said, "What a mutt you are! When one meets somebody, the usual questions are about the name, place, origin, family and so on. What made you throw such a question at me? Is it because of your broadmindedness or cunningness?"

I said that I was neither broadminded nor cunning. Frankly, I had no malice in my heart.

Moon said, "I know you are confused. You don't have to go by the knowledge about your female father. It's a song in the whole universe."

"I beg your pardon. Are you too facing fatherhood problem?"

"I do not have parents. I'm an orphan. I'm all alone and independent right from the beginning of the universe. But rumors are spread everywhere falsifying the fact."

"It's a pity that you have been provided with a charming body and a charred behavior. Don't feel that I'm finding fault with you." I said.

"It's a fact that I'm nature's watchdog. You can call me any names: Invigilator, investigator, inspector, interrogator or anything. I have to watch what's happening on the surface of earth. *Ipso facto,* my entire body is an eye. I came here for a random check. Whenever I appear on the sky, seeing my charisma all the individuals on earth should give ovation to me instead of getting frightened of me. My duty is to make a note of anyone adulterating the hormone of your mother that would pave the way to breaking of the law of nature and to report the matter to the Omnipotent."

"Who adulterates?" I inquired.

"You are intelligent as well as innocent. You don't know what's happening on the earth. You will come to know it later. You are a sensible tree-lad. That's why you raised question about my sex."

"By the by, what's the secret of your dual sex? Has the omnipotent provided you with a male member and a womb, sperm and ovum? Or do you mate with yourself? I'm anxious to know about this unnatural phenomenon. Is this a doom or a boon to you?"

My questions made no impact on Moon.

"It's not an unnatural phenomenon. It's something anti-natural. I have nothing in me as you said. In short, Moon is said to be male (he) and the Moonlight is said to be female (she). In this cosmos, I alone possess this peculiar fame. In our system Sun has solar energy. But I have no lunar energy. I'm a parasite. I have nothing to donate. How can a parasite that lives on somebody's mercy help someone? I maintain my astronomical status and I'm satisfied with it. One should be ambitious to reach the heights; one should not be greedy for attaining more heights, which latter may result in a fall. You'll only get what you deserve. Try not to lose that. I'm many times better and many times ahead compared to the condition of the stars."

"Stars! Who are they and where are they Mr. & Ms Moon?"

"You are quite intelligent to address me that way," continued Moon. "The stars are the subjects in the universal Kingdom. During daytime, they'll be working somewhere else. At night, when they come to take rest in the sky-yard you can see them."

"It's already night. I can't see them."

"They are under the custody of King Sun," said the Moon without interest. "They can be seen only at times. It's restricted."

"But why this discrimination?"

"Because they're the working class and we're the ruling class. As I'm also one of the higher stratum in the royal court of King Sun, I too enjoy ruling class privileges."

"How about my mother?"

"Your mother? She is his third wife. As she is a good dancer, she is his pet."

I recollected what His Highness Sun had told me.

Moon continued: "The labor class is neglected everywhere and always. They are treated as untouchables. If they fall in the spectrum of the ruling class it would harm them *ipso jure*. But I never think like that."

"What makes you to think differently?"

"See, dear tree-lad, after all they too are individuals created by the Omnipotent. You will be stunned to hear that each star is a much larger, powerful and energetic individual than it appears to be. Their voice is hi-powered and oscillating. They are always shouting slogans for their right to freedom and dignity. But as they are kept millions, billions and trillions of light years away, their voices do not reach the court."

"I see . . ." I sighed.

"It's time for me to retire. If you have to ask something more, better contact your mother."

Why should I ask my mother? She too belongs to the ruling class. I shall ask the King himself about this disparity, but not now. I will do it after seeing and studying the condition of the poor stars.

Days crawled by. I understood that I had crossed infancy when Mr. & Ms. Moon called me a tree-lad. But now I felt I had crossed that stage also. Moon had told me that the stars were companions to all the moving individuals during night. I too wanted to walk along with them listening to the stories of negligence.

During a cold night, shaking me up from my deep sleep, Moon said, "Hello, Master Tree-boy, wake up and see your complainants."

Waking up, I beheld the stars scattered on the background of the sky with Mr. & Ms. Moon on the foreground. Mr. Moon was smiling at me and Ms Moon bathed me with her soft milky white light. Stars blinked at me as though I was the judge and Moon the advocate.

Loudly I hailed, "Stars ahoy. If you can listen, could I speak to you? Or if you could speak to me, I can listen to you."

Eagerly I waited for their reply. But no voice came forth.

Then the Moon said, "Well, tree-boy, don't waste your time and energy. You can speak to them, but they can't hear you. They can speak to you, but you can't hear them. The waves of your sound won't reach them and their sound waves won't reach up to your place".

"Then what's the alternative?"

"I can relay your messages to them and their messages to you."

"Roger," I said. "First convey my compliments to them, then my message."

"I already conveyed it and they sent greetings to you for your companionship and kind-heartedness."

Mr. & Ms. Moon relayed the stars' heartbeats to me. It meant: All their eyes were focused on me. They could see me as a tiny-tot with their big eyes. They wanted to talk to me directly and were eager to hear my voice. They did not know whether a delicate tree-boy like me could plead for them in front of the cruel King Sun, who was always submerged in a pool of fire. And if at all I could, how much would I succeed.

My message relayed by Mr. & Ms. Moon to the stars was: "I wished to approach personally each and every star on the sky, listen to them and mark their grievances. But I was helpless. All I could do was to see them on the sky from a long way off. Keep no wrong impression of my capability to challenge His Highness Sun. They should not underestimate an individual by seeing his size; for the smallest of the small has the highest of high powers—a mote-sized seed could have the huge heart of a tree. They should not doubt my strength, vigor and vitality. They should not lose hope about the verdict of victory. At least, they could dream.

"No power on the cosmos can deny the right to dream, for that boon is given to each and every individual by the Omnipotent. You can dream without paying anything. Dreams are available in plenty everywhere and always. You can choose as per your caprice—irrespective of your dignity and valor. A slave can become a King. You can beat any number of Kings and imprison them. The enjoyment you gain through the real sessions with your most favorite mate could be lesser than that of the illusion in a dream. You can copulate with Miss Cosmos and can have a series of orgasms. No sentence can be framed in the figure-of-speech as a simile or a metaphor exemplifying the word dream. It's all alone—it is charismatic."

My words stirred their hearts. Further I requested them not to be crestfallen about keeping them very far away from this maddening earth. They should come forward with courage and faith and ask for their rights—shout slogans, raise protests, put up strikes, etc. If the solution was a revolution, make a revolution. 'Crying child alone gets the milk', they say.

After a long discourse on liberation to the stars, they resolved to unite to fight for justice.

Giving up even the last shades of timidity and collecting all the strands of boldness, I prepared to confront King Sun to demand the liberation of stars. Though he had shown me fatherly affection during my infancy, I was not certain how he would react now. I had all the best regards for him for he was the first individual I met in my life. He had instilled in me a courage that laid a strong foundation of principles in me. He was a gracious man-of-letters. As the teacher so the student. A good teacher can only produce good students. I thanked the Omnipotent for detailing King Sun as my instructor.

Gone were the days of meeting and talking with him. Whenever he passed over my head we both neglected each other. I was inclined to have contact with low-power individuals—wind, rain, clouds et al—roaming around the surface of the earth. Sun considered them short-living idiots of low value. So he might have thought that I too had fallen in those standards. Nevertheless, I decided to face him in a different manner but very decently. The style I adopted was this: Reduce praises to the minimum and to project facts to the maximum. So, instead of addressing him 'Your Highness', I started addressing him Mr. Sun.

I said, "Ahoy, Mr. Sun, Ahoy . . ."

Contrary to my anxiety, he kept better decorum.

Like an experienced King, Sun said to me, "Please erase those grievances from your mind. It'll not stand. The complainants, the stars, are many in number. I too hail from their family. One of your arguments is that I'm enjoying more privileges even though I'm smaller in size than the complainants. It is so because I'm their leader. I argue that I'm entitled to have more privileges in accordance with my duties and responsibilities as a cosmic King.'

"A King is not crowned for the size and type of his body, but for his wit and wisdom. A Kingdom ruled by a King without wisdom would bring boredom to the subjects and would leave them without freedom. Even otherwise, there should be only one King for one Kingdom. Can you imagine the condition of a Kingdom having a large number of Kings and less number of subjects?"

"But," I said, "they don't object to changing the King by turn and term. This will help them to become wise so that they too can get the opportunity of becoming Kings sometime in life, instead of your exclusive enjoyment of the whole lifetime as a permanent King."

"You are like a learned judge," Sun went on, "a King is for his lifetime. As per the royal rules, a successor to the King is chosen only after his death or he falls ill. And for your kind information, you know the consequences if I go sick-in-quarters. So the objection cannot be sustained and therefore is overruled."

Though I was the Justice of the Peace, and as there was no counsel to present the case of the stars as per the cosmic law, I argued for the complainants. But King Sun's strong statement put me in a dilemma.

King Sun said, "Hailing from the family of stars, I was given the throne. Why? The Omnipotent knew that I alone was fit to don the crown. That's why I have been brought to this place from the Milky Way and positioned here so that I could establish my empire in such a way that all the individuals in this universe should be benefited and looked after by me impartially.

"I alone possess the proper size and character among the many kinds of stars of all the galaxies. My Lord, you may be under the impression that I have been crowned by virtue of luck. Not at all. It's because I'm qualified.'

"My lord, though I am the defendant, I pity the complainants. That's why I took the oath not to harm anyone; I shall not show partiality to anyone; I shall not do injustice and I shall not disturb the equality and liberty or spoil anybody's peace of mind. The Omnipotent is the lawmaker. Only he can amend the law. He is intelligent enough to position everyone in his proper place as per the grade. I don't think he'll make any amendment or affect a reshuffle to show favoritism. I'm afraid, if he does that, that'll cause imbalance to the entire system of the cosmos and that will mark the start of the countdown to doomsday".

As the complainants had no evidences, exhibits or witnesses to substantiate their case, there was no way for me to pass a verdict favoring them. So I declared an adjournment.

Fibers of days were twisted into yarns of week, yarns of weeks into strands of month and strands of months into ropes of year in the machine of time by the craftsman of nature. The time machine was working non-stop and no one bothered to measure what length of rope had been made. I spoilt a lot of mental arithmetic formulae to calculate my age with the length of rope. I tried to measure the time-rope assuming one inch of time-rope as a day and calculating the time and speed like an inexperienced warrior ignorant of the method how of using sword and shield in a battle. I failed.

Then mother came as my tutor.

First she framed a question. Then she solved the problem and calculated my height, weight and age.

The problem: If the length of the time-rope was 50 feet from the date of birth of a tree and the speed of making the time-rope was one inch per month, what was the height and age of the tree? What was the weight of the tree if the ratio of height and weight was 1:20?

Like an astrologer, my mother explained to me everything. Despite the solution was not clear, yet I listened to her with pricked ears.

I was glad to know that I was fifty years old, fifty feet tall and weighed a ton. But I was sad to know that I was yet in my boyhood considering the lifespan of a tree. Only on attaining a hundred years of age I would become a youth. So I wished that the spinning of time-rope should have been made faster for I was impatient for the transition from adolescence to adulthood.

I was very much excited that I was the proud son of a mother, who was a mathematics expert with specialization in arithmetic. But learning my excitement, King Sun mocked my mother and me. He told me that my mother was not that much praiseworthy, for any damn fool could measure my physical standards with more ease. He had some practical applications to calculate my height by means of the light and shadow method and my weight by means of the gravity method.

Then he explained to me how he had found out my age: "I know pretty well that your mother had rotated me 50 times after giving birth to you. She takes a year for one trip and it's clearer than my light that you are 50 years old. And for your weight, it is calculated from the relative difference between the mass and weight and the gravitational force."

His exact explanation to this was: "Once I gave you a hint that your mother was a prostitute, who attracted any individual who came near her. She claims that it's a boon given to her by the Omnipotent. This attraction is named the force of gravitation. It's really a boon which I don't possess even though I'm a pretty sitting King. The heavenly bodies envy her for this peculiar property because they are still fixed in space where they possess only emptiness. Anyway, let's come to the calculation of your age. The law of gravity states that the attraction depends on mass and distance. To measure the weight of a tree, you can use the principle of gravitation. 'The power of your mother's attraction' varies from item to item and from distance to distance. There is an easy way to calculate your weight using the relative difference between the distance travelled by a fruit from your crown to the ground and the ratio between the mass and the weight of the fallen fruit. For this you have to consider the weight of the fruit as the unit of your weight.

I aired my doubt: "If it's a fruitless tree?"

"Then you can take its leaf as substitute and use the mass and weight ratio".

"If it's a leafless tree?"

"Then what's the use of measuring the height and weight? Instead of a physical check-up you should be sent for a medical check-up. A tree without fruits and leaves is good for nothing. Such trees are like impotent males and barren females."

"But," I said, "as they have no mouths to feed and no children to worry about, they'll tend and mend others. Living for others is more gracious than living for oneself."

"It's really gracious, young tree-boy, if they adopt such a system of living. But I find that most of such trees steal other trees' manure."

I did not want to argue much. To all good proposals he had his negative and suspicious opinions.

Seeing my devil-may-care attitude, King Sun went away.

After his departure, waiting a little, I asked my mother about the formulae stated by Sun. She told me that though King Sun was a genius, he was not trustworthy. "If you want to do the practical test of light and shadow, he won't provide you light on that day. If you do not want any light, he will throw more light on that day," she said.

Therefore I dropped the idea of conducting an experiment to take my measurement. It was quite confusing.

So, I was half a century old. I was satisfied with my health, growth and wealth. I was 50 feet tall. My trunk was strong and hefty. My roots occupied lots of room under the ground that made me stand firm. Branches full of leaves protruded to all sides. My friends, Wind, Rain, Clouds, Moon, Darkness, and even my mother regarded my growth as above average. King Sun alone did not comment. Thanks to my height, I could see a considerable area of my mother's body. The area was barren. During summer oasis could be seen. I stood amidst the vast stretch of land with oasis dancing around me during daytime.

But during the night, before going to sleep, I used to recall the petition filed by the stars. Poor petitioners! I felt ashamed for not giving them a favorable decree. I could not overrule the law. Helplessness was the only reason for the delay. Justice delayed is as good as justice denied. I could dismiss the petition. But every night they blinked at me earnestly asking for a good decision. But what would I do? When I received their grievances, I was under the impression that they were limited to the numbers in the Milky Way. But they were settled in different galaxies and each galaxy was inhabited with countless stars. If one penny worth more perks and privileges were to be given to these many stars, the exchequer would go bankrupt resulting in the closure of the cosmic treasury. Then I took the statements of King Sun into account. So, I thought of consulting the King for a compromise when he was in good mood.

Pertaining to my wealth, I was not greedy. I did not want to save anything for the future. All I wanted was some nutrition. I was content to have it as ration. I was sure that as long as the cosmos existed and as long as my mother would live I could get it with King Sun as the supply officer, and Wind, Rain and the atmosphere as the storekeepers.

One should be satisfied with what he deserves during his existence. He who seeks to save for future is ambitious. If you accumulate more than what you need, some others will be running short. Haves will keep on eating and have-nots will starve. There is no shortage of food, only shortage of hands to feed. Somebody's savings artificially create shortage. The mentality to save is selfishness. One should not bother about his past, should not discard his present and should not be anxious about the future. Whatever should happen will happen; whatever should not happen will not happen. So why savings?

Reading my mind, King Sun advised me that I should give up my negative thoughts and should think positively. In theory I was right. But in practice, without the habit of saving, there would not be any development. One cannot just live without a concern for future. It would create environmental problems.

I asked him what my saving should be. He replied to me that fruits were my savings. So from then on I thought of caring for my berries since they should be the children of tomorrow to preserve my race.

I would be a youth after a couple of years and then pass on to middle age. After then there would come the old age. Then I would not be healthy, wealthy and wise even if I get up early and go to sleep early. My condition might change to be very pathetic; I might become weak, poor and foolish. No one would be there to sympathize with me. Not even my children, if I had any. Therefore, to avoid disappointment at the final stage, I should carefully shape up a bright future.

One of the few points in the advice given by King Sun was very much attractive: One should never be a spendthrift. If you live lavishly your reserves will exhaust within no time and you will be as good as a living corpse. In such cases, King Sun is a stalwart. If he had spent his heat and light extravagantly, one cannot imagine what would have been the condition of all the organisms on earth. Without spending excessively, he regulates it benevolently for a long time for his neighbors.

Then I requested King Sun to grant an ex-gratia to the stars. My friends agreed to support me. But when they saw King Sun, they gave up their plans and vanished.

The King scolded me for approaching him with such silly matters. I replied that a silly matter to some might be hilly to others. He again got annoyed and declared that even if all the bodies in the solar system supported me he would not grant any ex-gratia privileges to the stars. He was not frightened of anybody and therefore would not render any excesses and mal-practices. And he further warned me that I should not try to become an advocate. I should not try to protect anybody in my shade from his heat and light because everyone on earth had to suffer these, he said.

Like a coward, I agreed to that with a broken heart. I did not want to spoil the good relationship with him. I did not want to earn his enmity. So, without delay I dismissed the grievance of the stars *ex-parte*. Likewise, somehow I unloaded the onus from my shoulders.

The wheel of time had kept on rolling giving chances to Sun and Darkness to rule the earth alternately. I could not find any change on the surface of the earth other than the change of seasons—spring gave way to summer, summer to autumn and autumn to winter.

Like competitors, all heavenly bodies took part in the nature's sports and games but none won. The Omnipotent did not give any prize to anyone in any event. He kept on reminding them that it was their duty. Their performance should be exemplary. I too agreed. You participate not for the sake of prize. It took me nearly a century to learn this.

All these days, changes have been happening to me. I had attained further height and weight. I worked out my height and weight as per the previous formulae of one-foot height: twenty times the weight per year of the first half century. My calculations were all wrong and again my mother came to solve the problem. She divided my previous height by two and multiplied my previous weight by two and added to the height and weight of first half century. That formula was unknown even to King Sun because it was based on the growth of my roots that had grown below the ground—the sum total was taken from above ground.

After attaining a height of 75 feet and weight of three tons of weight, I celebrated my transition from adolescence to adulthood on the auspicious occasion of the centenary.

I had invited almost all the very important and less important individuals for the ceremony but no one attended it. So I celebrated my hundredth birthday both as a host and as a guest—myself.

CENTURY 2

101 TO 200 AD

The venue of the centenary celebrations was the top of my crown. It was vast and convenient, and could accommodate a large number of individuals. I could accord a hearty welcome to all of them there. I gave various duties to the various departments like branches and leaves section and fruits and flowers section. All of them happily agreed.

I had instructed the branches to dance. They practiced 'roll-and-pitch dance', a fantastic piece. The leaves rehearsed a melodious, high-pitch low-pitch choir. I requested Mr. Wind to lend a helping hand by giving momentum to the branches and leaves for the song and dance sequences to grant the event a peculiar fervor as a favor.

The flowers volunteered to be presented themselves to the guests as bouquets, garlands and floral showers. It had rained the previous day and all the berries got cleaned themselves for consumption by the guests. I was very much particular about the feast—No guest should be left without food. So I instructed my fruits that, if there were too many guests and fruits were insufficient, each of them should break into two, four or even more. If it still fell short of the demand, each guest should be provided with at least one seed, so that they could take those seeds to their native places and deposit them in the soil. This way, we could be proud that our breed of a Banyan tree from this planet was represented in another soil. They also would be happy to have a presentation.

The time for the function was fixed taking into consideration the convenience of King Sun—from sunset to midnight. So King Sun as the chief guest could arrive first, inaugurate the function and could depart. Mr. Sky and his children, the clouds, would already be present,

30

followed by the Mr. & Ms. Moon. The stars of the Milky Way and other constellations, Mercury, Venus, Mars, Jupiter, Saturn, Uranus, Neptune and Pluto and their satellites would come. I invited even the rarely seen comets.

But none of them turned up! None . . . I could not understand why they did not come. Was it that my invitation was improper and erroneous? Or were they to be blamed? Did they have any dislike for me? Had I hurt their feelings in some way? No, not at all. In my knowledge, I had not done any mischief towards anybody.

Oh! The reason might be that I did not hail from the family of heavenly bodies. I was just a tree, depending on their mercy. I should not have mingled with the members of the celestial class. Then I recalled the words of King Darkness—racial prejudice! Yes, undoubtedly I too was a victim of racial prejudice. That was why the celestial bodies outcast me, staying away from my birthday party. Only poor King Darkness was present. He was prompt. But he had no part to play. He just remained silent.

He was ashamed to attend the party because his color painted the venue solid black. I had requested Mr. & Ms. Moon to provide light to illuminate the area. They betrayed me.

That afternoon Mr. Sky looked very gloomy. His color had changed from blue to ash. I wanted to ask Mr. Sky as to where King Sun was hiding. Was he behind the ash-smoke veil? He walked away, camouflaged, without paying any attention to me. I was not disheartened—he being a King might neglect a subject, a mere tree like me.

After his departure, Mr. Sky pretended to be asleep. He covered himself from head to foot with an ash-colored blanket. How could I ask him until and unless I saw his blue face? Moon was not there, the stars were absent. Not even a patch of cloud was there to witness my birthday function.

The absence of Mr. Wind made my branches and leaves melancholic for they could not perform their prestigious items. They had conducted a full-dress rehearsal the previous day. They were very confident and in high spirits.

The absence of light depressed my flowers and the fruits. Moon was responsible for that—he concealed himself in some dark corner of the sky. The fruits and flowers were ready for instantaneous serving remaining half-disconnected from the stalks. Therefore, the day that followed my birthday all the flowers had fallen and all the fruits had decayed.

I could not bear that. It was a great loss. My delicate heart turned heavy. I felt that the whole weight of my body was kept on it. I wanted to soften it. But how? To challenge them, to revenge or abuse them. Yes! Abuse! It is the most suitable way to lighten a laden heart: To liquefy a solidified heart.

Abusing someone is a wonderful experience. You will be relieved of your anger. It gives you relief. You get satisfaction. You will regain normalcy. No other non-violent act is so effective. It has two benefits: On the one hand, the abuser relieves his tension and on the other the abused realizes his fault.

The tension of cooperation of the party and tension of non-cooperation of the guests weakened my mind. I went to sleep.

I had made a blunder mistake. I did not invite my mother to the party. I forgot the *Guru-ship*. It was not deliberate. I just forgot. I begged her pardon.

She said, "Never mind, my dear tree-son. Sometimes we forget that we have a heart."

She was correct. I was said to be a holy tree, supposed to adhere strictly to precepts. Her words pained me. But when I thought that my mother was a paragon of patience, the pain relieved.

I got up in the morning. Sun was shining brightly. I felt he was the brain behind the conspiracy that spoiled my party. I fired him left and right. I used all the bad words that I had learnt till then to insult him. He did not utter a word. He knew, if he did, the shower of abusiveness would turn into a torrent. That was his trick. The elite class is not at all afraid of any weapon owned by the labor class other than the tongue. Right . . . Sun was sent away after an abusive bath.

Then I sprayed my anger on Mr. Sky. He remained there with guilty conscience, in silence. Listening to my abuse, the clouds ran away as fast as they could. At night Mr. & Ms. Moon appeared. I insulted Moon with words that *he* would not have heard in *his* whole life. I asked *him* to convey my anger to the thankless stars.

I was surprised. None of them responded. I became angrier. They smiled innocently as though they were deaf and dumb.

Hearing my inflated abuses, my mother scolded me. Then she cooled down.

"My good-mannered-man-of-a-tree", my mother called me. "Why do you behave unbecomingly to your elders? They are your seniors. Or your superiors. They are all venerable individuals, of course vulnerable as well.

Have you gone mad? Or are you mentally retarded? Let the Omnipotent save you from such handicaps! Don't abuse anyone. It's not becoming of a divine tree like you."

"But, *Ma*," I said. "That reduced the burden on my mind. It was an issue of my prestige. They ruined my party. What did they think? These fools should've thought that I was in need of their presence not indeed interested in their presents. My bloodless root!"

"For my sake, anchor your anger," Mother warned me.

"Otherwise? What'll they do? Eat us in one breath?"

My mother grieved, "They'll take revenge."

"Then I'll plead in the celestial court where the Supreme Judge, the Omnipotent, is sitting."

"Mind you, the heavenly bodies may file a defamation case against you."

"Why?"

"Don't ask me why; the sky is very high. You can't reach there. It's quite expensive and tiresome. They are all great bodies. Even otherwise, don't expect to win the case. You have committed a crime."

"I committed a crime? What the hell are you talking about, *Ma* . . . ?"

"Yes. You committed a crime. Boycotting your party is not a crime, but abusing is. Defamation is criminal offence. If it's proved, your life is spoilt."

"But this defamation charge is only on me?"

"Did you abuse them?"

"Yes," I admitted. "By that non-violent act, I got some relaxation, and they realized."

"You are misguided by someone. I'm sure of that," Mother continued. "You know, if you hit somebody with a weapon on his head, only his head is wounded. Hit somebody with a weapon on his hand, only his hand is wounded. But hit somebody with foul words, his heart is hurt. All the former wounds could be healed by treatment. But nothing can heal the wounds of heart."

Only then did I realize my mistakes. Seeing my reaction, my mother regretted. "*Chheyh*, I was very mean-minded," I thought.

I said approvingly, "*Ma*, they are great. They didn't lose their temper. They even didn't open their mouth. Really, they are great and venerable and I'm vulnerable."

Then mother told me about the deaf and dumb behavior of the celestial bodies. Any attempt by me to get a reply from them would be futile. Their faculty of listening to my language and that of mine of listening to their language were also lost forever. The day I turned hundred, I became independent. They did not attend my party. The reason was that it was my birth centenary. It was not even one-millionth of a second of their timescale.

Again I recalled my mother's scolding—the length, breadth and depth of it. She fumed: "Where did you learn this type of vulgar language! In my picture, there are no nutty-cracky friends for you. *Dhudh, dhudh, dhudh,* (Oh, no) I have forgotten that you are a child with a sophisticated thought system. You are a child who had demanded freedom in place of breast-milk the moment you were born. I gave birth to myriad of brainy children. They had never put forward such demands. And of course, at times, some children become textbooks for their parents.

"But this is a case of shame! At least you should have told me a word before taking this fallacious decision and reasoning. After all, I'm your mother. When the head is there, tail should not wag. You had a sharp intellect during childhood. Has the growth of your cerebellum overtaken your body growth? Did that brain instigate you to commit this vulgarity?"

I begged her pardon. I realized that it was a grave offence. Neither the brain nor the heart compelled me. None of the limbs forced me. All I knew was that those vulgar words were hidden somewhere in me. It came out as vomit that could never be cleared up.

I was sad. My sadness was not just the opposite of happiness. It was something more than that. If I were to be sentenced to death, I would have happily accepted it.

What was there for me now?

If you enter somewhere, there will be an exit. If you enroll somewhere, you will have to retire. One has to die if he is born.

The earlier the death, the happier I'd be. But this punishment was really cruel, as good as solitary confinement—curtailing my right to speak.

I prayed to omnipotent God not to give such punishment to anybody else. The power of communication was being switched off. How can I express my feelings? How can I understand their pieces of advice? How would we interact with each other? How would we send messages of affection, gratitude, or mercy?

I felt that my nervous system was collapsing.

Owff . . . ! What is the use of systems without a mind? What is the use of a mind without thoughts? What is the use of thoughts without speech? What is the use of speech without transmission? The freedom for transmitting and receiving of speech has been lost.

It was better to go to grave. I wished to die. There were no ways and means of suicide. So I altered my anger into agony. I further tried to alter the agony into ecstasy—in vain.

To show my protest, I shed lots of tender berries and leaves. Still I grieved.

Sensing my distress, my mother consoled me.

"Dear tree-son, don't be dismayed. Be brave. You should have courage and confidence to solve a problem that hammers your mind. In due course of your life, many hurdles, thorns, stones, dips, bumps, blocks, jams et al are to be by-passed—you'll have to complete your life-cycle painfully.

"You know, even The Almighty is in a whirlpool of problems. You have your own problems. I've my own. Problems are faced by your so-called friends—Atmosphere, Photosphere, Ionosphere, Space, Solar system, Galaxies, Constellations and Sky. The protons, neutrons and electrons of an atom have their own problems. To solve all these problems is The Almighty's problem."

I interfered, "*Ma* . . . What's the problem with these atoms being the smallest particles of an element?"

"You are not aware of it. You know, an atom has got three groups of children—Neutrons, Protons and Electrons."

I shook my head positively.

"*Ngaa* . . . They are fighting with each other."

"What for?"

"The protons complain that though they have a lot of positive charge, they are not recognized. Their names are nowhere. The electrons' complaint is that they, being younger, are forced to work always. Away from the home too. In a way, it's child labor. And the neutrons, being elders, remain inert; reside nicely in the palace of Nucleus as Kings. So the problems of working class, middle class and the upper class exist everywhere. Some are destined to have the spoon of joy in their mouth. And some to have the spoon of sorrow."

"Do you have any problem, *Ma* . . . ?"

"I too have many problems like pollution, excavation, depletion of the ozone layer etc. In one case you are very lucky."

I asked for an explanation.

She explained: "You have lost only the power of sending and receiving messages. You are allowed to speak. There is no restriction on your freedom to communicate with me. All these allowances also have to be curtailed. Stoppage of liberty to breathe. Mulcts on necessary gases and water particles. You understand what I say?"

I told her I understood.

"It's easy to say about suicide," mother continued.

"But, my dear, as death comes nearer and nearer, the one who wants to die feels to get away from it, even if he's very old and due for death. You are too young to think of suicide. There is a great stretch of life in front of you. When death comes very close to you with his warrant, I'm certain that you will sell not only your properties but also your kith and kin including your mother (myself) to bribe the devil of death."

I took a long breath and released it slowly.

Reluctantly, mother said, "Forget about the freedom of communication with the celestial bodies. At least, you have the freedom to see them. Sometimes the punishment will be so severe that you'll be forbidden to see them. Then what would be your condition? Just think about it! It will be as good as blindness.

"If you are dumb, nothing is lost; if you are deaf, something is lost; if you are blind, everything is lost even if your character is exemplary."

My mother's advice made me realize the seriousness of the punishment of living blind.

I said, "*Ma*, after all, The Almighty is great and kind. He gave me a very simple punishment. I was an egoist. I should have been awarded a summery punishment for that offence of abusing veterans."

"He is not just kind. He is very kind. This is not a punishment meted out to you. This is an award of 'Independence' to you," she said emphatically.

"An award of Independence!" I rejoiced.

"Yes, dear, yes. You do not have to be dependent on any celestial body. You are at liberty to take your own decision since the day you attained the age of a hundred years. Don't seek anyone's advice. You'll have to shoulder your responsibilities yourself. You were pampered till then. From now on you'll have to pamper somebody. They'll depend on you. You were a parasite till now. From now on you have to allow some other parasites to feed on you. It's your turn to help and save the weak—too young and too old sections of our society. The days are coming."

"But *Ma* . . . We can converse. It means, I could adopt your advice".

"Of course", said *Ma*. "But only in situations of extreme emergency."

So I again thanked god a great deal.

"*Ma*, there's an emergency; an essential question. Where can I find The Almighty?"

Mother answered my question passionately as follows.

The Almighty is found everywhere yet he is nowhere.

The Almighty resides in you, in me yet you don't feel him.

The Almighty lives in heaven and hell yet you won't reach him.

The Almighty shines in the sky yet you don't see him.

The Almighty is in all the visible objects but is invisible.

The Almighty exists in all the lights yet hides in the dark.

The Almighty is everything but is also nothing.

The Almighty is in sound yet he is silent.

The Almighty has no beginning and no end.

The Almighty has no sex but is very sexy.

The Almighty has nobody yet possesses all bodies.

The Almighty is ugly yet very beautiful.

The Almighty is medicine yet very poisonous.

The Almighty is very smart yet lethargic.

The Almighty is disciplined and non-disciplined.

The Almighty is obedient yet truant.

The Almighty is good yet very bad.

The Almighty is the satisfaction and dissatisfaction.

The Almighty is all the dos but also the don'ts.

The Almighty is fragrance itself but stinks.

The Almighty is soft and hard.

The Almighty is colorful and colorless.

The Almighty is kind yet very cruel.

The Almighty is food and shit.

The Almighty is bold yet a coward.

The Almighty is literate but illiterate too.

The Almighty is wise and yet a fool.

The Almighty is King and subject.

The Almighty is full and empty.

The Almighty is the science—physics, chemistry, and maths;

The Almighty is the language—alphabets, words, sentences, and grammar.

The Almighty is here, The Almighty is there;

The Almighty is this, The Almighty is that.

The Almighty is A to Z; The Almighty is Z to A.

"Enough *Ma*, enough," I exclaimed. "I shouldn't have asked you this question. I should have myself identified *The Almighty!*"

*   *   *

Seasons changed reluctantly. I passed my time. Nothing to think. Desperate days fell down as dewdrops. I was not much interested in living. I just lived on because there was a life in me—like a candle burning idly.

I wished to invite some external force to put out that naked flame by starving, smothering or by the cooling method—to finish my life. But no such force was available.

Then I thought about The Almighty's mercy. I desired I could have been provided with the privilege of communicating at least with darkness. That facility was also snatched away. There was no one to talk with.

Like a prisoner awaiting the termination of life, my mind wandered for my terminus.

Most of the nights, I did not get sleep. On those sleepless nights, my hobby was to stare at the sky. All the objects that appeared on the sky-screen blinked at me as if they were seeing me for the first time.

Even Darkness considered me as an unknown. That day onwards I considered them as mere inanimate individuals. That moment onwards I stopped cajoling them.

After my melancholic centenary, the next major event occurred when I entered the first decade of my second centenary.

Owing to my sleeplessness at night, I used to doze in the early hours of the day.

I heard a sudden blast. That chilled me to the marrow.

Sound followed by pelting of stones and spreading of sands. That wounded my body. Some wet things fell all over my body. There was no rain. Yet it was like a rain. Wet mud spread all over. Because of the shattering sounds I shivered from head to foot. I felt that I was going to be uprooted any time.

Some of my branches had fallen down with lots of flowers and berries. Panic-stricken, they wondered what on earth was going on. All of them tried to hold fast to the branches lest they should get hurt.

I could not see anything. The whole area was covered with dust. The clouds of dust travelled towards the sky. The atmosphere was polluted. I felt suffocated, and a little later fell unconscious.

For quite some time something was befalling. Suddenly a big rock hit my crown. That helped me regain my consciousness. But the hit caused severe pain.

I heard the hue and cry of my little leaves and fruits now lying on the ground. I did not know what to do and what not—I was intimidated.

What had happened? What is happening? What would happen? I had no answers to those questions. All I could gather was that there was an emergency.

I needed help. So, recalling the promise of my mother, I intended to call her. In the hustle and bustle, she did not even hear my high-pitched cries. I lamented. Soon my lamentation came as a lamentable song from my heart.

Come hither and help me;
Come hither and hug me,
As there is none to console me *Ma . . . Ma . . . Ma . . .*
Come hither and stop this halla-gulla;
Come hither and stop that hustle-bustle,
As there is none to save me *Ma . . . Ma . . . Ma . . .*
Come hither and conceal me in your lap;
Come hither and carry me on your shoulders,
As there is none to rescue me *Ma . . . Ma . . . Ma . . .*

Mother did not respond. I felt very sad.

Though the cluster of the clouds of dust was opaque, gradually it became translucent and then transparent.

I adjusted my sight at an angle of 45 degrees from the ground. I reckoned if my mathematics was correct and if my height was precisely 80 feet—exactly hundred-folds of my height—eight thousand feet away I saw that. Yes, really I saw a spectacular but a very terrifying scene . . .

Tons and tons of rocks, stones, sand, mud and many other materials burst out from my mother's body. All those stuffs travelled high into the air and fell down at a double distance (sixteen thousand feet) away from my dwelling place making a curved trajectory.

A series of serious explosions occurred. A series of replenishment also occurred. The sudden violent exploded portion of the earth was filled with water from where the rocky substance was excavated with loud noise. All those items were settled down and piled up side by side and lengthwise like a very tall dyke. The water-filled area was like a channel.

Thank God. The flight and accumulation of the earth was not towards my dwelling place. In that case I would have been buried inside the long and tall ridge of earth. I would have remained there like a hermit who would never be released to see the world without deliverance. Or without much ado I would have been swallowed by *death*.

The outburst continued with shattering effect and thundering sound. The outburst moved away by building the mountain and digging the river. At times the explosion compelled me to dance when the ground shattered. With great difficulty, I managed to keep my balance. When the earth shivered I quivered. When I quivered the earth shivered. We both shivered and quivered, quivered and shivered.

With each spurt, rocks and water jets from the ground gushed out simultaneously like fountains. Like the unending salvoes on a battlefield, the bursts continued for days and days moving further and farther.

Initially, I had counted the eruptions by counting the blasts. Later I had practical difficulty in counting and I gave up.

The broadsides of eruptions occurred on both sides and went out of sight after a few days. It seemed as if someone made a deep cut on my mother's belly. The cut portion was flooded with muddy water that resembled blood.

What on the cosmos was going on? I did not know whom to ask? My enquiry counter was Sky. I could not see his face. Mountains of black clouds were everywhere. They stared cruelly at me. No other bodies appeared during day or night.

Where were they? Were they absent? Were they hiding deliberately since they did not want to witness the catastrophe that was happening to one of their fellow beings? Or were they afraid that if they showed their faces, my mother might request them to save her from that calamity?

Oh, oh! What purpose would they serve even if they were present? For some time I had forgotten that communicating with them was forbidden.

For the past one hundred and fifty years, I had experienced all the four seasons. One season gave way to the other without any objection. Their precise presence and precise absence made me feel all right. I had accustomed to the climate of my native place. I learnt it was made up of temperature, wind and rainfall.

I never felt sick of weather changes. I recalled the body pain and uneasiness I was suffering from during my maturity period. That was something physiological. And on another occasion I had a mental shock—the boycotting of my birthday centenary by my dear and near ones. It was something unforgettable. But the magician named Time made me forget it.

ALL THAT GLITTERS IS NOT GOD

But, now this incidence tortured me physically and mentally. Something intolerable . . . It was not a fun. Something so serious and severe—my own mother was being hurt. That too right in front of me.

Who was the culprit? Some unknown spirit? Some celestial bodies? What for? Had she done something wrong? Had she misbehaved with them?

In my knowledge she had had no unbecoming habit. Then, *Ngaa*, I thought, "I'm a *mental crack*." I was a fool to forget what my mother had told me when I had abused the celestial objects. The vengeance! Were they taking revenge? Trying to destroy her? Or was it a duel between Darkness and Sun? Where they trying to bifurcate my mother to have a boundary for their individual territories? I could smell a rat but could not find the rat.

Sadly I sang:

"Will it penetrate deep into thy womb to reach the other side if it's a hit?

Will it propel up to the far end of thy sky if it's a burst?

Hit or burst it's horrifying me,

Transit me to a citadel *Ma . . . ma . . . ma . . .*

Then my mother said in a feeble voice: "Dear son-tree, erase your emotions and come to conclusions." My mother wanted to tell me something. But the shocks shook her body. Her attention shifted from me to her trauma.

Blasts continued . . .

Short blasts followed by long blasts,

Long blasts followed by prolonged blasts,

Prolonged blasts followed by long blasts,

Long blasts followed by short blasts.

Again blasts, blasts, blasts, blasts . . .

Left side blasts and right side blasts,

East side blasts and west side blasts,

Night-time blasts and day-time blasts,

Day-time blasts and night-time blasts,

Again blasts, blasts, blasts . . .

Blast continued for years.

Chheyh, really bad! Definitely, someone was poking my mother. Someone was shaking her. Her body was being cut all these days.

The water that gushed out like a fountain resembled her tears; the sounds produced resembled her cries.

As a son I wanted to help her. Even otherwise, it was my duty as a by-stander to help someone in distress. But save her from whom? Who was the culprit and where was the culprit? I did not know.

There was an interval. Sound was dead and silence was born. The whole area became quiet.

Suddenly I broke the silence.

"*Ma*," I shouted. "What's happening to you?"

She said in a feeble voice, "Son, this is *rarely*."

"Rarely?" I replied.

"Yes. Some female inhabitants of the earth have to undergo a natural phenomenon called *monthly*. Every month the menses takes place. During the menses period, there will be a monthly discharge of blood and other matters from the uterus of primates. Likewise, I too suffer from this process. It occurs once in a blue moon. That's why this is known as *rarely*. What you saw was the rarely discharged matters from my body".

"Are you benefited by this process known as *rarely*?" I asked.

"I'm not. You are benefited."

"I don't want any benefit that would inflict pain on you."

Mother said, "For one's pleasure, the other has to suffer. If I've plus with something you've some minus—it's quite natural. A mother suffers pain for delivering a baby."

"About what benefit are you talking, *Ma* . . . !"

"Can't you see? You have been provided with a river and a mountain."

Yes. Faraway, right in front of me, I could see a river with fresh water. And very far away I could see a mountain.

"What am I to do with this much water? What am I to do with such a bulk of rocks?" I enquired.

"After the air, your chief food is water. You could send your roots down to the river and fetch water. Water is the most essential food for living organisms. And about the mountain: Mountain maintains the climate of an area. Sooner or later the mountain would be covered by clouds. You could send your branches to pluck patches and patches of clouds. The plateau stretching before you has an active part to play in cultivation."

"Cultivation! This is a word that I've never heard, *Ma* . . ."

"It's not a mere word. It's an action packed with thrilling evolution. You are going to see it very soon".

"Explain it."

Mother explained, "You have air and water around. You are going to have a lot of subordinates. You'll be fascinated to see them. Your surroundings will be cherished. The soil can be prepared and used for crops."

"All of them my kind?"

"Different. Your kind and many other kinds."

"When are they coming?" I asked in anxiety.

"Wait and see," mother said. "It's a gradual process. I'll tell you a fact for your information. This very area had been fertile. The fashionable land had been occupied by all kinds of animate and inanimate beings— superior and inferior living creatures and attractive and fashionable inorganic things. Fully packed with the Kingdom of plants, the Kingdom of animals and the Kingdom of human beings."

"Then what and where are they?" I asked in surprise.

"Don't come before the bow while shooting, my dear tree-boy."

"I'm sorry. I will keep quiet," I gagged myself.

"Most of them had been superior to you, especially the human race. Years and years ago, there occurred a very bad and sad incident. This place was earlier a coastal city where an advanced civilization prevailed. All the heavenly bodies were jealous of me because this was such a marvelous city. I had valued that city like a diamond of my crown and was proud of it.

"Sun and Moon had jointly planned a monkey trick making the sea a monkey and me a stage. They ordered the nature to do the act, blaming darkness. In the hours after midnight, when the whole city was asleep, they created a depression at sea and hit the area with a cyclone.

"The tidal waves gained the height of giants and they were as long as the mountain in front of you. They rushed past the city, pell-mell, in lightning speed. The city was ruined! After the catastrophe, there was no trace of the city at all'.

"Where did the sea go?"

"The sea withdrew. It went miles and miles back. Waves behaved like hooligans trespassing a private property and destroyed everything they came across."

"Oh, poor souls!" I pitied.

"There were poor souls, of course. But sinners were there in great numbers."

"I wish I could have been one among the inhabitants."

"I wish your wish shall come true. Some symptoms are appearing. The first symptom you have already seen and experienced. Isn't it true?"

"Yes, yes. About the earthquake. Isn't it?"

"From where are those different kinds, different types and different patterns of pals coming? From Heaven or from Hell?" I asked.

"They won't and can't come back to me anymore. The saints went to Heaven and the sinners went to Hell. Gone means gone forever. Again, the area is to be repopulated either by migration of organisms from some other region or by creation of new organisms."

"OK," I said. "I understand the migration of organisms from some other fantastic and fashionable region after a catastrophe. It's my own case. But I don't understand the idea of the self-recreation."

"That's the theory of natural calamity. I had been, have been and would be subjected to natural calamities like quakes, floods and volcanic eruptions. I suffer cracks of crust, upheavals of mountain, landslides, formation of lakes, etc. Due to these catastrophes, the individuals in that region are destroyed. To understand evolution, the recreation of the organisms, you'll have to know my biography. Till now, have you acquired any knowledge about my origin?"

"I know it like a fiction—a tell-tale story told by the celestial bodies. But I don't know anything about your origin scientifically."

"I was part and parcel of my husband, King Sun. He gave me up when he married his fourth bride Mars. That time I was suffering from fever and my body was too hot. My temperature was more than 5000 degrees Celsius. I was pregnant too. I hate him because he threw me out in that condition. I lodged a complaint in the family court of nature. The verdict was: I should live far away from him; I should move around him; I should watch him lest he attempt violations on me.

"To compensate my services rendered to him, I should be provided with wind and rain to cool me down as alimony. I was given an assistant named Moon. I was pregnant and the embryo is still safe in the core of my body. My skin was cooled. The embryo is a combination of heavy elements like nickel, iron, copper, manganese, etc. The lighter elements like oxygen, nitrogen, hydrogen, carbon, etc occupied the air during my journey from the house of my husband.

"Normally, after a catastrophe, my crust is subjected to changes. If it's a place unfit for living organisms it shall turn to be fit and, if it's a place fit for living organisms it shall turn unfit. Your dwelling area, which was barren and where no organisms could originate and survive, turned good. All the unwanted solids, liquids and gases are evacuated and all the essential elements are introduced. All the harmful bacteria are eliminated and beneficial bacteria are created. Barren land becomes fertile and fertile land becomes barren.

"Development of micro-molecules into molecules and formation of pre-cell entities into cells would take place with the assistance of the atoms in the air, moisture and dust and photons in the sunlight."

"How did nature allow my birth and growth as this was an unfit habitat for living organisms?" I asked.

"That's the reason why you are said to be a celestial child. Maybe because you hail from a holy family of plants. Maybe because you are bold. Maybe because you are the most helping one. Maybe because you insist on justice. Maybe because you are a truthful tree-youth. Whatever be the reason, your birth and growth were the talk of the cosmos. Even the Omnipotent's secret eye couldn't trace it. That's why all the celestial bodies showered favors on you".

"Then why did they gag me?"

"The more you are growing, the more you a trouble-maker."

"Me, a trouble-creator! What are you talking about? If that is your impression, I didn't want to be earth-bound."

"It's not my opinion. You've challenged their authority. Though you demanded and advocated justice you gained their displeasure. That's why they gagged you. Make a note of this: Lawmakers are often law-breakers. They curtailed the extra-terrestrial properties awarded to you by The Almighty.

"Earlier, you had the ability to attain maximum growth and maximum size. You see yourself, not only your stem but also all your branches, leaves and fruits grew as per your internal urge. Your mind could have remotely controlled the growth as per your whim!

"But from now on you'll have to live according to the environment. If the land is fertile you'll lead a healthy and lavish life; if the land is not fertile, you'll be in Zulu condition. You may perish prematurely."

"It's better to perish rather than living like a corpse," I complained. "What are my duties? What are my hobbies? How'll I pass time?" I asked.

"Don't shirk away the responsibilities. You just forget your childhood, OK? You'll hardly have any time to pass. You'll be the senior-most in this habitat—the pioneer. Learn many things. Segregate good and bad things. Teach good things to others. Don't seek any kind of remuneration—even in the form of gifts. It's as good as accepting bribe. A teacher is a substitute for good.

"Now prepare yourself to receive your subordinates. From tomorrow it would rain for a week. The pollution in the atmosphere will be washed away. Rain will make wet the fertile soil. Next month, you're going to enter your third centenary. On that auspicious daybreak you'll receive newcomers. Don't treat them like fresh military recruits. Be polite to them. Help them in their growth. After a while they'll be known as the family of cultivation. Your habitat is going to turn into a most suitable dwelling place for all the creatures on earth. But watch your steps. They are in their tender stage. Don't try to seduce them into a life of crimes."

CENTURY 3

201 TO 300

The third daybreak of the third century of my life saw the opening of a new era in the plant life in my dwelling area. It was, of course, a very fine morning to me. It was quite the opposite for Sun. Sun, like a burglar, peeped from top of the mountain to the ground around me. He was reluctant to enter fearing that he might be caught red-handed by the newcomers. They had arrived the previous night. The amazing grotesque figures stunned the Sun. When he took his leave the previous evening there were no signs of the newcomers. As he departed, he had left behind nothing but the black and socked soil. To his surprise now, the newcomers looked like a column of green-uniformed regiment at parade.

The heavy downpour that continued for days had made Sun mad. He even forgot the fact that rainfall was one of his makings. He had listened to my dialogues with mother. He too had smelled a rat about the evolution that was due in my habitat. He did not like my mother's irregular menstruation at all. The conversion of her fluids into a river and the conversion of her solid matters into a mountain were not with his approval. He disliked the events.

My mother was watching her ex-husband whereas he did not bother about her dance around him. He disliked the progress of evolution occurring on her. It was against his desire that nature founded an evolution on my habitat. Once the foundation stone was in place, the construction would gradually get going. Sun had decided to play a monkey-trick again to ruin it all, but that would not be so easy always.

The Omnipotent too was watching. He knew that every nook and corner of the earth should be maintained according to the law of nature.

Polar Regions should be covered with ice and populated with penguins and pigmies; solar regions with humidity and human beings. It is his caprice to change a *terra rossa* into a plateau, a plateau into a delta, a delta into a desert, a desert into a sea, a sea into a mountain, a mountain again into a sea and so on and so forth.

Unable to challenge the authority of The Almighty, Sun finally decided to climb over the mountain and reached the sky. He panned his vision to the pageantry of my surroundings with a sullen face. The transformation of an infertile land into a fertile habitat disappointed him.

I could not confront him. I keenly and kindly looked down letting Sun go on his course. To a comprehensive view, the vast stretch of land resembled a green sheet of velvet, covering the length and breadth of my dwelling area. But for a closer view, the sight was not all that pretty. Undoubtedly, the land had become fit for cultivation. The formation of moss-type organisms, the newcomers, was a clear evidence of that.

Were they my colleagues? Were they my pals? Were they my relatives? Where did they come from? When did they come? Why did they come? For answers to the first three questions, I would approach my mother. The answer to the fourth question was that they came from my mother's lap. The answer to the next question was that they arrived the previous day. And the last question bounced on and off in my mind . . . Why did they come . . . ?

Were they extra-terrestrial? If they were, had they come just to see this world on a visiting visa? Or had they come to settle down permanently in this place with immigration certificates? Had they come as refugees? Were they gypsies on business tour? Were they carpet-baggers who sought fortune? My brain could not find out an answer to the question. So, without determining whether it was an emergency or not, I decided to get a clarification from my mother.

"*Ma*, in what way shall I consider these newcomers? As guests? As relatives, seniors, juniors, superiors, inferiors, friends or foes or . . . ?"

"*Dhudh* . . . *Dhudh* . . . *Dhudh* . . . stop it," mother got annoyed. "First of all, you should bear in mind that there are only two behavior patterns— decent and indecent. You should behave decently to all regardless of their dignity. And for *my* sake, always consider everyone as your friend. No foe is created by God. You may find someone as enemy due to the duty assigned to him by The Almighty. For example: Cats to rats and rats to grains; mongoose to snakes and snakes to frogs; frogs to mosquitoes and mosquitoes to man. All their activities of enmity are their activities for survival and sustenance.

"They prayed for their prey and God taught them the knack of preying. Thus population control also was achieved. Without this the whole world would have been jam-packed with all those creatures bringing in infinite increase in population."

"And, the newcomers," mother went on, "do not belong to any category you have thought about. They're also citizens like you. They are at liberty to live here like you. They shall eat what they get and shit when they want to. The only difference is that they are late-comers. And it's none of their fault. They were allowed to come only now.

"And being an early-comer, you have enjoyed enough and more facilities of this habitat. Let them enjoy too. It's their turn now. If you take them as your successors, they'll consider you as their predecessor. Give respect and take respect."

"*Ma*, whoever they are they make a pretty sight. Look at the ground."

"Now they look pretty. After a few days they would look prettier. A few more days later they would look the prettiest."

"I know you're their mother. Tell me something about their father. I didn't see any *Deserian* duck (duck from a desert), any crow or any vagabond bird that came to woo you?"

"They have no father. I'm their sole parent. You know I'm plural sometimes."

"How did they originate without a father? At least a process of pollination should have occurred. Am I right, *Ma*?"

"No, no, no," mother said. "It is a self or automatic evolution. In other words, transformation of certain inanimate things into animate beings. The Almighty has made a formula of a quadrilateral creation. The nature as a cosmic magician makes use of this formula without the knowledge of The Almighty".

"Which are the four sides of the quadrilateral creation, *Ma*?"

Mother explained. "Four essential powers are required for the creation of an organism from a non-organic entity. They are the air in the atmosphere (carbon dioxide, oxygen, methane etc), moisture (water particles), any raw material (soil, rock, dust) and the fire from the sun (atmospheric temperature to facilitate fertilization). For example, if you allow dust particles to remain undisturbed for quite a long period, you may find minute louse-like living things taking shape in the dust.

This is because of the absorption of water particles and heat from the atmosphere. This is a zoological example.

"Now an example for biology: You allow continuous water contact with any solid ground (rock, wood, sand etc). There would be formation of algae. They range in size from one-celled microorganisms to the giant weeds. They manufacture their own food using light energy. Another example: You see your skin (bark). You can find fungus on it. You are under the impression that it's your make-up. No. It's fungi. Fungi are a group of plants. They are parasites incapable of manufacturing own food. They absorb it from whatever host they are living on or in. It comprises a single-celled non-reproductive body. Reproduction of fungi is not known even to the so-called scientist 'nature'. It remains a secret with The Almighty.

"Another cryptogram is the bacterium. It is a unicellular organism found almost everywhere yet naked eyes cannot see it. It takes a variety of shapes like rods, spheres and spirals. Reproduction is usually by the simple splitting of a cell into two at frequent intervals at the required temperature."

Eagerly I said, "Can you narrate one more example pertaining to the spontaneous zoological evolution theory?"

Mother said, "You simply break one of your fallen berry lying on the ground and see what is inside. Among the many seeds you may find some germs. For all these developments the creation's quadrilateral formula is applied. Anyone out of these four elements is eliminated; there won't be life on me."

"I see," I said.

"For the transformation of inorganic compounds into organisms, a fifth significant power is required—the invisible force of The Almighty. Without this, the life in an organism is incomplete. Even if it is complete, it will be improper—some deformity, disfigurement, premature death and things like that occur."

"Do all these tiny tots hail from the same family, *Ma*?"

Mother said that the unfolding of these tiny tots was the first stage of evolution. The sequence of evolution: Gradual transformation of single-celled organisms into multi-celled plants. From plants to insects, from insects to amphibians, amphibians to reptiles, reptiles to birds, birds to mammals, mammals to monkeys and finally to man.

So, in a nutshell, these tiny tots might subsequently, slowly and steadily give rise to modified descendants of the simple life originated in the remote past. All the tiny and non-living articles on the earth are made up of atoms. The only difference among them is that the living things have life in it. Otherwise, all these organisms are as good as carbon at the end point.

Who is the giver of life? The Almighty. In evolution, the uninhibited power of The Almighty plays a significant role. Without that you would not have heard of ethics and epics. Some very prominent figures were born bastards. This is known as the evolution theory of spontaneous origin.

"So, I too can be proud of remaining a bastard," I said.

"That depends on the thoughts of a person. Actually, you are not a bastard. Yet you are said to be a bastard. There's a tendency in all the living individuals from remote past to spread rumors that won't match the truth. They pooh-pooh others. They won't even spare me though I am their mother." My mother lamented.

I sighed.

*   *   *

The platoons of plants placed in front of me stared pathetically at me as if they were not happy to have been enrolled in the academy of this world. I wondered what they would be thinking about me!

They were very small and I was very large both above and below the ground. I was certain that they could not measure my height or fathom my main root.

Like a parade commander, I wanted to deliver a lecture to them. But how would I address them? Dear pals? Comrades? No, no. All those terms looked very mild.

How about locking their hearts with timidity and hate by calling them, "You fools, you rascals, you bastards, etc", so that they would be compelled to pay respect to me? No, no, no. It is an uncivilized act.

The form of address should be civilized. It was not a single individual's meeting. They came *en masse* on this earth to live in a family of plants. I remembered that in the evolution theory, today's plants would be tomorrow's animals; tomorrow's animals would be next day's men; today's men would be tomorrow's ministers. There might be males and females among them. There would be production and reproduction. And they would form the society.

Taking all these past, present and future factors into consideration and without losing my dignity as an early-comer, I came to the conclusion that I should address them as juniors. No. Immediately I altered the course of my mind. If I call them juniors, they might call me senior. Why should there be this senior-junior complexity?

Though I was senior, I too hailed from a family of plants. So I was related to them. I should call them affectionately. Suddenly an idea emerged in my mind. I welded one male common noun to a female common noun: Brothers and sisters! Yes, if I address them so, what would they call me? Elder brother? No. Not at all. Possibly they would call me uncle. Good! An uncle had a respectable position in a family. In some societies uncle is the authoritarian. Finally, I intended to address them as brothers and sisters.

Before addressing, I wanted to alert them. They were in the stand-at-ease position. So, like a giant figure calling diminutive figures, I gave them an order.

"All plants, attention!"

No sooner did they hear my order than their loose bodies stood erect, bent leaves pricked, parted legs joined. They stood in a still and stiffened posture.

I called to them, "Dear brothers and sisters of the earth".

They listened in attention.

Again I commanded, "Plants, stand at ease."

They obeyed me by parting their legs sideways without relaxing.

Again I ordered, "Relax."

They relaxed.

Then, in a mild voice I said, "I'm Mr. Banyan. You may call me uncle. I welcome all of you on this habitat on behalf of my mother, sorry our virgin mother, Miss Globe".

"Good morning, instructor, sir. You may call us trainees," they said in unison. "Is there any objection in keeping a teacher-student relationship instead of keeping a (nephew) niece-uncle relationship?"

I wanted to burst into tears. I wanted to pluck my heart and throw it in the river. I wanted to break my useless brain into pieces. What a damn fool am I to see myself as an uncle of theirs!

It was mid-summer madness.

I decided to call them brothers and sisters because I felt it suitable. But, I could have addressed them as students. It would have been more suitable. And of course, as per their relation to me, the most suitable address was 'trainees'.

"You felt bad, sir?" They asked. "You being so big, we could see you only as a teacher. Teacher is next to The Almighty.

"Being so small, how do you know this?" I asked.

"Our veins—yours, ours and our mother's—carry the same blood. Don't you remember what our mother had once told you about the significance of a teacher?"

"Then call me teacher. Why this instructor?" I was a bit irritated.

"Teacher is the one who teaches, softly and mildly. He can only request the students to learn the lessons. Nowadays, the condition is such that the students may disrespect, disregard and discard the teacher, whereas an instructor does the job of a teacher with authority. He could command. The trainees are compelled to obey him even if they do not want to. We are new recruits and you are our instructor. We have to undergo training and you have to instruct us. This is the advice-cum-order from our mother."

Even though they were new recruits, they spoke as though they were senior cadets who had passed out from a military academy.

'*Chey*, at times, I'm just a fool,' I thought. I was too proud to have experiences of more than three hundred years on this earth. My intelligence, guts, health, everything was beaten up by these three-day-old shoots.

Owf . . . shame . . . shame . . . The shame made me think that a bulky character like me was fit for nothing but to be a pillar of a house.

Next week, I mustered them. "OK, trainees, contrary to my impression, all of you have good brains."

Some of them raised their hands intervening in my speech. "A high-brained should be highly trained, without which the personality of an individual won't develop. An untrained person is as good as a star without light".

I thought that they should have joined the cosmic academy and not the academy of the world.

I said, "You minors speak major philosophy!"

"Instructor sir, in special botany, a minor has got more thinking power. Take your case. The moment you were born you had thought of freedom. We have our regards to you for that kind of brave thinking. You're the harbinger of justice. You had left a landmark and we should steer by that.

'You have kept no stone unturned for the liberation of stars. We esteem you for that bold step. You challenged Sun for his partiality and prejudice. We respect you for that counseling.

"But as you grew up, the brain that was packed inside one shoot-tip was distributed among all the shoot-tips of all your branches, losing cohesion. So the concentration of your brain also scattered into fragments and subdivisions. In short, you have gained height, weight and bulk, but lost the power of brain. This is known as *disjecta membra* of the brain. We also have to face the same condition when we grow."

'My goodness,' I exclaimed to myself. This was new information to me. I did not know this because I was the only individual in this habitat.

Indeed it was a new knowledge given by the newcomers. A plant is born with a fully developed brain! As it grows into a tree, gradually the brain loses its power. A tree can grow for years and years, bigger and bigger. As the body ascends the brain descends.

Before reaching the zero stage of the brain, someone will fell the tree with an axe or saw.

There are two worlds on this earth—the world of environment and the world of entertainment. Biological organisms are the citizens of the environment world. Human beings are citizens of the entertainment world. The former never harms the latter. The latter always harms the former. The latter is never beneficial to the former. The former is always beneficial to the latter.

Nature hates the brutal killing of the biological organisms. To show the anger nature orders Sun to spread drought. In drought, human beings would die of thirst.

*   *   *

As all of them wanted to be trained as gentle plant-cadets to serve the world actively, I started giving them instructions in a military style. But I allowed them to choose the subject they liked most.

They said, "You being a disciplinarian please throw some light on *discipline.*"

The subject was as familiar to me as my foot (roots) without which I would not survive.

"Discipline is as essential to an organism as food is to a body because it is the system of rules and regulations of life. It is the instructions and exercises designed to train one to proper conduct and action. It is the punishment inflicted by way of correcting and training. It is the behavior in accordance with rules of conduct. It is an instrument of chastisement. It is a state of order and obedience by training and control with which to correct the trainee's way of life."

"Sir, we are not interested in your researches on the subject. We just want to know what's the importance of discipline in our normal day-to-day life."

I explained the use of discipline in practical life. "The foremost factor in a well-disciplined life is the turnout. You should dress well and that too correctly. Clean up yourself. When it rains, have a nice bath. Don't just let the water flow over your body and waste it. It's as good as wasting the chance.

"Do your make-up while Sun shines. It beautifies you. That action makes you grow to gain health, makes you bear more fruits to gain wealth and makes you think better to gain wisdom.

"Activate your branches and leaves, and if possible stem, when the wind comes. Don't stand like a statue and miss the opportunity. Welcome the wind and dance rhythmically. It's an exercise. It helps you to shape your body.

"The next important factor is the movement. All your movements should be very smart. One single blow of wind (light breeze) would create a small momentum, which would be amplified into a heavy wind by each one of you. Each and every momentum would be amplified to a heavy wind that could cool a wider area of our mother's body. Likewise we could serve our mother better.

"An individual is known by his movements. Everybody will praise you, if your movements are smart. Smarter the movements, greater the family, it is said."

They stood still as though they were listening to an unintelligible speech. I doubted whether they took my lecture as a factor or chatter. So, during stand-easy time, I tried to impress them by reminiscence.

When mother was free I met her and discussed the intellectual performance of the newcomers. In fact, I did not like their over-smartness. I was sure that they considered my lecture as gibberish. I hated their egotism.

Mother told me about their pathetic condition. Actually, they belonged to the family of weeds. "See how they have grown profusely. It's the nature's play to nourish valueless and troublesome creatures that inflict injury or make the life of valuable creatures miserable," she said.

Then I was annoyed with my mother for giving them that much lift.

Mother calmed me saying that they were also created by God. It was God who provided them the properties of a parasite. By virtue of luck I took birth as a divine Banyan tree. It is none of their fault that they have been born land weeds. That was the reason why mother had pampered them. After all, they were her children.

The more lamentable news about the weeds was that their life was limited to thirty days. They were guests for a few more days in this habitat. They should count down to their doomsday like cancer patients. But the matter was not disclosed to them. They were under the impression that they too had a pretty long life. After a fortnight they would be no more. I would find their dried up corpses everywhere.

From birth to death—with a short span of their life—they were ambitious to climb a mountain of knowledge. But the poor fellows did not know the fate to face. They were like participants in a marathon race, performing like sprinters. Being ignorant about their energy, they get exhausted before reaching the finishing line.

They complained to the mother that they did not have the terrestrial power of communicating with the heavenly bodies, as I had possessed the power once.

Their quest for knowledge was unending. But their life span was inadequate. Mother knew that. So, she transferred some knowledge to those little weeds, when they were in her womb. It was those arrows of knowledge that they were shooting me with.

When I heard about their history, I felt pity for them. How could I witness the sad demise of these many members of the plant kingdom? The whole habitat would undoubtedly look like *Kuruskhetra* after the *Mahabharata* conflict. The *Mahabharata* massacre was something tolerable. It had a purpose. It was a duel between *dharma* and *adharma*. But here, innocent plant infants who cherished their lives were going to perish without any reason and for no fault of theirs.

*   *   *

I wanted to rescue them from the furnace of fate. But Sun poured more oil into the fire. Sun had been gloomy since the arrival of the land weeds. The land weeds never felt the sunburn. They had not seen any damaging or destructive discharge of lightning.

They were comfortable in the air-conditioned climate. Within three weeks all of them grew up to be youths, eating and drinking the nutrients from the land as well as from the atmosphere. They passed their time learning lessons from me and playing among themselves.

Slowly, they cut short the study-time and increased the play-time. Excess of good things turns to excess of bad things. They played . . . played . . . played. Again played . . . played . . . played. Again and again played . . . played . . . played. They played till the play perverted to penalty. The penalty was such that no referee on earth could make a suggestion. Then the penalty led to offence. The offence was such that no judge on earth could pass a verdict.

They quarreled with each other. When the wind came they stretched their hands (veins) and pushed and pulled each other. The weak managed to fight with the strong. The weaker struggled with the stronger. The weakest surrendered to the strongest.

The riot spread like a contagious disease. The standard and status they maintained initially had been upset. They became the most non-disciplined and perverted beings on earth.

I recollected my mother's quotable quote:

Silence is best for the wise;

Violence is best for the vice.

So I stood block-headed.

Sun took advantage of their quarrel. Assisted by the clouds and Rain and with the consent of The Almighty, he decided to punish the land weeds severely: Massacre, total elimination, of the land weeds through drought. So Sun changed his policy.

He did not work properly. He dimmed his light to the minimum. He hid his boilers except one or two. Hence the production of steam from the water-filled area on the earth almost came to an end. The process of formation of clouds came to a standstill. Thus the chance of raining was ceased.

When asked, my mother replied that, it was a go-slow policy. As good as a tool-down strike. When one department of the cosmos was effected, the other departments and even the sections would also be affected by the movement. Because of their slackness, Sun could create scarcity of rain.

When all the storehouses of clouds were emptied, he looked down. He perverted the slowdown procedure by re-operating all his machinery to maximum capacity. He discharged intense heat to burn the land weeds.

He deployed many sunbeams to blind the weeds. He spread a blanket of humidity to make the weeds sweat.

I too was in a turbulent state by Sun's cruelty. Even mother was feeling uneasy.

He and his associates continued their wicked game for four days and postponed the cruelty. On the fifth day, the condition of the weeds became bad. They bent. On the sixth day, their condition became worse. They fell down. On the seventh day, they collapsed.

Their lives ceased. Their green color vanished. The color changed to a pale yellow. The entire habitat was filled with their dried up dead bodies.

Once upon a time they had been called the velvet-spread of the land. Now they were said to be the itching blanket of the land. Once upon a time, their presence had been a pleasure on the land. Now their presence choked the land.

Their glamour and guts were gone with the wind. Their life history became a fairy tale for the coming generations.

At last the mad Sun was happy to behold the sad fall of the land weeds. It was quite natural (or unnatural) that after a few days, when their corpses went back to the pavilion, the mother's womb served as their yard of germination as well as their graveyard.

Mother neither bothered nor lamented over the downfall of the downtrodden land weeds because it was nothing new to her. Because she had faced such situations many a time over many areas of her body.

I was the only one who attended their funeral and mourned their death.

During my life in the third century the birth and death of different kinds of land weeds with flowers and without flowers occurred about fifty times.

And it was the last day of the third century of my life when I heard the last post of their fiftieth funeral blown by the wind from somewhere.

CENTURY 4

301 TO 400 AD

After the fall of the land weeds, I was once again alone in the habitat. The solitude made me mad. After the massacre of the weeds, neither wind nor the clouds came that way. They too might have been repelled by the sight of the dried-up dead bodies. The weeds' space itself had become their burial ground. A sudden transition from beginning to end! A rapid transition from conquest to capitulate! A hasty transition from small heroes to big zeroes!

I wondered whether the land weeds could have built castles in the air. No. They did not have enough time to procure the materials for that. They were ambitious to grow. They were anxious to learn.

I recollected my mother's foretelling that I had good durability. Considering my durability, could I make durable castles in the air?

After witnessing the land weeds' doom, I determined to forget the past. I would think about the present and would never mind the future. So, giving up all hopes, well and bad, I thought only about my present and continuous situation.

The present situation vexed me. There was no one to talk to, no one to share the grief or the grace. Mother too did not care for me.

The presence of Sun harassed me. He knew that I was a perennial plant. He was annoyed when he created drought for I did not go frail. He disliked the fact that I did not lose my leaves. He always disliked me for providing shade to others. The land weeds beneath my shade had somehow withstood the heat for some time while those outside of my shade immediately succumbed to it. The fighters too surrendered finally. Sun misunderstood that I was making them confident.

What could I do? Asylum should not be denied to those who seek it. Chasing out a refugee is like throwing him into the mouth of death.

Contrary to my decision to forget the past, I was still thinking about the past.

I knew King Sun could do no harm to me. So I neglected him. My crown, like an umbrella, provided shade to my root system. My taproot reached far down to fetch water and minerals from the ground-water bed. My stem, branches and leaves enjoyed it.

Likewise, I lived merrily, spent time talking to myself, eating, sleeping and blinking at the vast unending land while awake.

One midnight, I heard a rhythmic beat of a march-past. As I woke up, I found that I was fully wet. It was raining heavily.

I wanted to ask a lot of questions to Mr. Rain. I wanted to know whether he had played any role in the massacre of the land weeds. But there was no way I could question Mr. Rain. The power of communication had been taken away from me long ago.

I wondered whether Rain wanted to tell me something to prove his innocence.

Sun did not come up. He used filters to dim his light.

It rained continuously and steadily for some days as though he was unloading some extra quota. Mother stored all the water in the water stores—the river nearby.

Then Mr. Rain went away.

I took advantage of the situation to take a nice bath, cleaning each and every hair (leaves) and soaking each and every limb (branches).

Though Mr. Rain stopped pouring himself down, I was dripping.

No sooner did Rain leave the place than Sun started firing all his guns. The sun guns showered extremely flat light everywhere.

After a couple of days the habitat turned a wonderland, like a cine dreamland! The whole habitat was packed with small, open, white umbrellas.

To my surprise, some baby umbrellas grew up to a height of one foot. The umbrella itself was half a foot in diameter. The umbrellas resembled whitewashed hutments with convex roofs. It was a spectacular scene! The transformation of a barren land into a dreamland.

Who manufactured all these umbrellas? I did not know. Who was the proprietor of this umbrella shop? What advertisement agency displayed all these umbrellas? Who was the sponsor of the show? I had no idea. I could not even know whether the umbrellas too belonged to a family of plants.

And the most astonishing matter was that they invaded my body besides invading the neighborhood.

How could they climb up my stem and establish themselves there without my knowledge? Are these creatures real? Or are they some spirits? I could not conclude anything.

Of course, one thing I could decide: Whatever they had done was against the law. It was not fair to trespass someone's property.

Angrily I said, "Aye, you trespassers, don't you feel shame to encroach upon private property? Who has given you permission? Let me know. Who the hell are you, boorish barbarians?"

There was an uproar.

"Do not call us barbarians. We're mushrooms. You got it, gaffer esquire?" They said in unison.

"Gaffer esquire!" I was stunned.

"Yeah, no doubt, you are our boss."

"Boss! Who told you this?"

"Who else? Your mother. Sorry, sorry, sorry, our mother," they mocked me.

I scolded them, "Did our mother advise you to intrude on other's body? Don't you know this is illegal? Do you know the exact meaning of the word trespassing?"

"We know pretty well. A wrongful entry upon the property of another with force: That is the exact meaning. But we have not committed any force."

They argued like real lawyers, throwing more light on the point.

But their law-point provoked me.

Angrily I said, "It doesn't mean that If A, B, C, D and E are operating an orphanage and you are the in-mates, and if the place and provisions are inadequate, you wicked fellows can make use of A's mouth as toilet, B's head as fire-place, C's chest as playground. It doesn't mean that if you are hungry, you will be industrious to use D's penis as water tap and eject the semen from E and make omelet."

"Oh! You have taken names of almost all the saints. We can only call you an esquire, not a saint."

"Esquire or four-square, I don't care. Tell me, will they thank you? That's the question."

"Understood, understood," said the mushrooms. "We have not encroached upon your body. It's the will of nature."

"I don't like such will. I'll take steps."

"You'll have to like it, Mr. Gaffer," they added. "You can take steps if a thief trespasses a house. But can you take steps if sea encroaches the land?"

I stood stunned.

"It's nature's will. As we are also the representatives of nature, you have to bear with us," they added.

"If so, tell me about your parentage," I demanded.

"You know that we are all the children of Miss Globe. *Ngaa*, about our father, nobody knows."

"Your instantaneous origin?"

"The production you mean? That was a monkey-trick played by fungi."

I told my mother that they should leave my body and mingle with others of their kind on the ground.

Mother explained to me with reference to the context: They might be argumentative, but they are harmless. I had no right to complain about their encroachment of the neighborhood. It was a no-man's land.

When I was born and occupied the spot where I'm standing now, no one questioned me. That was my need. When someone else needs the same, I should not object. Mutual help is inevitable. And so is mutual understanding.

It is God's policy that anything, a molecule or something bigger, has to occupy some space even if someone objects to it.

That is quite natural.

Long ago, a godhead, who was supposed to be born in a palace, was born in a prison. Years back another godhead, who was supposed to be born in a castle, was born in a cattle-shed.

I have a sturdy body. As parents take their children on their shoulders, I too should carry the mushrooms.

One must give support to those who need it.

I get support from the earth, Sun, Rain and Wind. So I should support the mushrooms.

I did not want to know whether the mushrooms could support somebody.

Eventually, I understood that a dwelling place is an individual's right. If one does not have it, the haves have to provide it.

So I asked mother whether I should render some other services to them other than supporting them on my branches.

Mother advised me to enlighten them with some lessons in ethics.

"I know," I said to the mushrooms, "that all of you are very proud of your white body. But you should not be so proud that you lose your prestige. Remember, you possess a delicate body. Color can't help you to be sturdy. It is better for your health to lead a moral life rather than an arrogant one."

"We don't know anything about moral life. Can you teach us?" They asked.

My gibberish was that the ethics of an individual should be model to others. "Be of better service to others and your moral sheen will be brighter. The more you polish your morality, the more will be the growth of your personality. You might not have heard of the eminent personalities who had sacrificed their lives for others' sake. They will be remembered. They are eternal. The rest are remembered as dead matter.

"Attach more importance to your subordinates' needs than yours. Save someone's life by giving up yours. Then only you will be known as life-savers. If you save your own lives who gets the benefit? You. Who'll thank you for that? Nobody. You can thank yourselves."

I taught them how to distinguish between right and wrong, good and evil, virtue and vice. "Try not to depend on others. Self-help should be the motto of life. About company: keep Company for the sake of companions. Work collectively. Work a little harder than other members of the cooperative. Collective effort can move a mountain, make a monster mourn.

"Do not neglect the weak and weary. Extend a helping hand before others do so. You should be the first to help a hapless person."

When I got up the very next morning I found the mushrooms taking a pledge to lead a life full of moral values.

I told mother that the toadstools were not only pretty but also prompt. I asked her whether she could foretell the future of the toadstools.

Mother said, "Let's wait and see. These are the different stages of evolution—from nothing to something, from something to a non-living thing, from a non-living thing to a living thing and from a living thing to everything."

I said, "I think, *Ma*, this is a stage of the living thing. When will the stage of everything come?"

"It's already started."

"But I have come across the land weeds and mushrooms only," I became curious.

"Actually, the stage of living things has got two divisions. One division comprises the family of plants—immobile living things. The other division comprises the animal kingdom—mobile living things. In other words, a biological stage is bifurcated into botanical and zoological divisions."

"Look, *Ma*, I too can move." I moved my branches to show my ability to move.

"Don't do the static run. Plants can move their body only from where they stand. Even for that the plants need the help of some external force, like wind or rain. Are you able to move from one place to another?" Mother got annoyed. She added, "For that someone has to uproot you. And if you are uprooted, your story is over."

Mother's statement forced me to think of my handicap.

I asked her with curiosity, "How many kinds of zoological staff are there? What do they look like? When are they coming?

"Innumerable," mother said. "They are of different kinds. Even The Almighty—the Creator—does not have the numbers. Some have already arrived as your neighbors. Why can't you see in your berries?"

I remembered what my mother had told me about the germs inside the berries.

I looked down at a fallen berry. I could not believe my eyes. A small creature was trying to come out of the berry.

Along with that I saw beings of many species crawling on the ground. They seemed to be escaping from a confinement.

Some of them were trying to climb on me. Some were already clinging to my branches. Some were making use of my leaves as double-cots and sleeping tightly. All sans my consent.

I was irritated. I shook my branches and leaves.

Coldly I said, "*Ma* . . . ! What on earth are these creatures? Are these you once called the *germs*?"

"This also is a process of evolution—transformation of a germ into a worm. A germ is the ancestor of a worm."

"Who is responsible for their germination? You?" I asked.

"I've no concern about their parentage. I'm not the mother of animals. I just accommodate them. They board, lodge and grow on me. That's all," she said.

"Then how will I find out? *Ma*, shall I ask them?"

"Little did you aware of your limitations. You can't communicate with them. They have their own language and hearing aids. Yours are entirely different from theirs. Even otherwise, how can a family of plants mingle with a family of animals?"

"Then who are their parents?" I persisted.

"May be the atmosphere." Saying so, Mother fell silent filling despair in me.

I knew that I could not communicate with the atmosphere anymore. So I pursed my lips.

An individual born out of the wedlock is said to be a bastard. One who has lost his parents is said to be an orphan. What is the term to refer to one who has had no parents at all? A dash!

I tried to invent a suitable word to add to the vocabulary. But my attempt bore no fruits. As I learned more about evolution, I inferred that most of the plants and animals were either fatherless or motherless, or without both the parents.

The worms crawled here and there like locomotives at a shunting yard. As I watched the process I saw that some other creatures were engaged in work en masse. They had a unique structure: Two bulb-like things mounted on six legs. The bulb in front acted as head and the rear one as tail.

I was fascinated to see their work. They were transporting a fallen berry. It was a joint venture. They stood around the berry and moved it with collective effort. The berry was made to roll. Though they were busy pulling and pushing the berry with great zeal and enthusiasm, the progress was very slow.

Their work resembled to that of the slaves who transported capstone for the largest pyramid in the desert. But there was a difference. There the work was compulsory whereas here it was voluntary. I liked the team-work of the six-legged creatures.

I was curious to know their identity. So, I asked my mother, "*Ma*, just behold those two-bulbed, six-legged creatures! I want to get their details."

I learnt from my mother that they belonged to the family of ants. These ants were black but there were ants of various colors. The Army were carrying their food stock. The berry must be very tasty to them.

I said, "Just see their unity."

"Their unity is unique," mother said. "Their energy and efforts are just wasted. If you observe them closely, you'll come to know of their foolery. If some are pushing the load in a certain direction, others are pulling it in the opposite direction. They have no knowledge of the laws of motion and so this idiocy goes on."

"Then how does the load move?" I asked.

"The load will move to the direction to which more force is applied."

"Are they brainless and leaderless?" I asked. "Though they are inter-acting well the efforts are counter-productive."

"They have brains. But they are not using it properly. They are leaderless, yet they are all leaders."

"So," I said, "the ants are a collection of fools. Isn't it, *Ma . . . ?*"

"A collection of fools or a collection of scholars—that is immaterial—there should at least be one idiot to lead them. Then only they can perform a task perfectly."

Then I realized the value of supervision. I pitied the foolish ants that unnecessarily wasted labor for lack of supervision.

Though the method was foolish, their work seemed funny. As I watched, I saw a peculiar type of creature from the animal kingdom. The creature was a quarter the size of a berry.

It moved from one berry to another without touching the ground. I watched that pretty-looking and fast-moving creature for a long time.

Mother told me that those creatures belonged to the family of birds, which my female father belonged to. They were winged but came under the category of insects, the flies. They sucked sweet juice from the berries using their stings.

I was fascinated by their free movements, now ascending and now descending. They landed and took off at will, fascinating me further.

Seeing their acrobatics a desire arose in me to have a pair of wings so that I could fly in the sky. However, it was just a dream.

Mother asked me to be cautious about some winged beings, especially the mosquitoes.

I knew the truth of mother's advice when I confronted their suicidal attack at night.

*   *   *

It was a fine morning for all the organisms, including me, of the habitat. But it was not so for the so-called toadstools, the mushrooms.

They were energetic the previous day. Now they seemed very dull and colorless. The next day they became weaker. After some more days, their piles shrank and stems bent and the umbrellas were torn.

When I expressed my concern, they desperately said that the day for their departure was nearing. There would be no massacre. It would not be a mass suicide. It would be a quiet and natural departure as mushrooms were just an annual breeding group. Sooner or later some other breed would eliminate them.

"For every encroachment, there is an equal and opposite eviction," they admitted.

Before parting, they wanted to pay respect to mother and me, thank other organisms that came to the land as their descendants, especially the moss and algae in the river, shrubs and the bushes of the mountain.

Prior to bidding farewell they sang a song flattering the earth:

Beauuuuuutiful! Beauuuuuutiful!!

My land iiiiiis very Beauuuuuutiful!!!

Looooved to live, Looooved to live

We Looooved to live on the laaaand of love.

Wiiiished to serve, Wiiiished to serve

We Wiiiished to serve on the land of love

Haaaappily, haaaappily

We haaaappily bid farewell to you . . .

We haaaappily bid farewell to you . . .

We haaaappily bid farewell to you . . .

As they sang, the volume of their voice decreased gradually and finally the voices faded away totally.

Even before they could complete their chanting, all of them collapsed—the strength, vigor and vitality left their falling bodies. All the organisms of the habitat mourned their death while the land was prepared to bury the bodies.

*   *   *

All these days, I was thinking about the area around me. The toadstools had mentioned in the anthem of agony about the algae and moss in the river and the grass and shrubs on the mountain.

I raised my head a little so that I could see the riverbed as well as the riverbank. I understood that the toadstools were correct.

Clad in moss, most of the stones there looked like bastard emeralds. Algae grew here and there on the riverbed. There was also some fodder along the riverbank. The grasses were dancing rhythmically in the wind. Snails and weeds also were playing in the fresh water.

The mountain was covered with shrubs and grass. The greenery there resembled that of a dense forest. To my eyes, the mountain looked like a sleeping dragon, covered head to foot with a made-to-order green blanket.

The grotesque mountain rejoiced me. I watched the bizarre scene till my eyes were overpowered by the sunshine. I zoomed in my sight from long to close range.

The neighborhoods remained still soaked in the heavy rain that had visited the area some days back. The earth was yet to absorb the decaying bodies of the toadstools. It seemed that some gypsies in transit had occupied the area and left without cleaning it. I insisted upon cleanliness because I hated dirt.

I decided to send all the stock of my stack as cleaning staff (brooms) to clear up the area. Thinking of the risk involved and apprehensive of the shame baldness would bring to me, I revoked the decision.

Thank God I did not send my cleaning staff. The scene of the land made me shiver and I shed cold sweat. The earth beneath the anchorage of the dead bodies of the toadstools was found loosening. The decayed bodies were moving!

Ngea! Was nature, the magician, trying to make the corpse walk? Was it a metamorphosis? When I observed closely, I saw a new kind of worms emerging from the bodies of the toadstools. Thousands and thousands of worms came out of the ground. They crawled over the ground like LPG trailers piling along the parking lanes of an oil refinery.

These too belonged to the category of worms, hailing from a different class. One class came from the heavens—aloft (from the berries). The other class came from the hell, from below the ground. What a wonder! The Creator, The Almighty and the Omnipotent—God—is great. What was the purpose behind the creation of these creatures?

To harm or to help?

I had ants in my pants. I asked my mother about them. She told me that they were also the ancestor stock of worms. Unlike other parasites that bored in to timber or ate dead bodies, this creature was not harmful. These worms were called the earthworms. They are said to be nature's plough, farmer's friend, growling person, etc.

They burrowed in earth and fed on earth.

After showing their presence, all of them went back to their dwelling place.

All the dead bodies of the toadstools got powdered and mingled with the earth.

Subsequently, some weeds with lots of flowers occupied the vacant lot. The flowers were very attractive. They always laughed. They never cried because they never knew grief. The only job they knew other than smiling was to say good-bye to the passers-by.

No sooner did a breeze come than the flowers waved their body.

As soon as a wind came, the flowers oscillated themselves like bidding farewell.

There was meaning in their actions. They were prepared to say good-bye at any time. The plants survived, the flowers fell. So they said good bye in advance as if they knew what was in store for them.

*   *   *

So many organisms were appearing on and disappearing from the habitat that I decided to prepare a nominal role of the inhabitants according to size, type and kind and as per seniority.

As the senior-most, it was incumbent upon me to keep a record of the entire fauna and flora. As the tidings spread out in the habitat, there were storms of objections among the fauna and flora over seniority. They were on the verge of a fight.

I interfered to put an end to their quarrel. I wanted the fauna to understand the need of the list. I was not sure whether they understood my speech.

They had their own zoological language. We had our botanical language. Plants and pests did not have a common biological language.

But one sure thing was that the pests could identify me as a tree, could recognize my berries as food and leaves as shelters. Plants could distinguish between pests that were harmful and beneficial and identify their sting and teeth as weapons. So an interaction was possible, after all.

Even otherwise, it was quite natural that the deaf and dumb, who had no viva-voce, understood each other easily. More over my experience of mingling with the fauna helped me to exchange ideas each other.

Hence I decided to hear their arguments.

The faunas' argument was that though most of them were not seniors, they had the ability to move; they were agile. The flora was immobile and lethargic. Who would serve the society better? An individual brimming with smartness or an individual constrained by laziness? Who deserved prominence? So the list should be made not as per seniority but as per ability.

The argument was genuine. I appreciated it. Still I had to consider the case of the flora too.

Being a flora family member and as the senior-most individual of the habitat, I tried to convince the faunas.

I said, "Senior is senior. An individual could be senior by a day. He cannot be made junior by any means. Not even nature can alter it.

"If I was born today and you yesterday, how could I be senior? A day lost is a day lost. It cannot be recovered. Till now, the theory of seniority has been that the early born is senior to the late-born babies.

"From now on, if you want to amend the formula of seniority, as last come will be senior to all those who have come already on the surface of the earth, you may. But if you adopt such a formula, when you become a father, your son will be your senior, when your son becomes an uncle, his nephew will be his senior.

"A senior is always respected. If not, a father would have to bow to his children. If not, a son would teach his parents such a lesson that they would have to repent. They would have to grieve for begetting a son, who is senior to them. He would teach his parents how to beget a child."

There came the fauna's reactions: "Does it mean that the parents alone are to be respected? And the children are only to be disrespected?"

"I didn't mean that. When the parents are alive, they are revered. Not the children. When children respect the parents, parents love them. What I'm trying to say is that elders are always seniors."

"What about our qualification?" they interrupted.

I said, "You mean your ability to move?"

They nodded.

I said, "Your movements may help you. It won't serve society. Immobile things can also help the society. Can you make your house move? Can you dwell without a house? Most of the plants provide shade and shelter to most of you most of the time. Isn't it? So, here, for making an inventory, I came to the conclusion that it is the seniority and not the ability that is taken as criterion. And I'm here to add that your ability will be taken into consideration for certain things and on other occasions."

All the inhabitants listened with great attention to my sermon.

And my preaching convinced them.

Yet, I did not want to harm the thorn as well as the leaf. I did not want to show favoritism to my family, the flora.

So I had drawn a circle in my mind, separating it into segments with radii. I started writing the biodata of the inhabitants in the segments like cardinal points in the compass card.

Likewise the senior-junior problem and the inferiority-superiority complexes were solved simply without any serial numbers.

The last individuals enrolled from fauna's side were the honeybees and the lizards. And from the flora's side came the plantain group from far end of the north and the citrus group from the mountains. They were not old enough to bear the fruits.

The first name I wrote on the circular list was that of the red rose. Everyone objected to it, even members of my own family. The reason was that it has a vine with thorns on its body.

"Our category is the biggest flower on our mother earth, so . . ."

"Oh, you're from Titan arum, isn't it? You're mistaken my dear. Firstly, Rafflesia is the largest; secondly, how can one stand your rotten rat smell!"

"Yes, yes," the members shouted unanimously, "we can't bear it."

And I saw the protesters' nausea.

"But it's none of our fault; it's God given . . ."

Somebody from the animal lot said, "God given bad smell is the result of your bad life in the past."

Others said, "We've no objection, let Red Rose be first on the roster."

But I knew that the harder and uglier they were on one side, the softer and more beautiful they were on the other. When they witnessed the blooming of the roses, they unanimously praised me and began to love the roses.

Thus the dispute was settled without much trouble.

*   *   *

It was a consolidated list. I did not know if the list was free of errors. New types and kinds of organisms, botanical and zoological, were coming in every minute. The birth rate was very high.

Some were self-germinated either by fungi or by bacteria. Some were reproduced either by pollination or by copulation.

Each carnivorous breed had its own way of living, a way of preying: Some by spreading their net (trapping method) some by direct attack (by force) some seizing by the claws as a kite (hijacking) and some by the hunting method.

Folks belonging to other races usually became prey to these folks. Some preyed on individuals of own race: They made omelet out of their own eggs, some cooked the meat of their own children and ate it.

What to say! There were plenty of highwaymen, thieves, burglars, hooligans, etc. Malefactors outnumbered benefactors in the kingdom of animals.

It was a tough task to computerize all these data. Somehow I managed to write down a biological list with the chalk of my memory on the black board of my mind. It was the first history ever made of the civilization of my habitat.

* * *

After a long period, I felt the desire to compile the geographical data of the habitat. Towards the east, I took the mountain as boundary.

The mountain stood there like a Chief security officer controlling entry and exit. I wondered whether a more civilized habitat existed on the other side of the mountain.

The river originated at the peak of the green mountain and flowed towards the west. I did not know where her destination was. She made her way busily as if she wanted to meet her lover residing somewhere in the west. During the rainy season she flowed passionately and pell-mell over the rocks like a rock-n-roll dancer making the spectators follow her curls and curves lustfully.

Seeing the river's milky color, some individuals in the habitat thought that it was the semen discharged from the manhood of the green mountain rushing to the vagina of the blue sea in the west.

Some others thought that any barren female, who drank that semen would develop embryo inside her. Any impotent male who drank the semen of the river would get sexual power, still some others thought.

I too believed this because of the egg-white color of the water. But my roots that drank the river water remarked: Unlike rain and groundwater, the river water was precious. My leaves also said they heard a flattering song sung by the citrons when they came to enroll. They sang:

Oh! What a water in our river!
You ask our mouths—it's sweeter than honey
You ask our hearts—it's better than fury
Oh! What a water in our river!

If your rain water is good,
If your groundwater is better,
Our river water is the best.
O! What a water in our river!
It's full of minerals,
It's full of medicines,
It's more balanced than your mother's milk.
O! What a water in our river!
It's thicker than the thickest
It's thinner than the thinnest
It's very easy to digest
Oh! What a water in our river!

But mother took away everyone's superstition: "The river is a gift from the nature to *fulfill* the purpose of cultivation and for the consumption of the inhabitants. Unlike so many rivers I have, this particular river has certain properties. The song sung by the citrons has more facts than flattery. All the citrons—orange, lemon etc,—contain citric acid. The fungus of these citrus fruits is an antibiotic that eliminates the harmful bacteria in the body of the water. That's why it's said to be medicinal. You may say the river is the circulatory tract of this habitat."

I agreed with mother. Still, I did not want to shatter somebody's superstition.

So, I let go all those ships with myths and facts.

Coming back to make a map of the neighborhoods, I considered the sea as the western boundary. The sea was not visible. I was certain; I might be able to see the sea when I attained more height, after a century or two, perhaps.

North and south had no landmarks. I assumed the respective horizons as the respective sides and the zenith as the upper top boundary and the top of the mantle as the bottom boundary.

A mandate was made: To safeguard the territories.

I chose a Capital—the place where I resided and its vicinity. I could judge. All the inhabitants agreed.

I marked my capital in the chart, selecting stretches of acres of land around my dwelling space. I detailed some tall plants to survey the area.

I named the capital *Massacre* for two reasons.

Firstly, the title was a combination of two words, mass and acre. The physical meaning pertained to nothing but acres and acres of land.

Secondly, these acres of land had witnessed three types of massacre.

No 1—the extermination of land weeds fifty times.

No 2—the annihilation of toad-stools many times.

No 3—the carnage of winged termites from the family of ants a number of times.

A pathetic story, as big as life. The most instantaneous and cruelest massacre ever occurred on the surface of the earth. Within a very limited time, unlimited number of winged termites were slaughtered by some unknown force leaving the world wars far behind in terms of casualties.

The whole habitat was asleep.

Like hearing an "attack-imminent" order, during action-stations, all of a sudden the winged termites came en masse flying like fighter planes from somewhere.

Nobody knew what had happened. But it happened.

The habitat woke up at daybreak. The flying squad was stained. Some without wings. Some without cockpit (head). Some without belly (abdomen). Some intact, but without life.

One thing was common. None had the black box (brain) without which an enquiry into the tragedy was impossible.

Silence pregnant with suspense prevailed.

There was unhappiness over the unfortunate incident. None of the inhabitants mourned. There spread a rumor like a wildfire—the termites were the secret agents from some other habitat.

No rescue party was sent. No salvage clearance party was formed. There was no Red Cross.

The opinion of the majority was: Let the bodies of the winged termites decay into manure.

The opinion looked like a bloodless eye. As it was the opinion of the majority, I had to agree with it. I kept quiet.

The fauna suffered a mono-massacre (only termites) and the flora a dual one (land weeds and toadstools). The area suffered a three-dimensional massacre. In fond memory of the dead, the capital was named after the stereo-massacre as *Massacre*.

All the mobile and immobile organisms were related to that mass massacre, and all of them agreed to name the Capital Massacre. All of them further agreed to assemble at Massacre to commemorate the threefold massacre.

That decision was the first to be unanimously applauded by the inhabitants. I appreciated their attachment towards their ancestors.

When I studied their hearts, I couldn't differentiate between my heart and theirs.

Coming back to the subject of sub-division of the land, there came the problem of representation from different parts, where my sight could not reach.

They sent messages by Wind and Rain. Demanding that the allocation of the sub-divisions of the land should be race-wise or branch-wise, so that they could develop their own culture and customs and also invent their own language.

I disagreed. That practice would develop a regional spirit of language, customs and culture in them. That might affect the strategy of the land. For the sake of patriotism, there should be a common custom, common culture and common language. This should be applicable to all the citizens of the country. Mixed culture, mixed language and mixed customs could lead to terrorism in due course. Physically and mechanically, we are from various families. Mentally and morally, we are from one single family.

"That may lead to boredom and suffocation in due course," some young Tigers remarked.

I replied, "As a citizen of this country, it is incumbent upon you to lead a unify-family life mentally and morally.

"Who knows that we're mentally and morally prepared to lead a 'one-family' life? Someone may pretend to. But some may wish to lead the physical and mechanical life of an individual family. Practically that's what's happening."

"My dear poppet," I said to them, "don't think my crown is a roof. Don't think each plant has a place left for each parasite to live. Plants too need roofs. Don't think each furrow is home, each trench a dwelling. Because they also need a ground to remain on". I went on, "You take it as granted, I'll prove that there is only one home mechanically, physically and practically for us. You look up. There is only one roof—the sky. You look down. There is only one floor—the earth. You see around. There is only one wall, the horizon. Here you have only one house, where we live in collectively."

My remarkable speech shook their minds. Again there was applause from the crowd.

Still they enquired, "Do we have any freedom?"

"Why not?" I exclaimed. "You write any number of lyrics. Sing any number of songs. But, the national anthem should be only one."

All of my botanical and zoological friends pricked their ears to listen to my patriotic address.

Little did I know how far my speech had won their hearts, especially some of the sons of guns. Whether they liked it or not, like a monarch, I declared the habitat as a sovereign country giving them more rights than duties.

Again I said, "You are at liberty to do any job which may bring fortune to our country. You are at liberty to perform any task, which may bring glory to our country.

"But mind it. I won't tolerate a mountain of glory to be adulterated by a stone of disgrace. I won't tolerate a sea of fortune to be adulterated with a drop of treason. Such cases shall be severely dealt with without delay."

I knew their habit. If I turned softer they would become harder. So, like an in-chief of all the forces, I commanded them.

"We have already named the capital Massacre. Now let's name our nation also."

I asked each and every individual to select a name. I asked them to write those names on leaves. Selection would be made by lot.

First day of the following week was the last day of the running year. We thought of celebrating that day with the "Naming the Nation" ceremony.

Everybody agreed to assemble on that day. That would be an auspicious day for the public and as much an auspicious day for me.

I kept it as a secret. The secret was . . .

CENTURY 5

401 TO 500 AD

It was no top secret. The day of Naming the Nation ceremony was my four hundredth birthday.

Everyone of the habitat was present. I disclosed the secret to them. Some were happy that the celebrations were on a two-fold purpose. Some were disappointed that they missed a chance for another get-together. They wished that my birthday be celebrated some other day. They were in a good mood. The interactions did not long last.

The weather was clear. A sunny day. But we heard the sound of a fast approaching rain. It was from the river-side. We focused our attention on a scene of anarchy. A collection of birds descended on the river surface. They drank so much water from the river that they seemed to be tired of completing many marathons at a single stretch.

Again there was pandemonium. More and more birds landed on the surface of the river.

The intruders were interrogated: What the hell . . . ?

They replied: Something's befalling. Something's befalling.

Again the question: Where the hell . . . ?

Not here. Not here.

Again the question: Then . . . ?

But there. But there.

Their eyes were filled with fear and confusion. There was din. Listening to their gibberish, I had ants in my pants.

"Come on; tell me specifically, who are you? What are you? And why do you intrude into our territory?" I asked them in a *forte-piano* voice.

They drank water . . . Took long breath . . . Relaxed . . . Then they said, "We are known as *Deserian* ducks. We're coming from Cheenisthan. A country with lots of cultures."

After a pose, they suggested, "By the by, if you can't hear us, we'll come close to your feet."

I said, "All mathematics."

"*Ngea*, what's that usage?"

"All the same."

"Oh! We see," they added after an expression. "In Cheenisthan, neither we could understand anybody's language nor could anybody understand ours. Here at least we can communicate with each other. So, we are very glad to visit this place."

"We are also happy to have you here. On behalf of all the inhabitants on this habitat, I salute you. If you would like to have, we have our famous berries for you," I invited them.

"No, thanks," said the ducks. "We won't take berries. It may cause diarrhea. We normally take grains. For the time being we don't need anything. We had enough of your celestial water."

"Our water is very famous," said the citrons.

"Indeed, indeed. We, Cheenisthanis also have heard that this river full of milk. It is believed that there is a river originating right at the Milky Way and falling on some part of the world. It is more balanced than any liquid on earth. The moment our beaks touched this water, we sensed its wonderful quality. And we're contended to have this juice of nature."

"Thank you for the flattery mixed with facts," I said. "Now you please go ahead with your narration."

"We belong to the migrating class. Whenever severe cold comes, we wander seeking warmth. When intense heat comes, we take off to cold countries."

A curiosity grew in me.

Is my father one among them? If so, I wanted to show him (her) the magic of my muscle, the magic of my mind. As a monarch, I arbitrated in the area. I wanted to show him (her) that a sand-sized seed from his (her) shit had grown up to touch the clouds of the sky. My taproot, once thinner than hair had developed to reach down touching the innermost wall of the uterus of the earth. I was in a reminiscent mood.

Four hundred years of steady growth. As a fatherless child, I had eaten enough cakes of defamation baked in the bakery of mockery. I fought the battle of life single-handedly, that too bare-handed—alone without sword and shield.

Now, I was the ruler of this country: A 100-foot tall king with a weight of twenty tons and a maturity of 400 years.

What if he (she) happens to know this? Will he (she) believe this? Or will he (she) wonder? The most unimportant matter (shit) from his (her) body once upon a time had caused the birth of a very important personality (me, the ruler)!

Would someone believe this? Even my colleagues would not believe the story of my parentage. They might lend their ears only with the interest of hearing a fairy tale.

If at all my father was among those numerous birds, the effort to identify him (her) was as tedious as counting the stars.

I was ashamed to ask the birds lest they should pooh-pooh me.

I was in doubt whether my father was alive. If not, what might have been the cause of his (her) death? Was it a natural death? Or did he (she) become the target of some hunter? I was morally and emotionally disturbed.

So, I let go my anxiety as well as curiosity. I was contented. After all, even if I could not find and talk to my father, I had seen, met and talked with thousands of my father's kith and kin.

"What were you telling me about something happening somewhere?" I asked the birds.

"We can predict the nature's behavior. Any moment, there's going to be a movement. A quake followed by an eruption. An eruption followed by a quake. Either a quake or an eruption. Or both simultaneously. No living thing will survive that. Even the strong will perish."

"*Aare*, how do you know this in advance?" I was surprised.

"The superior-most being on earth to date is the human being. Even they do not know about this. If you have something to write, you record our words: The country of Cheenisthan will change into *Registhan*, a desert."

No sooner did the birds say these words than there heard and saw an eruption far behind the mountain. Fire of gold was spurting like huge pillars coming up and collapsing quickly. The construction and the collapse of the pillars continued in quick succession—the magic of nature. And the last item of that magic show left us stricken with panic.

As I was very tall, I could see the golden fire behind the mountain very well from long off. It was like a group of giants with golden garments performing skip-jump at intervals in different parts of that country.

I witnessed it like a minor watching a *major* fireworks event.

The scene! The eyes and ears were fascinated. Really marvelous, fantastic, wonderful to the eyes and ears. What about the heart and nerves? To them it was unbearable.

All of us fell sick.

"*Aiiii aiii ooo!*" I exclaimed. "What would be happening in Cheenisthan now?"

The birds said, "Those capable of movement will be moving, flying, running, walking or crawling. Those unable to move will be shivering, quivering and trembling. Finally dying."

"Poor souls," all of us sighed in grief.

Somebody shot out a question in curiosity: "Where has the fire of gold gone"?

"It looks like gold and works like fire. The hottest matter on the globe, the lava."

"Laaa vaa!"

"Yes, lava," said the birds. "Its brightness can fuse your eyes if you look at it. You touch it and your hands will melt. The funniest thing would be, all the vegetarian food and non-vegetarian food would be cooked in one pot."

I said, "We can't follow you".

"Here, we think, you have only uncooked food. Why? Because this habitat is inhabited with only faunas and floras. No human beings."

"How do they look like? Beautiful? Ugly? Good? Bad? White? Black? Kind? Cruel?"

"Enough . . . enough . . . enough," The birds interrupted. "They are mixtures. They are poor in everything, can't bear much cold, heat or strain. Yet they are rich. Very rich. Very very rich."

"Rich in what?"

"Rich in the brain."

"Brain?" It was an exclamatory question.

"*Ngaa,* the brain. The brain can give answers to all the exclamatory questions as well as all the interrogative exclamations."

"Are they that superior?" I asked.

"Yeah. When we are known as non-thinking—beings, they are the thinking beings. They are very much sentimental and emotional. We just eat and shit. They . . . they create lots of things. Their power is boundless. Especially the power of thinking."

"We do think . . . ," some of the inhabitants interfered.

"You are right, partially," said the ducks. "Our greatest thinking is limited to just two subjects. Food and self-defense. Nothing more. We seldom care for other things. On the contrary, their thinking power will look like an ocean in comparison. Ours is just a few drops. That power comes out from the mind. The mind cares for one to all disciplines not only on earth but also in the whole cosmos."

"What's the weight of the mind and shape of the mind? If we eat it, we too will gain that power," a carnivorous creature put in.

"It is shapeless, and has no weight. Yet it is the heaviest, strongest, largest, longest and fastest in the whole universe. It is just a spirit. By the by, what's your name?"

"I have no name", said the carnivorous being.

"You nameless and shameless creature, don't be under the impression that you too can join the fall-in of the human beings."

"I just told you my ambition."

"Is it an ambition? It is greed."

After a pause, the ducks added, "So, we were telling you about the mind power of the man. The most significant power of the mind is the power of imagination."

Pointing at the carnivorous, a tree-lad said, "He also has wishes to become a man."

"What was his imagination? About eating. Can we imagine something creative?"

"Forget it. Man eats us both—fauna and flora. But we can't eat man."

I objected, "My mother told me once that there were man-eaters in the animal kingdom. Is it true, ducks?"

"It's very correct, your lordship. But man cooks food, makes it palatable and eats it. That's what is called creativity. He eats food with taste, and enjoys eating. We just eat to fill our stomachs. Is there anybody around here who cooks food and consumes it?"

Like preachers, they went on talking: "We can tell you of an extraordinary quality of man. He has a lot of senses. Among these, the feeling of shame is the most sensitive. For example: He mates in privacy. First he engages himself in foreplay, then he beds with his mate, and finally he copulates. But we don't feel boredom to bore our females in public."

"Who is this, mate?"

"For every man, there is a woman. For every woman, there is a man. Woman is the symbol of beauty. She is one of the most delicate being on the earth. One has to handle her carefully. She is the epitome of everything."

"Why is it so?" I asked.

"We have seen many cases in Cheenisthan. She could hide the water of the seas in her eyes as tears. If she opens it, the entire globe would be submerged. She is war and peace. A woman has tremendous will power. In a family, if a child is bad, nothing is bad. If the husband is bad, something is bad. If wife is bad, everything is bad."

"Wife! What is that?"

"Wife is the life-mate of a man. A woman married to a man is the wife of that man. He is the husband."

"Is it an abbreviation?"

"No. It's a word. We can use the word as an abbreviation of Wonderful Instrument For Enjoyment. The result of their mating is the fruit they bear—the child. The child is the most innocent and ignorant being on earth. Whenever a child cries the whole joy on earth solidifies into sorrow. Whenever a . . . ."

"Our kids also cry," a grasshopper from the crowd stated a fact.

"Indeed. We do cry. But can we laugh? If at all we laugh, who understands it? It's invisible and ineffective."

"Yes, yes. What happens when a child laughs?"

"All the solidified sorrows would melt like snow into a river of joy. It's the goodness of God."

"Is the man superior to God?" I asked.

"Everyone and everything is made and meant for man." Moving their beaks to indicate us, the ducks continued, "You, you, you and you . . . all are meant for him."

"Why so?"

"Because, you have to learn lot of things from man. He is the teacher. In Cheenisthan, a teacher is equivalent to God. So if a man is not God, he is not less than God."

"What does the man look like? Is he shapeless and weightless . . ." someone from the crowd asked.

"Ohooo! It's like asking who the hero is after listening to an entire story. Repeatedly we're telling you that man has got his own shape. Only the mind is shapeless. He has a head. This unit is comprised of two eyes, two ears, a nose with two small holes said to be nostrils and a big hole called the mouth. Coming down to the throat and abdomen unit, this comprises of two hands, two legs . . ."

Suddenly, shaking the whole habitat, shuddering all the inhabitants, sprouting water with a shrill, there gushed out a figure from the middle of the river amidst the ducks.

All the ducks flew away. The movements of their wings and bills shrilled as if they were saying: Here comes the man . . . Here comes the man . . . Here comes the man.

There is a general principle: the enjoyment that one gets while awaiting someone will not be there in the actual meeting. But this incident was something different. All of us were amazed at its sight. It was like sunrise.

Was he the son of Sun? A brother of Sun? A minor Sun? A second Sun? Or Sun himself?

The object filled the area with a blinding brightness. Made a mellow voice. He appeared for a split-second and vanished.

The birds hinted at the object, a man. So, that was man! We were anxiously waiting to have a glimpse. Yes, we had a glimpse.

Where did he vanish? In a nutshell, he vanished after vanquishing all of us. His disappearance caused the banishment of our amazement. He appeared from the water! Was he an aquatic? Was he an amphibian? By all means something incredible!

Let him be anything. But he *is* a great *thing*.

What for did he appear all of a sudden? To exhibit his physical features?

The ducks were exaggerating the merits of man.

Was he hearing our talk from under water? I wondered. Man! Man! Man!

What was the intention behind that man's instant presence? To alert us of some imminent catastrophe? To let us prepare for it?

Where did he hail from? From Cheenisthan? The ducks said that there are *myriad* of men there.

The ducks came by air. The man came by water. The ducks flew away. The man dived away?

Could I meet him again?

If he comes back, I would put to him a series of questions: About the tidings of his native land, about his wife, about his children . . . And I wanted to ask him if he could be my teacher, if he could enlighten me.

If he agreed, I would consider him my god. I would pray to him. I would gift my berries and flowers to him.

But, what was wrong with the ducks? Why did they fly away at the sight of the man? Were they afraid of him? If so, why did they flatter him? Or were the vagrant ducks accused of some criminal offence in Cheenisthan? Was this man bringing the warrant to arrest the offenders?

My mind was pregnant with lots of questions. But, without delay, the pregnancy aborted due to deficiency of answers.

*   *   *

The most astonishing incident was the disappearance of the assembly of fauna and flora. All my thoughts were centered on the man came out of the riverbed. With the appearance of the man all the inhabitants of my area disappeared.

Where did they go?

I was afraid that the bright halo around the head of the man had consumed them all. If that was the case, at least their ash should have been there. I could see around King Sun and Moon. They were celestial bodies. Was this man with the halo a celestial person?

I was worried that perhaps I was deserted again. In the whole habitat I was the only inhabitant.

The river did not alter her course. The mountain did not change his altitude. But I felt that both of them had amended their attitudes.

It seemed that she was hiding something inside her, like an adulterous queen. And the mountain looked like a king who keeps a *keep* in his chamber.

I wanted to know who those adulterer and adulteress were.

*   *   *

I grieved and cried. The habitat was vacant. There was not even a grass root. Even the atmosphere was empty. The air had been displaced. My breathing? Even my survival was uncertain.

Only the mountain and the river remained there, challenging me. They were the vanguards on earth. I hoped that some living organisms remained somewhere in the country. Therefore, I called out loudly.

"Ahoy . . . Ahoy . . . Ahoy . . ."

The mountain produced echoes of my call as if he was mocking me. The river also mocked me by producing a gargling sound.

The echo gave me an assurance: There was air in the atmosphere. My voice could travel only in a medium.

Neglecting the echoes, I waited. I was sure that some response would definitely come from the far end of the territories. My hope became uncertain.

Silence pregnant with suspense . . .

The name given to the capital was becoming all the more meaningful. The capital had already witnessed two massacres of flora and one of fauna.

O, ho, ho . . . ! Really pathetic!

Gone were gone . . .

What about me? Again I am in solitude. No one to talk to. No one to share my joy. Sorry. Sorry. Sorry. I have no joy now. There is no one to share my grief.

Areh . . . what a mutt am I? Who said that none was present? My mother, dear mother, was there. She would not give me up.

Let me ask my mother: "*Ma*! What's this all about? Always some bad things occur on this part of your body? Why? Why can't you take me back to your womb? I want to die. Die, die, die. I'm fed up of this harassment, and loneliness."

"*Dhudh . . . dhudh . . . dhudh,*" Mother said. "My dear tree-son, don't weep like a weak child. Don't behave like a barbarian. Don't babble like a baby. You have the responsibility of ruling this state. I couldn't think of a state where the ruler cried when the ruled laughed."

"Why don't you think of a situation of a state where the ruler rules without the ruled? What shall the ruler do? Rejoice? You know very well that the body of a king is made up of the cells called subjects. The most revered, the so-called man, came for a fraction of a second and killed all my subjects. I can't tolerate this. If he returns and stays here permanently, it would be a threat to my life. Is man a symbol of decency or a model of dacoity?"

"Hush, dear, hush," mother consoled me. "He's not such a character. He is a handsome debonair young man. He is the epitome of everything. Did you notice his halo? Those who come in the range of his sheen turn instantly insignificant. Those out of that range survive."

"Then why didn't they respond when I called to them."

"Henceforth, they won't respond. The inter-communication system has failed in this habitat because of his presence. Neither you'll hear their voice, nor will they hear you."

"But we were communicating!"

"We could converse till he steps on me. He just showed his face and disappeared. He didn't land on me. The moment he touches my ground, your freedom of speech would be buried forever."

I wanted to offload the weight of the numerous related questions on mother. All this development hurt my self-respect. But I controlled my rage.

Yet I said, "Your dearest man with the halo, who came from the water hole is not a holy person. He is a dirty devil. Who the hell is he to curtail my rights? It's unfair. It's contempt of God. Yet you consider him as the substitute of God. As a teacher, as a preacher and stuff like that."

"Shh," mother snarled at me. "Don't utter profane language," her voice was harsh. Now she did not seem pious.

I watched her very closely. I had never seen or heard her in such a state and stage! Was she changing to manhood from womanhood? Or was she becoming a masculine woman?

I had hallucinations. In the hallucination, I saw that she had lost breasts and they had transformed into testes at her groin. The downward displacement of her milk from the breasts into the testes as semen. I saw the protrusion of a penis. The chest turned to a field with hair. All these changes transformed her into an Amazon.

I asked her excuse.

Mother advised me, "You have already passed the metamorphosis. Your habit of losing temper will pave the way to your grave. The man with the halo is not an ordinary human being. He is supernatural. He knows metaphysics. If he reappears, you should kow-tow him. If he is pleased with your behavior, he'll bless you. Otherwise he'll curse you. With his blessings you'll bring fortune to this land in future. This land would be the most renowned country on earth. You'll be king at least of the plants if not of the human beings."

I was feeling prestigious.

"You'll be known as a sacred tree or a tree of divinity. People will give kudos to you," mother continued. "So, pray to be lucky. Luck is related with destiny. Destiny is determined by God. God's blessings are a must. So better abandon worldly affairs."

I repented for snubbing the man with the halo.

"Yes, *Ma*, yes. I'll pray to God," I said. "Years ago, there came a school of birds. Those chatter-boxes muttered many unbelievable incidents that had happened in a country called Cheenisthan. We saw major fireworks going on for many years far away, on the other side of the mountain. Now as there is nobody around, let's have a tête-à-tête about it."

"Whatever they narrated was correct word by word. There was a series of volcanic eruptions. In other words a perfect abortion. The fire of gold you saw was my bloody flesh (burning lava). Once I told you about my *rarely* (menses)?"

I nodded.

"But this was something different. An abortion."

"What would have happened if the abortion did not take place?"

"Then I would have borne a calm and quite child—a mountain. He would have been the tallest and the healthiest man of a mountain with highest ever erect penis (peak) on his body. I was dreaming about a child like him. What to say! He would have been a thorough figure. May be because of fate. May be because I was greedy. It was aborted."

Mother took a long sigh and added: "Instead of gift, I get grief. Actually the volcano erupted in the city of Chinching, the capital of Cheenisthan. It is a . . . I'm sorry. Actually it is not *is*. It is actually *was*. So it was the most cultured and most civilized city on my belly. All types of creatures inhabited there.

"The city was arranged with buildings like stone-built and fortified houses and timber-framed houses. Colleges with stone walls and cone roofs. Castles with plastered brick walls and bay windows with curved glass. Besides these, royal palaces and elegant bungalows were there. I ruined all.

"The city had many roads, bridges, stadiums, theatres and many other structures. I destroyed them all. The city also had many places of worship. I demolished them too.

"The people were mentally, morally and emotionally poor. There were teachers, scientists, artists, doctors, technicians and many connoisseurs of all the prevailing disciplines in the world. I killed them all."

"What was the reason?" I asked.

"Sin," mother quipped. "Even the fauna and flora were infected by a disease called sin. Priests and principals had no principles. Officials were offenders. The strong were wrong. No scientist had any idea of moral science. The wise were vicious. Traders were trespassers. All were sinners. Everyone indulged in sex and sinister games. So I killed them all."

"You shouldn't have killed them," I said.

"It was the whim of nature. Nature had given them sufficient time and chances to correct them. Warnings: To create scarcity of food, first there was a drought. Then a flood. But they imported the food and overcame the calamities. Thus the court of God ordered me to execute an eruption—the nature aborted me.

"I too incurred a great loss. I lost the largest mountain, with the highest peak in the world—all scattered into fragments."

"You might have killed lots of innocents!'"

"May be or may not be. I couldn't help it. But I was very much particular about saving a peculiar man: A transcendentalist who challenged me. I told him that it was the nature's caprice. He came to know that a volcanic eruption was a voluntary abortion. Seeing my ruin, he asked me whether nature could create a new earth and a new sky. It was impossible. So nature had no right to ruin the world. It had no right to break the peace of mind of the organisms."

I interfered, "It's really a macabre thing. I like his challenge."

"I too liked it."

"Did he escape?"

"Yes. He overpowered nature with his spiritual powers. He survived."

"Who is he, *Ma*?"

"He is the one whom you have already seen—the man with the halo."

I was dazed.

Mother said, "Some miscreants also escaped: The cunning birds who flew away from here at the sight of the man. And there were some more sinners who fled the city. I'm afraid that if those sinners land here, this part of my body also will get polluted. And my dear son, I have no words to express my grief to you."

"What's the matter, *Ma*? Why the reluctance?"

"It is . . . it is . . . You are going to lose your right to communicate with me forever . . ."

I knocked myself down senseless. Crestfallen, I remained still and stiffened like an earthen statue with a barren mind. But slowly I recaptured my mind that was now pregnant with thought: If God took away one right, he would gift me many other rights.

*　　*　　*

I let time run fast. I wished to complete the fifth century. The runner, time, completed his race. It took five hundred years for me to grow into this stage. I attained a height of 125 feet and many branches spread out of my body like railway lines from a main central station. The branches were packed with lots of leaves providing canopy to an area not less than an acre. My body (stem) was very hefty, occupying a space of radius not less than ten feet.

Sans doute I was growing bulky by the day. Mother advised me to avoid eating and drinking this and that as and whenever I felt like. Afraid of obesity, I controlled my diet by consuming one full square meal and two half square meals a day.

The following day, I was entering the first day of my sixth century. Overnight, I felt some abnormality inside my stem. As I looked down, I felt that someone was breaking my bark from inside.

All of a sudden, breaking open my belly, there came out a man. I was amazed to see him! The holy man with the halo!

Yes. He was the same man who had once emerged from the river.

CENTURY 6

501 TO 600

I realized that I had a big belly. Like a small cave, it was large enough to accommodate a small family.

What was the man doing inside my stomach all these days? Many years ago he had surfaced on the river. Then he vanished. Now he sprang up from my belly, and disappeared. My eyes were not fully satisfied.

How did he reach my belly from the river? Walking? Running? Flying? He might have neither walked nor run. If he had touched my mother's body—stepped on the earth—I would have lost my power to talk with her.

May be without touching her—by flight.

Exactly.

But when might have he been transported? During day? No. I had not seen him. At night, while I was asleep? Then also I would have been awakened by his presence. He, with his halo, is as brilliant as Sun with his corona.

Did mother see him? Judging by her reactions, she had not felt his presence. Was she pretending? Had she known the man's hideout? Did she willfully keep the secret shut inside my belly along with the man? My brain couldn't conceive anything.

I wanted to deluge her with questions.

Oh, God! What about my right to speak? Is it lost? Let me confirm.

I cried out, "*Ma . . . ma*, can you hear me?"

There was no answer.

I felt thirsty. The roots were at strike. They did not absorb water from the earth. I was sweating. The leaves were under Sun. They didn't absorb and assimilate light from Sun.

I became unconscious.

A soft shower came and wetted my head. I came to life again.

Then I heard a melodious murmur. "My dear child. Mind me not answering you. It is your mother speaking."

Gladly I said, "*Ma*, I'm happy to have not lost my right to speak. At the same time I am unhappy to have the halo—man. What business has he got to roam around here? That too hiding in the hollow of my stem?"

After a pause, I added:

"Who is he? How did he enter into me sans my awareness?"

Mother explained. "Spiritually . . . He is a *sanyasi* or sage. Very soon your body is going to be pregnant with the *sanyasi*. He'll be meditating in your belly. During that time you'll learn many matters of the eternal world. He will enlighten you. He'll remain in your pregnancy until and unless some major event would happen. Till such time you too will be under self-hypnosis. Please record my words; one thing is *sans doute*— you're going to be a divine tree.

Instantly, erupting the earth beside me, the *sanyasi* rose from the ground and slowly walked and impregnated me.

*   *   *

No sooner did he enter my belly than we both underwent a state of deep sleep in which we were the subjects and were responsive to suggestions—both of us became hypnotic.

In the sound sleep, I had a strange dream—I went back to my infancy. The *sanyasi* transformed me into a small plant. He planted me on his right palm. He carried me up to a delightfully wet basin on a golden peak of a silver mountain. The peak resembled the crown of King Mountain in the dawn.

The morning Sun was waiting to receive us with a garland in his hand. I was bathed in 'the' basin. Sun put the garland around my neck. He smiled at me. It seemed that he was marrying me.

Then he took me by air to the city of Chinching, the capital of Cheenisthan. The trip was very pleasurable. The panoramic view of the land below delighted me.

We landed in front of a divine palace.

The king, queen, their kinsmen and countrymen had gathered there to welcome me. The *sanyasi* presented me to the king. The king in turn handed me over to the queen. The queen planted me right in front of the palace.

Besides the hosts, there was an elephant kid standing beside the queen. The little elephant was impatiently waiting to have friendship with me. A sign order was given to the boy-elephant by the queen. He came, raised his trunk like a water-monitor and watered me with a soft shower from close quarters.

The court musicians sang their national anthem. The birds in the palace garden sang a greeting song in their fauna language. There was a fireworks display. It did not attract me much.

The *sanyasi* went to the palace with the king and the queen. The crowd had dispersed. All went back to their rest places and workplaces.

The boy-elephant gave me company.

He approached me and asked fondly, "Hello, *Mithra*, I'm *Hathi*. Your name please?"

"I'm a tree. My proper name is Banyan."

"No proper names here. Only common . . ."

"Then how will you find out a particular person?" I asked.

"Already we have first, second, third persons."

"Would you be clearer?"

"We use this *hathi*, that *hathi*. We avoid unwanted grammar, you know. No verb change in singular or plural subjects. Only, you *speak*, he *speak*. He is speaking. You *is* speaking. I *is* speaking. Your grammar?"

"Ours is entirely different. We consider singular and plural subjects, sequences of tense in verbs, etc."

The boy-elephant emphatically said, "We not use even what, why, which, when, how, etc, only the interrogation mark more than enough to distinguish interrogative sentence in writing. The talking tone enough to identify sentence a question or not. We use limited prepositions, interjections, conjunctions, etc, but very punctual about punctuation."

Listening to his gibberish, I got ants in my pants.

I said, "Grammar refines the language. A language without grammar is a language of the remote past. If we use such a language, we are as good as primitives. In the by-gone days, schools of scholars analyzed, framed and did structural works to make the language beautiful—that effort is grammar."

"Why waste time on grammar?" The boy elephant continued. "Communication our motto—just express ideas."

"If that's the case, why do we have palatable food. Why don't we just have something to fill our stomachs."

"You mean?"

I answered, "Language is as essential as food to any being. Grammar is the art of cooking that food. The more you research in cookery, the more tasty the food will be."

"You hear my example," he said. "If language a body, lot appendicitis is there. We chop it. Your statement add more appendicitis to language body.

I argued: "If language is body, grammar is the garment. A language without grammar is like a naked body."

"Nudity is true and natural, donning garments artificial."

"It differs from person to person. Do you have any literature?" I said.

"See, here no paper and pencil waste for such things. Our theory is maximum benefit with minimum time."

"Benefit?" I quipped in their style.

"*Haha* (yes). Material benefit. Here, everybody is busy making materials—rich want more riches. *Chor* (thief) steal more, *Mantri* (minister) is mean. *Thantri* (priest) more impure, *Devadasi* (whore) more sexy. King more unkind. This is country of sex, sin and sinister acts. Every one after wine, woman and wealth. Even fauna, flora too."

Though his language had no grammar, it was full of glamour. "By the by, what material benefit do you enjoy as a fauna?"

"Instead of eating coconut tree leaves, we steal jaggery from palace kitchen and sugar cane from the field. Now my mummy engage steal without time waste."

"OK. OK. In that case, what will the sugar cane have?" I asked.

"Instead of drinking dirty water, they drink pure water."

I was surprised. "Is there no one to check these excesses and mal-practices?"

"No. Nobody. In fact, they support each other, especially the human beings."

"Do you support this?"

"Except me and a man," the boy elephant said.

"Who is he!"

"Man who brought you here."

"Why did you greet only me? Why didn't you welcome him?"

"He is not guest; you is our guest."

"Then who is he?"

"He is one and all—the only son—of our king and queen.

"You mean the prince!"

"*Haha*. Prince."

"I want to know more about him. Please tell me."

The little elephant said, "It is going dusk. We talk *kal* (tomorrow).

The boy-elephant walked away, with the court dancer's buttocks that rolled and pitched sideways. I looked at Sun at dusk trying to hide himself beneath the desk of the earth as if he did not want to watch the walk of the elephant.

*   *   *

The next montage I experienced in the hypnosis: I had grown up a little. The man with the halo went back to his infancy—he became a newborn baby.

In the main court hall of the palace, there lay the baby upon a flowerbed on a golden cot. The king and the queen were sitting on either side, surrounded by many lords—princes from neighboring states, ministers, kinsmen *et al.* Their eyes were focused on the sparkling baby.

Camphor and scented sticks were burning.

A sage entered. Spectators bowed their heads in reverence.

Seeing the boy, tears of joy rolled down the sage's cheeks.

The sage exclaimed: "He will be as big as the world!"

The king said, "Please be clearer. I'm anxious about the future of my son."

"He will be a King of kings. He will be renowned all over the world and will conquer the world." The king and the queen rejoiced at those words.

They wanted their only son to follow the warrior tradition—conqueror of the world! They were contented.

At the same time, the sage told the king that the boy should be kept away from all sorrows and sufferings. Otherwise, instead of conquering, he will renounce the world. He was a divine child.

The sage named the child Sansara meaning *world*.

So the parents decided to keep Sansara surrounded by what was beautiful and charming. All matters of sorrow, evil and suffering were averted from his dwelling area.

Separate palaces were made to suit the changing seasons. Lots of lotus ponds and flower gardens were built around the palaces.

Prince Sansara led a posh life. Many guards and servants were employed to look after him.

One of his cousins, a little elder to him, was Sansara's merry-mate.

One day when Sansara was enjoying the beauty of lotus in the pond, a bird fell hurt in the pond, in front of him. He took the bird. He removed the arrow that had pierced the bird. He dried the feathers. He dressed the wounds and nursed it.

His cousin put up his claim. As he had shot down the bird, it belonged to him. Sansara refused. The claim was put before the king.

There was a trial.

The boy (cousin) said, "The bird was flying very fast. With great difficulty and accuracy, I shot it down. You have to appreciate my aim. I have proved my marksmanship in this tender age. So I should be given not just the bird but an award as well, or make me the Prince."

"I demand neither appreciation nor award," said Sansara humbly. "My cousin tried to kill the bird. I saved its life. He has failed in the trial for the bird is still alive. I have won it because the bird is not dead. If the bird had died I would have given it to him. Shouldn't a life belong to the *savior* rather than the *destroyer?*"

The king was very much impressed by the emphasis of the argument. He proclaimed Sansara as the owner of the bird.

From the very beginning, he was very fond of flora and fauna. The palace owned a royal garden. There were almost all the varieties of plants and trees in the garden. The woods served as a dwelling place for the animal kingdom.

The court *vaidyas* or doctors used to kill animals and pluck leaves for preparing Ayurvedic medicine.

The prince attained his boyhood.

Once a physician was ordered to prepare a black-monkey-*rasayana* (a viscous tonic for prolonged life). A crowd had gathered to see the killing of the ape.

Prince Sansara was also made to accompany the others of the royal family in order to prepare his mind and heart to face the bloodshed in the battle-field.

During those days Sansara was also a student of war techniques. He became proficient in the princely arts such as archery and fencing.

The best arrow-shooter of the court was detailed to shoot down the ape. The ape was feeding her child. The shooter strung the bow. The arrow accelerated towards the monkey.

Sansara with lightning speed sprang and grabbed the flying arrow.

The crowd was stunned.

The king asked him about the purpose of his deed. Sansara spoke softly: "The animal is innocent. What crime has she done to deserve a death sentence?"

"Let the animal be free." King ordered; turning to his son he spoke softly, "But your performance that we witnessed just now was of the occult type!"

"It's just a matter of will power, Your Highness. This power comes naturally if a man wants to do something good."

The people were happy in both ways. One way their prince would become a good judge because he is compassionate. The other way he would become a great conqueror because of his will power and boldness.

He was not sent to any school. Schooling was conducted in the palace by eminent scholars. Besides learning the academic subjects, the boy had learned some more with his inner knowledge.

One day, the royal family took the boy on a picnic in the royal gardens. Sansara's would-be-wife Sarayu, a voluptuous beauty, was accompanying him.

The boy was asked to kiss what he loved most.

The king expected a kiss.

The queen expected a kiss.

Sarayu expected a kiss.

Many expected a kiss.

Neither the parents nor his darling got the kiss.

Disappointing all of them, the boy kissed a flower. The next choice: He kissed a tiger. The third choice: A tree.

He neglected the supremacy of the human beings.

When asked, he said a child's heart will be pure. But as he grew up, he would change his character and his heart would lose purity.

But the characters he choose would never lost their purity. Their hearts—the hearts of the flower, tiger and the tree—remained steady. They did not know impurity. God provided whatever character they possessed.

During lunch-break, he was seated before various delicious dishes. He took an empty pot. He left the food. He left the place. He filled the pot with water from the lotus pond.

He climbed a nearby *neem* tree. Plucked some ripe leaves. He ate it. Then drank the water. He poured the remaining water back into the pond.

When asked, he answered that water should not be wasted. Green leaves were of benefit to the tree. Ripe one was as good as a dying leaf. Both water and tree were the gift of nature and one should preserve and conserve these.

His heart researched in disciplines like love, truth, reality and compassion. The kinsman never knew it.

He realized that truth was invisible. It came out from a true and a pure heart.

One who did not understand the truth could deny it as false. The reality was visible.

Once in the court he had arguments with the philosophers regarding truth and reality.

He said that the reality of his father as king was true because everyone in the court knew the reality of his father as the real king.

If his father—the real king—and his minister appeared without their royal robes before the subjects who did not know them, and if each one claimed as the king, the real king could lose the chance of being identified.

The subjects might fail to identify the real king and see the minister as their king.

*   *   *

Amidst the lavish life, he grew up into a handsome youth. The considerate and courteous youth was popular among all.

Sarayu was darling to Sansara. Certainly, Sansara was darling to Sarayu. But according to the custom of the country, the wooer had to win an archery contest to claim his love.

Princes from many provinces were anxiously waiting to take part in the contest. Rough, tough, strong, stupid, bold, coward, beautiful, ugly, kind, unkind—all types of characters had come to participate in the task.

Devadhanush (bow of God) was placed on the platform. No one could lift the bow up to chest-level to string it.

Sansara's was the last turn.

Sarayu prayed to all gods to let her have him as husband.

Sansara came on the platform. He was lean and sot.

Spectators stared at him sympathetically.

Suitors snarled at him sarcastically.

Mocking and joking rose from the crowd. He became the laughing-stock

Sansara bowed his head in respect to the bow. He prayed for a minute. He lifted the bow and easily strung it.

Spectators looked on expectantly.

Sansara shot the arrow letting it go on an infinite journey through the skies.

Sansara married Sarayu. Sarayu married Sansara. They married each other.

At the marriage ceremony his father-in-law asked, "Sansara, I dreamed that a delicate youth like you could render such a remarkable victory".

Sansara humbly replied, "With dedication, any delicate man could make any dream come true."

The king muttered in the ears of queen: "At this rate our son would, no doubt, become not only the conqueror of this world but . . ."

". . . but also the whole universe," the queen completed the sentence.

The king exclaimed, "He, at ease used the bow once owned by the God-of-strength!"

"This is the last but not the least evidence that he is matured enough to be crowned."

They decided to coronate Sansara on the occasion of his silver jubilee birthday function.

After the marriage function, special attention was taken to avoid his contact with lamentable matters. He had been told good things only and he experienced all synonyms of joy. He never knew that joy had antonyms too.

The newly married couple sailed on the ocean of luxury on board the boat of joy. They passed the time by merry-making.

The king was too old and frail to rule the country.

So Sansara was crowned. At the age of thirty he became the king of Cheenisthan.

Soon after ascending the throne, he decided to go around the country to visit the countrymen.

He started his journey on his four-horse golden chariot accompanied by his Chief Minister.

The chariot took them through the cleanest and best paths and parts of the city as instructed by the minister.

Countrymen stood in queues on both sides of the paths. They cheered, greeted and kow-towed the king.

The king ordered the Chief Minister to divert the journey to the slum area where the downtrodden people lived.

There were no banners of greetings. No posters on his arrival. No placards hailing him.

Every nook and corner of the slum was covered with dust. The place was crowded with cantankerous people. Young, old, filthy, orphans, morbid . . .

The atmosphere was filled with sorrows and sufferings.

There he saw a world of dull and colorless life. A life alien to him.

"Stop the carriage."

The horses came to a standstill.

Sansara felt that even the horses were pain-stricken by that lamentable life.

A hatless man halted. He stretched his hands. He said, "*Ai . . . ya . . . vallathum . . . tharane . . .*"

"What is he asking?" the young king asked the minister.

"He is asking for alms."

"Alms? Father and you had told me that I had learnt everything in the world. But this world is new to me."

"*Rajan* (Your highness)," The minister said. "I know. Not only is this word but this world also new to you."

"Let me see this world completely. Move ahead."

The carriage went further. Before it gained speed, he heard a groan.

A disfigured, deformed man was lying on the footpath. Passers-by neglected him.

"Stop, stop, stop!"

The carriage was stopped.

"Who is he?"

"He is sick."

"Sick . . . ?"

"Yes, Rajan. Sick. You have learnt only about the healthy condition of man."

"Why can't you nurse him?"

"He is suffering from leprosy. The disease spreads by contact."

"Please do the needful in the best possible way," said the king.

They moved farther at full pelt. It was time to return. The carriage turned back towards the palace.

After a distance, overwhelming the galloping sound, they heard the sound of wails.

They saw a moaning procession in the evening.

A body was being carried on a *charpoy,* followed by a big but silent crowd. A small crowd of women and children followed. Some were uttering wails, some kept silence.

"Is he also sick?" enquired the king.

"He's dead."

"Then do something for his need." The king commanded.

"Excuse me, *Rajan.* He doesn't need anything. He left life forever." The minister murmured.

"How? Why?"

"He's burnt to death—suicide—because of poverty."

"Now, where is he being taken?"

"From his charged-house to the charnel-house. It is pathetic."

"I found someone laughing and someone crying in the crowd."

The minister said, "It's quite natural—the more attached and more related to the dead will mourn. The less attached and less related will laugh."

*　　*　　*

In the dark hours of the night, King Sansara woke up. The sleep had gone far away from him.

He looked out through the wide-open window.

The stars, like spectators, snarled at him. The dazzling moon like a Chief justice, jeered at him. Unable to face them, he bowed his head like a criminal in the open-air court of the sky.

Some clouds came before the moon at times to produce some documentary evidence. At that time he looked up at the moon.

Yes. He is a born criminal. He averted his eyes. Yes, he was afraid to confront the moon.

The judge may pass an order against him for not favoring the weak, weary and withered. He was ashamed of his guilty consciousness.

Thirty years of life . . .

Enjoying a colorful and extravagant life in high places. It was not a petty crime to be put aside, when down in the street, the downtrodden people were leading a rock bottom life. He was a sinner!

O, ho, hoho! He lamented! Till then he had seen only the bright and heavy world of life. His repentance would not redress his sins. This had to be compensated.

He decided to go to the darker and lighter world of life, where old age, sickness, poverty and death prevailed.

He came to a conclusion—leave the palace.

But . . .

He was happy to say good-bye to the comforts.

But how to part with the part-and-parcel of his life? The dear and near? The kith and kin? Especially, his dear parents and his dearest wife?

It pained him.

He thought about the melancholic situation of the poor populace. He determined to leave the palace at once.

His wife Sarayu, like a fresh flower lay on the cot. Her butter-soft body invited him to embrace her. She was sleeping.

All the organisms on earth were sleeping. Even the guards on duty, who were not supposed to sleep, were asleep.

Sleep is like that—a natural boon to all organism.

Only he did not sleep.

He kissed on the temple of his wife.

He touched the feet of his dear wife.

He let go all lines of luxury and lavishness from the palace.

*   *   *

"*Haha*, you sleeping Master Banyan?"

I came to life when I heard the boy-elephant mocking me.

"*Aiyoo, illa.* (Oh, no) I'm listening. It was like listening a sacrosanct saga."

I was not interested in his narration in broken language. But I wanted to know about the king who had renounced all worldly comforts.

He agreed with me to converse in their olden grammatical language. He gave a lucid explanation of King Sansara.

Leaving the palace, the first and foremost thing he did was to give up his rich royal robes. He donned a simple saffron cloak. He cut off his lengthy hair and did a skull-crop.

Thus, he walked into the world of poverty and illiteracy. The scene he beheld there was horrible and nostalgic

People chopped animals, drank blood and ate the meat. They named the dishes—chicken chops, mutton *masala*, fish fry, beef boiled, pork *pollichathu* and what not!

Some people uprooted plants, plucked fruits, cut leaves and broke seeds that had not attained even boyhood. They cooked and ate it.

It was the people's custom; the so-called *Karma*.

He protested it; advised them to amend it. According to him, every object, a tree, stone, man or an animal had a soul.

He emphasized on *ahimsa* or non-violence—avoid hurting anything; avoid killing anything.

He knew the language of animals and plants. He used to talk to them. They used to understand him.

I aired a doubt, "It means he was neither a vegetarian nor a non-vegetarian. Then what was his food?"

He ate ripe fruits. Anything that is ripe is as good as a good for nothing. It was a burden to the carrier. Sooner or later it had to perish. A leaf, a fruit, a seed, a plant or anything just before decay could be used for benefaction. This gave satisfaction to both the eater and the eatable.

I again expressed a doubt, "This is the case of my family. How about your animal kingdom? Are you able to provide any ripe item as food to man?"

"As far as non-vegetarian food is concerned, no ripe matter could be provided as provision by our kingdom before the demise. *Ngaa*, nowadays, it's heard that some of our limbs suffering from cancer and sugar complaints are removed by operation. If we allow man to eat it, it may be infectious to him."

Hesitatingly I said, "*Kollaam* (good policy). You fellows consume men as well as plants as food. And nothing to contribute as provisions from your side."

The boy-elephant was annoyed. He turned red hot as if he had been taken out of a furnace.

"Who told you? Don't blame us unnecessarily. Who gives you milk, the most balanced diet on earth? Who gives you egg, the richest food. Who gives you honey, the sweetest of sweets. And stuffs like that . . ."

I complained, "Man may be benefited by these foodstuffs. We are not benefited . . . ?"

Again his temperature rose. "You don't utter such words of ingratitude. It's something disdainful. We give you manure. Our dung and urine are the best and natural fertilizers. Is there any doubt about it? In your Ayurveda, cows' urine use for some therapy; is it not?"

I apologized. "I'm extremely sorry, *yaar*. I just forgot it."

*   *   *

The transition from King Sansara to Sage Jaisara was instantaneous. People called him Jaisara. The name was a compound word: *Jai* or victory; *Sara* meant entire—Victory over everything.

He ate air and fruits; Drank water and milk. He practiced ahimsa.

He preached that clear belief, clear knowledge and clear conduct were the means through which one can attain *moksha* or salvation.

Jaisara wandered all over the country. Preached to anybody who came across. Some listened. Some did not. Some cared; some uncared.

He could not find truth anywhere. He met some sages. They gave him the lessons of penance to gain truth. He adopted the ancient method.

He went into the woods to become a penitent. He even gave up his ordinary clothes. The sacrament of confession was tough—putting his nude soft body to various hardships, keeping fast till the terminus of death.

Though he did not see even the shadow of truth in the woods, the penitential period paved the way for a privy physical life.

He grabbed a bridle to control the fast and random running horses of *Desire, Pleasure* and *Passion* in his body. Thereby he could do a lot of miracles. He gained the ability to fly in the air, submerge in the deep sea and walk on fire. All this because he had put his body to practice continuously with all the severe climates—hot and cold.

The wild animals became his friends, because he had continuous communion with each of them.

He gained the ability to remain without food for years through fasting. He fed only on air and water particles in the atmosphere. He did an experiment and proved that if a leafy tree was vibrated by chanting a *jala mantra* (hymns for water), all the leaves of the tree would absorb vapor contents from the atmosphere. The leaves would transfer the vapors through the branches to the stem. If you pierce a hole and place a tube, the tree would provide you pure water as if from a running water tap.

He further learnt that to attain *moksha,* one had to win two objects.

103

The visible object—the body.

The invisible object—the soul.

In the woods, through yoga exercises, he won the body. He could control it. Amend it. Alter it. Vary it.

Next object was his soul.

To handle the invisible soul, one should have the control on his invisible and inner power known as mind. Control of mind could only be gained by *thapasya* (meditation).

He wanted to select a suitable solitary place for meditation. He had a dream that far away, across his country Cheenisthan, there was a Banyan tree with a huge body and a bulky belly.

Jaisara the sage hurried out from the forest towards the tree craving to become a hermit inside the belly of the Banyan tree. (Me)

On the way he had to cross his country. So he began a cross-country walk of two thousand miles on bare feet. He wore two live serpents to cover his private parts. A small one wound around his waist as *aranjanam* and a big king cobra as *kaupeenam*. The *naga*s' hood concealed the *sanyasi's* private parts.

During the course of his journey, he taught the people his five-fold-path—clear living, clear thinking, clear words, clear view and clear action.

He advised the people to join his *sangha* to attain *Nirvana*. The villagers could not recognize him. Some learnt men accompanied him as his followers.

Most of the illiterates wanted him to perform miracles. Though he had the ability to perform various miracles, which he had gained through the *yoga*, he was unwilling to perform them lest it would be rendered as an effort to polish his halo.

En route, he reached his native place—Chinching city. There the people recognized him. He came to know what had happened to his family after his departure. His cousin (brother), who was jealous of Sarayu for marrying Sansara, captured the throne. He imprisoned Sansara's father. He tried to woo Sarayu. She refused. So, as a king he could spread a rumor like a wild-fire that Sansara was dead. The story was that Sansara was eaten by a tiger in the forest.

A widow had no right to live as per the customs and belief of the country. So the superstitious ritual, *Mathi,* was carried out. Sarayu was forced to walk straight into a pyre though her husband was still alive.

By the time the reformed Sansara appeared in the city as Jaisara the *sanyasi,* it was too late. He preached the noble truths. But his teachings made no impact on the people.

They did not want to abstain from the normal pleasures of life. They did not want to deny themselves material satisfaction. They were interested in *artha* and *kama.*

Some were inclined towards his asceticism. They became volunteers and changed their life-styles and practiced the principles of his discipline.

The king happened to know about the arrival of the *sanyasi.* He threatened his subjects. The subjects, in turn, turned against Jaisara. They chased him out. They mocked him, called him names, pelted stones and threw rotten eggs and vegetables at him—became a laughing-stock.

Still he did not perform any miracle to win over the boisterous crowd. Feeling pity and seeing the miseries of the sage, a voluptuous young woman gave him asylum.

She bathed him. She applied balm on his wounds and nursed him.

Before sleeping, he let the serpents on his waist take rest.

While he was asleep, the voluptuous beauty stripped her clothes and approached him lustfully. She tried to kindle the fire of passion in him. She took his genital organ in her mouth and sucked. The organ did not get erect. The limb remained limp.

The sage slept on. Temptations failed to touch him.

She, like a calf suckling milk from the dried-up udder of a cow, sucked his sex organ with fierce desire.

She took his scrotum in her hands and played with it.

Still the sage did not wake up. No responses came forth from him.

She wished to dissolve the organ like a piece of candy with her tongue, cheeks and saliva.

Nothing happened to the sage. He slept on not knowing the play of lips and tongue on his organ.

She became hysterical. The sucking and its sound became so wild that even the wild animals in the far away forest woke up in the dark hours. Small and big serpents got up from their sleep. They approached her straight away and bit her.

The *sanyasi* got up . . .

Once a queen of beauty, she lay at his foot with all her beauty drained, like a dry-fallen—flower. Bluish blood oozed from her mouth.

She confessed:

"I'm . . . a . . . sinner. I . . . want redemption . . . from . . . this . . . curse.

"I saw . . . the . . . inner light . . . in you.

"I want . . . to . . . succeed you . . . easily—not . . . by . . . penance, meditation, following . . . the five-fold . . . path. I thought . . . if I imbibe . . . the nourishment . . . in you *sub rossa* . . . I shall obtain . . . your . . . power.

"If not . . . nourishment . . . at least . . . your . . . excrement, please . . . your . . . urine . . . would . . . make me . . . holy. You are . . . that . . . holy.

Her condition worsened. The nude body changed its color from milky white to blue. She took long breaths as if her throat was choked. Her rock-like breasts rolled and pitched like two minor vessels out of command at sea. Blood streamed out of her mouth, ears, nostrils, vagina and anus. It seemed like millipedes creeping out of their burrows.

She needed to have water as if a lamp needed oil.

She, the *sanyasi* and the snakes were profusely sweating in the humid climate. The *sanyasi* with his index finger wiped his sweat and poured it in her mouth drop by drop.

Her mouth blotted it.

The *sanyasi* and the snakes witnessed it sympathetically.

Again she uttered her innocent and ignorant intention.

"I request you three things. Forgive my . . . wicked act. I wo . . . n't repeat this. The last . . . give back . . . my li . . . fe."

The *sanyasi* said, "I forgive you for the wicked act for there are people who do more wickedness than you. You can't repeat this kind of act for you are going to die now. The third but the last request is unnatural, for it is quite natural that one has to give up life when the time comes. Even God has to vacate his seat. The creator and the creation have to die. The creator can choose his death as well as the creation's death by all means, whereas the creation has no choice of death by any means."

She groaned desperately.

"It's the proper time for you to leave your body. You're not a female demon, supposed to have sexual intercourse with men in their sleep. You are just a woman with a great deal of lust—a prostitute."

The *fille de joie* succumbed to death.

The snakes took their places and joined duty.

Nature could not tolerate the insult on the sage by that place and people.

An eruption was the only lesson that they would learn.

*   *   *

The sage could have made his journey easily by air without being seen. For that he had to perform two miracles out of his *Ashatasiddhi* (eight powers). The *Aneyma* (power of diminishing) and *prapti* (power to reach anywhere without being seen by anyone). He wanted to use the minimum miracles. He did not want to misuse powers.

So he got sunk in the divine river that flowed towards the city of Massacre to reach this habitat where I—the so-called peepul or Banyan tree—was the king.

CENTURY 7

601 TO 700 AD

I came out of the hypnotic spell after my mother completed one hundred travels around Sun since I was hypnotized. When I came to, I saw that my figure had undergone great changes.

I was a big tree with a single sturdy stem. But by now, my branches had sent out adventitious roots to the ground to cover a large area. They looked like lean stems that supported me. There were four such roots.

I still felt that I was under the spell. Or was it the craft of some poltergeist? No. They were in wood and juice (flesh and blood). I was happy to have these roots. No, not just happy. Very happy. No, not very happy. I don't have the right word to express my happiness.

I was very proud of their presence. I was finding myself in a family. But what was my position in this family? How were they related to me? Were I the father of four children? Or were I the brother of four sisters? Or were I the husband of four wives? Or were they related to somebody else?

There was still another point to ponder: What was the secret of their coming into being? That too at my home? Who sent them? Were they friends? Or foes?

Pompously I asked, "Hoi, who are you? What are you? Why are you com . . . ?"

"*Bus, bus, bus, bus*, our dear hus," they said. "We are not your guests, geists or geisha. We are your wives."

"But where and when . . ."

"*Bus* . . . *bus* . . . *bus* (enough) our dear hus. The moment you harbored the man with the halo you too became holy. In lieu, he gave you a *varaprasadam* (boon). He ordered us to serve you as your wives. We are at your service. We are your part and parcel. And we'll share all your sorrows."

"Only sorrows? You know, I'm the king here. A king always enjoys life. So queens can share his happiness," I said.

"We are not queens. We are just your wives. We're like your *dasis* or servants. We are not married. The holy man with the halo has placed some restrictions on us. We are happy to have a husband like you. Yet we can't hug our Hus . . . All of us are *fille de joies* from heaven. Yet we can't woo our Hus. It's a curse."

"Well, as long as I am harboring the holy man, I too can't woo you. By the by, what are your names?"

"We are Uru, Mena, Ramb and Thilo, the superlative *sundaris* or beauties of the whole universe."

I wanted to ask them a lot of questions but something hindered. The howling of the wind from the mountain heralded the coming of some strangers.

It was a fine morning. I looked at the rising Sun. He stood on top of the mountain. This was, however, a regular thing.

But there was something irregular. I had not witnessed such a scene ever before. Some spectral images of human beings were coming out of the threshold of the sun.

They came down the mountain. They staggered all along the way. Then they fell down. They rolled, crawled and again they rolled, crawled and rolled.

There were two persons. They were approaching me.

When one rolled, other crawled. When the latter crawled, the former rolled.

After a great struggle they completed the descent. Somehow they managed to reach the sloppy riverbank. Both of them wallowed. They fell in the river, drank water. They drank water till there was no space left in their stomach.

After quenching thirst, they lay flat on the bank looking blankly at the sky.

Sun pierced their eyes.

They were two full-fledged human beings.

The exhausted human beings found the harsh Sun hard.

They got up. Arm in arm, they walked slowly.

My shade was their destination.

I watched them approaching. *Arey*! They resembled the man with the halo. But they had no halo.

One was about six feet tall. The other was less than six. Both were fair complexioned.

Both were in the peak of their youth.

Both had long disheveled titian hair.

Both were naked. Pubic hair covered their genitals. Their privates reminded me of tiny islands in a yellow river.

Their bellies were the shape of my leaves. The belle's belly was prettier.

There were some identical differences between them. The tall human being had hair on the lower jaw and between his nose and mouth. The figure had a flat chest.

The other figure had no hair on the face other than the two black linings on top of the eyes.

Spherical breasts filled her chest. The capping of the tiny peaks vibrated while she walked.

When they came at close range, I remembered the words of the migrating ducks: The human beings. Two categories. The man and the woman. Or the husband and the wife.

Which one was the man and which one the woman?

The tall one was the man. He looked rough and tough: a huge figure with a muscular wand below the navel. It was magical. A fleshy rod capable of performing *aneyma* and *mahima* (expand and contract). A miraculous organ capable of producing his miniatures! A pronoun *he*.

The other one was the woman, looking soft and beautiful: A figure with a gateway to let in the muscular baton of the man. If pregnant, she was a figure with a crater to let out their miniatures. As mother, it was a figure with two fleshy pyramids that served as the milk organs. A pronoun *she*.

But neither her gateway nor his magic wand was clearly visible. Black pubic hair covered the slit and the rod.

They picked up the fallen berries and ate. The taste satisfied them. They ate more berries. They continued eating till they filled their stomachs.

Exhausted, the lady leaned on me, legs apart. The man stretched himself horizontally between her legs keeping his head on her privy using it as a pillow.

The man hiccupped: "Ooooom . . ."

The spasm spread to her. She too hiccupped: "Ooooom . . ."

Oom (ॐ) is the *pranava Manthram*—hymn of life.

The moment the sound of the Oom oscillated, the air in the atmosphere vacillated. The sound waves woke up the sage from meditation in the hermitage. It was the herald of the human voice in the habitat.

Within a micro-second, he came to know that the *Oom Manthram* was not chanted properly by the proper person. It was not in hi-fi. It was dummy—the hiccup of the couples.

The duplicity hindered his meditation.

He wanted to go back to the meditation.

The present place—my belly—was polluted by the *pavithra paapikal* (the holy sinners)—the couples.

They were ignorant of the meaning of sin and virtue. So, the sage did not curse the couples.

He thought of quitting the place and selecting some other area for meditation.

The century-long meditation inside my belly had made him a super *sanyasi*. He had attained the power to control his *atman*. The last lesson in *sanyasa*—the waking up of the *Kundalini*—was yet to be learnt. It was pure divine power. The power of choice: death or *Samadhi*—the time, place and the reason for his death would be his choice once he attained that power.

All the might of his body and soul should be sold to buy that power. One who possessed that power was equal to The Almighty.

Leaving his body in my belly, his soul pierced out of my head and flew into the mountain.

My soul was also allowed to accompany him. That made me proud. Leaving my wood like a living corpse my soul flew alongside his soul. I was happy that I had attained the magical power. I was the first plant on this planet to achieve this supernatural power.

His soul and my soul reached atop the peak. We entered into duplicate bodies'—shadowy appearance, semblance of something or someone not physically present—and came back to normalcy.

We settled down near a cave.

The time of our arrival was noon.

He determined to begin his meditation at *Brahmamuhurtham,* the appropriate time, the next day.

We began to prepare the area. It was a great pleasure to work with him. The snakes too joined.

To disinfect the area, we fumigated the fragrant frankincense Boswellia gum, donated by Benjamin tree. The camphor tree provided enough camphor to burn to create light. The sandalwood tree supplied dried up logs of branches to kindle the fire-pit and to fuel it, inflaming the pit continuously till the end of the meditation period.

The flora, accepting my request, provided fresh fruits and flowers for the daily *pooja* or adoration.

The snakes requested the fauna to provide milk, honey and things like that to make *panjamrutham* or offerings.

In my humblest and sweetest voice I said, "I praise Your Almighty for blessing me with the supernatural power of separating the soul from the body."

"You have not attained that power. It's my side-effect," the *sanyasi* said. "A thorn neighboring a flower will have a little fragrance."

"Forgive me, lord; I shouldn't have compared me with thyself."

"It is the thorn that gives the properties to the flower. The more ugly, and stinging the thorn, the more beautiful, soft and fragrant the flower. Thorn is the owner of these qualities. But flower possesses them. You are superior to me in all the cases—stronger than me, bigger than me, with a life-span that is longer than mine. A normal man seldom crosses a century whereas you are now in your seventh century. You'll survive further and further.

"Man is easily perishable. His perished body is good-for-nothing and even harmful. But, even if you perish, you are useful in numerous ways. Yet man rules you because he has got the thinking power. The mind. Even if you flora think of something, you instantly forget it. If someone tries to cut you down, you don't protest. You can't defend others. You have no self-defense. It is *ultra vires*. Man reacts to attacks, reacts to justice as well as to injustice."

I said thoughtfully, "But, Your Lordship, you are the most eminent person to arrive in this habitat with an eventful life of more than hundred and fifty years. And you look too young."

"As you are exceptional in the plant world, I am in the human world. And, moreover, because of my *Thaposhakti* (power of meditation) I don't easily succumb to *Jaranara* (wrinkles and graying)."

The big snake came before the *sanyasi*, bowed to him and said, "*Brahmamuhurtham* is just a few hours away."

The *sanyasi* looked at the horizon.

The retiring Sun gave him an auburn salute.

The *sanyasi* called for a cluster of clouds and requested them to shower the area.

They obeyed. The wind brought fennel flowers and dropped them in the surrounding area.

He took a nice bath in the rain and allowed me and the snakes to do *shudhi* or clean up.

Further he instructed me that I should do my duty as a look-out outside the cave. The two snakes should serve him as two guards inside the cave in order to prevent any hindrance from outside to his *thapasya*.

I tried to do a trial as a lookout.

As I looked down into the valley, in the moonlight, I saw a vista—an array of penumbral grotesques marching along in fixed order towards my dwelling place.

The apparition startled me.

As I was about to clarify, the *sanyasi* said, "Your habitat is inhabited with all the kinds and types of creatures on this planet. They comprise of human beings, animals, mammals, reptiles, birds, insects, amphibians, aquatics, etc."

"Are there aquatics in that procession?"

"No. They are arriving from the ocean through the river."

"Ocean!"

"Yes. You have not heard of it. It's bigger than the sea. There is also a world beneath the sea where there are full of marvels and mysteries."

"My mother didn't say anything about this world beneath the sea. I'll ask her for details when I go back."

"You'll go back from here surely," said the *sanyasi*. "But you'll not hear from your mother."

I was dumbfounded.

"Your area is polluted," continued the *sanyasi*. "Don't you recollect your mother's words? The moment human beings step on her body in your habitat, you'll lose the power to communicate with her. That is what has happened."

I felt that I was hearing the news of my mother's demise. The state of no more communications! By all means the state of my mother is no more—remaining on her dead body.

I came out of my thoughts as the two serpents made a sound like the blowing of conches to alert the *sanyasi* of the arrival of the *Brahmamuhurtham.*

Meanwhile, the *sanyasi* churned the *arani* or wood kindled by attrition. The sandalwood *agnikundam* or the fire pit was lit.

In front of the *agnikundam,* the *sanyasi* sat down in *padmasanam* (lotus-posture). He began his *tapas.*

I stood outside the cave looking around vigilantly.

In that auspicious *muhurtham,* flowers showered, animals snapped conches, birds sang hymns, plants danced and many such extra-natural things happened.

* * *

Seventy years of my seventh century had passed like the fall of seventy dry leaves.

All this while the *sanyasi* was meditating.

His body was covered with an anthill. He was like a hermit in a termatarium. The bizarre object resembled a statue.

The serpents coiled up near the anthill. They relieved each other at intervals following a two-watch system. The one who was engaged on duty remained always alert keeping the hood up. It was as if they had got special commando training.

I had nothing to do except dozing. I too wished to meditate. But it was no kid's game.

Meditation was a simple word to pronounce. But to practice it was harder than lifting a mountain with one finger. It was harder than drinking all the waters of an ocean, harder than taking a bath in hot lava. It was harder than eating up all the solid matters on earth at a stretch.

It was the passage to the seat of The Almighty.

To meditate was to open the sanctum sanctorum. And if you could do it, The Almighty would vacate the seat for you. He would treat you as his reliever. He would hand over the charge of the universe to you.

But . . . no tools of mind had so far been found to pave the way to reach The Almighty.

Even the man with the halo was finding it difficult to attain the goal by maintaining the meditation in the proper manner.

To me, a simple *maram* (tree), the subject was unthinkable. So, I gave up the effort.

In one *Brahmamuhurtham*, I was in a drowsy mood. Then I heard a snap. Immediately I came to life.

The serpents raised their hoods.

I felt something wrong somewhere.

I looked around.

No object. No image. Not even a shadow.

But snakes upset me with their hiss.

It was like an air-raid warning.

The snakes snarled at me. Then they talked to each other. I could not understand their talk because their language was foreign to me.

After giving some instructions to the small snake, the big one came out of the cave. He took a round around me and moved into the darkness.

The round around me was an indication that I was not doing my duty properly.

I felt guilty.

But the guilt melted away soon.

I had not committed any mistake.

Then the opacity of the darkness waned and it turned translucent. I could make out the crawling sound of the scales of the reptile (big snake), followed by the sound of heavy footfall on the ground.

Yes. No, I could see their penumbrae.

Yes. Some human figures! The snake as a herald.

Being a reptile, the snake could sense even the faintest movement on the ground from far away.

I had no such ability. So, I could not know of the approach of the man. The sounds were coming nearer.

The big snake forced the sounds to a halt.

Meanwhile, the morning sun illuminated the mountain.

Three human beings! They were male human calves!

Yes. The so-called boys!

I examined their entire body.

None of them had reached adulthood like the *sanyasi* or the couples who came to the habitat.

I observed them closely.

The boy with the hollow cheeks was white-colored. The other with the flat cheeks had the color of wheat. The third with chubby cheeks had the color of meat.

They recognized our ghostly bodies.

Neglecting us, they tried to walk into the cave.

As I was the chief guard, it was my duty to prevent them from entering. I dropped down a branch to block their way.

They did not bother. They crossed the branch.

The big snake was angry. It unfurled its hood and hissed at them.

The snake, its hood and the hiss appalled them. They stepped back. They talked among themselves.

One said, "*Hey*, how would we enter?"

The other said, "The snake and the tree seem to be sentries. That's why they prevent us . . ."

The third: "But how to make them understand we've come from far away on foot to have the *swami's darshan* (glimpse)?

The first said, "What to do! They do not follow our language and we can't follow theirs."

Peeping into the cave, the second said, "But where is the *swami*? He is nowhere to be seen."

The third: "No trace of human beings inside!"

Cracking the anthill open, the *swami* woke up from his *tapas*.

The three boys were stupefied.

Many great changes occurred in the nature. The cave shone as if Sun had risen inside it.

The creatures dwelling in the burrows came out and danced. The lethargic creatures became energetic. Birds endured acrobatics. The river stopped flowing. Still waters stirred. The half-moon became full. The wind hummed hymns. The clouds played games. Animals pricked their ears. Wild beats howled and roared. Reptiles took out a procession led by a king cobra. Plants showered flowers. Trees tossed fruits down and played *ammanakali* or juggling.

In a nutshell, the earth was filled with *ragam, thanam, pallavi* and *thalam* and *melam*—music and dance everywhere.

Sorrow gave way to happiness.

The *sanyasi* stood up.

The snakes stood on their tale-tips to salute him.

The three boys hailed '*Swami Saranam*' (the lord was the refuge).

The boys paid their marks of respect.

The hollow-cheeked knelt before the *sanyasi*.

The flat-cheeked bent down.

The chubby-cheeked fell prostrate.

The *swami* blessed them: "*Swagatham Puthras*" (welcome, sons).

They came to their feet.

"Praise is to lord . . . ," the hollow-cheeked boy wished the *swami*.

"*Iss salam malik . . .* ," the flat-cheeked boy wished the *swami*.

"*Guruve nama . . .* ," the chubby-cheeked boy wished the *swami*.

"So, you have come in search of truth." the *Swami* said.

They said, "You're *antheryami* and you know our goal. We had had dreams about the three powers—*Brahesh, Vishma,* and *Mahnu.* You are the combination of all—the *trimurthis.*"

"The three powers you quote now are the fire, water and air, essential for any organism to exist on earth. The combination of all the three has got the ability to create, preserve and to destroy. Some who empowered those powers were known as the names you mentioned now."

"We too wish to gain these powers, *Guruji.*"

"No gain without pain. Anyway, you have reported here from different corners of the world to do good things."

"I'm from the land of Hova," said the hollow-cheeked boy.

"So you're Hova."

"I'm from the land of B'lla," said the flat-cheeked boy.

"So you're B'lla."

"I'm from the land of Eysa," said the chubby-cheeked boy.

"So you're Eysa."

So, the *swami* named them and said, "All of you hail from the land of one God. But he is known in different names. The lord is not one, two, three or its squares. The lord is zero."

"Zeeerooo!" exclaimed the boys in unison.

"*Haam.*" continued the swami. "Zero is the most difficult and valuable position to achieve. To attain that you will have to make your mind zero. The state of creating non-entity in your mind. For that you'll have to practice *yoga* first, then meditation. The beginning point of everything is zero or void."

Accepting the aphorism of the *swami*, the boys apologized. "Pardon us for hindering your meditation . . ."

"Don't be disappointed. I've curtailed the meditation voluntarily. I don't want to be on par with the Lord. So, I stopped vacillating the *Kundalini.*"

"*Kundalini?*" they exclaimed.

"That's the last lesson. You have to continue your studies for decades and decades to learn it."

"We'll be blessed to have you as our teacher," the boys requested.

"Anyway you have come in search of knowledge. Teaching shall not be refused and denied. Henceforth you may call me *guru*."

"We are blessed, *Guruji*."

"Alright," the *guru* said. "Today is the last day of your worldly life. Till *Brahmamuhurtham* tomorrow, you are at liberty to do whatever you want. Do even unnatural things or act . . ."

The boys were stupefied to hear that. They stared at each other.

The *guru* continued, "You betray yourselves and each other. Harm yourselves and each other. Cheat yourselves and each other. Brainwash yourselves and each other. Destroy yourselves and each other. Enjoy yourselves and each other. Rag yourselves and each other. Rape yourselves and each other. Drug yourselves and each other. This may be the first but it is last chance you have to experience what is said to be evil."

Again the boys showed dissatisfaction.

The *guru* added, "You should return tomorrow. Till that time commit whatever evil you want. You may experience all kinds of evils. Only then you can differentiate between *dushkarma* and *sat karma* or the vices and virtues. When you attain *moksha*, the reminiscence of your evil deeds will chill your marrow."

*   *   *

Obtaining permission from the *guru*, the three boys set out to the dense forest.

They had been starving during a week's journey.

Their alimentary canals were empty as dried-up canals.

Eating was their priority.

The forest was dense. Now and then they spotted a wild animal. They couldn't find any fig.

They walked, walked and walked.

They were thirsty too.

The river was far below in the valley. They cried in an effort to bring out tears so that they could at least make their lips wet. But their eyes did not open the tap.

They tried to urinate so that they could drink it. But the valves remained shut.

They cursed God.

They continued to wander for food.

They felt the smell of their intestines burning due to starvation. They thought they would even settle for a poisonous fruit. But they did not find any.

Again they cursed the Creator.

Eysa's leg hit a rock and it hurt.

He sat down clutching a plant to prevent a fall. The juice of the plant was smeared on his hand. He licked his palm. The juice was palatable.

The others also squeezed the plant and extracted the juice. They swallowed the drops till they felt nausea.

It was *a narcotic plant.*

They walked further . . . Eysa limped . . .

A mango tree with three ripe mangoes! They thought the mangoes were made for them. Then they praised the Lord.

B'lla climbed the tree and plucked a mango. He threw it to Hova to keep it.

The mango rolled down to the valley and a root stopped it. The second fruit also fell near the first.

Hova went down, picked up the fruits and threw them one by one to Eysa, who was in a foul mood because of the injury on his leg.

The third fruit also rolled down to the valley.

By that time Hova had already passed two mangoes to Eysa.

Three fruits for three men. One mango for each.

Eysa could not control his hunger. He ate his share before the other two reached the spot.

B'lla was descending the tree. Hova was ascending the valley.

As Eysa finished one fruit his hunger doubled. Without wasting time, he ate one more mango.

When B'lla and Hova approached, Eysa was beginning to eat the third one.

Angry and hungry, they caught hold of the third fruit. The fruit fell on the ground. B'lla and Hova fought for the fruit.

In the combat, the fruit got damaged. The flesh and juice of the fruit were covered with dust and mud. The mango became unfit to consume.

Anger tempted B'lla to hit Eysa.

Hunger tempted Hova to kick Eysa.

Leaving him there, B'lla and Hova made their way in search of fruits.

They found one more mango tree with two big ripe mangoes.

The sight watered their mouths.

B'lla climbed the tree. His idea was to eat the mango by sitting on the tree.

As he plucked the first fruit, an ant-cage nearby got disturbed. Ants attacked B'lla *en masse.*

In order to free his hands to remove the ants, he passed the mangoes to Hova.

B'lla jumped to the ground. He did a distress dance to remove the biting ants. It took time for him to get himself free of the ants.

Meanwhile, Hova, who was extremely hungry, was eating the second half of the second mango.

B'lla got wild.

There was an ant-cage lying down. He put it on Hova's head. Hova wanted to free his hands. He kept the half-eaten mango in his mouth and tried to remove the ants.

B'lla came and hit at the mango. It went straight into Hova's throat. That damaged his mouth.

By that time Eysa managed to reach the spot with great difficulty.

B'lla climbed another mango tree that bore a lot of mangoes.

Like a glutton, he ate many mangoes. He praised the lord.

He threw the mango seeds on the heads of Eysa and Hova.

They did not know the art of tree-climbing. They requested B'lla to give them one mango each at least.

But he only bared his teeth and jeered at them with a hiccup.

Annoyed, they threw stones at B'lla.

Hurriedly he dismounted. His legs slipped. He fell on his hands on the hard ground. Both hands got fractured.

So, all the three boys, one way or the other had mutilated their bodies and thereby were disabled.

The fracture made B'lla's thirst intense. Eysa and Hova were thirsty, hungry and angry. They jointly abused B'lla for his greed.

B'lla called names of their parents.

Eysa even abused those using words for the penis and vagina of B'lla's parents.

Hova even brought the ovary and ovum of their mothers into the abuses.

They snarled at each other.

They wrestled one another. Homicide tendency rose in them.

Then the drug started showing its effect on them. They became hilarious. They behaved like gays by making love like animals.

Sometimes they praised the lord. Sometimes they cursed. They sang, laughed, and rendered lot of frantic activities of fun and frolic.

When the intoxication of the drug increased, they felt thirsty.

To quench the thirst they travelled to the riverside.

B'lla and Hova had no injuries on their legs. They spurted as they reached the river earlier than Eysa. They drank enough water. Their thirst died down. But the thrust of revenge took birth in them when they remembered the troubles in the mango grove.

They dived into the water to get fresh. Their bare bodies chilled. The injuries burned.

But feeling of revenge burnt more.

Hova's hands were alright. He gripped B'lla's neck and clipped him. B'lla struggled hard to get off from the hands of Hova. He was helpless. His hands were fractured. He was on the verge of death. He prayed to the lord to save him from jeopardy. No response came from God's side. He was sure that he would be drowned. He saw the Satan of death under water with an anchor and cable in his hands.

He cursed God and praised the Satan.

The Satan seized and shackled his legs with his cable as if to moor him permanently in the fathomless waters of death. He closed his eyes to receive the darkness of death.

He did not like the cruel action of the Satan. So he cursed the Satan and praised the lord. He was on pins and needles when he felt pins and needles on his face.

He opened his eyes.

Yes! His savior appeared! Right in front of him! The savior's body measured half a foot in length and half an inch in radius. The savior looked at him and danced in accordance with the movements of his master.

His savior's master was his antagonist.

Yes. Hova was the master of B'lla's savior.

As he prayed to God, He came under water as a manifestation form the body of his own opponent.

So, B'lla experienced that God was everywhere—under water, in the air and on the land. He experienced that God would take every shape—animal, plant, human or any of the human organs.

B'lla's savior was Hova's *lingam* or the penis.

Yes. Hova's *lingam* appeared before him like an *avatar*.

B'lla snapped the tip of Hova's long and lean *lingam*. The loose foreskin was bitten between the teeth.

Hova writhed.

B'lla crushed the tip of the *lingam*.

Hova's groaning resounded: "Ohooo . . . ."

Hova loosened his grip. B'lla came to the surface. He took in air to fill his empty lungs through the mouth.

Poor Hova saw that his prepuce was resting on top of B'lla's tongue like a small pearl in a big shell.

B'lla was baptized by Hova and Hova was circumcised by B'lla.

Hova tried to hit B'lla. B'lla ran off to the bank. Hova followed him. But as he came out of the water, his injured penis started burning.

The gore-capped *lingam* bound Eysa in a spell.

Hova was irritated. He reached Eysa and tried to hit him. At the same time Eysa felt pins and needles on his wounded leg that was in water. He sank. He surfaced from the water with a fish in his hand. He threw the fish on to the bank. The fish writhed, stayed still for a moment and again writhed.

All the three assembled on the bank and watched the struggling fish. They were in company again and the death of the fish rejoiced them.

By that time they had recovered from toxemia but were overcome by exhaustion.

Like good friends, they slept on the bank using dry leaves as bed.

It was a cold night. Their bare bodies were chilled to the marrow. They overlapped and crossed legs to resist the cold. The heat of the body eased the cold to a certain extent. Still it was intolerable.

They hugged each other. Continuous hugging and crossing of the legs caused friction on their bodies. The hugging, the friction and the warmth from it made their penises erect. They became one body. They rolled.

Semen emitted like lava.

The second service of their sexual sequence made them sedate. But it weakened them mentally and physically.

They had gone to bed with guilt-filled heads. Eysa wondered what B'lla and Hova were thinking about him. B'lla wondered what Hova and Eysa were thinking about him. Hova wondered what B'lla and Eysa were thinking about him.

They stretched themselves separately and stared at Moon.

Moon gazed in an unfriendly manner at them with his eyes wide open.

The clouds rushed to report the malicious matter of the three boys to The Almighty.

Guilt made them unconscious—they slept.

Somewhere in the jungle, wild cocks crowed.

All the three jumped to their feet. Looked at each other as the rising sun looked at them.

"Aye, the *Brahmamuhurtham* is over, seems to be . . . !"

They ate crow.

"Common, on your toes. Let's take *shudhi.*

After the natural calls, they cleaned their teeth, tongue and mouth with a neem branch. They took bath in the river.

While taking bath, Eysa said, "We should not take anything. Not even a drop of water. *Guruji*'s instruction is that we should report at the *gurukulam* with empty stomach."

After taking *shudhi* they picked up some leaves, pinned with hard veins and made belts. Wore them around their waists. A big leaf covered the private parts.

Reaching the top Eysa urinated. The other two did not feel like doing that. They suspected that Eysa was preventing them from drinking water. But he had had enough . . .

And it was true!

Eysa infringed the ordinance issued by their *guru.* They wanted to punish him. They kicked around Eysa.

B'lla caught hold of Eysa from the back. Hova kicked at his testicles repeatedly.

The testicles were crushed! They wanted to hide somewhere.

The testicles crept into the abdominal cavity and stopped functioning. The genital organ had lost its sexual prowess and he became impotent— fit to be *brahmachari.*

Eysa was so tired that he had no kicks left.

He was dragged and produced before the *guru* by B'lla and Hova.

Each one tried to report the other's fault.

The *guru* raised his palm and said, "*Shanty, Puthras, shanty* . . . I saw the vistas with my third eye"

"The third eye?" they exclaimed.

"Yes. The inner and invisible eye or the *jnanadrishti*"

The three boys looked each other.

The *guru* said softly, "Eysa cheated you. You manhandled him. I think all of you enjoyed the stint with evil. Evil deeds are sweet and satisfying in the initial stage. But at the final stage they turn bitter and dissatisfying. On the contrary, virtues are the opposite. In due course of your life, you will have to compare the good with the bad and the right with the wrong and the up with the down."

The boys nodded.

The *guru* added, "The time is already up. So, today you can't start the lesson. Tomorrow we will start. Till then, don't go anywhere. Watch what the tree and snakes are doing. They do the daily routines. You too join them. Tomorrow onwards you will render all the services required for the smooth functioning of the *gurukulam*. Today all the three of you are as good as sinners. Tomorrow onwards you are going to become apprentices or *Vidhyarthis*. Best wishes!"

Ashamed of their acts and satisfied with the blessings, they *kow-towed* to the *guru*.

CENTURY 8

701 TO 800 AD

Fragments of peepul wood, sandalwood, devadaru or cadrus libin and pieces of my branches (Banyan) were burning in the homakunda.

The guru sat in front of the kunda in padmasanam. The three boys sat nearby to him cross-legged. Their bodies were smeared with sandal paste.

The Nagas and I eagerly watched the yajna or ritual performance.

The guru chanted, "*Om, Vighnes namaha.*"

The boys repeated, "*Om, Vighnes namaha.*"

The continuous chanting of the mantras or hymns and the rhythmic ringing of the bells in their left hands filled the forest.

They threw heaps of acqilaria, malaccenis, valirina wallichi and cardamom in the kunda one by one with the right hands. Those items were known as *Ishta samagri*. Milk and ghee *(pushta samagri)* were also poured in the kunda.

Honey, jaggery and dry grapes were *mishta samagri*. Other than these, grains like wheat, rice and gingilly were also added into the fire.

The fume and fragrance from the fire purified the forest.

Flames danced like *narthakis* to the rhythm of mantras and the ringing of the bell.

I fixed my eyes on the *Agni* or fire. With my mind concentrated on a particular spot, I forgot to indulge in all unwanted and wicked thoughts. I felt ease in breathing. The air was very light! No hot or cold feeling!

There was no noise other than that of the yajna. It seemed that all the noises of the globe mingled with the hymns at the yajna. They swept away sound pollution—even the horrifying sound of the sea waves and the hum of the heavy winds.

The soft and melodious sound of the hymns in low volume filled the whole place.

It seemed that all the air was sucked away from the atmosphere and removed the air pollution. The *homakunda* served as canister mask. It purified the impure air. It provided pure air to the world.

It seemed that the heat from the *kunda* evaporated all the water on earth, condensed it and eliminated water pollution.

The fire in the *homakunda* purified all the animate and inanimate things on earth.

A lot of physical and chemical changes were taking place owing to the yajna. The change enveloped initially the forest and then the entire earth.

The sound of the mantra and *Mani* (bell) echoed everywhere . . . everywhere . . . everywhere . . . The warmth of homakunda spread everywhere . . . everywhere . . . everywhere . . .

An idol had been placed in front of the *homakunda*. The deity's head resembled that of an elephant. The body was of a human being with a bulky belly.

Flowers lay in heaps in front of the guru and the three boys. Reciting the verses of the mantra, the guru picked up a flower petal and threw it on the statue. The boys imitated the guru's act.

The yajna concluded on the thirty-first daybreak.

The Guru chanted: "Om *purnamadah purnamidam,*
Poornal purnamudachyathe . . .
Poornasya purnamadayah,
Poornamewavasishyathe.
Ooooom Shanthi . . . Shanthi . . . Shanthi . . .
Ooooom Shanthi . . . Shanthi . . . Shanthi . . .
Ooooom Shanthi . . . Shanthi . . . Shanthi . . .

The boys repeated the hymns along with the guru.

They kept the bells on the ground. They stretched their hands and thrashed out the fire. The dancing flames were put out. Their hands did not suffer burns when they removed the torrid ash from the kunda.

The guru ordered, "Go and dispense the *bhasma* to the donors of the *pooja's* property."

The boys stood up. They swiveled their heads. Strong emotions seized them.

All around the *yagasala or evolution-hut,* animals were waiting anxiously. The boys distributed the ash and flowers to the animals under the supervision of the Nagas.

The Nagas requested the animals: "Respected donors please donate the *prasadam* to those who could not come here, especially the flora donors."

The animals stretched their limbs. They put the religious mark on their foreheads with the ash. It resembled an exclamation mark. They kept the flower petal on their ears.

The guru placed the idol at my foot. He drew three horizontal parallel lines ($\equiv$) on my trunk with the ash. That too was a religious mark.

Accepting the *prasadam,* the animals went away contented.

We were famishing since a month. I had some water and sunlight. They had milk and fruits. All, including the Nagas, filled their bellies.

Thirty days of non-stop yajna. The boys were tired. They slept . . .

After thirty hours of deep sleep, they woke up as if from a dream. The yajna in fact regenerated them.

They went to the river, had their *shudhi* and came back. They had not felt exhausted with the ascent and descent of the mountain as they had felt earlier.

When they reached the *gurukulam* they found that the guru had already completed his shudhi. He was ready to give them *vidya* or classes.

Then guru sat on an elevated rock. The boys sat on the ground. All sat erect in my shade.

The guru said: "Tomorrow, we'll start the lessons. Today I'll give you an introduction into the concepts of *gurukulam, Vidhyarthis,* guru and vidya. *Gurukulam* is the school. It covers the whole mountains, the river and the entire forest. You shouldn't cross the river and wander. Why is this out-of-bounds? The maintenance and cleaning will be impossible if the premises are large. You should consider your school as a place of worship and the cave as the sanctum sanctorum. And far away, across the river, human beings dwell. To mingle with them at this stage will not be deemed fit for your studies. It may harm your character. It may adulterate your behavior. You should be always a *satswabhavi.*

"You are a *Vidhyarthis* or student. In other words, you are the plants. I'm the farmer. Vidya the fertilizer—water, sunlight and other chemicals. The more you assimilate, the more you grow. The more you grow the more vidya you gain. Henceforth you'll be called—B'lla as Brahesh, Eysa as Vishma and Hova as Mahnu. You'll live here."

The boys responded approvingly.

The guru continued: And I . . . I'm your guru—the teacher. As per mythology, the teacher is next to God, sometimes parallel to God. You should pray to him. You should adore him. I don't demand that. It's up to you to decide. You need not be so obsequious to . . ."

The boys interfered, "We'll admire you till death . . ."

The guru went on: "I want only your obedience. If you don't obey me you won't follow my lessons. If you won't follow them . . ."

"We'll obey and follow you till death . . ."

"*Achcha . . . achcha . . .* (very good)," the Guru said. Now about *vidya. Vidya* is the knowledge you are going to gain during the schooling. Treasure of knowledge would be heaped in your heart-treasury. So you clean up your heart to keep those purest valuables known as the knowledge. And at the same time, you should sharpen your mind to acquire *vidya. Vidya* is like a diamond. To cut it, you need the sharpest blade of brain. For that you'll have to free your mind from unwanted thoughts and wickedness.

"Even if you possess that diamond, it does not belong to you. It is to be given to the ignorant. The more light you shed on them, the more your heart shines, the more your brain gets sharpened. That's the magic of *vidya*.

"Vidya is a gift given by Goddess *Vidayadevi* is *Saras*. We've to please her. Offer a pooja."

"Oh, is that what we've performed Guruji?"

"No. That's the *Vighnes pooja*. Prior to starting anything, we'll have to please the omnipotent of obstacles. He is very obstinate. Each and every moment and movement of our life is obstructed by different incidents, accidents, jeopardy and things like that. Hindrance is hidden here and there. Besides external obstructions, the body obstructs activities at times—we hit our leg on some stone or fall down while walking. The food particles go out of route while eating.

"Wind blows from the opposite side and reduces the speed of your life. Wind comes along with you and increases and damages the normal speed of your life. When you want to dry something rain comes. When you want to wet something the sun shines. Omens obstruct your sleep. The crow gets boils in its mouth while berries are ripe. When a tiger gets a stag, he suffers from a toothache.

"These obstructions do not make any difference whereas a minor obstruction will spoil a major education, especially where and when concentration is needed. Concrete concentration is very essential for practical classes of *pooja, yajna, thapasya* et al. You could remain without food and rest for thirty days. It was because of the concentration of your mind on the *Agni* of the *homakunda*. Epics tell us that the *munis* had meditated for more than a millennium in the dense forest. That's why we performed a *Vighnes yajna.*

"Then we'll collect properties for *Saraswathi yajna* also . . .

"She doesn't need a yajna. She is easily pleased. She never refuses boon to anyone. A simple pooja and a prayer are enough. She as your mother will take you on her bosom and breast-feed you with the milk of knowledge. You can consume as much as you can. She has a rich stock of it to provide the whole cosmos."

"Guruji, we're eager to embrace her . . . eager to embrace her . . . eager to embrace her . . ." the boys were impatient.

"*Shanthi . . . Shanthi . . . Shanthi . . .* (peace). Eat slowly and you can eat a mountain. Drink slowly, you can drink an ocean. To reach her bosom, you'll have to climb on her from the foot. If you're intelligent and enthusiastic, you'll reach there soon."

At the next *Brahmamuhurtham*, an idol of Saras was installed by the side of Lord Vighnes. A simple *pushpanjali* (offering of flowers) was performed. A simple devotional song was sung with the ringing of the bells.

"Saras is the great goddess of literacy.

Bless us to sing in Cosmolish . . .

Aaha Cosmolish . . . Ohho Cosmolish . . ."

"Do you know what Cosmolish is . . . ?"

"Nahi, Guruji, nahi . . ."

"It's the language of the whole universe. It's the vernacular of the faunas and floras too. As per *Saraswathy's* directives, Cosmolish comprises of four languages—the language of human beings, the language of plants, the language of animals and the language of inanimate things. And each language is subdivided by them. The other three categories won't understand what we speak. Likewise, we can't understand their languages. To communicate to each other one should know the common language—Cosmolish."

Pointing towards me, the guru added, "Here, the *Aalmaram* (Banyan tree), the Nagas (the snakes) and I only know it. As all the fauna and flora of our gurukulam are our staff, we have to communicate with them."

"Certainly, Guruji, certainly . . ."

"Achcha, let us call her, the Devi of *sangeetham* (music)."

Raising hands towards the heaven, they sang.

"O, Devi Saras, goddess of voice, goddess of noise, goddess of music! We hail you in our gurukulam.

This way . . . this way . . . this way Devi.

You're the *ragam*, you're the thanam, you are the *geetham*, you're the sangeetham. We hail you in our gurukulam.

This way . . . this way . . . this way Devi.

You're the *aksharam,* you're the *padam*, you're the *vachanam*, you're the *bhasha* (language). We hail you in our gurukulam.

This way . . . this way . . . this way Devi.

You're the *bhavi,* you're the *bhootham*, you're the *varthamanam*, you're the *charithram* (period and history). We hail you in our gurukulam.

This way . . . this way . . . this way Devi.

You're the art, you're the science, you're the commerce, and you're the business.

We hail you in our gurukulam.

This way . . . this way . . . this way Devi.

O! Goddess of knowledge, kindly come to our heart . . . home in our heart . . . home in our heart . . .

Devi *Saras's* voice came from the heaven . . . singing . . . swinging . . . shrieking the gurukulam.

All the nerves of all of them were regenerated. All the junctions on the roads of all the arteries and veins of all of them pulsated with blood. All the muscles in the flesh of all of them were flushed. All the bones of all of them turned as strong as bronze. All the bad ideas from the brains of all of them were drained. All the eyes' power of all of them was raised to the power of ten from the power of ten. All the ear-drums of all of them became capable of sensing even the sound of dry leaf movement from far away

They gained *gyanadrishty*—enlightened. They could make out the noise made by the *vriksha* (plants). They heard the dialogues between the two Nagas. They could understand the vernacular of maram and mrugam—the Cosmolish language.

The *Vidhyarthis* were happy to experience the magic of communicating with animate and inanimate beings. The Nagas were happier than the *Vidhyarthis* to have that magic. I was the happiest to regain that magic of communication.

First of all, they tried the language on me. They came beneath my parasol and asked me to bend a branch. I bowed a branch. Then they requested me to give some fruits to them. I shook a branch and the berries fell down. They opened the berries and ordered the germs inside to vacate the fruit. They vacated their quarters immediately.

Then the boys approached the elder naga, expressed their wish to show their poisonous teeth. The naga opened its mouth. I too was horrified to see the pointed poisonous piercing prongs in its cave-like mouth.

The Nagas and I asked the *Vidhyarthis* why their bodies were wet. They replied that it was sweat. We wished to taste it. They wiped the sweat from their temples with their forefingers. Brahesh dropped it into the mouth of the younger naga, Vishma into the elder naga's mouth and Mahnu dropped the sweat on my protrusive root. The sweat was salty yet tasty.

As Goddess Saraswathi gifted all of them with eyesight of a telescope, the guru instructed them to decrease the sight. They adjusted the focal length of their eyes so as to visualize the *gurukulam* premises only.

As Goddess *Saraswathi* gifted all of them with great audio power, the guru instructed them to reduce the volume to a minimum to cover the range of the *gurukulam* only.

The *Vidhyarthis* controlled the audio-visual faculties. On behalf of the *guru,* they called out:

"Do you hear and see there, do you hear and see there. This is the *Vidhyarthis* speaking. Calling attention of all the fauna and flora of the *gurukulam*. It is hereby informed that we are at liberty to communicate with you as and when we feel like and on an as-is-where-is basis with maximum convenience and minimum disturbance. As per the mutual understanding scheme, organized by our *Guruji*, we have to help each other. Aid each other. Details can be had from the *gurukulam*."

No sooner did the proclamation was over than many a fauna arrived around the *gurukulam* to have a glimpse of the *guru*, the *Vidhyarthis*, the Nagas and me. They too considered the *gurukulam* as the holy of holies.

Plenty of plants paid attention to the gurukulam on hearing the proclamation. They were very happy to have the opportunity of conversing with the human beings. Each plant prepared a composition in its heart about its agonies and ecstasies.

The past vistas of my native place and the occasion of Naming the Nation ceremony came as a flashback on the screen of my mind in montages. The proclamation and the gathering were not new to me.

Next day . . .

The *Vidhyarthis* followed the daily routine without the assistance of the Nagas. Many a morning the *gurukulam* woke up. The *Vidhyarthis* went to the valley and then to the river in lightning speed. After *shudhi* they collected ingredients for *nithya pooja* (daily rites)—water from the river, flowers from the valley, wood from the woods, fruits from the forest and milk from mammals.

A cow, goat, buffalo, a tigress or a lioness lined up to provide milk. They believed that if their milk was used for performing *pooja*, their categories would get *moksha* and their rebirth would be in human form. So every day, they used to fall in around me in five files after their natural calls and taking a nice bath in the cold river . . .

The guru welcomed them, "Dear fauna and flora, *Swagatham* . . . *Swagatham* . . . *Swagatham* . . . I understand that not only each and every *mrugam* but each and every *maram* also wants to sacrifice even its life for the sacrifices performed there. But every flower, every wood and every fruit cannot be taken for the pooja. As far as matter of milk is concerned, only cows are entitled to have that privilege."

The guru saw the dismay on their faces.

He added, "It doesn't mean that God is neglecting your contribution. Your goodwill is enough to please God. He will surely bless you."

Some tigers said, "We wish to provide some tiger skin of our deceased colleagues. It can be used as rugs."

"Thank you for your charity," the guru said. "But, the gurukulam doesn't use any kind of comforts. Not even body cover. No cooked food. Everything should be natural. Quite natural . . ."

The animals dispersed . . .

The guru instructed, "Goddess Saraswathi is a man-of-letters. She blessed us with supernatural learning powers. We should not misuse the powers. A person holding more powers will naturally lean towards pride and prejudice. It's not fair. The power is given to understand the agonies of others. Others are our *Sahajeevis*. Their sorrow is our sorrow. Their joy is our joy. Now fill up."

The *Vidhyarthis* filled up: "Their joy is our joy . . ."

"Pick out bad things from them. Make it good. Return to them."

"*Jee ham*, Guruji, *Jee ham*," the boys agreed.

The guru went on: "Now we will have our practical. That covers the performance of *Yajnam, Homam, bali, pooja*, etc. We have already completed Yajnam, Homam and some kinds of poojas. There are umpteen types of poojas—*nadakkal pooja, mula pooja, kumbhesakarkari pooja, Brahma kalasa pooja, parikalasa pooja* et al. And there are umpteen types of Homam—*thatwa homam, prayaschitta homam, proktha homam, Shanthi homam, adhivasa homam* et al. All these rites are for the installation of idols. Besides these we will go through in detail about Yajnam and bali. The benefits and blessings of God to a man to the mankind and his *Sahajeevis*.

"Before proceeding to the practical applications, we should learn something about our life. Literally, life is the animate condition of animals and plants proved by growth through metabolism, reproduction and adjusting to the milieu. But as per the human mythology life is the existence of an individual from a period of birth to death. This life period is governed by four *ashrams*. Do you follow?"

As one man, the *Vidhyarthis* said, "Jee ham, Guruji . . . ."

The guru added: "One: *brahmacharya*—the period of study of the sacred texts under a guru."

The boys interfered: "Is that what we do in gurukulam?"

"No interference—doubts may be cleared later. The second: *Grahasthya*—the period of domestic, married life. The third: *Vanaprastha*—a life of growing detachment and preparatory abnegation. And the fourth: *Sanyasa*—departing from the family, in self-denial and renunciation of worldly pursuits. The *ashramadharma* deals with man as a social being in the light of his *sramam* or natural training and development in the milieu of different stages of his life to pave way for him to attain the final goal of his existence—*Moksham*.

"Before we analyze *brahmacharyashramam*, unlike other social beings, you will not undergo the second and third stages of life, which is the *Grihastha* and the *Vanaprastha*, whatsoever. Because you are going to be the teachers of the whole world.

"You should be a bachelor, a chronic bachelor. A bachelor does not just mean an unmarried man. You should lead an absolutely celibate life. You have to avoid contact with women. You should not look at a woman lustfully or maliciously. You should not talk with her unnecessarily. Not even a mystic, a *nithya brahmachari*. You should not be even mythic. The ghosts of *Kama* (lust) *krodha* (anger) and *moha* (greed) should be evicted from the inner system of a *brahmachari*. In a nutshell, you will not lead a family life.

"As per the human mythology of life, the third stage—*vanaprasthasram*—also you will not follow. It is the stage of the hermit. As you will not become a householder, you have no period to practice and cultivate the two *purusharthas* viz the *artha* (material benefits) and *Kama* (enjoyment of senses). An ordinary person who completes his family and social life will enter this stage. He should linger no longer on the stage as a father and husband. He should withdraw at the right age, relinquish the responsibilities of life and hand over the charge of social life to his relievers—to the younger generation. He should devote himself completely to study and contemplation without any consideration. And he should pay attention to the pursuit of his last *ashram*—the *Sanyasa*.

"We will understand that *sanyasasharm* comes far later, because you are going to enter that stage in due course of your life.

"Tomorrow we will begin the discourse on Brahmacharya."

A whole day till the next day, the Vidhyarthis were engaged in collecting food and wood, flowers and fuels. The food items were fruits and milk. Essential wood, flowers and grass were required for the daily pooja. The fuels were camphor, galipot and resin.

Then for *sodhana* and *shudhi* they went to the river. The *praathal* (breakfast) would be only a handful of berries and a mouthful of milk.

After that the practical classes of all the prayers—*poojas, homas, yagnas, yagas and yogas*. The performances and observances will be strict and rigorous.

"There should not be any negative attitude. Every action should be affirmative and generated from positive thinking. You should be ethical. Not even a microsecond's thought in your mind should catch the spark of atheism. You should not snub God even in dreams. And you should keep yourselves away from dreams.

"Peace should prevail in the ashram. As you are Brahesh, Vishma and Mahnu—the three essential powers for the creation, existence and survival of the world—you should live in co-operation. If anyone power out of these fails or hesitates to co-operate, it would affect the balance of the world.

"Do not think about any comforts. You have natural accommodation—the sky is the roof, the earth is the floor and the horizon the walls.

"If you could successfully and willfully, enthusiastically and smartly pass out of the *brahmanashrama*, you will gain all the supernatural powers: The so-called miracle that an ordinary man can't perform. The normal populace would be enthralled by your miracles like *aneyma, garima, mahima, lahima, Iysethawam, vasythawam, prakasyam, prapthi* and what to say more, you may be able to control your own death according to your will and wish—the *Samadhi*."

*   *   *

Brahmacharya in thought, word and deed was insisted upon. That energized and channeled the *Vidhyarthis'* psyches and physiques into good course. They, in the gurukulam, led a simple life of honesty and modesty. Maintained cleanliness—kept their stomachs and tongues tight avoiding over-eating and chattering. Anchored their arms and moored their minds. They subjected to strict discipline. They paid the highest degree of reverence to the guru and regarded him as their spiritual teacher. The most striking feature of *gurukulam vidya* was that the moral culture in them was cultivated along with character-building and their intellectual culture in parallel.

There a test was conducted to check their mind power.

Brahesh, Vishma and Mahnu were made to sit beneath me. I hatted lot of dry leaves. Bunches and bunches of berries hung on my branches like pendants.

The guru sat on the elevated rock.

The boys were told to sing a devotional song.

They sang:

Saras is a great goddess of literacy!

Bless us to sing in Cosmolish.

Cos . . . . Cos . . . Cosmolish . . .

The guru ordered: "Change to some other language"

Varaveenaaa . . . vanalole, Varaveenaaa . . . vanalole

Vaaaney maney, varadaayini

Vaaaney maneeey, varadaayini . . .

The Guru, "Pray to Vighneswara, the Eliminator of Obstacles in another language . . ."

As one man they prayed . . .

Jai Janesh, Jai Janesh, Jai Janesh deva,

Maatha Teri Parvathi, Pitha Mahadeva.

While they were singing, I was ordered by the guru to drop berries on their shaven heads. Slowly, I dropped the berries one after another.

The Vidhyarthis were told to count the falling berries on their heads. One . . . two . . . three . . .

The guru told me to do it faster. I dropped the berries faster.

They kept on counting the berries in their mind while singing the prayer in various languages as ordered by the guru.

Further, I was ordered to drop some dry leaves in front of them. They were told to count those too.

The guru: "Change the language and song"

Samantha prapanjam rathichum bharichum
Muda samharichum rasichum ramichum
Kalichum pulachum mudakhora khoram
Vilichum mamananda dese vasichum.
Loka prapanja pravaaham sahajyothirachandratharam
Namasthe sivambo namaste, namaste.

It was a prayer to Lord Siva.

The elder naga was ordered to take clockwise rounds of the students while the little naga was asked to take anti-clockwise rounds. They changed their directions intermittently. The students were told to remember the number of rounds taken by each snake.

The birds were already asked to make mimicking noises. One bird made other bird's noise—they obeyed.

Some of the animals were asked to disturb the atmosphere of the *ashram* to divert the students' minds.

The lion roared . . . horses neighed . . . goats bleated . . .

The students were to find out the direction from where the sounds were coming.

They were given drops of milk from animals like cow, buffalo, goat, tiger, camel etc.

The students were to match the animal with the milk.

The wind sent various smells—fragrance and stink—to the nostrils of the students to sedate and nauseate them. They were to differentiate each smell.

The process continued for eight hours . . .

One by one, the students were asked the answers in-camera.

Each one answered as follows   : —
Berries dropped on head   : 28,800 per head

Leaves dropped in front	: 21,600
Rounds taken by elder snake	: 280 clockwise 200 anti-clockwise
Rounds taken by younger snake	: 400 anti-clockwise 140 clockwise.
Birds' noises (mimicry)	: Parrot made the noise of crow; crow made the noise of cock. Cock made the noise of duck; duck made the noise of nightingale.
Directions of animals' sounds	: Lion from Far East. Horses from Middle West and the sheep from rear and very near. Milk grading by viscosity, smell : First—cow; second—Buffalo; third—goat; fourth and sweetness Camel and fifth Tiger.
Sensing of smell while singing	: At first song—smell of jasmine. At second song—smell of rose. At third song—smell of lavender. At the other times bad smell . . .

Likewise the *Vidhyarthis' panchendriyas*—eyes, ear, nose, skin and tongue—were tested rigorously. They passed the tests with distinction.

Thereafter a painstaking test was conducted by pinning thorns on their skin. The blood that oozed out of them was collected in the respective *Kamandalu* or the ascetic's water-jug. They remained without blood for hours.

All of a sudden I heard hissing and growling. There came the Nagas followed by a regiment of snakes. They halted beside me. I asked: "Dear, why these many guests?"

The younger naga replied: Poisoning test for the princes of peace.

The guru said: "Well . . . Let go all the pins."

Each one helped the other to remove the thorns from the body. Then the guru said, "Now interchange your *Kamandalu*."

They did so.

"Drink the blood chanting the mantra of assimilation in mind."

They did so.

Their pale skin regained the flush. Brahesh assimilated the blood of Vishma. Brahesh's blood went into Mahnu. Mahnu's blood was drunk by Vishma. They opened eyes energetically. Thus the first ever blood transfusion was conducted orally in the woods of the gurukulam.

Guruji greeted the snakes: "*Namasthe*, Nagas. Please bite my *Puthras* with all your might. Let's see if they can withstand your poison. Vipers first."

The vipers, one by one, touched the guru's feet with their fangs as a mark of respect. Then they bit the Vidhyarthis on their feet.

After vipers, cobras approached the guru in single-file formation with their hoods up. Standing on their tails, they bit the Vidhyarthis on their heads. The monks' faces were pock-marked with snake-bites. Their bodies turned bluish.

"Enough, dear, enough. I thank you all for donating your precious property. Please remember to collect it back next week."

They kow-towed to the guru and marched off . . .

After a week, the same reptiles came back and withdrew their poison from the same bite-marks on the monk's bodies. It was surprising to note that the poisoning had made no physical or mental changes on the Vidhyarthis. They performed all the duties assigned to them.

The guru remarked with shining eyes: *Sabash pyaro, sabash*! You have proved that you are men-of-letters with high intelligence and great personalities. Why this rough and tough test is conducted? When you pass out from the ashram to the outer world to serve and save the society you should tolerate and withstand all the sound, air, water and visual pollution. The pollution should not adulterate your brain. You should not be distracted.

"The concentration thread of your mind should not be broken. You should strengthen it by constant practice. Here itself and now itself, it's safe working load should be to a maximum. The breaking stress of your patience should be maximum. In society life, a lot many incidents may irritate your tolerance. You should tolerate that irritation without fail. You should be your own masters.

"This eight-hour trial would pave the way for you for the attainment of *Ashatasiddh*i.

"As you know, the society is an organized state of living with individuals of upper and lower classes, people of fashionable and fashion-less manners, people with principle and no principle associated together for religious, benevolent, cultural, scientific, political, economical, patriotic and all other disciplines prevailing in a community.

"The society is a mixture of good and evil. It is a motley crowd beyond one's comprehension."

The guru described to them the reminiscences of his visit to his native place as a sage where he was the king . . .

"Mingling, uplifting and dealing with society are very hard job. But at the same time, serving the society is the most sacred rendering.

"An ordinary person can't render it. But you can! You are mystics. You are the missionaries to maintain the machinery of the society.

"You are the social scientists of the mankind. You are the social advocates of the mankind. You have to refer to the law of the mankind— the *Dharma*. You are the social architects of the mankind. You should develop dwelling spaces for the mankind with the stones of dharma and spiritual concrete.

"I will teach and train you . . . To capture the confidence of the populace, you should know all the mysteries and miracles that could marvel the mass. You should be able to alter their agonies to ecstasies. Heal their hurts using your instantaneous intelligence. Initially they may not listen to you. But finally they will regard you as their godheads."

Brahesh, Vishma and Mahnu bowed their heads.

The guru: "Right. Classes close for the day."

They retired for the day.

* * *

The guru walked backwards. The Vidhyarthis walked forward facing the guru. His eyes fixed in front of him, he had no difficulty walking backwards through the dense forest.

He taught while walking: "*Pyaro*, as you know, *mantras* are words and formulae to be recited during *pooja, homa, yajna, yaga* etc. *Tantras* are the esoteric doctrines pertaining to rituals, disciplines, meditation, etc. They are composed in the form of narration between God and his power. In other words, it is the philosophy of Siva-Shakhty. Shakhty is the wife of Shiva, the goddess worshipped as Uma or Kali—the universal mother.

"Tomorrow, I will let you know what *tantras* exactly are."

"Oooh! My god!!" I screamed out in exclamation.

All the *ashramavasis*, except the guru, looked at me.

The students and the snakes asked, "Why . . . what happened? Why this exclamation?"

I was reluctant to answer . . .

Calmly, the guru said like a soothsayer, "Tomorrow is the last day of our colleague's eighth centenary."

I sighed. Like reading an almanac, the Guru had read out my age. I wished to go back to my habitat. All my physical features were left over there. I wished to see my wives. I wished to see the naked couples seeking asylum beneath my shade. I wished to meet the faunas and floras.

I wanted to break all celestial obligations. I wanted to get away from the forest, fly to my native place. I wanted to enjoy the worldly life with my wives. But sensing my mind, the guru spoke to me softly: "My dear Maram, you'll get ample time to enjoy worldly life. But, for the time being you'll have to be with us. You're on our rolls till the students pass out from here. Or till I pass away from this world."

"Na, Guruji, na! We pray, such a date shall never arrive." All of us felt sad hearing Guruji's words.

So, giving due weight to his words, I buried all my wishes. I thought of remaining with them and waited for the beginning of my ninth centenary the second following day.

CENTURY 9

801 TO 900 AD

My stagnant mind began to roll. My body began to move as I heard the wholesome voice of the *Guru: "Puthras* . . . . , as we all know, today is the nine hundredth birthday of one of our staff, *Maram* . . ."

Brahesh, Vishma and Mahnu said: "Let's celebrate it, *Guruji.*"

I stood silent.

Enjoining the silence, the snakes exchanged glances.

Some milk-vendors and flower-vendors among the fauna and flora heard the tidings. But they did not react. They remained expressionless and still for the *guru's* reply.

Guru: "No. We're not celebrating the birthday. It is not that we won't respect or love him on the pretext that he is a mere *maram.* It's not that we have no regards to his service. He is the senior-most among us."

The *guru* looked at the *Vidhyarthis* and the *Nagas* with some concern. He continued: "You mark his merits. No living thing on earth will survive a lengthy life as his—*deerkhayus.* His horoscope says it. I'm not flattering. (pointing to me) This *maram* is great! Greater than you! Greatest of all of us!

"Then why no celebra . . . ."

The *guru* intervened: "Because great individuals never celebrate anything for themselves. It's for you too. He won't celebrate any personal dates. Any arguments?

"*Jeeham, Guruji, Jeeham* . . . Great people shall be remembered, won't they? Without a *jayanthi* (birthday) how can they be remb . . . ."

"Who are your so-called great people? Only one thing is great. God. So, God is to be remembered. That we can do by prayers."

"But you said our dear *maram* is great?"

"Of course. *Maram* is the greatest among us. He is not as great as God."

All the individuals present around the area appreciated the *guru's* wholesome advice. "Yet, in order to commemorate this auspicious day we will open a new subject—the *yoga*".

All of us were eager to learn *yoga*.

Guru: "To begin with, let's learn about our health first. Health is the wealthiest thing in the world for an individual. It is so dear, so celestial and so universal. Health does not mean the power of a small to uproot a big tree. He may dig a sea in a desert. He may pluck a star from the sky. Health is simply the proper state of mind and body to think and work perfectly: A standard state of strength, vigor and vitality, a balanced state of all the systems of the body and a sound condition pertaining to mental, moral or spiritual and physical freedom from infection, disease and jealous, anger and things like that.

"Someone may jump into a fire to show off. It's not a healthy act. If he jumps into the fire to save a life, he is mentally healthy. Someone may travel from one country to another with the speed of light. It's not salutary. But even if he travels with the speed of sound for his country, it is counted. It's a wholesome act.

"Our body decays even while we are living because the mind becomes infectious. Because we think badly. Inclined to do bad things. Brahesh, you say, who needs health?"

Brahesh: "Each and every object needs health. Right from I to the whole universe."

Guru: "From you to the universe. Just fill up this."

Brahesh: "I, you, family, society, country, continent, world, earth, solar system, Milky Way, the galaxies."

Guru: "Bus . . . . bus . . . . Now Vishma, tell me how can the earth be healthy?"

Vishma: "The land or healthy place, healthy climate, healthy atmosphere or pollution-free air and water. A healthy earth should have a wholesome nature."

Guru: "That's right. What happens, if the sun is not healthy, Mahnu?"

Mahnu: "Thus we will have to have a salutary fear of consequences— Sun may go weak, he may not shine, he may fall down, the atmosphere may change, the gravitation may get lost, solar system may collapse, celestial bodies may collide with each other."

Guru: "That's enough. So, all visible and invisible objects in the universe should be healthy. Then only we would be healthy. So, without the salutary effects of the milieu, human being can't maintain his health. Let's see how we can help ourselves to maintain it. Health of a person is the result of the interaction of items such as food, water, air, passion, body condition, work, rest, thinking, desire, doings, lust, mind, etc. If he would travel in a balanced vehicle with all the above-said wheels, he could maintain a perfect health. If any one of this is absent, then he loses his health—falls sick. No mercy on earth would forgive a person who breaks the law of nature.

"So, we should lead a natural life. Let us eat naturally. Dress naturally. Sleep naturally. Work naturally. A birth is natural with empty hands and bare body. Want to lead a natural life? Let us live empty-handed and bare-bodied.

"At the end of the life, it's quite natural that we'll have to leave even our body. If we are born we will die. The period from the birth to the death is the lifetime. So now, let us think about this period.

"Mahnu, how do we live naturally?"

Mahnu: "We should believe in the unity of all that live.

"In other words we should cultivate kinship with nature. Love the *mrugams*, *marams* and *malas* or mountains on earth. Regard the heavenly bodies, sky, atmosphere et al with respect."

Guru: "*Ham*, we should include everything in the nature in its fold. It is this harmony of human beings and nature that is the essential and basic idea of our life."

Vishma: "*Guruji*, we have experienced the birth. We are experiencing the life. What would be the experience of death?"

Guru: "To experience that, you'll have to know the genesis. Tell me how many *lokams* (worlds) are there in the universe?"

Vishma: "Three—*Devalokam* (heaven) on top, where God resides. *Bhoomi* (earth) in the middle, where we live and *Pathalam* (hell) where devils dwell."

Guru: "Well, the genesis—the first woman on earth was created in heaven by *Brahesh,* the Creator himself. The first man was created by Savi, Brahesh's wife. The pair of humans was made as an object of time-pass for the *Devas* and *Devis*. They were named as *Asuras* and were treated as puppets. The man and woman amused the heavenly beings.

"Turning noble living creatures into toys! Saras, the second wife of Brahesh could not tolerate this. Being the *devatha* of knowledge and enlightenment she energized the brain of the human pair. The dull mind of *Asuras* started working.

"Their minds were filled with lots of unwanted ideas. They started mingling with the gods. They wanted to live amongst the gods. The man wanted to marry a *Devi*. He tried to woo her. *Devi* refused. The woman wanted to woo a *Devan*. *Asuras* started asking wild questions and started harsh acts. They demanded the kingdom of heaven—the man wanted to be Raja and woman the Rani.

"This perturbed all the *Devas* and *Devis* in the heaven. Finally, the *Trimurthis*—the gods of creation, preservation and destruction—passed a full-bench verdict: Send the *Asuras* couple to exile on earth. They were ordered to be the king and the queen of the earth. Brahesh, the God of creation compensated for their losses with puberty, pregnancy and childbearing. Vishma, the preserver provided them with the provident natural items like air, water etc. To cater to the needs of their living he gave them various animals and plants. Mahnu, the destroyer was standing by to untie natural calamities like floods, earthquakes and volcanic eruptions in order to teach human beings lessons of life and punish them with diseases if they went astray.

"*Asuras* had all the amenities in heaven. Everything was good everywhere. The heaven was packed with the sweetest items in the universe—there, the sound was *Sangeetham*; air was *Pranavayu*; water was *Gangajal*; Food was *Amruth*; Love was *Dhyanam*; Work was *Prarthana*; Sleep was *Thapasya*. No suffering. No graying. No old age. Everywhere it was *Nithya Vasantham* (infinite spring) played. The wish, *Ayushmanbhava* (long life) had no meaning, for life was eternal. No hurting. No hurdling. Virtues everywhere.

"But, the man . . . He wasn't satisfied with mere virtues. Continuous consumption of the virtues couldn't be digested by the system of *Asuras*. They were inclined to evil. Slowly, they became interested in bad things. Mahnu, who was in charge of the earth, gave the *Asuras* ample sufferings like sorrows, lamentations, diseases, melancholy et al. The mind of the mankind needs both evils and virtues. It is like the equilibrium of opposites.

"Likewise, the human pair became complete and generations began from their children. And the humanity became like the stars of the sky.

When happiness came, they rejoiced. When disease and death came, they cried and prayed to God to save them.

"When *Asuras* were relieved from the heaven, the *Trimurthis* made a clause—all men shall die. He shall go to heaven if his *karma* is good. He shall go to hell if his *karma* is bad. So, it is the *karma* of a man—the deeds of virtue and evil—that decides his way to heaven—to attain *moksha* or salvation.

"Brahesh, you tell me how can one differentiate evils from virtues?"

Brahesh: "The evils and virtues of mankind differ from place to place and vary from society to society. If polygamy is a custom in some society, it is not in some other. If polyandry is common in some communities, it is primitive in some other. If *Mathi* is a custom somewhere, it is not so somewhere else. If *beli* or sacrifice is customary among some people, it is savagery among some others. In some place slaughter is divine and in some place *himsa* is sin.

"But irrespective of societies and places, there is a common form of evil and virtue. To help somebody—an ailing person, animal and plant. To feed an individual who is starving; to water a drying plant; give your blood to the weak; spread knowledge to the ignorant. All these acts come in the category of virtues."

Hearing this I felt ashamed when I had refused asylum to the mushrooms on my branches. I pricked my ears.

Brahesh continued: "You hurt a person bodily. You abuse a person to hurt his heart. You cheat somebody. You betray somebody. You become a spy. You turn a traitor and a terrorist—all these are counted as sins."

I again felt ashamed when I remembered that I had abused the heavenly bodies.

Guru: "*Dhanyavad* (Thanks). It's quite informative. So, the right and the wrong could be easily classified. A man will feel importance of goodness when he confronts a state of evil. We are here to do only good *karmas*. Not only that, to make others do good *karmas*. The human life has to have the *Purusharthas—artha, kama, krodha* and *moha*—to a limited level. But most men may go out of track. To have material benefits excessively for the bodily enjoyment they thrive. Hence they die too early."

The *Vidhyarthis* said: *Guruji,* kindly tell us about the experience of death and its consequence."

As I pricked my ears to listen to *Guruji*'s verses, I saw that the *Nagas* also had raised their hoods to hear him.

Guruji said: "Death is the total cessation of the life of an organism. You will feel the value of life when you are on the verge of death. A man who has got only one breath left will pray to God to bless him with one more. And he will pay whatever he has for it.

"Our body is an instrument. Any instrument needs energy to function. Once that energy fails, the instrument stops work. We call this *death*. If the instrument stops, the energy fails. Then also we call it *death*. So, for the proper functioning (living) of the instrument both the instrument and the energy (body and soul) should be perfect. They are inter-linked.

"The wear and tear of the body cause malfunctions. To avoid that we should maintain our body in a healthy state, and to avoid energy failure, we should keep our mind in good condition. For a human being has got two parts—physical element (body) and the spiritual element (mind) or the soul. To keep both body and mind in perfect condition, one has to become a *yogi*. To become a *yogi*, one has to learn *yoga*. A *yogi* never dies. He attains *Samadhi*. An ordinary man can't become a *yogi*. He embraces death. You asked what will happen after death."

Again, the *Nagas, Vidhyarthis* and I took long breaths to listen to the *guru*'s words.

The *guru* continued: "The spirit gives up its cage or the body. The body decays and joins the earth. The spirit straightaway goes to heaven if one's *karmas* are good. If he has done bad *karmas*, he would go to the hell or the abyss. And he would take rebirth in the form of an animal or a human being or a plant as per his *karma*. This cycle of life and death keeps on rolling unless and until he attains *moksha*.

"So, all of you have understood that the body is mortal and the soul is immortal. Now, if you want both the body and soul to be immortal, I told you, you have to learn *yoga*. *Yoga* is nothing but some exercises given to the body and mind. There are two types of *yogas*. The *Hatayoga* is for the body and the *Rajayoga* for the mind.

We exchanged glances in silence.

The *guru*: "Now tell me, what divine *mantras* you have sung about the glory of hard labor.

The *Vidhyarthis*: *"Na mrisha shrantam yadavanti devah"*

The *guru*: "Explain the verse in soft language and in the most befitting words to let the *mrugams* and *marams* understand."

The *Vidhyarthis* explained in *Cosmolish*: "God helps those who help themselves by the dint of hard labor.

"If you do hard labor physically and mentally, you will be healthy. Health is a precious pearl given by God. We should take pains to maintain health. Then only we can enjoy the bliss of life. Each and every cell of a human body is a human being. It has got its own individual system including the nervous system. So each cell thinks independently. Intentions differ from cell to cell. A civil war is always being waged inside a human body. Hence the body turns *disjecta membra*. Some cells may be agile while some may be lethargic. Some turn amok. Some adopt *ahimsa*. Some are normal. Some are abnormal. Some are moral. Some are amoral. Some are amorous. Some are cold. Some are cruel. Some are gentle. They fight each other. They always combat. The main brain or the capital *cerebellum* in the head of a human being gets fed up with aimless competition of other cells.

"One has to aim all the cells' intention distinctly. One has to advice the cells to concentrate together on the development of the human body as a whole. Regular practice of *yoga* will assemble all the cells and command them to fill the total body with new strength, vigor and vitality.

"Prior to doing *yoga*, maalish is a must. Do you know what it is?"

The *Vidhyarthis*: "Massage of the body with natural oils, waters, natural powders, sun rays, hands, legs, etc. Self-massage and mass massage can be done. Massage makes not only the body strong and supple but also it prevents *Jaranara* (the old age)."

The *Nagas* brought two coconut shells full of *vep* oil.

The *Guru*: "Now, let's massage."

The *Guru* dipped all his fingers in the oil pot and balanced them on his body. Brahesh, Vishma and Mahnu followed the actions of the *guru*. The *guru* did self-*maalish*, while the *Vidhyarthis* helped each other in mass *maalish* in oil from head to foot.

After the massage, they poured some drops of oil in their ears and nostrils.

The *guru* raised both his hands towards *Surya* (Sun) and prayed: "Oh Lord Divine! Lead us from mortality to immortality."

The students followed the *guru*'s action and prayed: "Oh Lord Divine! Lead *me* away from mortality."

The *guru* intervened: "Na . . . na . . . na. I wonder how from the first lesson itself you turned to be selfish!"

Not only *Vidhyarthis*, but the *Nagas* and I also did not understand either the command of *Guruji* or what wrong they had committed.

The *guru* went on: "Do not pray for self. You prayed, 'Lead *me* from mortality.' I pray you to pray 'lead *us*'. It is not just for all of us assembled here, but for all the animate and inanimate things in the universe. Let our principle be *Vasudhiyva Kudumbakam* or . . . tell me?"

Along with students, the *Nagas* and I said, *"Lokame Tharawadu."*

The *guru* asked, "Or?"

We said, "The whole world is *one* family"

The *guru* passed a remark: *"Sabash! Bilkul theek* (correct). You know already that work is worship. Let others too benefit from our work and worship."

We marked our folly in our mind.

I too repeated the hymn: "Oh Lord Divine! Lead *us* from mortality to immortality."

The *guru*: "Well, what is yoga?"

All of us looked at each other in ignorance.

The *guru* said: *"Yoga* is the bridle for the mental vacillation. It sheds light to pave a disciplined way for the spiritual horse of the man. Yoga covers eight portions. First the *yamas*—the pattern of social behavior. First pattern is *ahimsa* or non-violence. Do not ill-treat anybody. Pay only love and affection to everyone. All of you know the after-effects of violence. Don't you?"

Knowingly or unknowingly, words escaped our mouths: "Violence results in sorrow and distress while non-violence leads to joy and merriment."

The *guru*: "Next is *sathya* or the truth."

Hearing the word *sathya*, I felt horripilation for I knew very well what it was! The truth! It's like a gooseberry. Initially it will be bitter. As you chew on, it will taste sweeter and sweeter. Normally, truth is bitter for the speaker and the listener. But finally truth becomes sweet to both. I experienced it during my childhood.

The *guru* continued: "Your behavior should be a blend of honesty and truthfulness. You shouldn't be fraudulent and dishonest not only in deeds but also in thoughts and words. Never tell a lie even if it jeopardizes your life. There is a saying: When the *yogi* sets in truth whatever and whenever he says or does bear fruit."

The *sathya* told to me by my mother (earth) had some exceptions. That could be because my mother had got a treasure of experience. As per her maxim, *sathya* could be violated (lie) for the benefit of the masses. She had to think physically for the protection of the masses.

But opposed to nature, whatever, whenever and wherever might be the situation, *truth* should not be adulterated by any type of *exceptions* for a saint had to protect the mass spiritually. Yes. I too appreciated and adopted *Guruji*'s dictum wholeheartedly.

"Next one is *non-stealing*. Stealing another's property is wrong. One should make one's bread by the sweat of his body and be contented with it. One should procure things to meet the legitimate requirements by fair means alone. He should be neither prodigal nor a purloiner. So *asteya* is as essential as *sathya*."

I wanted to pass a remark on stealing that might not be a sin. The only precious thing you could steal was someone's *heart*. But I suppressed my urge.

"The next yama is *Brahmacharya* or celibacy. It is the preservation and conservation of the *virya* or the vital energy (semen). To observe this, a *yogi* has to be celibate. You have learned about *brahmacharya*. Explain it."

I, being a tree, *nithyabrahmachary* (chronic bachelor), was thorough about the subject in theory as well as in practice. But I only muttered in my mind: *Brahmacharya* is the abstinence from sexual relations. For a *yogi*, even from marriage. Then only a *yogi* could be free from fluctuations of mind and passions. Most of the time he should observe silence. He should follow his daily routine methodically. He should live in natural environment (and strictly be a vegetarian). He should not sleep during the first and last quarters of night or stay awake beyond limits. He may wear a *maravuri* (a loin-cover made out of bark) whenever he has to come into contact with the common people in society.

"And the last one in the vow of *yamas* is non-hoarding: Giving up vanity and hypocrisy, detachment from wealth, name and fame. Then he leads a solitary life. Then he matches his past life of violence and wrong doings with his present life of righteousness and truth contributed by the vow of non-hoarding."

Panning us with his external eye camera and reaming us with his internal eye, Guruji advised us with a concern: "So, you should shoot from your bow of heart, arrows of *ahimsa, sathya, aparigraha* and *vyayama* or work—exercise—(instead of *brahmacharya*) to mould a good society. As we are the teachers of the society, *brahmacharya* is exclusively for us. Society is like students. It can't observe *brahmacharya* lest the cycles of its race should be pedaled and pedaled to keep the world moving.

"Now let us take the social integration pledge."

The *guru* and the students stretched their right hands forward, parallel to the ground, keeping their left hands on chest. The fingers of both hands were tightly clenched. The *Nagas* raised their hoods to the maximum possible height and looked straight, their eyes concentrating on my body (stems). And I . . . I gave maximum strength to my longest branch and instructed my leaves to prick their ears.

The *Guru* read out loudly. We avowed the pledge aloud in *Cosmolish* that meant: We . . . we . . . in the name of god . . . in the name of god . . . solemnly swear . . . solemnly swear . . . to shoot from our bow of heart . . . to shoot from our bow of heart . . . arrows of *ahimsa* . . . arrows of *ahimsa* . . . *sathya, asteya, aparigraha* and *vyayama* . . . *sathya, asteya, aparigraha* and *vyayama*. The arrow-heads shall be made out of . . . the arrow-heads shall be made out of . . . an alloy of kindness and compassion . . . an alloy of kindness and compassion; shafts out of love and affection . . . shafts out of love and affection; and tails out of joy and happiness . . . and tails of joy and happiness . . . . For the goodness of the society . . . . For the goodness of the society.

Then, all of us closed our eyes and chanted a *mantra "Om shanty, shanty, shanty, om shanty, shanty, shanty"* (Om peace, peace, peace. Om peace, peace, peace.)

After a minute's silence when I opened my eyes, I could see a large number of large trees nearby and huge animals waiting to attend the class. Sensing their wish, the *guru* said, "You don't bother about this class of devotion. After all we are practicing it only for your benevolence." Satisfied with his advice, all the *marams* and the *mrugams* dispersed.

"The next stage of *yoga* is the *Niyamam*, consisting of the duty's consistency of an individual. A *yogi* should be always contented. All the sorrows should exit and happiness should enter the stage of his heart. He should ensure a state of activation and cheerfulness. Thus, *santosh* grants the highest of happiness. Then comes the *tapas* or discipline."

When I heard about discipline, the panorama of my life with the land weeds returned to my mind. I was anxious to know about the *discipline* from *Guruji*'s point of view.

He went on: "A *yogi* should be disciplined both physically and mentally. He should discharge his duties with devotion, to his utmost satisfaction. Do well to the society without seeking reward. Remember the saying: "To work you have the right, and not for the fruit thereof". Free his consciousness from fault and guilt. Rectify the mistakes hidden in him. Always keep his mind unruffled to do righteous deeds. The divine verses say that physical and mental discipline brings power to the organs by removing the impurities.

"Now the *Swadhyaya*, the study of spiritual wisdom. The practices of introspection by examining one's own mental and emotional state. He shall process his mind by chanting *mantras* beginning with Om . . . . and perform *tantras*. Thereupon he shall acquire the ability to concentrate the mind on God. *Swadhyaya* is like a burning torch to a student who is searching for *yoga* in the darkness. It leads him to the realization of self and enlightenment.

"Another *Niyamam* for attaining the goal of yoga: One should have good faith and profound love towards God. All of us know that the Omniscient is our father and helper. He is kind and just to us. So, we should worship him. Obey his commands. We should be submissive to the will of God. Thereby *Samadhi* becomes perfect.

"And lastly, I m going to explain to you about *Saucham*, which I was supposed to teach you as first lesson of the *Niyamam*. *Saucham* signifies the cleanliness not only of one's body, living space and the environment but also of the inner body. A *yogi* should possess a clean heart, clean brain, clean blood, clean bones and marrow as well as clean veins and arteries. *Saucham* has to be practiced. Tomorrow at *Brahmamuhurtham* I shall show it and you shall follow it. Till the time of *nidra* (sleep) you may augment your knowledge through self-study."

All of us recited 'Om . . . Om . . . Om' till the beginning of the first quarter of the night. Thus we retired for the day bearing in mind that we would learn the practical class of *Saucham* the following day.

I woke up a little early as it was raining. The *Nagas*, who were sleeping beneath my parasol using one of my protruded roots as pillow, woke up before me. They went to a clear spot in order to have bath. As *Guruji* woke up, the prostrated students also got up. They went into the jungle to answer the call of nature.

I marveled to see myriad of *marams* and *mrugams* lined up along the path towards the valley. All of them had something or other with them. When *Guruji* and the students returned after the nature calls, they were given the gifts.

One of the *neem* trees said, "*Guruji*, kindly accept these twigs. You can use them as toothbrushes. It's a use-and-throw type."

Guruji said with contentment, *"Dhanyavad,* my dear *maram* (thanks dear tree). Accepting gifts is forbidden in the *Niyamam* of *yoga,* whether it's a tooth-brush, a diamond or a decayed tooth."

A lion turned his thunderous throat and humbly said, "We too are part and parcel of nature. Shall we escort you up to the valley by clearing the obstructions and obstacles on the path during these dark hours of the morning? Kindly note that I am not issuing a command as a king. I am representing the *mrugams* and it is a request."

"Dear Rajan (king)", the *guru* said softly. "Thank you for your uncalled for helping mentality. Obstructions and obstacles should be more in number than the easiness and comforts in life, which are also the lessons in the subject of penance. So thank you for waking up in the sleeping hours with a helping heart along with your subjects."

All of them returned to their shelters with contentment.

Then the *Guru* and the disciples walked downward to the valley. On the way they took ripe mango leaves that had fallen on the ground. They rolled the leaves and cleaned their teeth with it.

Rolling the leaf the *Guru* pronounced: *"Pazutha mavila kondu pallu thechaal, puzutha pallum navaratnamakum".*

I remembered the meaning of the saying: If one would clean the teeth regularly with ripe mango leaves, even decayed teeth would turn into diamonds.

They took bath in the river after cleaning their bodies with soft clay from the riverbed. They fetched water in earthen pots and returned to the *gurukulam.* On the way they collected some fruits, berries and leaves for food.

The *guru* said, "These stuffs are considered the pure and most acceptable eatables for a *yogi.* This will maintain the protein-calorie blend and at the same time eliminate *Kama* and *Krodha*—lust and anger—as this kind of food won't awake your *indriyas* or body elements.

The *Nagas* had already swept the *gurukulam* and its surroundings clean with leafy branches provided by me. The *Guru* sprinkled some water inside the cave reciting a *mantra.* The students did the same outside the cave. They fumigated the area burning some sandalwood and benjamine tree wax.

Then they stood erect, facing the east. They prayed for a time of 15 degrees of my mother's movement (earth's rotation for an hour). They were praying in the name of Mother Earth. As *Surya* (Sun) woke up and beheld them, they stopped chanting the name of Mother Earth and started chanting the name of *Surya* to provide them the cosmic fire of light, heat and energy, which are vital for survival during *yoga* practice.

Before breakfast, they gave me some food (they poured three pails of water on my stem). They gave enough berries and two pails of milk to the *Nagas*.

The *guru* said, "Prior to taking food, we should always meet the requirement of our subordinates even if we will have to starve. So, from now on, we'll feed the *maram* and *mrugam* first."

Then they sat down for breakfast. They ate some leaves and fruits.

The *guru* said: "Food should not be taken hastily. You should grind it properly with your teeth."

At the end, each of them drank a handful of river water. I could see the satisfaction on their face. The distribution of breakfast was really a great experience in my life, because nobody had ever served me any food during my long life. Till now I had my food on my own. The nature had allowed me to have a cafeteria self-service. The *Nagas* were also contented to have been served food before them for the first time in their lives. That too by the superlative creatures on this earth—the human beings.

The *guru* ordered, "get up."

They got up. I too became alert.

He said, "Now, we are going to have the practical lessons on *Asanas* or postures of prayer. Are there any questions?"

Brahesh asked, "Which is the best venue for practicing *yoga*?"

The *guru*: "We have a waterfall, a riverbank, a meadow, a forest filled with pure aromatic air. We have already instructed all the fauna and flora not to obstruct, disturb and interfere the arena. They may fumigate the area with the purifying smoke of *Agnihotra* or sacrificial fires. Any other queries?"

Vishma asked, "What's the procedure for . . ."

The *guru*: "Well, the first posture we are going to render is *Sheershanam*. Our body should be in today's state—it is compulsory that our body should be completely cleaned, especially the bowels."

The *guru* swiveled his head towards the *Nagas* and commanded, "Provide *inja* (bark of acacia intsia)."

The *Nagas* climbed on me and took the pealed *inja* that was kept hanging for drying on my lower-most branch. All of them wore the *inja* as *kaupeenam* as demonstrated by the *guru*.

The *guru* said, "One has to secure his testicles and *lingam* while doing the exercise of *yoga*."

They followed the *guru*.

The *guru* rolled some *inja* fibers and kept it on the ground. He sat down with bent knees. Placed the fingers interlocked around the *inja* roll. He kept the head on that in such a manner so that the forefinger space of the forehead resting only on the rolled *inja* without exerting pressure on fontanel of the head. He lifted his knees slowly and straightened the legs with toes touching the ground. Allowing the weight of the body to be supported by the hands and the front position of the head, he brought the legs towards the face by keeping the body straight. Thus he balanced the body, bent the legs so that the knees were lifted upwards and gradually raised the legs so that the body became upside down. He carefully kept his body straight. Now the disciples too had come to the posture of *sheershasanam*. They silently remained in the post for 5 degrees of Mother Earth's rotation (20 minutes). They kept their eyes open. Initially their eyes focused right in front of them and later at a distance of one footstep from the head.

I saw that the disciples were having difficulty in performing the *Asanas*. But later on they were steady by observing the practice of *pranayamams* (breath control).

The same procedure was adopted to bring down the legs. Thus they raised the head from the ground. They remained still and stiff for some time. Thus they lay on the ground in the state of *savasanam*. They relaxed their bodies and gradually slept dorsally and ventrally.

They stood on their feet. The *guru* asked Mahnu, "Could you guess the benefits of *Sheershasanam*?"

Mahnu glanced at his colleagues. He studied them and said, "Regular practice of *Sheershasanam* makes man's body solid. Extirpate grey-hairedness and effects of old age and to preserve eyes".

The *Guru* said, "*Bilkul theek* (correct). *Sheershasanam* is an exercise for eyes also. (He rotated his eyeballs) If you do this methodically, your eyesight will improve immensely. Any other advantage? Brahesh . . . ?"

He said, "*Sheershasanam* improves sound sleep and eradicate bad dreams. It enables one to retain memory. It lightens the stomach. It prevents all the ailments of blood and skin as well as abdominal diseases. *Sheershasanam* promotes the good condition and proper order of the body system for ever . . ."

"Yes. You'll never be a patient. Any other benefits, Vishma?"

Vishma said, "Protection of vital fluid is a prime advantage of *Sheershasanam* is that by doing it the blood, instead of flowing towards the spermatic glands, makes its way towards the head where brain is secured. It enables the doer to remain a *brahmachari* (celibate). By preserving the seminal energy, wet dreams and wind—trouble disease are rooted out. The concentration of the vital fluid increases *ojas* or the glow of the body. Hence the doer gains strength, vigor and vitality. Old age never comes on the way of life and he leads a prolonged life . . ."

Contented, the *guru* commented, "*Bahuth achcha* (very good). And consequently you gain victory over your *Kala* (death) provided you practice all other *Asanas* which will be demonstrated tomorrow."

The next day, after completing the *Sheershasanam* session, the *guru* made them do *Urdhva padmasanam by* bending and folding both the legs in the posture of *Padmasanam*.

The *guru* said, "The title *Padmasanam* is given to this *asana* because this has the appearance of a *Padma* (lotus). Now you shall go to *Padmasanam* as I instruct. Sit down."

They sat on the ground.

"Close your eyes."

They closed the eyes.

"Stretch the legs forward."

They stretched their legs.

"Keep them together."

They kept the legs together.

"Place the right foot on the left thigh."

They did so.

"Place the left foot on the right thigh so that the heels of both the feet touch your abdomen on both sides of the navel."

Seeing them struggling, the *guru* helped them to do it properly.

"Now keep your hands on the knees."

They kept their hands on the knees.

"Keep your body, back, chest and head erect."

The *guru* corrected them.

On completion of each *asana*, the *Guru* told them about the benefits. In the evening they went to the riverbank.

"Now let's practice *Sidhdhasanam*", the *Guru* said. "It's for attaining supernatural powers like *Ashatasiddhi*."

They performed *Sidhdhasanam* as told by the *guru* by pulling up their anus, the genital and organs in abdomen upwards by exerting intra-muscular pressure. On the following day, the *Guru* taught them *Swastikasanam*. This *asana* was for prosperity and success of the doers. The method was: They kept the soles of each of their feet pressed against the thigh of the other leg. They sat straight keeping their necks, chests and backbones erect.

The *guru* said, "The specialty of this *asana* is that one can sit comfortably. This is for those who are unable to sit in *padmasanam* while meditating or observing *pranayamams*. They can do so conveniently in *Swastikasanam*. This paves the way to devotion towards God."

The following day he showed them *sarvangasanam* by lying on the ground and raising the whole body upwards. The entire body rested on the head and shoulders. The peculiarity of this *asana* was that it accelerated the seminal fluid towards the brain and stimulated life. Also it kept the body young and glowing.

After that he taught them *Chakrasanam*. This denoted a circle. The disciples stretched themselves flat with backs on the ground. Then fixed their hands and feet on the ground. They raised their middle portions upwards. They remained like a semi-circle and their heads were kept between the hands.

The *Guru* explained about the *Bhujangasanam* or *Sarpasanam*. It was the posture of the cobra. Each disciple's body resembled that of a cobra when he was in *Sarpasanam*.

The next one was *Pavanamuktasanam*. It was for the relaxation of the gas formation inside the body.

After learning *Matsyasanam*, all of them went to the river. The *Nagas* followed them with the permission of *Guruji*. I remained there. But I could see clearly what was happening. They were floating on the water for a pretty long time performing *Matsyasanam*, which meant the posture of a fish with the aid of *Plavini Pranayamam*. I saw that the snakes on the bank were stunned.

They went to the meadow the next day and did *Yogamudrasanam*. That *mudra* was of paramount significance in the *yoga* practice because it ensured the awakening of the *Kundalini*.

Then they conducted *Dhanusasanam* that gave the body the shape of a bow.

Further they practiced *Hridayastamthasanam* which was related to the heart. That not only cured the chest, neck, back and abdomen ailments but also energized the heart and prevented shocks.

They carried out *Purvottanasanam*. After lying down on the ground, they took both feet and hands backwards. This removed the physical deformities and disfigurements if any, breathing trouble, cough, etc.

After that they learnt *Nabhiasanam* by giving the entire body weight on the naval to curb seminal disorders and bulging of the belly.

When they did *Hansasanam*, their bodies looked like those of swans. The muscles of the arms became strong, increased the charm of the face and they looked very smart and alert.

The *guru* made them do *Sankochsanam*. The disciples lay flat on the ground. They raised the legs towards the sky. As in *Padmasanam*, supporting the waist, each of them lowered one knee and touched the nose by doing *Rechaka*. They repeated the same with the other knee. The posture converted the body into a compact mass.

Mrugasanam was very simple. First they sat in *Vajrasanam* by bending and resting the abdomen and chest on the thigh. Then they brought back both hands and straightened them up. They gazed forward. They put the weight of the body on the knees, inhaled and raised the buttocks slightly. That *Asanas* helped in reducing fat, removing gout and making the neck strong.

Special attention was given to *Dhruvasanam*. It was as good as performing penance for attaining *sidhdhi*. "Let's go to the riverbank to do this," the *guru* said. "Stand erect." They stood erect.

"Bend the right leg touching its heel with the groin above the left leg." They did so.

"Inhale and hold the breath."

They inhaled and held breath.

"Fold both hands and hold them in the middle of the chest."

They obeyed.

"You may close your eyes."

They closed their eyes.

This *asana* obviously helped in concentrating, chanting *mantras*, doing *tantras* and establishing communication with the Omniscient.

They went to the peak of the mountain and practiced *Khagasanam*. They lay on the ground on abdomen in *Padmasanam*. On both sides of the body close to the trunk each placed his hands. Took long breath; raised the head and chest upwards. Holding the breath, they stared at the sky. After some time they resumed to normal position by bringing back their chests and heads to the ground.

When they were in *Konasanam*, I could see their body bent in an angle.

Again they sat down in *Padmasanam*. Filled the lungs. Lifted both hands upward contracting the arms. They held the breath sufficiently. In that posture they resembled mountain peaks.

Before packing up, the *guru* said, "I'll let you perform *Asanas* like *Tadasanam*, *Ekpadasanam*, *Mahavirasanam*, *Trikasanam*, *Dhanusasanam*, *Janushirasanam*, *Tulasanam*, etc. But prior to practicing these *Asanas* you'll have to get acquainted and accustomed with *Pranayamam* or the breath control. Hurry up; we'll have to reach the *gurukulam* as early as possible."

They set out on their way to the *gurukulam* . . .

MILLENNIUM

901 TO 1000 AD

After the normal routine, all of them assembled beneath my parasol. Guru sat on the rock beside me and said, "Despite our principle—*entire* world *is* one family—we have our own individual necessities. It is so because all of us have inherited different habits, hopes, ambitions, anguish, animosity and things like that from nature. Though we are all created by God, (pointing towards the disciples) you are categorized as *manush* (human), that too male. (Pointing towards the snakes) You are *Mrugams* (animals), that too reptiles. (Touching my stem) You are a *Maram* (tree), a Banyan. Thereby each of you has your individual mind. That mind may be wishing to have an earthly life of your own. If someone among you is interested in leading a worldly life, please come forward . . ."

Guruji swiveled his head to see all of us.

"We have not even dreamt of it, *Guruji*. We still stick to the universal dictum *vasudyva Kudumbakam*. We do swear in the name of God, you and us."

"*Theek*. Why did I warn you? If you are unwilling, before practicing *Pranayamam*, we may disperse this divine school. All these *yogas* and *Asanas* you learned are more than enough for you to lead a healthy life. No disease will touch you. You'll be model men in the society. The only drawback will be that without further study (spiritual knowledge) you can't become supernatural. And that study is significant and magnificent. During that period no problem, sorrow or confusion should distract your mind. Prior to commencing the spiritual class, all of you should have void minds. You shall wash your mind with the spiritual waters. Mind that, myriad of *bhootham, pretham* and *pisach* (devil, ghost and poltergeist) would appear in the form of *mohini,* attired in the ornamental garments of *Kama, krodha* and *moha* to instigate you to lead an earthly life. They'll try to boil your vital fluid. If you allow them to enter your mind, then mind that, you won't find even a speck of space for the spiritual volume in the vault of your mind. Mind that the voluptuous devils will spread their nets in such a way that they'll steal the gratification of senses. And mind you that, you can't evict them. Mind that once they occupy the space in your mind, it's registered there. You follow me?"

Prevailed upon by the magniloquent preaching of Guru, they bowed their heads positively, *"Jee ham, Sreeman.* We'll be with you till the end of the world."

Guru retorted, "The world never ends. At least for the betterment of the world, you be with me *till the end of me.* Now, no more questions. Let the *Maram* stand fast while the others and I go to the riverbank"

Ignorant of the hidden meaning of—*till the end of me*—Guru's words, they went to the riverbank. Guru said lovingly, "My dear *Maram,* you know, I'm glad that the three *Students* represent the entire human race, the two *Nagas* represent the whole of animal world and you represent the greenery of the world. I'm grateful to you for sharing the major part of your youth with me, living away from your family. I know you have four wives, in fact, queens. You were a king commanding all the flora and fauna in a habitant. You are very much senior to me. You have more experience. You are a divine tree. You're a pet child of Mother Earth. For certain subjects, knowledge and thoughts, you are superior to me."

I couldn't bear a man like *Guruji* having the power of a star (falling down to the earth) to joining me when I was not having even the power of a satellite. Respectfully I interposed, *"Guruji!* Don't make me shy. Why this flattery? I'm merely a *Maram.* You too know that a life of even more than a millennium for a *Maram* is in no way equal to a decade's life of an ordinary *manush* (man). You . . . you are equivalent to the whole mankind. You are the ocean of nature where I'm only a drop. You are unique. Each word you utter is heavier than the world. Am I divine? If at all I turned divine, I acquired that divinity only from you."

"Hush, dear hush. Why am I obliged to you? You've forgotten a fact. Yesterday was your nine hundredth birthday. Today your tenth centenary wheel started moving. Already you have spent your three hundred years for me. Again . . ."

"We won't leave you. We promised you that. And we mean it *Guruji*. A word given to you is a word given to God, and at the same time a word given by you is a word given by God. All of us can see the glittering of your halo having God"

"You know, all that glitters is not God. Anyway, I'm contented." Taking a long breath, *Guruji* sympathetically continued, "I would have given deliverance to you and Nagas. The *Students* have to remain here. But, I want you, especially you, here to witness an incident. You are the *time*. Please wait and watch. Do not ask me anything about it. You may witness it personally."

Saying so, *Guruji* went to the riverside leaving a gigantic question mark before me. Yes. I had forgotten my age. I did not want to celebrate any more centenaries as *Guruji* had once told us: Celebrating one's own birthday is selfishness. It is the *ahankar* (egoism) in us that prompts us to do so. Yes, I was grateful and obliged to him for remembering my birthday. Actually, I indulged in the enjoyment of the spiritual atmosphere in Gurukulam whereas he was busy creating the spiritual air everywhere. He did not forget the physical data of his associates, beings he had a lot of concern about. He considered that I was the king of the plant kingdom. He considered that Nagas were the kings of the animal kingdom. We considered that he was the king of humanity, the most superior kingdom. Yet he gave us the chance to maintain the same superior statuesque.

It was so because he understood natural phenomena—the world won't survive without any one of us. It is the joint venture of all the three of us that makes the earth livable. In a nutshell, one way or other we are the *Trimurthis*—three powers—named Brahesh, Vishma and Mahnu who creates, preserves and destroys each and every object on this earth respectively.

The celestial bodies taught me about the physical life on this earth in my childhood. My mother taught me about the moral life on this earth in my boyhood. And now, *Guruji* was teaching me the spiritual life in my youth. I would definitely continue to learn this from him till my last breath. No power on this universe would be able to part us. If at all such a situation comes, I would not part with him voluntarily. Let the destiny do it. I had never seen my father and enjoyed his love. Who knew *Guruji* was not his substitute? He might be my father's reincarnation.

I came to life when I heard noises from the riverbank. I saw the *Students* and Nagas floating on the water in *Matsyasanam* when *Guruji* reached the spot.

They came out of the water and lined up before *Guruji*.

He gave a lecture: "The fourth part of the spiritual discipline is *Pranayamam* or the control over your breath. As you have maintained the buoyancy of your body for a considerable time, it's quite clear that you are already well acquainted with some aspects of *Pranayamam*. Until and unless you acquire mastery over the inhalation and exhalation, you can't attain *Pranayamam*. A *yogi* doing regular practice of *it* is capable of holding his breath internally and externally at his caprice and capacity. There are eight kinds of *Pranayamam*. First of all, we'll do *Surya Bhedi* practically. Spread your seat." They spread the aromatic cuscus grass (*Ramacham*) on the ground as seats.

Guru went on: "Another thing I want to make clear to you is that *Pranayamam* means life or *Shiva* or the combination of creation, preservation and destruction. That means *Pooraka* is the act of inhaling of breath (*Creation*). *Kumbhaka* is the act of Retention of breath inside (*Preservation*). And *Rechaka* is the act of exhaling of breath (*Destruction*).

After a pose, *Guruji* said with a stress: "Note down this equation on the pad of your heart with the nib of your mind and with blood as the ink:

SHIVA = SANKARAN = SAN/ KAN/ RAN (break up of three stages)

SAN/ KAN/ RAN = Creation/ Preservation/ Destruction.

Creation/ Preservation/ Destruction = Inhalation/ Retention or absorption/ Exhalation.

Inhalation/ Retention/ Exhalation = *S*ankara or Pooraka/ *Kumbhaka*/ *Rechaka*

Therefore *S*ankara or *Pooraka* + *Kumbhaka* + *Rechaka* = *SANKANRAN* = SHIVA

"*Surya Bhedi* can be performed in three postures. Brahesh, you be in *Swastikasanam,* Vishma in *Sidhdhasanam* and Mahnu, you be in *Padmasanam*."

They assumed the *asanas* as told by Guru. He helped them to keep their necks, heads and bodies erect.

"Now all of you inhale through your right nostrils and retain it inside as long as you can."

They held the breath for a long time.

"Very good." Guru said. "This process is known as *Pooraka* and *Kumbhaka*. Now, through your left nostrils, all of you exhale by and by with force. And this is *Rechaka*."

They exhaled with a noise.

"If you practice this during winter, your body gets warmed up and you can withstand any cold. Next one is *Ujjayi*. Now change round your postures."

They changed postures.

"All of you exhale fully with force by making a snoring sound."

They exhaled.

"Now inhale fully."

They inhaled.

Not satisfied with their performance, Guru commanded, "Come on, this is an endurance test. Inflate your lungs fully and let the chest be expanded."

They did so.

"OK. Let go the breath very slowly."

They relaxed after exhalation.

"We are going to do *Sitkari*. Change your pose." They changed the posture.

"Bite your tongue and let the lips be kept open. Inhale the air through the mouth forcefully and hold it."

When they took air through the mouth, there arose a hissing sound. After waiting for some time and watching them, Guru instructed, "Now perform *Rechaka* through the nostrils by and by."

After relaxing a little, all of them sat in *Sukhasanam* for doing *Shitali*. Guru instructed: "Shape your tongue like the beak of a crow." They did so.

"Let it project. Now fill up your belly with air through this passage." They obeyed.

"Now close your mouth and hold the breath."

For a long time they remained in retention.

"Perform *Rechaka* as you feel uneasiness."

They released the breath through the nostrils.

"Well, now to engage *Bhastika*. This can be done in any habitual posture. Breathe normally through the nostrils with sound. Lungs should be filled and emptied fully while inhaling and exhaling. This process helps you to awaken the *Kundalini* very quickly . . ."

They obeyed *Guruji* word by word . . .

"Next is *Murchha*. This should be carried out with utmost care. All of you come to *Sidhdhasanam* ". They assumed the pose and sat erect. "Take a long breath and hold it inside. Now give a twist to the vacuum beneath your chin." They did so.

"This is known as *Jalandhara Bandham*. Now keep all the fingers down and close eyelids softly with the index fingers. With the third finger, press the nose from both sides." They did exactly as they were told.

"Close your mouth with the fourth finger. Form *Mool Bandham* and *Udyan Bandham* by maintaining *Kumbhaka*." They did so.

"If you feel suffocation, you may remove the fingers and breathe and breathe in as usual through the nostrils.

"Next comes the *Plavini Pranayamam,* a miraculous exercise. If a *yogi* practices this systematically and regularly, he can float on swelling waters like a buoy; plunge in fathomless waters like a fish and even walk on the waters."

The disciples' eyes widened in surprise and aspiration.

Guru continued, "The method is very simple. You sit in the posture of *Padmasanam*. Perform *Pooraka*. After *Rechaka* compress your abdomen. Again do *Pooraka* and repeat this process for some time."

The whole day, Sun witnessed the performances of the aspirants and their *guru*. When he was retiring in the evening, on the way he met the golden clouds. As he magnified about the *yogic* activities of Guru*kulavasis*, the clouds also commented on the excellence of the exercises they saw on the riverbank.

Guru ordered, "All right *sons*, it's time to retire for the day. On the way we'll perform the *Brahmana Pranayamam*."

Guru walked backwards leading them. The aspirants walked forward in a file facing Guru.

Guru said, "Your body should be erect while walking. Do *Pooraka* through the nostrils by counting one, two, three, four . . . in your mind. Then do *Rechaka* through the nostrils by counting one, two, three, four, five, six . . . in your mind. When you exhale, the belly should be completely deflated."

By the time they conducted the exercise for ten times, they had reached *Gurukulam*. They came straight towards me. They gave me a full square supper by pouring more water on my foot-base. When I glanced at Nagas, they told me that they too enjoyed a good meal as a simple celebration of my ninth centenary."

The *Students* constantly practiced *asanas* and *pranayamams* maintaining strictly the *Yamas* and *Niyamams* under the keen supervision of *Guruji*. The teacher and students were wholeheartedly involved in their duty. Nagas too were immersed in the day-to-day affairs of Gurukulam with great zeal and enthusiasm. And I . . . I witnessed all the incidents in and around Gurukulam. Not even a single dry leaf was allowed to move without my permission. I prevented all the unnecessary movements other than the motions of the heavenly bodies. No motions could let loose the concentration or hinder the studies. I always tried to keep up a spiritual and aromatic environment.

Only three-quarters of a century were left for me to complete a millennium. Out of this lengthy life, more than two centuries I spent with Guru in Gurukulam. That's the reason why Guru considered me as the *time.*

Guru was doing a noble thing. He was trying to light up *three torches* (three students) that would shed light on the darkened world. They would purify the hearts of the motley masses of human beings. They would be the guardians of nature. Contented with our performance, I kept on counting the time correctly.

Yes . . . Precisely, Mother Earth travelled fifty times along her orbit since the disciples started performing *asanas* and *pranayamams* and they turned perfect in it. Creating confidence in them, *Guruji* decided to take the second semester of the spiritual course—*Pratyahar, Dharana, Dhyanam* and *Samadhi,* which could be taught only by a universal chancellor like *Guruji* to the aspirants like his three disciples for the course was the passage to the seat of The Almighty.

The disciples were called up. They lined up before *Guruji.* He deluged them with flowers of questions pertaining to their past study.

"How many stages are there in *Suryanamaskaram* and which are they? Mahnu . . ."

Mahnu confined his answer to the subject proper, "Ten in number of stages. They are known as, first stage . . ."

Guru intervened: "The last stage?"

"The last stage is ditto of the first stage. Plus standing erect by pressing the knees together. Then do *Kumbhaka.*"

"Then first stage . . . ?"

"It is *Avasthanam*"

"Middle stage . . . ?"

"Fifth stage is *Sashtangam.*"

"Let me know, how do you perform the last stage but one?"

"The ninth stage is similar to the second stage plus deflating the belly, touching the knees in the middle with nose and forehead and proceeding to *Rechaka* with a noise."

"The second stage is known as?"

"*Janunasa.*"

"Now, Vishma, tell us about the benefits of performing the fourth stage of *Suryanamaskaram.*"

"Due to the weight of the entire body falling on arms, palms and toes in *Tulitavapu* stage, hands and feet become sturdy and rigid."

"The advantage of *Urdhavekshanam?*"

"It is an exercise for the waist, back, neck and throat. The forward and backward movements of the legs build pressure in the liver and make the internal organs strong."

"What about the eighth stage . . . ?"

"It's a close copy of the third stage—*Urdhavekshanam.*"

"Explain the seventh stage."

"This stage is *Kesheruvikasam.* While proceeding through *Kumbhaka*, straighten the legs. Keep the head between the hands so as the chin touches the chest, and simultaneously stretch the arms forward. Make sure the soles and palms are touching the ground straight. Do *Kumbhaka.*"

"Now, all of you execute sixth stage, *Kesherusankota.*"

All of them stood firm on the ground with straightened arms. Inhaling deeply, they brought their chests forward and bent back. Then they bent their backs backward and performed *Kumbhaka* at the same time staring at the sky.

"Right, go to *Savasanam.*" After doing so, when they were fully relaxed, *Guruji* again showered questions on them: "Brahesh shall narrate the advantages of *Sidhdhasanam.*"

"*Sidhdhasanam* is the foremost stage in awakening *Kundalini*. This *asana* purifies all the seventy-two thousand nerves. It also refines the vital fluid. With the aid of *Pranayamam*, we could transform the *virya* (semen) into *ojas* (glow) and mental acumen that would clear the passage to perception and apprehension of self."

"Any other *asanas* that lead to the arising of the *Kundalini Shakhty?*"

"*Jee ham. Bhujangasanam* springs up the *Kundalini.*"

"How?"

"It tones up all the parts and ligaments of the vertebral column. It not only activates the circulation to the spinal cord but also suppresses the sexual urges. Constant conducting of the *Yogamudrasanam* also shakes up the *Kundalini* and will power."

"Very good," *Guruji* commented. His eyes and teeth were gleaming and the chambers of his heart were filled with the fluid of contentment. "So, the first term covering the lessons pertaining—practical and theory—to the *Hatayoga* has been completed. I'm confident that you have gained confidence to perform some miracles like walking on fire, submerging in water and flying in the air. The *Hatayoga* has influenced you and induced very much in you. The evidence is that, all of you are still living and looking very young. You landed here a quarter to last to last century plus the last full century plus half of this century, and that too at the age of fifteen. Therefore you are now quarter-to-two-centuries old. Hence, it's obvious that the lessons worked on you bodily and mentally.

"But unless and until you attend the second terminal class, the lessons on *Rajayoga*, you can't perform any miracles perfectly before a motley crowd. You may lose your concentration. The performance may fail. The people will lose trust in you. If you go before them as reformers, they won't lend their ears to you. In spite of spreading flowers on your path, they would spread thorns. If you fail to walk on the thorns, they would stone you. You should apprehend their attitude and appetite when you approach them. Despite you fool them; you cool them. Never be corrupt; ever be correct. If your followers would ask for water in a desert, you'll have to provide it. You follow me?"

The disciples said with reverence, "*Guruji* has taught us to perform miracles with our body and mind. But a miracle like spurting water from the earth's bottom of a desert is something unreal, unnatural and unscientific. Nowhere in *yoga* study, we learn this portion; not even in *Ashatasiddhi* (eight divine powers). Magic and witch-crafts are forbidden to the monk-hood."

Guru retorted like a scientist: "It can be executed in quite a natural way even in summer—it's the science of nature itself. God is the scientist of nature."

He took the *Kamandalu* and said, "You pour the water from this *Kamandalu*. What happens?"

The disciples unanimously said: "The water will fall down naturally on the earth."

"And our Mother Earth drinks it. It's because of her gravitational force or magnetic effect. You know that our Mother Earth has an elephantine portion of her stomach filled with water. She has attracted all these waters. We have lots of loadstones lying hither and thither. God (nature) has provided them with this peculiar property—a medium-sized load stone will attract a small-sized one. If you keep a big one on another side neglecting the middle-sized loadstone the small loadstone will naturally attract the big one with relation to its poles and place. Likewise all the waters attracted by our mother by her magnetic force could be pulled out (attracted) using a greater magnetic force. Then the water within her shall spurt like a fountain irrespective of time and place. But it depends upon the magnetic force within you and as per the like the 'like poles repel' and 'unlike poles attract' principle. Is it clear to you, *Sons*?"

"*Jee ham, Guruji*. But how could we procure and possess properties of a magnet? We are men, not metals. And if at all we turn to metals, the physical science says that no metallic magnet could attract or repel (challenge) the magnetic force of our Mother Earth."

"Correct," Guru said, "a magnet is produced by arranging its molecules in north-to-south direction."

As I was hearing the description by *Guruji* with immense interest, I saw the elder *naga* coming into the open-air-class with a coconut shell full of some black powder followed by the younger *naga* with a tubular stalk of a plant.

Guruji filled the powder inside the stalk. He kept the powder-filled stalk on top of the rock in front of him. He placed a load stone rod beside the powder-filled stalk. Nothing happened. Then he rubbed the stalk smoothly with the load stone rod. And repeated the process a number of times. He then placed the rod near the powder-filled-stalk. There was an attraction.

The disciples, *Nagas* and I watched the experiment amazingly.

"You know," Guru said, "I filled the hollow of the stalk with load stone filings. As I ran the load stone rod which is a natural magnet, the particles of load stone inside the stalk got arranged to north-south poles (directions) themselves with the help of the magnetic power of the load stone rod. By this process, the tube filled with the particles of loadstone *acquired* the properties of a magnet from the *innate* magnetic properties of the load stone. You can see that nature has gifted some creatures, like lizards, the power to overcome the gravitational force by creating their own vacuum force. How does a chameleon change its colors? See the eyes of a cat. See the smell-sensing capability of dogs.

"So, how can you make a magnet which is not at all a magnet? You are also like a tube. Your bodies are filled with particles as good as load stone filings. I'm the bar magnet that rubs you. All the cells in your body reside random, lumpish, lethargic, lunatic, lurking, macabre, etc. All these cells should be ordained to a particular point of concentration. Thereby they get arranged with agility. Hence, you would be like in an electrically charged state. You in turn will become a powerful bar magnet. This will create a magnetic field around you. And that would be many times greater than that of our Mother Earth. In other words, *yoga* and meditation make you obtain this power."

After a pause, *Guruji* went on, "But remember, do not misuse this power. This may be used only in extreme emergencies or on compassionate grounds. That too for the benevolence of the masses. Not even for your self-defense. The more you make use of this special effect (by doing and showing miracles for gimmick to attract the public) the more quickly you will lose this power just like a magnet loses its magnetism because of its repeated usage. Without the magnetic field around you, you'll be as good as a living corpse. The cells in your bodies will not respond extraordinarily and start deteriorating. Thereupon you'll go back to *Manushyavarsham* (year of man) from *Devavarsham* (year of God)."

Yes. I recalled my mother's age as told by her during my childhood.

Her age was one *Kalpam*, 157 *Deva yugams*, 4888 *Deva varsham* and 320 *manushya varsham*.

Where 360 Manushya *varsham* = 1 *Deva Varsham*
12000 *Deva varsham* = 1 *Deva yugams*
1000 *Deva yugams* = 1 *Kalpam*

And I calculated my age. I was nearing three years of *Deva varsham* and *Guruji* and Nagas had completed one *Deva varsham*.

Guru went on: "Our Earth Mother rotates. Her one rotation is our one *Ahorathram* (a day). Her three hundred and sixty-five and a quarter rotations make her one revolution—our one year. This period, one revolution of the earth, is a day for God. So, a day for God is a year for us. (Gazing to the disciples) Actually, you have not yet completed half a year *Devavarsham* of age. If you achieve more spiritual magnetic power, you would live a prolonged life of the *Devayugam*. An ordinary man in ordinary case may complete a century of life. *Hatayoga* helps you to live extraordinarily. If you practice *Rajayoga* your lifespan would be further extended."

He took one dry teak leaf from the ground. He fanned it. That caused a small stir of air. The disciples also did the same.

Guru said: "Wind is produced by nature. We too produced a small wind now. Likewise, we too can produce the magnetic power within our body."

They kept the leaves in their left hands. *Guruji* asked them to blow on it. The leaves flew away.

Guru: If we practice *Rajayoga* we would attain the *Ashatasiddhi*. Then we could blow off all the trees. To obtain that, we, like *Irishis* (very senior monks) have to remain in meditation for centuries and centuries. During such period, of *Japam, Thapam* and *Manthram* would feed our mind as spiritual food. Air and water particles in the atmosphere would be fed to our body as physical victuals by the nature. But they won't know about it for our mind and bodies are fully concentrated on God. That's what *Thapasya* is. The more we are engaged in *Thapasya*, the more we gain maturity. A *Irishi* doing *Thapasya* doesn't need any foodstuffs at all. No waste of time on all that. No nourishment. No excrements. In nature, there's nothing coming in as new and nothing's going out as old. Everything (whatever you see) is already there—only the shape changes. There is only one nature. But it manifests in different forms. There is only one natural phenomenon. But there are different processes."

The disciples enquired, "But, what about the new-bourns of the human race, animal kingdom and the forest?"

I chuckled in my mind hearing their childish query. Even Nagas knew that fact.

Guruji coolly retorted, "Dear *Sons*, you should have known this universal truth in the initial lessons that *Manush, Mrugams* and *Marams* are nothing but *Panchabhootham* (viz earth, water, sun, air, ether). All these already exist in nature."

Guruji's followers understood their folly.

He continued, "So the nature is only one. A *Thapaswy* joins the oneness of nature. He's only one. But in different forms. He takes different shapes. Like viewing his *self* in all and all in his own *self*—the self—knowledge or self-purification. This can be attained only all by ourselves. Not with any support. So from now on, unlike other periods of your leisure time, your minds should be de-conditioned perfectly by yourselves.

"For self-purification, we'll begin with self penance—the performance of *Panchathapas*."

The next day in a clear and sunshine area, the disciples constructed four big *Agnikundam* (fire-pit) as instructed by *Guruji*. I arranged the firewood. Nagas collected ingredients like grains, oils and aromatic articles.

The three disciples were made to stand in the middle of the four fires with the hot sun overhead considered as the fifth fire. They were told to chant *Hari Ommm . . . Hari Ommm . . . Hari Ommm . . .* mantra non-stop. Every day from dawn to dusk, they performed the *Panchathapas* and continued it through the summer paving the way to the expulsion of the impurities in the ocean of their mind.

On completion of the course, Guru fondly asked: "Well. I told you that all the articles in nature are made up of any or all of the five elements such as earth, water, air, sun and ether. Then where is the oneness? *Panchabhootham* is a combination of five, not one."

Just like senior monks, the disciples replied: "Though the human body has five senses, the body is only one. Likewise, all the five elements are the body of *Brahma* or God. God is the only one. The air we feel, the water we see are the magic of nature. God is the magician and his variety show of illusion is the nature—all his magical transformations and transitions.

Guru's eyes expressed satisfaction.

*   *   *

All of them went to the bank of the river. *Guruji* said, "All of you have already observed *Yamas* and Niyamams. Perfectly practiced the *Asanas* and *Pranayamams*. Now over to *Pratyaharam*. You know, our mind is a scattered force. To assemble the mind by controlling the sense organs is the act of *Pratyaharam*. I have already narrated to you the procedure of making a magnet. The only difference is that *Pratyaharam* is the method of gathering and arranging your mind stuff by self from outer to inner inclinations. When I say, all the three of you walk straight on the riverbank closing your eyes. Turn by turn you'll chant and hear the devotional songs glorifying God. Make certain that in the end of each *Anupallavi*, the *Pranavamantra* (*Om*) is recited internally. We are going back to Gurukulam. You should come back only after your dejection is over if there is any. Now . . . all of you . . . on your way . . . set, go . . ."

As the monks started their onward journey, *Guruji* and Nagas started their return journey.

*   *   *

For some days we felt that Gurukulam was like a desert without the three monks. My heart throbbed. So was the case with Nagas. Their eyes were thirsty to have a glance of the monks. And Nagas and I could guess the pain painted on the face of our *Guruji* due to their absence.

Guruji followed his normal routine. Nagas served him. I had nothing to do except thinking deeply about the monks. I wondered what they would be doing. I could have easily seen them even if they were at a greater distance. But *Guruji* prohibited me from looking at them for fear that the monks might lose their attention on prayers.

On the third day, *Guruji* said to me, "Before dusk they'll come. But, before that I want to put one thing into your knowledge. Very soon— before the end of this century—you're going to witness an important incident. It would be the second-most significant event in my life. It would be the end of an old episode and the beginning a new episode. Do not ask me much. But bear in mind that you're going to lose a thing which you love most; you are going to lose a thing which you never want to lose. You console yourself that it's the will of God."

By the time I prepared to ask what it would be, there came the three monks with closed eyes, singing prayers.

Straightaway *Guruji* went beside the home coming monks and greeted them "*Aayushaman bhava, sons, Aayushaman bhava (long live . . .)* Let your eyes be opened to behold a new world."

When they opened their eyes, I could see the compact constellation concentrated in their eyes.

They kow-towed Guru*ji*.

Next day onwards *Guruji* taught them about the sixth step— *Dharana* i.e., concentrating the mind upon one spot. "The mind can be concentrated on any particular object such as your job, hobby or even an evil object. That would make you perfect in that discipline. But a *yogi* should only *practice* or exercise *Dharana* exclusively on God. It's as good as transforming your body into a perfect and permanent magnet by which you could repel all the unwanted desires pertaining to worldly affairs and attract the object of God in any form such as an animal, a plant or a human being. Or any natural elements such as earth, water, air, fire, sky or any heavenly bodies. If you concentrate your mind on a thorn, the thorn will appear before you as a flower of God. Initially, *Dharana* could be practiced by giving the God any shape in your heart and mind. And in due course, as the *Dharana* progresses, God will be an attribution. Finally you will feel God without figure and attribution and as an absolute being.

And that's the pure consciousness. Carry out concentration of mind on the umbilicus.

"*Dharana* is interrelated with *Dhyanam*. It establishes meditation. Contemplation is very difficult, as it is passage to the pure conscious state. During *Dhyanam*, a *yogi* fixes his mind always on the point meditated upon. Thereupon his mind repels all mundane affairs and he cultivates his attention to God. The alpha point of meditation is the mystical heart situated inside the naval region. Years and years of perfect meditation make the bud of mind bloom into a flower of mind. Then the heart becomes clearer than crystal. So the impurities of ego are distilled away from the ocean of the *yogi*'s mind and he transforms himself into a pure being. Eventually he feels only his having communion with God.

"*Samadhi* is the omega stage of *yoga*. It is nothing but the close relationship with God."

Guruji sent the three monks to three different locations—Brahesh to the riverbank, Vishma to the dense forest and Mahnu to the peak. They were told to sit in the *Sidhdhasanam* posture, absorbed in their own thought and to hold the consciousness on the top portion—between the eyebrows—of the *Sushumna,* the most significant and a mystical *nerve* begins from the base of the spine to the brain centre. Performing *Bhastika Pranayamam*, they chanted the *mantra* inwardly: 'I've no body. I've no mind. I'm independent. I'm separate. I'm contained. I'm knowledge. I'm absolute. I'm *atman*! I'm *atman*! I'm *atman*!'

Then they beheld a glazing figure of a white lotus like a full moon emitting soft white light. They felt that each and every particle of their being was being homogenized by that light. After that they felt that the lotus had changed into red and was encircled by a disc. It had also transferred its location to the base of the spinal column, in an upward position. On the disc, there appeared a triangle. The monks concentrated their minds on it. It was the cosmic power on the earth. The monks prayed to attain that strength of Mother Earth.

At dusk they secured the meditation and reported back to *Guruji*.

Guruji deliberately advised: "Upon completing the exercise of *Samadhi padam*, i.e. after awakening of the *Kundalini Shakhty*—the generation of electric power in your spinal column or charging of spinal cord, you are no more monks. You will be transformed into *Irishis* (holy men). You'll be superior to all the animate and inanimate articles in the universe. You'll pass out from here as prophets. You shall be the 'thought-airs of the atmosphere of the humanity. You shall be the thought—oscillations of the ocean of the society. You shall teach the mankind the spiritual hygiene. You shall treat the society for curing the infection of their bad thoughts with your medicine of good thoughts."

Before dawn they again went to their respective seats and sat erect. They caught sight of a lotus, which had six petals within the spine near the area of genital organ with vermilion color surrounded by a disc. They felt that the cosmic waters were oscillating within them.

Next they sighted another lotus in the naval region within the spine. On the scarlet disc there was a triangle. Its apex pointing towards the body. The brilliance of it was the cosmic fire. The monks prayed to acquire the power of fire in order to purify themselves as well as others, through them.

After that they saw a lotus in their inner sight in the spinal column on the spot of heart. It had twelve blue petals. Its disc was comprised of a six-armed star. It was the symbol of cosmic air. They prayed to The Almighty to inflate them with the qualities of cosmic air as the medium of contact between the individual minds.

Again they visualized one more lotus inside the spine at the neck in grey color with sixteen petals surrounded by a disc. It had a white circle representing the cosmic ether. The monks affirmed and chanted the following *mantras* individually: "O, cosmic ether! Come and fill up every pore of mine with your brilliance. As you are the universal substance, give me thy power to serve the rich and the poor, strong and the weak, ugly and the beautiful, wise and the ignorant, the highest creator to the lowest creature irrespective of time and place. As I'm the strength of cosmic ether so am I the entity of existence."

*   *   *

Days became weeks; weeks swelled into months; months turned to seasons and seasons gave way to years.

I continued to witness the unbroken performance of *yoga*, the light of the spiritual life. They surrendered themselves to the will of God in *Samadhi padam*. The inner *yogic* practice of *Dharana, Dhyanam* and *Samadhi* altogether converged on a particular object—*Sanyam*. They made *Sanyam* on the relation of body with ether, they gained the supernatural powers of seeing, hearing, touching and moving plus control over the gravitational force—*Ashttasidhdhis* in *Vibhudhipadam*. They continued their practice glorifying the body.

* * *

The monks went to their respective seats of *yoga* to awaken the dormant *Kundalini*. They assumed the spinal cord as a vein of an imaginary lotus on which there were seven stages of consciousness divided right from the root to the petals such as *Muladharam, Swadhistanam, Manipuram, Anahatam, Vishuddam, Ajnam* and *Sahasrasam* or sacrum, lumbar, gluteal, thoracic, cervical, lattissimus dorsi and trapezius on the other way. They gently started the *Pranayamam* and simultaneously visualized the glazed *Sushumna*. Due to the breathing power and thought power, the blocked bottom of the *Sushumna* got cleared and the Kundalini stirred up like a serpent from its sleep, raising its hood.

They experienced subtle heat and light in the figure of the eight conduits called the *Ida* on one half and the *Pingla,* the other half. That energy of spirituality slowly journeyed from *Muladharam* through *Sushumna* channel to the region of genital organ or *Swadhisthasanam* where all the animal forces were spiritualized.

As the monks concentrated their mind further, the divine light of *Kundalini* moved further upward to the *Manipuram,* the third lotus heart centre where they gained the spiritual knowledge of everything pertaining to material enjoyment. When they were surpassing the stage of *Manipuram*, there occurred a natural tendency to suppress the *Kundalini Shakhty* to the initial stage again. They felt some uneasiness. Darkness was trying to capture them disturbing their determination. But they somehow managed to keep *Kundalini* moving aloft the stage of *Anahatam*. In that centre the spiritual current was overpowering by which the monks attained *Ashta sidhdhi* (the eight-fold supernatural powers).

Happily the monks woke up from meditation. They wanted to show the effects of the *Kundalini Shakhty* they gained to *Guruji* as well as to their colleague—Nagas and me. A spark of urge arose in their minds and their hearts poured more oil into the arson to conduct the load test of the *Kundalini* current generated in them.

I let Nagas to climb on my crown to have an aerial view. They looked around from atop as if from a watchtower. *Guruji* could visualize through his third eye, from the cave itself. Yes, we saw Monk Brahesh spurting from the far away ocean. Vishma erupted from underground. Mahnu broke open the ice-clad peak. All of them flew to Gurukulam like soft cotton floating in the air but in their own forms and figures. They came before *Guruji*. With folded arms they said, *"Pranamam, Guruji, Pranamam.* We have passed the *Manipuram* stage."

Guruji said matter-of-factly: "Yes. You indeed overcame gravity."

The disciples asked, "What's the secret of this *Satyashastra* (factual science) behind the *Kundalini Shakhty, Guruji?*"

"Assume your vertebral column as the tube to be magnetized and the meditation as the strong magnet. Meditating is as good as rubbing and arranging the spine inside the vertebral column. As soon as the *Sushumna* gets a spark by rubbing the spine by the spiritual magnet, the first wheel of spirituality starts cranking. The first cranks the second . . . The second cranks the third . . . The third cranks the fourth . . . The fourth cranks the fifth . . . The fifth cranks the sixth . . . The sixth cranks the seventh . . . All the movements of all these seven stages of the lotus heart will electrify or charge the *Kundalini*. That electrification of your body produces the magnetic field around you and it further develops into a halo.

"That's why a saint has a halo around his head. And *he* is said to be godhead. That's why he becomes supernatural. He can do miracles. Physics fails before him. But to obtain this mystical power one has to absorb all the voltage in the entire universe like a spiritual transformer comprising contemplative coils. One has to accumulate all the light, heat and energy in the entire cosmos as Sun. One has to preserve all the waters of the earth within him. One has to inhale all the air in the atmosphere. One has to comprise in him all the ether above the earth.

"Yet the most prominent and paramount factor is that he shall not use all these physical matters! He possesses all these physical properties, yet he lives without enjoying them. That's the secret of a saint. When he walks on fire, he uses the ocean as water concealed in him to extinguish the fire. That's why God has made all the substance on earth as flammable and water as non-flammable. When a *yogi* is submerged in water, he uses the air concealed in him as *Pranavayu* (life-saving gas). When he remains on the icy mountain as a hermit, he uses the fire (heat) in him to withstand the cold. When he passes through the dark, he makes use of the light within him. When he resides underground without food, he makes use of all the energy within him. All these actions or processes are counter-balanced. That's the *artha sathya* or fact behind it.

"To gain these powers through *yoga* and meditation, one should be the owner of a pure body, pure heart, pure mind, pure soul and pure spirit. If you allow any atom of impurity to enter, the rivet shakes. The power goes off. Hence, you go back to the state of an ordinary man.

"With the awakening of *Kundalini*, your inner eye will be opened. With the inner eye, you can visualize the inner things consisting of our mother's body. You can scan her body with this instrument. You can mine and geologize the earth's strata—the water belt, oil belt, minerals, metals, etc.

"I'm seeing," after a pose, Guru continued, "that our staff has some inclination to disbelieve. As masters of monk-hood, kindly clarify it."

The monks said: "We too are seeing their undecided frame of mind, *Guruji*. They're at full liberty to air any doubt. We're at their service. On this planet, we're next to them and coming on the fifth position only."

Looking at me, the masters of monkhood asked, "Reverend staff, it's our privilege to share our knowledge with you."

I said, "Please pour your milk of knowledge on my crown that could heal my disease of doubts. If Nagas and I are in the fourth position, who comes in the first, second and third positions?"

The monks said matter-of-factly, "First God. Then *Guruji*. Then the Mother Earth."

I said, "There are numerous creatures on the lap of our mother. Why do you want to hold the fifth position? Why can't you leave it and think you are in the last position?"

"We stand in the last position for the achievements of any advantages or benefits. But, in the society, we have to hold the first position lest the society won't lend their ears to us. After all, our motto is to plunge into the ocean of humanity and save the sinners, the sufferers and the disabled. We have to teach them lessons of goodness. A teacher or a preacher should have a position in the society. If we stand in the last position, it's the tendency of the society to disrespect us. Respect is the unknown or imaginary power between a teacher and a student. That's the reason why when *Guruji* would send us as prophets, we'll maintain the first position among the public. Not from pride or prejudice and not because of egoism or egotism. The first position is exclusively for fighting against *adharma*, preaching and to love the hated."

The elder *naga* had a feeling of uncertainty pertaining to the time difference: "Please shed a little light to the time variation. E.g.: Our year is equal to just a day for God. About 365-folds of difference! Unthinkable!"

The monks said: "We're only bothered about the earth's rotation. So, we limit our daily work from dawn to dusk. We normally take rest from dusk to dawn whereas God has to bother not only about our planet but about all the other planets, satellites, solar system, galaxies, milky way, constellations, the sky, so on and so forth as well. Some heavenly bodies take Mother Earth's rotation and revolution rise to the power of many-folds and many-many-folds of time. So, God waits for all the heavenly bodies, especially the last one, to complete its movements."

*　*　*

Sitting beneath my parasol, *Guruji* said, "I'm contented *sons,* contented. You have killed all the devils within you—*Ashta kashtas* (the eight woes viz desire, anger, avarice, haughtiness, envy, egoism, greed and quarrelsomeness) with the swords of your *Ashta karanas* (the eight senses viz the mind, intelligence, soul, pride, imagination, determination, self-respect and assertion). You have achieved the *Ashta Sidhdhis* (the eight miraculous attainments through asceticism)."

The disciples prostrated before *Guruji* touching the ground with their heads, legs, shoulders, the breasts and the foreheads.

Instantly *Guruji* became weak and weary. He lay on the ground, his head resting on one of my protruding roots. It seemed that it was his deathbed. He called Brahesh, Vishma and Mahnu around him. Both *Nagas* stood on either side of him cautiously. All my branches along with their leaves looked downward at him. The elder *Naga* poured a few drops of holy water into the dried up mouth of Guru.

Guru said to his disciples, "My most respected *Gurujis* . . ."

All the three disciples looked in surprise at each other and stared at their *Guruji*. They were ignorant about the secret of their own *Guruji* addressing them as *Gurujis*. Though they could find out the secret by opening their third eye, they did not want to experiment it on their reverend *Guruji* by awakening the *Kundalini*. They behaved like normal, ordinary and common men.

Guru went on: "Dear *Gurujis*, this *Brahmamuhurtham* onwards, all the three of you are my *Gurujis*. I've given you all that I had within me. Now I'm an empty cage filled with darkness, where my heart throbs like an injured bird that may die any moment."

As one man, the disciples said: "*Guruji*, you've donated your knowledge to us. You taught us that knowledge never ends—the more you give, the more you gain. That the giver and taker and the knowledge would shine brighter than Sun; that the minds and hearts of the giver and taker would develop to have infinitely long lives definitely."

Guruji's voice became feeble: "That's when teaching a student any subject on our Mother Earth. The giver gives knowledge to the taker and both are benefited. This case is distinct. In this case, I have poured all my stock of power into you, especially when you gained the *Kundalini* power. I took lessons of *Kundalini* shaking. You were doing it. I was not doing it. I was making you do it. If someone is climbing a tree, the tree remains there; the climber reaches aloft. If someone is making way, the path remains there; the walker goes ahead. If someone crosses a river, he crosses; the river remains there. I could cope up with you to move the seventh wheel of meditation. The movement of that last and final wheel is the climax of meditation. But someone has to direct the scene. If I too had acted to gain the *Kundalini Shakhty,* then none of us would have attained that power. I was supervising your exercises. If any step were misplaced during that period, you also would have suffered my prevailing state. When you were in meditation to stir up the *Kundalini* I was awaken pouring oil in my eyes in order to scrutinize all of you.

"Thus I lost all my power and you have gained it. I told you earlier that a person who wins that power is a master or a *yogi.* A person who won't win that is merely a patient or *rogi.* It's time for you to quit this island of knowledge (*gurukulam*). You shall plunge into the ocean of humanity. You shall drill out crude things from there. You shall refine it and fuel them so that their vehicle of life should make its way smoothly."

Brahesh, Vishma and Mahnu took long breaths and felt sympathy for him. Guru said in broken words: But, I . . . am . . . con . . . ten . . . ted . . . I . . . pro . . . du . . . ced . . . three . . . Gu . . . rus . . . Each . . . one . . . of . . . you . . . wi . . . ll . . . ha . . . ve . . . ma . . . ny . . . fo . . . llo . . . wers . . . Do . . . not . . . for . . . get . . . Marams . . . and . . . Mrugams . . . Do . . . not . . . po . . . llu . . . te . . . air . . . fire . . . wa . . . ter . . . ear . . . th . . . and . . . sky . . . *Aa* . . . *yush* . . . *man* . . . *bha* . . . *va* . . . to . . . all . . ."

Guruji was finding difficulty in breathing. Somehow he continued muttering: The . . . ta . . . xi . . . of . . . dea . . . th . . . is . . . wai . . . t . . . ing . . . fo . . . r . . . me . . . Yes . . . ter . . . day . . . *he* . . . tra . . . vell . . . ed . . . To . . . day . . . *I* . . . To . . . mo . . . rrow . . . *you* . . . The . . . des . . . ti . . . na . . . tion . . . at . . . the . . . dis . . . cre . . . tion . . . of . . . God . . . Let . . . me . . . go . . . go . . . go . . . Om . . . san . . . ti . . . san . . . ti . . . san . . . ti . . .

As *Guruji* raised his right palm to bless them Brahesh, Vishma and Mahnu, one by one they poured divine water drop by drop into his mouth from the spoons made out of my leaves. As he swallowed the water drops, his lips quivered, eyes rolled and chest stood still. He was dead. He embraced a choice death—attained *Samadhi*.

The disciples hugged *Guruji* and wept. Their eyes produced streams. Both the dismayed *Nagas* hit their heads on my stem, their hoods sustained injuries and suffered gores. Crestfallen, I remained there like a stagnant object sans photosynthesis, sans process of chlorophyll.

Their hearts broken, they sent a condolence message to all *Mrugams* and *Marams* of the whole universe. The message was: They considered the incident not as a death; they considered it as a transition from everything to nothing.

The wind was the messenger of the news of the sad demise of their universal *Guru* to all the floras and faunas. Immediately they stopped merry-making. They became modest. It was a liver-melting message to them. Yet they made arrangements for the funeral courageously. While most of the floras were busy making the wreaths, most of the faunas wanted to become the pal-bearers. They were on the verge of a fight to have that right.

But when the senior-most lion happened to know about it, he interrupted, "It's the right of royal animals and we are there to render it."

The activities of all other animals came to a standstill. Their minds were filled with sorrow.

King Lion again commanded: "Let me tell you one thing clearly: It's the time for taking flowers, not weapons. Now all of us will mourn by observing silence for five degrees rotation of our Mother Earth. After that, all of us shall go to Gurukulam and take part in the funeral ceremony. Lots of rites have to be carried out for the *moksha* of our *guru*'s soul."

*   *   *

I was made to shiver. When I came to life, I saw two elegant elephants shaking me, their trunks clenched around my trunk. My empty mind earned energy. I felt tickling and scratching all over my body—myriad of monkeys, bats, birds and so many flying creatures had lodged on my branches and leaves in order to have a clear view of funeral rites from aloft. Though their acts disturbed me, I did not protest. I welcomed them. I looked down. The three disciples were trying to bring *Guruji*'s body into the *Padmasanam* posture. Nagas were helping them. The animals made sounds.

Seeing the hustle and bustle, the disciples pleaded: Co-operate please . . . Co-operate. This is no time for fun. This is the time to mourn. So, stop showing your *shakti* and please maintain *shanty*."

Lion King said modestly, "We are aware of the situation and circumstances. But, you should understand our condition. We're not human beings to act with patience."

"We understand your grief," the disciples said. "We know that your hearts are pounding for want of blood of tolerance. Your lungs are throbbing for want of air of love. Your ears are eager to hear the voice of courage. And your eyes want to see the scenes of compassion."

One deer said in fast soft voice, "Our sea of love is dried up; land of peace is flooded; atmosphere of compassion is emptied. Can you resurrect him?"

"No. It's against the will of *Guruji*. And not only that, it will amount to challenging the nature as well as defeating God."

"Then what shall we do now?" A peacock asked.

"Just pray . . . pray for *Guruji*'s *athma* . . ."

I saw all the animals looking down and standing still and stiff. They prayed for the soul of their beloved *Guruji*. After observing the silence, they rushed and assembled in and around Gurukulam in order to have a glimpse of his body. Their livers melted. Yet they obeyed the instructions given to them by Nagas to facilitate performing funeral.

Then I saw all the floras were weeping, dropping all their belongings viz buds, flowers, fruits, berries and even leaves as it was our family way of removing the ornaments and decorations from our bodies to mourn for the dear and near. Actually I too was supposed to follow suit. But Brahesh, Vishma and Mahnu, the successors of *Guruji* requested me to preserve all my stock in order to feed the motley crowd on the second day of the funeral to break their fast. However, I was immensely pleased with the profound love of the *Mrugams* and *Marams* towards the deceased *Guruji*.

Brahesh, Vishma and Mahnu started singing the prayer song. The animals added symphony. I chanted the song in my heart.

O! God! Lover of devotees!
O! God! Your grace shall be shed on the soul . . .
The soul that's given us up and went away somewhere
O! Omnipotent! Bless . . . Bless . . . Bless . . .

O! Blesser and omniscient!
O! Giver of kindness!
Your blessing is the only way for the wandering soul.
It is null and void to cry for the dead
Alas! Eyes are not agreeing sans crying;
The liver compels the tears to shed.
O! Omnipresent! Men are nothing before thee
Knowingly or unknowingly, all the sins done by the soul
Shall be forgiven; and give a bit of your grace to the soul.
Prominent personalities in the whole world
Are mere burning flies in your fire of death.
O! You multifarious, mourning for the dead is meaningless
O! God! Parting of the dearest is flooding our eyes.
The soul that's left the cage of the bones and the flesh,
Thee, pave the way for his soul to reach the altar of the Almighty . . .
Emperors also have to embrace death indeed.
O! You Omniscient, we're just particles before your proximity
O! God! Lover of devotees! Let the soul receive your favors.
O! God! Your grace shall be shed on the soul . . .
O! God! Pay the soul incessant peace . . .

*   *   *

Guruji's Samadhi was kept in *Padmasanam*. The body was placed inside the cave on a rock like a statue. Except the face, the entire body was covered with *Ramacham*. The mourners were allowed to pay homage to Guru. Animals queued up outside. One by one they came forward; gave salute; turned left and retreated. When they came out of the cave, some were in sad, sad condition; some were in bad, bad condition and some were in mad, mad condition.

Many *Mrugams* assembled beneath many *Marams*. It was the largest convention ever held in nature. I could hear the mourners flattering Guru in murmuring voice. Some mother *Mrugams* sat down with their children and sang sad songs. Children joined the choir. The song comprised of verses of deep thoughts. The song was so passionate that even rock hearts would melt like wax.

Floras prayed to me that they also should have the opportunity to have a glimpse of their beloved *Guruji*. I promised them that I would make arrangements. I was anxious to know what was happening inside the cave.

I bent down my lowest branch to the maximum and peeped inside the cave. I requested the *Trimurthis* about the floras' wish.

"Why not? By all means they're entitled to have the *darshan*." Disciples said, "We're taking *Guruji's Samadhi* for a procession to the riverbank and back to facilitate *darshan* to all the animals, plants, aquatics as well as to the celestial bodies."

The *Samadhi* was fleeted by Nagas at the front and *Trimurthis* as pal-bearers. All the animals followed them in a slow march. All the plants bent their bodies. A platoon of monkeys played a funeral pathos with the available instrument they gathered as if a Military band set.

All the heavenly bodies appeared on the sky and looked crestfallen. It was the largest procession ever held in the history of nature.

The *Samadhi* was lowered on the riverbank. I was amazed to see the array of underwater creatures anxiously waiting on the surface of the water to behold the *Samadhi* of their *Guruji*. Schools of fish surfaced on the water; stayed a few moments in the air; seen the *Samadhi* and dived down. Myriad of turtles and snails crawled on to the bank, protruded their heads, gave salute and withdrew to hermitage. Each and every creature paid melancholic marks of respect to the universal *Guru*. The most shocking incident was that the water level of the river had immensely gone up due to the shedding of the tears by aquatic creatures.

I could not bear the sorrow. Yes, there it was—the great *Samadhi* of *my guru*! Yes, this time I used the word *"my"* knowingly that the word *"my"* was a word denoting selfishness. For in this particular case, I was selfish. I wished he were my property. I wanted him in my possession. I wished if he were born on this earth exclusively for me. Yes, I was selfish. I did not want any others to have any right to his body. I was jealous of someone else's claim on him as his relative, friend, *guru* et al. Even as someone else's enemy. We were made for each other. I loved him more than anybody else on this planet. I did not even love Mother Earth as much as I had loved my *Guruji* because my mother gave me the love of a mother whereas he was like my father, brother, friend and above all my teacher—benefactor.

I felt giddiness as I thought about the funeral rites of a *manush* (human) as per the lessons taught by Guru—the corpse should be kept on the pyre and burnt to ashes. The ashes had to be sprinkled in the divine river water that flowed to the sea. One sea met another. Thus the human being became the part and parcel of the entire earth.

I remembered his foretelling: "You are the *time*! You shall witness an incident; you're going to lose a *thing*; please remain here to witness it." So, this was what he had in mind; he himself was the *thing* that I was going to lose.

How can I bear the parting of my *Guru*? At least his physical body could be left free forever for the eyes to see at the time of agony. A glimpse of his body would be more than enough to heal a hurt heart. A thought about him would be more than enough to shed all the sorrows. What else a living creature wanted on this earth? What else you could expect from a living creature?

I trembled as I thought about the disposal of his dead body. I could not stand it. On the contrary, I could not contradict the discretion of the three ascended *gurus*—the *Trimurthis*. As I stared at the sky, I saw the late setting Sun, the early rising Moon, the clouds, etc.

They too were crestfallen and gloomy for they too did not want that body buried. I could see denial on their faces. I wondered what the other *gurukulam* staff—Nagas—might be thinking about the parting of Guru. Will they be willing . . . ?

They were engaged in funeral *mantras* and *tantras* in front of the *homakunda*. Everywhere camphor was burning. Everywhere frankincense was fumigated. Everywhere sandalwood burned. Everywhere sadness prevailed.

My mind was again pregnant with madness. At daybreak the body would be cremated. I took a concrete decision—to fall down into the burning pyre of Guru . . . ! All my hair stood on end. Tired and frightened, I dozed.

I came to life when Nagas shook me up.

They asked me, "What's your decision?"

I said, "I'm going to die."

"Why?"

"Without Guru, I have no life."

"You think, if you let go your soul, Guru's soul would come back?"

"At least can't we preserve the body?"

"Who is going to destroy it?" the snakes asked with concern.

I was stupefied, "So no cremation?"

"No . . ."

Again in anxiety I asked, "No pyre . . ."

Nagas interrupted: "No cremation. Unlike an ordinary person, Guru has voluntarily left his cage. He attained *Samadhi*. His body will be preserved in the posture of *Padmasanam*. There are a lot of changes going to happen in this habitat. It's proved in *jyothisham* (astrology). The *Trimurthis* will tell you later. All the funeral rites are over and so is the dispersal of all the *Mrugams* and *Marams*. Now be alert and concentrate on the final funeral prayer. We've to alert all the mourners. The prayer is a choir to be attended with concentration".

As Nagas left towards the crowd of animals, I sighed in relief. When I heard the *Trimurthis* reciting the final funeral prayer of *Pithru yagyam* (the main obligation to the deceased ancestor), I too joined the prayer with my sharply concentrated mind.

The *Trimurthis* said, "This place is going to be the holy of holies—a would-be pilgrimage. *Guruji's* body, which we have installed on this rock, would be the most famous monument in the world. Like bones in a body, his figure also would be transformed from flesh to a fresh substance as hard as bones. His *atman* or inner man (soul) has already attained *moksha* in *paralokam*. His outer man (corpse) became a *smarakam* or monument in *ihalokam*.

After the installation of Guru's solidified body at the shrine, I declared to the *Trimurthis*: "Reverend prophets, there is a last wish—the Will—verbally told by our beloved *Guruji* while you were engaged in *Kaivalya padam* away from Gurukulam.

"Please narrate it," the *Trimurthis* asked in terrific curiosity.

I said: "The tête-à-tête was a *Sruthi* (viva voce). The exact wordings are: To the creator, the preserver and the destroyer, Brahesh, Vishma and Mahnu, this may concern. All the three are identical as one—the cycle of life—the wheel of nature . . .

Para one: I aged four hundred fifty revolutions of the earth namely Jaisara meaning the *Victor of all,* couldn't win or earn all. I could win everything on earth but not the universe. Because I supplied all that I won and gained my physical and spiritual magnetism to my above-said disciples in order to make them perfect and permanent spiritual magnets. I'm contented that they achieved the goal by attaining the powers of controlling the heavenly bodies also.

Para two: I'm the proprietor of all the—animate and inanimate—men and materials, animals, plants as well as the earth, air, water, fire and ether. I appoint the *Maram,* namely *Banyan,* as the guardian of all the sizes, types and kinds of plants. I bequeath a quarter portion of my property such as earth, air, water, fire and ether to Rev Banyan for the free use of his subordinates, and treat them as sublimate.

Para three: Likewise, I appoint the *Mrugams* namely the elder and younger *Nagas* as the guardians of all the sizes, types and kinds of animals. I bequeath another quarter portion of my properties such as earth, water, air fire and ether for the free use of their subordinates, and treat them as sublimate. Likewise, I appoint all my above-said three disciples namely Brahesh, Vishma and Mahnu as the guardians of all sizes, types and kinds of human beings. I bequeath the remaining half of my properties such as earth, water, air, fire and ether for the free use of their subordinates and treat them as sublimate.

Para four: I hereby charge the above-said disciples with the additional responsibility of overall command and control of all the animals and plants as also the subordinates of Rev Banyan and respected *Nagas* and the immovable and non-thinking creatures.

Para five: Other than the movable and immovable properties, I also bequeath all my personal assets such as my knowledge, practices, mind and my physical body to the disciples. They shall use indiscriminately all these assets for the betterment of all the human beings, animals and plants on the earth. They shall similarly serve, protect and preserve the nature and nature's belongings sincerely.

Para six: The entitlement to and emolument for their services are that they have the right to live on this earth by free utilization of air, fire, water, earth and ether. The moment they cease to serve the earth, their entitlement will be severed. They are at full liberty to hand over all the assets to any staunch and suitable sages, who consider the whole world as a single family, as their successors. The same regulations are applicable to them also in succession.

Para seven: This Will is exhorted and recorded in viva-voce on my most exhaustive day at my direction under the nature's notary Rev Banyan and witnessed by the respected *Nagas* both elder and younger.

After a pose, I said, "I still remember, it was on a moon-lit night and all the stars on the sky were witnesses to the reading of the deed." The *Trimurthis* and the other listeners admired their *Guruji*'s sublime self-sacrifice.

As one man, the prophets promulgated: "As the sons of nature, as the disciples of *Guruji*, as the lowliest of all the creatures, we hereby declare that we earnestly and entirely execute the expectation (*Will*) of our eternal *Guruji* with enthusiasm and esteem. It's not necessary to scratch and to calculate the carat of his divinity and directives. Needless to say, he was the epitome of nature. If any creature of nature wants any further amendments to his Will may come forward. We're particular that none should be disheartened."

To their surprise, no representation of objection came. The listeners unanimously and whole-heartedly agreed to execute the easement of their ever-loving *Guruji*.

The *Trimurthis* went on: "The next thing we would like to declare is that we're going to close down this *gurukulam*. As you know, *Guruji* has assigned us distinct tasks. We must wander the nooks and corners of the world, preach and teach the people, spread the message of mercy and propagate the importance of peace. This is to enable us to live like family members on the floor of the earth and beneath the roof of the sky welcoming bright days to work and dark nights to rest. So, at this rate and stage, we can't man Gurukulam. If anyone has any objections please come forward."

None came forward. All the animals looked at their king—the lion. King Lion said, "All of us very well know that no faunas or floras, including the respected *Nagas,* can be the head of this institution. Yet, it's a pity to break the spiritual environment of this forest. But, we're ready to break up even our hearts for a decision pertaining to the betterment of the entire world."

Turning towards Nagas, the *Trimurthis* said, "Well, then, the respected *Nagas* shall execute the Will of our *Guruji* from the part of the animals. And the Reverend Banyan shall execute the will of our *Guruji* from the part of the plants. We're parting to seek our goal without any farewell ceremony. If nature (God) permits, all of us would meet here annually to observe the death anniversary of our *Guruji*."

All the mourners, including the *Trimurthis* and Nagas, dispersed and slowly disappeared. I watched the spectacular scene of their fallout. Tears poured in the area like rain. It made two big bangs in my mind during my busy packing-up hours from there. One: The closing down ceremony of Gurukulam—parting of the dearest colleagues. The other was because that day was my unceremonious birthday—I was completing a millennium. I could not know whether I should believe in a millennium expecting another millennium of life ahead . . . .

CENTURY 11

1000 TO 1100 AD

O, my good God! What was this? My home coming? A resurrection? Or a reincarnation? Or a reinstatement? After more than four centuries in exile the spiritual bird in me was coming back into my physical cage—a replenishment, or transmigration of soul.

Did any transfiguration befall me? I did not feel any. Was I sleeping? Or was I unconscious? Or had I been hypnotized? Or had I been dead? And now a re-birth! I could not understand anything. The only thing I was aware at that hour was that I was in *wood* and *juice* on my pretty body. I appreciated my physique—taller and sturdier than all other trees on earth. Supposing that the earth was a ship, my habitat the poop decks, I was the main mast.

Anyway, I felt absolutely healthy though I did not know about it. Who helped me to keep up my health? Who mended it all these days? Who nursed me? My mother? There was no question of finding the answers to these questions because we could communicate no more.

Then who serviced me? My wives? Oh! I forgot them. I should have cared them the moment I came back. But there were four of them. Whom to call first? Their hearts were so fragile that if I ranked my wives, no one on earth would be able to put together the fragments of their broken hearts. The saying is, "Frailty, thy name is woman".

Finally, I decided to call them in Cosmolish alphabetical order. "Uru . . . Oh, Uru . . ." I called her softly like a husband murmuring in his wife's ear on the wedding night. No reply came forth. I raised the volume. Yet there was no answer. Was she sleeping? May be.

I called another wife. "Thilo . . . O, Thilo . . ."

There was no response.

I called, "Mena . . . O, Mena . . ."

No response at all.

Like from a loud-hailer, I hailed, "Ramb . . . Ramb . . ."

She too did not respond.

Repeatedly I called them but there was no response. One thing was quite clear. It was not that they did not hear me. They did not want to answer me. Was it that we too could no more communicate?

I was depressed. The high spirits that filled my renovated body were reduced to low degree. I felt I was deprived of the enjoyment of family life.

Suddenly I thought about *Guruji.*

I realized that whatever I dreamt of *my* family life (wife, children, society of a tree), it was all just *Maya* (unreal), just a fantasy. I further apprehended that my consciousness had five more subordinates namely sub-consciousness, deputy-consciousness, associate consciousness, assistant consciousness and additional consciousness. All these mental faculties were performing myriad of *Maya* and *Mohini* (Beauties) acts on the stage of my mind.

I had no wives or children. All I had was my own body. Uru, Mena, Ramb and Thilo, my so-called wives were just *Mohinies* (non-existing). They were four associated stems around my trunk and were just some among many of my adventitious roots. So I suppressed the ambition of leading a self-contained family life. Thereupon I put out the egoistic selfishness from the field of my mind and sowed the seeds of *Vasudhiyva Kudumbakam* (world is one family) by ethnology which burst open many buds of euphoria in me.

Another thing I learnt thoroughly was that I was able to think of, understand and participate in the feelings of other creatures of the world. But I did not know whether the other creatures were able to think, understand and participate in my feelings. The loss of communicating power compelled me to conclude that I, mere a tree, was nobody to meddle in the matters of others.

Instantly my thought got nullified. When some women came before me and lighted up Cut-coconut oil lamps at nightfall, some men and children also came there and sat before me. They started singing poems praising my glory. I wondered. "Am I praiseworthy?" They named me the *Bodhi* tree—the enlightened one. They flattered me as their benefactor. They believed that I was their guide to Benthamism.

I was just standing still there. My feet and heart were numbed. Was that a benevolent action? Of course. That was enough for them. My shade was shelter to them. My crown served them as a place of safety and security. They sang:

Giving us shade, giving us shadow, giving us shelter
You're our home.
Giving us courage, giving us cradle, giving us crutches
You're our savior.
Giving us name, giving us fame, giving us game
You're our character.
Giving us lessons, giving us seasons, giving us blossom
You're our teacher.

I could understand the vernacular. So I was home for them. I was the cradle for their children—they hitched my hanging roots and used them as cradles. I was the crutches for the cripples and the old—they used my broken branches as staffs.

In the morning they offered *pooja* to me. The consideration was that I was the symbol of fertility. The land had indeed turned fertile. But its credit should have gone to Mother Earth. People considered her also. They offered *Beli* (blood sacrifice) to keep her fertility. But *Beli* was totally a superstition. That too in the form of *ahimsa*. The populace, without knowing it is poppycock, their minds clad in clay, was ever ready to render any wicked thing out of superstition—even self-destruction.

What a change! I had left the habitat with pure-minded animals, plants and human beings (the naked couples). A half a millennium had changed the habit of the inhabitants of the habitat. It was a transition from innocence to guilt and from gentleness to wildness.

And immediately I learnt that the exclusive spiritual world, which I had seen in *gurukulam* had disappeared from my life and there appeared the exclusive physical world of the habitat where *Cosmolish* was foreign to the inhabitants.

I could neither advise nor argue nor abuse them for their absurdity. Their prayer turned to perversion. I pitied their perversity. I could not connive with the insanity.

The transgressors' act was the most wicked I had ever witnessed, and heard from my mother, during my life. That too right around me. While singing the prayer, all the ladies, men and the children were drinking country-made liquor. Intoxication made them dance by hugging-and-clasping. They hugged each other. Some men with women. Some women with men.

Some kissed mouth to mouth till the stronger ones bit away the lips of the weaker ones. Men urinated on the faces of women. They drenched their faces in it. Men made their palms as piss-pots. Women pissed in them and the men drank the urine.

Instantly I learnt one thing: The perverted ideas of wrong pervade faster than the right ideas.

They indulged in sex and sin, liquor and lust. Should they be blamed for leading a sinister life instead of a sacred life? No, not at all. For them that sinister life was sacred. They regarded that lifestyle as custom and culture. They felt those activities as duty-bound because they were born and brought up in such an atmosphere.

Like animals running amok, human beings always altered the atmosphere of life from *ahimsa* to an Aceldama—a girl, two boys, two men and a woman were killed on the second day of my home-coming. There was no trace of love in their activities. There was not even any dust of decency in their sphere.

I wished they had at least one irritancy.

But my spirit that went on the voyage to the *gurukulam* understood that the atmosphere there had not been polluted like this. All living and non-living things were bona fide. Now everything had changed from boon company to a boor company. How did this adulteration occur? Was the culprit a person or a situation? Or was it just an accident?

What should I do about their boorishness? I could only lament. So I lamented. After lamenting for a while, I felt that I should do something better than lamentation. So I wept . . . wept . . . and kept on weeping till my physical body caught a flashback of the habitat during my absence.

Scene 1

Midway opening
Sub title: 1000 years—400 = 600 A.D

Scene 2

Beneath the Banyan tree—outdoor; **daytime**.
Man, woman, a dog, a bitch—all naked.
The couple eating some fruits (combination shot).

Dog mates with the bitch—close-up.

Couples watch the mating curiously.

They throw away the fruits.

Woman takes the position of the bitch.

Man kneels behind her buttocks. They imitate the dog's action. Dogs get hooked up (Mid-close shot).

They stand coupled, facing opposite with tongues hanging.

Couples try to take the position of dogs.

Coupling gets disconnected.

Seeing the couples, dogs trail away to distance (panning shot). Couples on knees in opposite direction with lustful reaction.

Scene 3

Same location.

Lying on ground, they hug. Her bare bosom dents on his bare chest (close-up).

They kiss so deeply as if to suck out some hidden substance from each other's mouth (close shot of faces and lips).

They roll on the ground.

They stop rolling.

Woman beneath the man.

They copulate. They produce lustful sounds.

While man works on her, she pinches and pricks his back and buttocks with her nails.

They are exhausted. Their chests heaving heavily, they lay flat . . .

Scene 4

Same location and time as Scene No II.

Man, woman.

Woman is sitting, resting her back on the Banyan tree.

She is pregnant (close shot of her bulged belly).

Man enters with a bamboo jar in one land. The other hand is full of fruits.

He sits beside her.

He pours water into her mouth.

They both eat the fruits.

Scene 5

Hollow of the Banyan tree—Indoor. **Night**.

Man, woman, a child.

A wooden torch is tied on to a vertical root. It lights up the insides of the hollow (zoom forward).

Scream of woman . . . . Aaaah . . . . Oooh . . .

She is in labor.

Her vulva (tight close shot).

The hairy head of the child protruding.

Man's reaction in amazement.

Again the wailing of the woman . . . *Aiiiyooowh* . . .

Man is frightened.

Delivery seems difficult.

Man pulls out the child.

He throws the child away as if it is an unwanted thing.

Scene cuts.

Baby falls on a heap of dry leaves nearby.

Scene cuts back to the hollow of the tree.

Woman stops screaming. She is relieved of pain.

Rain falls.

Cry of the child.

Inter-cut to the hollow.

Woman's hands search her sides for the child in vain.

She gets up. Her disappointed reaction.

Crestfallen, she staggers towards the child.

Man watches her with innocent eyes.

Scene 5 A

Woman breast-feeds the baby lying on a bed of wet leaves.

Baby enjoys it with closed eyes.

Baby's legs start cycling and hands start horning the free breast of the mother.

Man watches them in fascination (another frame).

The heavy rain disturbs them.

Man enters the frame and kneels down beside the mother and child and bends his body over their body so as to prevent the rainfall.

She smiles at him and combs his hair with her fingers as if approving his intellectual act serving his body as an umbrella.

Strong wind blows off the wooden torch (another frame). Total blackout. The sound in the background is the creak of crickets.

Scene 6

Beneath the Banyan tree; outdoor, morning.
Couple, baby daughter, peacocks.
The family is asleep inside the hollow of the tree.
Many peacocks come and peck at the fallen berries. They do random actions.
They make noises . . . crock . . . crock . . . crock . . .
Satisfied, some peahens dance.
(Inter cut to hallow of the tree).
The man wakes up.
His dissatisfaction seeing the peacocks.
He jumps out of the hollow.
(Cut back to outside)
Peacocks sense his approach.
They run away through the open field.
Man runs behind the birds as fast as his legs could carry him (panning shot).
He catches one bird (inter-cut).

Scene 7

Beneath the Banyan tree; door, daylight.
Man, Woman, child, peacock.
Peacock hangs upside down in the man's strong hold.
Inter-cuts of peacock's struggle and savage reaction of the man at intervals.
Woman enters the frame running.
Her daughter rests on her shoulders cross-legged, clasping her hair.
Man gives one leg of the peacock to the woman.
They heave the legs of the peacock in opposite directions like in a tug-of-war. Their frantic reactions.
Close-up shot of the bird being torn into two parts. Horror music.
Pool of blood.

Man keeps the bifurcated dead bird on his chest.
Woman collects the oozing blood in a bamboo jar.
The liver hangs out in close shot.
Woman plucks the liver and hands it over to the daughter.
Daughter chews it like chocolate.
Reaction of satisfaction on her face and in eyes.
The couples enjoy eating the meat of the peacock.
All characters sit on the ground and eat.
Daughter's throat chocks.
Mother strike on her head slightly with her palm.
Daughter coughs.
Mother gives her some blood to drink.
Daughter's throat clears.
Couples also share the blood.

Scene 8

River bank; Outdoor
Noon.
Man, woman, girl (daughter), child (second daughter)
Woman and girl watch the water.
The child is belted onto the woman's back with a vine.
(Cut to the river).
Man surfaces (close shot).
His hands gripping two fishes.
He throws the fish on the shore one by one.
Cut back to the shore.
Girl picks up the fluttering fish.
She strings the fishes into a midrib of a coconut leaf blade.
Fishes flutter (close shot).

Scene 9

A huge anthill.
Evening.
The family.
They are walking.
The child is secured on the back of the mother.
The bunch of dead fishes is hanging in the hand of the girl.

The man carries a long dried up stick under his armpit. He has got two pieces of rocks in his hands by which he tries to burn the end of the stick by sparking the granites while walking.

In their long view, there is an anthill like a spot.

They reach the anthill having the height of a big tree.

A snake crawls out of it.

Man catches it by the tail and pulls strongly backwards.

Like a hammer-thrower, he throws away the snake.

Long shot of snake in the air.

Several termites fly away from the anthill.

Wind and rain arrive.

Sleeping infant cries.

Man pierces the earthen mound of the anthill with the stick.

He crawls inside the mound and removes more earth from inside.

Girl and woman help him clear the sand.

They make a cave-like hollow within the mounds.

Scene 10

Inside the anthill.

Night.

Whole family is in the anthill.

Man fixes the wooden torch on the mound at a height.

Girl keeps the bunch of fishes on the ground.

Rain stops.

Family goes out of the anthill.

The torch falls down on top of the fish-bunch.

Man senses the burning smell of fish inside the cave.

Family enters the cave.

Man takes away the torch.

Woman picks up the fish.

She smells, bites and tastes it.

Man takes the other fish and inspects it.

He tastes it also.

His eyes shine.

They enjoy eating the burnt fish.

Man touches up the unburned portion of fish.

He gives it to the elder daughter.

All of them laugh.

Family's reactions of contentment of their invention of baking the food accidentally.

Scene 11

Beneath the Banyan tree; outdoor
Night.
Man, woman, elder girl, six girls younger to her in series.
Family is sitting around a bonfire (combination trolley shot).
The glowing fire illuminates all the characters' faces.
A pig is hung over the fire for baking.
Elder grown up girl stands up.
Menses oozes out of her vulva (tight close shot).
She wipes away the discharge with leaves.
She throws the leaves into the fire.

Scene 11 A

Same location, time and characters as Scene XII.
The fire is live without flame. It resembles a heap of gold (mid-shot).
Children are sleeping.
Man lies on his back.
Woman approaches him.
She kisses on his navel.
She takes his testicles in her hands and plays with it.
She climbs on him and starts working on him.
Rattling sound of the dry leaves where they lay and hissing sound of their breaths.
Elder daughter watches the sexual activities of her parents.
Her lustful reaction—She presses her breasts.
Inter-cuts of the couples at intercourse, burning logs and the lustful actions of the girl.
Woman gets exhausted.
She rolls away.
Girl gets up.
She views his manhood.
She skirts the father.
She takes his erected genital in her mouth.
He hugs her.

Lying on top of her, he starts mating.
Woman wakes up.
She screams and prevents their action.
Man gets up and strikes her.
She still protests.
Tight close-up of fire.
Man heaves the woman by her hair.
He throws her into the fire pit.
She falls amidst the fire.
Ash, flare and glare generated in the fire pit.
Woman jumps out of the fire screaming.
Man again pushes her into the fire ridiculously.
She tries to escape again.
He again pushes her into the fire.
Inter-cuts of the ghastly reaction of the woman and the look of rage on the face of man.
Woman runs with the blazing body (panning shot).
She collapses. She screams. She dies.
He triumphantly drags her into the fire.
Bakes her body by turning this way and that.
The elder girl helps him in poking.
The noise of hustle and bustle shake the other children.
The roasted body of the woman is hung on the branch of the Banyan tree by the man and the elder girl from head and feet.
Man bites the burned bosom of the woman's body and munches it.
The children share the roasted flesh of their mother.
Their actions resemble those of famished, voracious and carnivorous creatures. Their hoarse laughter.

Scene 12

Open field; outdoor
Dawn.
Men, monkeys.
The scene opens with the long shot of the man's approach from far away. The background is the rising sun in the horizon. Foreground is the stretch of open field.

Scene 13

Beneath the Banyan tree; Outdoor.

Day.

Lady, children, baby, dogs.

The lady is breast-feeding her son.

The son sucks and presses the breast.

A little away, the three girls are sitting in the background.

In the foreground exposure, they are shitting. Simultaneously they are eating some fruits.

Three dogs are impatient.

Scene inter-cut.

Two grown up girls are trying to skin a rabbit.

One holds the rabbit. Other skins. Like in a tug-of-war they pull.

The sixth girl is engaged in baking a skinned rabbit.

Inter-cut to mother and baby.

Baby urinates.

Mother collects the urine in a bamboo jar.

She drinks the hot urine as though it's the refinement of her milk in the form of urine processed in the unit of the body of her son.

Inter-cut.

The three shitting girls stand up.

Close-up of the excrements like steaming cakes.

Three stand-by dogs eat it fastidiously.

Inter-cut.

Two girls hand over the skinned rabbit to the baking girl.

The removed skins are hung on the lower branch of the tree for drying.

All the children come around the baking place.

They look at the rising sun.

In their view, mid-close of their father.

He enters into the frame.

Children are surprised to see the two monkeys he brings along with him hitched by a dry vein.

The man fastens the monkeys to a root.

The amusement of monkeys. Their jumping and scratching.

Children's reactions of amazement. Monkeys' ridiculous actions.

Dogs bark ferociously at the monkeys.

Monkeys bite.

Man beats up and chases away the dogs.

Scene 14

Beneath the Banyan tree; outdoor.
Day.
Family members—men, women and children.
Some chiff-chaffs warble from atop the tree.
The mother imitates the birds by uttering musically as if to sing a nursery rhyme to lull her son to sleep.
The chirping of birds comes from the background as if one bird is questioning and the other answering.
Family members also chatter, clatter and babble as though they are learning the alphabets of a viva voce language (combination shot).

Scene 14 A

Some pigeons peck at some small sticks, big leaves and long flexible veins scattered on the ground.
They fly atop the tree.
They repeat the action.
Family observes the play of the birds.

Scene 15

A platoon of army ants marching in marshal order from one root to the other (panning shot).
They carry a piece of bone with effort.
The whole family members watch it in fascination.
The senior-most man shows an action that meant means the family too should adopt the ants' collective method.

Scene 16

Beneath the Banyan tree; outdoor.
Night.
All the family members.
Elder girl is pregnant. She massages her stomach.
Senior-most man (old man) rapes the next girl.

She shrieks.

Scene 17

In the woods.
Day.
All the family members except the pregnant woman.
A herd of deer go through the woods.
Man hides behind a large tree. He's holding a stick.
The herd is chased by the girls.
A deer comes near the tree. Man hits it with the bar
Deer quivers and dies.
The man skins the deer.
Inter-cut.
Girls are cutting bamboo.
Inter-cut.
The boy shoots an arrow at a honeycomb. The arrow is tied with a thread.
Honey flows through the thread (panning shot).
Boy collects it in a bamboo jar.
Inter-cut.
Girls collect palm leaves.

Scene 18

Mid-way opening.
Beneath the Banyan tree.
Day.
All the family members.
Ten cradles made out of veins are hanging from different branches.
Cradles are being swung by a small girl.
Many boys and girls are engaged in different jobs.
Cut.
A boy climbs on top of the tree.
He brings some eggs from the birds' nests.
He breaks open the eggs and pours it into the infants' mouths.
Cut.
A girl carries a dead python.
Old man chops its head.

He cuts the skin of the snake's belly.
He wipes out the fat and stores it in the snake's skin.
He chops the snake into pieces.
One grown up girl put the pieces into an earthen pot.
Pour some water, starts boiling it.

Scene 19

Surrounding area of the Banyan tree.
Day.
Family.
Young man with the help of some ladies rebuilds the thatched huts nearby.
All the grown up members have covered their private parts with rabbit skin.
The old man and the young man in deer skins.

Scene 20

Thatched house—Indoors.
Night.
All the family members except the young man.
A wooden torch lights up the location.
Family sleeps.

Scene 21

In the open field. Outdoors.
Night.
Young man.
He is humming a tune.
He is following a herd of sheep.

Cut back to Scene 22

Effects of wind and rain in the background. Old man gets up, removes his deer skin-wear.

He daubs his entire body with the python fat. His bare and oiled body shines in the glare of the torch. He massages his long and erect manhood.

He approaches his granddaughter lustfully.

Scene cut back to 23.

The moon in the sky is covered with black clouds.
Young man's reaction of fast approaching wind and rain.
He chases the sheep and starts running . . .

Scene 24

Thatched house; indoors.
Rainy night.
All the family members including the young man.
Young man enters breathing heavily.
The visuals of the rape.
Young man's beetle brow.
He pulls his father away from the girl.
The terror in the eyes of all the female members of the family.
They point their fingers towards the old man as if he's a swindler.
Young man beats the old man.
Old man vies with his son.
The defeat of the old man. He runs out of the house.
Young man follows.

Scene 25

Beneath the Banyan tree; outdoors.
Night—downpour.
All the family members.
Lightning and thunder at intermission.
Fight of old and young man (long, mid and close shots.)
Family members watch the fight. Their uncontrollable mirth.
Young man beats the old man with a beetle.
Old man falls down near the stem of the tree.
Son strikes the old man's head on the stem.
Shivery reaction of the old man.
Fierce reaction of the young man.
Old man dies.

Scene 26

Thatched house; Indoors.
Night.
All the family members.
The atmosphere is full of fun, frolic and fucking.
Some are drinking *toddy*.
Some are smoking *ganja*.
Some are making love.
The young man copulates with his grown up sister.

Scene 27

Beneath the Banyan tree—Outdoors.
Day.
The old man's corpse is still lying beneath the Banyan tree.
Vultures come around and bite at his body (various angle shots)
Young man shoots down the vultures with arrows.
Ladies pick up the birds.
They remove the feathers.
They bake the birds in the open fire.

Scene 28

Woods; outdoors.
Day.
All the men, women, boys and girls of the family.
Inter-cuts of the various actions of the characters—Dissolves.
Some men tapping toddy from the palm trees.
Some women collecting fruits and plantains.
Some boys collecting honey.
Some girls fetching water from the river in wooden barrels.
They hook those articles on separate bamboo stumps.
Each pair carries the load and walk.

Scene 29

Beneath the Banyan tree; outdoors.
Day.

All the family members.

The decayed dead body is being pecked out by myriads of birds—(close, mid and long shots).

The family members' unpleasant reactions to the stink from the body.

They close their nostrils.

Some pregnant women nauseate.

The young man drags the corpse holding its legs through the open field to a distance.

Visuals of birds' sorties over the corpse.

Scene 30

Around the Banyan tree; outdoors.

Day.

Scene opens with the visuals of several old men, old women, young men, young women, boys, girls, infants engaged in various actions.

Many huts in the background.

Then wiping the movements of the domestic animals—fowls pecking out insects from the ground.

Cattle are secured on the roots.

Dogs are running at random.

Monkeys climbing the tree.

Scene 31

Mid-way opening.

Open field—Outdoors.

Day—downpour.

Few men and few women—Costume—Private parts are hidden with hide.

A forked log is moving on the soaked soil.

Tilt-scene is elevated from the clay-covered legs of two men to their heads of the pulling man and the pushing man.

Many men ploughing the field.

The zigzag lines made by the ploughs.

The farmers are all wet.

Cut.

Women scatter seeds on the earth—Different angle shots.

Scene 32

Graveyard; outdoors.
Day.
Plenty of skeletons are lying open on the ground.
Two men fence the yard.
Thunder and lightning.
Men look at the sky with folded arms and pray.

Scene 33

The river; outdoors.
Daybreak.
Many women.
Midway opening of sunrise.
Sun's rays fall in the river through the branches of trees.
Ladies taking dip in the water.
Take water in their folded-palms.
Show it to the rising sun.
Their eyes are closed in devotion.

Scene 34

Beneath the Banyan tree; outdoor.
Day.
A young man, a young woman and many others.
Young man is engaged in picture-writing on the stem of the tree with charcoal.
Close up of the drawings of goat, cat, monkey, human beings etc.
Others watch and try to read the hieroglyph in confusion—They look at each other.
Cut to . . .
Young woman is playing a fiddle-like instrument.
Others enjoy the music.

Scene 35

Open paddy-field; outdoor.
Day.

Two roaring elephants approaching.
Paddy plants sway in the wind in the background.
Echo of the elephants' roar.

Scene 36

Beneath the Banyan tree; outdoor.
Day.
A boy.
A baby elephant is shackled to a rigid root.
The boy is feeding the elephant with palm leaves.
The roar of the approaching elephants on the background.
Elephants enter the frame.
The boy is frightened.
Cut to . . .
Elephants destroy the hutment, plantations and vegetation (visuals in various angles).
Barking of dogs.
Boy in despair.
He climbs the tree.
Inter-cut.
Boy takes shelter on a branch where a honey hive is hanging.
Elephants break the shackles of the boy elephant.
The branch of the tree shakes.
Cry of the boy.
Elephants alter their attentions towards the boy.
Elephants try to pull out the boy from the branch by stretching their trunks.
Boy wants to repulse the elephants.
Unknowingly he catches the hanging honey hive.
Honey hive falls exactly on the head of one elephant.
All the honeybees rush out of the comb—close-up.
They prick the elephants.
The repulsion of elephants. Their roars.
They run away with their kid.
Boy remains on top still afraid.
Scene cuts to ground.
All the family members enter.
They witness the topsy-turvy situation.

They unload their articles.
They are afraid as well as angry.
The senior man walks through the debris.
His reaction ruffled in temper.
The cry of the boy from top.
Boy explains the flashback with gestures and noise.
The senior man inspects the honey hive, He breaks it open.
The bees fly hither and thither.
A big queen bee is seen.
Family watches in fascination.
The senior man explains the members with gestures that he is like the big bee and the others are the workers and fighters. The reactions of the family members indicate that they have learned the system of the social insects and they would follow it.
Crowd lifts the sturdy, tall senior man above their head as if they are making him their head—their cheers.

Scene 37

Paddy-field; outdoor
Day.
Two young men, a girl, other field workers.
Grown up paddy sways in the wind like waves of the sea.
Various shots of the workers in the field.
Camera moves from long shot to mid-close—Two young men working. Their muscles. Their sweat—(Dissolve). A beautiful girl stands there working—(Tight close-shot.)

Scene 38

Beneath the Banyan tree; outdoor.
Day.
Senior man (head), some ladies.
The headman is lying naked on a wooden cot.
He pulls on the hookah.
Ladies sit around him.
They apply python fat on his body.
One young lady rubbing up his genitals—close-up.

Continuation of Scene 37

The girl is removing the weeds—(sharp focus in the foreground).
The two youths work, standing—(out of focus in the background)
A young man comes in and removes her bottom-wear.
She stands erect.
He hugs her.
Other youth also approaches.
He pulls out the first youth with actions and voice that the girl belongs to him.
The men's malicious reactions.
The second man kisses her left cheek and consoles her.
The first man kisses her right cheek.
He takes her right breast in his left palm and squeezes.
The second youth sucks her left breast.
He uses both his hands to release the first man's hands troubling her breast.
Girl's reaction of helplessness—close-up.
First man removes his skin-under-wear.
He slips his prong-like organ into her anus.
Girl's shrill cry (special sound effect).
The second man also gets naked in a hurry.
He propels his organ into her from the front.
He hits the first man's forehead.
The shrieking girl tries to escape from their grip in vain.
The echo of the cry alerts the other workers.
They start running from background to the foreground.

Continuation of scene 38

The headman is lying on the cot.
Both the youths and the girl are standing on the leg-side of the head with folded arms—(combination shot).
Motley crowd is around in the back ground—(out of focus).
The girl complains with gestures and voice that she is being troubled by both the youths.
Sitting on the cot the headman makes a sound—Shhh . . .
One harpy closes the girl's mouth as if women are not supposed to speak before the headman.

The first youth shows with action that the girl belongs to him.

The second youth also claims the girl.

They pull her from both sides gripping her hands.

Girl's wailing . . . (Special effect—sound).

Headman jumps from the cot and stands before the youths.

Youths release the girl.

Girl's wailing reduced to low noise.

The headman points at the youths with his finger.

In their vision, two spears are fixed on the ground like prongs of a pronghorn.

Each youth takes a spear.

They start fighting.

The crowd steps back to provide them sufficient space.

Freezing and dissolving visuals of their spear-fight.

Inter-cut.

The headman compels the girl to bed with him.

She tries to escape.

Some harpy type women push the girl towards the cot. They show action that the custom of breaking the virginity of a girl is the head's right.

Head rapes the girl—(Dissolves from different angles).

Harpy type women stoop to witness the wicked act.

Inter-cut.

The first man hurls the spear at the second man.

The man is nailed to the ground with the spear on his chest.

His profuse bleeding—(close up).

He dies.

The victor (first man) is being carried by the jubilant crowd towards the cot.

The headman hands over the naked girl to the victor.

She bleeds form her private part (close-up).

One harpy hands over two garlands made out of leaves with flower pendants to the headman.

He garlands the bride and the bridegroom.

He keeps his palms on their heads.

The crowd makes actions and noises of joy as if the marriage ceremony is being blessed by both the gods of sex and violence (various long, close and mid shots).

Scene 39

Beneath the Banyan tree; outdoor.
Day.
The headman.
Boys.
The headman is sitting on a platform (close-up).
Boys are sitting around him on the ground—(Dolly shot)
Midway opening.
Headman is teaching the boys (combination shot).
Boys' rhythmic learning of alphabets invented by the head—their vocal study.
Head—Aaa . . .
Boys—Aaa . . .
Head—Eee . . .
Boys—Eee . . .
Head-Uoo . . .
Boys—Uoo . . .
Head—Ae . . .
Boys—Ae . . .
Head—Hi . . .
Boys—Hi . . .
The thirty nine scenes I watched in the imaginary video theatre of my mind was as lengthy and as wide as not less than a three-hundred-and-ninety-episode television serial telecast in three hundred and ninety installments covering three hundred and ninety years. Or the vistas seemed to be a film full of vital visuals. The film operator was my physical body and my spiritual body was like a wide screen.

It was felt that the film broke before the climax. I was very much interested in that for the location for most of the scenes was my dwelling and its surroundings. But I was very much dismayed about the story and the characters because of the crudeness. Yet I enjoyed the scenes. It was the historical play of nothingness to somethingness of a habitat—brainlessness to brain-fullness. A transformation of mindless and will-less automation into the starting stage of minding and willing.

A simple synopsis of my analysis of the serial was like this: The arrival of the nude couple from Cheenisthan with blank minds. Their brains had all the blends of human beings but without mental discernment. They had forgotten all the knowledge they acquired from their native land because of the natural impact on their mind power due to the earthquake that destroyed the civilization in Cheenisthan. They were heedful when they quit their native place. But the sight of the last quake made them heedless. Their minds were void. On reaching the habitat the first lesson they learned was voracity. They were able to eat and excrete. Was it ability? Even if it was ability, it was not to their credit. That credit went to *nature* because a newborn baby would search the bosom of its mother for food and would excrete.

So they blindly walked from their area of calamity and came down to my habitat of calm state. Refugees took asylum beneath my crown. They settled down, learned the process of reproduction from the animals, and learned how to collect food from the insects. They learned a babble language from birds.

Their social life was nothing but a life in a group. Their chief customs were eating and shitting. Their chief cultural aspects were fucking and forgetting. Slowly they enriched their minds. They appointed a head (chief) following the model of the queen-bee. As the queen-bee was larger in size and form, they mistook it for a male bee. It was just an invention by incident after the fall of the honey-hive. The strong and bold man became the chief of the inhabitants. Bees became models to their lives. They learned many aspects of duties watching the bees and ants. They started hunting and cultivation. They cooked the food, made cells to live in, nursed kids and conducted marriages. The chief made a language sans script. He taught the selected boys vocally. They started singing folklore. The people started communicating in the common dialect. Gradually the phonetic language was followed by lithograph—a sublimation of study.

They were afraid of the power of Sun, thunder and Rain. So they regarded them as gods. They respected the trees and the earth, as we were their erstwhile and primitive shelters. As they saw me daily, they made the area around me their arena for the evening get-together and sang praises for me. It was their leisure period. But their only leisure was eating, drinking and mating.

Their single-minded devotion towards their malicious activities surprised and depressed me. The flown-out pigeon of pageantry of the scenes came back again and again into the pigeonholes of my mind.

I wanted to save them with civilization from this random state at least to the rank and file state in a society. I wondered whether I would succeed.

I was not accustomed to their lifestyle. They were leading a barbarous life. Though I was the oldest member in the habitat, I felt that no one felt concern for me. They just wanted to enslave me with their songs under intoxication. The evening leitmotif defiled me. There was no benevolence. Only malevolence. No merry. Only cruelty.

They continued their leitmotif around me every evening. Slowly I got used to the sights and sounds. As far as age was concerned they were like my great grandchildren. So I thought of opening a class to teach and reform them. But it was a foolish thought. They were human beings. All animate or inanimate articles, however big, old or hard, were always junior or inferior to the human beings. So, I gave up my plan of pedagogy and intended to open a school of Andragogy. My intention was to teach, educate and to develop them. Develop what? Their personality. What kind of personality? Their behaviorism. I just wanted to make each one of them a proper human being. I found that they did not behave even like ordinary men. They behaved like barbarians—a life diametrically opposite to that of a decent man.

I was thorough about the life and behavior of proper men. Once, I had lived among them. I was even more than a man—an epitome of ethics. That certificate was given by the holy man, my *Guruji*. And his disciples had unanimously approved me as a proper man.

A man should have some social and moral values. He should be able to differentiate between what is wrong and what is good. Unlike plants and animals, a human being should have a culture—humanity. Humanity is like daylight. No screen can dim that light. But the light of humanity can be emitted only by a proper human race. Improper human beings can only produce darkness to make the world blind.

The inhabitants in my habitat were blemishing the meaning of humanity. So I wanted to humanize them. As I was preparing mentally to inaugurate an Andragogy school of culture and morale, a pigeon of thought entered the pigeonhole of my mind.

What a fool was I? I was as good as a deaf-and-dumb being. How would the inhabitants understand me? I wished they ate my berries so that my knowledge could be transferred in them as food and further transubstantiate as my feelings and concern for them. But would they assimilate it? Even otherwise who was I? A mere *maram*. How could I deviate the lifestyle, alter the attitude and amend the ambitions of the superior creatures of planet earth? Whatever they perform, wicked or crooked, it had to be accepted as superior to all actions by all the plants and animals. As I pondered more and more over the efforts of a *maram* trying to reform men, I found zoology and botany laughing at me. And my psyche compelled me to withdraw. So I gave up that mountainous blunder of planning to educate the human race.

CENTURY 12

1101 TO 1200 AD

On the first dawn of the twelfth centenary of my life, refusing to settle in the hole of my mind, my dove-of-thought (spiritual phoenix) flew off with downcast wings from the treeless atmosphere towards to the tree-filled *gurukulam*. Sitting on the *Samadhi* of the great *sanyasi* (my *Guruji*) my dove of thought preened its feathers. The dove had become elegant and smart. The dove was exultant. The dove was proud of *Guruji*. The atmosphere of the forest was such. It was the place where my *Guruji* lived. He is no more. Either death had captured him or he had conquered it. He alone knew it because he attained *Samadhi*. Was it a death? No. It was a consummation of life and no consumption of life. I wondered if his soul was somewhere around. The dove hovered over the *Samadhi* babbling for the soul in vain. Soul was not a slice of something floating in the atmosphere. It was an invisible and immortal entity blended with everything everywhere. So my dove could not find the soul.

Then my dove wondered where the large *naga* and little *naga* were. Were they dead? Had they settled in some part of the forest trying to reform the animal kingdom? They too were experts in human physiology rather than in zoology. I wished to know if they were also in a dilemma like me. So I prayed to the Almighty: Wherever they were and whatever they were, they shall be happy.

Afterwards, my dove's concern was about the three holy men, the disciples. *Guruji* had asked them to travel around the world that was doing bad things—because they knew what was good and what was bad—for doing good. First by themselves, then to do good to those who were proper persons who could know right and wrong, beautiful and ugly and bold and coward characters. Unlike *maram* and *mrugam*, they were men, deemed fit individuals with distinctive identities and characters to educate the society—teach about supreme action and sublime behavior. They were professional prophets. They graduated from the omnibus university of humanity. They were awarded the degree of 'Master of Truth'. They had learnt by heart the code of conduct taught by *Guruji. Yoga* and meditation had steeled their physical and mental health. With it they could challenge any difficulty. Their renderings were excellent. They would not wait for ideal weather. They never wasted their time and energy. They could deliver homilies to men, *marams* and *mrugams* because they were conversant in *Cosmolish.* My dove-of-thought wanted to narrate to them the sad and bad conditions of the inhabitants in my habitat. But where to search for them? My dove could see the sea far away. The dove set a true course in its mental compass and set out across the sea.

Mind is after all a mind. Faster than any other phenomenon. It is neither ultrasonic nor ultraphotonic—It does not need time to travel. It is omnipresent. Not taking my time, my dove reached the seashore of an unknown State in the West.

Standing on tip-toe, I could see the sea from my habitat. During monsoon, I could hear the roar of the sea. At leisure times I used to look at the sea and enjoy the swells approaching from far away, shouting slogans and protests as if they wanted to capture the land. The shore easily took them. Reaching the shore, all their strength, vigor and vitality ended up leaving chance to the succeeding waves. It was a panoramic but pathetic vista.

*   *   *

But contrary to my hypothesis, my phoenix (dove-of-thought) witnessed and understood the actual relationship between the shore and the sea. There is no enmity between them. They are real lovers. They are always engaged in love-making. The waves are like hands of the sea patting on the chest of the shore. Their genuine love is an example to other lovers.

My dove saw a crowd on the seashore at a distance. She flew to the spot and settled on top of a palm tree. There was a hubbub among fishermen. They were anxiously staring at the horizon. The dove too looked towards the unseen limits of the sea. She could see only the waves dancing pell-mell to the frightening music. But all of a sudden the sea became calm, and the noise died down. Something was approaching the shore. What on earth was that? Some figures! Figures of what? A little while later, a man-like-figure came on the shore from the sea towing two men by their legs. The figure had two short horns grown from his temples like those of a bull. He was besieged by the crowd with folded arms. The two towed men were attended by some women.

The women said, "Oh! You Son of Satan, we admire you. You've saved our husband. You're the paragon of promise."

The Son of Satan said proudly, "You don't know. All the men aboard the boat drowned. I went to the bottom of the sea to rescue these men."

One man said, "It's a risky job".

"Taking risk is my work. It intoxicates me."

Another wailing woman came running, "Oh, Son of Satan! I adore you. Where's my husband?"

The Son of Satan replied, "Why do you beg me now? You adored Hova, the Son of God, the so-called hypostasis. Go to him if you can. He's drowned in the sea. See the state of the sea now. Come on, go and beg to him if you can."

Yes. The sea had again become rough. The crowd desperately stared at the cruel sea. But easing their hopelessness, Hova appeared the sea carrying a victim on his shoulder. The woman prostrated herself before Hova. He stooped to lay the victim on her lap.

The woman said in grief, "Oh, prince of light, please wake up my husband."

Hova sympathetically said, "He's not sleeping. He's dead. Please bury your husband's body before it decays."

The Son of Satan confronted Hova. He said in a challenging voice to the public, "He can't do that. He doesn't possess any powers. We both brought fishermen from the same wrecked boat. I rescued two men from the bottom of the sea alive whereas he just picked up a floating dead body from the surface. He's just a swimmer. And a swindler too. I challenge him to make this corpse walk."

Hova said patiently, "Without the will of God, one can't make a dead person alive. (Pointing to the dead body) This man's days are completed. He has been summoned by God who gave him life."

"OK, OK," the Son of Satan said. "Can you make this sea clam? (Turning towards the crowd) You might have seen the state of the sea when I had landed and when he had landed."

"It's the nature that makes calmness and calamity. Man shouldn't interfere. It's against God. I can't do that."

"Then why do you mesmerize the men to follow you if you're not a man of miracles?"

Hova replied, "I don't claim to be a superman. I just advise the people to follow the words of the Lord."

An old man from the crowd commented, "What's the use of Lord's words if they are not useful to the people?"

Hova answered, "God's words are useful in the end. They are bitter initially but sweeter lastly."

Another man asked, "We're fishermen—illiterate, ordinary and ignorant populace. You're always speaking about God and his words. Just let's know what's this all about!"

Patiently Hova said, "God is nothing but *goodness*. He is the supreme and the eternal being. He created you and rules you. God's deeds are always good to you, and me—kind and beneficent in quality and quantity."

Another man asked, "Then who is bad?"

"Satan is bad."

"No," the Son of Satan shouted. "Satan is your friend in need. See, I came to help you now. Hova didn't help you. He's a cheat. You follow my path. I'll give you happiness."

The wailing woman said, "You said that a friend in need is a friend in deed. If that's true, give life to my husband."

The crowd shouted as one man, "Yes. Yes. If you do that we all will be your slaves".

The Son of Satan pointed his magic wand towards the dead body and said, "Look now."

All the three rescued fishermen lying on the beach in a stupor got up and started walking away from the crowd like somnambulists. This stunned the crowd. They looked at each other approvingly. The wives of the three fishermen threw sand and seashells at Hova. He stayed there with a serene look on his face.

Some fishermen shouted at him: "You and your goddamn God. We don't want to hear you and see you. We praise the Satan."

Hova tried to make them understand, "No. This is magic. Satanic efforts are temporary. It'll perish very soon."

Satan's son shouted, "He's a liar. Don't listen to him. You fellows follow me."

He walked to the opposite direction where the corpses had gone. The flaccid fishermen followed the Satan. Relatives of the dead fishermen followed the corpses. Hova stood still.

The crowd disappeared from the sight. All the three rescued fishermen—the so-called corpses—staggered for a little time and collapsed on the shore dead. It was confirmed that the Satan's efforts were temporary—mere magic, unreal and false. Whatever Hova said was true.

The wives of the dead men prostrated before Hova and prayed: "Forgive us. We're little folk of this littoral. We shouldn't have snubbed you. We don't know liturgy."

Hova lifted them by their shoulders "My dear little ones, wait a little. I'll teach you. Do as I do."

He knelt down and raised his palms towards the sky. Staring at the heaven he prayed silently. The fishermen followed suit. More people joined the prayer. They were trying to imbibe as much knowledge as possible from the preacher.

*　*　*

The dove watched Hova closely. Oh! Really wonderful! A man attired in ordinary clothes—an immaculate long cotton cloak. His long and curly hair was well kept aback. His short beard had short steps. God had specially given him an ornate face. His eyes were nothing less than two pearls kept inside the oysters of eyelids. And the look of his face! How kind it was! Like a gem emitting gentle light, it illuminates the world that was dark with sin.

He had achieved more vitality than when he was in the *gurukulam*. It seemed that nature had administered doses of invigorator to him prescribed by God the Physician. In a nutshell, each and every part of his body was elaborately made under the craftsmanship of The Almighty. He was the king of the day and subdued all the lights—a luminary on the earth for the people. A living saint, undoubtedly.

The dove flitted very near to the preacher. Seeing the dove myriad of sea birds came to see him. The dove further saw umpteen aquatic creatures gathering to have a glimpse of the master. They were immensely inspired by his personality and politeness. The dove was imbued with his immaculate behavior. The dove also beheld numerous domestic animals attending the prayer as if they were also his followers. Hence the dove understood that all the animals and plants were immersed in the preaching and prayer of the prophet.

Hova walked along the seashore. Some disciples followed him. He was besieged by some lepers. They prayed to the preacher for a cure to their disease. At a distance, some womanizers were running after a woman. She rushed to Hova. She knelt before Him. Hova took her face in his hands. The rolling sweat from her face and tears from her eyes resembled beads. She was frightened as a rabbit that was chased by a herd of wolves. Her cloth was torn. Her bare breast was covered with her disheveled hair. She was a voluptuous beauty. Hova threw his shawl on her to cover her nudity.

Womanizers came running.

One of them said, "Leave the lady to our leader."

"Who's the leader?"

"Can't you recognize me?" The leader said with pout, "Oh! You don't belong to this place."

Hove replied, "I belong to all places. I have no particular place."

"The world may belong to you. But the woman belongs to me."

"But she doesn't agree to it."

"I don't need her consent. I purchased her. I paid coins of gold to own her. She's for me to flirt with. Leave her to me. *Ngaa*! On one condition— if your god-ship can woo this woman in this condition, I may let the woman go."

Though the leader's reply was flippant, Hova said calmly, "Look leader, I'm not a godhead. I'm just a messenger of his—an ordinary person like you. I'm afraid of making merry with this leper lady. Are you ready to flirt with this lean leper lady?"

Looking at the covered body of the lady, the leader answered in anger, "A leper? What the hell are you talking about? She's a voluptuous beauty."

Hova stared at the heavens and said, "Oh! God the greatest! I praise you for creating men like this." Then he stared at the leader in astonishment like staring at a star that had been fallen on the earth. Hova said, "You're really great—your eyes are so graceful to see beauty in an ugly leper lady; your lips are so literal to kiss the deformed lips of a leper lady. Your body is so humble to hug the body of a leper lady. Your heart is so merciful to make love with a lean leper lady. Your behavior is so gentle to show geniality to a groaning lady with a grim heart. Certainly you're an *avatar*. So please take care of your beach beauty."

Hova grinned when the leader grimaced. Hova walked away while the leader drew the shawl off the woman's body. It was a grisly sight—the beauty queen had been transformed into a chronic leper. Her face, lips and breasts were studded with patches and sears of leprosy. Her aquiline nose had become flat. Her chubby cheeks had become hollow. Her stout body was now gaunt.

The lotus-like lady had been transfigured into a lout! She sprang up, looked ferociously at the leader and tried to embrace him with her deformed hands. The leader and his gang quit the scene.

All the lepers approached Hova. The leper lady knelt before him and prayed: "Oh! Man of miracles! You saved me from those wolves. You're my redeemer!"

Hova humbly replied, "No, sister, no. Lord in the skies is the savior. I'm just his messenger. Now I'll redeem your disease."

"No redemption please, man of miracles. I know that no efficacious cure for leprosy has yet been discovered. Yet you can heal this disease because you have supernatural powers: To spread leprosy and to cure it. But let me remain as a leper with you. I prefer it rather than becoming a victim to those brothel brokers."

"Dear sister. You're a temporary leper. You won't need any cure even. A few minutes' sunrays shall cure you. But I have some advice to the real lepers. Lend their ears to me."

All the lepers pricked their ears. Hova continued, "I can cure the leprosy with our God's help and I need your help. To cure any disease, it requires two treatments—physical and spiritual. I'll treat you physically. You'll have to treat yourselves spiritually. That's through charismatic prayer to God."

Hova asked them to take dry sand from the beach and scrub their skins with it till their body became gory. Then they should have a long bath in the sea. And they should stand on the beach still—exposed to sunlight—concentrating their mind on Sun with closed eyes. They followed the instructions whole-heartedly. The lepers continued the physical and spiritual treatment for a few weeks. And their leprosy vanished!

The lepers said, "Your miraculous treatment is an exclusive excogitation! It cleaned our epidemical epidermis and provided us with proper vascular and sensitive skin. Do you really belong to this planet?" They started merry-making in excitement. Their exhilaration exceeded the limits of exclamation—they started to rampage.

Hova said: "Calm down before you exhaust yourself. If you go on being rampant, you may be ruined."

An old man among the crowd said, "My lord, you've healed us and we're not exaggerating. We're exalting you for your exquisite action. We've to praise you. Let many more be aware of your miracles. Hail Hova, hail! You're a son of God indeed!"

"Am I praiseworthy?" Hova asked. "No. The credit is not mine, but God's. Do not expose the fact that you've gained fruits from Him. More sick would come to seek fruits, not faith. Faith first; then the fruit. A fruit earned without faith in God—no matter how big it is—is always sour and a fruit earned with faith in God—no matter how small it is—is always sweet."

Hova described the method of treating lepers: "Every result follows an effort—the sand rubbed off the wounds because of its abrasive effect. The bath cleaned up the wounds because of the ingredients like minerals, salt and other chemicals in the seawater. The heat of the sun dried up the wounds because of the ultraviolet radiation in sunlight. Above all the faith in God has cured your disease."

The listeners agreed with that principle.

Then Hova chose four men—Chackoppy, Kuriappy, Thaomappy and Lonappy—from the admirers. They bowed to him.

Hova asked them, "Who're you?"

"We're your admirers," they answered.

"I'm not the one to be admired. There's the Lord in Heaven. Anyway, thanks for the honor bestowed upon me, God's messenger. From now on, the four of you are my disciples. God will make your minds capable of delivering homily lectures. This country is *Britana*. Chackoppy shall go to the countries of the west, Kuriappy to the east, Thaomappy to the south and Lonappy to the northern countries. I charge you with the responsibility of propagating the Good News from Heaven. You have the full authority in the matter of keeping the moral law and mental order among the people."

There was a tense silence. The chosen disciples were unable to speak. Hova could see total willingness in their shining eyes and quivering lips.

Hova continued, "Well. Silence normally implies consent." He walked straight into the sea. He turned about to confront the public. He stayed on the surface of water—above the waves facing the crowd. The people stood stunned. Hova smiled at them.

Some youths rushed forward and demanded, "We too wish to become preachers. We're healthy, wealthy and wise. We are also bold and brave. You've chosen wrong men as your disciples. They are not only weak and meek but also goblins—nothing less than scarecrows. Teach us some miracles; we'll spread the Good News. We expect the people to show implicit obedience."

Hova came to the shore and humbly said to the gang: "The mission is very irksome. I want preachers, not princes. Should the princes go on foot miles and miles treading over thorny, stony, fierce and chilly terrains instead of walking over flower-strewn floors? Should the princes forget their feast and be fascinated by famishing? Should the princes partake in penance considering it a pleasure? You know, it is incumbent upon a disciple to guide the people along the right path. How can blind disciples guide others? You know, a disciple should inculcate only good ideas in the minds of the people. How can disciples with minds full of devilish ideas inculcate in the people's mind divine ideas? It's incongruous!"

The gang seemed to revel in recrimination. Their leader said, "So you're finding fault with us. What are the merits you find in the men you've chosen? We're not blind. Our eyesight is sharper than theirs. Our bodies are stronger than theirs. Our will power is firmer than theirs. We too know that preachers have to have three qualifications—to talk well, to walk well and to do well by showing magic. We too can perform these activities better than the men you have chosen provided you teach us some magic. We are sure we can prove it."

"Of course," Hova replied. "Do any activity with innocence, not with nonsense. You're blind with pride; strong with envy and brave with egotism. *Ngah*, you can walk, talk and mock better than them indeed. But you can't walk, talk and mock even normally in need."

The gang angrily retorted, "You bet?"

"Yes. I bet."

"Then let's put a test?"

"Well. What test do you want?"

The gang leader said, "You conduct the test. Any test will be easy for us."

Hova announced aloud to the enormous crowd: "An open recruitment is going to be held. Anyone can participate. There's a very simple task to overcome. Somebody may regale with it. For them the test is refreshing. And somebody may regret themselves at their inability. For them the test is rigorous. But I give guarantee that anybody who possesses a faithful heart can easily qualify. Those who are selected may be appointed my disciples—the agents of God."

The gang leader asked, "If we pass the test, would we be able to walk on the water, lie in the fire and fly in the air?"

"Certainly. If you're ready to die for your faith."

The gang members were impatient. They could not wait. They shouted: "Come on, then. Why the delay? Announce the test fast. We're ready and rigid to face any test. We want to complete as fast and as smart as we can before others do. We wish to become magicians as early as possible."

"You have to do nothing great. Just follow me on foot, talking. Those who cease to walk and cease to talk will lose the chance to be my disciples."

Hova simply started walking along the sea line. Hearing the announcement, myriad of people of Britana—lame, blind, deaf, dumb— joined the task to test their fortune to become his disciples so that they also could travel around performing heroic acts. Their aim was to gain easy popularity and prominence.

Hova walked very fast. The gang was very close to him. The crowd followed. Some fell back. Some discontinued in dismay. Some were in distress. The gang continued to walk behind Hova. They were talking ceaselessly ("Give us mystic powers; make us magicians; make us wizards so that we could do marvels and wonders"). Hova appreciated their energy and enthusiasm.

The gang leader said proudly to Hova, "You want us to overtake you? We won't get exhausted."

Hova said calmly, "If you go ahead of me how you can follow me?"

"We'll follow you. But when are you going to teach us the technique of magic?"

Hova retorted, "Let all the weak and weary retire."

The walk continued . . .

Chackoppy, Kuriappy, Thaomappy and Lonappy walked slowly and steadily. They muttered while walking: "God is great; He'll save us. Hail God . . . Hail God . . . Hail God . . ." Some participants tiresomely walked murmuring, "Make us disciples; give us mystical powers." With the passage of each minute, more and more people retired.

Hova stopped for a moment. He turned back. The gang was just behind him. Far behind they could see the four chosen men making their way—waggling.

The gang leader sarcastically said: "You, man of miracles. They have no stamina. See how they are staggering."

The second man in the gang said, "Let's forget and forgive them. You make us your disciples."

The third said, "We're bodily and mentally prepared to learn the lessons of the magic. Please teach us."

The fourth man said, "We're losing our patience."

And the last man in the gang said, "We're anxious to walk on water."

"Follow me for just one minute," said Hova. He walked straight into the sea. They could neither walk nor talk. Their legs went under water the waves choked them. Slowly, swells started swallowing them.

When Chackoppy, Kuriappy, Thaomappy and Lonappy reached the spot, they saw their son of God walking over the sea. They too simply started walking on the water with courage and faith. They followed Hova chanting praises of God: "*Hail God . . . Hail God . . . Hail God . . .*" Hova moved ahead. They trailed him.

God sent a big wave that swept the drowning persons towards the shore. Reposing on the beach, the greedy gang repented for their folly. Meanwhile they heard an admonition: "its faith and not health or wealth that leads to heaven. A heart without faith is a heart full of filth. The door of the heaven is permanently closed to owners of such hearts."

They regarded the voice from the sky as an advice.

Waves died down. There was no aqueous movement. The surface of the sea resembled a mirror. Hova moved further and further. The four followers followed him. They were far away from the fishermen and the shore. The sea seemed to be an aquamarine aquarium. All the aquatic creatures were appraised to appear on the surface in order to greet the great Son of God, Hova and the sons of men, disciples. Their approach was applauded. The aphorism of Hova was appreciated by all the aquatic living things. Even the algae at the seabed approved of it. They too regarded it as something unique. Hova, the harbinger of peace gave his apostles some sermons at the sea:

1) No disbelief. For your belief will save you. Thereby you can save others.

2) No profanity. For it is contempt of God. Thereby God won't help you and you can't help others.

3) No violence. For it will create cruelty in your own heart. Thereby you shall inflict injury to others.

4) No adultery. For all the women except your wife shall be treated as your mothers and sisters.
5) No deception. For it will betray you. Thereby you may cheat others.
6) No Divorce. For a spouse is a permanent life-partner.
7) No hatred. For love is the light of life.
8) No affliction. For assisting others is holier than supporting oneself.

Hova's eight-fold sermon was obtained by his disciples at an exorbitant price—their hearts. It was with great pleasure that they pledged their lives for the propagation of his message.

Hova advised his disciples: "You preach in public, but pray privately. For prayers come out of the heart—God sees it. Give due regards to riff-raff. Do not perform miracles for showing off. Do not neglect the sinful; make them sinless. If you stretch one helping finger, let the nail not know of it. You should behave like wise men; no addiction to vice. Do not hurt the milieu. Don't snub anyone. Your wife is not less than a friend to you. Treat all the males as your own fathers, brothers and sons; and all the females as your mothers, sisters and daughters. They may be (there may be) raw hands. You may drill out crude things from them. Refine it. Fuel them so that their vehicle of life moves smoothly towards the heaven."

Before bidding farewell, all the four disciples bowed to Hova and vowed never to turn away from their mission. So, Chackoppy went to west, Kuriappy to the east, Thaomappy to south and Lonappy to the northern lands as gospel-preachers.

Hova went back to the beach to preach and teach. As a prolific preacher, he professed an ideology exclusively built by him. His orthodox views were already acclaimed by almost all the people. Hearing his homily lecturers, some priests asked him: "What's your intention?"

Hova said: "I wish to transform heterogeneous vicious people to homogeneous wise people." People pealed with legitimate pride: "Hail Hova, hail . . ." An enormous crowd followed him.

The priests envied him. He was arrested by the temple police and brought before the priest who had the power to punish any person who condemned priesthood. Hova was pushed into the trial-box.

The senior priest complained, "He's a prig. But, by the name of our temple, we can't tolerate his behavior. He's misguiding and bewitching the people. Whatever he does is magic. He's an impostor who claims to be

God. The mass is marveled by his glittering magic; and you know, all that glitters is not God."

But Hova's innocent look impressed the Prime priest. He was a man of principle. He asked Hova, "Please identify yourself . . ."

Hova humbly replied, "I'm not God as your religious leader or the so-called priests alleged. Pride goes before a fall. And I'm not the son of God. I am a messenger of God."

The Prime priest said, "There is no *prima facie* reason for instituting a plaint against this preacher. So, I must say that your accusation stands invalid."

But the plaintiffs were not ready to withdraw the complaint. The senior priest adamantly argued on behalf of all the priests: "Objection, your lordship. This man is a liar. He has a propensity for stealing the hearts of the proletariat by propagating fraud. The prime prop is witchcraft."

The Prime priest asked Hova "Is it . . . ?"

"No witchcraft. No magic. It's metaphysics."

"Could you heal the sick with metaphysics? If you can, please cure my dying mother. And if you cure her, you'll be set free. And that too inside this temple before the altar. Agreed?"

"Disagreed," Hova said. "Caring for and curing the diseased are divine activities. It can't be performed publicly."

"Then perform it in a secluded place. Now agree?"

"Disagree. Divine activities are not carried out under compulsion."

"No compulsion. I leave it to your will and wish. Now you agree?"

The audience babbled among themselves. They were eager to hear the reply.

"I disagree," Hova answered. "The Divine activities are not carried out on conditions."

"No condition at all. Now you agree?"

The public anxiously waited for Hova's answer. Carelessly, he answered, "I disagree. Divine activities are not carried out on contract."

"Oh! Ho! Break the contract and cure my mother. Still you won't agree?"

"Still I disagree. Because, if you break the contract how can you set me free? That was the reward promised by you—my liberation."

Anger contorted the Prime priest's face. Yet he controlled his rage and said, "You, being a messenger of God, must learn to serve without any hope of reward. You should serve, not render."

"That's on compassionate grounds. This doesn't involve any sympathy."

People went into rhapsody over their argumentative performance in the prayer hall of the temple.

The Prime priest acted as if he had ants in his pants. His cries rent the air, "You're not competent to cure my mother's illness. You're a fraud. You, son of Satan! I'll make you do it willy-nilly."

Taking undue advantage of the situation, the Senior priest brought wild religious charges against Hova: "Your priest ship, he promulgated an order, not to cooperate with the prayer in the temple by the people, to deny the monetary contribution in the *hundi* and to refuse the commandments of our Chief. It's against our faith and worship. If his plan progresses, then even our progeny would be prone to fits of disobedience. Hence, we pray to our priest ship to prohibit his programmes and pierce him with our holy prong till death."

Hova argued: "Who is this Chief who commands? Man commanding man! It's profane! God has provided all men with the same flesh and blood. I found evil-hearted priests with weak bones keeping whole-hearted bonny slaves. Man ill-treating man. It is against the will of God!"

The Prime priest mocked him: "You're very proud of delivering homilies. But don't you feel mortified at your failure in reviving my mother? By the by, let's know who you are?

"I'm neither God nor the son of God. I'm a messenger of God."

"Just tell me who your God is?"

"There is no *your* God or *my* God. By God, there's only one God—that's our God."

"What you mean by God?"

Hova posed question: "What do you think?"

"God, we think, is a *power to fear*—power from top that the men below fear."

"If you believe in this definition, then why should a man fear another man? He should be only God-fearing. Here, man is afraid of man; man bluffs man. Somebody is bloated with pride. There's bad blood among neighbors. Society is bifurcated into friends and foes, haves and have-nots. It has a bicameral ruling system—the upper chamber and the lower chamber. Dual employment—the laborers and the overseers. Each one is afraid of the other. They can't live beyond fear. Still your dictum says man should fear only God. But I found there is no God-fearing man here. I could see only man-fearing men. Your philosophy is in letters and not in practice."

The audience appreciated his erudition. But the priesthood envied him. One among them interrupted, "Now stop your babbling. How do you define God?"

Hova said: "God is nothing but *mercy to mankind*. Even the feeble doesn't have to fear him. God is such a fellow that instead of filling you with fear, he'll feed you with facility. God keeps fellowship with even felons to guide them to righteousness. God even looks after his enemy— the one who snubs and denies him."

The Senior priest said, "But you're poisoning the people's belief. And they refuse to make offerings to God."

"What do they gain with such belief? God does not amass wealth by foul beliefs. He himself is a treasure. God is always a giver, never a taker."

"Why don't you speak practically? Will God come down from heaven with his treasury to act as a cashier? Will he say, 'Come on, take this much money for the maintenance of my house, the temple? Will he say, 'Take this much money for the payment of the priest who offers prayer to me and the police to protect my place of worship'?" Hova became the laughing stock of the priesthood.

But Hova threw back an incisive reply: "God doesn't need a place of worship. He's everywhere. He doesn't reside in a temple. He resides inside the hearts of his devotees. He doesn't want any protectors. For he is the protector of all the forces on earth. He doesn't like priests as mediators. For He himself is the peacemaker between the earth and the heavens. He hates those who render service to him seeking remuneration. They're as good as employees on wages; not devoted to duty—without fruits. There's no room for a single penny inside his treasury. For its pent up with love. Does wealth conduce to happiness? Only peace and prayer are conducive to happy life. If you're that God-fearing, stop your perfunctory praying and start painting the walls of the temple. Otherwise why waste your time?

"What's the use of this temple where only superstition prevails? Level up this temple if you can't maintain it. Build up a temple in your heart which doesn't require any maintenance. Your mind will maintain it, your blood will paint it and your breath will clean it. And I'm of the opinion that all the panic-stricken panjandrums—priests and police—should descend to the level of poltergeists."

His logical arguments had created a counter-effect upon his opponents. The priests shouted, "Your priest ship, kill him, not let him go. For he is condemning the clergy and the temple. And above all, he's reluctant to cure your mother because she is the mother of a priest whom he considers as his enemy. He's taking revenge on the whole priesthood. Kill him, not let him go."

Hova did not lose his composure even when his opponents submitted severe charges against him in public. He humbly said, "I feel caring and curing of the disabled as compassionate services. But really, I'm not competent to revive your mother who has fainted permanently."

"Tell me the truth," the Prime priest pleaded again. "Can you do something for my mother?"

"Of course," Hova said. "The only thing I can do for your mother is to express condolence."

The priests shouted, "He's a real Satan! Instead of extending a person's life when pleaded, he has great pleasure in curtailing it. Condemn him to death, not let him go."

The Prime priest opened a book and read out, "I, the Prime priest of Britana, abiding by the rules of this country, sentence that as per the last and final article of our law book that every person subject to the law of Britana, who willfully wishes the death of any person, unless he has committed any grave crime if proved, that may cost his life, shall be condemned to death if the offence is proved. As the offence is proved, I assure the priesthood of this country that this man named Hova shall be sentenced to death."

The audience hung about the entrance to ensure the genuineness of the verdict and to ogle the accused, Hova. But maintaining his calm, Hova said, "I'm happy to hear this. But prior to that prepare yourself to mourn."

The Prime priest said sarcastically, "I' don't think that someone would mourn your death."

"You don't have to mourn over my death. You mourn on the demise of your mother!"

"You, son of Satan! Telling me about the sad demise of my mother . . ."

"Yes. She's no more."

Just when Hova expressed his sympathy, there came a messenger from the Prime priest's residence with a message stating that his mother had expired.

The entire audience was stunned.

Hova calmly said, "Can your communion extend the life of the expired? Think of one thing. Death is the only truth in the world. No one can refuse it. When time comes, it stops the mechanism of our life-clock. No mechanic can restart it."

The prime priest as a judge was in a dilemma because whatever Hova proclaimed was true word by word. His conscience did not allow him to cast Hova into the death-well. But on the contrary, he had to execute the guarantee—the death sentence—given to the priesthood for it could not be amended by any means. Moreover he had to propitiate the priesthood lest they should impeach him under the law of Britana. So, at any cost, Hova had to be handed over to death. The only concession Hova deserved was a choice of the mode of death.

So, the prime priest asked Hova, "I permit you to have your choice—when, where and by what method do you want to die?"

"The concession made to me would be as good as inscribing your name on your own tombstone, for my request may lead to stop the execution of my death sentence. If I demand that the time of my death shall be after a hundred and one years, will you agree? And if I demand that the place of my death shall be only in the open sky in space, can you guarantee it? And the last choice—the method of my execution: What's the use of a towel to a person who wishes to drown? Let my death choice be as per your caprice and not guided by my whim."

The priesthood uttered the ultimatum, "Then let him also be drowned to death for he himself has indicated his death choice. And that too right now in the open sea. We will make necessary arrangements as early as possible.

The Prime priest looked sympathetically at Hova and said, "I'm so sorry to toll your death bell at so young an age . . ."

Hova asked, "Could you please approximate my age?"

"By look, you may be around forty years or so."

"Your statement is correct provided you add a zero to the right side, and then add the age you mentioned now, plus four days less for your years—the sum total is my age."

The audience sighed in astonishment. One among them exclaimed aloud, "My Goodness! You're aged four hundred and forty four years? We can't believe this!"

"You'll have to exclaim for four hundred and forty four times if your priest ship would allow me to live for another four days—I'll complete exactly four hundred forty four years of age."

"Allowed! Yes, it's my franchise to declare in this open court of our temple, that on compassionate grounds I confer an extension of four days as an ex gratia to him to live. I've promised the priesthood only to execute him. And not when, where and how."

His arbitrary decision was not acceptable to the priesthood. They warned him that Hova might outwit them and escape. And if such an incident occurred the Prime priest would have to resign and face impeachment for an infringement.

As this was the established law of Britana, the Prime priest was again in a dilemma. Seeing the pathetic condition of the Prime priest, Hova consoled him, "You do not have to lament. I want only four hours' extension from your side. I'll have the rest from God's side."

Hova was set free for four hours on self-bail on condition of surrendering himself at the temple yard before the completion of four hours, before dark. In the meantime, temple police were detailed to make necessary arrangements—constructing an iron chest, riveting of chains, making of locks and keys—to shackle Hova inside the chest and throw right into the rock bottom of the sea secured with a heavy anchor.

During those hours, there was a great shout outside the temple. The execution committee was adjourned. An ocean of human beings was formed outside the temple—some to have a glimpse, some to seek blessings, some for getting cured—the lame to walk, blind to see, ill to get cured and the dying to live. People, especially those from the labor class, ran amok to take revenge on the priesthood.

Hova advised the people to keep their pocker up against possibility and speculation. He became the friend of the penitent people. He further advised them: "Do not take liberties of libido."

For others, he was like the pebble on the beach. When the level-less lewd man approached to attack the level-headed Hova, he levitated; then turned to be a leviathan and further levitated with his *yogic* power gained from *Gurukulam*.

The hilarious crowd hailed Hova: "Here comes the godhead. Hip, hip, hurrah!" Hova humbly said, "You're wrong, my dear men. I'm not godhead. I'm His messenger. The only difference between you and me is that I'm a man for the masses and you are for yourself."

The multitude again cried out, "You're our savior. We're your adorers."

Hova denied: "God in the heaven is your savior. We should adore Him." Saying this Hova started walking towards the beach. The crowd cleared the way for him. Soon a mother came running and bowed to him.

She laid her son at his feet and requested, "I pray to your sacred heart to have sympathy on me. Please give life to my dead child as he's the only one . . ."

Hova enquired, "What happened actually?"

The mother replied, in one breath: "He, all of a sudden wailed, then shivered, had a stroke, then fainted, fell down, and became silent and died."

"When . . . ?"

"Just a few minutes ago."

While she was explaining, Hova sat on his knees beside the boy. He pressed the chest of the child and intermittently blew his breath into the mouth of the child. He repeated the process for ten times and the child started groaning, then opened his eyes and feebly asked for water. There was no source of water around there. The tears of joy were gushing out of the mother's eyes. Hova wiped the rolling tears from her cheeks with his finger-tip and dipped it into the mouth of the child to cool his dried-up tongue. The boy got up and hugged his mother.

"Do not waste your tears; it's useful in exigencies like this."

Saying thus Hova proceeded through a gangway made by some of the gang from the crowd.

Then Hova witnessed a horrible, inhuman, incident on the coast. A voluptuous lady was besieged by some personnel from the temple police. She was convicted of infidelity. Her husband was the complainant and he gained a verdict. She was to be stoned to death. The punishment was being executed by the police. Innumerable spectators had gathered there to witness the execution.

The policemen carried bags full of granite pieces. The lady remained naked amidst them. She was shy of her nudity and was afraid of her fate and she trembled like a lamb cornered by lions. She covered her private parts with her palms and arms. She closed her eyes and prayed to God to spray the shower of mercy on her.

The head of the policemen was standing by to give the order to stone the woman. Hova could not tolerate it. He cut through the crowd and reached the woman. He covered her body with his shawl. She opened her eyes widely. He could see the ocean of innocence there. She wept.

"Don't cry," Hova said. "Are you guilty?"

"Your kind heart," The lady said feebly. "I'm innocent. By God, I've not committed infidelity. My unfaithful husband compelled me to go to bed with a priest, who is the tax collector. I refused. The charges are fabricated. The allegations are false. I do swear in the name of God, that till now I've never given myself physically or mentally to anyone other than my husband. But unfortunately he's greedy for money—a mammonist."

The head of the police warned Hova: "You're no one to poke your nose in this case. It's time for stoning. Anyone who wishes to save her life will also lose his life, for stones have no hearts or heads to show pity on you or the lady. Better clear out."

Hova approached the police chief and said, "Yes! You're right, my dear brother. Stone does not have heart and head, but the thrower has. The lady—our sister—is innocent. Please leave her alone."

"She's not my sister," the police chief said curtly. "Moreover I've my orders to execute. You don't know. No power on earth can alter the verdict of Britana."

"I didn't mean that," Hova added. "Let the law of this country be carried out fully. Let it be as strong and unshakeable as a mountain. But you don't know. Humanity can provide hearts and heads even to the stones that may kiss an innocent rather than hitting hard . . ."

In the meantime, the crowd swelled until hundreds upon hundreds were pushing and pulling about and crushing each other. And there were great lamentation and gnashing of the teeth among them—some in support of the execution; some against it.

The head of the police cruelly commanded, "Throw . . ."

No sooner did the policemen hear the command than they started throwing granite pieces at the lady.

Hova comforted her, "Don't be afraid, I'm with you . . ."

The stones thrown at her were transformed into flowers and fell on her body softly. All the stone bags went empty. And the throwers felt exhausted. The spectators, who were in favor of the punishment, were in a state of exhaustion after the unbelievable scene.

The lady stood there smiling, covered in flowers. She seemed to be an angel surrounded by clouds. The police chief reached her and inspected the stones, now turned into flowers. He felt the flowers were as soft as butter and as light as cotton. All the policemen came and scented the flowers and fainted on the shore. Some of the spectators also smelt the flowers. They did not faint.

Hova declared, "It's the smell of their sins that made them unconscious. Those who had not sinned didn't."

There was a heavy rush of people who acted on impulse to possess at least a single petal of the flowers that covered the woman. Those who succeeded, kept the flower close to their chest as if they had gained a fresh heart pumping pure blood in replacement of a frozen heart and finding difficulty in pumping impure blood—a subtle scene! The multitude named it the Great Floral Function. They indulged in merry-making. They named the area Merry land.

Hova said, "After some time, the unconscious will recover and repent. The rejoiced may follow me."

They all wished to be his followers. He walked straight into the sea and took a bath. The crowd also did the same.

Hova reminded them: "All those who're inclined to the God's verses— Live and let live—shall be cleaned physically and spiritually by this bath. The remainders shall be cleaned physically only." And all those people took part in that mass bath and regarded it as a Great Bath.

Hova saw that some lame and crippled people were hobbling to reach the sea to partake in the Great Bath in vain. He approached them; took their legs in his hand; heaved and straightened them. He made right one leg of those who were lame by two legs. He made right both legs of those who were lame by one leg. He gave light to one eye to those were blind in both eyes stroking their eye-lids with his fingers. He gave light to both eyes to those who were blind in one eye. The totally disabled were blessed as partially disabled and partially disabled were blessed as totally able and advised them to be content with whatever redressal God had given.

*   *   *

Hova liberated the lady. She did not want to live with her husband anymore and she wanted a divorce.

Hova counseled her: "Dear sister, none can break the bond between the husband and wife unless one of the two commits infidelity. It's not proved here. Marriage is a boon to man and woman by the society and God himself. It's not to be broken over silly matters. And moreover you're a woman—the strength of a man, his right hand. Only a woman can make and mend the mind of a man. Woman combines the dispersed. Woman regularizes the irregular. Only a woman can heal the injured heart of a man. I can see that your beloved husband's heart is profusely bleeding. Arrest that flow with the bandage of your profound love. And here further, don't even think of a divorce. May God bless you both."

Her husband came running to confess before Hova. The mob wanted to stone him to death. But Hova's advice was: "Any person who willfully confesses and repents for what he has done or left undone shall start his journey towards the seat of the supreme—God in heaven. If the confession is confirmed, God may condone him and allot a suitable position to him in the palace of heaven."

Then Hova counseled the boorish husband: "Don't blame your wife unnecessarily. She's your bonded wife; not a bond woman. You should live like a boon and not a boor companion till your death. If you start hating your wife, just think about God. He has plenty of love in him. He'll provide you with some love from his liver. Make use of it. Then you'll again start loving your wife. Or, if you still detest your wife, think about death. For only death can do apart what marriage has combined."

* * *

Soon after the funeral ceremony of the prime priest's mother, all the priests assembled in the temple, with the Prime priest in chair. He was very terribly annoyed and angry with Hova for he denied the request of a prestigious person and accepted the request of a poor fisher-woman. The Prime priest imagined: "Yes. The priesthood was very correct. His pride! I'll put an end to it. He should be killed in the cruelest way, inch by inch. His lungs shall throb for want of air; his throat shall dry for want of water though he would be surrounded by water; his brain shall become empty for want of ideas to escape from the death trap but there won't be any escape; his stomach shall starve for a small fish where there are myriad of marine fish around him; his heart shall hate his so-called god who would be helpless to save him. The people will use their common sense to believe in the priesthood and the temple rather than Hova and his homily."

But where was he? The time was up. All the eyes were fixed at the entrance, hoping that Hova might appear any time. But Hova did not show up.

The Prime priest banged on the desk and coarsely commanded, "Guards! Where's that culprit? Only a few seconds are left for the expiry of his parole!"

The chief guard said, "Your priest ship, he's not seen anywhere."

"Has he escaped?"

There was muttering and gnashing of teeth in the priests' gallery. The confused crowd outside the temple turned boisterous.

The senior priest got up and hoarsely said, "I told my priest ship he has tricks to evade the law. He may have reached somewhere else by now."

No sooner did he complete his statement than another priest sitting next to him got up and said, "I had told my priest ship that I won't go anywhere else and I'll be present here well before my parole ended."

All the eyes and minds of the people in the crowd were focused on that priest. Astonishing! The man who sat clad in priestly garments among the other priests was none but Hova!

The senior priest pushed Hova down and said, "Don't pollute the priesthood, you shaming Satan!"

Hova fell down on the floor.

Hova retorted, "I'm not a sham. It was your illusion."

As he was getting to his feet, the Prime priest asked him in annoyance: "How dare you boor sit with the sacred men of the temple?"

Hova replied humbly, "I couldn't find a suitable place to accommodate myself."

The Prime priest scolded, "You scoundrel, you're no one to sit comfortably in the gallery of priests by shaming. You're supposed to stand in the accused person's box—You're an accused and a convict."

"That's the reason why I said the gallery of priests was the most suitable place for me to sit. The other persons gathered here are far more gentle and civilized than the priests."

All the priests protested in one voice, "It means we're also criminals?"

"If there's a meaning to it," Hova said soothingly, "how can I change it? Let the meaning be as it is."

The prime priest proclaimed, "Let me say one thing clearly that it's a disgrace to all of us that we couldn't recognize a person who was in disguise. We should have identified him before he polluted the sacred priestly seats. He'll be given severe punishment even before his death."

Then he turned to Hova and said vehemently, "You deserve it. Because the law of Britana wants to punish you for breaking it and the people of Britana want to take revenge on you for misguiding them. The whole priesthood is vindictive of polluting them. Moreover, I have a personal vendetta for insulting me—you've saved the life of a beggar's son and neglected the life of a priest's mother. Can you vindicate, you villain?"

Hova calmly said, "I neither want to uphold your accusation by arguments nor justify it with evidence for the sake of forgiving and saving my life. But I want to stress on one thing: God has no discrimination. He uses the same effort to make a *beggar* and *a bishop*."

The Prime priest furiously said, "He's comparing me with a beggar. How dare you devil . . ."

Hova interfered, in a devil-may-care attitude, "The poor boy! He was just a bud on the tree of life, yet to be blossomed! Not even had the chance of consuming enough sunlight, air and freshwater—the natural alms provided by God. Your mother had polluted more than enough of it. Your devilish mother had enjoyed a devilish (worldly) life for decades. She married a devil and gave births to many devils like you. She was fully satisfied with your performance of putting many innocents between the devil and the deep sea. For what else she wanted to live further and farther to the end of the world? She has gone up to the skies and now down in the hell. Every devil has a day to die. So your mother died. You say I'm a devil. I have only four days remaining."

As Hova spoke, the Prime priests became violent. He banged the gavel so hard on the desk that it severed the head of the gavel from its handle. He said hoarsely, "To hell with your four days. You'll die now itself. You'll not go up into the skies. You'll go down in the deep blue sea to measure the fathoms where you'll be a delicious dish for the marine beings . . ."

"They'll be friendlier to me than you foes. Send me . . ."

The priests raised their hands and shouted: "Let's not waste a single minute. Yes, yes, kill this boor brutally. Yes. yes . . ."

This time the Prime priest banged his palm on the desk. He didn't feel pain on his soft, sinful palm for his mind was impregnated with vindictiveness. He angrily gnashed his teeth and promulgated, "This man named Hova has been sentenced to death for the grave offences he has committed. Let's prepare his grave. He will drown at sea. March off the accused to the beach where the execution arrangements have already been made. He should be launched into the open sea before dusk. As the Sun is the representative of our God, the setting Sun shall witness the launching ceremony (the execution) so that the Sun'll convey the good news to God when the sun reaches up in the sky the next noon. Our God will be satisfied for we have eliminated an evil-spirited man from the surface of this earth forever. Come on, take this man away . . ."

The guards paid marks of respect to the Prime priest. They chained Hova and pulled him out of the accused-box and into the temple yard. Hova followed them like a calf calmly trailing behind a herd of cows. A donkey was kept ready in the yard. He was asked to sit on the donkey—an insult. As he sat on, the animal felt horripilation. The donkey behaved very distinctly from its usual characteristics as an animal of a family of asses. It acted like a solid-hoofed ungulate with flowing tail and mane.

The members of the clergy laughed. They asked him mockingly, "Are you the king of priests?"

He said mildly, "No, I'm a kingpin for the poor . . ."

"Are you the prince of the people . . . ?"

"No. I'm a prince of peace . . . ?"

They again mocked him, "Anyway he's a king. Let's give him thorn instead of throne."

They put a crown made out of long thorn-lined barbed wire on his head and scoffed at him: "Here comes the king of thorns. Hip, hip hurrah . . ."

People thronged to witness the scene.

Some other guard's mighty roar prevailed: "Here comes the king of stones. Welcome him and let's give him stones . . ."

The throng thought that the stones thrown at him may alter its shape to flowers. But it did not happen. Guards jeered at him: "Where're your flowers? You fool."

Drops of blood dripped from the wounds on Hova's head. He said, "Collect my blood and make use of it, for it will heal many diseases."

People thronged to collect the blood with their finger tips. Guards again started throwing stones at him. The crowd ran pell-mell lest they would be hit. A big stone hit right on the left side of his chest from where the blood oozed out of his wounded heart. He became weak.

Numerous grief-stricken women trailed along. They could not tolerate the sight of the wound on the heart of Hova. If their nails were lengthy, sharp and stiff enough, they would have torn off their chests, plucked their healthy hearts and planted them in his chest as spare hearts.

They wailed: "Poor soul! How cruelly he's being tortured! Oh, you tormentors, even Satan won't save your soul!"

An old woman plaintively but loudly said, "Why can't you son of God save yourself! Do some miracles, please . . ."

Hova said meekly, "Miracles are not to be performed for one's own benefit. They are meant for others and that too in extreme emergencies."

One of his fans—the helmsman who got a good catch, whose boat Hova had once blessed—began to boom in favor of the holy man in distress, "It's for us, the full crew, for your life is dearer than ours. Please give all your pains to us. Tell each stone to fly towards us and tear us. We're going to resist the guards."

Hova peacefully said, "Oh, able-bodied men! I appreciate your feelings. But at the same time I doubt your resistance and tolerance power."

The fishermen rushed towards the stone-throwing guards. They hindered their action with force. But the mighty guards, many in number, flogged them fiercely with leaded whip. They wailed in pain and surrendered to the guards with folded arms. The fishermen were forced to throw stones at their holy man. Thus, his enemies stopped and his friends began throwing stones at him.

A crippled woman whose one leg had once been restored by Hova cried in agony, "Oh, cunning and shaming friends of his. You act like friends and work like cheats. You dishonest, regardless sinners . . ."

Hova soothed her: "Don't curse them. For human beings have limitations in tolerating pain. It's none of their fault. It's quite natural. And after all, what difference does it make? Whether X throws or Y throws is insignificant: A throw is a throw. The so-called foes are tired; the so-called friends relieved them. There's no friend or enemy as such. After all they're all alike in distress."

Another woman exclaimed, "But how could you bear the pain! It's a wonder!"

"I have to," Hova answered calmly. "I'm not an individual. I'm independent. I took birth for the mankind. They've myriad of painful problems. I'm a sum total of it. So, forget about my problems and pains please . . ."

By this time the *great journey* of one mile came to a halt at the execution point. An iron chest with lot of tiny holes on all the sides was kept ready on board a vessel. The sea was very calm. It resembled a big blue sheet of glass. Hova was heaved into the vessel and was thrown inside the box.

Simultaneously the donkey deserted the beach. It joined its herd to tell the sad story of the sage; the mad, mad behavior of the guards who had tortured him; how fortunate he was to get the chance to carry the holy man on his back; the experience of walking over the floral gangway and the throw of petals.

Hova was very weak and weary. Still he managed to raise his chained arms to bless the crowds. They lamented badly. "Don't lament," Hova consoled them. "We're just going on a bon voyage. I'll come back."

One guard roared: "Unless you go, how can you come back."

Another said, "First let's go; then let's see who comes back."

Many slaves were ready to push and launch the vessel into the water. Hova was hooked up inside the iron chest. The lid was locked by the executioner. He confirmed that the hinges were intact. Then he threw away the key into the ocean. The chest was further secured with four granite blocks tied to all the corners and was kept ready to be cast into the sea by shoving.

Two rows of rowers were seated on the thwarts. The coxswain at the rear gave order to the crew: "Oars forward." The crew stretched their hands fully and forwarded the oars.

Next order: "Give way together." They rowed the boat in a row as per the timings given by the coxswain by beating a drum. The vessel did not pick up speed. The blades of the oars shed tears; the shaft of the oars cried inside the crutches. What to say, even the vessel itself was reluctant to make its way like an animal jibing to a slaughter-house.

The coxswain roared: "Battle speed."

The crew put their maximum effort but the vessel did not gain even minimum speed. It moved inch by inch.

The chief guard alerted the crew in rage: "What the hell's happening! The sea is so quiet; the weather is so calm; the pull is so fast and why the speed is so meager? It's going to be dusk and we'll have to cast the chest at least ten nautical miles away from the shore."

Meanwhile, there was a stampede. A mighty roar that rose from the crowds on the coast boomed as one voice: "Take us too along with the son of God!"

Some rushed into the sea in protest of the wicked act of the priesthood. Some were fascinated by the gruesome event. People ran pell-mell . . .

There came a wind. The coxswain said immediately, "Secure the oars and rig the sails!"

They rigged the sails as fast as they could. The pulling vessel turned to be a sailing vessel. It instantly gained speed for the wind turned into heavy wind immediately and a tempest was imminent. All of a sudden the sea became very rough. The resemblance of the blue sheet of glass was broken and now the sea was violently dancing. The coxswain could not control the helm of the vessel. It was flying as if out of command.

The chief guard coarsely commanded, "Cast off the chest. Let's go back."

The guards got up unsteadily to shove the chest outboard. As they were engaged in the job, the coxswain ordered, "Jibe . . ." The tack man changed the tack instantly and the vessel capsized with the crew, the guards and the chest. With the weight of the iron chest and the granite blocks—the securing chains had got entangled with the vessel's fittings—the vessel sank into the bottom of the roaring sea.

Huge waves carried Hova's followers, who volunteered to drown, back to the shore. They were saved. Due to the inclement weather, the crowd on the beach returned to their hutments. The head of the family in each hutment prayed: "If there's a power named God, have mercy on the prince of peace!" The others of the family chanted: "Amen . . ."

The head: "If there's a power named God, save the soul of the Prince of peace!" The others: "Amen . . ."

The head: "If there's a power named God, resurrect him if he's dead!" The others: "Amen . . ."

The priests, including the Prime priest, did not go back to their residences. They assembled in the temple, anxious to get the details of the execution team that had set sail to the sea. Dusk was already over and darkness crept in. None of the seafarers came back. Anxiety and fatigue pushed the priests into sleep. At midnight they felt that they too were at sea. All of them woke up. Yes, it was true! They were floating on water! Total darkness prevailed. The earth wept by flooding—she shed all the tears in her reservoir of eyes. The sky horse-laughed by thundering—shown all the teeth in its mouth of lightning . . .

A cyclone hit Britana. A gale, like a giant, came out of the sea; ran up to a mile on the land and uprooted the one-time prestigious land mark—the temple. When the great giant gale withdrew, it not only razed the temple but also most of the palatial buildings of the princely people.

*   *   *

The dove-of-thought took shelter on a palm tree—the only one plant remaining in the area—all others had been uprooted—and witnessed all the evil events that happened on the coastal region of Britana. The dove understood that Hova was a Prince of peace and was the deemed fit person for the redemption of its native land. The dove was so obsequious to him; wished to call him. But, it was obvious that he had been thrown into the open sea. How about and what about his obsequies?

But he had promised the people about his resurrection! How far it'd be true, only he and God knew. The prediction was not clear. Should one wait for him? Or should one scud from there in search of another saint out of the trinity?

The dove passed a message to its master (Banyan) asking whether the disciple sent by Hova had reached there. Like a flash, the-dove-of-thought got the message: Negative. Fly north in search of B'lla. Invite him to our land for redeeming the people.

So, the dove-of-thought rushed to the northern region saying farewell to the seabirds on the seaboard. They did not like the dove's relinquishment for they were waiting for the return of the Prince of peace since the sentence was executed. They said *good bye* to the dove reluctantly giving counter-countenance to the outgoing bird.

CENTURY 13

1201 TO 1300 AD

I counted and calculated. One out of the Trinity was no more—Hova has been havened! And that too on the first day of my thirteenth centenary. His death came exactly as he had predicted—four days after the *execution*. He remained sunk in the sea for three whole days! A solitary confinement inside an iron chest on a false allegation of social evils. What a wonderful law designed by some blockhead engineers of human beings! If you do good effort, you are convicted as atheist; if you do bad work, you are acquitted *godlike*!

All the aquatic animals assembled around his chamber requesting him to accept their help to save him. They wanted to welcome him to their underwater paradise. He refused. His presence delighted them. They did not want to leave him—to send back to the land—for he had turned their water world into a holy place. They were very much contented with his presence. They felt horripilation—their scales stood on end. All the immature beings under water became mature! All the imperfects turned perfect! For example, the pearls shone more brilliancy. His presence brought a wave of prosperity of the water

A senior whale ordered each and every one of its subordinates to search out the key of the chest as fast as they could. A school of sharks put up a mass submission that they could easily break open the chest with their tails to release the holy man. But the dolphins wisecracked it and suggested that it might hurt him and hinder his meditation.

All the while Hova was immersed in meditation. It was no new task for him. He had undergone such types of evolution under the strict and earnest guidance of his *guru* during the *gurukulam* life. I was confident of his *Thaposhakti* and *yogashakthi*. These *Shaktis* gave him the power to hold the breath during seclusion, power to withstand famishing and destitution and the thermal energy to survive in severe cold. But Hova kept his promise to the *Guru*. He did not perform any miracle to end his sufferings and for cheap popularity. The meditation under water made him a powerful magnet. Thus the chest too became a giant magnet. The key made out of iron, which was lying far away was attracted to the chest due to that magnetism. He opened the chest and came out.

On the third day of Hova's easing off, the tempest died down and a temperate weather prevailed. The sea became calm. The weather was very pleasant. The sky became clear. The people in a bad temper (priests) cursed Hova for causing the havoc and distressing the people. The people in a good temper (populace) praised Hova.

The labor class, especially the fisher-men, were starving. They went for fishing and easily got a good catch—the havoc had given rise to a mud-bank. Sun was about to set. But as they returned to the shore and secured their boats and nets, they were amazed to see another *sunrise* far away on the coast in the east! It was precisely sunset time in the open sea in the west. All of them rushed to that spot.

They went; they saw; they confirmed: It was Hova! They recognized him! Their prince of peace in blood and flesh! His prophecy turned true! He resurrected!

He was standing on the damaged altar of the ruined temple. His smile sent invisible shower of kindness to the whole mankind. His halo emitted visible power and vigor to the disabled. His breath blew the wind of wisdom to the ignorant.

There was great hustle and bustle to touch him. An enormous *fleet-footed* crowd swiftly moved to the temple to see him. A great section of the people of Britana gathered around him. They chanted hymns praising Hova. They knelt down to adore him. The time passed by . . .

It was almost dusk time. Hova walked slowly towards the beach. The crowd gave way to him. He blessed the people raising his right hand. He commented: "Those who give good will receive good things. Those who believe in me are my own blood and flesh." He walked straight into the sea. The halo around his head gradually faded into darkness. Thereafter the people of Britana constructed a prayer hall known as *Purch* where the erstwhile temple was situated; they prayed and paid homage to Hova. Thus, there originated a religion named Hovaism among the people who believed in him . . .

*   *   *

I wondered where Kuriappy had gone! He was one of Hova's four disciples exclusively sent to preach his messages in the eastern region. I was earnestly eager for his arrival for the revival of the people of my country.

The situation in my habitat worsened day by the day. All the men were affected by morbid growth in their morals. I felt mortified by the morose behavior of the so-called mankind. Sorry, how could I call a collection of unkind men *mankind*? It was a common collective noun. But it should be amended to a suitable and concrete noun *man-unkind*. The activities of the animals around me were far better than the activities of the human beings. During daytime the men worked at least like cultured beasts. But ho! ho!! ho!!! During the dark hours they were spiritually blind and deaf and dull in morale.

Prior to starting the leitmotif, if I had a cover large enough to cover my face, I would have done it. If I had plugs large enough to close my ears, I would have done it. But due to non-availability of those things, I was compelled to tolerate their audio-visual activities. The performance of those dramas was like pouring poison into my mouth, like thrusting prongs into my eyes. It polluted me. After each play, I wished for a rain to clean my body. I prayed for a wind to blow my eyes to take away the contamination.

What could I do! I was a mere *maram*, whose communication power had already been lost. To divert the inhabitants from that remoteness to civilization, some apostle or his successor should come and announce an aphorism. Locking up superlative degrees of expectations in the vault of my very-less-thinking mind, I longed for my dove-of-thought, who had been given the lion's portion of my thinking power, to search for a preacher to solve my problem.

*   *   *

When the bird-of-thought was sky-borne, it saw its physical body—the Banyan tree in a flash. I as a tree was not growing at all. Not even an inch of height or a pound of weight was gained in the past few centuries: A state of waning—due to the desperate condition of the mind, due to the decayed state of the morale of the people. The-dove-of-thought stopped thinking about me—its physical master and started thinking about the next spiritual master—B'lla.

So, leaving me past bearing, the phoenix altered its course of flight to the magnetic north by taking a true bearing in the compass of its mind. The bird endured a non-stop flight far away from Britana into the unexplored distances. The dove sighted a desert. It looked like a sheet of silver. The dove slowed down and reduced the altitude. The place was filled with sand. There was nothing but sand.

Ngea . . . ! What's there? Some things were moving like millipedes. The bird reduced altitude further. What's that? The dove identified the moving objects through the clouds of rising dust. Yes, human beings and animals! Men posed themselves in an array finishing arrears of revenge. Most of them were on camelbacks.

A little away, the dove saw a wounded camel. Unable to stand, it was lying. The dove landed on it; but the animal did not know its presence because dove was invisible.

There were cracking sounds from breaking bones and blood-shed. Men wielding swords and shields were fighting at close quarters—on one side professionals and on the other clumsy fighters. The former was an attacking army and the latter the defending villagers. The army-men were in their uniforms and head-gears. The villagers were in their ordinary clothing with turbans on their heads. After killing and wounding too many, the army marched ahead.

The phoenix was shell-shocked to see the battle. More shocking was the reason for the battle—no reason at all!

One wounded man asked: "What for do you fight?"

The other replied: "I found you fighting. So I fought."

Another said: "I found everybody fighting. That's why I fought."

The phoenix felt pity for their ignorance but not on their distress.

Leaving the battlefield, it followed the soldiers lumbering ahead.

*   *   *

The sparkling stretch of the desert seemed to be an ocean in the hot sun. The army was deceived by the mirage. The Captain of the army was angry with his subordinates for the misconception. They lumbered and lumbered further and further with thirsty throats and dirty thoughts. To their surprise, there appeared an oasis. It was, of course, a village.

The army reached there. They were happy to see a fresh-water pond. The area was filled with date-palm trees full of fruits. There were large numbers of huts made of palm leaves. They owned a cattle flock (camels.) The inhabitants were hard-working and peace-loving. Selling dates to the neighboring areas—away from desert—was their main source of income. They exchanged their product for other essentials in kind. They were god-fearing, yet they believed in superstitions like witchcraft and poltergeist.

At times, thugs looted the village. While crossing the desert, the village was a boon to the thugs. In periods of boon, the villagers had made a good profit. Smelling a rat about the good harvest, the thugs looted the village and enjoyed the booty. In order to prevent and protect themselves from the looters, the village had organized a protection force—all the able-bodied male members—trained in shield-and-sword fight. But there was no leadership, proper guidance and battle tactics. They straightaway went to face the attackers without any planning; and often the enemies straightaway pierced their chests. Those were more or less suicide attacks. This had been happening for years and years. Many men became martyrs for the sake of their village.

The army arrived from Pakkana, the capital of the desert. Its intention was to demolish the village and to massacre the men in the village. The reason was that they were harboring a self-styled holy man named B'lla, who had migrated from somewhere and was misguiding the people of Pakkana. He assembled the common people, rendered pedagogy and andragogy service—a transition from ignorance to enlightenment. The populace turned riotous and they tried to drive the populists by mob action. But before the mobocracy climbed to its peak, the rulers put all of them behind the bars. As the law-and-order situation was handled by the military, the Marshal ordered the Captain that B'lla be arrested and brought before the Court-of-Marshal.

Army started destroying the village. The villagers bore the battle. They were borne back by the army's swords yet they bore the onslaught themselves straight. There were just a few men who survived the numerous attacks and mostly there were only woman and children left. The women were voluptuous beauties. This stimulated the army personnel's sexual desire. They were starving for sex; they made use of the situation. The army-men gang-raped the women. Some were homosexuals. They did the unnatural act with the boys and the under-aged. They ate the entire ration stored by the peasants; they drank all the liquor collected by the villagers for consumption during extreme cold and inclement weather conditions. They slaughtered camels and made hot dog. After annihilating myriad of people, the army started searching for B'lla. They raided all the huts but could not find him. So they set fire to the huts. The flames danced like giants celebrating a festival of fire. Next, they dived into the pond in search of B'lla. They did not find him. The angry army agitated the pond to make it muddy. Then they climbed on top of the palm trees and cut the leaves. They did not find him. They chopped off the trees.

The devil of death vanquished the village. Unwilling to witness the situation, the evening Sun took his leave early. Moon hid behind a big dark cloud lest he also should be killed. No stars came out. Even the atmospheric air wanted to escape. But poor Darkness! What could he do? He had to take over the duty in the absence of the Sun. So he came, he saw and he lamented.

The villagers raised their hands and cried out in distress messages to heaven! O God! Save our souls! Save our souls! Save our souls!

The soldiers thrust their swords in spots from where the prayer was sounded.

All of a sudden they heard an echoing voice: "Basta . . . battlers . . . basta!"

Hearing this, the Captain gave an instant order to his men: "Enough!"

Voice: "What on the globe are you doing?"

Captain: "We're doing our duty."

Voice: "Duty! Do you call unmanly, unkind, unhealthy, unholy, unfriendly, unfounded, unequal, unfaithful, unrefined, unfavorable, unlawful and unforeseen undertakings duty? If so, what do you call manly, kind, healthy, holy, friendly, faithful, refined, favorable and lawful acts? Is it just a function of pretence?"

The Captain shouted: "Just let me know who the hell you're on this globe!"

Voice: "I'm love."

The Captain asked in confusion: "Love? What love?"

Voice: "Love . . . Love can't be explained. It has got the smell of flower; taste of honey, color of azure sky, depth of heart, width of mind. And above all, it's omnipotent. But it's cheap and available in plenty with everybody. It's unique and universal."

Captain: "Let us see you physically and decide whether we could assimilate you and your so-called love."

Instantaneously, there appeared a man from a sand dune. It was B'lla, their wanted holy man! He said, "I'm B'lla, your pet."

Pitch-dark condition prevailed. There was no naked light or torch available to identify him. So, eager to kill B'lla, the soldiers slew whosoever came on their way and into their hands.

The Captain proclaimed: "What's the use of carrying all these qualities if you can't appear before the warriors? If you're that powerful why are you not bold enough to face the men of boldness like us?"

B'lla's idea was to propel internally rather than compel externally. Yet he took the Captain's challenge.

He said: "*Fiat lux.*" The light came around him like a halo. He became visible.

The army Captain asked in astonishment: "If the globe is rotating and if that science is correct, tell me who on the globe you're."

B'lla said: "I'm a force one cannot resist, like the rotation of the globe."

Captain: "Even if you are the force that drives the globe, I'll kill you."

B'lla: "You can't."

Captain: "It's the command of our chief. It's unchangeable."

B'lla: "So, if you can't kill me, *memento mori* and you'll become memento mori."

The Captain angrily shouted: "Yes. I do remember that I must die and serve as a skull of death; but, before that *memento mori.*"

B'lla: "Still there's time for that. Your time has come."

The Captain went beside B'lla. The glare was blinding him. He ordered a soldier to behead B'lla. The soldier whirled the sword to chop the head of B'lla. B'lla vanished, and the light too went off. Darkness captured the area instantly. Nobody could see anything. In that confusing condition, the sword swished through the neck of the Captain, chopping down his head. Again B'lla appeared with the halo amidst the amazed army.

The confused crowd curiously stared at the beheaded Captain.

B'lla remarked with pity: "God has ordained that he shall die. The court of God condemned his disgraceful deed. It's a lesson to all of us. Bear in mind."

The second-in-command of the army threw a question: "If so, what about the innocents who were slain in the homicide? Were they wicked? We can't take your statements as axioms."

"No," B'lla continued. "They were not wicked. They were not slain by God. We're the homicide squad. We slew them. And, they didn't take pride in challenging God about their death. They'll be welcomed by God. We don't have to bother about them. We don't have to mourn for them even. They're safe in the hands of the savior."

Hearing his homily lecture, the crowd besieged him and bestowed honors on him. They knelt before him thinking that he was beyond all powers.

They shouted: "B'lla is *Ultra Vires*. He is the strongest. He came, he saw and he conquered our hearts."

The army personnel without their Captain were as good as oxen without horns. They could be tamed. B'lla made them gentle. They made B'lla their spiritual Captain. *Ante bellum*, the village was an *ashram* of *ahimsa*—a place of peace; post *bellum*, it became an Aceldama—the field of flesh and bloodshed. B'lla restored it to the previous condition! So the villagers considered him a prodigious person.

All was grist that came to B'lla's mill of mind. He intended to create a new generation by filling up the generation gap between the evil-doers and the virtue lovers. The genius wanted to eliminate the grisly situation in the village and bring forth a gracious and gorgeous life. He was determined to transform the village into a storehouse packed with a gentle community by reforming the multitude that was once interested in genocide.

There was a famine in the village. The people were starving, and there was no water. As the army had stirred up the fresh pond the water became unfit for consumption. There was no stock of food as the army consumed it all. Most of the wounded people were bedridden. They were to be cared for and treated. Their village had been the only fertile spot in the desert. Though it was far away, the nearest inhabited place was the capital of Pakkana. They could not go there lest they should be arrested for treason.

B'lla instructed the people to take the dead bodies away from the residential area to the open air. Some were hugging their beloved and crying.

B'lla said, "Leave your sentiments and come to the senses. We have no time to mourn for the dead; let's spare our time and tide for the living. Gone are gone. Forget them. Think about the living. Let the vultures come and eat the carrion and let us eat the vultures. There are lots of snakes burrowing around our dwellings. Catch them; cut off their heads and consume."

Some of the villagers said, "We're afraid of snakes and we hate vultures. How can we . . ."

B'lla gave them a satisfying answer: "A carrion-eating vulture is tastier than a carrot-eating bird. A snake sans head is as palatable as a fish sans gills. At times, a cow has to eat meat and a lion has to eat grass if needed for their sustenance . . . However, killing of animals shall not be encouraged, at this rate you'll be compelled to eat your children, and then your own hands and legs. That's what famine is."

Though the people were starving, they did not want to slaughter the remaining camels. Life without camels was unthinkable for the desert-dwellers. Yet, eating the flesh of vultures and snakes was also unthinkable to them—a problem of scruple. But when they felt the smell of cooking of their own intestines, they saw eye to eye with him on social matters. Initially half-heartedly and finally whole-heartedly they started consuming whatever they could get. B'lla did not eat. When asked he said, "Let it be useful to someone else."

B'lla advised the surrendered soldiers to shoulder the responsibility of renovating the village. He engineered the reconstruction of the hutment with the leaves and wood that had been cut by the soldiers. The patients were sheltered inside. He extracted the juice of date seeds and daubed it on the wounds of the injured. He fanned the deep cuts with the dried pinnate leaves. He invoked rhythmic prayer songs of love and affection. They enjoyed the music. For music was the best treatment for all the hurts including the hurts in the heart. He hung some stumps of the palm tree inside the pond. That acted as filters by absorbing all the filth and mud in the water. There was a heap of charcoal expelled from the hearth. He threw it in the pond that accumulated on the bottom, cleaning the water. Thus the pond-water became fresh and sweet. Then he encouraged the able-bodied men, women and children to work hard with clear vision for rehabilitation.

He advised: "You toil. You may not get the yield. But God watches your deeds. He'll give you enough when you're really in need. For God is a friend indeed! Can I entrust you with this task? Or are your ears just holes with no hearing quality? Or are your eyes just two beads of stone which have no power of seeing? Remember that lethargic life of a coward is ephemeral. So, enroll your names in the epic of this village by rendering heroic acts."

Hearing his enunciation, the people earnestly took pledge to obey him. They worked shoulder to shoulder; held arm in arm, amused heart to heart and slept chest to chest. Their lethargy gave way and gained energy. Devil's domination ended and God took over the hearts of the villagers.

He wanted to turn the village into a paradise. Prior to that, he had to reform the villagers. So he gave them moral education. He succeeded in the mission for he had great knowledge in ethics, and the charismatic power inherited through *yoga* during his life in the *gurukulam* was of great advantage. He recalled the principle of his *Guru*: "Good manner is one of the properties of man". He taught them the code of conduct and to be always pro-social and never anti-social. Thus they were committed to society. They gained physical and mental health. The moral classes molded them into fine individuals from the raw material of immature individuals. They changed their way of passive, dependent, narrow-minded, negative and subordinate life into one of active, independent, broadminded, affirmative, abiding and equal feelings.

A fine social weather prevailed in the village. Breezes of peace flowed through everyone's mind, extinguishing the arson of malice in their hearts. Women in the village rubbed balm of love on the livers of the army-men. They, in turn, gave the women sweets of safe returns. They interacted.

The army personnel became part and parcel of the village. They did not want to return to their unit in the capital of Pakkana. They were marked *run* by that time. Forgetting the past army lifestyle, they toiled for the prosperity of the village. Instead of physical training and parade, they performed hard labor on the land.

They expanded the pond, planted more date-palm trees, reared more cattle, prepared more wine and married more women as per the norm of polygamy. As most of the bona fide male members of the village were slain in the onslaught, in the present statistics, the number of women was four times larger than that of the men.

B'lla's sagacity was remarkable. He was like a physician who had a cure for every malady.

He advised: "Women should be protected properly by the safe and strong hands of men. So polygamy should be promoted—a man is at liberty to marry as many women as he can as per his strength, vigor and vitality, provided all the wives of that husband are willing to co-operate. If any spouse does not agree with it, that spouse can divorce the other spouse simply and voluntarily by reciting: Deliver . . . deliver . . . deliver. The dissolution of marriage is very easy when the husband and wife find it difficult to live together. And any man can marry any woman and any woman can remarry any man irrespective of age after their puberty and maturity. People must be encouraged to produce maximum number of offspring to raise the population. All those who believe in me shall be cleaned mentally and bodily.

The villagers whole-heartedly listened to his counseling and lived peacefully accordingly. Likewise, making the belief of the people—"Once a desert, always a desert"—meaningless the desert gradually turned into a paradise by the grace of God. But, again breaking their firm belief—"Once a paradise, always a paradise"—their paradise was again turned into a desert by the devastating acts of the devils.

The devils were the military contingent arrived from the capital of Pakkana in search of the pioneering force sent to the village to arrest B'lla the Seer. The contingent was prepared to face all contingencies; they brought sufficient men, arms and animals with them.

When the contingent reached the village to seize B'lla the Seer, the villagers' hearts scorched in the hearth of their chest. A Major commanded the contingent.

He identified the renegades. He was astounded to see the coalition and collaboration of the villagers and the ex-servicemen—their resettlement in the village! It was an anti-climax. The Major felt fury. He tried to create antagonism between the villagers and the former army-men. But he failed.

The Major ordered the contingent to line up in battle order. He climbed a pulpit and said: "You, deserters, the sand in this desert will never end. Prepare your mouth to eat it."

The villagers kept mum for they did not understand the meaning of his command. They did not react.

He again commanded: "Come on, make them fall in. The ex-army in the front, rest in the rear."

After the fall-in, he continued: "Demonstrate . . . you fall out."

The man came out of the fall-in was made to sit on the pulpit. One militant shoved sand into his mouth and another poured camel urine into his mouth. He was forced to gulp the stuff.

The Major gave them a red warning: "You should sever all connections with the villagers and come back to your former life to serve the Army. Otherwise, you'll be condemned of quisling."

They said unanimously, "We're pleased with this peaceful, peasant and pleasant life rather than a forced life."

"Then you'll be seized as slaves."

B'lla the Seer rose amidst the crowd and said, "I'm there for the liberation of slaves . . ."

"Catch him," the Major cried, "and don't kill him for his death shall be in the city before our Marshal."

The army platoon marched towards B'lla. People hurdled. The army made gangway by killing many. It was a terrifying event. The animals and even the plants in the village were horrified by the homicide.

The Seer said, "I'm surrendering; please stop the killing."

The Major ordered, "Halt!"

The homicide squad became still. B'lla was brought before the Major on sword-point.

The Major studied him from head to foot and hastily remarked: "So, you're that culprit, the so-called Seer who transformed our men of PT and parade to peace-loving peasants. The task of army is land fighting; not for land-fertilizing. You understand?"

Seer: "Land-fighting?"

Major: "Yes. Means, fight for the land."

Seer: "It would be beneficial to mankind if you amend the term to *fight with land.*"

Major: "You've no right either to *fight for the land* or *fight with the land* for the land belongs to the government."

Seer: "Who told you?"

Major: "Each and every person of Pakkana knows that the lord of this land is the Marshal—the chief who governs this country."

Seer: "Each and every sand of this land knows, each and every plant of this planet knows that we're the lords of this land."

If plants and sands could speak, they would have shouted that the statements given by the Seer were true. However, a wind rose, the sand whirled above the ground, the trees swayed crowns. It seemed that they were raising hands in support of the Seer.

The Seer continued, "The earth, air and water do not belong to any other lord except the lord in the sky. He's our father and we're his children. So, we're at liberty to reclaim it—if not the entire land, at least the unoccupied area."

The Seer's precise speech raised a blush on the Major's cheeks. Major used his megaphone again: "Spoil his father's earth, air and water."

The army advanced and usurped the village—they jumped into the pond; bathed, urinated and defecated in it. The force forced the villagers to excrete; daub the night-soil on their bodies and have a dip in the pond. Some extremists compelled the villagers to eat the excrement. The militants compelled them to cast the dead bodies into the water to pollute it. The cunning contingent chopped off all the plantations, destroyed vegetation, torched all the huts and threw all the available inflammable materials into the arson. All this changed the paradise-like village into an inferno.

Stink of burning flesh and spreading smoke polluted the air. Children cried; women wailed; men mourned; animals bleated and the birds chirped, smelling the rat about the bleak future of their village.

B'lla's hands and legs were fastened and secured behind the horse-drawn carriage of the Major. There was a heavy wooden stump of a palm tree tied to his legs.

The Major battered B'lla with his baton and barked: "All those who're supporting this sheepish and stupid marsh-shell may fall in on my left and all those who support our standard Marshal fall-in on my right. And again I'm giving you the last warning—supporting this petty Seer is an anti-government activity and it'll be severely dealt with."

Neglecting the consequences, all the people supported their Seer. They shouted as one man: "We can be anti-government but can't be anti-social. Good or bad, right or wrong, friend or foe, we choose this simple shell-in-the-marsh—B'lla the Seer and not your malicious Marshal."

The ex-army men came before the Major en masse and declared unanimously: "We can Marshal all the secrets of your Marshal. He's not a friend; he is a fiend."

In fuming rage, the Major ordered his men to disrobe the villagers and smash their sexual organs with the blunt side of the sword. But some barbarians used the sharp side. The robes were thrown into the fire. Further, nothing could be seen and heard in the melee. People *started* feeling suffocation; all were amid reek and squalor.

Mounting on the carriage, the Major moaned: "We've no time. Leave them as they are. They'll be starved to death, chilled to death or burnt to death. The devil's on his way to take charge of 'em. Now; chop, chop; let's go; we'll hale him."

His carriage moved forward trailing B'lla on the ground, dragging the Prophet. The contingent followed their Major on their horsebacks. It was a melancholic event. The villagers could not tolerate the wicked operation of the attackers. They too followed them in nude. They did not bother about their shame; they bothered about the pathetic state of their

Prophet. Seeing the movement of the mob, the animals and birds in the village joined them. If the flora had the ability to uproot themselves, they also would have gone after the fauna.

Thus, the Major was followed by the military; the military was followed by the multitude and the multitude was followed by myriad of fauna. The former two wanted to destroy B'lla while the latter two wanted to deliver him from ill treatment. They trailed and wailed . . . The march continued . . . continued . . . and continued. Some staggered, some waggled, and some collapsed on the way. Yet the rest kept on moving ahead like a cavalry with no commander in a battle field.

*   *   *

B'lla was invited to an Epicurean feast in the military mess. B'lla being the chief guest and the Marshal being the chief host, the occasion was supposed to be a grand gala function. The dining hall was not less than a volleyball court in the area; the dining table was as elegant as a billiards table. The menu was exorbitant—many kinds of domestic animals and birds were cooked and fried with various spices in different oils. The food was pre-set in the dishes for each chair except for the chief guest.

The mess was near the open-air detention quarters where the political prisoners and internees were starving to death. At intervals, the garbage from the mess was thrown at them. Then, there would be an internecine quarrel among them. The scene would be inexplicable. Taking a recumbent pose on their chairs and watching that most inhumane event was the most exciting recreation of the military authorities. There was still time for the chief guest and chief host to arrive. So the early-comers passed time watching the sinister scenes of the concentration camp.

There was a hail—a soldier called out loudly—"VIP and VIP arriving, sir . . ." B'lla and the Marshal arrived on a five-horse carriage. After the salutation both the dignitaries entered the dining hall. The Marshal was a terrific figure in his ceremonial dress—grey uniform with glittering shoulder stripes and decorations. His cap had ornamental beading. Still, the ornaments on his body were unable to banish the malice on his dark face.

B'lla was robed in a simple black cloak that covered the injuries he sustained when he was dragged through the desert. His face was full of bruises and scratches. Each wound seemed like an ornament of gentleness emitting sparks of kindness.

The invitees bowed in order to pay mark of respect to their Marshal.

Then, turning to B'lla, they said as a man, "hay, you blacky prisoner, see our glittering Marshal, he looks like a god; and you, you seems a devil in our desert."

B'lla said softly, "all that glitters is not God."

"Please take your seats," the Marshal said politely.

The invitees sat on the side seats. The Marshal sat down on the head seat where the full form of VIP—Very Important Person—was written. The only seat left vacant was the one at the foot-side where another full form of VIP—Very Important Prisoner—was written. B'lla sat there.

"Serve our VIP," the Marshal softly said. "Prior to cremating we shall serve him some excrement."

An invitee next to him bit a piece off a fish. He put it on B'lla's empty plate and politely said, "Please have it."

All the invitees chuckled. B'lla understood that the function was a mock-feast for him. He was given half a glass of yellow-colored liquor.

The Marshal said sarcastically, "We're not lucky to have this precious urine of a dying, for we could procure only this much and all that is exclusively for you. Cheers!" Raising his wine glass, he continued, "come on, say cheers to our chief guest."

All of them sipped the wine. B'lla again became a laughing stock. He too participated in the other participant's merriment.

B'lla calmly said, "Urine, I like the Major content in it; the remainder I hereby reject."

He closed his eyes and meditated for some moments. He became electrified. He dipped his pointing finger into the urine. As the finger acted like an electrode and the urine as electrolyte, all the other ingredients in the urine dissociated and accumulated on His finger. After removing the precipitate, the liquid was converted into water. B'lla drank it. He sprinted his finger. The precipitates scattered and fell in the glasses of other participants converting their matured wine into waste matter—urine.

His empty plate became a cornucopia. All the other's full plates became empty instantaneously. All the dignitaries grinned at B'lla. The hungry chief asked him in anger: "Where's our food?"

B'lla: "Hey, glutton, the obesity will increase. All of you need fasting instead of food. For excessive food is palatable only to the tongue. It is harmful to the body. So why waste food? Millions in your country need it. If you don't mind, look there. They are in need of food to stay alive."

When they looked out, they found the poor prisoners in the concentration camp consuming food.

B'lla commented: "Watch how they eat. You learn eating from them—they're consuming less food taking more time. Food should be properly masticated. You may do any activity fast. But eating is the only activity to be performed slowly and steadily."

The invitees crushed hands and gnawed teeth. They were suffering from sitophobia—morbid aversion to food. They controlled their rage by keeping mum, continued beholding the prisoners.

B'lla continued: "*Sursum corda* please, *Sursum corda,* if you're that hungry lift your hearts and follow me. I'll feed you with the cream of creams."

Though they had aversion to food, they asked him with sarcastic reflections: "Just let us know what your menu is?"

B'lla replied: "Starvation. Starvation is my menu; famine is my food. You too practice fasting. It helps lengthen the period from birth to death and it develops your strength, vigor and vitality spiritually rather than physically."

*　　*　　*

B'lla was brought before the court of Marshal. He made a tirade against the military rule in the court—bitter criticism against the government and the cruel governor, the Marshal.

He said: "You claim that this is a sovereign country. You should know that there are two kinds of sovereignty. One, the legal sovereignty that exclusively belongs to the rulers or the power of the rulers and the other is the people's sovereignty—the power of the people. Do you incorporate both?"

The Marshal argued: "We don't follow duel sovereignty. We insist on mono sovereignty—the supreme power of the Marshal who governs this country. You identify me, for I'm that supreme power."

B'lla: "Because this's a coup country. Sooner or later, there's going to be a *coup de grace* against your *coup d'état.* It would be a decisive stroke to finish your pride and power."

The rulers hated his pomposity. He was charged with contempt of court. The Marshal wanted to give him warrant punishment. He deluged B'lla with questions. But people knew he was not quisling.

The Marshal quizzed him: "You've no address. You're a bastard."

B'lla: "If you're my elder brother, your statement is correct."

The Marshal: "You're a dastard. That's why you ran away from here and took shelter faraway. You will have to face the consequences by combating with court."

B'lla: "Anyway, I'm a little bolder than you."

The Marshal: "How the hell?"

B'lla: "You and your court are afraid of me, the women and even the children of the village. That's why you've arrested them too. It's a dastardly action."

The Marshal exclaimed: "Oh! They're your pets. You keep all the women as mistresses? You want to produce more children to form an army against us? All of them are as dear as your wife?"

"Nothing of that sense. They're also human beings. They're innocent. Why should they be punished for the crime if I've committed it? You punish me extremely and let them go for I love them as dear as my life."

"That's the only reason why they'll be sent to the abyss before you. For we hate most what you love most. There's no scarcity of space in the desert of Pakkana for a graveyard. You'll be given the golden opportunity of enjoying the spectacular scene of burying your beloved people alive. Above all, your last post will be sounded at the last so that nobody would be remaining to respect your relic."

"If that's your verdict," the Seer prophesied politely, "you listen to God's verdict: Your last post will be sounded at first and I assure you that, there won't be an inch of space available for your reliquary on this earth."

The grisly Marshal said, "You've no right to spread a new religion amongst the people. This country has got a particular system of faith and worship. I govern them; therefore I'm their Supreme Being. So, you Prophet relinquish your prophecy and relieve them. And for doing so, if you're interested, as a reward, I'll enroll you in the court of military as a subordinate judge above the rank of a Major provided you'll assure me that you'll be in our good books forever."

"I've no interest. I've relinquished all the worldly affairs. Moreover, I'm interested in the heart of justice and not in your court of injustice. And again, I'm not interested in fanaticism."

B'lla was good at repartee. The Marshal of the court suffered an ignominious defeat in arguments at the hands of the Prophet.

So B'lla the Prophet was sentenced to death. On that melancholic occasion, the color of the walls of the court hall faded with agony. The roof beams chilled. The floor quivered in anger. In a nutshell, his misfortune saddened each and every stone of the court hall.

*　　*　　*

Numerous trenches were dug in the desert to accommodate the offenders. Awnings were rigged; seating arrangements were made; officers and their families sat comfortably beneath the shade. Prisoners were deployed to fan the area—dignitaries enjoyed the current of air. People of Pakkana came to the desert from far and near. They lined up around the field of massacre like a human fence.

B'lla was brought followed by the other offenders (villagers). They were shackled among themselves. They were made to fall in before the Marshal, with B'lla in the middle.

Marshal proclaimed again: "There's no excuse for B'lla. Because he's a fanatic. He'll be killed. The other offenders will be exempted from execution provided they do exactly what I say."

Pointing to a soldier, he continued: "Petty officer, give them the order."

The petty officer bowed and said, "I've my order, sir." He turned about and in turn gave order to an ordinary hand to unshackle the villagers. B'lla was dropped into the trench right in front of the Marshal's seat. The petty officer further ordered all the offenders to take sand in hands and to line up near B'lla's trench.

They obeyed. They anxiously awaited with handful of sand thinking that they would be told to eat the sand so that they would be suffocated to death with choked esophagus. It did not happen.

The Marshal got up from his seat and promulgated: "Now all of you throw the sand in your hands into the pit of your pet, so that the Prophet will never volunteer to take a rebirth if he ever got a chance for it. It's an act of double—benefit: You all will be set free to see your village and he'll be sent to see his forefather's world. A handful of sand each from many men may make a mountain. Come on . . . start . . . one by one . . ."

As most of the male members of the village were slew in the onset, most of the villagers were women, children and the aged. The offenders were in a dilemma. They were reluctant even to move.

B'lla cried out from the pit requesting them not to pity on him and to empty their hands over him.

He howled: "Please, for heaven's sake, do as you wish and save your life. Don't hesitate, please."

The people of Pakkana were eager to know the reaction of the offenders.

The first turn was of a woman. She was very courageous. She resembled a beautiful flower tanned in the sun of tumult. She confronted the Marshal and boldly declared: "If all of us throw the sand over you, you'll be buried alive beneath a mountain of sand. But we're not that cruel to kill a living person by virtue of his evils. And, of course, you may not know that, we've another easy method of murdering the one who tries to defile our chastity—if all of us spit at you, you'll be submerged in an ocean of our saliva. But we're not that hard-hearted to drown a man. It'll blemish the gentleness of the whole human race and the generations to come will hardly believe that a multitude pardoned a man who wanted to kill a multitude of men."

The *houri*'s elaborate speech stunned the audience including the Marshal. Shell-shocked, his mouth remained open. It moved the tranquil minds of the public to turbulence.

The nymph loquaciously continued: "Your hobby is massacre. If that makes you happy, we're ready to bury ourselves alive. But before that you should taste the breast milk of your mother."

She spat on the face of the Marshal. The jet exactly went into his open mouth like a bullet hitting the bull's eye. As he recovered from the shock, he closed his mouth unknowingly and he felt exactly the taste of his mother's milk in the spit of that village woman of virtue.

The offenders took the *houri*'s declaration as a decree of justice. And the villagers were in the first degree of readiness to face the third degree method of the Marshal and his military men.

The sheepish Marshal burnt with rage. He burst out: "Belie the last regarding offenders' burial to death. They'll be burnt to death. Pour oil and burn them at random. Let the burnt go and hug the unburned. Let, B'lla be the last one to be burnt; he has still got time to join us. Behead the belle of the ball and hand over her head to B'lla the Benedict, as a gallantry award for he himself is a gallant in many meanings and forms.

ALL THAT GLITTERS IS NOT GOD

And let this be a lesson to the mob that if someone renders a gallant action or speech undermining the coup, that gallant would be given a greater award than this, by parting and parceling the gallant's limbs."

The Marshal's rude and unfair words provoked not only the offenders but also the poor populace of Pakkana. They threw the sand at the face of the sitting dignitaries. They became riotous. The military swung into action to suppress the mob. First of all, they buried B'lla alive in a trench by turning the trench into a big sand dune.

There was a melee. The people ran pell-mell. There was a hue and cry. Crowds crumbled. The dignitaries were puzzled. Their wives cried for help. They had never seen warfare like this. The offenders took shelter inside the trenches. The traps dug for their pit-falls turned their palaces. It was a boon to them. But the militants poured oil over them. They lighted torches to burn the multitude.

Unable to bear the sight, the clouds vanished. Unwilling to witness the melancholy, Sun tried to leave the area as early as he could. The sky stood still.

Fight . . . fight . . . everywhere fight!

The desert turned into a power house.

Physical power versus mental power.

The former had armed arms; the latter had armless arms.

Yes, yes! Powerful fight and powerless fight!

Fight . . . fight . . . everywhere fight!

Blood . . . blood . . . everywhere blood!

The desert turned into a vampire.

It was thirsty, for ever since it was born.

Quenched its thirst by sucking hot blood.

Yes, yes! Human blood as well as animal blood!

Blood . . . blood . . . everywhere blood!

Flesh . . . Flesh . . . everywhere flesh!

The desert turned into a dragon.

It was hungry, forever since it came into being.

Ate enough meat as in an Epicurean feast.

Yes, yes! Human flesh as well as animal flesh!

Flesh . . . Flesh . . . everywhere flesh!

The dove of thought should eschew violence. That was the instruction given by me, the *Bodhi* tree. Yet, the bird wanted to write some verses. So, it wrote the above-mentioned lines.

Anyway, there were gory sand patches here and there and the limbs of the dead scattered everywhere. The desert resembled a large plate of hotchpotch. And the flies and birds that came over there to enjoy the great feast of fresh flesh and hot blood, behaved like gluttons in that battle-field. Once a tranquil area, the desert turned into the biggest slaughter-house on entire earth.

Nightfall was nearing.

In the meantime, B'lla was meditating under the sand dune. He was electrified by his *yoga Shakti*. Gaining the power of a mountain-magnet, he rose from the trench. Bursting the sand dune open, he appeared in the open with a corona. Eagles circled aloft; jackals lingered around. They arrived from far away to eat carrion.

B'lla raised his hands. An invisible magnetic power transmitted. All the trenches were filled with water. The offenders' bodies went under water but the heads stayed above water. The army could not burn them. The force fancied. There was a *coup de main*.

The Marshal was trying to flee. B'lla grabbed him and said, "The government should be as pure as milk; if one dirty drop like you're in it, the whole milk becomes impure and unfit to be consumed by the public."

B'lla bifurcated the body of Marshal. He tore him by catching his legs and parting them apart. Then he separated each of his limbs and threw into the sky. The eagles were eager to have it. They pecked the flesh pieces from the sky itself and flew away.

The people were surprised to see this and remembered B'lla the Seer's prophecy: "No monument is required for the Marshal. His body also vanished along with his spirit."

B'lla's trembling body belied his calm. He jumped into a waterless— trench. It was time for him to leave this world. All the people including the dignitaries ran after him. They wanted to divert him from the misery. Sand came and covered his trench automatically. The task force tried to remove the heap of sand. But more and more sand came to the trench from all sides to cover him. More and more people also came to prevent the sand-fall but in vain. Someone's intention was just to touch the Seer. But couldn't find him. Still people went on digging till they were unable to dig further. The trench area was transformed into a water reservoir.

Thus the anarchy ended in a fiasco and the social feuds ended forever.

The people of Pakkana believed B'lla was their savior and they followed B'llaism—a new religion giving due weightage to his teachings and preaching. They started propagating it throughout the world by deploying volunteers.

After the downfall of Marshal Law, all the military personnel merged with the other multitude. They became the followers of B'lla and believed in B'llaism.

The dove-of-thought hurriedly scribbled the most significant scraps from the scripture told by the Seer and rushed to send a quick message colubrine to me, Banyan. But prior to that the bird received a lightning message from me asking it to cancel the campaign and return home forthwith.

CENTURY 14

1301 TO 1400 AD

I was longing very badly for the homecoming of my dove-of-thought. For a century, my brain-house was vacant. I was capable of peripheral thinking only because I had handed over the major part of my intelligence to the bird. Though my bird might be soaring higher and higher and flying from continent to continent gathering news to report to me, I wanted to discuss with my paragon of smartness some matters regarding the folklore of a paragon of peace who had landed in our motherland.

A saga of sacrifice by a sage! A fight between his sagacity and the society's sadism! An unforgettable story of a poor but powerful *sadhoo* or saint and the tale of the people who forgot their duties and had gone to dirty acts. A state where people had once been maddened by his presence and where people were now saddened by his absence. There was a time when people of my habitat regarded him sardonically. But now! Now they remember him as a saint ironically.

My paragon of smartness might be eager to know who this paragon of peace was! No sooner did the bird left Britana than the man appeared. When the bird happened to know who that man was, it felt that he was dear. No, he was dearer. No, he was the dearest of all others on this earth. He was nobody other than one of the close, very close friends of mine—Eysa, the ex-student of the *gurukulam*.

When the bird returned and house-warmed my lofty home of brain, I narrated episode by episode the epic of the *sanyasi*, who had devoted his life to the renaissance of Indana—our native place.

"The people are so promiscuous," the bird said. "They never think they are short-living and prone to pronounce profanity towards the ever-living maker of men and everlasting baker of their bread."

"What to do?" I consoled the bird with gentle caresses with my leaves on its feathers. "It's the society's propensity. They react at first and realize at last."

"Of course. That's what I too experienced with the Britans and the Pakkans. May I've the permission to pry out the past events of the protagonist?

"Why not? That's an account of something to be remembered through life." I said.

It so happened that when the inhabitants of my habitat were indulged in the wicked evening games, a mighty gale lashed in. The evening game was nothing but the usual entertainment of wining and womanizing. Son copulates with his mother, mother copulates with her father, father copulates with his daughter, daughter copulates with her brother and so on like in chain reaction irrespective of their blood-bond and other relationships.

Prior to doing the priapian activities, they would smear themselves with wine. Their wining was: The myrmidons put myriads of myriapods into a giant wooden vat containing country liquor and fermented the stuff to attain stronger intoxicating effect. Then the chief would come. A new-born bonny baby would be kept ready. Holding the legs, the chief would invert the baby and immerse the baby's head in the liquor till the baby died of suffocation. In the meantime, the people sang profane songs praising Priapus to win the boon for procreation. After that they boiled the baby's body. Finally they would enjoy the evening with feast and booze. The common belief among the people was that they would be renewed like a baby if they consumed the baby's crumb. But, this was the only one occasion when and where one could eat human flesh. Otherwise, cannibalism was forbidden.

They boozed up to the nose with liquor-punch irrespective of age. A child of five years had at least five ounces whereas an adult of fifty years of age consumed at least five bottles. Thereafter they sang some meaningless lyrics in coarse voice sans rhythm. The essence of the verses was purely profane.

And at the end of the show, as they were cantankerous, there would always be bloodshed. In the pandemonium, the children usually used to be trampled beneath the feet of the mob. But the parents did not bother for they were not aware of their attachments. Normally, the riot would end up on the basis of the 'stronger survives' principle.

Yes, about a century back, one day, during the course of their wicked games, there came a giant gale. Its velocity and range were so awesome that even the strongest fauna and flora could not withstand its thrust. The condition was too Zulu—their merriment came to a standstill. All the torches went off. Darkness conquered the area. Most of my branches fell over them, killing and wounding many. Those who did not cling or hug to some strong points were carried away by the wind. The wind whistled like prolonged blasts from fleets and fleets of steamers signaling *Save Our Soul*.

After a while, the wayward gale went off its way. The area became still and silent. Then there occurred the miracle. Bursting open my belly, the colossal monk appeared from the hollow of my stem, with a nimbus that blinded even me. The sight of the giant naked body with a corona filled the people with consternation. They stood awe-truck. But soon, the Chief came to his senses.

He bowed and prayed: "Oh, God of Priapus! Grant us the boon of procreation." After the request, he fell unconscious.

But no sooner did the holy man hear the unexpected human voice than he disappeared and darkness wrapped the area. Horrified and crestfallen, the people who saw the miracle went back to their dwellings lest they should be cursed, with terror in their hearts.

I looked at the monk cap-a-pie and instantly recognized him. The monk also stared at me as though he already knew that I was the same Banyan tree who was one of the staff of his *gurukulam*. When Hova had gone to Britana and B'lla to Pakkana, Eysa just followed me without my knowledge. He settled down in my hollow in an intense *thapasya*—a prolonged meditation to reach the seat of God. But he was destined to be a reformer to make the people of Indana perfect. So, in between, he was compelled to break the meditation for the sake of his mission.

Oh, that night! That night was very special to all the inhabitants. A peculiar night for all the fauna and flora. An uncommon night even for the soil, rock and all the inanimate articles of the habitat. They had seen, heard and experienced many catastrophes during the course of their lives and right from the origin of the non-living things. But this wind on land, like a whale in the sea, spelt destruction to the habitat in various ways and forms. All the hutments collapsed. Most of the weak trees were pulled up by the stump; some senior trees were uprooted; some minor trees broke by the stem; some plants fell down; the cattle fled from their sheds at random. The wind carried some men with it, and they fell in the dense forest.

The wild beasts were frightened of the high-pitched roar of the falling men. They were seeing human beings for the first time. They mistook the men as some extra-terrestrial creatures. All the animals of the jungle came around and watched the strange creatures' fallen half-dead and dead. Animals were afraid to approach the shattered bodies. But some bold lions and brave tigers dared to come forward to investigate the matter. The gory men's smell created in the beasts a yearning to eat that extra-special flexible flesh. They felt that the human flesh was the most palatable food and the human blood was the most delicious drink they had ever had. Thenceforth the beasts loved to eat human flesh and from then on they were said to be cannibals.

Then on, the desire to fight each other like human beings grew in them—the consumption of human blood and flesh instilled in the animals' cruelty and carnivorousness.

It was a sleepless night for the people of Indana for the gale was so intense and destructive. Though many men managed to escape with their skin intact, most of their material properties were wrecked. The Indans had survived many natural calamities associated with wind, temperature and rainfall. But this time, they could not even breathe in the heavy wind! They were chilled to the marrow in the cold downpour! They felt that their bodies were burning in the intense heat emitted from the monk's strong and long *lingam*—a powerful penis!

I heard eerie shrieks coming from everywhere.

Who would he be? Was he the son of Sun? Or was he Sun himself? Was he a sex pot? Where had he gone? All those sentences were swinging from the terminal of exclamation to the terminal of interrogation in each and every one's mind. But soon their mind gained the answer—a superstitious discovery.

Yes, he was none but their Priapus. Undoubtedly an *avatar* of procreation. There was evidence. How large was his *lingam*! How firm and fiery it was! Its energy could provide offspring to all the barren women and make potent all impotent men.

But they could not discover the reason for his fiery temper. *Sans doute*, he was angry. That was the reason he had unleashed a gale. He was dissatisfied. But why? Was the libation polluted by some means or the other? Priapus might not have been pleased with the preparation of the potion. Was it potable to him? The offering of a new-born baby should have been with the consent of the parents. The father and mother should offer their baby happily for the preparation of the potion. Daily, a pot of that special liquor would be kept on the pulpit of my feet (root area) as libation to Priapus. The people considered the potion as *Amruth* or ambrosia—a drink of immortality, in other words, the vital energy for procreation and prolonged life.

I wondered, rather chuckled, at the way the people imagined things about my chum. By God, he was my chum, chum. And I was prepared to chant a million, billion, trillion times that he was my chum.

His personality as imagined by the people and his reality were comparable to the similarity between a star and a satellite or a mountain and a mustard seed. He was neither Priapus nor a procreator. Above all he was not at all interested in libation. He was just a simple person feeding on air and water particles in the atmosphere. Oh! His nudity? For perfect performance of proper meditation a *sanyasi* had to be in his natural form. Even a single thread on his body would make variations in his mind that might hinder the progress towards The Almighty. Yes, he ran amuck for his meditation was disturbed by the merriment of the men and for making the divine field their amusement park. And about his strong and long *lingam*: That's the storage area of vital energy of a man. Even after the passage of centuries, not even a single drop of semen had lost from him. His genital organ was always strong and erect like an inflated balloon. It was the seat of the human energy and if a *sadhoo* wanted, he could operate his organ like a volcanic eruption that might spurt seminal lava that could melt anything on its way. This monk was a celibate in total control over lust—a celestial celebrity.

And his nimbus! Unlike Hova and B'lla, Eysa had a powerful and luminous head. The reason was that he had undergone profound *thapasya* for centuries, even after passing out from the *gurukulam*. Our *guru* was next to God. And Eysa was next to *the guru*. And there was no one next to him. One could fear whether God was jealous of him. Had he continued his *thapasya*, God would have been forced to vacate his seat for Eysa. That was why, prior to that he was assigned the job of reforming Indana. God gives; man takes—Eysa accepted the mission.

God wanted to show Eysa—with his physical eye—the wicked games played by cruel men. God gave him liberty to render the service by way of miracles or by advising and teaching the unrefined people. Eysa did not want to be a man of miracles. So he chose to be a teacher rather than a mystic. He had had a good teacher, the *guru*. He was a good student to him. Now he himself was to teach myriad of men. So he was determined to shed light on their darkened minds.

I analyzed Eysa, the monk closely and scientifically: Of course, he was in a fiery temper when he was compelled to give up that solitary and confined life inside my hollow, when he lost his monasticism. Instead of a fine face, he had fiery face and eyes. I could not find fault with him. He had never been angry. He was a harbinger of peace. I recalled his verses: 'if you get angry, you won't get anything from anywhere; if not, you'll at least get peace-of-mind from everywhere' But now he was like a fire-eater. It was because his meditation was disrupted when his *Kundalini*—the divine power of force—was about to wake up. It was the saturation time and point of his *thapasya* for more than a quarter of a millennium. His soul and whole were totally concentrated on God. There were no sound and no thought in his environment of enlightenment. The people polluted it with their entertainment—the wicked evening games. Meditation needed perfect stillness—a state of no body and no mind from which the entire universe should disappear and where God alone should exist—a tranquil trance.

When the awakened *Kundalini* power proceeded further and unfolded the *aniana*—the space between the eyebrows—and as he was about to see the effulgence of The almighty—even a small degree of disturbance could hinder his meditation—he was disturbed by the hilarious hubbub of the inhabitants of the habitant.

Meditation is no fun. It is a serious performance—a case of subtle spiritual sense, intense heat and emanation of light. Unless it is performed properly it will end up in a tragedy. A meditator who would become a *yogi* or a monk would have to lead a life of tragedy until his *Samadhi,* whereas he could give comedy to others. He's a comedy to the others. His each and every action has an equal and opposite reaction—when he burns himself, he cools others. That is the formula. Seeking other's happiness he donates his happiness and fortunes. That is his profession. A person who volunteers to put his physical and spiritual bodies to that profession should only adopt the discipline of *sanyasa*. That is the real sacrifice. A mentality to help others who face problems. It is not common to all human beings. An average person cannot achieve that. It is not natural. It is something mystic. It has to be acquired by processing and reprocessing the crude form of selfishness or the *mine* in man to a fine and finished product of benevolence. Even the residue after the refinement should have the quality of charity. For such a refinement, a *yogi* needs unlimited calories of heat that he acquires by the breathing and yogic exercises. Through this the *Kundalini* is stirred up; an explosion takes place in his body generating tremendous heat and light energies.

Eysa's body was like a refinery. His heart was the vessel, his head the control room, his bones the pipelines, his blood vessels the product lines, his liver the storage tank and his penis was the outlet of flare. Flare is the most important factor. In an emergency, due to malfunctioning the outlet has to be opened through the flare tower. The people's wicked game distracted the mind of the monk paving the way for the malfunctioning of his physical machinery making the flare fierce. That was the heat emitted from his penis. If that heat was not discharged through the penis, he would burn himself into ashes. The *Tantra* system of *yoga* would fall into disrepute.

Eysa was like a spiritual refinery under shut-down. God was the only technician who could do the maintenance works on him. But God wished to divert Eysa's spiritual capacity to refine the people of Indana. Instead of keeping on distilling himself, let him distill the people's mind into intermediate stage, middle distillate stage and then to moral stage till they were distilled to the spirit to run the motor of society.

Though his determination was to reach the highest spiritual goal and enter into the super conscious stage—the transcendental plane— giving due weightage to God's discretion, Eysa divested himself of such thoughts. So, relinquishing all his supernatural powers of heat and light, he attained the normalcy of an ordinary person of my habitat—a transition from heaven to hell.

He appeared as an average man—transfiguration. The people rejected Eysa *prima facie*.

Let me take stock of the three previous centuries: The years of self-reformation of my habitat—a period of evolution from primitiveness to the present state of Eysa's appearance. Out of the whole, it was a separate chapter in the history of my so-called motherland. If I went back to the dim past of my native place, I could recollect that I was the king and all the faunas and floras were my subjects and that our land was named *Massacre*. But I could not recollect, when, how and why the name *Massacre* was changed into Indana. Perhaps the human beings who named their nation were not aware of the name *Massacre* for it was the dialect of faunas and floras. Enormous transformations had occurred to the shape and style of land as well as the people. Let me narrate it one by one.

The land—nature had made Indana a separate geographical entity. Its physical features were distinct. It was a triangular peninsula. Out of the three boundaries, two sides—the west and the east—converged in the south at a cape in the ocean of Indana, where waves frequently washed the shore from both sides. The third boundary was blocked by the icy heights of a mountain with a perpetual snow-capped peak in the extreme north.

Between the highest peaks and the longest coast, there were some hottest, coldest and wettest regions. Besides, there was a dense forest where many varieties of rare animals dwelled.

The people, the cloth-less, shameless and senseless couple, were the first inhabitants. Since their arrival, till now, man has made tremendous advances to cover his body with bark to animal skin.

Their language—the thoughtless couples inherited the knowledge of the power of speech from the birds and animals. It is the tendency of human beings to relay whatever knowledge they gained to the next generation. And, they in turn added new knowledge attained the ability to speak. The process of transmission of expression and ideas paved the way for a dialect. Usage of dialect subsequently sowed the seeds of intelligence in them. With the birth of intelligence, they gave up the crude tools made from bones, wood and stones and acquired the art of using axes, spears, bows and arrows.

Now about their livelihood: I still remember the first meal of the nude couples: The river water and the berries provided by me. How gluttonous they were to have it! Then from fruit-gathering and drinking of water, they shifted to hunting and consumption of blood. During hunting, they could easily tame some animals. This paved the way for domestication of animals like cows, goats and buffalo. They ate their meat and drank their milk. They kept dogs as security staff, donkeys as carriers and horses as transports.

Their occupation: It was obvious that the chief occupation of the first couples of my habitat was nothing other than copulation. Their main tools were legs for walking, hands for eating and genitals for mating. But with the invention of implements like ploughs and sickles, they learned to prepare land for agriculture. The beginning of farming gradually changed their occupation from food-gathering to food-producing. I could see farmers sowing and re-sowing plots and plots of land year after year. The fields were fertilized every time with manure accumulated from floods or decayed matter. They treated the soil with manure.

Their dwellings: The inhabitants settled in an infertile area. There would be no unwanted growth of grass or weeds. They abandoned pit-dwelling and started living in mud-houses. Thereafter, they shifted to safer and more comfortable homes made of wooden planks and beams with thatched roofs. They had shown their skill in architecture by building a bungalow for their chief on top of a flat rock that served like granite flooring with lot of air passages and comforts. For the inhabitants of my habitat, the people of Indana, I was the first natural wonder; the second was the chief's bungalow though it was artificial.

Their beliefs: The primitive inhabitants of Indana appeared to have lived around me. I was the only shelter to them. So, being a tree and their rectory, they revered me as *Yaksha* and my big branch roots or my so called wives—Uru, Mena, Ramb and Tilo—as *Yakshis*. We were their tree spirits. There were many snakes settled in burrows beneath my roots. The *Nagas* and *Naginis* were their snake spirits. Besides them, there were enormous invisible *Jinns*, dryads and hobgoblins. Above all, they were afraid of the visible natural powers of sun and storm. Any type of gain or loss or any kind of good or bad was superstitious to them.

In my habitat, all the inhabitants' heads of inferiority were crushed by the one and only feet of superiority of the chief. They were forced to stoop even before his shadow. No king of any country had availed of such type of entertainment and entitlement as enjoyed by this chief. He always indulged in festive array; his armed kinsfolk always roamed with him en masse *en fete* like honey bees around a hive. He was the visible omnipotent to them, or audible omniscient or physical omnipresent or whatever world you may flatter him unnecessarily with a suffix of Omni.

He had the right to hobnob with any virgin he chose. He could hocus any person. Always there would be a swarming multitude beside him to marvel with his hocus-pocus. His hold was the only Hobson's choice for the hive. Though he was hoary and hoarse, his hoax hypnotized even the hobble decoys of the habitat to hobble behind him—a hobgoblin sans any holiness. Actually, the present chief was a tiny-figured man with big brains. The others had been giant-figured with small brains. They used to obey him word by word and move inch by inch as per his command. This was so because they had set up a society on the model shown by the honey bees.

The only difference was that the hive was commanded by the queen wasp, an enchantress, whereas the chief of the habitat was an enchanter. In the hive, the female played the dominant role. In the habitat, the male played that role. Another peculiarity was that in the so-called society of my habitat, other than the chief, everyone belonged to the labor class. There were only two types of jobs. These were: The commands from the chief and the carrying out of the command by others. There was no confusion. The former ordered, the latter obeyed—whatever, whenever or wherever the jobs might be. Whosoever came in his sight, the chief issued him a job card of a nature of his choice.

Hence there was no profession to any specific category. A hunter was a farmer too. A farmer was a fighter too—a multi-craft system. A pick had to do the work of a poniard; a poniard had to work as a spade; a spade had to do the work of a spoon; a spoon would do the work of a pin. It was an unskilled working system.

As there was no profession, there was no perfection in any kind of job. Therefore, rice had the taste of rat; rats had the smell of rice. Sugar had the effect of salt; salt was sweet like sugar. Flowers were hard like seeds; seed had the softness of flower—a hell upside-down effect. Yet some way and somehow they lived.

*   *   *

Ignorant of Eysa's significance, the inhabitants of my habitat considered him insignificant. They ill-treated him under the influence of their Chieftain. Arguments and identification parade were held.

The Chieftain interrogated him: "Who the hell are you?"

Eysa: "I'm the monk you saw yesterday."

Chieftain: "Are you a monk or monkey?"

Eysa: "Monkey was our forefather. We're the ramification."

Chieftain: "If you're the previous day's monk, come in that rig."

Eysa: "I'm neither a fire-eater nor a fire-walker. You better give up your flamboyant jugglery."

Chieftain: "The people enthroned me. I entertain them in return. The People of Indana reject you. You can't do any good to them."

Eysa: "You're not entertaining them. You're enthralling them. I'll enlighten them and I don't need any enthronement in return."

Chieftain: "You're not a colossus."

Eysa: "But, you're a colubrine."

275

Chieftain: "I'm the Chieftain."

Eysa: "Agreed. But you should not be a cheat."

Chieftain: "You came from somewhere to inflame them."

Eysa: "You flagitious . . ."

Chieftain: "We won't need flagrance. You better retreat. Or you would be flagellated."

Eysa, the most significant man, could not win the mind of the most insignificant man, the chief. Neither could he capture the hearts of the people nor the hearts of the animals or the plant kingdom. They too were inclined towards priapism and intoxication. All the members of my family (plant kingdom) were indulged in fertilization rather than fruit-producing—leaves kissed each other; flowers discharged pollen from one another. And everywhere and every time there was process of pollard.

Animals did not care for their little ones. The he-animals were interested in plugging and plucking their partners. The she-animals were interested to get plugged and to get plucked by their partners. And the little ones, they too influenced by their elders, jumped upon each other's back trying to fix their plugs without success.

In a nutshell, even the rocks and sands of my habitat overlapped each other as if all of them had tight-fixed their plugs for ever and were never willing to unplug.

Turning to the multitude, Eysa said, "You should have cardinal virtues. Priapism will lead you to the prim rose path. Finally, you'll suffer from malady. Give up this malefic life and follow me. I'm your protector who seeks your prosperity."

People roared, "We want a Priapus who could procreate. We hate frauds like you."

Eysa utterly failed in passing his confidence into the hearts of the masses. It was a war between a one-man Salvation Army (Eysa) and many-men savage army (chief and his men). It was a combat between a VIP and VIPs (very important person and very insignificant persons). A conflict between morality and immorality.

After the verbal warfare there commenced a fight with hands and legs. Enormous people crowded around Eysa. The chief sat on the pulpit beneath my parasol. A scoundrel was deployed to scourge him. He hit Eysa with a spade. Eysa wavered. Again hit . . . again and again hit . . . hit . . . hit . . . the hitting continued.

I felt sad. It was really bad. I pitied his condition. What could I do? I wished to screech an eloquence, flattering the divinity of that innocent man who was being flagellated. But it was unfortunate that my silent eloquence remained in my mind.

He was bleeding profusely. Why could this man of mystic powers not perform some miracle? Why could not he open his inner eye and spread its fire in the entire habitat and turn the whole men and materials to ashes? Why would not he open his inner tap to flood the whole of Indana? Why would he not cut the earth to size to cast all the cruel creatures of this world to the netherworld? Despite performing some supernatural acts, he simply suffered the pains as though he was welcoming his doomsday.

O, fooh! I forgot the command of our *Guruji*: The mystic power is meant to save men; not for self. That was the reason why Eysa was tolerating the bodily injuries.

The people's hearts and thoughts differ from person to person. Some are good at times; some are bad at times. Some are good all the time; some are bad all the time. All are not bad all the times; all are not good all the times.

The enormity initially enraptured the enormous crowd; but seeing the enigma's danger, some from the crowd muttered *en rapport* and supported him *en masse*.

The supporters said to their chief, "Please spare him." Their livers melted for they were not under intoxication at that time.

At these words, the chief wavered. It was the first ever *protest* I had heard from the mouths of many men. What a surprise! How fast was the formation of a *union*! What a magic inter-linked the hearts and thoughts of the people instantly! In the by-gone years, I had heard protests from the faunas and floras during the Naming of the Nation ceremony. On that occasion, I had not felt any excitement as I felt now.

The chief commanded, "Well. If he supports lust, we'll leave him".

Eysa said firmly, "No. I don't support lust for battle. I support only love and peace. It's unalterable".

Enraged, the chief ordered, "Come on, continue chastise . . ."

The beating restarted.

During flagellation, Eysa was about to flag.

All of a sudden, there rose a spasm of energy in him—God acted as a resuscitator. Though his gory physical body lost vigor, his spiritual body gained vigor. Thereupon he could keep both his bodies in a steadfast state. Eysa steadied his legs. He stood amidst the crowd like a metal statue. The man who was scourging him lost his vigor and finally drooped. Then some men who favored Eysa scoffed at the scoundrel and towed him shouting ridiculous slogans against their Chieftain.

The Chieftain detailed another strong man to scourge Eysa. He lashed him drastically. After a time his interest in chastisement flagged; he too went down. A third villain came voluntarily; after lashing for some time he too collapsed. All this while the crowd jeered at the villains. All the while Eysa remained there steadily. More and more men favored him. Women lamented. It was the very first moment in their lives that their concrete hearts were moved by compassion. A huge crowd formed on his side.

Eysa said, "Prices soar here for peace because of its scarcity whereas prices are slashed here for violence for its available in plenty!"

"Peace!" the people exclaimed. "What's that? How much we've to pay?"

There was no such word as *peace* in their dialect. They wished to experience a piece of peace from the prince of peace.

"Those who come with me shall be given peace free of cost. We shall go to a place where there is plenty of peace," Eysa said.

By then, more men joined his side.

The Chieftain's face flamed up with anger. He commanded, "Anyone who follows him shall be killed. Those who love their lives stand fast. Let's see how the corpse can walk."

Eysa retorted, "You've no right to strike off any one from the register of life. That power is vested in the console of *time*, controlled by The Almighty."

The multitudes were in a flurry of alarm when they heard the warning of their chief. But some did not bother. Fracas between the followers' side and the rival side occurred. The Chieftain was plotting a war against Eysa—a battle between cold blood and cold heart. Eysa wanted to avoid bloodshed. So he decided to vacate my neighborhood. He walked slowly and steadily towards the riverside. The mob—his followers—followed him in god stead. On the way the scoundrels who scourged him joined the exodus. Leaving the promiscuous crowd behind, the prominent crowd, like a mob, moved like a promenade.

*   *   *

The martyr and the masses marooned—nested amidst lush flora and the bewitching backwaters. There they could reveal the breathtaking view of the maroon sky-roof and a marshland floor. A perfect living place where all the elements of nature were accumulated for any settler might marvel—pure air, pure water and pure land plus pure-minded people. There was no masquerade or masochism. Instead of a masochist to command them, there was a mascot to control them. People marveled at the marvelous mind of Eysa. He introduced innovative morality. It was a practical method to rear the marshland worthy of cultivation and cattle-rearing as a nature's receptacle.

He added science to mysticism. Natural + unnatural = supernatural. He advised the people to dig many narrow channels to collect all the accumulated water into a pond. Lion's portion of the marshy area was reclaimed. A part of the place was reserved and prepared for residential area. Some wet land was reserved for grazing the domestic animals and cattle. They cleared the woods and planted fruit-bearing trees. Despite taking respite, they responded to the obligation and suffering of their expedition.

Eysa, the martyr, advised, "Explore this piece of land. We must exploit its natural resources for the good of each one of us."

Seeing the exploits of Eysa, the people were exulting as they labored on the land, shoulder to shoulder in exuberant spirit. Thereafter, Eysa, the saint, sanctified the land and it became the sanctuary of refugees. Those who were fed up of sanguinary life quit my neighborhood and took sanctuary there. The refugees regarded the newfound land as a sanatorium for the treatment of masochism and Eysa as their Samaritan. Some sect considered the sector not merely as a sanctuary but as a sanctum sanctorum and Eysa as their saint. The place turned an on-the-way shelter to the successors of my forefathers, the migrating *Deserian* ducks. Since so many years, they never surfaced on the river lest they should be shot for food. Now they again floated on the sanguine pond water and sang melodies in sang-froid. The birds were surprised to see plants with exuberant foliage and people with courage.

The people constructed a wooden palatial building for their reformer. But he stayed in a shed made out of creepers. That place was an abode of peace. They made a soft straw bed. But refusing the pallet, he slept on a plank. They manufactured a palanquin for his transportation. He preferred to travel by foot. They made a moccasin for him. He used wooden sandals that he himself made. They prepared palatable and delectable varieties of non-vegetarian dishes. But he refused the palate and ate fruits and drank river water. He advised the people to stick to strict vegetarianism.

Eysa taught the people the science of development and nature as well as the laws of human life. They learned to live a friendly and sociable life in an organized community. The forming of society eradicated the cantankerousness and brought rays of culture to the people. The cultural life in turn helped them construct a civilization. It was the first social, economic and cultural life in my habitat. I was amazed, in fact happy, to see such a human race in my neighboring area. The people who had not had any name and address once, had by now.

The marooned men were on a new thoroughfare of history. They altered their barbarous routes of past life to an enlightened present continuous life of Eysa's socialism. In the erstwhile history of Indana, there was no evidence of the use of clothing. The fine cottons grown in the forest was as soft and white as snow. The main wear of the women was *sari*—six to eight yards in length and two to three yards in width. Half the portion of the sari was wrapped around the waist; the other half was used to cover the upper body by tucking the tip into the waistband. Wearing a sari was comfortable and the woman looked graceful in that.

The men usually wore two-piece garments. The elaborate dress, the *dhoti* was the lower garment and the other piece was the shawl for covering the shoulders. All those costumes were easy to wear and comfortable for doing any kind of job—suitable to perform the duties of a preacher or a peasant. The innovative costumes were quite a fascinating sight for me for I had only seen the old-fashioned animal skin and feather decorations worn by the wild inhabitants in my habitat.

He taught them a lingua franca—*Indi*—which was easily digestible to the populace. He further detailed some intellectuals to teach the language to the common people.

Eysa further divided the society into five categories as per the choice of profession that required for moving the cycle of society. The division was on volunteer basis. Anyone could join any category to select a profession, suiting to the natural abilities, tendencies, attitudes and dispositions. No compromise was allowed to the chooser—his performance in that particular category should be perfect. The categories were: The *Jyothyshies* (teaching class), the *Toojaries* (divine class) the *Rajashrees* (ruling class), the *Vyaparis* (business class) and the *Savas* (working class).

Before the selection, Eysa elaborately explained the duties and rights of each category to the people. He said: "Those persons in whom truth and light are predominant shall be selected as *Jyothyshies* and they would be the teaching order of the society. The first and foremost duty of a *Jyothishy* is to study the lessons of spiritual, intellectual and cultural knowledge. Then he will spread the light of his knowledge to the society. His rights are converted and regulated as his responsibilities of teaching others without any remuneration. He has to render a selfless service to the society for uplifting the moral values. And above all, he has to relinquish comforts of life—*artha* and *kama*—to a certain extent. The status of the *Jyothyshies* in society shall stand atop the flag pole of prestige. As a teacher he is equivalent to *guru,* a *guru* is equivalent to God, a *Jyothishy* is to be revered if not corresponding to a god, not less than a godhead. They would hold the highest ranks in the society; they would be regarded as the upper class or the most learned class. All the other classes in the society should respect them. Irrespective of the seniority and superiority, none would challenge a *Jyothishy* even if he is weak and weary."

The next category was *Toojari.* He shall perform the rites as a priest and practice austerities or *tapas.* His main means of livelihood would be preaching and priesthood. He's allowed to take alms or *Dana.* He should always lead a life of serenity, purity and austerity. The significant features of a *Toojari* were good nature, forgiveness, kindness, wisdom, pure heart, charity and devotion to God. "In lieu of his duties, he shall not enjoy any rights pertaining to the worldly life. They were considered as the mediators between God and man.

Everyone was seeking admission to the *Jyothishy* and *Toojari* class as everyone wanted to become the status symbol. It was not possible to enroll the overwhelming volunteers in the teaching order. So, they were put to an aptitude test. Only a few could pass. Eysa conducted only a test-dose of the training he had had in the alma mater.

An instantaneous spark of the reminiscence of the by-gone days in the *gurukulam* resurfaced in my mind like a lightning—getting up many a morning, performing the yogic exercises many a time, learning many a hymns, chanting it a great many times, famishing for many days by fasting, relinquishing a good many facilities of earthly life, observing self-penance for many days.

The many-sidedness and engagement of the mind for many hours continuously in such activities made many-headed beast to fall out from the teaching order in the enrolment stage itself. The very few selected in the preliminary test were transferred to the hill top and given special training in serenity, self-control, uprightness, forbearance, knowledge, insight and devotion. In addition to the above, they studied *mantras, tantras,* and other rituals pertaining to prayers and *poojas* in *demple* or temple style. Though female candidates were also selected in the *Jyothishy* and *Toojari* class, they were forbidden to perform *poojas* in the *demple* for they could not maintain cleanliness always for their bodies would remain *unclean* during the menstrual period. However, they were allowed to become the fellow pilgrims on the path of knowledge as *Yoginis* or *Sanyasinis.*

Thus, lacking the stringent qualifications and qualities and fearing the hardships of the *Jyothishy* and *Toojari* class, many tried to choose the next category, the *Rajashree* class.

Eysa proclaimed: "Those who have the predominant characteristics of action-packed, thrilling and adventurous life would be chosen for the *Rajashree* or the ruling cum defense class. They should have strength, vigor and vitality. They shall show courage, bravery and alertness. A *Rajashree* is the custodian of the society and the defender of the state— one who struggles for the freedom and peace of his people and the land from filibusters. He shall fight bravely and be ready to spare his life for keeping up honesty and justice sans shedding blood. He will be given rigorous training in martial arts without any type of arms—physical combat with strength of hands and legs—with strict instruction to adhere to *ahimsa.* Killing of a living thing is strictly prohibited. With that sort of an art, a *Rajashree* could easily grab the weapons from the hands of his foe skillfully. The most valiant, vigorous, firm, generous, just, forgiving, merciful and majestic hero among the *Rajashree* will be selected or crowned as the King of the land. He should love his subjects as his own blood and flesh—if they are hurt, he's hurt, if they starve, he's starved. He may indulge in a jovial life giving due weightage to the happiness of his subjects."

The selection of *Rajashrees* was like that of the *Jyothyshies*. A lot of people wished to become the king, or his minister or a courtier or an adherent or just a sepoy in the royal class. But most of the candidates failed in the personality and physical tests. And the cadets recruited did not dare to complete the training. They lacked some quality or the other to become a perfect *Rajashree*. If one was bold, he was not polite. If the other was strong, he was a coward. So, very few were selected to the ruling-cum-defense class. They were to shoulder the responsibility of ruling the country and defending its territories from alien attackers with non-violence. However, the peace-keeping force was given training in *Kaiamkali*—a martial art of self-protection with bare-hands. The main armaments were the god-given hands, legs and head. Even a poke with the pointing finger would have the effect of piercing with a poniard. A kick with the leg will have the effect of beating with a rifle butt. A slap had the effect of a sword-thrust. A thrust of the head had the effect of a cannon-ball hit. A *Rajashree* would do such kind of action-packed performances during emergencies that would damage the properties and persons of their country not with the intention of giving sufferings to the enemy but to make the enemy surrender.

The rush for recruitment waned when the aspirants were brought to bear the physical tests like cross-country race, mud-walk, day-long trek in torrential rains without food, mountaineering in torrid climate, jumping, swimming against the current, obstacle-crossing, wrestling, etc. The torments made the weak and weary fallout from the *Rajashree* class. They were dismissed from service with disgrace before passing out the course.

Women were not permitted to join the course. However, the female relatives of the men recruits were allowed to join the royal class and right to rule the country was admissible provided they mirrored all the abilities and qualities of a ruler, inherited from their royal father, royal husband or royal brother. If the country needed an immediate king, his mother or wife or sister or daughter would become his reliever as queen.

Those who had fallen out rushed to join the agricultural-cum-mercantile class called the *Vyaparis*. Skill in oration and cunningness plus intelligence made a *Vyaparis*. The torrent of words, expression and images were the secrets of his success. Otherwise, his business would fail. He must make use of his creative ideas of publicity, politeness and sense of humor to attract customers.

Eysa declared: "As a *Rajashree* has to command the country, a *Vypari* has to control the economy of the country. He should be perfect in arithmetic and a master of economics. His main profession shall be agriculture, cattle-tending and trade. It is his responsibility to settle the production, distribution and disbursement of the wealth properly. He is the in-charge of *artha* or money matters. A good *Vypari*, who is firm on the principle of *dharma* or righteousness and seeking *moksha* or salvation, shall use the wealth for the prosperity and general happiness of the society. He should never take any undue advantage by misusing the wealth for his personal pleasures. In a nutshell, he is the kingpin of the wheel of economy. If the pin is incorrect, the movement of the community stops.

"This profession did not need any physical exertion. So all the weary, weak and the lethargic people rushed to become *Vyaparis* thinking they could enjoy *soubhagya* or material happiness. But most of them were dull in calculating even their age. They did not know how many ears, nose, eyes or fingers they themselves had. Some said they had one eye and two heads; some said they had two noses and one ear. Some thought they were walking on their hands and working with their legs. Some were not aware that they owned a heart.

Sensing the danger in investing the responsibility of the economy with a pack of fools, Eysa segregated the ignorant and the idiots from the group. Otherwise it would be like giving a floral bouquet to a monkey.

Cunning with a make-up of politeness was an essential factor for the survival of the business class. Their profession was such that they did not have to wet their hands for catching fish. In other words, they were the brokers. They used their intelligence to win the hearts of the buyers. They could earn enormous wealth through corruption if they wanted. But it was against *dharma* and *karma*.

Eysa's dictum was: "The real enjoyment of life of a *Vypari* is in the business he does for the profit of the community without any regard for his own fortune—maximum profit to the customers and minimum profit to oneself."

The bullish as well as the dull were enrolled in the last category of *Savas*. Theirs was the menial occupation since they were the labor class. They did not need much intelligence. They never shouldered any responsibility. They were free birds: Nothing to bother. Just eat, work and sleep. They could spend their spare time indulging in *kama* and virility. The traders used to take their yield and they got essential commodities in exchange. They did not bother about any profit or loss. They just wanted to live because they were born.

Eysa said, "In short, the *Jyothyshies* acquire their status by knowledge; the *Rajashrees* by their martial capacities; the *Vyaparis* by wealth and the *Savas* by their labor. It doesn't mean that the *Sava* class is less significant than the others and as such they are to be given equal honor. I insist that the degree of dignity shall not vary from *Jyothyshies* to *Savas*. Each category has got its own significance—without one, the other can't survive. Let anyone render any service, a labor is a labor and dignity of labor shall be maintained."

He further explained that all the classes were parts of a body in which the head was the *Jyothishy*, thorax the *Rajashree*, *Vypari* the abdomen and

Sava the legs. If any limb was weak the whole body suffers. So the feet or *Sava* was as essential as the head or *Jyothishy.*

Thus, Eysa devised a social system engaging the various type of human strength, vigor and vitality and channelized them as per talent to each individual streaming all the social force towards one target: The development of a stable and progressive society.

Eysa thus transformed Indana into a rich and diversified garden of society where he sowed the seeds of cultivation and civilization. The people of Indana enriched the cultivation. They enjoyed the sweet life giving sweet fruits of fundamental values such as truth, non-violence, universal love and hospitality. They also enjoyed the scent of integrated knowledge and spiritual wisdom. The hearts throbbed with the dynamism of peace.

*   *   *

The Chieftain of Old Indana came to know of the tidings of New Indana. He could not digest, rather tolerate, the progress and prosperity of the people who deserted his land. His land remained a fool's paradise of priapism and superstitions. Eysa and his people were proud of their land; the Chieftain and his people were jealous of the others' success. There was a torrid tussle growing because of the neighbor's pride and the owner's envy. The Chieftain planned a war gathering all the men and collecting all the tools and implements to annihilate New Indana. He announced stoppage of all works like agriculture and construction and ordered compulsory military training. He named the professional users of specific instruments such as Ur Picket, Ur Poker, Ur Poniard, Ur Sickle, Ur Knife, Ur Sword, etc. Ur was the abbreviation used for *User* as a title prefixed to name of man or woman with skill to use that particular tool. For the first time in my habitat men were named. Prior to that they were denoted with sounds like, ai, uu, hoo, foo, and the like.

The Chieftain prepared all the available horses, donkeys and auxiliary forces to convey provisions. Declaring no war, Chieftain, with his infantry and cavalry, proceeded to New Indana. His plan was to attack them while they were asleep. And it was the first and foremost battle strategy that I had ever witnessed.

The Chieftain declared: "You've the practice of flooding our barley field with water. Make use of that procedure for shedding enemies' blood in the battle field. You've practice of reaping the crops. You must use that skill to reap the enemies' heads."

His intention was to add New Indana to his territory, to loot the fortunes of that land and to take revenge on Eysa, his rival. He ordered all the people, including the disabled, to join the force. Even the lame, deaf, dumb, blind and sick were made to move by force. From Old Indana, the attacking force led by the filibuster marched all day long and reached New Indana at midnight.

I was ablaze with anxiety. I wanted to inform the people or at least a plant of New Indana about the imminent attack. I tried to send a message through a heavy wind that passed by. But it did not bother. Then I asked some low-moving clouds to warn the people of New Indana. They too did not listen to me. After that I requested each perching bird to render a courier service by flashing the message of emergency. The ungrateful birds neglected me as if telling that it was their time to roost. I felt very bad; in fact very sad. Every day they came to me to roost as though my body was their home. I too treated them as my dearest friends. Very often I served them with my berries. They not only spent all the nights comfortably on my roost but also used it as comfort stations. But what was the use of a friend who did not listen to me in need? I did not want them to rule the roost. Therefore I quivered so roughly that all the roosting birds took flight from my roost in search of other roost. The neighboring trees refused them shelter and chased them away without giving the roost as a punishment for disobeying my order.

At last I begged the bats to do something to save the people of the neighboring state. I felt like they saying curtly, "Why do you ask for our help, that too to help human beings? They always blame us and cast us out saying that we're the representatives of the devils and vampires. Yes, we admit that we're interested in bloodshed and blood-sucking. Let's enjoy this rare chance. We're on our way to that God-fearing land to see the bloodshed."

The cruel reply of the cruel creatures broke the boundary of my patience. What could I do? I wept, dropping many of my berries and shedding many leaves.

The attack at night was totally unexpected! The New Indans could not prepare and defend themselves in short notice.

No sooner did the animals of Old Indana step on the land of New Indana than they began to breathe the air of civilization. They could even see civilized bears there! Most of the beasts that were supposed to be carnivorous were strict vegetarians due to adoption of *ahimsa*. They liked and appreciated the distinct culture of that country. They marveled at the behavior of the animals of that country. They greeted them as their guests! They allowed the enemy animals to have a nice bath in their best bathing pools get rid of the fatigue after the long journey. They gave sumptuous vegetables to the enemy beasts to eat.

The beasts discussed among themselves and took a decision. They should bear in mind that they were from the animal class and were opponents by no means. They should not interfere in the quarrel between men the reason for which was known only to them. It was the men's caprice, not theirs. Instead of bearing arms in the war, they should bear up the good *karma* and extend a helping hand to *dharma*.

Yes, I appreciated and applauded their decision for it was appropriate.

But the men? Owff . . . The men remained uncivilized beasts. Though they were two-legged they were four-fold worse than the four-legged animals. I wondered how a man could be called a social being. He was undoubtedly un-social. But, sometimes, some men are undoubtedly more than social. Expecting that exception only is considered the man as a social being.

So the strike during the silent hours was like a thunder shower on a summer night! At first, the cattle of that country smelled a rat about the approach of the storming cavalry. They heard the horses' neigh and the cry of the mules. Actually the animals from Old Indana did not wish to be involved in the combat. They were compelled to do so. They were favoring New Indana with their hearts because they knew it was an unjust conflict. There was no reason at all! An attack from a cultureless team on a cultured group. The brainless animals realized it. And the animals lamented; whereas the brainy social animals, the so-called men, did not apprehend it. They applauded the approbation.

The attacking force of the Chieftain obeyed his orders word by word. All of them straightaway rushed into the dwellings and started their "Operation Reap and Rape" beheading all the male members and raping all the female members regardless of whether they were young, old or disabled. During the whipping and whirling of the war, other whimsical and wicked acts were also worthwhile—some men raped women; some women also raped men. Chieftain's war tactics was "might is right". But Eysa's people did not have any tactics. They believed in the axiom "Almighty is right".

The Old Indans cultivated violence very rigorously. They set fire on all the hutments and other constructions. Out of the countless cruel perils of the war, I would like to quote one of the most unkind deeds—a very old and ugly looking lame man from Old Indana crept over a sweet and soft *Jyothishy* girl of sixteen, disrobed her pointing a poniard and did a priapic and unnatural act on her. He compelled her to work hard in order to get his long, limp organ erect. It took an hour for him to get an erection. He took yet another hour or so to reach orgasm, that too without ejaculation as there was no semen left in him to secrete. The persistent goring with the muscular horn of that social animal into the anus, vagina, ears and mouth of the girl made wounds in all the above-mentioned parts. She fell lifeless. A priapic fight between the hard and the soft in which the soft was vanquished totally.

Another cruel sight, even from far away my eyes could not bear was: A voluptuous beauty was breast-feeding her crying baby busily in the hustle and bustle of the havoc. A rough and tough man who was very thirsty after the day-long foodless journey snatched the baby and threw away. He then sucked all her milk. His sucking was so fierce that when the milk got dried up blood streamed out of her breasts. And his thirst was so severe that he continued sucking till she turned white without blood!

I am describing another event here just to show the perils of war: The new-born baby thrown away by the ruffian had fallen in front of a savage and hungry woman. She snatched the baby like a bird pecking at its prey. She simmered the baby alive in the fire of an arson. She ate the burnt flesh so fastidiously as though it was the most delicious nourishment she had ever had in her life, blemishing feminine gentleness.

I thought deeply: It would have been better if she could have cut both her bosoms, boiled and had them if she were in such a famishing state. When The Almighty had made the first, foremost and the finest creature—woman—of the whole universe, he would never have thought that this noble and modest creature could ever do this kind of notorious and noxious act that could humiliate his creativity. While naming that creature as *woman,* he might have thought that she would be simple and splendid. God had studied thoroughly the science of semantics; selected the very best word and called the adult human female, *woman.* It was because he had confidence in her to show all the best qualities like self-mortification, self-renunciation and even self-sacrifice and not the worst qualities of self-importance, self-indulgence and self-feeding. That was why God provided woman with womb for conceiving and bosom for nourishing a child till birth. After the birth of the child an invisible and spiritual oracle has been provided to her as a mother to love, care and consort her child till death. But this woman! My goodness! Though I'm a tree, as the senior-most member of Indana, I have seen many wishy-washy womenfolk; but I have never seen such a harsh harpy. She had tarnished the wombs of all the women in the world and treated all the children as tumors. She had the semblance of an angel and the heart of a devil.

Now let me describe the steps taken by Eysa's group, the New Indans. There were no precautionary measures. For they never had any intention of extending and expanding their territory. They had excitation in exhilaration and exhortation of non-violence—*ahimsa*. Their principle was "Let peace prevail." They had only an armless force for self-defense, maintained by the ruling class, the *Rajashrees*. They tried to play their role at the level best to defeat the enemy with *Kaiamkali*. It was an extempore defense. So it did not succeed as they had expected. They had the tactics of tackling the enemy with *marmaany*, a process of taming any attacker with the thrust of a finger at a vital joint or part without wounding. But it was practical only dealing *mano a mano* fights. When one *Rajashree* was engaging an enemy, another enemy came from behind and beheaded him.

Besides this, another reason for their downfall was that the people belonged to the *Jyothishy* class was purely adherent to *ahimsa* and was never of the attacking type. They prayed to God to save the country and the people by performing *pooja* and *homa*. I could witness some more humanitarian and less humorous scenes when a giant-sized enemy came to behead a *Toojari*, instead of throwing the burning wood at him or at least running away, he gave him a pot of sweetened milk and ripe plantains and offered his head to be cut by bowing before the enemy humbly. Seeing his decorous treatment the enemy giant's liver melted. He put down his arm-held arm and hugged the *Toojari*.

Another incident I beheld was: A troop of non-swimmers from the enemy's side fell down in the pond by chance. Some people from the *Sava* class threw a rope at them and pulled them out to safety. *Savas* were illiterate but robust. They were innocent, not indecent. They were sturdy, not stylish. They were hard-working, not hurting. They were constructive, not destructive.

After all, man is not made out of metal. He—a friend or a foe—has blood and flesh. He has a mind hidden in his cage of brain. That makes his heart feel, liver melt and blood boil. That causes him to recognize his consort, differentiate between good and bad, exchange love for love, transact help for help and activities like that. The same thing happened in New Indana during the conflict.

It was a war between *himsa* and *ahimsa* or a tug-of-war between violence and non-violence. Initially, the winning-mark had an inclination towards the side of *himsa*. The attacking team won as the death toll on the battle-ground of Indana's worst-ever clash rose unaccountably with countless panic-stricken individuals on the side of the attacked abandoning their dwellings and fleeing their village.

But slowly and steadily, the winning mark started moving towards the side of *ahimsa*. A wonderful phenomenon brought about by the power of love. And finally, the team of *himsa* collapsed. The affectionate effect of the New Indans' behavior forced the Old Indans to accept whatever happened as inevitable. Foes turned friends. For the first time, the people of Old Indana experienced the sweet taste of love. Till then they knew only the bitterness of hatred.

The Chieftain and some of his soldiers deployed to deport or destroy Eysa could not succeed in identifying him in the hustle and bustle of the crowd. When the Chieftain advanced right into the struggle, he saw the sheer nonsense of his combatants' attitude towards the enemy side. Apprehending the dangerous situation of surrendering his full fighting force including the fauna before the love and affection of his rivals, he proposed a treaty.

He proclaimed: "I do not wish to shed the blood of either the Old or the New Indans. I just want Eysa, the so-called saint. He's not the property of Old Indana or New Indana. He belongs to both the states. As both the parties have equal right on him, he shall be bifurcated. I appeal to the people of New Indana to give the people of Old Indana either his head or his body. We want a portion as *spolia opima*. It's up to you to choose the part you want—head or body. My people would regard his organ as the richest booty. There would be bloodshed if my demand is refused. It is better to agree with me before my request turns into a command."

Some of the stalwarts from the Chieftain's own side who were now very much attracted towards the humble activities of the people of New Indana declared openly: "If that's the choice of the chief, we'll make a treaty of exchange—an exchange of the body above the neck for a body above the neck or an exchange of a body below the neck for a body below the neck."

The Chieftain said in anxiety, "Sounds OK! But exchange with whose head or body?"

The antagonists flatly announced, "We mean with your head or your body."

The Chieftain stunned as if hearing a court-martial verdict against him for the charge of treason.

The monition from the mob made the Chieftain monstrous. He suffered from monomania. The conciliation dialogues had reached a deadlock. How to unlock it? He pondered for a point. Yes, he found a way. Yet another mobilization was the only solution to get out of the mob-law for he had never faced any mobocracy against him that far. For the first time in the whole of his monopoly life, he felt fear. He trembled in the wind of horror like a solitary dry leaf on a branch while all the other fresh leaves on all the other branches of that very big tree were waving good-bye when he was about to fall off the tree of his world.

Somehow he gathered the guts and said, "Kill them."

All the fingers are not equal. So is the case of man. Though man has mind, heart, liver and blood, sometimes his mind will not think, heart will not beat, liver will not work and his blood will not run. He turns as hard as a rock without life in his body. Such men—the staunch supporters of the Chieftain—again took up arms and jumped on the multitude. Again hurly-burly broke out and chasing out the prevailing peace, violence reigned there sowing perils of *himsa*. Everywhere, there were flesh-cutting, blood-shedding, wailing, stampede and many other sob-stuffs.

Then there appeared Eysa, the Nob of *ahimsa* amidst the mob like a nova. In that blood-flowing battlefield, where a fluid situation prevailed, he had a significant role to play.

Eysa said, "Unlike in the natural calamities caused by God, our land is facing an unprecedented calamity caused by man. It is quite unnatural. The artificial cataclysm caused the fall of men and material. The cause of this is nothing but the envy on the crest of the wave of this land. The continuance of severe devastation is acute causing grave damage to innocent lives and property. Besides, this is a serious detriment to fauna; loss of crops and cattle. It's inhuman to get fascinated by fatality. Life is dignified. But, we men destroy it by denouncing and denigrating God."

The multitude was moved by his oration. He continued, "I deeply deplore the sheer magnitude of the situation. I know that all the creatures of this land are crestfallen due to the denial of the deontology."

I could see people crushing their fingers and gnawing their teeth with impatience. To cool them down, Eysa again said, "I appeal to all my fellowmen to adopt *ahimsa* and it should be gratefully practiced around the orb in order to deodorize the wicked and shameful deeds of *himsa*. Apart from this, I request you for demobilization. If I'm the demagogue and if the demolishers want to demit me I'll depart voluntarily for the denouement of this combustion of conflict.

There was *vox populi*: "Sage, it's not you; the culprit is the Chieftain. He is the force behind this massacre. So, he should be punished for wrong-doing."

Eysa said, "A sinner should not hope to escape from the nemesis."

The Chieftain tried to speculate, "As chief, I believe that disobeying my orders is the real sin. You say that murder is sin. If that's true, I only said that these people only committed sin by killing."

His vindication violated his own reputation. The violent mass turned vindictive. They vilified, "You, villain, you only persuaded us to sin. From now on, you're not our *persona grata*."

Eysa interfered and explained, "Motley people are more sinned against than sinning. You, as their Nob, should have turned the mob away from sinning."

The Chieftain shouted, "I don't care for sinners."

Eysa said politely, "Actually, there's no one known as a *sinner*. If at all there is, he's not your enemy. He should be taken care of for he has committed sin for your sake. You can easily cure him."

Someone from the gathering eagerly enquired, "We're sinners for we've worked as per his words. How we could be cured? We wish to sheer off our present life. Please spare some sense, seer."

Eysa replied, "To cure the human being, two great visions are necessary: Medicine and Meditation. If you practice it in spite of sinning, you would be singing oratorio."

Eysa's instruction inspired the gathering. They, as one man cried out, "Yes, We'll do that. We'll do that, if someone teaches us. We'll definitely do that."

Eysa's oration created oppugnancy against the Chieftain. His own kinsfolk became his opponents. They performed an orchestration with the tools they held as ordnance. He felt bitter contemplation of Eysa's success. The slip between the cup and the lip made him mad and confined to his objectives. He did not wish to vanquish.

He said vehemently, "You rascal, you're not a seer, you're a sinner. I won't spare you."

Like a monolithic person, he raised his weapon—a long spear—and sprang foreword to pierce the chest of Eysa. But smelling a rat about his monstrosity, the mob besieged him and protected Eysa.

There rose a monotone from the mob, "Kill him. Don't let him live any more for he's an insidious enemy of the entire people. He's the worst element in our society."

But Eysa's protest protected him. Eysa consoled the crowd, "*Om Shanthi . . . Shanthi . . . Shanthi . . .* Don't be destructive. His death has been adjourned *sine die* by the God. So, please free him."

Thus, the ferocious fellows freed the fiend. Broken down, he, then and there, retreated from the scene and rapidly fled to the forest along with the remnants of his rigid rioters.

Eysa continued, "I understand, there's a statement. Let me give you a key of suggestion to open the deadlock in order to partake in the ambition of your Chieftain. Instead of parting my body into two parts and keeping the parts of my body by both the parties in this part of the world, why can't you concur with my views?"

Again there was a monotone from the masses, "Go ahead, you sage. We're ready to concur with whatever you suggest."

Eysa, their *persona grata*, had condescended to seek the consent from the common people. He firmly asked them, "You *promise . . . ?*"

"*Sans doute*", they said unanimously. "Doubtlessly, we agree."

Eysa said with determination, "Once again I request you that you should not swerve from the consensus for I give due weight to the common agreement."

"We're ready to face any consequence of any of your suggestion even if it's foolish. You say, shall we die *en masse*? There would be self-annihilation. For we're certain that each breath of yours is for the common good of this country."

"Well. Then I'm going to depart from this world," Eysa said enthusiastically.

His exaltation did not enthrall the public. They stood awe-struck.

They pleaded, "No sage, no . . . Please belie the last regarding your departure. You shall not abandon us. If you do it, we too will depart along with you. We didn't mourn for the other departed in the agitation though they were our dear and near ones. Unlike their demise, we can't tolerate your demise."

"All fatalistic fate! God had already struck off the names of the martyrs from the register of death. Now he has taken his pen—I can see—and opened my page and is now counting down my doomsday. Unless otherwise he counts down someone's doomsday, nobody can depart from this world—without his will—even if he's thrown in the open sea, buried in the mud or pushed into a pyre. Fate is decided by God. We're just clients. Now, as he has ordained that I shall die, I must die. It's my turn. I can't evade that. I can already hear his call clearly."

Eysa closed his eyes and raised both his arms, palms facing his face. He stood still and stiff for sometime chanting some *mantras*. Motley people favoring both *ahimsa* and *himsa* stared at his posture. His body became electrified due to the spiritual exercise—*Rajayoga*. A radiation was generated. Suddenly he opened his eyes. Two beams of light emitted from his eyes! They had radioactive effect. The rays inflamed his palms. The flame spread from his hands, engulfed his entire body, belching more and more fluorescence from his body. He remained there like a firestone.

Some people again tried untiringly to extinguish the fire on his body by pouring water on him. But it only intensified the fire, transforming the water into an inflammable liquid. Witnessing that terrific scene of the inferno, the people wailed as if their own bodies were blazing while Eysa remained tranquil. In spite of crying, he chanted: O! God! I'm departing . . . departing . . . departing my part and parcel—my people and my place for ever . . . Let peace . . . peace . . . peace prevail (*Om shanty . . . shanty . . . shanty . . .*)

CENTURY 15

1401 TO 1500 AD

While it was the beginning moments of my life of the fifteenth century, it was the last moments of Eysa's life of a quarter to one millennium. Prodigious people prayed for the prodigy.

I too was bleeping for my best and blest friend, Eysa. The blaze on him was nothing less than an arson that blistered my entire body. What could I do? I knew the fate of my friend was bleak—God's will. I could only blare out a sad song of agony inside me.

While Eysa's blaze of glory, the air in the atmosphere transmitted that awful news to all the areas where air was available and unavailable. Hearing the news, eagles came from the east, vultures came from the west, savage kites came from the south, nightingales came from the north and above all a *Garuda* (Haliastur) came down from the heavens. All the winged beings on earth respected the noble bird as their Nob. They had seen the *Garuda* in hallucination only. When asked by the nightingales—news reporters from the press trust of the birds—*Garuda* said that seeing the nimbus and feeling the magnitude of the monk, Vishma, the preserver of the earth sent him to investigate the havoc. Eventually, the bird took Eysa on its back. Fanning its wings it soared. The people stared at the wonderful bird. As the bird and Eysa disappeared, their minds were pregnant with a question of suspense—after Eysa, who? The same question was hammering in the same way in my mind also.

After the miscreants, especially the Chieftain, left the land, the masses enjoyed a good time for they had Eysa as their principal to teach the principles of life. The Chieftain had done much mischief to the country. He was none but a rodent that gnawed the liver of the people. Anyway the rogues were rightly punished for their misdeeds. Nevertheless, after the close shave the Chieftain had, their seer swerved swiftly to some other world of God's choice, leaving them in a stalemate. There was no alternative. As his spirit was gone, he had to part with the purse of his body.

They could not bear the heat of the rays of their memory of his demise. There were umpteen arguments, protests and much mourning from the motley masses.

Some requested, "Don't leave us, sage."

Some pleaded, "Please don't make us orphans."

Some said, "You're our blood."

Some said, "You're our flesh."

Some said, "You're our breath."

Eysa said easily yet with an ebullience, "Yes, dear ones, yes. It's something pertaining to my breath i.e., someone's going to stop my breath."

The huge and heterogeneous crowd cried uneasily and in excitement: "Who's that culprit other than the absconding Chieftain who wants to stop the breath of a celestial and celibate person like you?"

The essence of *vox populi* was: He was their patron who polished their patina-painted hearts. They had pawned their hearts to him; He gave them an amount of pax in return. His position was still vacant because of the paucity of a prodigy.

"Hush, dear, hush," Eysa said. "If you censure him, you may turn to stone. Only blithering fools can blaspheme him. He's not censorious."

"But, don't we have the liberty to know that celebrity? Please, for God's sake, let's know who that person is having the right to judge you!"

"All of you know him very well. You just now uttered his name. It's God . . . Yes, He is the . . ."

The people's hearts turned calm on hearing the will of God, their minds were in confusion. Someone even thought that God was so cruel to cease the breath of their censor. Yes, *sans doute,* Eysa was their judge to quell what was immoral, seditious and inopportune. He was the censer placed in the centre of each one's heart from where perfume with incense burned to evacuate centuple of centipedes of malignity. His epilogue was an eclogue with éclat. Nevertheless his relics were elsewhere, they decided to erect a cenotaph of Eysa the late casuist.

Each one enshrined Eysa in his heart. That much enthrallment he had. But what to do? After the birth, there is only one unavoidable and unforgettable truth—yet we try to avoid and forget it. It is death. No one can escape it.

Still people ran pell-mell to fetch water, mud, sand and other such materials to put out the fire, in vain. It was his inner body that was burning rather than his physical body. Therefore it was a formidable task. Some fire-fighters sprang forward and embraced him *en masse* to smother the air that fanned the arson. He blew them off prior to palpability. They fell very far from the fire with palpitating hearts.

Even now it still rises in my mind—the echo of Eysa's epilogue: "Moreover, I'm the oldest human being living on this earth. There's a consort, who is very much senior to me—the Banyan. Then the people from both the Old and New Indana started respecting rather worshipping me jointly. I could not enjoy the dendrolatry for I was immersed deep in the ocean of agony over the demise of my close mate, Eysa.

One's mind begins to be a burette filled with abnormal grief when some close fellow is closed down. Initially, the level of the liquefied lamentation never comes out even if someone opens the stopcock. However, as the days pass by, the level of grief gradually comes down even if the cock remains closed. And in due course, the dismay would be refilled with normal delight. My case was different—my grief solidified like granite, its mass and weight remaining intact—no power could liquefy and drain it. For unlike my other two close classmates—Hova and B'lla—Eysa was closer to me all those days.

He obtained more power of our *Guruji* by self-mortification than the other two. He was a depository from where one could draw anything at anytime for survival. He lived a century longer than B'lla and two centuries than Hova. He administered all the principles of *Guruji*, especially total *ahimsa*. He was firm about vegetarianism. He never promoted meat-eating. He never encouraged the hurting of even the harmful insects, thinking that they too had the feeling of grief and pain just like human beings.

I admire him many degrees higher than Hova and B'lla. If I were an adjudicator to award them, the first rank would go to Eysa. Apart from the above-mentioned extra-special flexible qualities of Eysa, I could chart out the common qualities mentioned below—as sons of God against sons of Satan—of all the three disciples of my *Guruji,* giving due weight to the reports submitted by my dove-of-thought, I hereby declare those in the form of nouns, adjectives and adverbs.

Sons of God	Sons of Satan
True	False
Paragon of kindness	Dragon of cruelty
Corroborative	Corrosive
Preaching	Philippic
Prince of peace	Prince of world
Serene-looking	Sensual-looking
Penance	Primrose
Cardinal	Carnal
Ahimsa	*Himsa*
Spiritual master	Spiteful master
Tardy yet permanent protector	Temporary yet fast protector
Cares waifs and strays	Steeping people in superstition
Sacred heart in simple clothing	Filthy heart in festive clothing
Virtue and virtuosos	Virulent and villain
Imploring	Imposing
Important	Impious

Consequently, all my contemporaries—first *Guruji*, followed by Hova, B'lla and Eysa—suffered contempt some way or the other, by someone or the other, for something or the other—and eventually attained *Samadhi*. And I must think of all the fauna that also passed away during the passage of time. Notwithstanding, some members of my family (flora) are still living here and there in the forest. And ultimately I kept on living beholding the present and yet to behold the future of my habitat renamed as United Indana.

Now, the saga of the old and new states has begun to be the past pages of the by-gone history of Indana.

Yes, the lands of Old and New Indana were united by the people of Old and New Indana. Hence, the united people arrayed on one floor—United Indana. They enjoyed the sweetness of truth, non-violence, universal love and hospitality. They were enlightened by the teachings of Eysa, they praised him as godhead. But I firmly believed him not as a deity but as a great philosopher, teacher and a reformer. Despite his being a spiritual master, for the smooth moving of the wheel of the society, he did not ignore the desire to earn material good without which there would not be any social welfare measures. He advised them not to deviate from the course of prosperity—financial and worldly status as shelters, adequate sustenance such as cattle, food and progeny. Besides travelling along the spiritual path, one should travel on the parallel line of material path maintaining same pace to acquire earthly fortune also. One should work hard to search, gather, produce, conserve, consume and organize all his worldly pleasures. Then only one can be a clean drop in the ocean of society. A single individual cannot shoulder the weight of this heterogeneous and complex labor. That is why Eysa divided the society into four professional categories as per their aptitudes and abilities.

But, as the axis of time turned in the clockwise direction, the wheel of the society started moving anti-clockwise as if the kingpin fixed by the kingpin Eysa was gradually loosened. The law of equality made by him diverted its direction to the law of inequality made by his followers. They segregated the five professional categories as four classes—first; second, third and fourth classes of people were made in the society with the introduction of the caste system in the United Indana.

Jyothyshies and *Toojaries* were considered as the superlative degree in the grammar of society; The *Rajashrees* were in the comparative degree; The *Vyaparis* were in the positive degree. And what about the last and the lowest class—the *Savas*? They were having no degree at all to compare with, because they were not treated as human beings! Not even as an animal's excreta—for certain purposes the dung was useful to the elite classes. They even handled it with hands. But the lower class *Savas*, though they were human beings with the same blood and flesh, were considered as *polluting the upper classes*! If, by chance, a *Sava* touched any upper class person, it was believed that he was polluted by the *Sava*. The pollution varies in many ways—if they touch them, their bodies were polluted; if they see them, their eyes were polluted. So, they were to stand far away, so that their eyes could see them from a long range or a diluting distance in order to avoid the concentration of the pollution.

The distance of unapproachability varied from class to class according to the rules of untouchability. *Jyothyshies, Toojaries* and *Rajashrees* could mingle from close quarters. A *Vypari* must maintain not less than fifteen feet and a *Sava* was restricted to more than fifty feet from upper class individuals.

In all the classes, there used to be sub-castes within the caste. They too maintained different distance-keeping rules and schedules within their castes. *Jyothyshies* being the learned and superb class, they made the rules and table of untouchability and unapproachability. The *Rajashrees* being the ruling class executed the law and order. The table was so complicated that even a master of mathematics could not hide it in the precious pigeonholes of his mind. But, the poor and illiterate people of the *Sava* class were supposed to remember the law and table of inhumanity for they were duty-bound to obey and maintain them by guessing the exact distance. The lowest sub-caste among the *Savas* would keep a distance of a hundred feet from the highest sub-caste of the *Jyothyshies*. The distance shall reduce to zero till he confronts his own family member. The maximum-to-minimum distance-keeping-chart was by heart to each and every one lest they should be severely punished if failed to abide by the law.

*   *   *

My bones were still chilled to the marrow with the reminiscence of a botch that had happened once: An engagement ceremony of a *Jyothishy* was supposed to be held. The thoroughfare leading to his house was an embankment parting a paddy-field. The monsoon had damaged the path. An old man from the *Sava* caste was detailed by the manager of the *Jyothishy* to reconstruct the ridge in order to prevent the inflow of water. The ridge also served as a barrier. The laborer labored very hard to gather mud and sand with a shovel. Somehow, he managed to make the bund. The water flow had just been arrested.

All of a sudden he heard a rhythmic voice: *Hoooi . . . Hooooi . . . Hoooooi . . .* A young man from the *Jyothishy* caste was being carried in a palanquin by his bearers. The howl was the warning to the untouchables to hide at the unapproachable distance. The laborer went up to a distance of not less than a hundred feet. The bund made with difficulty was thrashed by the palanquin-bearers. Water again stared flowing. The penurious man again made the embankment.

Then there came a *Rajashree* followed by his henchmen, wailing the siren of unapproachability. Again the laborer disappeared to keep the desired distance. The bund was crushed as the walkers walked over it. The water began to flow with more force than before. The unfortunate man once again made the bund.

Later, there came a *Vypari* and some of his errand boys with loads on their heads. He gave way to them also keeping proper unapproachability distance. The several men's treading severely severed the bund—the continuous discontinuation of the work made the reconstruction incomplete. The water again gushed through the broken breakwater barrier.

The farmer was famishing. He neither had his breakfast nor his lunch. He was supposed to receive a measure of rice as wage only on completion of the work. His starving family was anxiously awaiting for the rice rather than him to prepare the gruel lest they should be starved to death. But what to do? The excessive exertion exhausted him.

On the other hand, if he would report back to the *Jyothishy* executor, with an incomplete report, in lieu of food, he would be supplied with his own foot chopped off. The executor did not like any excuses. He liked only one formula—"Others should work by hook or by crook"—for his work was off the hook. His fear-filled mind joined his weak and weary body—both lost the buoyancy. He fainted.

The engagement party was arriving, the executioner in the rear. With great difficulty, they were transporting the *Jyothishy* on a palanquin. The ridge was full of ups and downs. *En route*, the ridge narrowed and the bearers could not get foot-hold. They fell down in the mud-filled field with the palanquin of the superb *Jyothishy*. Somehow, he managed to come to his feet. But the mud-clad superb resembled a scarecrow.

The *Jyothishy* never had such an experience—other than his body excreta—for he had never come into contact with mud, clay, sand and stuffs like that. Though he was supposed to be a divine person in the society, he felt pollution by touching the most divine earth. He was supposed to be the most polite person for he hailed from the holy class, yet he lost his temper. As he turned towards his executor (manager) he beheld him in a healthy and clean condition. So he became barbarous. Though he was from the learned class, he abused his executor bombastically blemishing his bonhomie.

He scolded, "You bonvirant bastard, just gormanding all the yield of the temple and standing like a bobby dazzler! You bobby bastard, I'll make you bolt on a bobbin in public."

Sensing his boiling point, the executor hailing from *Naya* caste—the lowest sub caste of *Rajashree* class—requested, "Oh! Forgive me, your divinity. I had detailed a *Sava* to make and mend the ridge. That booby's a bohemian. I guarantee that, I'll award that bonded man all the bondage of this land with a bonus. I think he's absconding." *Jyothishy* bumped, "Then chop, chop. Stop your bunkum; go and buckle that absconding bonded servant fast."

The boisterous atmosphere made the bonded servant come to life who was bogged a little away. His mind was filled with devotion to the duty which he had been assigned to. He came to his feet and took the fallen spade to continue the work.

"*Ngea*! There he is! The bohemian bastard bonded slave." The executor boiled explosively, "Catch'im and buckle'im immediately."

Some of the *Naya* youths from the fighting class, who were accompanying the engagement party as guards, reached for the bonded servant while others carried away the *Jyothishy* back to his palace for seeing a *Sava* would make his eyes sick.

Far away from the ridge another farmer (of *Sava* caste) was ploughing the field. He was summoned. He came along with his race oxen. The bond servant was buckled behind the oxen. They started racing on the bog.

By then, many spectators came from far and near the village to witness the consequences of bohemianism. Each category kept his unapproachability and untouchability distance as per the dictum.

But, breaking all the bonhomie, a girl—a voluptuous sweet-sixteen black beauty—transformed into a bohemian, made a gangway through the crowd and sprang forward in front of the racing oxen. The ferocious oxen instantly became lethargic. They stood rooted to the earth. They recognized her. She was their nurse. They were twins. Ever since their mother expired—during delivery—she served them as their mother. No, more than a mother. As animals, they never deserved love from the social animals. But the twins consumed an invisible stuff, *love,* tastier than the green fodder and other cattle feeds.

She knelt down between the cattle; bestowed caresses with her cheek just below the eyes of the oxen affectionately. Then she whispered something in their ears. They shook their heads as if they had understood the message. They protruded their lengthy tongues and licked her on the cheeks as acknowledgement of affection.

The anxious spectators stood contemplating the noteworthy scene. Her action held them spellbound. The executor, the executioner and executives from the upper classes could not speculate anything for they were stupefied by the suspense of the spectacle. Satisfied with the reaction of the cattle, she got up and unbuckled the victim. Then she pointed out the antagonists who were standing petrified on the ridge as targets in a firing range.

The bulls rushed towards them like horses do while nearing the finishing point in a race course. Seeing the scuttle of the cattle, the upper class men scurried for their lives were at stake. But their scud came to nought. They could not bulldoze ahead for they were bull-dozed. Like two marksmen hitting the bull's eye, the bulls pricked the notorious antagonists with their stiff horns killing two of them. The dead bodies were strung on the horns!

The people ran pell-mell. They could easily make their way for they were used to the marshy fields whereas the people from the upper caste who came to enjoy the funny carnival of trailing a man to death were in jeopardy. They were crushed to death by the feet of their own caste fellows in the stampede. Within seconds, the field became empty like an open air theatre after the last show.

I was watching all the long-shot scenes from far away. All the scenes were tragic except the last. The playwright (God) ended up the drama by destroying the villains so as to teach the audience a lesson—a message to the evil-doers. The drama written and directed by God was adhered on the back of the mind of the masses. Of course, the last scene was tragic, notwithstanding it had blended with comedy—like a horror comedy. For the first time in my life I laughed beholding horridness though I was horror-struck.

By all means, once again, God made his mark as a great impresario. I thought the holy caste also would learn something from that event; nevertheless they did not assimilate anything good into their social system. And it was another sub-story of the girl, the heroine—a second part of the part-I.

Who was she? She was none but the only offspring of the bonded servant, the victim of the story.

In the remainder of the society, the higher castes weighed like all the weight of the globe whereas the lower or polluting castes did not weigh even the weight of a granule. They had no mass or weight in the society. He was not allowed to occupy any space for all the space was allotted to the upper castes. The elite were the essence; the others waste. The elite were pure and white; Savas were impure and dark. The polluting castes were not marked in the scale of status. But the upper class was marked in bold on that scale. They enjoyed the exchequer. Others had no rights. The only right they enjoyed was the right to work; they never reaped the fruits. And in case they asked for any fruit as right or any right as fruit, *death* was the only allotment. But the purse of the public was always pilfered by the privileged class. The polluting class would pay the tax in cash and kind on a banana leaf maintaining the distance of untouchability and unapproachability.

The funniest thing was that if there would be a voluptuous beauty in the polluted—*Sava's*—family then the distance would come down to zero automatically. The upper caste men could use her keeping her close for teasing, kissing, biting, ticking, plugging her from the rear and fucking her from the front by breaking all the rules and tables of casteism. Some priapic upper caste men even drank the piss of the polluted women when they came in the saturation point of lust. They would be willing to consume her night soil as candy. They were ready to sniff a fart keeping the nostril close to her anus considering it as a fragrant flower. They considered such women as prodigy and they became prodigal sons. But as and when the priapism is over, the prodigy again becomes a polluted prey for the Priapus.

What a paradoxical principle made by some principal people of the society! Raping was the birth right of the upper caste men; to be raped was the duty of the lower caste women. Adultery was the privilege of the former; involuntary prostitution was invested with the latter. *Sava* was a tumor in the economy of society; a stink in the fragrance of society. *Sava*, whatever he said was stultiloquence; whatever others said was statutory eloquence, though it was worthless.

I wanted to inhume the inhumanity of casteism. But I was helpless. Who understands my language? I wished if the inhabitants knew *Cosmolish*. I wondered whether the heroic girl knew that language. She had communicated with the cattle! I appreciated her for she had done something practically against casteism. I wished to present her with a garland and ear pendants made out of my softest leaves and hard berries for her brave performance. What had happened to the beautiful and bold girl?

* * *

Her father was no more. He was dragged to death! She was sad. She was sadder for her bullocks also were no more. They were slaughtered. Simultaneously, she was happy that some of the executors also were no more. But that unit of happiness was subtracted from more units of sorrow for many executors were still alive. And that sorrow was multiplied by more sorrows for the *Jyothishy*, the chief culprit behind the catastrophe, was intact in flesh and blood enjoying the flesh and blood of many virgin girls. The exquisite girl exhaled exquisitely.

She too was brought disrobed before the *Jyothishy*. She wanted to exscind the executors for they were exploring her exposed body's exquisiteness. But she was helpless for her hands were tied together. She seemed impaired. The snow-white jute rope around her black wrists looked like bangles. Her eyes resembled two pearls studded on her granite-like body. Her lascivious lips were zipped up like those of a wallet where all the thirty-two sparkling white teeth were hidden and secured safely like costly diamonds. The Amazon's tongue resided inside her mouth like an aquatic anaconda. She owned a pair of extra special flexible breasts like rubber air-horns. Her belly resembled my leaf (of a banyan tree). Coming down to the vital part—the vagina! She had a special clitoris that peeped out of the vulva like the beak of a parrot.

The impalpable girl stood in an impassive posture in the courtyard of the *Jyothishy's* palace, besieged by the privileged caste people. Her impassionate look provoked even celibates into lust. Members of the priestly caste who were so adamant in maintaining the unapproachability theory came very close to her eagerly to see her bare body, especially the exquisite private parts. Some desired to suck the impalpable girl's breasts. Some turned impatient to lick the fluid dripping from her clitoris like honey dews because their wives seldom had such peculiarities!

Frankly speaking, I did not look that side. All the arboreal animals did what I did. Of course, it was an episode of chivalry and we mean it. But it was not well to see such romantic incident remote from everyday life. All the narration I made here was the tell-tale I overheard from two celibates who took rest on my pulpit on their return from the scene. I had trained and elevated my eyesight towards the sky where I saw Sun peeping through the clouds like a spectator peeping at a carnival through a peephole without a ticket.

Comparing with the dialogues of the travelers, I could guess the event was a comedy but Sun did not laugh. I could make out from his peevish face that he was peeved; wondering how could some men bump power upon some other men breaking Eysa's consideration of treating all men as peers.

The *Jyothishy*, the bumptious bumble beheld the lascivious lady. The bum type priest was attracted to the bum of the black beauty.

He sympathetically commanded to the executor, "Untie her clove hitch; I'll tie her with my hand hitch."

He tied her with his hands by hugging and said to her, "Let's amalgamate ourselves. What do you say, sweetie?"

She was invited inside the impassable palace to bed with him. It was impossible to escape the impasse. So she followed him in anguish with a concentrated concern in the centre of her heart.

The onlookers had a rollicking time. They enjoyed the crudely romantic scene. Everyone's mouth became a wet basin ready to receive a ship.

After a little while, there arose a prolonged plaintive cry of pain from inside the palace. The high, higher and highest castes people who were impatiently waiting outside for their turn to mate with her enjoyed the wail. The wail was followed by a series of wails as if they rose from a steamship blasting distress signal.

Instead of feeling sad hearing the lamentations, a womanizer said mockingly, "How sweet are the lady's screams!"

Another supported him by passing a rollicking remark, "Of course, as sweet as her body!"

But to their surprise, the *Sava* girl savagely rushed amuck from the palace. Her mouth was bulged as if an apple was kept inside. Her vagina was covered with her right hand serving it as a chastity belt, while the left hand hid her bosom. Still, a wailing was waning inside.

Smelling a rat about the unsuitable situation, one bodyguard jumped before her to tackle the exotic dancer. Like an exorcist, she spat on his face. Something like a frog flew out of her mouth. The expelled item was nothing but his master's genitals, including the testicles. Then she swallowed something from her left fist. That was nothing but his master's diamond ring—she died.

*　*　*

Eysa had introduced a sound social principle creatively for the principality of New Indana pertaining to the character—various aptitudes and abilities—and the *function*—diverse opportunity and work. As per the natural tendency, the division was to be fixed for the betterment of humanity. But the priestly and majestic divisions dehumanized Eysa's doctrine to devastation that paved many paths to social, economic, political and many other discrimination.

If I subtract one century from the many centuries of my age, I still remember, it all started with the great battle of Indana as there was an immense loss of life and defilement of New Indana's sanctity. It produced in the New Indans' minds and souls a deep desire to take revenge on the Old Indana immigrants who were illiterate, uncultured and uncouth barbarians. In the by-gone days, all of them were like cattle under the bridle of a single Chieftain ploughing their lives in his field of monopoly.

When both the states were riveted to one nation, the people of Old Indana were purposely conquered by the people of New Indana by all means of human qualities—mental, moral, physical, political, economic and social. They never enjoyed any above-stated social status in their old life. They regarded New Indana as a paradise and its people as parsons. The occultists took undue advantage of the innocence of the Old Indans. The innocent masses were happy to have deliverance from their ex-chief. They were happier to have been ruled by the New Indans. They were the happiest to have the permission to remain slaves under them because it was far more than what they dreamt of, for they felt New Indana was a dreamland. At least they were allowed to live there; at least they were permitted to see the sacred people at a distance. They felt that it was more than what they deserved.

A grain is more than enough for the famished, a drop of water is more than enough for the thirsty, a thread is more than enough for the nude, a straw is more than enough for the drowning, and an alphabet is more than enough for the illiterate. Their illiterate and helpless hearts throbbed: "something is better than nothing." Initially, at the time of the introduction, it sounded like Benthamism both to the Old and New denominations of Indana. But in the long run, it led to poverty to the *Old* sect and fertility to the *New* sect. The existing *Sava* caste of New Indana was upgraded to *Naya* caste—attendants to upper castes.

So, all the Old Indans voluntarily joined the lowest class of society and thus they became *Savas*, the polluted caste, satisfied with the social designation as *Sava* for they never had any designation at all. On the other hand, unaware of the fact that they were as good as grit in the grains, unfit to consume as food for the society and if consumed by mistake, it would cause indigestion—they were treated as outcastes.

If you keep on keeping a black thing unexposed to the weather it may turn white. If you keep on keeping a white thing exposed to weather it may transform its color to black. Because of their hard work in the sun and rain throughout the life, hereditarily all the *Savas* were dark-complexioned. And the high, higher and highest castes of New Indana were fair-skinned for their profession was teaching, ruling and skilled works. Hence, people of the highest caste (*Jyothyshies* plus *Toojaries*) being white in color were seen as symbols of purity; the higher caste (*Rajashrees*) men being reddish in color were symbols of vitality; the high caste (Vyaparis) people being yellow in color became symbols of cleverness and the lower castes (*Savas*) workers being dark in color were symbols of dullness.

Thus the transition from divisions and sub-divisions of the society as per the choice of occupation to castes and sub-castes was as per the choice of the occultists.

So I laughed. What a paradoxical comedy! Man may command man for reason. But what's this? Color commands Color for no reason. Pathetic! I wanted to compose a pastoral elegy on the subject of the pathless dark-skinned men's life till they found a pathfinder to pave the path to a new *pasturage* of social life equivalent to the patent of the fair-skinned men.

Obviously, repeatedly I emphasize here, though Eysa segregated the society as sacred section, ruling section, business section and construction section for the creative development of each and every individual with indiscriminate mind with the passage of time, it reached the worst stage of racial prejudice or casteism.

Speaking matter-of-factly, all the three castes from top were fair in color *ipso facto* because their work stations were indoors and cool-areas. After the training they did not have to work outdoors. The *Jyothyshies* being the teachers opened many schools exclusively to educate upper caste pupils and *Toojaries* being priests made many *demples,* the worshipping centers for Esyans throughout the country. The installation of idols and performance of *poojas* were their profession, in fact right. The *Rajashrees* being the rulers and warriors built up palaces here and there dividing the country into different districts. They ruled the people under the law and order made by the so-called learned *Jyothyshies*. The *Vyaparis* being business men constructed trade centers like markets and ports and owned the lion's portion of the land. In a nutshell the upper castes had the exclusive right on all the revenue of the land; it was patent that lower caste men could never be patentees for even a handful of soil.

The *Savas* were mere tenants without any tenement. Earth was the floor and sky was the roof of their abode. They were just peasants or laborers or construction workers for the infrastructural facility. They could be used for miscellaneous sweat-emitting jobs for the upper caste, weather-proof people. *Ipso facto* their skin was tanned and gradually they became dark. Hence they became a *dark* generation and the others a *fair* generation. The generation gap between the dark-skinned and the fair-colored became great.

The upper castes could not be kept away from social activities whereas the *Savas* were kept out of all the functions. However they were allowed to come even at frictional distance for lustful activities. They were subjected to imperial imperviousness which imperiled them.

An upper caste lascivious lady might seek a strong *Sava* youth for her undying desire. If caught the immorality was imposed upon him. If an upper caste priapic man sought a *Sava* beauty for his passionate enjoyment she should obey him. If caught the immorality was imposed upon her. The immodest upper caste individual turned innocent and the innocent lower caste person was immolated. If a stone falls over a mirror or mirror falls over a stone, it is the mirror that shatters. Such was the law of the land against the Savas. On such occasions, the imperious law and order machinery of the country turned in reverse gear. Yet the *Savas* were lascivious instruments for the lascivious upper castes people.

I wanted to make use of all my stalks as pen and all the leaves' extractions as ink. But, I waited to compile more miscellaneous events to include in the eclogue. As the wheel of time rolled on, I eye-witnessed another event of pathos pertaining to the prejudice against the dark-colored by the fair-skinned.

This was very close to my angle of sight. I doubted that the law of gravitation was also anti-lower caste like the law of the country. I felt that even my leaves and berries were getting detached and were soaring.

As Sun came to Indana to wake up its people, his head drooped. The mood of *good morning* was gone when an angry wind came from far away. I felt that its drone was scolding me for the inhumane activities of the land. The sea waves jumped up to have a glimpse of the wicked act. A human head was pronged on a spear and placed on a fallow ground like a device to scare people. An act of deteriorating humanity! It was a dreadful to the decent; it was droll deed to the indecent upper castes. The kind-hearted kept their fingers sympathetically on their noses; the hard-hearted horse-laughed for they had done that horrendous deed in order to sow scare among the dark-colored, notwithstanding the fact that it was an erroneous act towards an innocent man.

A passionate and lusty lady from the *Naya* caste had been kept as mistress by a *Rajashree*, who was old enough to be her grandfather. She was his pet prostitute for she was skilled in lustful tactics of *kamarathi*.

Her abode was an out-house, a little away from his bungalow near the bathing pool and on the way to the cattle-yard. The cowherd was at the threshold of his youth, just a sapling, yet with strong muscles secured inside his charcoal-colored skin. Every day after grazing the cattle he would put them back in the cattle-yard at dusk.

The doxy had desire towards the dark youth. She used to spy on his sturdy body, exquisite looks and his overall elegance whenever she went for her evening bath in the secured pool. She wished to make him her paramour. But she could not fool the old man's golden eyes.

Once a prince of a state, now the prince of the world, the old Rajashree one day went to the king's palace to collect his weekly presentation (priapic pills) or an *ayurshastric* preparation with the desire to thrust his powerless prong into the fleshy pit of his pet prostitute. He desired to show his *ayurshakti*—strength, vigor and vitality—to her that night. It was her turn to prepare the bed for him. His long grey hair and beard and his thick loose-skinned body made him look like an old monk but in fact he was nothing less than a punk. Though he was eighty he had been keeping eight doxies.

As a matter of fact, both young prostitute and the old punk were the instruments of experiment in *Kamavedam*—a treatise on sexual science— conducted by Kamananda, the royal sexologist.

If you dip your finger in the honey, you are sure to lick it. Indana's upper classes' hands were always in the honey pot. After the departure of Eysa, as the time passed by, devaluing all the principles taught by him, they engaged in exorbitant *artha, kama, krodha,* and *moha.* The royal class—*Rajashrees*—abandoned the principles of *ahimsa.* There was a transition from unarmed self-defense of Indana to armed fighting force of the individuals. They trespassed all the abodes of the Old Indans leaving them astray. The *Vyaparis* earned excessive profits. Even the *Tundits* were indulged in priapic life instead of living as a *Toojari* or priest.

The *Rajas* established a royal academy where different disciplines were taught. This was exclusively for the upper classes. The teachers were the *Tundits.* One of the disciplines was *Kamavedam* under which sexual science, erotic and salacity were taught. With the aid of herbal medicinal science—*jeevaveda*—they invented some priapic pills for perfect and prolonged enjoyment of masculine sex. The medicated men normally turned to a musk mustering more muscles to his mollusk-type manhood-mutating the dead as mutton genitals to mutton on hoof. Most of the female victims were the libidinous ladies from the lower castes and some volunteer doxies from the *Naya* caste.

Actually, the research was conducted to study the function of the priapic pills on the old human body. The old punk had to submit a sexual infatuation report about its practical effects on his own body. The cloying power, duration of performance, excitement in orgasm, amount of semen ejected, its throw, its fertility count, level of gratification of the lovers and many other aspects pertaining to libido were to be checked.

But for the *Naya* doxy, the old *Rajashree* was a good-for-nothing even as a drone. She intended to conduct an experimental verification with young blood to cure her malady caused by sexual frustration. Hence she was longing for the *Sava* youth without any regard for his caste and creed to quench her sexual thirst with cost and greed. And she waited to avail of that facility. Her dream came true! On that evening . . .

The cattle marched ahead, their stomachs full with green fodder and belly filled with river water, with their master, the *Sava* youth in the rear. Then it was time for their roost. He came near the bathing pond on his way. High walls secured the pond from the sight of the untouchable and unapproachable outcaste. It had a covered gate also for the oiling and soaping of the bathing ladies.

"Aiiii ooo . . . ." There was a moan.

"Aiii aiii ooo . . . ."Again came the moan.

He listened. The moaning of a woman! Without listening he started walking further. He had no concern with human wailing for he was acquainted only with the blaaa . . . and burrr . . . of animal's right from his childhood. But the singular wail grew to plural wails. Neglecting the cry, he walked away . . .

"Hey, you pretty, please stop and help me . . ."

He was stunned! He stopped and stooped to listen. Kneh! The wail was now welded with words! He could not detect where the agony-clad melodious voice was coming from and to whom it was meant for. As he stopped, his cattle also stopped; as the commander waited the commanded waited too . . .

"*Havoo*, come and save me you black pearl. I pray."

Yes. Someone was requesting something from him! Someone was in danger! Someone was in the pond! It was a great social crime for the polluted to focus his eyesight on the pond of the princely class. Yet he went and peered through the gate.

There she was, the *Thampuratti*—the *Naya* doxy—the fair-colored beauty, lying flat on the step of the pond. All her limbs were symbols of sex. The soaked condition added sexy lustre. The sympathetic situation gave her added sex appeal.

Through half-opened eyes she looked at him. Through the half-opened mouth she requested, "Come on sweetie, give me a hand. I'm fractured."

A *Thampuratti* requesting a *Sava* boy! It was as if a goddess was praying to a devotee to save her from distress! He could believe neither his ears nor his eyes!

"*Thampuratti*, I'm an outcaste. How can I approach you? It's forbidden!"

He was right. He was not allowed to enter the social circle. If someone came to know of it, he would be cast out from this world.

"But I am telling you. Come, lift me."

"*Thampuratti*, looking at you itself is a great crime on my part. Hearing your voice is a greater crime and touching your body is the greatest crime for my type of men. So, how can it be possible to approach and touch you?"

"Let your unapproachability and untouchability drown in the pond. I hereby command you to come to me. Nobody will condemn you."

"If someone sees . . . !"

"There is nobody around. The old punk is away."

"But the cattle?"

"They're your comrades."

Yes, they were his friends rather than his relatives. They mattered to him. They too were watching him and the woman through the gate. They too were anxious to know what was going to happen for they too were aware of the prevailing social system of the state. They did not shake their heads in support of obeying her command or denying. As their commander looked at them expecting an affirmative or negative answer, they did not react. They remained neutral.

A command or a request, a help is a help. A woman seeking help from an able-bodied man! He should extend his hand especially when she is in distress.

Thampuratti again cried, "I curse your cattle; help me a little."

Neglecting the consequences, he reached for her. He sat on his knees beside her. Instantly, she grabbed him, locking her hands over his shoulders and making him lay over her body. She felt the warmth of real manhood on her soaked cold body. The taste and smell of his sweat were sweet and that appealed to her senses. The up and down movements of her breast made his chest to throb sideways. She hurriedly stripped her thin crape and his coarse loin cloth. She pulled all his weight inside her. There was an inflammation in his body. He could not feel his inferior color. His black eyes were confronting her white color. His black body was making friction on her white body producing sparks in his biological senses. When she ate his lips and when he sucked her tongue both were in a licentious mood.

She squeezed the *Sava*'s body savagely breaking all the bones of untouchability. He too squeezed her, bleeding all the blood of unapproachability. For some time, he too was a member of le beau-monde temporarily, dropping his polluted anchor of vitality into the sacrosanct wet basin of the demi-monde. His hard, fleshy rod made its way into the soft-walled fleshy cave repeatedly to move further and further into an unknown dreamland. The action was cloying!

There was a flooding with an explosion. She had never experienced such a luscious excitement during the course of her career as a mistress of *Kamavedam*. As far as he was concerned it was neither a biological necessity nor an enjoyment. It was just an offence. He had destroyed the purity of the inner-container of an elite lady by pouring his polluted vital fluid. Notwithstanding the compulsion behind his deed, it might cost him his life if someone had beheld it.

And it so happened . . .

"*Poonana, Poorana . . .*" Someone called some names of some god. Yes, human voices of a male inhuman being were heard over his head. Simultaneously there was a shrieking of a female inhuman being. The latter was the *Thampuratti* and the former the *Thampuran,* her husband.

"O God! This dirty untouchable devil has dirtied my milk!"

The black youth jumped to his feet. He tried to snatch his loin cloth in vain. The demi-monde reared her head; hid her face and squalled.

Further she spoke amidst sobs, "This cowherd cowed me. He's worse than an animal. You dear, you just allowed this dirty devil to roam astray? Push him into the cattle-shed and castrate him."

For the first time in my life, I saw a real case of betrayal. The presentation given for persuasion! A perfect perversion! That too by a woman, supposed to be the most humble creation. Women are created to sacred the finest universal nutrition—milk. But this woman secreted venom of ingratitude. She denied her cloying paramour as a dirty devil faced with the risk after the gratification of her sexual desire. Really a cupboard love! She pretended to be in arson of agony; to escape from it she pretended to end her life.

She sobbed, "Now I don't wish to live on this earth."

She pretended to jump into the pond to commit suicide. The old man whisked her away saving her in time.

He commanded to his *Naya* bodyguards who were standing by with swords to obey his orders word by word.

"Behead him . . ."

The nude *Sava* youth ran away from there as fast as his legs could carry him. The bodyguards ran swiftly after him. But the youth's legs were stronger and faster than theirs and his young blood, flesh and bones were working very well to save his life whereas the guards being womanizers—sans vital energy—and boozers, were lethargic—sans stamina. On top of that, guards' minds were still concentrated on the nude beauty of their master's mistress and the hard genital rod of their master's servant. So, the sapless guards could not sack the sapling. Yet they kept on pelting behind him, like a wild goose chase because they were duty-bound.

The victim's parents were summoned before—a hundred yards away—the king. A proclamation was read out: "Your son, the convict. The wild boy is to be beheaded on the charge of sowing his wild oats. If he surrenders, only he would be killed; if someone harbors him, they too will be killed. If he does not surrender, he would be caught and killed and you will have to pay your life as interest for the punishment pawned by your son. In addition to this, in order to sanctify the pond polluted by your pet, you and your clan have to collect the funds in cash and kind by working without wages. The only sustenance you'll get is half a square meal thrice a day."

He surrendered in order to save the lives of his father, mother and his two sisters and the stomachs of the members of his clan. He knew the pros and cons of the proclamation—he could expect only cons and not pros from the princely class. If they could not gather the funds, the sustenance would be cut from three to two, two to one and one to nil. They would have to survive only on water. So he surrendered.

He could have easily escaped into the jungle with the cattle; they would definitely have filed behind him. But he did not do that. Why should the innocent suffer? So, he voluntarily donated his head to protect many heads. But the execution was too cruel! The son was beheaded by his own father forcefully! As if coup de grace!

Thus, the lower caste wild who committed a lesser degree of offence was awarded death punishment. His mate, the higher-caste woman, who committed higher degree of offence, was awarded an appellation as "the Brave Dame of Indana". The conclusion being that she had withstood the situation without submitting her chastity! No principle on any principality was parabolic to such kind of partial and paradoxical paralogism.

Along with many paragons of the fool's paradise (Indana) the paramour also arrived to see the exhibition of her deceased lover's head. She had donned all her paraphernalia to add more beauty to her exhibitionism. All the paramount persons stood afar. She fell back to the rear rank. In delitescence, she peered at the head of her one-time lover. Her eyes could not stand the sight. Instead of being delighted, she became delirious.

She suffered from paranoia. It not only subtracted all her artificial beauty but the natural beauty also drained out from her body and it turned ugly. God's dexterity on her body deliquesced due to the *demi monde's* delinquency. Yet she did not repent her wild youth! It was because she was the owner of only diabolical and biological thought; not the owner of kindness and genteelness.

I felt like hearing a silent horse-laugh from beneath-the-neck of the body-less head of the youth, pondering mockingly about the comedy of collecting funds by the poor peasants for the purifying the pond. The reason being, his loin—cloth had fallen in the pond.

A committee was formed and the proceedings had already started. The pond-water had to be emptied to evict the bale by reciting hymns while to the ringing of sanctum bells. A *homa* and *pooja* were to be performed. As the pond was filled with fresh groundwater, pots and pots of incense water and sandalwood oil were also poured.

The *pooja* and *homa* and the pouring of the scented articles were carried out by the priests or *Tundits*. The bailing of the battle-pound water, polluted by a washed loin-cloth of the polluted caste, which was already polluted with the urine, fluid matters from the private parts, sometimes night soil (in case of emergencies) and the foul wind from the anus of the princely people, was the responsibility of the poor polluted caste. Still some submissive type of the polluted caste considered the urine-mixed water as their holy river water; the floating shit cakes as sandal paste and they felt pride in rendering the purifying task even though they had no pride in the society.

Besides, the manpower to render all the physical work and money to gather all the ingredients for the purifying procedures had to be met by the youth's parents and the members from his destitute clan.

His clan was basket-makers by profession. They used to go to the forest from the village, cut rattan reed from cane-brake, treat it, and make baskets and mats for various domestic and agricultural purposes. Above all they were perfect artisans who made artistic cane-bottomed furniture.

The punishment imposed a heavy burden on them. They could not raise the fund. So, one day, all of them went to the wilds in a procession. The princely people were under the impression that they were trying to raise the fund as early as they could by doing by more work by more workers. But they did not return.

They travelled far into the woods. In the long run they turned to be the children of the jungle and were known as the Tribe. The dense wilds and willful settling in the wild transformed them from wilds to civilized, brought them from slavery to freedom, led them from insufficient life to self-sufficient life and delivered them from their dependent situation to independence—they gained deliverance! Unshackled from the chain of society, they lived merrily in the wild, consuming honey and wilding in the initial stage. The forest flock sang folklore flattering the fauna and flora as their friends and food.

Ohooi . . . Ohooi . . . . Ohooi . . . .
Living in the wild areas means living in the nature;
Living with the wild animals means more than living with men.
Means far better than out in the wild.
No strain, no pain—only joy, joy, joy . . .
Ohooi . . . Ohooi . . . Ohooi . . . .
Consuming the wild cherries as food is palatable;
Donning the wild beast's skin as cloth is fashionable.
Means far better than out in the wild.
No famine, no shame—only fame, fame, fame . . .
Ohooi . . . Ohooi . . . Ohooi . . .
Working in the wilderness is most satisfying;
Mating in the wilderness is most exciting.
Means far better than out in the wild.
No fear, no hear—only fair, fair, fair . . .
Ohooi . . . Ohooi . . . Ohooi . . .

Later they cultivated sensuous and scented spices like cardamom, cloves, pepper, ginger, tea, coffee, etc. Further they planted tuberous roots and bulbs with more calories. Thereafter they fixed tropical trees to produce plantains.

In their plantations, there were tobacco and marijuana. Other than the cultivators and planters, some took to hunting; some went out to the sea through the river flowing out from the forest. The Indans never used to go to the sea for they considered the sea as impure and devilish. They were afraid to see the tribesmen floating in the sea on catamarans, silhouetting their body as figures made of ebony.

The tribal exchanged their articles in kind—fishermen exchanged their catch with planters and hunters. The hunters exchanged the meat with fishermen and planters. The planters exchanged their vegetables with others. Likewise, they changed round their products in rotation and as per seasons. They ceased believing in coins; considered the coinages as token of detestation.

It was a noteworthy achievement that they framed their own social norms which were much nobler than the law made by the nobles of Indana. They respected the skilled, cared for the old and children, married and created confidence to spouses. Marriage was through consummation. Above all, they loved each other holding respect and dignity of labor.

*   *   *

Another discipline in the Royal academy was *Gyanashastra* or the study of religion or the Eysaism. The structure of the religion was casteism where the rights and duties of the castes were the performance of *poojas*, making and maintaining of demples, *yogas* or sacrifices. There was a department for *Rastrashastra* or the rules and regulations of the rulers plus the law and order were included in it. The third department which covered the *Vanibhashastra* was for the trade and commerce people. The last one was the *Manavashastra* or the study of humanity. It comprised the impartial treatment of all the social injuries of all the castes and the maintenance of dignity of labor—no human pollution pertaining to untouchability and unapproachability, the attachments of dark to fair and fair to dark. Breaking all the essential parts of Eysa's caste structure, the so-called elite class constructed a separate framework for their own purpose. They, instead of educating the *Sava* caste, held them as downtrodden and enjoyed the elixir doses of society from the hospital of casteism.

The deans of all the departments were *Tundits* from the *Jyothishy* castes. The *Toojaries* from the same caste also had the exclusive rights of installation of idols and performance of *Togas* for all the Gods and Goddesses. The *Jyothishies'* pet godheads were Brahesh as male and Saramy as female; *Rajashrees's* had Mahnu as male and Kali as female godheads; Vyaparis' godheads were Vishma as male and Lakswathy as female.

The fair-skinned built demples throughout Indana and installed filigree idols. Having the installation and recitation rights, the *Jyothishies* established ideal idols of godheads of creation and knowledge, godheads of power and destruction, godheads of preservation and prosperity. The *Savas* had no right to install, pray or even to approach the area of the ideal demples lest they should pollute the sanctum of the ideal gods and their ideal wives—flagrant injustice! Prohibition of praying! Segregation of gods!

However, the *Savas* themselves prayed to some imaginary objects. Those were some idiot godheads such as *Pay, Chath, Maruth* etc. They performed some witchcraft as *pooja.* Their main offerings were chicken blood and toddy to satisfy the devil-heads. They had no *demples* at all. Their major worshipping places were the platforms beneath my family members (the banyan trees). To evict the evil spirits, they struck long nails on the tree stem with their heads and sometimes buried men alive in pits as human an act of sacrifices.

Woman had a distinct social status in Eysaism. On the one hand they enjoyed and entertained the safety and security from men flock but on the other they had certain restrictions. Though they were regarded as the purest human beings during normal days, they were considered the most impure during menstruation days. The noble castle ladies were transferred to isolated outhouses. It was considered that all that biological dirt from a woman might pollute the men doing sacred duties. During that period the woman was not allowed to go to the demple or to contact men. She should take rest. She should be always neat and should keep herself clean by applying turmeric paste on her entire body. She should keep clear from the dirty gore discharged from the uterus.

This system of restriction was applicable to all the primates of all the classes and castes. But, contradicting it, the noble caste contrived a deceitful practice of making use of lower caste immature girls to clean the ejected dirt from the genitals.

Eysaism also held that all the men from all the castes should take care of and give support to all the women from all the castes. The women should in turn obey and respect the men. They should be gentler than men. They should be submissive. In short, they should appreciate the masculine command. The only one occasion a woman could command over men was when she was enthroned as a queen at the juncture of her husband's, the king's, demise. Then the power comes to her naturally to hold sway over the entire people. She could easily find fault with the crooked, condemn them and punish them drastically. On no other occasion she would have the opportunity to punish either a man or a woman because a woman was supposed to possess the qualities of forgiveness and only love, love, love. Ultimately she was mother.

But some noble women with sharp tongue and long clitoris were more powerful than men with strong bodies and long rods of reproduction. The unnatural power came naturally to them to hold command over and control their subordinates.

Let me narrate the sinews of a high-caste harpy who wanted to be happy and for its sake committed an act of sex and sin during her menstrual period. The nasty story might fill you with nausea. It is a story somewhere between the lilies and roses and little and thorns.

A newly married *Sava* girl was detailed to look after the *grande amoureuse*, neglecting all the norms of unapproachability, untouchabilitiy for the job itself was a polluting one. So the noble castes gave an opportunity to the polluted castes for approaching and touching them on such occasions. When noble caste men suffered from small pox, chicken pox or other contagious and infectious diseases, lower caste men were detailed to look after the patients. The poor caretaker would treat the patients by absorbing the disease as if he were a blotting paper. Often the poor servants were glad to give gratuitous services to their rich masters. The masters thought that it was gratis and was a right to them.

The rich and noble *grande amoureuse* had no qualities of the accepted characters of a woman. She had a grandiose mind, grandiloquent mouth and a granite-like heart in a grate-type bony body. The grass widow was reluctant to attend to the dirty duty of cleaning the menstrual fluids of another woman.

She requested, "*Thampuratti*, if I attend to your menstruation, I too will become dirty. I too have a husband. After the duty, if I touch him he too will be polluted. So, you may swab your menstruation with these flowers I brought for you. These are lilies".

She handed over some grandiflora to the *grande dame.*

The *grande dame* grappled the girl with her grapnel type of hands. She grandiloquently grunted, "How dare you grumble such questions in one breath? You're not a woman of the society. You're like a worm in the soil. Now you hear the answers. All these customs are not applicable to you type of downtrodden for you don't have any sanctity as a human being in the society. You won't get dirty by me for you're already dirtied by God. If you touch your grass widower, nothing will happen to him for he's already polluted by God."

The grass widow said in anxiety, "Why! Though he's graphite-colored, he takes bath twice a day."

"You senseless drab, talking nonsense. His daily bath won't purify his social pollution."

"Social pollution is made by you, not by God. Social pollution doesn't stink; it's the body that stinks."

The society lady retorted, "Fishes live long lives in the water. They are always in bathing state. Yet they stink. They are also God's creation. You're polluted by virtue of your birth in the polluted caste."

"But *Thampuratti*, your delivery hole also stinks. Please don't ask me to clean that area."

"You bitch," she said furiously. "I don't have to teach you all this for you belong to that cheap class, which you're not to be taught anything at all. You know I'm a *Thampuratti*; my top secret part is so sacred that even my husband being a *Toojari* regards that part as sanctum sanctorum. As a punishment for your arguments, you'll mop my secret secretion with your mouth."

"Mouth . . . !" the maid stupefied.

"Yes. There's a mop in your mouth."

"A mop?"

Seeing the servant's amazement, she said, "You stupid don't stand in stupor. It's the most beloved part, the tongue."

"The tongue!" It was a stunning blow. "That would be a stupendous folly, madam."

"You're just a bride. Let me give one more lesson to you. This lesson would help your grass widower to satisfy you provided you teach him this practical application. I must teach you and you must learn a dictum. All the sexual desires or the lewd activities are just a stupendous folly. Yet it's a tremendous jolly. The more the folly the more the jolly. In our mythology, lots of gods exercised lots of follies for sexual gratification. And, we admire their sublime lewd jollification."

She stripped off her clothes exposing her sturdy body. Her formidable look frightened the female servant.

She ordered, "Now you strip off your covers."

"No, *Thampuratti*, No. I've learned from my mother that willful showing of the secret parts of a lower caste woman to an upper caste individual is a sin; seeing the secret parts of the lower castes by an upper caste is also a sin!"

"Is she still alive?"

"My mother's no more."

"You thank your God. Otherwise I would've made her hike throughout this state in her birthday suit. Anyway, as punishment for listening to your garrulous mother's misguiding lessons, I'll submit a submission before the ruler that henceforth no lower caste woman will wear any type of upper cover."

"But it's forbidden," the peasant woman pleaded.

"All the forbidden facts are forgivable for the sake of fun and fucking."

"But *Thampuratti*, it's sinful to strip our cloth."

"Before the sex," *Thampuratti* said, "sin vanishes. You learn one more lesson from me that sex is *supreme*. In fact, sex is a blend of sin and sinister acts. Moreover, you're not showing your private parts willfully; I compel you. Disobeying the command of a high caste person is greater than any other sins. So strip, baby, strip."

The maid tried to secure her lower cover with one hand and the upper cover with the other protecting her clothes from stripping. But the priggish *Thampuratti* reached for her and stripped her. Staring at the nude servant, she savagely said, "And what I said, Yes. The tongue. As a punishment for the refusal of cleaning my refuse with your so-called pretty hands provided by God to do works, let your tongue do the job. Like a cow cleaning the mucus on her calf, you'll clean my genital area. You know why do the animals use the tongue? God didn't provide them with hands."

"But that's the case of animals. We're human beings," said the servant seriously.

But the society lady said mockingly, "No. You lower castes are of lesser status. You'll have to take many rebirths to fall in the category of human beings. For that you'll have to obey the orders of the sacred castes.

As you do not wish to use your hands as hands, you're also as good as an animal. So make hands forelegs and come to the pose of an animal."

By that time, the *Thampuratti* was bleeding badly. It resembled a miniature of just-erupted crater. Contemplating the volcano-like vulva and lava-like menstrual fluids, the maid tried to run away. But before taking a step ahead, the *Thampuratti* pulled the head of the maid towards her private parts and made her kiss the lips of her vagina with the lips touching her crater-like vulva and lava-like menses. The latter felt the smell of quicklime and the taste of lemon and iron.

She tried to escape from the grip. But the malevolent mistress held her so tightly that she could not get out of the grapnel hand; she pressed the maid's mouth deeper into the cave-like vagina. Maid's tongue came out automatically from the mouth and brushed the vaginal walls of her mistress. *Thampuratti* sang a lascivious song.

Maid sensed the dangerous situation. *Thampuratti* was in a jovial mood. She was joggling the servant's head into her under-pit keeping both her hands as joggle. All the while she continued the song in jubilation.

"Luck, luck, luck your luck, luck, luck,
You unapproachable are allowed to approach me!
For you're no one to approach me . . . .
Suck, suck, suck sucker suck, suck, suck,
You un-suck-able are allowed to suck my sacred secretion!
For you're no one to touch me . . . .
Fuck, fuck, fuck mare fuck, fuck, fuck,
You un-fuck-able are allowed to fuck my unfathomed womb!
For you're no one to fuck me.
The only one who has luck to
Lick, suck and fuck me is my spouse
Who's a holy doyen.
The one who communes with God.
The one who communes with God.

All the while the *grande amoureuse* was involved in merry-making vulgar sex, the maidservant's mind was transmitting the silent signals of mayday, mayday, mayday. No one could hear the distress signal. I could hear the di di di . . . da da da . . . di di di . . . because one of my long roots was residing beneath the outhouse of that *Thampuratti's* palace. But what to do? I could not save her soul. Frankly speaking, I liked the lilt of the *Thampuratti*; I did not like the last limerick. It was quite luminal.

The servant's nose and mouth kept on rubbing in the *Thampuratti*'s cave-like vagina under the stronghold of her grapnel-like arms. This suffocated the maid but *Thampuratti* enjoyed multiple clitoral orgasms through this. When the servant was released, her face was gory— menses-clad. She fell down like an uprooted tree: motionless, breathless, senseless and then lifeless—smothered to death.

*   *   *

Grass widower and the grass roots were called upon from grassroots. The grass widower was smoothed away of the sadness of his grass widow's smother-to-death news by a grasshopper-looking *Naya* solider. He advised: "Sucking the impurities of a holy caste woman will make the unholy caste pure. Your wife's havened." Subsequently, an act of admonishment was read out to the lower caste assemblage.

The grasshopper-type man read out the prohibition act to the grassroots. "I buy your ears to this holy act of prohibiting two-piece body cover with effect from today. This act is an amendment too. No person of the unholy castes is allowed to wear any type of upper cover including head cover. It shall be considered as a mark of disrespect to the holy castes. However, the unholy castes are at their liberty to wear loincloth as lower cover for the sake of concealing their genital organs."

He discontinued reading and looked meaningfully with mean-mindedness to the innocent assemblage. Seeing his pride over the prejudiced class, I compared him in my mind to a foolish commander of a platoon of idiots.

He continued: "The prohibition of wearing ornaments by the unholy castes is still in force. If anyone in any form from the said castes denied the order, he or she would be punished with mutilating of the ears of the male and nose of the female."

Likewise, theoretically and practically, the suppression by the upper castes created depression in the minds of the lower castes. Though it was harassing, everyone yielded to it—some happily and some painfully. Some easily succumbed to the slavery; some succumbed to death by the social injuries sustained to their hearts.

Still, all the Indans regarded Indana as a *Shastra Bhoomi or* the land of treatise, a *Veda Bhoomi* or the land of knowledge, a *Deva Bhoomi* or the land of God and above all a *Punya Bhoomi* or the land of divinity. Let it be any land of diversity, I longed to see the unity of the people. For that I wished I were an anatomist who had a knife to cut the unwanted appendicitis filled with casteism from the body of society that harmed humanity.

Hearing of and seeing all those sad sacrifices of the sub-standard castes of United Indana, I was unaware that my journey of life was nearing the time-stone of my sixteenth century. I came to know about it only on completion of my fifteenth century of life.

CENTURY 16

1501 TO 1600 AD

Agony is an antagonist who kills the joy. While telling the story of the antagonists' attack on United Indana, I am proud of unfolding the pages of the political, economic and practical developments of the country rather than remaining depressed about the social under-developments of the country.

Besides the developments of arts and culture, the higher castes built many schools of scientific thought all around the country. Eysa taught them the classification of the universe into five basic elements—earth, air, fire, water and ether by intuition and logic. The *Tundits* carried out experiments and laid the foundation of atoms and its research. They developed the *Shastra* of zodiac too.

Admission to and promotion at the institutions of studies were allowed to all the subjects irrespective of their caste, creed and color—including the *Savas*—as per the social instructions of Eysaism. But the nobles made use of all those facilities exclusively for their benefits.

One day, a *Sava* youth, who went to the forest to gather the ingredients for the *homa*, happened to see a star-like object falling in the sea in the dark hours of night.

Though he was fascinated by the sight, he chose to neglect it. But in the forest, alone at night, climbing on trees to cut branches, his eyes fixed at the star-studded sky, he saw it. Subsequently, he frequently beheld the same sight at nights. He jealously watched the jade-like shower. The shower of jadeite passed by him as if it wanted him to identify it. It was like a suicide of stars: By jumping straight into the open sea. He could see their attempt clearly from atop the tree.

I too watched this and guessed the imagination of the *Sava* youth. I identified the objects without interest. But I was interested in his incorrect imagination. I kept on watching him, chuckling at his folly. As the whole of Indana was submerged in the sea of sleep, no one had the rare chance to see the shower.

The *Sava* youth did not get scared. He was at a loss to know what in the universe they were! He shifted his eyes from the sea to the sky, point-blank. The stars stared scoffingly at him twinkling their eyes in anxiety. It seemed that they wanted to know whether he was intelligent enough to distinguish the objects debarred from their home. Then he stared at the moon. The moon mocked at him. It seemed the moon knew the objects very well, but was unwilling to disclose their identity.

His anxiety grew into curiosity. Were those quasi-stellar objects also out-castes like him from the holy population of the heavenly bodies? He wanted to find out the myth and matter hidden in it. He wanted to approach them and have an interview to know what had happened. Therefore, he took a pledge to search for the truth behind it through a great research.

They were some quasi-stellar objects, he was sure. But they carried some peculiarities that helped one differentiate them from the stars. He wished to see them very close. Once he experienced a magnifying effect when he looked through the round bottom of a broken glass bottle. It acted as a lens. He collected some broken glass bottles and glass jars from the garbage area. He took them to the forest. On completion of collecting the *homa* items from the jungle overnight, daytime was spared for him. He scraped the glass bottoms of bottles and jars, shaped them into perfect optical lenses by rubbing those glass blocks into spherical sections. As he viewed through it, he could see a beetle as big as an elephant. Astonished by the magnifying effect, he looked through two lenses keeping them in his hands at a distance. It was strange to see the distant objects appearing larger and nearer.

Overwhelmed by the wonder, he experimented further. He took a big bamboo, hollowed it and fixed the quasi-lenses. Again keeping the lenses this way and that and looking through this end and that, he succeeded in seeing the stellar objects larger and nearer. Likewise, the reflection of the quasi-stellar object was enlarged and he viewed it very well for the terrestrial use. The remote strange objects were super luminous!

He exclaimed, "Viva . . . !"

Yes. I wanted to congratulate him for his exploits. It was an exceptional advancement! An exquisite exploration of the sky! An exemplary achievement for the fellows of his caste! He believed that he revealed comets by inventing a quasi-telescope.

He wrongly supposed that the objects he saw encountering the earth as comets were meteorites. The shower which destroyed themselves before falling on the earth, in the streak of luminosity was meteors. He named both the former and the latter as *shooting stars*. And I appreciated him for selecting such a suitable name.

He wished to expose his exploits, his remarkable experiments and research works to the world. But how? Who would appreciate the exploits of a *Sava* caste boy? The learned class would scoff at the invention and discovery of the illiterate class. Would he be rewarded or reprimanded? What would he do?

Yes. He contacted the demple attendant who belonged to the *Naya* caste. He had a soft corner towards the youth for he was very prompt in bringing sufficient items for *homa*.

As usual, the youth placed the items outside the temple. The *Naya* came and sprinkled holy water thrice on the items in order to sanctify it.

The youth spoke to him with mouth covered by his palm keeping the distance of unapproachability: "*Thampra,* I've committed a crime. Please forgive me."

"Did you kill somebody? If you kill someone from your caste and or another caste below yours, it could be settled; if you kill someone from my caste or above, tell your beloved head to say *goodbye* to your body."

"It's got nothing to do with *himsa.* It's something else."

He narrated the true story of his discovery and invention. The *Naya* sighed.

He said with a concern, "Owff, what've you done? You limb of the devil! You looked at the sky during night hours! You've committed a great crime. And you stared at the stars with your dirty eyes. You know, they're *our*—not your—heavenly bodies. Even I don't dare do that. Looking at a star is as good as quasi-raping a noble woman!"

"But, *Thampra,* I've looked at the stars not with bad intentions."

"You drop a drop of urine in the milk with good intentions. Will it not be polluted? You've defiled the whole sky by looking at it with your polluted eyes. You don't know, even our caste—the lowest among the high—is prohibited to see the stars. The stars are the lucky symbols of the holy castes. However, you're permitted to view the sun. But how long can you keep your eyes on the sun?"

"But somehow, these discoveries are to be disclosed to the divine dignitaries. Otherwise, it would remain a myth rather than truth."

"Well," scoffed the Naya. "If you're so much interested in cracking open the nut of your so-called truth, then show me your instrument and tell me about your thesis. I'll take the patent so that your life could be saved."

"But, *Thampra*, I am not afraid of the punishment. Let the patent be mine."

"OK, OK. If you're prepared to donate your head, I'll proceed with your proposal."

The theme to be discussed and proved was a statement. The proposition prepared by the *Sava* youth was propounded by the *Naya* youth before the *Tundits* of the palace—with the *Naya* as the sole proprietor of the proposal.

The thesis read: "The sky is not studded with sun, moon and stars alone. It's a playground for other heavenly bodies like plenty of planets, series of satellites, countless comets, millions of meteors, myriads of meteorites and assemblies of asteroids.

The head of the *Naya* youth deflected to delinquency. Due to that the *Tundits* or the learned class suffered degradation. The *Tundits*—notwithstanding they were all nonsensical persons—were regarded as the most deliberate, delicate and delicious maxims for people of Indana. A *Tundit* was not less than a living deity. Nobody else had the right to discover, invent, explore, find out or even think of the natural phenomena or unnatural falsity. And if any higher caste person wanted to try such cases, they would have to obtain permission from the academy of *Shastra* run by the *Tundits*. A *Tundit* was the title awarded to the exclusively learned class from the *Toojari* caste.

The *Naya* youth had defied the *Tundits*' clan. It was true that he too belonged to a high caste. But that was the lowest organ of the body of the higher castes—it was as good as an overgrown nail or hair—an insignificant item. His sound body was counted in the society, not his sound mind. Often he was cunning. Usually he was permitted to explode his cunningness to exploit the lower castes by making them work hard without wages for the higher and highest castes. But he had utilized his fox-mind against the officials of the society. It displeased them. He deserved punishment. He over-reacted himself. Smelling foul, the defrauder expressed his innocence and forwarded the real culprit, the *Sava* youth and asked pardon for copying someone's misconceptions.

The *Naya* youth was admonished, sent out of service from the demple and given the job of milking fifty milch cows a day. He was cut off from the communication with the society. A plebiscite, (exclusive high caste affair) he was declared as a plebian.

This was no punishment when you hear of the punishment awarded to the *Sava* youth without a plea.

"Plug out all his communication systems."

The King's vindictive verdict was vindicated by all the *Tundits* of the royal court. They as one man said in falsetto, "Me lord, it's a perfect plebiscite. Here-after he and his caste fellows won't look at, hear or talk about our heavenly bodies denoting our destinies."

And it was confirmed when the *Sava* youth's eyes were plucked out so that he would not see heavenly bodies or the other bodies on this earth. His tongue was pulled out so that he would not talk to anybody on this earth. Molten plumbago was poured into his ears so that he would not hear the voice of his own cry.

I mourned. The villains! Plucking the pluck of a plucky peasant plugged by the God as a present to every person. He lived for some more time on this insidious earth's surface in insanity. Some scolded him, some scorned him, and some scoffed at him. But some wept for his misfortune. They believed that posthumously he was transferred from this planet to some other part of this universe and transformed into a transcendental star that served as a sun to some other solar system.

But that consolidated and confidential concept was concealed inside the tranquil minds of his caste fellows only. Thus the so-called astray *Sava* youth turned astral for his caste fellows.

The learned class had a concept that the shining shower seen in the sky had nothing to do with astronomy and it had everything to do with astrology. They regularly conducted the study of occult influence of heavenly bodies on human affairs. The luminous objects seen during the dark hours were the flying serpents from the heaven, unable to be seen with naked eyes. They always soared in the space. Some of them did random patrolling in the atmosphere. Some rarely came down and took shelter on top of tall trees like me (Banyan), coconut and palm trees. Some serpents would rarely abandon the jewel on their head, especially when they flew over the sea or river. And sometimes someone would get it. That jewel was said to be the most precious, sacred and lucid stone in the whole universe.

The person who earns such a jewel was considered the most luckiest and honorable on this earth. He would gain prize money. But, whoever it was, he had to hand it over to the state treasury—to the King's palace—the most sacred and safest place to keep it. It was believed that the rays of the jewel could pass through even a leather case. So none could conceal it. If someone was caught for such an act, he would have to relinquish his head along with the lime-shaped stone to the state.

The lucky stone would be brighter than Sun and as big as a lime. It could be seen even during daylight, provided the serpent opened the lid on its head. Usually, they opened the lid during night hours.

And the learned class had another concept—superstition or not—that the moon, sun, planets and stars were objects denoting the destiny of human beings according to their apparent positions. *Tundits* extensively practiced astrology to find out the lucky stars of the princely people.

Another belief they kept pertained to the eclipse. There was another belief. Sometimes the moon swallowed the sun when the moon turned a python and the sun became a frog. This was called the solar eclipse. The lunar eclipse was believed to be the revenge of the sun when it swallowed the moon. During the total eclipse, one should not look at the sky. However, they might view the magnificent sight indirectly by looking into plates filled with water mixed with cow dung.

I could only chuckle on their mysterious and irrational fear of unknown things. I accepted the statements of the *Sava* youth because I avowed myself that after awhile, it would turn automatically into an axiom. Neither Hova, B'lla and Eysa nor our *Guruji* ever mentioned a legend related to the flying serpents carrying and sometimes catapulting sacred stones from their heads.

As the wheel of the time rolled, it achieved the goal—the wrong thinking of the learned class came to a halt. Further, they accepted and approved the concept of the *Sava* youth that they were not serpents but meteors or shooting stars. They developed his invention of bamboo monocular into a giant telescope. They made decent developments in the science of the sky giving due weightage to astronomy rather than astrology. The science of stars shed more light on the dark corners of their minds eradicating the obscurity of ignorance. Yet, the prejudice against the polluted caste prevailed upon the *Tundits*—they did not prefer the preciousness of the *Sava* youth whereas some of the *Tundits* hesitated to approve the legendary *Sava* youth.

*   *   *

I would like to emphasize how the men of Indana felt the need for numbers; how they started numeration; how they gained the numerical ability and how they invented numerology after Eysa's demise. It was quite funny yet fantastic while I counted and calculated in my recollections, because I and most of the fauna and flora were very much familiar with the arithmetic from the remote past of my habitat.

The *Tundits* established an academy of arithmetic. All the formulae of counting and calculation were taught there to the upper caste students. The history of the discovery or invention or exploration or anything you may call to find out the values of the digits and figures was another story.

As the human being is credited with a single (one) body, they knew only one figure—they named it as digit 1 (one). Whenever they wanted to count two persons—a married couple—they counted as *you* and *me* or whenever they wanted to give three fruits to somebody, they gave him one each thrice by counting one, one, one (1,1,1—three times). Then they felt the need of number two (2) they had two eyes, two nostrils, two hands, two legs, etc. After that they were in need of the number three (3) because once a man had to give two coconuts to a *Rajashree* and one coconut to a *Vypari*. So he had to gather two + one (2+1). Thus they found out the digit three (3). The figure four (4) came into being because they saw most of the animals had four legs followed by figure five (5) as human beings had five fingers on each hand. The introduction of number six (6) came into the rolls because the queen had six fingers on her right hand (5+1) became six.

In a sword-fight practice, a prince lost three fingers from his left hand. To count the remaining fingers, they invented the new number 5+2 = 7 (seven). Once the king's fingers got whitlow except the thumbs. The fingers with whitlow had to be explained to the *Vaidya* or Physician as *eight* (8). After inventing the figure 8, one day, one *Jyothishy's* little finger was bitten by a snake. So the physician wanted to isolate the remaining nine (9) fingers. Afterwards, the total nails of both hands were to be polished for the high caste ladies with the Athena. They could not get a number for that. Actually, they had ten digits already starting from zero (0) to nine (9). Zero denoted nothing or empty or vacant—not valid at all. The *Tundits* of the numerical *Shastra* struggled hard to find out a procedure or formula or a theory or a way to establish the numbers like ten and its folds like hundred, thousands, etc . . .

An old *Naya* caste person, who was an attendant in the academy for providing the *thaliyola* or Palmyra leaf and *narayam* or an iron-tipped stiletto for writing, was fascinated by the *Tundits'* experiments in numerical activities. It was he who suggested the method of putting the zero to the right hand side of a number to add its value to tens, hundreds, thousands, so on and so forth. Thus the Indans paved the path to have void *zeroes* as valuable heroes in the field of numismatic. Thus they succeeded in building numerous numerical castles and sky-scrappers in arithmetic like fractions containing bricks of numerators and denominators. Prior to that they computed and fractionated by inventing addition, subtraction, multiplication and division. That in turn led them to learn mathematics, algebra, geometry and trigonometry. Subsequently coins become popular among the populace.

So, cash took the place of kind. The common people fancied themselves dead. They were extravagantly fanciful about the medium of exchange! You gave many sacks of grains and you got money! Just a small coin as substitute! You gave back the coin; you could take back the same sacks! What a wonderful acceptance among each other! They considered the currency as their own parents. So they named it as an abbreviation—*Famo*. They made coins of small denominations. They denominated the denominations as *feeds* for they regarded the smaller coins as good as their food. The subdivisions were: four feeds made quarter of a Famo. Half-a-Famo and one-Famo coins were made out of copper; five and ten Famo coins were of silver; differing in their values as per their size. A hundred Famo coin was made out of Gold. The former inscriptions on the coins were of the heads of the godheads like Brahesh, Vishma and Mahnu. Later, these were changed and the marks of the monarch's head of Indana took that place.

All the castes had the liberty to handle the coins without fear. It was the trick—suggestive idea—of the higher caste, especially the *Toojaries*. Their intention was: Let the lower castes work hard; earn some money. After all, the same had to come to the treasury. The high caste kept the exchequer. Though the polluted castes were prohibited to enter the *demple* and pray to the exclusive godheads belonging to the holy castes, they were permitted to give their offerings to the *demple*. Earlier the offerings were in kinds like milk, ghee, jaggery, grains, sandalwood, and other *homa* items. It was a difficult job to get those items purified especially the consumables. The holy caste considered it as abhorrent substance and neglected it as trash. That incurred great loss to the *demple* funds. But with the introduction of the currency, instead of consumable substances, the *Toojaries* suggested money. The suggestion in turn swerved to demand. The poor and innocent polluted caste wholeheartedly welcomed the suggestion. At least it was an opportunity to supplicate before the holy godheads for pardon and their sufferings, if not from close, at least from, long range. It was as good as a reformation to them.

Hundis were installed at unapproachable distances. So many drops of small coins became heavy rain of currency. The *hundis* were flooded with money offered by the common people especially the superstitious woman devotees of the *Sava* caste. The *Toojaries* sprinkled some holy water over the haphazard coin collection. Then they hugged it close to their hearts as though that was dearer than their children.

Anyway, with the introduction of the currency, the illiterate common people automatically learned to count the coins from one to ten. But, while counting, at times they were chilled to the marrow. Such was the horrible and terrible ending of the man who found out the value of the *zero!*

Stealing was the charge. Stealing what? Stealing knowledge. A new crime! Any unauthorized persons (of the lower caste) who willingly or unwillingly tried to acquire knowledge should be punished for stealing. If caught, they should be treated as thick thieves. The punishment was "brainwashing". The brain trust of the country ordered, "Shave off his head; keep a heap of camphor on the crown of his head and burn."

The unlawful, unsafe, unreasonable and unworthy order was exactly carried out. Thus the brain trust showed incivility to that brainy *Naya*.

A *Sava*, being from the depressed caste, though born great, was considered as without any greatness. Normally, they had only greatness thrust upon them.

*   *   *

The drought descended upon like a dragon. Its tongue of heat licked up all the vegetation. Unsatisfied with the prey, it kept its mouth open to swallow all the creatures of Indana. Cattle collapsed day by day due to non-availability of fodder. Inhuman men split open the throats of all the available animals, collected blood and quenched their thirst. They cut the flesh and kept the lump on hot rocks for drying and ate it.

Acute shortage of water prevailed everywhere. All the water sources, including the wells in the palaces and demples, dried up. Though the river dried up patches of water were seen here and there. The bodyguards of the noble castes protected them for the exclusive use of the palaces and places of worship. But rumor spread that water was unnecessarily wasted in the kitchen and bathrooms of the noble castes.

As animals were unhealthy to carry the loads of water, able-bodied young men and women from the downtrodden sects were deployed for the purpose. They carried water-filled tanks right from the riverbed to the royal beds. They touched the water with their hands. Some sipped the water like animals did. In normal course, such was considered polluted. The noble castes never used such water even for cleaning their undergarments. But in the drastic situation, they gladly got used to it.

They regarded it as pollution-free. They provisionally lifted the prohibition on pollution till the end of drought, until everything went back to normal.

Some carriers urinated into the drinking water for the holy people as an act of vengeance. The holy caste, unaware of this, drank it as holy water thinking that it had more mineral salts than usual due to the drought. Those who were aware of it simply used it as sweet water for the pollution was nil before the famine.

Palmists, astrologers and fortune-tellers were ordered to assemble in the palace court. Astrological calculations were conducted. The soothsayers declared that the God of *heat* had to be pleased to end the drought. The only solution was that the young prince of Indana should marry a prostitute! She should be a whore, yet a virgin! She should be from an unholy caste, yet a holy girl! She should be in her sweet sixteen!

What paradoxical and funny conclusions the *Tundits* had reached at! How could a prostitute be a virgin? How could a *Sava* girl be from a holy caste? If one had never attended a school how would she be a scholar? Where to search for such a girl? The prince had to search for her by travelling all over the country.

Alone, the young eighteen-year-old prince set out on his journey. He wandered through many populated areas, he crossed many deserts, and he passed many forests. He had the liberty to do anything with anybody. He ate and mated with many unmarried.

Before reaching the big sea and before getting out of the forest, he saw a hut made out of creepers. He heard a crescendo. Yes, a human voice. But there was no one around. Only the crescent in the sky was present. The waxing moon smiled at him. He peeped through a crevice.

A sweet sixteen! A *Munikumari* or daughter of an *Irishi*—a scholar in divine science. She was sitting on a vine crib. She was uttering something in low plaintive tone into the ear of a deer. They were some stanzas pertaining to twilight. The crepuscular song reverberated in his ears. The prince could see the reaction of the deer. The deer sniffed. She patted on its body. The deer's setulac stood on end. Priapism prepared in the *Panchakarani* of the prince. All his five sensory organs got stimulated.

He entered the hut. She let go the deer. Oooh! What a beauty! She got up. He studied her from head to foot. Her genitals were covered with a big banyan leaf, all other parts of the body were exposed. He had never seen such a charming creature in his life. His eyes were sure about it. He touched her breast. He had pumped a lot of breasts including his mother's. He had never felt the softness of those breasts anywhere before. And her nipples? What a spring effect! His hands could sense that.

She slowly walked away from him. The shining black strands of hair were so lengthy that they swept the ground while she walked. The Mother Earth felt horripilation as she touched her. Yes, this was *the* beauty. Even the creator would go crazy over her. The most beautiful girl of his kingdom would seem to be an ugly woman before her. He wanted to deluge her with questions: What on earth she was . . . But his lips just quivered; there was no sound. His throat dried up. He did not have the courage to ask her anything lest she should disappear.

So he plucked a green leaf from the creeper, wrote with his thumb-nail "*I love you*" and held it in front of her.

She said softly as if reading a poem, "Oh, you paramour, paramour, I don't know love for I'm an unholy, holy girl."

He murmured, "I'll teach you. It's very simple."

The *Munikumari* asked, "How?"

The young prince replied, "Practically. Just touch me. You can hear the music of love. Just kiss me. You can consume the honey of love."

Munikumari: "The job of my hands is to do the *pooja*; the job of my lips is to chant *mantras*. Love's forbidden to me."

The prince: "Love's life. How can you live without love?"

Munikumari: "Your love's not pure love; your love's full of lust."

She turned away from him. By this time the prince was panic-stricken with his priapic mind. Her luscious, bare back maddened him.

He grabbed her from behind. She resisted. But his paroxysm overwhelmed her. He forcefully laid her on the leaf-strewn ground and raped her.

During the course of his forcible intercourse with the *Munikumari*, the *Muni*, her father returned from the woods after his daily *yoga*. The *Muni* closed his eyes. He raised his hands. Instantly the hut was filled with fumes, fragrance and flute music. Besides, a bed of flowers sprang up. The *Muni* came out of the hut.

All the while, the young prince was raping the *Muni's* daughter. After the rape, he looked at the girl. But seeing the rareness—fragrance, fumes and flowers—inside the hut, he became cautious about his rashness. He got up.

The *Muni* again entered. He pointed his right hand's index finger against the prince's forehead.

As if hearing the rappel, the royal lad tried to draw his rapier. But he could not move his hand. His respiratory organ rasped against his ribs.

The Muni said, "*Kumara*, you broke the *Niyamam* of the *ashram*. You're a rapist."

Prince: "*Guruji,* I'm not aware of the *ashram's Niyamam*. Please don't curse me for violating the chastity of your daughter. She is that charming and luscious."

"*Kumara*, I know. Even The Almighty feels ardency towards her. But a sin is a sin. No repentance would save you. The only cure for your ailment is to marry the *Kumari*."

Prince pleaded, "*Allayo Guruji*, I'm not a rapparee. I'm from the royal family. I can marry only a chaste girl, not a whore. And if she is a whore, she should be a chaste girl."

"Areh!" the *Muni* said in surprise. "Dear royal lad, tell me about your conditions clearly."

"My would-be wife should be a prostitute, yet a chaste girl. She should be from an unholy caste, yet a holy girl. And she should not be less than fifteen and more then sixteen. Above all she should be a scholar without schooling, especially in divine discipline."

"If you want to honor all these conditions, then your would-be wife is my daughter. She's the same chaste prostitute. The profession of a prostitute is to do adultery. She'll lend her body voluntarily for the sake of the gifts. My daughter has not been a professional that way. It was you who deflowered her. So in a way she lost her virginity. So she's a whore. And the other way she's not a whore. She's as good as a chaste girl provided you marry her."

"But that is irrelevant to my problem. She should be as holy as a priest as well as unholy as a polluted caste person."

Pointing to the girl, the *Muni* said, "That same holy yet unholy girl is standing before you. She's unholy by birth for her late mother was from the *Sava* caste. I am her father and as I am a *Tundit* she was brought up as a learned lady. A holy person is none but a learned person. I taught her all the rites of *poojas, homas, mantras* and *tantras*. She's as intelligent as Goddess Saras, as powerful as Parva, as prosperous as Laksh and as beautiful as Urva.

"You know, she's devout as well as diabolic. She could have easily devastated you for your dirty trick. But she recognized your diadem."

"Oh! What a deuce am I!" The prince deplored. "I'm not to be pardoned. Please punish me for my devilishness. I'm a *paapi*."

"You're a *Pavithra paapi* (pious sinner). We won't punish you. Whatever happened is destiny and your meeting was inevitable. You're made for each other. Marriage is a mark by The Almighty, not by the men."

The *Muni* gave the prince a pot of julep. When he drank it, the prince in depression felt vitalized again.

The shocked *Munikumari* took a long breath and regained normalcy.

They were married before an *agnikundam*. The Muni was the priest.

* * *

They reached Indana city. The *Munikumari* chanted *varsha mantra* or the hymn of rain. All the subjects joined her. A *varsha homa* was conducted at the courtyard of the palace. Many rites were performed in the *demples*. Rich men carried out various religious ceremonies to please the god of rain. The heavens opened.

The fumes emitted from the *homakunda* and the voices of the *mantras* reached high in the sky disturbing the clouds. Rain started pouring. People danced.

Jubilant crowds sang, danced and rejoiced. There was fun and frolic everywhere. Irrespective of caste, creed and color, they enjoyed the jubilations.

The jocund company of royal and the *Tundit* class felicitated the young prince for his achievements. Their purpose was fulfilled. The great problem had been solved—they got rain. The river flowed jovially. The wells and ponds were filled with water.

I found that all the Indans were in a jovial mood. Even animals, after filling their bellies with water, joined the jocund company. I was also happy to have a nice bath in the heavy rain. My roots drank enough water.

In a nutshell, the whole of Indana rejoiced except the young bride, *Munikumari*. Yes, I watched her curiously. She was in agony. As the downpour began, the *Munikumari* seemed devitalized. Her physical and spiritual powers transformed into water. Gradually she became weak and weary. No one cared for her; no one congratulated her; no one consoled her. She was jostled by the crowd. Like a fallen flower she collapsed on the ground. Everyone repudiated her as if she was a repugnant object to them. Lying on the ground, she was squeezed and smashed by myriads of feet. She squirmed; none saw it. She squeaked; none heard it.

Thus the divine bride was devastated in the dense forest of the human devils.

In the meantime, away from the merriment, a man stood on the balcony of the *demple* tower. He was extraordinarily tall, fat, and healthy and he was above normal in every physical aspect. Besides all those 'extraisms', he owned long grey hair, tied on his pate, tied with threaded Ilion cooperies. His long gray moustache stood projected to both sides of his face like the pointers of a balance. And his long grey beard! It had grown long enough to touch his feet. Though he had just celebrated his centenary, his eyes had the experience of a millennium.

In short, he was the symbol of masculinity. He was none but the *Maha Kama Vaidya* or the great physician of the Indana Academy of Priapism— the dean. At this age he still used to take classes for the students who underwent specialization course in *Kamashastra*. He invented medicines for expanding and reducing the *lingam*—a small plantain-sized penis to a big banana-sized *lingam* and vice versa. He possessed an anodyne tactics to augment a pin-hole *yoni* to a pond-sized vagina and *vice versa*.

Maha Kama Vaidya was mesmerized by the magical beauty of the *Munikumari*. He, the one-time gratuitous, was said to be the greatest fucker of Indana. The size and strength of his manhood was said to be unparalleled. The performance test on him—duration, throw, volume and matters like that—had produced fantastic results. Procreation was the predominant feature of his research. He entertained unlimited number of voluptuous wanton beauties, presenting lovely babies to their wombs and filling their mind with merriment.

In the first glance itself, Maha Kama Vaidya guessed that the *Munikumari* was the pre-eminent and precocious one above all the women he had mated with. Seeing the girl's unpleasant situation, he ordered his attendants to save her from the predicament.

I too suffered the prick of conscience witnessing her pathetic condition.

The downpour was in full swing clearing the arrears of the period of drought. Fed up of the flood, people returned to their dwellings. A spate was growing.

Yes, the unconscious *Munikumari* was carried inside the chamber of Maha Kama Vaidya. She was laid on a sandalwood cot. Yes, it was indeed a compassionate deed by him to save the life of a great woman. I appreciated him for his magnanimity.

He kept his hard palm on her forehead. She was wet and cold. He stripped her of the soaked clothes. He removed his dry saffron cloak and wiped her soft body with it. She was as cold as snow. She should be warmed with human heat. He lay down on top of her—not giving much weight on her chest—and covered her with his long beard and hair, making them a woolen blanket. He pinned his hot penis into her cold vagina, thrust his hot tongue into her cold mouth and sucked her tongue, rubbed his palms on her palms producing heat by friction. His hot breath sent sparks of heat into her brain through her nostrils. His hot saliva steamed up her mouth. Series of his orgasms injected ounces and ounces of hot semen into her cold womb. The culmination of the sexual act shook up her senses. Her cold body started gaining heat from his body. The transfer of heat thawed her and she woke up. She began to breathe heavily; her heart throbbed passionately. She opened her eyes.

When her senses came alive, her eyes attained crystal clear vision. She stared at him still lying on the cot. She was astonished. Who's standing beside her? A theophany! No. If not, is he a man? If so what a figure? The more she exclaimed, the more she was puzzled. She was all the more shocked when she saw his strong penis pointing at her like a cannon—something preeminent!

She swiveled her head. Many men were standing around her naked. Then she looked at her organ of orgasm. Owff! It resembled a shattered target shot at by many hits. She looked at their faces. There was contentment.

"Where's my husband?" She enquired in utter despair.

"Can't you see us?" Maha Kama Vaidya replied.

"All of you are my quasi-forefathers. I want my hus . . ."

"Hush, baby, hush. He's your prince."

"Yes, the prince. He's my husband."

"He was. Presently, he's the husband of somebody else."

Then, there appeared the Prince along with a beautiful bride clinging to his right shoulder. Unable to get up, the *Munikumari* said in agony, "Ho, my paramour, save me from this distress."

Looking at the rapists, he said to her, "They'll save you."

She said, "It's the husband's duty to save his wife."

Patting on the shoulder of the accompanying lady, Prince said, "Yes. By all means. At present she's my wife."

"Then what about me?"

"You're my ex-wife."

"Mind that I'm a *Devakumari*, as good as the daughter of God himself."

Maha Pujari said, "We're also not less than *Devas*. The priests who communicate with God. Now onwards you're our *Dasi*."

"Daa . . . *sii* . . . !" she screamed.

"Yes. *Devadasi*. The one who would entertain us with songs and dances and by exposing the body for our desire. Then only you'll attain *moksha*."

Likewise, she became the entertaining slave for the holy and royal persons. She gave birth to many daughters. In the long run, all those dolls became the grand dames—*Devadasis*.

Having come to know of the doom of his daughter with the *gyanadrishty*, the Muni in the jungle flared up. He cursed the entire Indana and the Indans: "*Om Siva Shakti!* Let the power of entire Indana be grabbed by someone other than Indans. Let all Indans be slaves of the invaders.

And that happened exactly. The invasion of Indana by the foreigners, first the followers of B'lla, followed by the followers of Hova.

* * *

When I rose with the sun, I was so puzzled to find that Indana's sun was set: Bands and bands of rough and tough men had arrived in Indana. They were slim, tall, wheat-colored, though sun-tanned, with trimmed beards and cropped hair. They wore turbans. Attired in *chudidar* and *pyjama*-type garments, they wore leather belts around the waist and swords hung from them. The owner of the sword had no idea how many heads he had chopped off and the sword did not know how many swords it had confronted during the battles fought on their way to Indana from Pakkana.

They arrived during the night. They stayed in the demples. They got up in the wee hours of the morning though they had completed a very hard cross-country race during the last day. They knelt down, spread a sheet on the ground, bent their bodies, touched their foreheads on the ground and then shouted: "B'llaaaaa . . . ."

The shout woke me up. I watched their activities. I had no idea who they were. Everything was foreign to me. Where did they hail from? What was their motto? From their repeated actions and *fortissimo,* I could guess that they were praying. But that system and style of prayer were alien to me. Immediately, I recollected the epic of Pakkana told to me by my dove-of-thought. So my dear friend B'lla the great might have introduced his own way of praying. The *guru* had never taught us such a method. Anyway, I appreciated their *fortissimo* hailing. It was as loud and grandiloquent that the voice could be heard in heaven. After the prayer, they dived deep into the demple pond, swam at random and had a nice bath. Then they went in search of food.

When the *Toojaries* came to the *demple* to perform the morning *pooja,* they saw the demple doors of the surrounding block and the sanctum sanctorum ajar. Instead of the usual fragrance, the place stank. In the place of sandal paste, they could see night soil in and around the shrine. Instead of rose-water, they saw urine even beside the idol. It seemed that someone had rubbed his wet urine-stick on the idol. All the brass utensils such as plates, glasses, goblet, censer, Sanctus-bell et al were missing. The most astounding deed was somebody had sat on the top of the *demple* coffer kept outside and comfortably completed his call of nature. The shit scattered all around. The urine travelled right into the coffer through the hole. In short, the entire area was polluted totally. No amount of sacrifice, *mantra* and *tantra* would purify it again. Besides that, the crystal clear water in the pond was churned with filth and sediments.

I recalled the purification proceedings of the pond when a clean cloth of the executed *Sava* youth had fallen in the pond. It took many days, great manpower and much money to mend it.

It was a private pond. Indana's religious reference said that if a *demple* pond was polluted thousand-folds of expense and exertion were needed to purify it. And if a *demple* was polluted, even ten thousand-folds would not be enough. Just think of purifying ten *demples* and their ponds! That too all dirtied with faeces.

I could not calculate the manpower and the expense it would need. So I handed over the job to my branches. They attempted their very best to calculate it but failed. The reason was very simple—relinquishing all the essential activities of day to day life, let the entire Indana population work through their lives aided by all the treasuries of the exchequer. Even then there was no guarantee that purification would be completed! A Himalayan task indeed!

The *Toojaries* pathetically prayed to all the godheads they knew of— Lord Brahesh, Lord Vishma, Lord Mahnu and goddesses Parva, Laksh and Saras. None of them responded. Not even the nemesis. The idols remained silent as if they had no complaint against being polluted. The godheads (idols) seemed to be enjoying the stink of the excrement as if they were censed. Idols, after all, were just statues. Stink or perfume, could they sense? Nevertheless, I could see a smile on their lips.

Indana was known as the brightest land by all its meaning to the invaders. Their religious leader, B'lla, had flattered the divinity of this land. But Pakkans could not see any magnanimity. Very soon they realized that Indans were nothing less than clods. Notwithstanding their expectation of glory, they were gloomy. They possessed a totally different culture. The Pakkans' *modus operandi* and *modus vivendi* were distinct from those of Indans. They never propagated casteism and racism. Maybe because they were all white-washed by God himself. Socially and economically all of them were in *pari pasu*. Or it could have been because of the proclamation of B'lla: "All men are created equally."

But Pakkans were wayward and perverted when compared to Indans. Their sexual instinct was perverted. There was something unnatural. For them, the most vital organ of their body was the external organ of generation. It had to be kept clean always.

The idols inside the *demple* were mere whim-wham for the invaders. They brushed their urine-stick on the idols made of smooth rocks after urination. While rubbing their organs, some men felt sexual desire. They hugged the life-size idols of naked goddesses of ideal beauty. Thus, instead of sublimation, the objects of worship were subjected to stain. Idol-worship was alien to the invaders.

But to their surprise, unlike in Pakkana, the earth of Indana was a paradise to the Pakkans, the invaders. Deserts formed most parts of their country—a sandy waste, interrupted by bare rocky hills and arid valleys. But here, ha, everywhere there were rivers, lakes and ponds! There the ground was often bare. But here, ha, everywhere there were trees, plants and green fields! There the rainfall was generally very less. But here, ha, drizzle, rain and downpour round the year! There the desert villages were almost uninhabited most of the times. But here, ha, the villages were always vivacious with cattle and men! There the climate was always too hot in summer and too cold in winter. But here, ha, how very pleasant is the weather! The invaders undoubtedly understood that Indana was rich in the demple of fame.

Prior to narrating the invasion, I would like to quote the status of women in Indana as a whole. *Guruji* had taught: *Janani Janmabhumischa Sawrgadapi Gariyasi.* Eysa taught all Indans that all the women were mothers. The mother and the motherland had to be venerated as worthier of adoration than heaven itself. The first place was given to the mother. Any pain-suffering person would naturally wail *Maa . . .* I could hear even animals crying calling mother: A calf would cry *Aamma.* A cat cries *maaavoo.* This meant all the beings called their mothers when in agony. So, it was quite natural that the *guru* gave women the first position in the society. They were symbols of modesty. Thus, a woman was addressed as *Devi* or goddess, *sakhi* or friend and *sumangali* or the auspicious with deep respect. The *guru's* advice memoirs are very celestial. I remembered that the *guru* educated all of us—*Vidhyarthis, the nagas* and me—in the name of Saras, a female godhead of alphabets.

So, during the regime of Eysa, women of Indana seemed to enjoy profound respect by men. As the wheel of time turned and turned the corruption of the original pure doctrine of woman's status suffered a gradual wear without the bearing of Eysaism.

*　　*　　*

With their bodies made clean and fresh, invaders now needed refreshment. So they marched ahead with swords held aloft. As they moved, they hallucinated that they were moving through a never-never land. Crossing a mango grove they ate ripe mangoes. Then they went across gingilly and mustard fields. After that they passed through paddy fields. There they saw men and women cutting and tying the straws in bunches. Men lifted the bunches onto women's heads. They walked with those loads of paddy straws along the narrow ridge in single line. The marching invaders followed them in formation.

The last man in the line was straggling; he wanted to urinate. A little distance away he pissed behind a mango tree. A lady was plucking mangoes. Timidly, she ran away through the field of grown up sugar cane. As she ran, her loin-cloth-covered buttocks ascended and descended alternately; her bare breasts pranced up and down. Her sex appeal overwhelmed the straggler. Being left behind, he thought of following the running lascivious lady. There was a chase, the former like a stag and the latter like a lion.

At the far fringe of the sugarcane field, there was a two-room thatched hut. As the lady entered the house, she saw her husband asleep there.

She cried out, "Come on hus, get up fast. A *Rakshasa* (giant) is trailing me. Please hide somewhere."

She pulled him from the sleeping mat. He could not stand straight as he was a cripple. She handed over the walking stick to him. Simultaneously, the invader intruded.

"What is this creature? Does this belong to this planet?" Panic-stricken, the cripple took a chopper to protest. The intruder gave a riposte with his long sword. The chopper flew off and fell near a wooden pillar in the centre of the room.

Sensing danger; the woman came to a conclusion: Time called for tactful action. Here, sagacity would be more powerful than sanctity. Safety of self and her disabled spouse was in her hands. She did not want to take any risk. The intruder being a strong sadist, succumbing to his wish was the only congruent alternative to save their lives.

"If not, he will kill my husband, I will be abducted and gang-raped by all the invaders," she thought.

So, she lustfully smiled at him and coaxed in a sweet voice, "Allayo, beauty and sturdy, come, let's enjoy."

Her language was alien to him; but he understood the meaning.

She removed her loin cloth. Ha! He was stupefied by the sight of her stupendous body structure! The disheveled tress of her long hair and the curly pubic hair maddened him.

As she invited the intruder into the kitchen room, the cripple barred the way. The intruder pushed him away. He fell down near the pillar. She threw a rope at him. Intruder tied the cripple to the pillar. She said succinctly: "He's a loggerhead. Good for nothing. I hereby subtract him from my life. Would you please add me to your life?"

The intruder understood the succinctness from her gestures. He was contented with the contemptuous attitude of the lady towards her husband. That increased her trustworthiness. He joined her for enjoyment in the other room.

The disdainful words of the able-bodied wife hurt the disable husband. It was something that could spoil the congeal happiness. He heard the hissing and kissing audio of adultery from the other room. He turned back the pages of the book of his married life.

He, who belonged to the top branch of the social tree, broke the social hierarchy by marrying a voluptuous *Naya* beauty belonging to a lower branch. The intercaste marriage dictated the prohibited degree of relationship. He had the liberty to maintain her as a mistress, not as a Mrs. The social villain broke his legs making him a cripple. They were outcast. Thus the anathemas settled on the outskirts of the straggling village. They were enduring a happy conjugal life by farming and cattle-rearing. She undertook the outdoor activities; he looked after the domestic matters. They were akin. He was her god; she was his goddess. Both of them were like *multum in parvo*. He learned the lessons of love from her, considered her as the redressed forum of life. But now . . .

She has shown a subterfuge! He could see an underground chasm in her character. Perished by the fornication of his wife, he cursed her: "Owff! This woman! She's a sadist. She can split up even splice. She has become the spolia opima to an unknown intruder!"

He contemplated: "I shall die. Prior to that I must kill her."

He grabbed the chopper lying beside.

Covering her nudity with the loin cloth, she came beside him from the other room. Her sweating body seemed vitreous. Her chest throbbed; eyes were full of fear but they reflected contentment as if she had won a war and confiscated the spolia opima.

Here comes the impostor, he thought. He also should act as she acted. He pretended love to her: "Where's our guest?"

"Resting," she replied.

"You've saved my life."

"It's the duty of a wife to save the life of a disabled husband.

As she was untying the rope to release him, he grabbed her neck, bent it and locked her head between his thighs. He fumed: "You cheat; I don't need you anymore. Now you're as good as a spittoon. You should have killed yourself rather than entertaining him. You spoiled, now I'll kill you."

Without much ado, he riposted her neck with the chopper. The gushed out spray of blood painted his face red transforming him into a devil.

She tried to elucidate with quivering lips: "I've not spoiled my love . . . I've killed . . . him. He's . . . res . . . ting . . . in . . . Peace . . . My endear . . . ment . . . wa . . . s . . . fa . . . ke . . ."

The cripple husband did not know what had happened in the other room—as per the custom and procedure; the invader had to clean her genitals before an intercourse. He made her stand erect, sucked the succulent vulva. She gripped his head close to her private parts and stabbed him to death with the long knife she hid behind her back.

In deep regret the crippled husband consumed poison and embraced death.

My vitreous wish to congratulate that particular woman of Indana for timely action of using her intelligence to save her husband's life and hers plus her chastity. But unfortunately fate fragmented it by swallowing her.

Ending the mad and sad sagacious story of one of the invaders there let me concentrate my mind on the saga of the other invaders' fortunes and misfortunes as well as the fortunes and misfortunes of the inhabitants of the union of Indana.

The farm workers and the infantry of invaders reached an *illom,* the palatial residence of the landlord of that district. There was an idol of *trimurthis* in the centre of the wide yard. The landlord, after the paganism, opened his eyes. He saw the invaders who had intruded into his compound with swords in their hands. The other pagans were also puzzled to see the foreigners.

The landlord asked the labor chief in surprise, "You've brought the crops. OK. Are these thugs also yields from our fields instead of weeds?"

The chief answered with decorum, "Yields or weeds, they're not grown in our fields. They seem to be foreigners."

It was the day for celebrating the grand gala birthday of the landlord.

Almost all the village dignitaries and families were invited.

"What the hell do they want? They have polluted our compound," said the landlord.

"These poltergeists polluted our demples and ponds also."

The *Toojaries* from the *demple* came panting and narrated the *demple*-hunt.

By that time the invited and uninvited multitude had arrived in and around the *illom*. They arrayed themselves obeying the unapproachability dictum. Prior to enjoying a full meal, they wanted to catch a glimpse of the invaders. Panic spread through the people when they heard that the invaders were at large. The people tried to skulk from there. The invaders swung into action, covered the *illom* compound and thus blocked the escape efforts of the people.

The invaders felt pangs of hunger. They expressed their desire and demand through gestures. Half of them had birthday feast while the other half remained on guard holding their swords in both hands.

After the feast, it was time for prayer. Half of them prayed while the other half remained on guard. After their prayer, they compelled all the assemblage to perform prayer as per their style *au pair*.

At times, everything surrenders before sword point.

Those who resisted were annihilated; those who were reluctant were beaten up. Seeing the gory situation, others obeyed the sword-command of the invaders word by word, inch by inch and act by act . . . Soon after the prayer, they ordered all the male members to quit the place and the female members to remain there.

They wished to marry the women of Indana. Their hair, eyes, ears, nose, throats, bosoms, bellies and buttocks intoxicated them. They selected pairs. Some selected teenage girls as their brides. In the evening when all the available men and women prayed to B'llaaa the hail echoed in my ears. I just had the feeling of witnessing a mass *PT* (physical training).

The landlord sent his messenger to the district headquarters demanding a protection force to curb the hostilities and chase the invaders out of Indana.

Without much ado, a platoon of men with swords and shields arrived. But without more ado, they were defeated by the invaders for they were born fighters brought up in torrid zones. They were such a type that they did not know what fatigue was. They needed only food. They would work like machines, perhaps better than machines, because machines halted due to wear and tear but the Pakkans never faltered. Nobody could stop them. Moreover, the indigenous force could not stand the tropical climate. As they had never sweated before any attackers they had to bleed before the invaders.

The landlord was fastened on to the life-size statue of the *Trimurthy*.

Afraid, he passed his stool over the idol, polluting it.

The matter of malice was reported to the king. He immediately summoned the *Jyothishies* from all the branches in the capital city to verify the antecedence of the antagonists. They were identified as Pakkans. The *Tundits* found out the precedence—the names of Pakkana and Pakkans were mentioned by Indana's *guru* Eysa in his holy texts. It was said that the Pakkans in the neighboring country on the other side of the snow-capped mountains were to be treated as brothers as they were the followers of B'lla, the *gurukulam* mate of Eysa.

Hence the king ordered the district authorities not to take them hostage but to treat them as guests. Those misappropriate orders paved the way for causing more infliction upon the Indans.

Men who came to witness the mass prayer were circumcised; good-looking women were raped. They were forcefully enrolled in the religion of B'llaism.

Gradually the B'llaists started moving to the other districts spreading their religion by cutting the foreskin of the genitals of all the males and marrying the women in *Rakshasa* style: Capturing of the maiden from her residence, enjoying the agony of the victim after slaying her kinsmen. People obeyed the antagonists lest they should be annihilated. The door of B'llaism was opened for all regardless of caste, creed and color. Some were volunteers for they were attracted by the purple color and distinct culture of the Pakkans. The black women thought that they would have reddish offspring if they went to bed with the purple Pakkans had the art of using their genital spikes on the Indana women was appreciated.

Within fifty years of their invasion, they had conquered fifty districts—about half of Indana. And within that short period, about fifty thousand families—about a quarter of the population of Indana converted into B'llaism. The Indans were adhered to monogamy; the Pakkans were polygamous. So they enjoyed sex with many women at the same time. They hated zoomorphic and dendrolatry. They only believed in monotheism—B'lla. B'lla was their only God. They never performed idol-worshiping. So they destroyed all the idols of Eysaism they came across. They looted many *illom* and razed many *demples*. They erected myriads of *purches* in the place of *demples* and installed their holy text to read and worship the words of B'lla. All the *purches* had huge dome-shaped roofs. Three times a day, prayer was compulsory to all the B'llaists.

Having come to know about the grave damage caused to the country and its belief, the king swung into action. But it was too late.

A battle was fought: Almost all the northern part of Indana went under the custody of B'llaists and the people under their control. They prided themselves in their victory. They intended to attack the capital of Indana, my birthplace. They conquered the area up to my shadow. They camped beneath my crown pitching tents. I heard the antagonists preparing a plot for attacking the palace. And if so, the Pakkans had nothing to do other than beheading the king. And if so, I had nothing to do other than wiping out the name Indana from the history of the world and annex the area to Pakkana. And if so, the people of Indana had nothing to do other than forgetting their traditional faith in Eysaism and believe in a foreign faith B'llaism.

Though I believed in *Vasudyva Kudumbakam* (world is one family) this was something unjust. After all Indana was not Pakkana and Pakkana was not Indana; after all Indans were not Pakkans and Pakkans were not Indans; after all Eysaism was not B'llaism and B'llaism was not Eysaism.

Though all men were equal, their thought and faith differed from person to person; though all tongues and saliva were of the same composition, the taste varied from mouth to mouth. Compelling to accept the disliked taste and faith would make men mad. That was what the Pakkans were doing. So I had to register my protest against unfair attempt.

Let the King play any kind of war tactics, I was certain that it would be ridiculous—the victory would be far away. The only one tactics to defeat the Pakkana immigrants was known to me alone—not by any sort of metal clash or bloodshed. It was by a natural force which was intrinsic. The indecent invaders, their successors and followers intrigued for toppling the kingdom. Simultaneously, stronger intrigues were going on within me and my wives to chase the totalitarians out of the country.

We held a conference. In fact it was a conspiracy. It was for the first time in my whole life, I had donned the garment of a conspirator. My family members and relatives—my wives and all my branches, adventitious roots and other nearby trees—whole-heartedly joined the conspiracy for they too knew the purpose was the eviction of the evil-doers. The aim was the uplift of *dharma*. Frankly speaking, we, the flora never believed in annihilation. We were born to help and develop the life of living creatures. So, there was no question of beheading or slaying the antagonists. It was just a sting. A sting that caused a sharp, smarting pain, enough to divert the antagonists from the attack.

Who would sting them? With what? When? And where? We could do it at any time; we could do it anywhere; we did not have to gather any stings for that. Then how? We had a task force. A force which was not even as large as a fly. They had the stings. It was like a minute pin. But it had the power of many swords. It could create even acute mental or moral anguish. We planned to use our task force at the right time. We anxiously awaited to watch their movements. As we waited, the flower of the last night of the sixteenth century of my life fell down and there blossomed the fresh flower of the first morning of the seventeenth century . . .

CENTURY 17

1601 TO 1700 AD

The memory of the events of this century is not at all sweet to me. It still stings.

All living things directly or indirectly help man. There is a great deal of interdependence of give and take, and insects play a significant role in this. But the thankless man always rejects the fact.

Our task force was composed of insects, the wasps. Almost all my branches had wasp hives hanging like pendants. They were comfortably breeding in those elaborate homes not only on my branches but also on most of the hollows of the trees in the surrounding area. Our intention was only to compel the intruders to disperse by fulminating the masses and masses of wasps in order to rebuild the kingdom. I was very nervous for I could not reckon anything up. Therefore, I handed over my commander-in-chief position to a nearby young jackfruit tree supported by all other members of the plant kingdom in the vicinity. They advised me to wait and watch until the expected event occurred. As the second-in-command, I waited.

The invaders' intention was to attack the place in the dead hours of the night. So, the whole day they were spending time in wassail and merry-making. Some tied my aerial roots with reef-knot, sat on it and swung in the air. Some used them to stand like on swinging bridge; some did rope-climbing; some jumped from one branch to another like in a circus; some made use of the branches as parallel bars in a gymnasium; some jumped from tree to tree like monkeys.

Those who climbed up the branches were fascinated to see the wasp hives. They mistook them for black-and-brown jackfruits. The act of

A.K.B. KUMAR

swinging, the sweep of moving bodies and the oscillations disturbed the peace of the wasps. Besides, some miscreants broke small branches and killed some wasps.

Losing the safety and tranquility, the swift-winged wasps abandoned their homes. They swiftly spread around. They stung the tyrant's group point-black. They had never expected and experienced such an attack by the unidentified flying creatures. Some of the ufologists among the attackers misunderstood the insects as UFOs.

The *en masse* attack of the wasps forced the felons to flee. Lemon-sized swells developed on the bodies where they were stung. Due to the acute bodily and mental pain of the pungency, the speed of the exodus reduced considerably. The avenging insects hit them like miniature guided missiles. Without looking back, the original Pakkan-blood flowed back to Pakkana renouncing Indana and leaving behind some miscegenation of B'llaism to the renegades of Indana.

Yes, the misfeasance had their misfortune for their misdeeds.

As an ancient member of Indana, I still remember the first human race—the arrival of the young couples from Cheenisthan. During those days, the only cultural stream flowing around my habitat was for faunas and floras. The men had no philosophy of life like social organization, rules of conduct or law comprising social, economic, cultural, scientific or religious elements.

Indana had a distinct faith, Eysaism. When people of Pakkana came to Indana and settled down here and there with an entirely different faith, B'llaism, they could not absorb the vast fold of Eysaism.

While the wheel of Indana's society was moving freely, the Pakkans applied brake on it. For the early rule of the B'llaists described how it utterly spoiled the religion and culture in the religions of the places they took possession. B'lla fanatics defeated and insulted Eysa society. Yet they showed iron will to withstand and to uphold Eysaism. Still, due to compulsion, some of the Essayists assimilated B'llaism. Slowly and steadily, there grew apostasy. Sooner or later, the renegades absorbed all the alien culture fully. The merging had its merits and demerits. The most unhealthy feature and adverse effects that led to deteriorate the concerned status of women.

The intentions behind the Pakkans' invasion of Indana were looting and fucking. They had already looted more than enough. They had already fucked myriads of women from all age groups. They were very much interested in raping. They liked women when they wailed. The defeated

352

men who fought against the invasion were either killed or put in prison. Their mortified wives were tortured and raped. One such incident still stings my mind.

A young Indan warrior fought against the Pakkans in the battle over my neighboring district. Soon after the victory, the Pakkans declared all the Indan fighters who sustained more than fifty per cent injury as good for nothing—dead bodies. The young warrior was also one among them. Though he had sustained only ten per cent injury, he too was declared equal to the dead.

A mile away from me, there was a field. It served as the ground for the state's annual fair, exhibition and games. The conquerors arranged numerous pyres to burn their rivals who were declared dead. The above-said youth was also placed on the pyre. Logs of firewood were piled upon him. He screamed like other victims who were also alive with throbbing hearts and running blood.

I stood *rigor mortis*.

Their wives came and gathered around the pyres wailing. As per the fighting force's rule in Pakkana, no fighter was supposed to have sexual affair during the war. This was to preserve the stamina. When the war was over, they had the liberty to fuck anybody in order to quench their sexual desire.

The screams of the martyrs, the sight of the blazing pyres and the wails of the widows served as scenes of a horror movie—so horrible and pathetic to any hard-hearted human that he would feel like lamenting for them.

On the contrary, the warriors felt this funny. It was the right occasion for them to celebrate the peace-time rules; it was the right time for the fanatics to fuck the widows of the defenders. They found pleasure in mating the sail of their vessels of frenzy in other's ocean of agony.

Warriors caught widows, stripped them, and threw the garments into the burning pyres. They were laid beside their husband's pyre. Some worked on the widows' comely bosoms as though they were interested in uncooked meat; some sipped the vulva like gourmets interested in the wine hidden in the vagina; some raped the widows for hours on end as though their semen valves were out of order. The rapists changed rounds and the widows were raped . . . raped . . . and gang-raped!

The above-said brave fighter's bold and bonny widow did not submit easily though she could not resist much. So, escaping from the grip of a rapist, she ran straight towards the pyre of her husband and jumped into the blazing bed of the corpse. The flame welcomed and swallowed her with pleasure. I saw a flash of happiness on her face.

Thenceforth, in order to save chastity, the widows of Indana welcomed wholeheartedly the process of *mathi*—the vernacular word meaning *enough* i.e. They did not need life on earth anymore for them after the demise of their husbands. They felt more sacredness in sacrifice than in the widowed life. It was better than becoming victims of the rebel fanatics' sadistic lust. As the days passed by, mathi, the women's joining the husbands in death by climbing onto the blazing pyre became popular.

I consulted with my family members about the anti-Eysaism war.

A deep-thinking tree in its youth complained: "I agree that the disaster of the human race was unpleasant. On the contrary, what about our family members? Was it not atrocious? They too were chopped down and burnt!"

Though I too was angry like them I chided, "Hush dear, hush. Don't be so heinous and hostile to our patriots. It's we who became the fuel to burn them. After all, we should be grateful to them for they fought for our motherland."

I was crestfallen over the B'llaists conquest of Indan women by the *purdah* custom of Pakkana. This custom was to prevent the women from molestation and teasing. A veil-less woman was regarded as a shameless and inviting woman.

One day, an elite class Eysaist lady went to the demple. On the way, a lewd B'llaist was attracted by her beauty. He straightaway worked on her by hugging her fast, kissing her lips and inserting his organ into her genital passage. Though he was impotent, he was an important person in the B'llaist society. Though his standing shot was very short, the public fucking created a huge impact on the Eysaist society. Her lips were injured by his bite. To conceal the bleeding she covered her gory face with the tip of her sari. Then on, all the Eysaist society ladies other than the ones from the downtrodden sects started veiling their faces. Subsequently, the custom of *purdah* became popular in the B'llaist-occupied areas as well as other parts of Indana. Consequently, by the observance of *purdah*, the women were secluded in the dark and denied the light and pleasures of the external society. Eventually, they suffered from physical, mental and moral ailments.

I was surprised to see the tremendous change in observance of the foreign culture by the Indans in the ceremonies and mannerisms, dress and drink. The Pakkans too assimilated some aspects Indan culture and fashion in return. Indans blended the Pakkan music and dance with *Indanattam* and *Keerthanattam*. Thus many new rhythms and melodies were born. B'llaist women wore ear rings. Eysaist women wore nose rings. Likewise sari and salwar-kameez were exchanged.

I felt pity for the people who broke the principle of *ahimsa* and encouraged the slaughter of animals and killing of birds. Once a pure vegetarian *Tundit* was invited for a marriage feast of a B'llaist. He was immensely interested in the taste of the non-veg preparation. He had cloyed *Biriyani* and chicken roast. During the satiation, the glutton consumed liquor also. His experience paved the way to meat-eating by many bonvirants belonging to the upper social strata of Eysaism. Having come to know of the pleasant taste of the vegetable masala, the Pakkan gentry also started consuming Indan food at their festivals. Day by day pure vegetarians became gourmands and gourmets.

I appreciated the B'llaists' belief in monotheism. It influenced many Eysaists who were fed up of appeasing of and praying to innumerable idols. The monotheistic ideology led them to the revival of equality, fraternity and universality.

The Pakkan language, *B'llia* was sweet. It added a great number of words widening *Indi* vocabulary. Initially, I used to laugh at the nasal pronunciations in that foreign language; later I came to like it more than the language of my own country.

Other than the astronomical signs and the dated calendar, another contribution from their scientific culture that I liked most was the medicinal field, *Paknani*. The system was useful in the treatment of ills of the fauna and flora too. They were masters of architecture. The arches, minarets, domes and turrets added style to the buildings. The Indans also began to adopt that style to beautify their constructions.

The last but not the least significant change Indana accepted from the Pakkans was the replacement of palm-leaf and the stiletto for writing. They began to use slates and graphite rods as materials for writing.

Thus the Pakkan society accepted the Indan culture and Indan society adopted Pakkan culture forming an innovative society of Inda-Pakk culture on mutual understanding.

In a nutshell, the life cranked slowly and steadily with the aid of mutual understanding gears of the B'llaists and Eysaists. The oil of social interaction smoothed their movements with the help of love and brotherhood. Reports of rare incidents blocked the movement at times. But it picked up speed again. The mutual adjustments and joint ventures opened the door for building a strong society and carving out a peaceful life.

I'm not a historian but I have many memoirs in the form of chronicles and short stories in my mind that serve as records of the B'llaist rule of Indana. After the initial conquest of the districts and the states, they annexed the entire northeastern region and established an empire. Out of the many B'lla military conquerors and empire-builders, I corroborate the concise biography of the most acclaimed emperor, Raziyum the great, who had secured a place of distinction in the history of Indana.

He was born in Pakkana in the early years of this century. In spite of the study through books aided by tutors, he wished to learn the real and practical life himself. The boy enjoyed his days hunting, camel and horse-riding and animal-taming. He was the successor of the famous king Kakker, the founder of B'lla dynasty in Indana.

His uncle Barasher killed his father. His mother was put in prison. Barasher declared himself as king. However, the nephew was looked after by the uncle. A homosexual, he was deeply passionate to the handsome nephew. He liked to remain a chronic bachelor for he hated women. He was the brain behind the *mathi*.

The king said, "Dear, you would be my successor for your boldness. You didn't mourn your father's death. You're loyal. You didn't resist your mother's imprisonment. You're sweet, you didn't dislike my desire."

At the age of twelve Raziyum was appointed governor of a nearby state after defeating a *Rajashree* king. The puppet prime minister, Jairam, joined the B'llaists. He was appointed caretaker.

He advised the young governor, "Your uncle is a cheat. Beware of him. Better uproot him before he cuts your stem."

They waited for an occasion.

The smart scion of the defeated king was against B'llaism. He joined hands with the neighboring states, marched towards Barasher's palace with thousands of war elephants. A historical battle was fought. Raziyum was present there. He played a trick with the help of Jairam.

Instead of sword and shield, all the men in the Barasher's army carried bunches of plantain and jaggery in one hand and a cage of biting ants in the other.

When the enemy elephants came near, they were amazed to see the rivals without arms. The hungry elephants were fed with the most delicious item. Simultaneously, the men tactfully inserted ants inside the trunk. The huge animals became angry, threw away the fighters and mahouts, ran at random and created huge distress and destruction to their own side. In the hustle and bustle, the nephew sent an arrow into the eye of his uncle. He fell down from horseback while the running elephants' legs crushed the king to chutney.

At the age of sixteen, he was proclaimed King. On the occasion of coronation everyone paid tribute to him. Jaimala, the beautiful daughter of Jairam, became the playmate of the young and handsome king. Later he married her as per the norms of B'llaism as well as Eysaism.

He had a great quest for conquests. Over half a century, he continued his annexations, expanding his dominion to entire northern and eastern Indana. During his empire-building, he happened to conquer a kingdom which was ruled by a widow queen. Her charm and valor were laudable. She fought heroically. But her fighters could not withstand the overwhelming deluge of arrows—they fled. Eventually, the eventful combat ended. He defeated her country. She defeated his heart. They got married according to the Eysaist custom. On the first night, they had free and frank curtain-lecture:

Queen: "I' am forty."

King: "I' am fifty."

Queen: "You're my fourth husband."

King: "You're my fortieth wife."

Queen: "All's your grace."

King: "How?"

Queen: "You encouraged widow marriage."

King: "I foresaw that a brave widow like you would come to my bed."

Queen: "I too foresaw a valorous king like you were there to bed with me."

King: "Anyway, our face-to-face fight in the field is over. Now let's start the battle on the bed and see who's braver and stronger."

They unrigged their dresses and started rigging their organs of lust considering that she was his first wife and he was her first husband. Like young married couples eager to break the celibacy and chastity in their first night they played love games.

The vision in the royal bedroom was vague. But as they came out of the valance, after the battle of the bed, I frankly evaluated: Both the erstwhile valentines were equally strong and bold in bed.

Another king from the *Rajashree* dynasty was defeated. The army stole all the wealth from the state's treasury. Soldiers snatched the jewel ornaments of the surrendered King's daughter.

Emperor ordered, "We drop the booty and take the beauty."

King gladly offered his daughter to the emperor. Emperor restored the state to him. He took the princess on his horseback and galloped to his place.

She was well-versed in *Kamashastra*. The emperor enjoyed with her all the postures described in the text. After her arrival, he stopped playing with his other wives. They were neither allowed to mate with anyone else. Out of his fifty years of royal rule, he had fifty wives of different ages, castes and creeds.

His senior-most wife belonged to the B'lla religion. She could not digest the total consumption of her dear husband's love by a young bride belonging to the rival religion. Moreover, her only ambition was to make her son the successor.

She murdered the new bride. The emperor was dismayed.

The mother and son were paraded naked in the court. The emperor provided a poniard to his criminal son and a sword to his cruel wife.

He ordered, "Son, you put the poniard into the genitals of your mother. Wife, you cut the genitals of your son. Let's see who does it first. It's your choice. The faster and smarter between you would survive."

To the surprise the whole courtiers, the mother and son, so eager for their lives, committed their assigned jobs simultaneously. Both of them bled to death.

To commemorate his intense love for his young bride Jaimala, he built a famous marble flower of architecture *Meeramahal*. Consequently he ended his quest for conquests. Instead, he started making finest monuments, pillars and gardens throughout his dominion.

Other than his administrative reforms such as central government— holding of his unlimited powers, provincial governments for decentralized administration, reasonable revenue reforms, currency reforms, trade and commerce development, judiciary, communication facilities, security and military and art, architecture and literature, I'm loquacious about the religious policy of Raziyum. His catholic approach and liberal idea pertaining to religion resulted in myriads of virtues. I admire his efforts to bring about the synthesis of all religions during his reign to curtail religious rivalry. He constructed a conference hall, summoned the learned priests of both the religions and used to preside over the deliberations. He never made any attempt like his predecessors to force his religion on others because he was a universal lover. He discouraged *Mathi* and allowed widow marriage as well as inter-religious marriage. He himself was the pioneer and example in marrying widows and ladies from other sects. His vision of the national idealism led to the establishment of cultural as well as political unity in the empire.

*   *   *

Before I say something about the decline of the empire of B'lla, I would like to describe the literary contributions of the Pakkans and the Indans. Other than the holy book, the Pakkans had only a compilation of nine-hundred-one-night stories. But if I cumulate all the amount of literature deposited by Indana in my bank of memory, there were two major accounts which had become the passbooks of memoirs. Those passbooks were issued with cheques by which any writer could draw any amount of facts, formulae and ideas for ample use of story-making even in modern times—The four main tactics and the four objects of human pursuits, i.e. virtue, love, wealth and beatitude.

The first and the best passbook is the *Mahapurana* written by Gyanananda, one of the devoted disciples of Eysa. On completion of his monkhood, he went into the deep forest. The hermit wrote episodes and episodes pertaining to the *dharma* and *adharma*—the revolutions and solutions in the practical earthly life of the human beings. The work became the holy book of Indana.

The other one incorporates love, affection and romance among all the beings in the nature. His work's zoomorphism and dendrolatry became the conceptions of animals as deities and worship of trees. They became the doxologies for Indans. The author, Kaladhara was an illiterate boy. The goddess *Shakthima* blessed him. He rose to the position of the palace poet. Most of his writings were master pieces, especially *Munikumari Mangalam.*

The drama version of the poetic story had been staged many times before me. I liked the performance of Mangala, a *Munikumari* who fell in love with Mukundan, a King. Their platonic love became an example to the cupboard lovers in beau monde.

In short, the golden works contributed by both the authors were nothing less than wisdom banks for the whole world—the moral and model stories pertaining to wine, women and wealth causing all the troubles of sex, sin and sinister. The readers learned from these texts the principle "Giving love and taking love are the most profitable businesses in life."

Though the B'lla society was feudal-oriented, it has had its brilliance and dullness. The emperor was the head. He lived a lavish and luxurious life. They passed the time in indoor games like chess and wrestling.

I still remember the introduction of chess by a learned *Tundit* of Indana in the early days of Pakkan invasion. It was nothing but the application of the last tactics of human pursuit.

A small force was attacked by Pakkans. The petty chief had only a small force of sixteen men, camels, horses, elephants, one administrator and the chief himself. The *Tundit* converted the four kinds of forces— cavalry, infantry, elephantry and chariotry—into a game of chess played by two men (kings) with dice symbolic of the above-mentioned four kinds of forces. He divided the army into two groups, arranged on either side of the sixty-four columns, tactfully broke the martial order by making each move intelligently and tactfully. Thereby he could win the game with one or two outstanding moves.

The small army of the district defeated the big army of Pakkans diligently with chivalry as in a chess game. Notwithstanding the failure, the intruders apprehended the *Tundit*. He received appreciation from the conqueror's side. On the contrary, some of the sorcerers sardonically yet seriously said, "Well, he's intelligent as large as life. If we eat his brain, we too shall become intelligent like him."

Their misconception was approved by the chief conqueror. His plan was to mince the *Tundit*'s brain, stuff into a gut and eat it all by himself.

So the savage summoned the sage-like *Tundit*. Before breaking the skull the *Tundit* was asked, "Tell me bright, your last wish?"

"My wish would be very costly to you."

"A dying man having so greedy a wish?" said the conqueror in surprise. "OK, open your mouth."

The harbinger humbly said, "Assume the sixty-four checks in the chess board as a granary. Kindly keep one quintal of wheat for one square; keep the double for the next square; keep double of that for the next square. Keep on keeping the double of the grains of the previous one for the next-to-next and next-to-next squares till you store the granary for the sixty fourth column."

"So simple a wish. Give it to him," The conqueror sauced the sage. "But, I can't understand what you are going to do with all these provisions! This is your last day. One quart of grain is more than enough to cloy you."

"This is for the people of my village who suffer from famine; nevertheless I too am at a loss to know from where you are going to provide this much provision."

"More than quarter of your country is under my control. My word has the weight of the world. If I can't, you'll be set free."

They tried hard to fulfill the wish of the *Tundit*. But they could not comply with it even though the conqueror chief ordered his cavalry to bring forth all the grains of Pakkana.

By the by, the conqueror became desperate, he kept his word—the *Tundit* was set free. But the jealous sorcerers murdered him. In order to pay homage to him, they recognized the game of chess. Chess was gradually developed. Eventually it became the royal game for the royal people. They made black and white dices of King, Queen, Rook, Bishop, Knight and Pawn. The chess notation, in which each move is registered as a particular dye moving to a particular check occupies the titles for many checks. And each check is known by two titles, one from the position giving superiority in defense or attack of White, the other from that of Black. Each player makes bad moves and good moves according to the skill and the opponent's response.

Likewise, wrestling took birth from the fight between two stout Pakkan army men. It all started with a lecherous lady inviting two of her lovers to her bedroom at the same time. Enraged, one lover said to her, "You cheat, why you loved him?"

Inflated, the other lover also blamed her, "You should have loved me alone."

She replied, "Cool down hotty, cool down. Both of you ordered me to love. I obeyed. Now you decide whom shall I love."

First lover: "You love me."

Second lover: "No. You love me."

Verbal quarrel turned into physical fight. They had a combat. The first lover killed the second one. It was free-style wrestling.

A soldier was killed by another soldier! The news spread and fell in the ears of the Pakkan Provost Marshal. He was surprised to hear it: How could a man kill another of equal qualities without any arms? He wished to witness the demo. Another man was engaged with the killer on the condition of not to kill each other but only to fight. The fight was witnessed and cheered by all the invaders. I too beheld it as a by-stander. I did not enjoy, but they did. Thenceforth the fight was named wrestling with certain rules and regulations—the one who makes the antagonist to lay flat on the back would be the winner.

God creates man; man creates trouble. Often he wishes to trouble others; but it comes back as his own downfall. Such was the case of the decline of the B'lla dynasty.

After the demise of Raziyum, a series of puppet emperors occupied the throne. They were fanatic and involved in various types of atrocious deeds on Eysaists like imposition of religious tax, demolition of Eysa demples and dismissal of non-B'llaists from government services. The unimportant rulers were far away from virtues. Neglecting the administration, they got addicted to depravity. Good became bad; bad the worst. B'lla's' court turned into a market for conspiracies and civil wars. Their own kinsmen became their own rivals.

Gradually, the defeated and the expelled Eysa rulers gained power. They encroached upon the empire in the north under the command of the so-called tiger of the forest Balaji. This created a desire for cutting out independent kingdoms helping the rapidity of dismemberment of the B'lla officers as well as Eysa chiefs. The frequent rebellions led to the pilferage of the treasury and the empire exhausted.

B'lla rulers were proud of having a vast coastal line as a territory sans any threat. They left the area unattended, never bothered to protect it. One fine morning . . .

*　　*　　*

Unlike other days, I woke up early in that morning not knowing that it would be a day that would turn all the stones of Indana to face a new test. I confirmed it. I wished I could melt all the gold of Indana to ink. I should point all the diamonds of Indana to pens to write the forthcoming history of Indana in golden letters.

As usual, the fishermen plied their boats to have a good catch. The calm sea resembled a green glass sheet. It was clearer than crystal. Then they saw . . . Far in the west a huge figure appeared. It was approaching the shore. Securing their nets, fishing hooks and floats, they ran back to the shore fearing the figure was a sea-monster that surfaced from the marvelous and mysterious bottom of the sea.

My top-most branch could clearly see the object. Undoubtedly it was a vessel as described by my dove-of-thought during its journey to the land of Hova. The only difference was that this particular vessel was bigger in

 size and was called a ship. The news spread from the coast to the interior
regions. The District ruler was Karithiri, an orthodox Eysaist from the
Rajashree caste.

He proclaimed, "On to the sea shore. On the way summon all the
villagers and their kith and kin. Let them carry all the available weapons
including the household tools to combat with the strangers from the seas."

* * *

The seafarers were surprised to see the forest along the coast behind
the white sandy beach from far away.

Grabbing the throat of the captain, one of the crew said cruelly, "You
bastard, you told us Indana was a land of gold and silver. It's a land of
fragrance and spices. It's a land of art and culture. But what the hell,
where the hell and why the hell you landed!"

Main-sheet man bounced, "It seems only forest, forest and forest
everywhere. You want us to feed on leaves and stalks? We're not asking
for butter but just a piece of bread. How many days have passed without
a drop of fresh water touching our throats? How many days have passed
with our eyes beholding not even a single woman?"

Maintaining peace and patience, captain politely said, "I can
understand your starvation. But, I can't understand your imagination. The
food's cooked. Wait till it gets cold." They unrigged the sails.

* * *

The natives lined up on the coast ready to raise the weapons to attack
the appearing object. To their astonishment, the floating and dancing
object anchored about a call-distance away. They saw moving bodies on
board. Then they saw a boat approaching the coast. A foreign party landed
on the coast.

The dissimilar dress of the aliens—the boots, pants, overcoats,
waist-belts, long hair, beards, moustaches and whiskers—fascinated
not only the people but also the animals and coconut trees which were
witnessing the remarkable occasion of the invasion by sea.

A stray dog snarled ferociously, bared its teeth and jumped on the
captain. Swiftly he took something from his waist-holster and pressed a
lever. A blast was heard and some smoke with a peculiar smell streamed
from a hollow tube. The dog howled and went flat. Witnessing the magic

of the foreigners, the villages stood thunderstruck. They dropped the tools involuntarily on the sandy beach.

The navigators were brought before Karithiri.

Communication was by action like in the television newscast for the deaf and dumb.

I got the points which read:

Captain: *"We're friends. Not enemies. We wish to have trade and commerce with your land. We admire this land . . ."*

As the crew took sand in their hands and kissed their fists in order to respect his land, Karithiri nodded as though he understood the foreign (Hovan) language. He said in Indi with similar gestures: *"What will you give us in return? If you behave badly, we too will play wicked. I heard you killed a dog with some fireworks!"*

Captain: "That's for self-defense. It's my pistol."

Karithiri: Please demonstrate it. We've plenty of dogs here."

The captain took his muzzle-loading pistol from his hostler, loaded it, and aimed at a dog standing away barking. The moment he pressed the trigger, the dog fell down dead.

Gladly Karithiri said, "Well, we give you a piece of land for use as your base. You give this lethal stick to me."

"It's not a lethal stick; it's a pistol . . . a pistol . . ."

Karithiri said, "What's there is in the name. It's the performance that matters."

The captain was compelled to hand over his only gun to the District Chief Karithiri, lest he should sweep the sea. He was happy to have the fire-arm like a child who just got a doll.

"Right. Now walk around and select a suitable place to make a base for trade and commerce purposes."

Thus conciliation took place. They were given tender coconut water.

The foreigners walked into the interiors.

They exclaimed. Oh, God! The coastal village of Kalabar, Indana! Really marvelous! The forest on the coast line they saw from the sea was the swaying coconut trees! Everywhere there were canals, creeks and lakes that stretched like fingers from the palm of the sea! Fields of dancing paddy leaves beckoned them! An unspoilt paradise with pure and quiet nature. On the waterfront were situated myriads of thatched huts providing natural air-conditioning. The fittest and finest place for boating, fishing, trekking and bird-watching. The land resembled a pictorial sheet.

The navigators, after appreciating the beauty of the land and remarked as one man, "Really, this is God's own land . . . More valuable than gold!"

The Hovans liked the hospitality of the people. The dress of the natives—the elite class attired in clean white double-dhothies tucked in at the waist as lower cover and a bordered shawl worn around the neck as upper garment. The people of the downtrodden classes were clad in half lion-cloth of hard fabric. This fascinated the foreigners.

The farmers working at the paddy fields and toddy-tappers climbing the coconut trees like squirrels were wonderful vistas to the visitors from Britana. The caste, creed and color prejudice of the predominant people of the peninsula were not at all that familiar to the foreigners. They loved the country and countrymen of this wondrous part of the world.

On the contrary, in a short span of time, they felt the wondrous land and marvelous landlords transformed to thunderous men and ponderous material. Initially, the Indans were also eager to share happiness with Hovans. But very soon they understood the exotic men were white-skinned but black-hearted. Their cunningness came to light. Hence the curiosity of the natives turned into animosity towards the guests.

One day, the white men were summoned.

Karithiri cried, "You cheats, we complied with our custom of hospitality towards guests or '*Shatruvum than grihea vannal, vazhi pol salkarikkenam*'. But you're worse than enemies. Though you are modest in speech and behavior, you are not at all decent. Now no more straightforwardness from our side."

Hovan captain humbly asked, "May I have the liberty to know what's the accusation?"

"*Thondy konduvaru.*"

A dark man was brought before the lined-up foreigners. He carried a casket.

"*Thurakku.*"

The casket was opened.

The pistol which was presented to Karithiri and some spare parts of the gun were seen! The ruler took the pistol, he loaded it. He said, "I gave you the gun to kill a stray tiger because you had good aim. But you cheat; you gave it to this blacksmith to make a duplicate. Not one or two. But many duplicates. You gave me only four pellets and a little gun powder. You liar, you've lots of pellets with you. You want to kill me? Kill all of us? You conspirators, you did not know that this blacksmith is my spy. Get lost from my land."

"Please return the gun. We'll leave this land and go to our home."

"It's better to leave from this world and go to the grave." Handing over the only gun to Karithiri was a folly on Hovan's part. He fired.

The captain fell down and died on the spot.

His colleagues ran for life. They jumped into the sea, swam like swans and boarded the ship at anchor already loaded with spices. They set sail running free as they got a good westward wind.

The people gathered on the coast to see them disappear and dissolve in the horizon along with the sinking evening sun.

*   *   *

Without the captain, with a full load of condiments, the ship entered the harbor of Britana. Even before embarkation, the bidders boarded the ship. Buyers made a hue and cry on the jetty. In order to have a glimpse of the favorite foreign items, there broke out pandemonium.

Samples of black pepper, cardamom, cloves, turmeric, tamarind, dried ginger, citronellas oil, etc were sent to the Queen. She was surprised by the pungent and aromatic quality of the stuffs.

She exclaimed, "Really these are God's eatables!"

The above-said nature's produces with their attractive smell, color, taste and medicinal effects, were more valuable than precious diamonds in their land. Diamond cannot be consumed. But these items! Ha! It was something foreign to the foreigners. The land of Indana was a wonderland to them. They regarded Indana as God's own land. Stepping on that land was as good as landing in heaven!

The Hovans were already aware about the Indan produce through the Pakkan traders who came by land route. Since then, they had dreamt of discovering a sea route to Indana to establish their sovereignty in trade and commerce.

The Queen of Britana promulgated, "Congratulations crew, congratulations. I hereby declare that the maritime relationship between us and the Indans would be our monopoly."

There was a publicity-cum-demonstration of the produce from Indana in the capital city of Britana.

A merchant: "This's cardamom. Just smell it and enjoy the aroma. Just bite it and enjoy the taste. Just one piece is enough to relish ten pounds of cake!"

Hearing the merchant's magniloquence, people came and purchased the merchandise.

A clove-seller from another stall advertised: "Just bite and see the effect."

One miser: "What's the cost?"

"Ten pounds apiece."

"Whaaatt? Ten pounds?"

The shopkeeper said with sarcasm: "Don't buy. Just put the coin in your mouth; chew and enjoy the taste of metal."

A turmeric-seller announced the healing power of the turmeric paste on the skin disease as well as the odor and insect repellant qualities of the citronella oil. A buyer who consumed a little eucalyptus oil mixed with warm water was relieved from his stomach ache. Another man who was suffering from tooth ache chewed a clove and got instant relief. And the zedoary qualities of the medicine created a great zeal in him.

The marvels and magic of the important imported produce of Indana rang many mystical bells in the minds of the people of Britana. All of them carried cinnamon pieces always in their hands to smell and bite. Among the college students, it became a fashion symbol.

*　　*　　*

The next contingent of the Hovans arrived in fleets of huge ships under the command of a capable captain named Hardest. The voyagers carried a lot of guns with them. Their aim was the establishment of a company in Indana. The captain requested trading concessions from Nezeeb, a B'lla ruler. Initially, his mission did not succeed. But later he was granted permission to open a factory a little away from the neighborhood. It still hangs in my memory.

Captain Hardest was a successful surgeon in the Hovan Navy. The B'lla King's only daughter was a very chubby and bonny girl. Unlike the other women on earth, she had a vulva that hung from the crural joint like the tail of a puppy.

B'llaism had by then bifurcated into B'llaist origin and the B'llaist Indan. Though there were protests, the latter followed many customs of Eysaism and neglected many customs of B'llaism. On the contrary, the former was adamant on the religious rites, particularly in marriage regulations in the royal class.

The first and foremost pre-marriage procedure was that both the man and his fiancée should go into a private room to converse and expose their genitals to each other for verifications of the form and hygienic state. It was believed in the royal class that such a meeting would help in checking the virginity of the princess and the celibacy of the prince.

King Nezeeb came to know about the surgical efficiency of the captain. He commanded, "You may show your skill on my daughter. It you cure her, you'll be rewarded. If not, you'll be beheaded."

Captain could cut off the extra vaginal growth of the princess with a minor operation. He needed a pot of boiled water, a pair of sterilized scissors, cotton, turmeric powder and eucalyptus oil.

During the course of treatment and convalescence, the princess allowed the young captain to make love to her. She enjoyed the painless mating with the bold and handsome Captain. Eventually, they fell in love and consequently they got married. King gave the coastal village as dowry to his son-in-law.

Captain Hardest named the place "Kalibay".

So, I threw the name "Massacre" in the basket of the past with the consent of all the floras of my neighborhood.

Captain laid the foundation stone for a factory there. The factory purchased spices from the farmers, cleaned them and made them fit for export. The factory reclaimed vast areas of land to cultivate spices. The coastal region was not fertile enough for such cultivation. So selling out some part of Kalibay to some foreign private businessmen, the factory acquired hectares and hectares of forest area on lease. Further, the factory built many warehouses to store the raw as well as the processed product prior to shipment.

Every year, a fleet would come with boarding parties, who were volunteers to settle down in Indana. Most of them had come as fortune-seekers. On return they loaded the ships with the precious produces from Indana to sell in Britana.

To facilitate the ships' berthing close to the shore they constructed an embarkation jetty and pier. As ships at anchor got harbor facilities, they seldom stayed at anchorage. The weak and weary crews needed boarding and lodging. So, not only the company but many private parties also started hotels. Hotels became duty-free shops as well as brothels. The rich visited the hotels to enjoy the facilities.

There occurred a remarkable social change in the sociology of Indana. *Sans doute,* I could call it a golden era for the lower castes. On the contrary, it was a corrosion era for the status of the upper classes of Indana.

The occurrence was not all that noteworthy. A *Sava* caste man opened a fast food stall on the street side. The controversy was that the shopkeeper had contravened the social law. It was of course a wonder in the society of Indana. How could a *Sava* have the guts to commit such an act! A person who was not supposed to enter an ordinary thoroughfare had opened a shop on the side of the main road that too foods stall. In short, as per the Indan social policy, he had polluted the whole street. Who would go to that polluted place and have his polluted food? His own caste fellows? They were not allowed to enter the area. They could not afford cooked food.

The intelligent *Sava* had an iron will and good foresightedness. He was eyeing the foreign navigators. They were not at all accustomed to untouchability and unapproachability. In their country, slavery was in full swing. The Blacks were supposed to cook food for the Whites. So, the *Sava*'s fast food stall was the appropriate place for their grub. Moreover, they were also interested in country liquors. The *Sava* provided that too. After the booze, some gluttons ate there; some stayed there; some Lucifer slept there for they were provided with the cheapest and best food, accommodation and also prostitutes.

The foreign invasion cooked delicious social food in the pot of Indan history. This *Sava* hotelier also had the chance to consume food paying his hard work. He and his family—wife and two daughters—were plantation workers of the Hovan estate. All the four worked hard; earned a lot by refusing to be spendthrifts.

Once a flood hit the valley. The plantations ruined. The company declared a lock-out. The laborers were suspended. A white supervisor got attracted towards the elder beauty as she was his cook-cum-keep in the farmhouse in the valley. He brought her along with him to the port city. He suffered from malaria. As malaria was a contagious disease, everyone isolated him. But, the *Sava* family looked after him round the clock. They considered him as their savior. They were even ready to eat his shit, drink his urine and lick his spit if it would have a remedial effect. It was not a cupboard love. Their master's life was indispensable to them. Likewise, their love and care was *cine qua non* to him. The sincerity and loyalty of the family amazed him. The White saw the real beauty of the Black in his deathbed. He did not get sufficient words to praise them. So, he surrendered his spiritual property to The Almighty and all his material properties to his caretakers.

The *Sava* family became the owners of the properties once owned by the white man! They were the first landlords of Indana. The most profitable business in those days in the port city was the sale of cooked meat of the animals and uncooked meat of the women. He opened an eating-cum-fucking house.

Other than the fun-and-frolic facilities, another reason for the foreigners to visit his eating house was that they could purchase Indan spices directly from the local cultivators at cheaper rates—tax-free—rather than from their own factory. They did not have to pay Indan money for transaction. They exchanged goods like foreign soap, shaving kit, talcum powder, mirror and other fancy items which were foreign to the Indan market. Enormous people from all the sects came to purchase those items. The *Sava* traders gradually became rich, richer and the richest.

One day . . .

A rich *Toojari* youth visited the port city. As a villager and as a *Tundit*, he was supposed to enjoy only minimum earthly extravagance though he had unending lust not just for foreign articles but towards wine, women and epicurean non-veg food as well. He watched the boards hanging on the street-side.

"*Toojaries'* Hotel and Teashop"

Another board read: "*Rajashrees* Restaurant"

Customarily, customers used to go to the eating joints of their respective castes. But this hungry *Tundit* did not want to go to his people's joint for non-veg food was not available there.

He saw a board:

For Indan and Foreign Food

HOVAN FOOD HOUSE

There was a foot-note also.

Veg and non-veg meals ready.

The *Tundit*'s mouth became a wet basin. The meat masala's smell from the chimney made his nose a red rose. He entered, sat at a comfortable table and ordered his choice.

"Beef kawab."

When the supplier served the stuff his mouth turned to a dry dock. A *Sava* who was outcast from his house was standing before him, smiling. Is it a wrath! The ebony-colored, excommunicated man was looking at him like an executive! "Huuummm."

The *Tundit* had ants in his pants. Though the food was epicurean, he felt nausea. How could a *Tundit* of the high castes consume food prepared by the lowest of the low class families? And see the idiot's forbidden look? Watch his pride! No prejudice at all!

"Huuummm . . . It is all the fault of the ebb of time."

The *Tundit* threw the plate on the waiter's face.

Recognizing the *Tundit* and his punishment, the poor plebeian stood perplexed.

"You *Shumbhan, Mleachan, Adhaman*," the *Tundit* roared, "You untouchable tribe, step back to an unapproachable distance from me." As the bearer was going to the washbasin to wash his face, the Tundit murmured to himself: "Siva, Siva, Wah . . ."

"Did you call me.?" The bearer turned back to the *Tundit*.

"I called Lord Siva., You're not Siva; the lord made you *Sava* . . ."

The plebeian was the personification of patience. But now he got angry: "Here, I'm not less than Lord Siva. But, you're worse than a *Sava*," The bearer approached the *Tundit*.

The *Tundit* shouted: "Yei, you don't pollute me. You know the punishment for it."

"Let me see what would happen to you if I pollute you. All these days we were afraid that something would happen. Let's see practically whether it's an omen or miracle."

The *Sava* servant hugged the *Tundit*, kissed him on the lips and transferred saliva into his mouth for quite some time. Then put the curry bowl on the *Tundit*'s head like a foreigner's fashionable hat.

Shouts of human beings fall of benches and desks and crack of plates created sound pollution inside the restaurant. Three rooms were curtained off as brothels. Three white men appeared before the *Tundit*. All the three were carrying ebony-bodied women in their stretched arms. All the men and women were naked.

I wondered how three pairs of Adam and Eve arrived at the same time and at the same place as though they were about to attend some seminars on pioneer men and women on earth. I had not felt that shy of seeing the premier nude couples who arrived in my habitat but the new pairs at the restaurant were different. The former pair was gentler than the latter. The ladies were writhing in pleasure under the customers' teasing acts.

Making the scene funnier, the prostitutes put their index fingers inside their rectums, took out some shit and stuffed it into the *Tundit*'s mouth as though they were administering some oral medicine to a baby. To add further comedy to the scene, the white customers smeared their semen on the *Tundit*'s face with their long penises. The comedy did not end there. It rather turned into a tragedy. Disheartened due to the defamation, the young man's dead body was found at the jetty. Was it a suicide or murder? However, the real cause of his death remained a mystery.

At that time Kalibay was under a full-fledged government governed by the Hovan Captain Hardest. As the event had occurred under his jurisdiction, a case was filed against the owners of Hovan Eating House. The complainant was the widow of Mr. *Tundit*. She was a resident of a far away village under the jurisdiction of an Indan ruler. The to-and-fro expenses of all those journeys, boarding and lodging, lawyer's fees and other costs of the case were unbearable to her. She sold her property. Her wealth ebbed very soon. She was ready for a compromise. But the accused did not agree. It was a counter-case.

In the Hovan by-law, if an accused was no more his or her next-of-kin was responsible for the charges against the deceased—a substitute respondent.

The final verdict read as follows:

"Defendants 1, 2, 3 and 4 are joint owners of the Hovan Eating House on Fifth Jetty Street of Kalibay. The above-mentioned defendants' venture is their livelihood. Defendant 2 is the wife and defendants 3 and 4 are daughters of defendant 1. At about noon hours 17-7-1677, the complainant's deceased husband visited the shop and ordered a dish. The food was brought and served to the *Tundit* with hospitality by the first defendant.

"But the *Tundit* abused and ill-treated the first defendant. The second defendant requested the *Tundit* to go to some other restaurant. But he refused. The *Tundit* lathy-charged the second defendant. Hearing the hubbub, the third defendant came to save her mother from the hard hands of the *Tundit*. He raped her. When the fourth defendant came to defend the cruel action, the Tundit took a table knife and threatened her. Scared and tormented, the fourth defendant ran away. Defendant 4 is still missing.

"When the three Hovan customers appeared in the restaurant as witnesses, afraid of his guilt, the *Tundit* committed suicide by jumping from the jetty into the sea.

"I have studied the reports and evidences from the prosecution and from the police. I have also heard the arguments of both the learned counsels. The arguments of the *Tundit*'s side were that as he was a *Tundit*, he had to follow certain customs and religious rites pertaining to his personality cult in society. I am here to say that all those pride and prejudice he enjoyed were in his jurisdiction. This is a separate jurisdiction. We don't follow unapproachability and untouchability. No human being pollutes another human being here. However, we command slaves because slavery is allowed. As he hailed from a learned class, he should have studied the maxim: When you're in Hova, live like Hovans.

"So, I am under the impression that all the misfortunes happened to the family of the so-called *Sava* caste members, i.e. the defendants 1 to 4, were because of the misdeeds committed by the above-said miscreant *Tundit*. He could have gone to some other restaurant to avoid the mis-happenings rather than ordering the defendants to close down their shop. It is understood that he intentionally came to avenge the animosity towards the defendants.

"Therefore, law of the Britana's Hovan criminal procedure code 101, 119, 142 and 186 the above-said *Tundit* is hereby proved not as a complainant, but as a convict for trespassing, ill-treating, raping and causing the missing of a person. Besides, the said *Tundit* humiliated the defendants who were peace-loving adamantly believing in social evils.

"As the convict is no more, his window, the next-of-kin of the *Tundit* is declared as the substitute respondent. I hereby award her five years of rigorous imprisonment and five years of simple imprisonment. But considering that she is a widow, a time of one month w.e.f. today is given her to approach the appellate authorities for revision."

"No, jury, no . . ." My shout made my voice quiver and my body shiver. Then I took a long and deep breath and said openly, "What's this barbarism! A substitute convict for the crime committed by someone else? Judiciary is *not* able to maintain whatever it stands for? The law and order are already dead letters. Then why these additional bye-laws? The dead is dead. Let his sin also be buried with him. Why does that sin turn a dead to the dead's next-of-kin? Sans doute, this is injustice on the part of justice." I just kept on arguing grandiloquently to amend the by-laws.

"Hush, husband, hush . . ."

There came a voice, familiar to me in the dim past of my younger years. I asked in anticipation: "Who's that . . . ?"

"It's me. One of your wives."

"Wife . . . !"

"Yes. It's Mena, your wife."

"But my wives have been mum for years and years."

"Yes. We were always hearing you. Now we felt like talking. After all we're your part and parcel."

"Just what do you want to say?"

"It's all about your jumping out of the earth unnecessarily." It was Ramb's voice.

"You say it's not necessary. Didn't you know, an innocent lady was summarily punished for an offence committed by her husband who has gone to the grave."

"It's quite natural. You only told us about the wheel of *Karma* as taught by *Guruji*. Could you please step down the ladder of life to the fifteenth century? Do you remember a *Thampuratti* with a granite heart who made a grand-hearted maidservant clean her menses with her tongue? And when refused, the *Sava* girl was suffocated to death."

"Yes, yes, yes. For that the society punished her grass-widower. Isn't it?"

"Yes. This convicted widow is the same *grande amoureuse*. And please go back further; you may recall an ebony-type *Sava* youth who was victimized for intentionally raping a *Naya* doxy of an old *Rajashree*."

Remembering the deceased object of the past I said, "Ooo, the one whose chopped head was exhibited?"

"Yes," she continued. "He has been reborn as the shopkeeper, the first defendant. Both of them are still travelling on their cycles of birth and death. Their spirits are the same inside different forms of physical bodies. That's why they're not aware of their old life. But as per the doctrine of *Karma*, righteousness and unrighteousness in one life are rewarded or punished in the next."

I agreed with her arguments.

After a pause, she said again, "Moreover, practically we see it daily—the combat between The Almighty's virtues and the unforeseen catastrophes and inequalities in the world. Multitudes of innocent *maram, mrugam* and *manush*, living beings, are destroyed and many constructions, human efforts are demolished in various calamities. Don't you remember the massacre of the land weeds, toadstools and the termites during your boyhood? Why did you name your capital 'Massacre'? Were they not innocents? What were they accused of?"

I observed silence . . .

She was saying in the low tone of a flute: "It's all the fate, dear . . . The learned and righteous God can create such disasters. The ignorant men make laws and the bye-laws."

I nodded, "You're correct, my dear Thilo. I just forgot the teachings of reincarnation, the doctrine of the immortality of the soul and the construction of the law of *Karma*".

"It's because of your *Karmas* are quite magnanimous that we're safe from misfortunes."

I recognized the voice of Uru.

Mrs. *Tundit*'s counsel advised her, "That shopkeeper alone can save you. You should know one surprising fact Mrs. *Tundit*. It was that *Sava* who arranged your interim bail on the guarantee of two of his customers. You may file a petition praying appeal and request him to compromise. Do it within a month or your bail would be cancelled. Then, don't tell me when the police are after you with cuffs to arrest you."

Mrs. Tundit pleaded to the *Sava*: "Please don't drag me to the prison. I've an innocent grown-up daughter as you have. You're my lord. So please . . ."

The *Sava*, deeply moved, patted her on the back. That action did not create any pollution on her, rather it purified her.

The *Sava* said with a determination: "Your husband did not agree that I'm a god. At least you . . . All right, let's forget it . . . You told me that you're an excommunicate from your house?

She nodded.

"Then stay with me as my own sister. Your daughter is my own daughter. Let's all live happily working hard."

No sooner did Mrs. *Tundit* with her daughter unloaded their luggage in the Hovan Eating House, she was loaded with many foreign customers' cocks. Very soon her daughter also followed suit. Her first customer was her mother's counsel.

I judged. Advocates—they are paid by us and we are fooled by them—belong to a shameless tribe.

Thus I wrote a footnote pertaining to the sociological changes that took place in Indana. How a holy caste non-swimmer was pushed into the sea, how a holy caste woman and her daughter were transformed from the inmates of a one-time wealthy and prestigious priesthood family into prostitutes merely for livelihood: was it a transition from pollution to purification?

And one more jolly yet folly thing—I want to mark it with an asterisk—was that the unholy *Sava* also ceased to be her brother. He did not keep his word. He kept the holy widow as his mistress—a transition from enticement to entanglement!

Hence, I became bewildered how bitterness tastes like honey for want of money in time. But here, all due to a report of criminal case sans any veracity.

I felt contented for the fact that my wives were my memory bank. I was so happy about the analogy between my physical body and their spiritual bodies. So, I thought of thinking anything in consultation with them and doing anything with their consent only from the next centenary on because I had completed the seventeenth century of my life.

CENTURY 18

1701 TO 1800

I felt fresh. Fresher than a bibulous man who has turned a bibliomaniac. I was protected. More protected than a military chief who has been transferred to a citadel from a bivouac. My wives were here to serve and safeguard me from confusion in thought over matters about the betterment of all the living creatures on this earth.

If I disclose a fact, the Hovans would feel bad. If I do not, the Indans—the Indan origin and the Pakkan settlers—would feel bad. Let anyone feel good or bad, I have to disclose it for the hypocrisy would inflate me so much that I might burst like a balloon.

When the Hovans landed in Indana, they brought a very non-precious item, which could blemish the humanity, along with them. I mean carrying on their body, one of their organs. The organ was nothing but their reproductive organ—the penis! The item was nothing but a contagious disease—the venereal disease! There were reasons for suffering from such type of sexually transmitted disease. Most of them were sea-going adventurers who did not see the land for months and months together. Women were not allowed as crew on board. The crew could only enjoy sexual union as and when they went to the harbor. Their slogan was: "New port; new wife." Someone's slogan was worse than that: "Any port; any wife." Another reason was that mating with many maids made the men go mad over sex. Some more reasons were: The temperature variations inside the vaginal passage; the penis did not match the vagina; lack of cleanliness on both the organs due to shortage of water on board as well as on shore. Notwithstanding, almost all of them were carriers of both syphillis and gonorrhea. It remained latent because of the cold climate in Britana. But the tropical climate of Indana blew up the disease.

One of their senior physicians prescribed a treatment for an easy and early cure. The sexual disease could not only be transmitted but transferred permanently if the patient had intercourse with immature girls. My spouses wept. How can the disease be cured when the germs are in the blood?

The fake and floppy treatment made multitudes of tender girls as scapegoats. It became the right of the Hovan men to drop anchor-of-flesh into the flesh-basins of the Indan girls angrily (rape) because the former were said to be the masters and latter the slaves. Some of the Hovans, who were not affected by the venereal disease, also followed the same path just for fun.

In order to escape from this unnatural and unbecoming act, the parents married their female children in very young age. So, child marriages became very popular in Indana. On the one hand it was a boon to them; on the other it was a doom for the poor and innocent teenagers who became parents in their young ages. How could a small girl take care of a child while she herself needed care! The boy-fathers were pondering for livelihood and even for their daily bread. The teenage parents became weak and weary even in their adolescence—like fallen buds. Some of the husbands of the little brides were as old as their fathers. Chubby and bonny baby-brides were wedded to devil-looking skeletal grooms.

The Indan girls who lost virginity and tightness were of no use to the Hovan VD patients. But I came to know that the disease was only transmitted, not transferred.

One day, a young girl approached a good-looking VD patient in his military tent.

She requested, "*Sar*, I'm a virgin. Please use me."

"Tomorrow you would be a wife . . ."

She wept: "After the marriage, I would not be alive for my groom is not less than an ugly devil, older than my father. I hate even to look at him."

Likewise, there were many girls who secretly surrendered to the foreigners for want of fund and fun. Unlike Indans and Pakkans, the Britans gave handful of silver coins and made the dames' wallets and wombs bulge. The cold Britans gave strong strokes to the dames' hot vaginal walls that created great friction and spark of sexual stimulation giving indescribable satisfaction.

The young captain Hardest took initiative to transform the remote village to a paradise on the west coast. Slowly and steadily, Kalibay grew to be more and more prosperous and became a significant Hovan trading centre. He built his palatial residence, lived lavishly as the governor of the Hovan occupied land. That laid the keel for the ship of Hovan Empire. Gradually they tried to fix longitudinal and latitudinal as the framework for it. The settlers and traders who landed from Britana went in search of plates to facilitate the construction of that vessel. They reached the south. Established trading centers in Malcutta. Further they spread their activities to the eastern littoral also.

After the death of the King Nezeeb, most of the rulers of the states became rebels against the Britans. The B'llas wanted to chase the Hovans away. So, with the consent of the King of Britana, they formed a force to fight against the threat rather than conquering. More men, arms and ammunition disembarked. Multitudes of row hands were recruited to the Hovan army. They marched towards the north to combat with the B'llaists.

I had an anxious time. I raised my head in annoyance that increased my wives' anguish. The company's policy was going out of its track. A company which was supposed to do peaceful merchandise was inclined to a political-oriented establishment with the intention of introducing political dominance over Indana—the transition from mercantile community to ministerial community. Breaking the mercantile law, fleets carrying men-of-war berthed on the harbors of Indana.

The mercantilism prevailed in Indana favored the wind for this transformation. The downfall of the B'llan Empire and the weak knees of the one-time brave Balajis' kingdom misused the strategy. Thus the integrity was lost. Besides conflicts spread for power and prestige among the rulers of different states. They were jealous and suspicious of each other.

I wanted them to unite under one roof, but I could see only disunity, chaos and confusion. The Britans exploited this golden opportunity. Though there were encounters and opposition from many bodies of state, they succeeded in interfering and intriguing in the internal matters of Indana.

In the course of time, I really appreciated the brain of the Governor General of Britana ruling that time.

One of the Eysaist Rajas was in despair. His neighbor, a B'llaist Nawab challenged him, "You monkey-brand, you'll be beheaded tomorrow. So, as a last chance, tell your head to think maximum; tell your eyes to see maximum; tell your mouth to eat maximum; tell your tongue to talk maximum; tell your ears to hear maximum within this minimum time."

That open summons to a contest was an insult to the Raja's power and prestige. Though he had very less power he had more prestige. On the contrary, the Nawab had more power than prestige. He had unlimited force. The King had a limited bow-and-arrow force plus some sword fighters. These were nothing before his rival.

He said to his minister, "If we could get one rifle from the Britans, we could finish that son-of-a-pig."

"How, Your Highness?" asked the confused minister.

"Shoot the Nawab at the battlefield from a distance."

"We don't know how to shoot!"

"A rifle includes a marksman from Britana."

The conspiracy intoxicated the minister. "Shall I go and request the Governor General, Your Highness?

"Tell him we'll give him half of our kingdom."

* * *

"Nooo, nooo, nooo," Governor General said. "We are not that greedy to have your home. We just want some rent as *taxes*. What do you say in your vernacular?"

"We say *Kappam*."

Biting the tongue, the general exclaimed! "Yes, yes. *Kappam*. Your king is known for charity. Let him meet the expanses of my army. I'll deploy the army to defeat your rival."

A contract was signed between the Eysaist King as the subsidiary ruler and the Hovan Governor General as the sovereign power. It stated that the Raja would pay *Kappam* as tribute in token of vassalage as part of a subsidiary scheme.

The Governor General summoned his resident and commanded: "Make him understand our bye-laws." The resident started talking and walking towards his bungalow. The minister followed him, pricking his ears.

"Our alliance has certain understandings and characteristics."

The resident continued, "Now, listen to me carefully. One of our representatives would stay at your capital as a resident. You shall not have any connection with any of the foreign or indigenous officials. Do not ask for any help from any other forces without the prior permission of the company's forces and representatives deployed in your state."

After a pause, he went on, "In return, the company shall detail the required contingents to protect your territories and the people. The company shall also undertake to maintain peace and refrain from any external and internal aggressions".

The resident turned around, patted the minister on his back and admonished him, "but mind this. Once the company takes over the administration, you and your king cannot interfere in our matters."

Satisfied with the salient features of the subsidiary scheme, Raja blindly joined the military alliance of Britana. Moreover, that was the only alternative to turn his rival, the Nawab to kawab.

I was dead sure. The Governor General foresaw the future of the scheme only for the company. In a nutshell, the maintenance and practice of his force would be done by someone else thereby his tardy force would turn a task force.

Raja was virtually not a king; he became the company's vassal. The alliance really meant the transfer of the rule into the hands of the Hovans in lieu of all the grains and vegetation on his land as fees to the company's army. The resident and his staff not only ate the flesh of the animals (they were meat-eaters) but also enjoyed the flesh of the beautiful women in the state. An old officer wished to go to bed with the King's mother.

The Raja became bankrupt. Subsequently his state was annexed to the Hovan dominion. Eventually the Raja atoned his faults for wounding the life of his subjects by hanging himself on a piece of rope.

Likewise, several weak rulers and petty chiefs were annexed to the Hovan Empire after trapping them in the subsidiary alliance. I strongly say, in the historical truth, it was really a "pennywise and pound foolish" system. The system trapped everything into the Hovan's net. Thus, they could make and maintain a tough troop with the expense of others' funds!

How cunning! Still, the innocent Indans did not realize its perils for quite a long time. They were mesmerized by the hiring of the subsidiary force; they were attracted by the glow of the Hovan sheen not aware of the reality that—all that glitters is not God—they were nothing but blood-sucking bugs. But rarely, the subsidiary scheme helped to subside the treacherous conspirators.

I recall an example.

The southwest province was ruled by a middle-aged, windowed queen named Nallarani. She loved her subjects profoundly. They loved her more than she loved them.

The country and the countrymen were of peace-loving nature. So there was no so-called army. The peninsular state was gifted with seashore on both the territories and the third one was strewn with hills. So the peace-lovers did not need any defense forces. The only defensive and offensive force she had was ten *Naya* youths who were masters in martial arts. Their one heart and twenty eyes were focused on money and power. The gregarious brothers' greed for the throne had made them dishonest. They were ready to commit any offence to hit the target.

Their chief duty was to carry out the security of the queen as and when she went out. The other routine was to look after and teach her five sons all sorts of martial arts.

One day, as usual, all the princes, except the elder, Ponnuraja, were taken for swimming practice in the lake. But the boys never returned. They were killed by a crocodile!

Only I knew it was a human crocodile. The confidential assistants turned cheating attendants. They were just thugs who wanted to rob the rule. The secret Will of the deceased King was known to them. It read: "After the demise of my wife Nallarani, in case, if by any reason and by any means if all my sons expire, the elder out of the ten attendants shall take the kingdom and shall become the bona fide King. Otherwise my sons will rule in succession."

So, the aide-de-camp, forgetting bohemianism, thought it would be faster, safer and easier to kill all the princes. But unfortunately, the elder prince, aged about fifteen, was left alive. They sharpened the knife of conspiracy to kill Nallarani and Ponnuraja.

It was the time the Hovan subsidiary scheme had become popular. Left helpless, Queen Nallarani requested the resident for help. By that time, the conspirators also formed on indigenous emergency force. But the sound of cannon was more than enough for the untrained army of the conspirators to disperse. Ponnuraja, the elder son of Nallarani, was proclaimed King. The treacherous men were hanged to death publicly. It was the first penal punishment ever given to the royal class of Indana. Nallarani suitably rewarded the Hovan officials by providing some part of the land and a huge sum with the consent of her son. Thus the company could gain a strong foothold in the southwest part of Indana.

By subsidiary scheme, I really saw the need of mercy to both the provider and the receiver. It would be an aide-memoir. When the young princes were suffocated to death under water, they cried for mercy; when the defaulters were hanged, they too cried for mercy. O! Mercy, O! Mercy, you're really wonderful though you rarely do wonders!

*   *   *

Always a battlefield is such a field where cruelty grows like coconut trees and mercy falls like dry leaves. One of the inhuman incidents that crush my heart is the capture of the Madicut city of the northeastern coast. The Whites intended to cast out the B'llaists from there with the help of the exiled Eysaist ruler of that state. But the Vazir received a report of the move well in advance.

One hundred and fifty Hovan soldiers marched to capture Madicut with arms hanging from their shoulders and ammunition in haversacks. They reached the Madicut coast. The place was deserted. It was midnight. It was monsoon. Rain started pouring down. The troops wanted a shelter not just to protect the men but the arms and ammunition as well. They saw a large caravan-type container mounted on four wheels on the shore. It had only a small door that served as a narrow entrance.

The major commanded, "Common, get inside this damn thing before the ammunition gets damp. I don't mind the men getting wet; but I won't tolerate if the materials got wet."

Actually it was an air-tight wagon meant for carrying coffee packets from the embarkation jetty to the city towed by the slaves. Due to the whirlwind, all the soldiers rushed into the wagon with the major in the head. The goods wagon was just a sick container and was unfit for any living creature. It had space enough for 25 men to lie down or fifty men to sit or a hundred men to stand. But all the hundred and fifty men somehow managed to get in. The soldiers' action had a multi-purpose intention—to escape from the blowing sand on the beach and concealment.

"To hell with the sand and wind. Close the door only half . . ." the major shouted.

All of a sudden the half-closed door was slammed shut by someone hiding behind the wagon. The Whites inside were jam-packed like logs of wood. There was no ventilation. Forget about ventilation, there was not even air to breathe. Slowly, the wagon started moving. The trapped men started screaming. Each soldier's scream was overlapped with the other's making echoes upon echoes. A single sound amplified by many sounds breaking their ear drums.

The major felt suffocation. He ordered, "Fire . . ."

There was random upward firing without any aim or target. The wagon rolled from the littoral towards the sea. The metal had no heart and ears. The iron walls of the wagon could not understand the agony of the attackers.

The B'llaist slaves pushed the wagon into the roaring sea. The cries of the soldiers were swallowed by the sea. It came to be known as the Coffee Box Tragedy.

Despite the cruelty of the act, I could feel only a slight sympathy towards the dead for it was a lesson to the greedy men intruding others' motherland.

The peace-lovers should beware of the war-lovers because, often, battlefield is as good as a market place where you will not get kindness even if you pay your life as price.

But disunity, division, jealousy, hate, pride, prejudice, confusion and chaos are available in plenty on payment of power and prestige.

I don't feel either happy or unhappy while speaking about the influence of Hovan culture on the political, social, economic, religious and artistic walks of Indan life. In the political field, the impact was immense as my country was a vast stretch of land, a triangular peninsula surrounded by seas on both sides and a huge snow-capped mountain comprising many moon-touching peaks on the third. She had inherited distinct local customs and cultures as per her physical features and regions. She had twenty states with different vernaculars. All those states were sub divided into districts. The Kings ruled the states independently and the districts were administered by independent petty chiefs.

The Britana rule resulted in a uniform centralized system of government, oneness of the official language, Hovalish, making Indi and Pakkani as the mother tongue and the second language respectively. It also introduced a uniform administrative and coinage system, *Rooba*.

This drive of Britana's moving culture on the stationary culture of Indana opened the doors of her contacts with the external world. We were pioneers in the fire world, but we were ignorant about the fire-arms. They were the first to implement the art of using muskets in battlefields. The native Indan troops were also trained in shooting and combating with guns and cannons by enrolling them in artillery, infantry and cavalry. Unlike the primitive Indan fighting force with conventional weapons, he Britans modified the Hovan Indan army and navy with mobile lethal weapons to combat any land and sea warfare.

I would like to state another result of the Hovan rule: Making the caste system very stiff.

The enthusiasm of the Hovan missionaries to convert Eysaists by persuasion strengthened like anything. The victims were the lower caste people who were being roasted in the hot oven of socio-religious oppression by the higher caste Eysaists. The politico-religious despotism of the Britans made many downtrodden people embrace Hovaism by sprinkling water on their body and putting a rosary around the neck. The conversion gave deliverance to the renegades from social insult, injustice and injury.

Well, the Hovans were tactful in trapping the desperate outcasts and converting them into their religion by giving petty jobs. Some were given only some alms or donations such as imported milk powder, crushed wheat, soya bean cooking oil and tinned meat produce, which were foreign items to the Indans. Some of the dark-skinned Indans, especially women, were attracted by the purple color of the body and purport of the Hovan's holy book. The women who prowled about the proximity of the Bosque were taken to the zenana. After feeding and bathing, the priests, military offices and other Hovan dignitaries extinguished their desire of flesh on those women. In return, they were given a packet which contained quite a good sum, a holy book and a rosary. Those dark Indan pussies had keen interest and satisfaction in joining lips to lips, chest to chest, genitals to genitals and foot to foot with the Hovans' white bodies. Some children were fascinated to have used loin clothes, underwear, banians and knickers. But they too were put rosaries around their necks and holy books in their hands after baptizing. Anyone who went to the proximity of Hovans was converted!

I am very proud. On the contrary, I am very much ashamed to note an incident of insult suffered by both the socio-religious parties.

A middle-aged man belonging to the *Sava* caste was beaten to death for running beside the residence of an upper caste Eysaist. The body was dragged and thrown at the doorsteps of his hut in the *Sava* colony. The residents were rigorously reprimanded for repeating the social offence.

Then and there, the son of the deceased, a bonny and bold youth boisterously barked, "I, on behalf of my dead dad and other poor people, take your challenge as null and void."

The ruffians, headed by the castellan who brought the body raised lathys to charge on him. But the youth swung a sickle to reap their heads.

Like a desperado, he added, "Now I order you to take back your order to your so-called *Thampuran*; read out my order loudly to him. If there is a tomorrow then by this time I'll cross his gates. Let me see who'll prevent me. And if any one does . . . Now all of you run away from here like stray dogs and bark before him my order. Let him prepare his men and materials to obstruct me."

The ruffians ran away from there.

The news of the bold man spread fire in the area like conflagration. I too was amazed to know the news like other villagers. All of us anxiously awaited. What would happen the following evening to the *Sava* youth?

I told my wives, "It shouldn't have."

They reminded me unanimously, "It should be. If incidents like this do not occur, how can reformation take place? We like your dislike for the sake of his health. But we want to abolish the superstitious norms of the society. So, let's wait and watch what happens."

So we waited. Tension mounted by the moment as the evening neared.

For the human beings, the best method of easing tension is to have private sex. For that, I saw many men including gentlemen hiring taxis. The best method of easing tension for the faunas is to have public sex. For that I saw many animals including infants climb on their mothers. And the best method of easing tension of floras is to have chlorophyll sex. But for that I had no phototaxy for it was dark. So, I and my wives simply indulged in conversation. I could not remember our dialogues as my mind was filled with anxiety.

Uru said, ". . . . . ?"
I replied, ". . . . . ?"
Mena said, ". . . . . ?"
I replied, ". . . . . ?"
Ramb said, ". . . . . ?"
I replied, ". . . . . ?"
Thilo said, ". . . . . ?"

That way, they said, I said; I said, they said; we all said; said, said, said, while Sun got up early from the bed as though he too was aware of the challenge declared by the *Sava* youth. By that time, we beheld an enormous crowd coming to witness the fortune or misfortune of the challenger. Elite caste people lined up at close quarters, lower castes at unapproachable distance and some cowards stood at life-saving distance or they were certain that there was going to be a conflict—if not a battle, nothing less than a battle.

From far end of the thoroughfare, there appeared a white spot. Slowly it grew into a small moving figure on the deserted street. The people assembled near the landlord's residence did not care about the figure. They thought that it might be a Hovan coming to witness the struggle. But believe it or not, as the figure reached nearer the assemblage heaved a sigh: It was the same *Sava* youth, the challenger! Attired in white muslin fabric! That too a dhoti for the lower part and a full-sleeve shirt as upper garment!

One from the crowd said, "From where could he arrange this dress? It's funny but fantastic!"

Another said, "I too wonder. Even our *Thampuran* can't afford a dress like this"

Like an ambassador, the *Sava* youth came and halted in front of the landlord's residence, breaking the unapproachability barrier. No one could believe his eyes for it was unthinkable.

Someone said in surprise, "From where did he gather the guts?"

Another said, "I too wonder. Even the *Thampran*'s alter-ego has to bow to him!"

Yet another remarked, "The youth is supposed to genuflect before the *Thampuran* . . ."

A ghoul said, "There's going to be genocide. The *Thampuran* will annihilate all the *Savas*."

It discomfited the *Thampuran*. He shouted, "Cut his throat and pack his body in his silver cloth.

Naya goondas jumped on the youth, with swords at the ready. But the *Sava* youth roared like a lion, "Don't touch me, you ghouls. I'm a desperado."

"Common, cut the head of this son-of-a-gun," the landlord ordered.

The *Nayas* swung their swords.

It kicked up a row.

Excepting a bloodshed, the crowd stepped back

Like a commander, the *Sava* youth shouted, "Hold on . . . Before cutting my throat, you should cut this."

Slowly, he inserted his right hand inside his shirt.

An unknown item! The crowd anxiously waited to have a glimpse. I too felt the same anxiety.

The people were silently asking: What would it be? Is it a gun? If it is . . . ?

The scene and situation became boisterous.

Patient people said, "Keep patience. Let's see."

Yes. He pulled out the item he mentioned: A rosary with a locket hanging at the end with a star on one side and Hova's head on the other.

The *Naya* antagonists withdrew as though they were suppressed by the bogy of Hovaism. As they stepped backward, the youth stepped forward to challenge them.

"Common, what are you waiting for? My throat is eager to wed your sword."

Silence pregnant with suspense. The people in the crowd looked at one another in confusion. They blew out their checks in relief.

"Owff, thank God. It is not a gun."

I felt shame. I should not have thought morbidly.

Pointing his finger at the landlord, the *Sava* youth howled, "Now I'm not a cheap *Sava*. As big as life, I'm as big as you. You can't maintain your status quo before me. You don't know—if I make you eat my shit and if I make you launder my shirt, none will ask me because now I'm a Hovan. You know, if one drop of Hovan blood is shed, a pool of your blood will be made because we rule you, slaves. One bullet of ours is more than enough to pierce holes on ten bellies of your people. Now I've some official matters to attend to; I'll deal with you later severely."

So he was the first *Sava* to become a government servant! I appreciated his harangue.

As he walked away with pride, like a cock, the crowd gave him way like a herd of hens.

Really strange! Yesterday's helminth has gained hegemony overnight by becoming Hovan!

A hecatomb is avoided.

I was amazed to see the strange social reformation! My wives praised his transition from an insulted lower caste youth to a dignified person within a short span of time, with the help of the Hovan rule. All of us approved that surprising event as a social wonder of Indana.

But at the same time we analyzed his dialogues, verified his reactions. It was more an anti-climax rather than a climax. He said that he was a desperado. In other words, he was a destitute who lost everything—a desperate condition. We could see that his face was coated with the varnish of dissatisfaction. His reactions were as if he had pawned his personality, first as an Eysaist, then as an Indan. In short, he had sold out his favorite faith and purchased another faith which he did not like at all.

Actually, I was still in doubt whether he earned any status in the society. Though he could shine among the Indan natives, he was dull and sham among the Hovans. He was called and considered as a convert. Besides, he was trapped inside their aquarium like a fish out of the sea. Earlier, life had breadth and depth; now it was limited and compact.

As he was a paddy-field worker, he had been given a part-time job as grave digger. In the remaining hours of the day he was the in-charge of a charnel-house. The payment and the tips he received were lucrative. But somewhere in a corner of his heart there was discomfort. A discord between his heart and head. A feeling of discrepancy in his biology. He had discontinued his ancestral faith in Eysaism by disowning his principles. A feeling of committing *less-majeste*. He lost his discretion. On Wednesdays he was compelled to attend the mass prayer in the Bosque which suffocated him.

The moment they were converted, there started the movement of building a new Bosque. The manpower of the converts was compulsory for the construction. The Bosque had a prayer hall with an altar at one end and a huge and elegant arch door at the other. Side walls comprised many arch windows. The roof usually protruded with a dome as if it were a crown to the building.

Huwwa . . . Iillassa . . . Huwwa . . . Iillassa . . .

Eala . . . Elella . . . Eala . . . Elella . . .

Not only had the human beings in my neighborhood but all the faunas and floras also woke up. What the hell that rhythmic voice was! Very few trees had attained the age of more than a century, and I went back to the by-gone years. We polished our memories. Yes, it was during the B'llaists' golden period that the Indan manpower was utilized for constructing buildings. They were the human cranes to lift heavy blocks of rocks aloft.

But now . . . at this dead hour of the night . . . . ! I beheld that many men, women and children were pushing and pulling lined-up carts carrying bricks and timbers. I identified the supervisor's nocturnal task. He held a burning torch in his raised hand. The converted *Sava* youth! Oh, I realized that it was a group task for collecting the materials for erecting the largest Bosque ever built by Hovans in Indana.

During the B'llaists' conquest, there existed many Eysaist demples. Their plans and construction were distinct from those of both the B'llaists and the Hovans. Comparatively, its area was very limited; they were cylindrical in shape with a conical roof. The building had only a small doorway and had no other opening. The deity was installed here inside in seclusion. The devotees stood outside the sanctum sanctorum for worship.

The B'llaists constructed innumerable purches. It was a place of worship with large enclosures, rectangular in plan resembling a castle. Each Purch had a built-in pond for ablution.

But, the Hovans stood first in building large number of their centers of worship.

*   *   *

There was a big rush of missionaries from Britana. Their vigorous propaganda attracted and attacked some high class people in general and downtrodden in particular. The prominent pastors preached to sow the seeds of Hovaism in their hearts. The work resulted in the multiplication of the converts.

So the Britans added conversion to the trading for the purpose of their survival in Indana. Not satisfied with all this, the staunch militants wished to add one more purpose. So the strategy became three-fold, i.e. business, conversion, and annexation. To fulfill their many-faced intention, they adopted all conceivable methods including the third degree. Those who hindered their moves were annihilated.

Alas! I felt sorry. What an annihilation for the cause of annexation! I may summarize it. The Governor Generalship of Mr. Cruel, the lord, was noted by a vigorous portion of history of Hovan Indana. He thrived in the Hovan Empire in Indana by conquering many states. As per his whims and fancies Mr. Cruel became a great imperialist. He implemented a dogma called 'termination of adoption', which said that the sovereignty of an Indan state could not pass on to an adopted son without the consent of the Hovan's suzerain ship.

The Prince of Bhatpara passed away leaving behind no natural heir to the throne. As per the erstwhile doctrine, his adopted son was supposed to ascend the throne. But Lord Cruel proclaimed the adoption illegal on the false reasons that the Prince of Bhatpara had not obtained permission in advance. He annexed Bhatpara to Britana dominion.

At the deathbed, King of Mangapuri said to his queen, "Dear, my last wish is this. Crown my nephew. Don't delay it."

After the funeral, the coronation was going on. Conches and *nagaswaram* filled the air of the palace with music. Piercing the *ortissimo,* gunfire erupted. Two soldiers and a Hovan officer came and handed over a letter to the young King. It read: "You are not a natural heir to the late Raja. Surrender the state to the Crown."

By order of the Imperial Lord Mr. Cruel."

"But I'm his nephew, and therefore I am the legal heir," he said in surprise.

"You're not his son. You're his sister's son."

"I'm as good as his son."

"There's no son named as 'as good as son' in our doctrine," the Hovan officer said. "You could be considered as his real son if he had had sexual intercourse with his sister (your mother) and if you were the product of his semen."

This declamation made the young King furious for the officer had abused the relationship between his uncle and mother, which was supposed to be very sacred under the Esyan's tradition.

"Behead them and send the bodies to their Lord." The young King's order was carried out instantly.

Mr. Cruel the Lord marched with three hundred armed soldiers. He made bullet holes on three hundred royal men including the King—a 1:100 revenge.

Raja Namohar of Hansi died without leaving a son behind to succeed him. Prior permission had been taken from the Crown to enthrone an adopted son. Even then the Hovan Crown refused to recognize him and annexed the state. The late Raja's wife Mahalmani was deported.

Another funny annexation I remember related to the Vazeer of Nehar. He had failed to maintain the contingent of the Crown. It was not a term in the treaty signed with him as the term of the subsidy had expired. Mr. Cunning, another lord, nevertheless, took possession of his fertile land as substitute to the subsidy.

*   *   *

The Hovan revenue system meant mainly the collection of land tax from private landlords. Very few landlords were there. Most of the people were tenants and peasants. The Crown had unlimited hectares of barren land in its possession by way of annexation and auction through the subsidiary scheme. So they played a trick to enrich their treasury by making use of those wastelands.

On a hot summer day, I heard a trumpet. The platform around me usually served as a pulpit. A Hovan official along with some Indan servants stood on it. The natives gathered around them. A zamindar read out a declaration in the vernacular through a loud-hailer: "Do you hear there, do you hear there . . ."

"This is a declaration from the Hovan Government which wants to improve the status and standard of the poor of the society, especially the peasants. All the hardworking adult peasants interested in owning a piece of land shall be provided with a plot not less than a hectare in area."

The landless people jumped on the land in jubilation. I too felt horripilation. A poor peasant turns to be a landlord! That too without paying a single penny! My goodness! It is a dream comes true. Some greedy landlords and stout-looking adolescents also registered their names.

All were given plots of land.

Actually, the terrain was rocky, the soil salty and the land was barren. But some patches of land were rock-free and had loose soil. So there was a hue and cry to own that land. A decision was taken. The rocky land would go to the men and the remaining to women. Many beautiful women, including housewives, were ready to hug the Hovan totalitarians to avoid their huff and to make them happy by any means. Greedy to possess the soft land, they surrendered their soft bodies to them.

I saw a lot of excesses and malpractices in allocating the plots. The land revenue officers enjoyed many fair ladies.

The process of registration went on for more than a month. The stock of the tea and coffee powder they brought had exhausted. These unaffordable items were alien to the villagers. There, the chief fluid for drinking was goat's milk.

Some cunning deeds make us cry; some funny deeds make us laugh; but, some funny-cum-cunning deeds make us passive. Such an event occurred in that village which put me and my spouses in a state of confusion. We did not know whether to laugh or cry. The *modus operandi* was named as milking-the-married-maid.

It was the hottest summer of that century. Due to dehydration, the registrar always felt thirsty. Every now and then he wanted to have liquid food. Unlike other officers, the registrar was a childish guy who never cared for etiquette. He refused to take the pond water lest he should suffer from some bowel complaint. He was ready to consume fresh milk. Other than goats and donkeys no animals were bred in that village. He disliked

.he milk of these animals. Then what milk he wanted? Human milk! That .oo udder-fresh!! He preferred to have fresh milk straight from the breasts of young mothers.

The women in the village were well-versed with a character named Turvasa in the *Mahapurana*, the holy text of Indana. Turvasa, a sage, had the habit of giving boons to anyone if he was pleased. But as he was habitually given to anger, the devotees offered sacrifices to please him lest he should curse them in a huff.

The registrar was not less than a Turvasa as far as women were concerned. They were lined up in a separate queue. The tender babies in their hands were crying and grasping their mothers' breasts. But the babies were handed over to their husbands who were standing in the men's queue.

One by one, the women were invited into the records room. They were his cows. He, like a calf sucking the milk from the udder of its mother cow, sucked human milk from the women's breasts with his lips.

I became envious for the first time in my life. It intoxicated me. I wished to push my biggest bough through that Lucifer's lacto lips. My four wives were also very much depressed about that inhuman act. We were deeply dismayed especially while the mother was weeping in the private place, her child was screaming in public.

The allotment of land was on 'more the lactose, more the land' basis!

Other land revenue officers poured their hot milk into the sex-pot of many many village maids and broke their maiden-hood.

After a month, all the landless villagers turned landlords, thanks to the mercy of the Hovan lordship. The villagers kept the title deeds close to their chest—some as dear as their children, some as dear as their spouses, some as dear as their kith and kin and some as dear as their kennels and pets.

Thus the wasteland of the government was fragmented and handed over to the hard-working peasants.

Days passed by. The cruel sun became calm. The sky called in the clouds. The earth invited the rain. The cold rain water of the nature and the hot sweat of the peasants made the tenacious fields soft. All the families worked industriously on the field. They cultivated the land. They sowed seed for the seasonal crop. Some did combined farming. All of them reaped a good harvest. The yield of paddy was remarkable.

Time moved on to receive the next monsoon. One day, after a heavy rain, once again I heard the sound of a trumpet. The same revenue party had arrived again. They read out another declaration: "All the landlords are hereby warned about the non-payment of dues to the Crown. Anyone who fails to pay the land tax with arrears i.e. two half-yearly installments for the revenue year 1787-88 shall pay the penalty or they shall be inducted as company laborers or imprisoned for life. In order to facilitate the easy payment of tax the company's tax collector would be visiting the village next week."

The stump speech stunned the peasants. However, they tried to hoot. But the vox-populi was suppressed by the howls of the Hovan soldiers' rifles—they fired in the air.

In a huff, a limb of the law howled, "Hey, you mob, we'll trim your limbs to shape your character."

He drew his dagger from the scabbard.

The man standing in the front row of the grassroots was a grass widower. The limb of the law grandiloquently asked grass widower, "You follow me?"

He nodded.

"Well. You follow me, but do you obey me?"

He remained mum. Pin-drop silence filled with suspense. The grasshopper-like limb of the law had ants in his pants. He howled: "Common, you idiots say something . . ."

His threatening command had the sharpness to inflict wounds in their ears and noses. "If you don't like to pay the land tax, be prepared to go beneath the land."

Politely, the grass widower said, "It's not the likes and dislikes of the likes of me. It's the exclusive likes and dislikes of the likes you, because *we're* born for that".

The-limb-of-the-law sprang forward and gripped his neck. His mouth opened widely; the tongue came out and hung like that of a dog. The soldier placed his dagger on the victim's tongue.

He howled again, "You limb-of-the-Devil, how dare you utter the word *we*! You're you only. Even less than that. You're not even counted as *one*. You're not even half; you're quarter of a man. Then how dare you use the word *we,* the collective pronoun when you're a singular. Mind that you devils have no grammar either in the language or in the monde."

The widower quivered, "Is this *sine qua non* only for me? If so, please pardon me. If not, I just spoke out everyone's mind."

Releasing him, the soldier said, "Oh, you wanted to ease my job. Still, remember one thing. The word *we* can only be used by a Hovan ruler or he's the master of all you Indan slaves even though he's singular. In other words, he's the sole owner of all the men and materials of this land. n future if you commit such an offence you'll have to pay your tongue. t's funny to see a slave without tongue. But the tongue is spared for the reason of getting the reply to the orders given to you. Now, without any questions, disperse quickly and open your granary to pay the debt."

While this entire hubbub was going on, the registrar, with his Lucifer's eyes, was eagerly searching for a lascivious lady who had breasts as large as earthen pots and had as much volume of milk in it.

Haaait! There she stands staring at him!

He had consumed the milk from the breasts of one hundred and one mothers from that village. Of course, all of them yielded balanced fluid. t was as big as a diet in which all the food factors were compressed in a fixed proportion. Yes, that is what milk is!

But this particular lady! Something peculiar!! Really and truly *pyari, pyari, pyari*—lovable. Her bosom! Really and truly sweet, sweet, sweet— luscious! It comprises more SNF (solids not fat) than that of any other woman. He still felt the warmth of her lukewarm lactose in his large lips; still he felt shy to confront her. But her lustful look lured him. Again he experienced the glucose in her milk. As she ogled; he too looked amorously at her. Nobody noticed the nods. Once again they went inside the record room of the registrar's office after the gap of a year.

She unrigged her upper rig. The big breasts stared at him as if they have been longing to invite him for very long time. The rig closed his face to her bosom like a starving baby. He drew in a nipple and sucked. He spooned the other one with his fingers. He quenched his thirst and lust. He could enjoy all the tastes of the breast milk. But he felt a little distaste. Though he could not judge what that distaste was, he was satisfied for certain reasons. Perhaps she might have passed a year after her delivery or he might have sucked her blood or she might have not cleaned the papillae or it could have been because he had not cleaned his mouth that day.

However, an immobility was overcoming him. The distaste developed into disquiet. He vomited. Again he vomited. Again and again he vomited. He vomited one hundred and two times, one vomit corresponding to the breast milk he consumed from one mother. The last vomit was the breast milk he had sucked from his own mother's papillae in his infancy. The queer immodest person went flat.

Frightened to see his bluish body, she fled from there. She straight way went to a pond. She had a nice bath, cleaning thoroughly the poison-smeared papillae with coconut fiber and herbal shampoo. Then both her breasts inflated more than their size as if they were proud on providing *quid pro quo* to a humbug as retaliation for the result inflicted on them.

Well. Fine or not fine, fair or unfair the retaliation was, I was certain that the yeomen of the village would have to face the dire consequences of it, *sans doute.*

"Come on, who's the culprit? Or who are the culprits?" Pointing the pistol to the lined-up men of the village, the grasshopper-looking limb-of-the-law enquired: "Singular or plural, come forward. The transgressors could be put on trial. Otherwise we will annihilate all the villagers."

The people remained mum. Silence pregnant with suspense. The limb-of-the-law was irritated. He continued, "It's better for you dirty devils to heed my advice."

Still the mass remained reaction less.

"So no one. OK. If you *do* not want to avoid a homicide, I don't mind."

In a huff, he shot the first man in the row. He fell down. A little while after, the echo of the firing died. Then he pointed the pistol to the next. Instantly, reverberating the tranquility, there heard a voice.

"I killed him."

All the Hovan officers stared at him.

Another man from the crowd came forward and said. "No. I killed him."

"No. I'm the killer."

"No. It was me."

Many men wanted to own up responsibility.

I was dozing . . .

The shouts of the mob were greater than the sound of the firing. Usually Indans faced many stereotyped events from the invaders. But this stereophonic uproar startled my spouses. They shook me up.

The soldiers again fired some rounds killing two or three villagers lest there should be a mobocracy.

As I started out of my sleep, I observed not only the human beings but also all the objects in and around the pandemonium sniveling.

There was a stampede.

"Don't run." A panic-monger threatened the panic-stricken public. "Those who run are running to their graves."

Again there was firing. The people remained pinned. My heart went pit-a-pat. But the grass widower interfered.

He quivered with palpitation, "*Saar*, you have robbed ten of our lives for a single life from your . . ."

"Shut up, you interloper. You know, a Hovan officer is equivalent to a thousand Indans."

Seeing the fury of the soldier and fearing a further firing, an officer interfered. He said calmly, "Well, altogether you're two hundred men. Still we need to shed another eight hundred men's blood."

Another officer said in his sweet voice, "Add the women and children also. The law commands that the substitute for one human blood drop of Britana is a thousand human blood drops of Indana."

Another learned officer politely said, "The sub-clause advices that men for men, women for women and children for children. However, it's up to the discretion of the regent who would be arriving day after tomorrow."

"Well. Make a temporary concentration camp; till then let them be in it."

The villagers refused to pay the tax under the leadership of the grass widower who was a learned youth from a *Tundit* family. He was held as the first accused.

I always appreciated the grass widower as the forerunner from as orthodox *Tundit* family who always interceded with the higher sect on behalf of the lower section of the society. Frankly speaking, he had nothing to do with the registration and the tax disobedience; nevertheless he interacted socially with the peasants.

Actually he was highly educated and wealthy. He was the biggest landlord of the village. That is a strange story. He was always involved in quodlibet. He was quixotic. He sold out his entire quantum for the sake of the poor. Consequently, the benefactor turned bankrupt. His caste fellows quizzed him. Eventually his bride left him. He became a grass widower.

There was a drama actress in the village. She loved the *Tundit* youth from all the angles. She was from the *Naya* caste. As a regular heroine of the dramas staged in the village, she shone brighter than Sun. Her name was Kamini.

I saw many times after the drama, her erotic looks eroded the peace of many men's nights. They lost their body essence for they masturbated keeping her amorous acts in the mind.

More armed men arrived. A special land tribunal was established. Mr. Fraud was appointed the special judge. The case was under trial. Indana's national festival *Soly* came in between. The inmates of the concentration camp pleaded to the judge to let them celebrate it. The judge was very much interested in seeing the art and culture of Indana. A special programme was conducted in the camp. The inmates were given a full meal. There were fun and frolic. At night, the famous drama "*Munikanya Mangalam*" was staged. Mr. Fraud, the judge, was the chief guest.

The judge was perplexed to see the voluptuous heroine of the play, Miss Kamini, the profound lover of the *Tundit* youth, the first accused in the tax disobedience persuasion case.

After the play Mr. Fraud ordered to his adjutant: "I want her."

"What for sir?" The adjutant very well knew that the judge was a *persona non grata*.

"I want to learn *Indi*, the vernacular from her."

I chuckled to myself when I thought of the funny character of the Hovans. They pay more marks of respect to harlots than to any other human being.

Next evening, she was invited to his tent.

Mr. Fraud said with deep respect, "I know Indi a little; I heard you know Hovish a little. Let's put little into little to make more."

"More what?" she trialed him.

"More fun."

"You mean fuck and forget?"

"No, no, no." The judge was embarrassed by her question. He managed to continue. "I like you very much."

"Like my what?"

"Like your everything."

"Suppose if I give my everything to you what you'll give me in return?"

"Anything. Anything you want."

She started undressing. He interrupted.

"No, no, no. Leave this job to me. I can see your sex appeal inside your garments."

"Then tell me what I should do?"

"You tell me what you want from me?"

"That I'll let you know at the climax."

"Well. Then tell me the climax of the Indan dramas you played so far. And translate the lyrics also. You could make me a Priapus only by reciting a poem."

So she sang as follows by combing the gray hair on his chest with her fingers.

O! You Prince showing honey in my tent of love permit me to be the paramour in your parasol.

Shall I unlock the door of lust?

Shall I show the window of passion?

In this night while each flower of flesh is blooming.

Shall I pull my love boat in your lascivious lake?

Shall I push your love raft in my luscious sea?

In this never never world of ecstasy,

You shall pour your lustful juice in my hot pot of passion

I shall receive it with utmost impression.

For I'm born to bear your fruit.

Oh, my bosom friend! Oh, my bosom friend! Oh, my bosom friend!

My meditation came true as you cropped up before me.

Oh, my amorous cupid! Oh, amorous cupid! Oh, my amorous cupid!

While she was delivering the ditty, he was undressing himself and stripping her as well. He moored his muscular anchor in her wet basin. When the first drop of his vital fluid hit her vaginal ravine, she murmured in his ears: please acquit my brother, the first accused in the tax disobedience-cum-provocation case.

Thus, the accused, the *Tundit* and Miss Kamini were emancipated and saved from imminent death. Like a practice firing in a firing range, all others in the concentration camp were shot dead on the false allegation of murder, defamation, civil disobedience, immoral traffic and many other charges.

This untoward incident was a heavy blow to the Hovan inhuman administration. It hurt the world conscience. A commission of enquiry was held. The excerpt of the enquiry read:

"Notwithstanding the judgment to shoot to death the men convicts ingrained, it is dolorous to quote that the annihilation of the women and children is iniquitous."

I could not bear the genocide; I was melancholic for many days.

Miss Kamini along with her bosom friend, the *Tundit* youth, fled to another village where Hovan regency was not in force.

Mr. Fraud was dismissed and deported. He went back home. There also he continued his womanizing. He had a pet harlot. He told all the stories narrated by Miss Kamini to her. The harlot had another chronic customer who a dramatist was named Mr. Quiver Spine. He grasped the excellent epitomes and epilogues of the stories from her, retold it blending Indan heritage and Hovan culture, made dramas to remember which comprised innumerable unforgettable situations, quotable quotes, fantabulous fancies and fairy tales. Those mixtures added to his fame in performing plays pertaining to the universal subjects—platonic love, romance, mercy and cheating. Mr. Quiver Spine was acclaimed as the greatest dramatist of the globe. *Sans doute* he was a unique genius; I was jealous of his fame. What a meretricious merit!

*   *   *

The heat of the genocide did not subside. The wave of that inhumanity was inextinguishable. Even the Indan soldiers who earned Britana salary were discontented. Everyone's heart turned to be a hearth hot enough to bake the Hovan administrators.

Miss Kamini and the *Tundit* youth reached the state of Murugapura. Its ruler was afraid that the Britana government would sooner or later annex his territories. Murugapura was the asylum for many deprived kings, deserters and other banished personalities. All of them wished to drive the Britans away from Indana. The persons in exit had divergent reasons to rebel against the Hovans viz religious, social, economic and political. Miss Kamini and the *Tundit* youth arranged all the affected princes, priests, peasants and landlords under one roof to raise a revolt. All of them were Eysaists.

The erudite *Tundit* gave a vibrant speech: "Dear patriots, the heritage or the cultural slogan of our country is that *Sathuruvum tan grihe vannal, vazhi pol salkarikkenam* (hospitality should be extended to a guest comes home even if he is an enemy). Well. For the past hundred years and more, these foreign foes are enjoying our hospitality. We don't need their rule. They give us nothing back except vice and violence. For example, let's take the political cause. They annexed our states through certain treacherous policies known as the subsidiary scheme, lapse of heir ship, etc. Royal titles and pensions were abolished. Besides, many privileges were curtailed by paralogism. I know many people in this assembly sitting

400

before me are parabolic victims. They made us paupers! Now you tell me, are they our papas?"

The assembly shouted, "No . . . . No . . . . No . . . ."

The youth continued, "If not are they our patrons?"

Again the assembly shouted, "No . . . . No . . . . No . . . ."

The youth continued, "If not, are they our patriarchs?"

Again and again the assembly shouted, "No . . . . No . . . . No . . . ."

All of sudden there heard a female voice. "Then tell me who're they?" It was the grandiloquent voice of Miss Kamini.

The crowd cried, "They're nothing."

Kamini said, "No, dear, no. They're something. Dear patricians, they're patricides. If your eyes are not affected with papilloma, you must look at all the Hovans from an angle of enmity."

"Sure. Sure . . . . They are our enemies, *sans doute*." The assembly became white with rage.

"Please don't break the rope of patience. Let's confirm whether they're our true foes by analyzing these matters". She continued her eloquence. "Let's look into the economic head. The Hovans' land revenue policy is very much disagreeable. The discriminative tax collection: The expatriate farmers and landlords pay very less. The indigenous pay very high. This is disastrous. They're discouraging our cottage industries and encouraging mechanization. Our markets are packed with their machine-made goods. This resulted in unemployment. Not only the princes and the higher section but also the yeoman and other lower strata of Indana are reeling under the Hovan rule."

The gathering approved her speech. There was loud applause.

"My dear esteemed patricians, the worst example to remember our Indan friends and the best example to condemn our Hovan foes are the camp tragedy of last month. You don't know, that day, even the cruel sun was so ashamed that he did not shine. The pure white sand inside the camp drank so much human blood that it turned red. The wails of the women and the cries of the children echoed above the galaxies. You know, even the B'llan butchers showed compassion towards the animal victims: They prayed before slaughtering where as these Hovans have not even heard the word *compassion*. Now, think this over. It's up to you to decide whether the Hovans are our best friends or worst enemies."

The assembly listened to her speech intently. They grew angry. They started murmuring, "Cheaters! Ruffians! Revenge!"

But the *Tundit* youth restrained them. He said smoothly, "Please don't drop your anchor of anger now. I beg you to lend your ears to me."

The crowd became calm.

He said, "There are other sentimental reasons to take revenge against them. As all of us know, side by side of our each and every social custom has the purity of religion. Our social vehicle has the religious chassis. It has the wheels of the village community fixed on the axis of joint-family system. The foreigners are blocking its smooth movement. Their recently established tribunals have swallowed all the powers of our *Panchayats*. The vigorous efforts of the Hovan missionaries to convert our people into their religion have the support of the foreign government. The compulsory teaching of Hovaism in our *pathasalas* (schools) has had drastic effects. The construction of cathedrals or the so-called bosques is a cataclysm. Wherever you go, you've to meet and mingle with meat-eaters. Now, you decide, shall we accommodate the Hovans in our homeland? Shall we allow them to make us homeless?"

The sitting people stood up. They avowed to cut at the roots of the foreign government.

I too watched the exclusive meeting. I saw that numerous people were joining the assembly. The stump speeches stirred their hearts. Secretly, the native recruits also developed dissatisfaction with the army. They were forced to have beef in the menu. Cow was their sacred animal. The Eysa soldiers concealed their hatred in their hearts. They too availed the conspiracy as the best opportunity for avenging.

The participants were ready to give up their lives to save their country from the foreign hands. The assembly was now out of all command and control. They said as one man, "Please provide us weapon."

He advised, "Let the princes carry swords; peasants take their tools. Let's face them boldly. Our desire is to deprive them. We're not killers; but purges."

Thus the decision "A revolt was the only way to throw the Hovans out" was passed. The assembly determined to begin the revolt on the daybreak of the thirty-first of December 1800. Fortunately or unfortunately that day was the last day of my eighteen hundredth birthday and the first day of a new era of freedom struggle.

I wondered whether I would be petrified, peevished or prided in the forthcoming century.

CENTURY 19

1801 TO 1900 AD

How could someone enjoy birthday when his motherland is in trouble? So, in spite of celebrating it, I and wives were deeply discussing about the revolt anticipating an Aceldama.

Urva uttered, "Does this aggression lead to aristocracy?"

Mena mentioned, "No. It may lead to bureaucracy."

Remb remarked, "No, no, no. It'll lead to democracy."

Tilo told, "Certainly, it'll lead to only mobocracy."

"You're exactly correct Tilo, I too sure about that." I intervened.

Other wives enquired inquisitively "Why . . . ? How . . . ?"

"Because hypocrisy is involved in this insurrection".

Let it leads to any ~ crazy, the so-called crazy revolt utterly failed to he ground level . . .

Initially the uprising seemed formidable. Hovans chilled to marrow. The native army personal or sepoys participating in a civil meeting!

Though, the uprising was organized from Murugapura, it broke out rom Kalibay. I was puzzled to see the mutineers beheading the Resident ind raided his residence. Some miscreants hung his headless body on the irch of the main gate. Some took his chopped off head to the Kalibay ground. Their prediction was the Hovans' perdition. They controlled the operation from there.

Per contra, a bold Brigadier, named Tactics—as his name, so his leeds—used his wit and wisdom. He suppressed the militancy with his military experience and his tactics. He deployed the army in such a way that he could depopulate the mutineers; he used his diplomacy in such a way that he could depolarize the dependency.

The chief reasons for the failure were the insurgents couldn't secure the support from all the rulers of all the states. Their weapons were very conventional. They had lack of leadership. They had no military tactics. Their movement was as if a rudderless ship.

However and whatever the case may be, I really appreciated Miss Kamini and the Tundit youth for the valorous actions in the insurrection.

I agreed with the dogma, the life of a man is in the hands of a woman. But no, I've to agree at times, the life of a country also falls in the hands of a woman. Many feudal vassals and B'lla chiefs tried to help Hovans. But Miss Kamini's pretty eyes prevailed upon them. She even submitted her hot flesh to have their confidence motion. All her good or bad deeds meant for the betterment of her country and its people. She was indomitable to the Hovans. She was more agile and efficient than a real soldier!

The Tundit youth also fought bravely against the Britans. He was not a soldier; nevertheless he shined like a man of military skill and experience! But all their efforts had no effect before the Britana riffles and their storming. Both the rebellious hero and heroine of the appraisal embraced a soldier's death. Hence the rebellion had been completely suppressed and tranquility was restored once again in Indana . . .

I was dead sure that the revolt shook the foundation stone of the Hovan Empire. It was a bolt from the blue. Many alterations and amendments in the systems and devices of the government came into force directly from their Homeland. Whatever and however poor was the rebellion; it was a curtain-raiser cum eye-opener event for the coming generation to think about the independence of Indana.

Brigadier Tactics named the aggression "Recruits Revolt". He was not at all bothered the pressure of the civic oppugnancy. He was restless due to the soldiers' unrest. He minutely studied the reasons behind it. He got it. The Eysan soldiers' religions feeling were hurt. A cow is considered and deeply revered as a sacred animal, in fact mother. How could a believer of that faith be compelled to consume his mother's flesh?

Brigadier immediately delivered a verbal order "Here further, no bloody beef business in our brigades. Any bloody well compels the sepoys to consume beef will be severely dealt with. The meat ration of the military is hereby changed to bloody mutton".

His bloody message helped to save a heavy bloodshed. It was passed instantly to all the military units as fast as they could by all the available sources of communication.

Having satisfied with the order, the participants from the military withdrew the mutiny from their side. Most of the mutineers were ignorant about the cause . . .

One young sepoy was asked, "Why did you follow the mutiny?"

He said, "I du'nno. As everybody followed, I too followed."

B'llans had already decided to fall-out from the line of freedom struggle for beef was their palatable food. So, the so-called Recruits Revolt was a problem exclusively for Eysaists . . .

It created communalism. An isolated religious feeling for the protection of the particular faith was prevalent. Following the suit, I witnessed a communal riot for the first time to add some bad pages in the history of Indana.

Sans turning some historical pages backward, the exile of the excommunicated Sava awakened reminiscences of my mid-fifteenth century . . . The furniture makers who settled in the hills and forest area—now known as the tribes—climbed the snow capped mountain, Mahalaya. They reached near the remains of the Gurukulam. They saw the obscure mortal remains of the Guruji. They regarded the solidified granite like statue as their Udayappan (the excommunicated Sava who invented the telescope and quasi—stellar objects) or the Sun God—a separate form of Eysa. During heavy winter, they used to vacate the area for the snowfall used to be terrifying and terrible. The tribes believed that it was the time three months—Udayappan goes to the heavens to assimilate more heat and light in order to spend the energy for the forthcoming seasons— nine months. Hence, for three months—during this absence—the sector remained misty, foggy, rainy and windy.

I gave more weight-age to the tribes' belief; though I knew scientifically sun didn't go anywhere and he rose from the mountainside itself; but he was good for nothing during those three months in the eastern ghat of Indana. The cold climate was unbearable to any normal skinned human being.

Per contra for Pakkan intruders from the mountainous boundary— western ghat inhabitants—seldom care about any climate. They were born and brought up in the valley of the Mahalaya Mountain's other side boundary. Nature had cursed that region, as a barren area comprised of rocky sandy and dusty stretch of infertile land. Where even a grass would refuse to shoot up.

The almighty has favored the Indans by constructing the mountain in such a way that during summer, all the snow of the Mahalaya melted and flew towards Indana, making her fertile. The famous divine river Manga and her tributaries were the blood circulatory system of the body of Indana. Indans enjoyed and cherished with it.

Where as, during monsoon, all the excess water in the Mahalaya over flew towards Pakkana. This unwanted water plus the rainwater made the whole of Pakkana to a pond—flooding the entire region, making the men homeless and animals to die. The nature always sows seed of catastrophe in the ecological field of Pakkana.

But Indians didn't face any natural disaster for the excess water easily found access to the sea through the rivers. Unfortunately, Pakkans never saw a sea for the great digger; the God did not provide Pakkana with a sea. For Pakkans, the area atop the mountain was safer than that of their flood affected valley. So, during the winter and monsoon period, Pakkans reached on top of the Mahalaya. They took shelter in the cave, where the erstwhile gurukulam functioned. They regarded the statue as the monument of their front-ranking intruder named Kaiber. That pioneer was considered as another form of their beloved B'lla. Thus, the statue of my Guruji was revered by both Eysans (tribes) and B'llans (intruders) on half yearly basis sans harming the harmony. A handing and taking over ceremony used to be held atop while each group vacates the sanctum to the other.

I couldn't rub the memory by any means how people of both the countries—both the religions—celebrate the festival colorfully with great zeal and enthusiasm.

But Hovans invasion harmed the harmony among them. Hovans, especially the military officers were deeply interested in mountaineering and trekking. Moreover those operations were a part of training to sweat more in peacetime to bleed less in wartime.

The commandant of the border infantry was Major Mount. He was truculent yet a trumped up historian. His name was in harmony with his deeds—Major Mount was keen on mountaineering. His greatest wish was to become greater than any other Hovan officer by making any great historical event even if it was a trumped up one. So, he intended to climb on the highest peak, Himarest in the ghat of Mahalayas. His last but not the least ambition was to fix the Hovan Jack atop the peak to grab the worldwide acclamations.

He had conquered many many mini mountains in his homeland. But Mahalaya—its geographical and climatic conditions—was entirely different from those. In the initial stage itself, he experienced difficulties. He neither could accomplish his mission nor acclaim his name. Somehow the spearhead and his subordinates managed to reach the tryst, the Gurukulam. They were amazed to see the crowd; the spectacular festival of Indans handing over the sanctum and the statue to the Pakkans! As if that time and place were arranged clandestinely by the Eysan and B'llans lovers!! Major was envious.

He couldn't tolerate, "Hum, Both paying homage to one idol of an idiot! Like brothers from a family!! They and their bloody statue!!!"

He was inflated with jealousy . . . He fired his pistol. Celebrations calmed . . . Silence captured the area.

He howled, "Such a ceremony is taboo according to the Hovans". He straightaway went before the statue; performed a front-salute. His subordinates also did as he did. He then adorned the statue with a festoon made out of bullets.

Major Mount made a high-flown proclamation, "Do not trump up history. The *defacto* history says 'This is the monument of Kuriappy, the first and finest disciples of our lord Hova."

"No." A monk remembered, "This is the *Samadhi* of our sun God."

"No, no, no." This's the *Kaiber* of our Moon God." A mull came forward and demanded.

"No abrasion of your tongue with the teeth." Major Mount grandiloquently ordered, "your sun and moon do not shine here. This tomb exemplifies the outstanding attribution of our God of Stars. So, humbly quit this tryst and simply cook your tit bit in some other pot."

The Eysans and B'llan devotees didn't like the Major's stubbornness. They as one man cut his stultiloquence with their grandiloquence as in 'tit for tat' they deluged the Major with abuse.

The area was illuminated with sticks of burning greasewood. The devotees transformed to dare devils. They took the burning torches and attacked the army men. Army men transformed to antagonists; they fired left and right jeopardizing the huddle.

Screams . . . wails . . . shout . . . Then darkness . . .

I didn't know how many got killed, how many got hurt. Even in the darkness, I could assume that hot, red blood of men was unsuccessfully trying to melt the cold white snow. Any way, it was the outbreak of the first communal disharmony that too a triangular religious riot. The *modus operandi* of the quarrel was on the basis of a tri-formula: Hit first by Hovan army, hit hard by Eysan tribe and keep on hitting by B'llan infiltrators.

In the following morn, I saw the body of Major Mount was lying flat in the valley of Mahalaya. Remuneration for his high-handed action! Thus his desire to become a hero in the Hovan religion also remained unaccomplished . . .

The Hovan Government published an out-of-bounds order to the *Gurukulam* prohibiting the entry of all the persons belonging to Hovaism and Eysaism and its castes.

All these religions had some similar factors pertaining to certain characters; nevertheless they had distinct tendencies pertaining to their sacred fauna and flora, custom and culture and many other symbols. To exhibit their favoritism I'll have to mention one more table to differentiate it.

RELIGION	HOVAISM	B'LLAISM	EYSAISM
Guru	Hova	B'lla	Eysa
Bird	Eagle	Crow	Pigeon
Animal	Pig	Goat	Cow
Plant	Olive	Pudina	Vep
Element	Water	Earth	Fire
Food	Non-vegetarian	Non-vegetarian	Pure vegetarian
Medicine	Allopathy	Herbal	Ayurpathy
Superstition	Witchcraft	Sorcery	Mysticism
Marriage	Monogamy	Polygamy	Polyandry
Liquor	Allowed	Not allowed	Not allowed
Smoking	Allowed	Not allowed	Allowed
Praying	Kneeling down	Prostration	Bowing
Sanctorum	Bosque	Purch	Demple
Principle	Violence	Violence	Non-violence
Heavenly-body	Star	Moon	Sun

*   *   *

On the previous day of the Mahalayan massacre, Indana witnessed an unusual social drama—a real incident!

A monk clad in yellow garments came from somewhere to the outskirts of Kalibay. He was very weak and weary despite travelling hard from sun to sun. He was very thirsty. On the way he saw a black teenage beauty pulling water from a well belonged to Sava caste society. He approached her and requested some drinking water.

She didn't run away lest the spate bucket should fall into the well. Seeing her astonishment blend with puzzlement, the monk asked, "Please gi'mme some *sheeth jal* dear dame."

Hurriedly, she pulled the water and kept the bucket on the parapet. She covered her mouth with the right hand palm, bowed and pleaded, "Allayo sanyasi, asking *jel* from me is as good as asking my *jaan*. It's not that I'm reluctant to spare my life for you. But consuming water from an untouchable is as good as consuming poison."

"The poison you're talking about," said the sage, "has nothing to do with the biology; but, something to do with the sociology."

"You may be a nihilist. But I've to follow it."

"Voluntarily . . . ?"

"No. Forcefully."

"Then vivaciously gi'mme water."

She provided him water, he hiccupped with satisfaction.

He said, "On the way, I drank some water from the well of the well-known caste. It was so impure, that I suffered from diarria. Even if your polluted water is impure, I may suffer from constipation. I love constipation rather than loose motion."

As he cracked the joke, she laughed; as she laughed he clothed her upper bare body with his long shawl. He further taught her some viva voce mantras and asked her to chant it continuously. The sanyasi made the polluted woman a sanyasin, a holy woman! He broke the social norms and customs of Indana.

"Siva, Siva a Sava girl joining the order of sanyasi!" The whole holy castes protested.

Enraged by that action, one Tundit interrogated, "Allayo swamyji, you're a holy man. You're supposed to have holy book beside you. Why do you want a woman?"

The sage said, "You're a learned man. If you've a woman beside you, why do you need a holy book? There's nothing equivalent to woman."

"If so how about god?"

"In the breed of God, nothing is equivalent to Goddess."

"But, hay you fraud friar," said the Tundit, "here, nothing's equivalent to me. I'm the wholly solely."

Sans saying anything, the sage set off from the scene . . .

The Tundit's flippant reply made me angry . . .

The sage, even in his boyhood, as a cherub was concerned about the religion and being sensible in his views; he carried out experiments into religious truths. He was disgusted the fight of various religious denominations. Thereby apprehended the rational unity of all religion.

His "Operation unity in Trinity" was an example . . .

It's easy to correct a major mistake; but difficult to correct many minor mistakes. I give you great evidence how a major mistake—disobedience of Hovan government order—was smoothly corrected by the same sage . . .

I saw a bizarre bivouac! Darkness captured the Mahalayan mountain range. Myriads of devotees assembled in many bivouacs atop the *arête*. There was a bonfire. The yellow monk conducted a camp meeting. His *bonafides* was to refine the crude Eysaism by adding catalysts of B'llaism and Hovaism. He intended to synthesize the three cultures for the oneness of mankind.

Military arrived; camp meeting banned. Then and there he was trialed by the military court. A colonel was the judge advocate. He was quite reasonable.

He asked, "Just what's your name?"

"Naran."

"Any specific meaning in the vernacular?"

Monk replied, "Means human."

"Does it mean, I'm not a human?"

"You're a man."

"Just what are you?"

"I'm nothing."

"I behold you in the form of a perfect man before me."

"Within minutes, you'll kill me. You know what happens after the death. He remains nothing other than remembrance."

The judge malignantly accused, "You're always arguing and winning."

"It's not to argue and win; but to know and make known."

"Alright. Why do you arrive this *arête*?"

The saint said, "We're conducting a requiem, a mass for the dead."

"Just let me know your religion?"

"Humanism."

"Humanism!" exclaimed the judge, "I've heard about Hovaism, B'llaism and Eysaism. Just what's this religion Humanism?"

"To understand Humanism," said the sage "first learn what a religion is. It's a faith or thought. This system concerning with man is said to be Wumanism."

"It means, "Judge asked him mockingly," other religions are meant for animals?

"That I don't know. My religion Wumanism is not designed for animals; it's exclusively for men."

"Just what does it signify?"

"Wumanism signifies that essence of all religions is same. The study of all religions would reveal that there is no difference in their basic principles. The religious beliefs thus revealed is the *one religion*, that's Wumanism."

"Is there any God in your . . . ?"

"Why not. It's you, he and me . . . The man. He himself is the God."

"Just funny . . ." The judge chuckled, "I don't feel a god in me; is there a god in you?"

"It's the germ or the atom that acts as the almighty. Imagine your body and my body subjected to division and sub-division. We can imagine that we thus reach that which one would be tempted to conceive as nothing."

The judge enquired curiously, "So God is nothing . . . ?"

Sage replied, "One way. On the other hand, you're born, living and will die by the chain reactions of atoms. The most powerful authority on the whole of universe is the atom. It's the energy. We won't see atom; we won't feel atom. But the effect is right with us". The listeners reacted with full of confusion . . .

As the sage continued, the crowd prided up their ears, "see the campfire burning; feel the breeze blowing. Stars staring at us sans falling down. We get heat and light from the sun. Now it's dark; after few hours it would be day. We say there is gravitation. We eat, digest and excrete. I speak; you listen. All these are the power or energy of atom. Atom is almighty. It's omnibus; it's omnipotent; it's omniscient; it's omnipresent Etc . . . Etc. So atom is our God; God is just power; God is energy. *And all that glitters is not God*"

411

The crowd looked each other as if they understood his explanation word by word. Tranquility prevailed . . .

The Judge blew out his checks. He asked, "By the by you didn't mention anything about your caste?"

"I'm casteless."

"Didn't you know this *arête* is an out of bounds sectors?"

"That's for Hovans, B'llans and Eysans. Isn't it?" The monk remonstrated "I'm not that. I've no caste, creed or color bar. I'm a man. Your order doesn't promulgate the prohibition of man entering this sector. Isn't it? Moreover, this is a mountain range; not a private rendezvous. This is not your property. This belongs to our mother Earth. Earth is for everybody and the devotees are not renegades. They're more men. So our entry is not termed as trespass."

The Judge asked, "Just let me know your aim?"

Sage replied, "I just want to convey a message to the people about the oneness of caste, oneness of religion and oneness of God or one thought, one faith and one power for the men. *And all that glitters is not God*"

"Are you a sort of trinity?"

"No. I'm telling about the triune."

"Just what are you going to do?"

Pointing to the statue, the monk said, "This may be the relics of some bonhomie an age old alter ego of all of us. Notwithstanding the complexity, we must think of the magnitude of this problem. In spite of annihilation and prohibition we must find out a solution."

"Have you any?" Judge asked.

"Of course. You may see it practically."

The sage summoned one *swamy* who had a yellow bundle with him. He took out a full sized mirror from it. He handed it over to the monk. Monk closed his eyes. He walked straight into the cave. He installed the mirror inside, *swamy* followed. He stretched out an earthen pot before the monk. Monk took out a little sandal paste with his pointing finger. He wrote on the glass surface: OO HH MM. THUT SAUT. He stared at his reflection in the mirror; folded his palms and prayed to himself for a few minutes.

All the while continuous ringing of the bells, blowing of the conchs and burning of the frankincense were performed by devotes outside the cave.

The monk came out after finishing the prayer.

Another devote took position before the mirror and started praying his own image. All the devotees followed suit.

Dazzled by that performance, the Judge asked, "What's the scribbling on the mirror?"

The philologist monk replied philosophically, "*O* denotes memory. You forget what you're—good or bad. Before the mirror you see you; you remember you. You exclaim the short comings—disobedience, cruelty, indifference, negative attitude etc. Or *O* is your confession to yourself.

Judge nodded . . .

"*H* (uu) denotes anger in you—your challenging and shouting mentality. *M* (ma) denotes your age. You think your time is running fast away; you must work today and work now itself sans emitting the poison in you."

Again the Judge nodded his head approvingly.

The monk continued, "Mirror says that you're the universe, and you're the supreme soul. You can do anything. In short you're the fetish for you."

Monk pointed the snow-capped peaks and said that you can melt this snow, and make a sea here; you can remove the mountain and make a tableland here if you want. All you need is determination and will power to render services for the betterment of the mankind. *SAUT* denotes you yourself are noble, apt, handsome, honorable, real holy so on and so forth. There's a school within you. You're the teacher for yourself as a student."

Judge exclaimed, "Excellent elucidation! I pray to myself. A built-in God in me!! But Guruji, would this lead to egotism and pride?"

"No. This procedure of praying is a form of self-respect. You'll get refined yourself from the crude form to a fine product of humanity, provided you're sincere to your own conscience."

On the outside wall of the cave, the monk scribbled; "This is a tryst where only one caste (mankind) one religion (a faith) and one God (the atom) believers live in fraternity."

The Judge bowed his body before the bonhomie monk. Other army personals paid mark of respect by salute arm. They marched off . . . The multitude stupefied till they faded away from their sight . . .

I was stunned how the monk handled the complex issue of communalism, resuming the liberty and restoring the peace. He transformed the hardhearted army to harbingers of peace. I really appreciated the *bons mots* of the bonhomie.

He once said to a suffering motley crowd, "Be vivacious; very soon the people who denied mercy to the receivers would cry for want of mercy; people who were denied mercy from the givers would deluge them with mercy—a transition from mercy receiver to mercy giver".

The yellow gowned monk was a memento to my memory. I wondered which monastery he belonged! I've come across numerous men from the order of monks. I've seen innumerable aldermen, Judges, clergymen, Chancellors etc attired in gown. But this monk! He was worth wearing it. I've seen and heard lot of theists, atheists, theologists, nihilists, monotheists and fanatics; they were nothing less than social eagles; but, this monk was a social dove.

Proudly saying, I was the tallest tree in the entire Indana. By standing from Kalibay, the southern coastal city, I could see the activities of the monk on the ridge of the Mahalayas at the northeastern frontier. I'm not heightening the fact, what a *modus operandi!* That resulted to a *modus vivendi!!*

Indeed he was a mogul of the monk hood. I evaluated his bons motis: There's only one kind of man i.e. *Human;* there's only one religion i.e. *Faith;* There's only one God for man i.e. *Atom.* And in total: *All that glitters is not God.*

Once the sage was besieged by a group of leaned Tundits who were very adherent to casteism.

One said, "*Allayo* Guruji, Humanity is a tree. A tree itself has got different size and type of leaves. So men also . . ."

"Understood," the sage quipped, "You pluck those leaves and chew it; the extraction is same. Likewise human blood or the essence of the men is same.

Another asked, "We've a distinct religion. How can you say that Hovaism and B'llaism are same as Eysaism?"

"Well, what's these religions say? Every religion's goal is faith in God. So I say there's only one faith."

Another said sarcastically, "Swami, don't compare our Gods with theirs. We can't imagine it. We hate to see their grotesque gods.

Sage remarked, "So you say your God has more voltage. If so, why there's rise and fall in your religion? I find other religion-believes also became magnets in many fields."

"That's because of one's *karma* and bad deed" Another Haunted.

Sage retorted, "Then why wastes time on religious matters? Render good work. To work you need energy. Energy is God. You store energy by eating. To eat, grow food. Eat less and work more. All the inert atoms in your body would become agile. Working is better than worshipping. If at all you want to worship, worship the work.

The Mahalayan pact was a marvelous achievement for peace lovers. I gave the full credit to the monk. *Sans doute* the sage was genius *loci*. The paragon established a pantheon at the mountain range where memorials of illustrious dead—semblance of Hova, B'lla and Eysa—were carved on the rocky walls. He presided over the function of the assemblage of all the religion under the religious leaders.

The harbinger of harmony hiked the length and breadth of the country. He delivered obtrusive moral advices; people observed his preaching.

He advised, "The real blessing of the God is to gain knowledge for knowledge is almighty. To achieve knowledge, you've to go the school. So, the real temple of a man is the school."

Even the government officials were moved by his advice. Many schools were built in cities and towns. Volunteer groups from all walks of life organized *padasalas* in many villages.

Besides these, he advised the people to abolish the unwanted funeral rites and perform it unceremoniously.

He said, "Forget the dead; love the living."

On some occasions he remarked, "It's worthwhile you mourn for the dead once in a while, not all the while."

And once he replied to a question, "The most suitable and peaceful place for unbosoming oneself is the burial ground."

He tried hard to transform many graveyards to horticultural gardens.

Multitude became his followers . . . Many turned apostasies.

By the time I became his votary and wished to hail "Viva sage, viva!" There came the day of his *Samadhi*. The legendary sociologist who swayed the emotions of millions of people with his profound human loving qualities died on the Siva hills in north Kalibay, early morning on the end of the first half of this century at the age of seventy following a prolonged meditation.

Enormous crowd who assembled in the rendezvous to pay the last respect to the humanist despite bad weather, were seen trying hard to control their emotions. The coffin was kept on my platform for solid one day. Public from far and near besieged me. Some queued up for paying homage; some climbed on top of me—squatted, hung, stood on all my branches—to have a glimpse of the Samadhi of the sage. The body was taken to the pyre in the next morning. When the mortal remains were consigned to flames, I too mourned. I dropped all my flowers to pay homage to the holy man.

Yes. His era was a period of renaissance as large as life!

Actually, the antecedents of the apostle were arcane. But I knew it; I un laid it . . .

Naran was born in a small village in my district, Kalibay in the third quarter of the eighteenth century. Though it was surprising to note that the cherub didn't cry at the time of his birth, little did the parents know that their son would become the hero of the renaissance of their country. He was worthwhile to everyone in his childhood, for he was a question bank where all amount of answer-cheques were bounced.

In his boyhood he rose in protest against orthodoxy by making a stump speech. The fanatics excommunicated him. I still remember his school days: Enroute, he used to teach his colleagues. His classes contained tremendous out burn of intellectual, social and religious lessons. It was something modern, which I couldn't assimilate.

After the schooling, he went through all the religious texts and acquired profound knowledge. Traveled extensively and experienced about various customs and cultures. He started his reforming activities. Even though he hailed from a high caste family, he had no caste bar in his life. He dined and mingled with lower caste.

One of his junior classmates, a Sava youth named Dasan was incited with that revolutionary ideas. Dasan accepted Naran as his Guru. Guru changed Dasan's name to Devan for *Dasan* denotes *servant* and *Devan* denotes lord. Devan became a great poet. Both the contemporaries stirred the high society in general and the lower strata in particular. The contents of the poem opposed the anti-social activities, which resulted to the transformation from superstition to science and geared the movements of development.

Enormous people became renegades despite of the poet's ardent devotion, great zeal, elegant eloquence and marvelous manners.

Notwithstanding the Sage Naran sphere headed the renaissance of Indana, many other great reformers came as his successors. Their progressive ideas paved the path for the total abolition of *Mathi*, child marriage, untouchability, degradation of women and many other social evils. They advocated education of people. A great reformer founded a mission. His disciple Ananda has rendered significant services not only in the country but also abroad. The mission worked for the benevolence of all the men indiscrimination of caste, creed or color.

Thus, during the first half of the nineteenth century, I witnessed tremendous outburst of great cultural renaissance pertains to the religious and social movements of modern Indana. Though I, as a tree kept aloof from religious revivals, from close quarters, I watched how humanists did innumerable research works in the sociological laboratory to blend the essence of the three religions to an extract of oneness.

Besides Eysan reformers, some B'llan and Hovan reformists—both exotic and indigenous—came forward and stretched hands to give momentum to the communal harmony movements and cultural unity. Myriads of women, children and men joined in their organization and mission. The volunteer staffs taught the illiterate members not only the vernacular but also Hovish. As a result, the ignorant turned to be learned. Thereby almost all the Indans moved forward from middle age to modern age.

*   *   *

Time may sub the record of any untoward social behavior; but still some letters of it would remain as a reminder on the board of memory. The reminiscence of the Recruits Revolt still stung the Hovans . . .

After beheading the Resident of Kalibay, the rejoiced revolt-makers kicked and kicked, passed and passed his chopped off head each other on the ground. That action of the fanatics gave the way for finding our football game for the first time on the ground of Indana.

The mutineers had trespassed Hovan officers quarters, captured large number of Hovan women and children, took them as hostages, kept them aloof, pushed them into a big dried up well, poured barrels of ghee over them and was ablaze them to death. Hovan government renovated and protected the area, making the well of death as the "Innocents memorial".

*   *   *

When the Indans played first football, little did the kid—the only one child of the beheaded Resident of Kalibay—know that the ball rolled on the ground was his father's head. He was a preparatory school student at that time. His mother told him all about the cruelty. As a child, he didn't take it seriously. But as the time rolled and rolled, his heart gathered more and more moss of revenge. When he grown up, he too became not only a fan of football but also turned to be the best scorer in the soccer in the Naval Academy of Britana.

The sport light of service proved to be outstanding in all the fields—passed out as the best *gentleman* cadet. But, was he gentle? No, Not at all. When he was graded to Lieutenant, his behavior got degraded to harsh, graded to Lt. Commander, simultaneously degraded to cruel, graded to Commander, simultaneously degraded to wild and as a Commodore when he became the Governor General to Indana, he became the crude form of rude too. As a ruler, he was unrulier than any other rulers I've ever seen. Even his own Governors of states couldn't tame him for he was intractable.

Thus Commodore Powerfill disembarked at the port of Kalibay.

Well, on his appointment, he was received to Indana ceremoniously. As he was a football fan cum player, a football union match at Kalibay recreation ground was programmed to please and entertain him.

Football . . . I unrolled the gruesome scenes—It was in the wee hours of morning, I heard the mourning of women and children. I broke out of my sleep; saw the howling mutineers kicking something on the ground. The oval thing rolled and rolled as they kicked with their army booted legs. A stout fellow kicked it so hard, that it took a short flight and fell near to my stem. I saw the item. I chilled to my *wood* and *juice*—the head of the Resident of Kalibay! My goodness! Both the eyes stood ajar. They looked sympathetically at me to save the head from defamation. The mouth too was slightly opened as if asking me to join the head to its body. Perhaps the head hesitated to request the plea to any human being for they only separated the head from its body.

Yes, God never created a man—a body sans heads, a head sans body. A human body is said to have the combination of both. I knew, unlike the living men, the dead are very innocent. They do no harm to anybody; nevertheless I couldn't help. I and my consorts watched the men running and humming after the rolling human head till someone kicked the head to the river . . .

Next day onwards the boys started playing the same way with unripe bread—fruit. In due course, adults took over it for evening time-passing cum exercise. Hovans were also fascinated by the game. They played inside a boundary lined field with an oval ball, which they kicked, carried and thrown. The ball was made out of wool filled leather shell. Out of the fifteen players on each side, one each was detailed as the goalkeeper. His duty was to safe guard the goal post. Others played hard to place the ball on the opponents' goal line to score more and more goals. If the goalkeeper fails to defend the goal, another player takes over as the goal-keeper and the former joins the latter's place till the time exhausted; or all the goal-keepers were replaced. The winner was selected accordingly . . .

Thus Britans founded the game *Footty bally* in a scientific manner like in Britana which became the most popular game in the field of Indan and foreign sports.

Mr. Powerfill, the Governor General was offered the velvet covered chair as the chief guest. Where as he refused to receive their hospitality. He didn't sit. He summoned the secretary of the *Footty bally* club. The match was Hovans versus Indans. The secretary, a Hovan origin bowed before Governor General.

Mr. Powerfill said, "Arrange for a sports rig. I'm on my toes to play. I'll play on my men's side. But before that everybody has to sign a contract."

There was applause . . . followed by hails "Viva General, viva!" Aaha, what a magnanimous man! See his verve—to play with common men! Is he the Governor General of the Hovan Empire? Man, a man should be like this! The players flattered him unaware about the fury concealed in his heart. The contract had a furtive condition—a very dangerous terms as large as life.

My spouses sensed it . . .

Urva uttered, "He's trying to counteract the machinations of his opponents.

Mena mentioned, "There's an arbitrary decision in that contract."

Ramb remarked, "The general can never forget the atrocities committed by the Indans during the mutiny".

Thilo talked, "The match would be a comedy as large as life; but I smell a tragedy as big as life at the end of the game".

The match was marvelous . . . !

Though middle aged, Governor General, the center forward was as flying as anything on the ground. Sometimes he battled for the possession of the ball, most of the time the ball was magnetized by his foot as if a domestic puppy licks his master's foot. He alone scored fifteen goals on Hovan's side. Not only the hilarious crowd but my family too appreciated his brilliant and excellent individual performance. Mr. Powerfill, the player was loudly clapped for his each kicks. Few minutes before the half—time, the game was over as he defeated the Indan team by giving chance to all the fifteen players as goal—keeper as per the terms and conditions of the Machiavellian contract.

As the referee blew the long whistle, Mr. Powerfill, the player left the court, stripped his sportswear, worn his Governor General's ceremonial rig boarded his golden chariot and took off . . . Crowd shouted, "Three *jais* to our General. Hip, hip, hurree . . ."

No sooner did the Governor General leave; than fifteen military police men came forward and arrested all the fifteen Indan players who were relaxing on the oval ground. Seeing the untoward scene, the thinning crowd again thickened so eager to know the cause of the apprehension.

"What's the matter?" The team captain enquired.

A Provost Marshall in-charge of the police squad quipped, "I've my orders."

"What orders?"

"Death warrants for all of you."

"Whaaatt the hell?"

Provost Marshall gibed, "Don't ask me what the hell; ask me what is hell? And you'll come to know when you reach there."

The handcuffed players started running random . . .

Provost Marshall grandiloquently ordered to his constables, "common, take off their heads from the necks."

Policemen drew swords form their sheaths; ran behind the victims; swing the swords above their necks—the heads of the players fell down as if plucked jackfruits from aloft the tree.

All the fifteen heads were suspended on the beam of the goal post. The cause of the grisly incident was established as suicide—voluntarily taken their own lives as per the third clause of the fourth Para—a furtive one—of the *Footty bally* game contract made by Hovans and Indans. When the contract was signed, little did the players know that each goal was costing each player's head? Thus fifteen Hovan goals were paid for fifteen Indan lives by decapitation.

Governor General was not satisfied with the 1:15 revenge ratio. The iron entered into his soul was irrevocable. There was no iota of love or mercy in him. He intended again to strike the Indans while the iron was hot. But it was not that easy. The merciless incident damaged the hearts of the Indans irreparably. Especially the headless bodies of the dead were left lying on the ground itself. None of the relatives came to claim the crops lest they too should became headless.

Vultures came from the hell . . . They were happy. Might be the Governor General too. The carrion crows also enjoyed the feast . . .

I saw personally. Those who came to know the disaster were sunk in the ocean of agony. The luminous objects refuse to throw light for they too were lamenting for the dead. I could feel. My roots ran beneath the earth chilled to their juice. What to say, the grass in the recreation ground itself stood on its ends with fear.

The chopping and displaying of the innocent players' heads incited a wake of indignation among the people especially the youths. Spontaneous demonstrations were held in and around the state of Kalibay. Violent canaille carried placards showing "Depower Mr. Power" and "Powerfill go back to hell." Hundreds of men from both the sides were killed; thousands of men and women were arrested. The unrest continued despite the ruthless repression from the Hovan army and police. The Hovan officials had pins and needles.

Governor General was staying in the district headquarters of Kalibay, some miles away from the ground. Demonstrators surrounded his building. They pooh-poohed him.

Sitting inside his chamber, he thought deeply: How to handle twenty corores of Indan natives with strength of two thousand Hovans in Indana. That was only in the ratio of 1:2000. He wanted to induct some educated and efficient Indan employees. They should obey him. They should harass their own countrymen. He wished to introduce lot of reforms related to administrative, political and military . . .

As he was about to lit a cigar, Kalibay State Governor entered in his chamber; took attention position; gave a smart salute keeping the palm vibrating like a spring for more than a minute . . .

G.G. Powerfill reluctantly replied the salute and threw a question "What's happening?"

"The mob demand your quitting or and *amende honorable* from your honor *al fresco*."

"Why can't you suppress them?"

"They're multitude; we're a few."

"Recruit the force immediately; train them instantly."

"Past experience says it won't do any good."

"Why!"

"The recruits do not know our language; the rioters would convince them in their vernacular. They may join with the rioters."

"Does this riot disease spread to other states . . . ?"

"Not yet your honor; Contagious chances are there."

"Get the force from other states."

"Acute shortage of transport. Till then? The canailles are ready to burn our office and prepared to kill our officials. After you, I'm their first target your honor. We may escape now; but Kalibay . . ."

"Before an odium, How about shifting our capital to Deltan?"

G.G proposed, "Staying in Kalibay seems dangerous."

"That's a nice idea. But Deltan is quite far—near to our northeastern frontier hills. Moreover it's not a port city. Our conveyance facility is very poor."

"Had the railways come into practice?"

"Only some suburban trains are running."

"Express it from Kalibay to Deltan and Deltan to Mulcut."

"Linking the lines is not that easy your honor."

"Why? We've sufficient iron and coalmines in our empire. Exploit somebody to explore it."

"It costs . . ." Governor said politely, "Moreover our postal system is also poor. It takes more than a month to reach a letter from here to Deltan."

"Improve and innovate that too."

"The funds . . . ?" Governor asked in a very low tone.

After a thought, G.G. asked "What's the chief food of these bloody pin-holed people?"

"Majority takes rice and wheat." Governor replied surprisingly.

"Impose tax."

"It may create further . . ."

"We're not disturbing the peasants; they're at liberty to saw. We're not disturbing the farmers; they're at liberty to reap. We're not disturbing the merchants; they're at liberty to sell. All we want is just twenty percent commission as tax. We're interested about this land; not landlords.

*　　*　　*

Sans doute Mr.Powerfill was the marksmen of Modern Indana. With a sort of fierce zeal he was adamant on his dictum: "Suppress the strike, repress the riot and depress the deceit." Sometimes he was as stubborn as a mule. At the same time he was the magician of the marvelous developments. He was immensely able, energetic and untiringly industrious. His absolute honesty and devotion to the greatness of his motherland and her imperialism were displayed on Indan land during his Governor Generalship. In short he was the culmination of many reforms.

Though he was seldom cared for the social reforms such as human sacrifices and infanticide which were prevalent in Indan society—instead of abolishing and making such acts punishable by law as a ruler, he encouraged those cruel practices—yet, he was a gem of ruler in many other fields . . .

I too was amazed to see, some years back, the inaugural ceremony of the first train—Kalibay Queen. Its maiden journey to the town of Moona was news as large as life. People called it *steel horse*. Haa! The marvels of steam!! After consuming coal and water, the steel horse galloped on its parallel path, trailing three wooden bogies. There was a separate compartment exclusively for Hovans. They were 'A' class passengers. They enjoyed lot of comforts. The others were 'B' class passengers with fewer facilities in their compartments like wooden seat and urinal without water provision. The most paradoxical fact was the ruling class had to pay half a rooba for the ticket and the ruled class a full Rooba as fare! The down trodden of the 'C' class travelers ran behind the slow moving train as they couldn't afford the ticket. They were happy to have the railway track. It made their journey to the city quite easy. The erstwhile thoroughfare was a passage to the hell.

But now, how fast the fifty mile journey in the by gone days extended to five hundred miles. Train gained more than the speed of racehorses. It linked Kalibay, Deltan and Mulcut metropolises. There were three weekly *up* and *down* trains—Kalibay Fast, Deltan Express and Mulct mail—plying with ten comfortable compartments each comprising First, Second and Third class distinctions.

I was fascinated by the crawling of the train. It resembled a millipede while climbing on the hills . . .

Likewise, a new type of communication device knows as a telegraph was also introduced along with the old and conventional postal system. The mailbags also traveled by trains. The first telegraph line was opened from Deltan to Kalibay in the opening of the last quarter of the last but one century of my life story. The first telegram sent by the Governor General from Deltan to the Governor of Kalibay read: *All safe here Are you safe there*. The telegraphy has had its own language sans any grammar and punctuation. A full stop was charged as a word . . . ! People called the invention as *Horce code* . . .

The estimate of the development policy was settled . . . .

Governor General called a conference. All the Hovan capitalists—settlers—attended the emergent and extemporaneous meeting.

G.G made a stump speech "Dear white gentlemen, we the Hovans are the rulers; they the Indans are our slaves. Our inefficiency of men—if there is—and our insufficiency of money—there is—should not be known to them."

As the rich men looked each other G.G continued, "Well. This is a gathering to gather some funds. As you're aware that enormous cost is required for the development of administrative, reformative and public works. Our strength is limited. We need some assistants and attendants. Aren't we?"

The capitalists said as one man, "Of course, your honor . . ."

"The natives are illiterate. They've to be taught Hovalish. We could make them our puppets in our offices, residence and even for espionage provided they know our language. We need to open educational institutions . . . Next is about our strategic problem. Our troops are very thin. We've to recruit some natives in the regular Army as lower ratings so that the Indans could be annihilated by Indans in case of revolts. We've to strengthen the Navy also. I requested the crown to dispatch some men—of—war. It's for your safety. These bloody idiot Indan are not less than cannibals. I don't have to tell you the story of my great escape from Kalibay . . ."

A retired magistrate remarked, "Your honor was trapped as if in a Padma chakra in Indan epic."

"You are exactly correct". G.G continued as the other nodded their head in appreciation to the learned magistrate's knowledge in Indian epic. "Ok. Next, regarding railways. Some new constructions are going on other than the live lines already we have. Most of you're traders. Steel horses could replace your bullock cart transportation of men and materials. And now about the P and T. Unless you improve this system, you can't know the market of each trade centers instantly. You could immediately send the merchandise to a higher demanding center by sending and receiving telegrams. And the last but not the least item in the agenda is the public works. The condition of our roads, bridges and water supply is very deteriorating. Next steam ship would arrive with consignment of motorcars from our motherland. Without proper passage and adequate access, what's the use of it? So a public works department should be set up. All the engineers and officers would be from our side."

The capitalists were more interested to own a car rather than to improve the public works . . . A business magnet couldn't assimilate his enjoyment. He was neither timid of the glittering of the top brass.

He stood up and asked, "We're ready to invest. The return . . . ?"

"I know, "The top-brass replied, "your positive answer has a negative question. You'll be paid interest if possible. There is lot of salient features—I'll make a free-trade policy for you people. The merchants of Indana would be levied. We could collect toll from the users of our roads and bridges. You'll be exempted. I'll declare all the ports as duty-free. Only our traders and manufacturers would hold the import export license. We'll impose heavy duty on Indan articles. This would give an impetus to our economic interests. All of you know very well that the Industrial revolution is spreading fast . . ."

Another rich-gun, a narcotic racketeer rapaciously enquired, "How about the opium trade?"

G.G. answered, "To collect funds, we imposed tax on wheat and rice. Despite of it, the populace started eating some root-food like tapioca, yam, colocasia and stuffs like that. Somehow that tax policy failed. However we're going to import opium from Pakkana and would find out market in the metros and cities of Indana. But remember one thing. If the government does it, it's a legal trading; if you do it, its smuggling and illegal. So better to cooperate with us."

"Of course we'll co operate your honor. Thus we could make the Indan youths opium eaters. Thereby we could transform them from energetic to lethargic."

Another rich man remarked, "Then they would be as good as living corpse."

"But for Hova's sake, you should not be addicted to that and transform to real corpse." As the Governor General cracked the joke, one to all of them laughed unanimously . . .

*   *   *

I used to wake up at the silent hours while hearing the long and short blasts from the port of Kalibay the steam ship gave way to old sailing vessels in the history of navigation.

The innovative transport and communication that came with the industrial revolution helped spreading the imperialism easier. Britans built many miles of railways, highways and waterways with cheap labors.

The capitalists were happy. They could get raw materials out of the interior and send their finished product into new markets. Capitalists made more capitals . . .

University of Kalibay, University of Deltan and University of Mulct were established to facilitate the degree level studies to Hovan and the students of their henchmen. The economic tenet was organized to cater the needs of foreigners only.

On the contrary Indans' interests were left uncared. Thereby natives suffered from economic diseases. They were to pay levies, tolls and high fares for all the needs. The mechanization made many middle class men jobless. The populace of Indana felt and lamented at the unalleviated economic exploitation of their motherland by the exotic men. The heavy duties imposed by the government on Indan articles had blocked the business of Indan merchants.

Besides these, there was a lot of discontentment among the Indans—Hovans; the *haute couture* had full of haughtiness in their heart and full of malice in their mind. They had a bad impression about the Indans' character.

*   *   *

A pair of sandals, black goggles, a miniskirt, a full sleeve shirt and a hat saved the life of Mr. Powerfill magically.

My wives were ready to bet with me that some untoward incident would happen in the office of the Governor of Kalibay. But I bet I was certain that there will not be any such incident.

I had watched each and every movements of the G.G. right from his ship secured on the embarkation birth. A black car carrying that white man rolled out of the specially made gangway. I was beholding a car for the first and foremost time! People called the car a motorized monster!

On the jetty itself, he was presented with a single line arms guard by naval personals. A band played the music 'Standard'. The guard commander shouted orders. Men obeyed. The sequence of drill was very smart and conspicuous! People called it 'Guard of honor'! Any way I was seeing it for the first time. My spouses were afraid of rifles. Later we came to know that the rifles were just dummy—unserviceable for drill purpose only. More over the sailors were not trained for land fighting and musketry. Also there was a ceremonial parade on the ground in front of the Governor's office. Participated by two platoons of army and one platoon of the local police—the total strength of the Kalibay force.

No sooner did the dispersal of parade than the soldiers were sent to construct a temporary bridge—which was collapsed while the car was passing over it—over a creek on the cracked way to Deltan. The limited police force was provided with swords and batons. G.G's gunman who was standing outside the office building afraid of the wrath of the agitators took to his heels and joined with the car driver for he was very much bothered about his own life. The car was concealed in a locked underground garage. So any attack from the Hovan's side was impossible.

G.G. had never thought the people will rise for a riot. It was not practicable to recall the army already marched for more than two hours. Moreover he left his revolver inside his car. He repented to have the gun and the gunman by his side. Instead of cursing his foolishness, he accused others as fools . . .

So impersonation was the only solution. Attired in those dress he escaped with the Governor pretending as his wife. The extremists were anxiously waiting to kill the black bearded G.G, unaware he had taken a *presto* shaving.

They shouted, "Where did the G.G. hid?"

Governor of Kalibay said politely, "He's not hiding. He's preparing an explanation. He'll come to address you soon."

People waited . . . waited . . . and waited until all the ants in their pants started biting. Finally finding the folly, some of the angry crowd turned murderers—they thronged the nearby police station and killed one to all constables including the provost marshal . . . others kindled the Governor's office.

That brutal and boisterous rebellion boiled the G.G's blood like lava in his volcanic heart. Mr. Powerfill patiently waited to use his power hammer impatiently when the iron becomes hot.

Deltan Central became the biggest railway station of Indana. Kalibay Express was ready for departure on platform No. I. As the train moved, a throng of thugs like unemployed youths thrust inside the 1st class compartment. There were thuds and thumps. Train gained speed . . . They threw all the Hovan passengers outboard. They wrote heterodox slogans everywhere on the train walls: *It is not fair to accommodate full-fare-paid Indans in 3rd class; it is also not fair to accommodate half-fare-paid Hovans in 1st class.*

There was no "emergency stop pull chain system" in those days. When the train reached the next station, they were welcomed warmly with warrant of arrest. The newly introduced telephone facility helped Hovan police a lot to vanquish the agitators.

There came a telephone message from the G.G's office to produce the youths before the G.G.

They were produced . . .

Sanguinary Governor General stormed, "You black heathens, stop worshipping stocks and stones; start worshipping me. I'm your Godfather. It's I who reclaimed this land. All these developments are my boon to you swinging bees on bamboos."

One valiant youth took out a blade and snapped, "Yuuu, white skinned and black hearted bastard, this land and labors belong to us. It's better to root out your rail and jail and quit quickly from our land. Otherwise . . ."

He couldn't complete the last sentence for he was given the last sentence—shot then and there. The smell of gun powder from the G.G's revolver chilled the crowd to marrow . . .

He sneered, "Common, Marshall, I don't want to devastate my bullets and time for these devalued targets. Throw these inferior breed to the gallows."

And G.G's order was promptly and properly executed . . .

* * *

Shifting of the capital pained me. My sensorium ached. It was true that I was senile. It never made me slip-off. But this evolution! I felt I lost my address. Entire energy drained out. My consorts consoled me to assimilate some nutrients.

I said, "No, thanks. I've no appetite. You please go ahead."

They unanimously said, "It is cultureless to have food before the husband's consumption as per our customs."

"Huuummm, the customs?" I muttered myself.

There was argument—*you eat first, you eat first*—among us. At last all the consorts came to a consolidated and consonant conclusion—not to consume any food but consult about the customs.

On hearing the word customs, my sorrow recapitulated the reminiscence—how Kalibay rose to be the first and fantastic city of Indana—again and again. When asked, I said to my spouses "You don't know. The rise of Kalibay leads to a series of far reaching evolutions.

In the remote past, there was none around here. It all started with my birth. Now look everywhere full of faunas and floras. This is the most populous city now-a-days. This is the center of Indana civilization. Kalibay's advancement has a unique feature in its own contribution to the human progress. Kalibay's present maturity has had many wonder tales of organized political and social system, trade and commerce affairs, complicated religious beliefs, writing and literature and art and science."

I studied my spouses. As I continued eagerly they were listening earnestly. "You may not know. Now the city of Kalibay faced a transition from nothingness to everything except peace."

"We know it Hus, we know it." All my wives said as one man."

"Anyway the city is lacking peace. You calculate yourself: Kalibay + Peace =?"

"Paradise!" Unanimously they solved the problem without any problem. Because *sans doute,* it was clear that if you let in the air of peace in the atmosphere of Kalibay, her people would breathe it and would become healthy, wealthy and wise.

Now that G.G Powerfill, who claims to be a heaven-return couldn't recognize Kalibay as heaven. Because he only minuses the peace from this district to make a devil's paradise. I don't know what the hell he's going to do in Deltan city, making it as his capital . . . !"

Many gold, iron and coalmines were exploited. Myriads of native men were labored to death in those mines. Dowry system was prevalent in Indana. Gold was the chief item. The demand was so much that the mine owners—Hovan capitalists—earned enormous profit. The iron ore was exported to Britana. From there, all most all the heavy machineries plates and vessels were manufactured and shipped back. Coal was indeed used for all the steam propelled utilities indigenously.

The hinterland of my state was a land of coconut cultivation. The carpets and mats made here were popularly known as Koir was in great demand as the Britana was a very cold country. All the villagers including women and children employed in the cottage industry for separating coconut fibers from the husk, spinning and weaving. The *modus operandi* was by manual labor. They had spinning wheels and hand and lug operated looms. They ran the business under co-operative societies. The village chief, being the secretary looked after it. He sold the product to the Hovan merchants. They imported it to their homeland making huge profit.

One day . . .

Large numbers of cartload finished products were taken to the shipping center at Kalibay port. The exporting agent refused to receive the consignment.

He said, "Until further orders, the finished Koir goods are rejected by the government."

"Then what about our cottage industry!" The Village Chief was thunder struck.

"We're not interested about your cottage industry; however we're interested about your coconut industry."

"I didn't get you . . ."

Patting on the Chief's shoulder, the exporter said, "Don't worry man. As we're lovers of your coconut, you get any amount of its husk and seed. We'll accept and export it."

"You take this order at least; if not, our families will be at sea."

"Lie mere lie." Continued the exporter, "during my voyage, I've not seen a single Indan family at sea."

The villager implored, "I mean they're in trouble."

"I beg you earnestly. If I take your order I'll be in trouble, I mean at sea." The sarcasm in the Hovan trader's answer had the complete sense of rejection.

Sadly the chief returned to his village. He cursed the exporter. The animals also had ants in their pants. They too listened the dialogues. They cursed both the Chief and the exporter. They were sadder for they had trekked all the way taking two solid days and nights shouldering the heavy loads. They were so tired that they couldn't withstand the loaded return journey. It would lead them to the dead end before the half way journey.

Due to the adverse import export policy of Hovan government, many people were famishing for one time meal. Especially I still remember the Kalibay famine took a heavy toll of human lives. That's one of the reasons why I and my consorts refused to consume food to give a moral support to the hungry men.

The industrial revolution appeared before the working classes as if a man eating monster. In Britana, they invented steam driven power looms and automatic spinners. The mechanical oil expellers milled maximum oil out of the coconuts. You add sugar even to poison; your mouth and tongue would easily go for it. Hovans knew it very well. They fleeced Indans of their golden fleece—the coconut oil cakes were powdered, blended with some sort of cheap flour, added sugar and baked into biscuits. Ignorant Indans paid money and present it to their children. Innocent children liked it dearer than the breast milk. Thus the foreigners exploited the innocents by inhumane and indecent method.

The reforms and renovations of the G.G. helped to make true the Hovan capitalist's dream of making money. Parallel to that it also helped to make true the Indan masses' dream of nationalism. The conveyance and communication system made easy for them to assemble and exchange ideas each other in the nooks and corners of Indana more conveniently than ever before.

It was Hovans folly to teach Hovalish to the natives. It filled their heart with new blood of Britana's ideas and breathed the air of Britana's philosophies. Setting aside many of their vernaculars, they had a thirst for learning Hovalish. It influenced the Indan youths more. It was this medium which contributed more than anything else to the growth of freedom movement in Indana.

I saw all the self respecting Indans joined hand to hand the freedom struggle. Deep thinking individuals came forward as national leaders. They formed a party. Their speeches and campaigns kindled ardent zeal among the populace also consequently the number of the members in the Freedom Struggle Party (F.S.P.) increased like anything. Party offices started functioning even in small towns. Sub committees, state committees and central committees meetings were held frequently. Great national leaders like Mr. Mal, Mr. Dal and Mr. Kal led the state committees at Mulcut, Deltan and Kalibay respectively. And the central committee was presided over by Mr. Dosh. His blood contained full of extremist corpuscles, his heart pumped militant spirit, and he inhaled the oxygen of nationalism and exhaled the carbon-di-oxide of terrorism. All his speeches and writings had an inclination towards revolution. Eventually extremism took a gigantic shape in the body of nationalism.

One of the chief profits to the Hovan exchequer was through opium smuggling. Some soil of Pakkana was very suitable for growing narcotic plants. The contraband good was transported to Indana by thousands of head load workers through a hilly access. The majority of the workers were Indan B'llans.

If any of the membrane of my memory is not damaged, I was certain that the first and foremost *union* in Indana was of the head-load workers under the leadership of secretary Mr.M'ulluddin. He was also an activist in F.S.P. Mr. Dosh, as the President of the F.S.P. promulgated a strike by the head-load workers as it spoiled the career of the carriers for they too were opium consumers. That hindered the Hovan's profit business. They employed Pakkan laborers as substitutes. But they were not allowed to enter the Indan boundary. There were clashes—Firing . . . killing . . . looting. As an alternative, government planned a very big project to convey the contraband good by convey of trucks. But the roads . . . ?

The Mahalayan Mountain range had a low attitude portion—only about 5000 feet M.S.L. Government wanted to construct a hill highway to Pakkana, known as *Pakkana Pass*. It had a stretch of 500 miles from Deltan to Malachi, the capital of Pakkana. Mass petitions were submitted by F.S.P. to protest against the construction with the exclusive Indan revenue collected by way of extra, special and compulsory taxes exclusively from Indan Individuals. The contents of the petitions were few questions and its proper answers.

Q. Why do you need a highway in the inhibited uninhabited hilly area?

A. To smuggle opium from Pakkana.

Q. Why you're so interested about laying roads in some other land where our land has lack of roads?

A. To promote opium smuggling from Pakkana.

Q. Why do you want to spend Indan revenue for the development of Pakkana where we've plenty of under developed areas?

A. To compensate the profit.

Q. Why do you bring opium to Indana only, instead of importing to your country?

A. To annihilate the Indan activists.

Q. Why don't you bring nuts instead of narcotics?

A. To spread famine.

There was a foregone conclusion: "Stop this Project forthwith; Or . . ."

More than one lakh of people signed on the petition. Government regarded the properly answered questions as improper. They used that bundle of papers as inflammable material in their bedroom mantle-piece.

Not only I, the whole world knew that the *union is strength*. The head-load workers' union was as good as a *splice*. Each and every worker was a fiber in the rope of their union. They were the forerunners to shout the famous slogan *"Union zindabad, Union zindabad"* slogan. The echo of it horripilated all the hills in the boundary range. The government feared the union's growing strength.

Bribe is a bridle for any bright person. Mr. M'ulluddin was an example. Hovan officials prevailed upon him. As a union leader he could do lots of mischief. Mr. M'ulluddin was a militant also. Besides injecting communalism, government offered him many favors. They gave *sir* title,

432

offered him huge prize money and made him a member in the Hovan cabinet. Betraying the workers, he easily yielded to Hovans—The union spitted . . .

His dogmatic explanation was that he hadn't yielded to any fore-gifts. He was after all a B'llaist. A Pakkana migrant. He loved and liked Pakkana and its people more than that of Indana and her people. Out of the four chambers of his heart, three were reserved for Pakkans. Moreover, his mind was filled with hatred and dislike towards Indan's culture and custom. So he fell out of the freedom movement of Track and Opium strike.

In the same period, B'llan communalism aroused by him found its culmination in the organization of B'llan *Masdoor* League. With the support of B.M.L, Hovan government earned a *Mahalayam* mountain of money by selling opium in Indana at a four-fold price where Pakkana sold it only for quarter price.

Nominated member Sir M'ulluddin demanded in the cabinet for more privileges to B'llans as they're the minority community of only two corores among a twenty crore Indan population. They were placed comfortably in government employment and as licensees, venders and agents.

Mr. Dosh couldn't sleep since the fall out of Sir M'ulluddin. He took a pledge: First, I'll kill Mr. Powerfill, the G.G. Then Sir M'ulluddin, the B.M.L. leader . . .

Out of all the incidents—good or bad, fortunate or unfortunate, glorious or inglorious, advantageous or disadvantageous, happy or unhappy, believable or unbelievable, decent or indecent—the city of Mulcut faced a most cruel incident. Actually, it was bellicosity between the rats and the rioters . . .

But I smelled a rat that the bellicose G.G. was the brain behind it. He played a prominent roll to annihilate all the antagonists from the Eysans world of cruelty.

Splitting from F.S.P, Mr. Dosh, militant leader founded a National Revolutionary Army. Many volunteer youths joined in his force. He was the chief-of-the-army-staffs. His headquarters was at Mulcut. Out of the many officers and men in N.R.A, there were two valiant lady Brigadiers, Really, I had never seen such type of belligerent ladies! Even after giving them cent percent marks in the practical examination of extremism, I gave them some bonus marks also.

N.R.A. received provisions from the peasants, clothing from the cotton workers. What about arms and ammunitions . . . ? They captured many police stations and that booty of musket was more than enough to fill their armory. And the funds . . . ? They looted many banks. One out of it grabbed the front pages of the newspapers of the country as well as the foreign.

On all the last Wednesdays of every month, dispatch of money used to be held from the Mint of Hovan government situated at Mulcut to the treasuries of Deltan and Kalibay. From there, the money dispersed to different districts' funds as salaries and other needs. This time the security press authorities didn't transport the amount in the train—they usually do—lest it should be looted be the extremists.

A truck with an armor plate body. Packed with ten lakhs of *Rooba*—Indan currency—moved as if a pregnant lady going to her residence from the spouse's house. Two trucks—one at the front and other at the rear—packed with ten soldiers and a Hovan officer in each truck escorted it. They had to cover precisely six hundred fifty miles to Deltan. They needed precisely two days and two nights. The convoy moved . . .

Many a morning on the first day, they reached a village. They halted for the morning routine near to a convenient place. Some distance away, peasants were laboring in the mustard fields. Drivers went in search of water to fill in the coal boilers of the trucks. They had chitchat with the women peasants. It was an intense hot summer. Even the sun couldn't bear his own heat. After fetching water from the well, the drivers pleaded to the peasants for some cold drink.

An elderly woman replied, "We villagers drink butter-milk, milk and toddy. You prefer which, *sahib* . . . ?"

"Oh, toddy! Toddy is good for body." One said.

Other said, "OF course, we want toddy."

The women rushed to the hutments a little distance away.

The third driver called out loudly "Common sirs, lets quench our thirst. Common."

They too joined. All the soldiers sat beneath the shade of a coconut tree. Making sure the key of the truck was safe in his belt, the senior officer also relaxed with his subordinates.

If you want to experience love, its only with a woman provided it shouldn't be cupboard love. Women are substitute to happiness provided she's willing. Otherwise you'll be like one among the money escorts suffered from a slip between the cup and the lips.

One of the militant ladies—Brigadier, Miss Chapatti came to know that the drink was for the escorts. She took over the mission of making the soldiers' merriment.

"I've mixed a little marijuana juice in this drink." She said merrily while handing over the glass full of liquor.

"Owff, fine. It's a pleasure . . ." The senior officer said, "It'll eradicate our tiredness. Owff, what a long and tortuous journey it was! Anything else to present to us?"

"O, yes. Mango marinade."

The junior officer asked "Only that? No fleshy items?"

The driver commented, "Saar, she is full of flesh. Let's eat her"

"Nooo, nooo, noo." She lied, "tomorrow is my marriage. My flesh's reserved for someone else."

"I'll marry you." Another driver said.

"Tell that to the mariners . . . It would be a mis-alliance . . ."

The rendezvous became lively, cheerful, full of laughter, joyous and slightly tipsy. The soldiers made mirth, hilarious enjoyment, fun and frolic. The jovial peasants watched the visitors' jollity.

It seemed—too much of merriment results to mishap. Irrespective of respect, rank and seniority, one to all soldiers collapsed on the ground. Really a misadventure during their adventure of escorting!

Miss Chappathy was a lascivious lady as large as life. Her soft body! Vaaa, vaa, va! More soft than cotton candy. Nevertheless there was a lioness hidden in her. Her laser emitting eyes pin-holed any hard man's heart. She intentionally adulterated the drink to kill the adulterated soldiers—they were poisoned!

That remote village was the harbor for all the freedom movement militants—many vulnerable areas were infested with the extremists. The villagers provided them hut to sleep and food to eat. Mustard seeds had a great demand. Its oil never solidified even in extreme chilling climate. The military men needed it for *massaging* their body. So there was price rise. Thus the villagers could afford the antagonists' expenses. They also acted as auxiliaries.

G.G once again became bloodthirsty. His thirst couldn't be quenched with the lives of the militants. He intended to annihilate the entire village.

He shouted, "Common, switch on the motor of cruelty."

G.G's physician, who used to be always with him as if his shadow, spoke softly, "Your Excellency, use the soft side of the sword. If you use the sharp side, the people would become a turbulent sea. I don't want to spare your head as a football like your father's. You've to grace the inauguration of the Pakkan pass in the next week. If you take the responsibility of any more disaster, I presume it would be your disaster."

"Then? What shall we do? Let leave those Indan beggars to pick pocket all the Hovan's hearts? I want revenge. A horrible revenge of homicide that human history had never heard."

"Please don't smoke your head Your Excellency, please. Leave this dispute to me. I'm not only a trouble-shooter but also a trouble-creator also at times. And, Your Excellency, if I create a trouble, I'll transform to a destroyer sans thinking that I'm a protector as a physician."

If the killer is a Hovan nominee—soldier, policeman or any hired man—it would be a test of testing the patience of not only the extremists but also the peace loving people. So G.G didn't want to take any flying arrow in his anus.

Then who'll kill? How? When? All those questions rebounded in his mind as if balls on a billiard table. It was the duty of the G.G's physician to look after and treat the mental worries of his ruler. Mr. Panic was the G.G's roving doctor. He was a good reader and a traveler as well.

"Burry your worry." He said firmly" I'll get some killers."

G.G asked with a concern, "From where?"

"They're foreigners . . ."

"Foreigners! From Britana, our homeland? The Crown will scold me like anything.

"No. Leave it to me."

"Roger. All should be safe and secret from our side."

"Even the killers won't know they're killing."

"Fine. I'll pay this year's budget to them."

"Nooo, noo, no. Not even a single penny is needed as remuneration. The only expense is that your Excellency may provide some trucks. I'll make a trip to Mulcut."

"You take a fleet of transport. Only thing is that the homicide should not be leaked out."

"Only you, I and God will know it. I give you guarantee."

"Mind Doc," Powerfill said, "all that glitters is not damn God."

I chuckled myself because I too could smell a rat of his plot.

The suggestion of the physician was exactly executed. The killers were transferred in the transports from Cheenisthan via Pakkana. The convoy movement perplexed people. It was propagated as a trial run before the opening of the Pakkan Pass.

436

The trucks, on the way halted at the Village of Militancy in the dead hours of sleep. I and my spouses didn't sleep. We were anxiously waiting to see the killers. Yes. We saw them. Our conclusion was exactly correct. Within few moments the trucks started its onward journey after unloading the killers. As the trucks left the village, the killers entered the village.

Trucks reached the Headquarters of Mulcut. The Resident welcomed the Physician.

Shaking hands, the Resident said, "Hallow Dr. Panic, I received a wireless message from the G.G. By the by, are the killers safely landed in the village? How about their food, accommodation and clothing?"

Dr. Panic, the physician answered, "I arranged everything. Otherwise also they don't need anything. They never change the cloths; they live anywhere; they eat anything. They're quite natural."

"Look doc, I'm afraid. The village is an extremist's dominated area. If your killers are killed?"

"Let's wait and see who'll survive."

To our surprise, nothing happened . . . Neither a villager nor a killer was killed.

A week passed by . . .

The marriage ceremony of Miss Chappathy was nearing. All most all the militants assembled well in advance except Militant's General Dosh who was issued with a warrant of 'shoot-at-sight'. The bride groom's party was also sheltered in the village . . .

The wedding day . . .

None of the invitees came to the venue. Neither the bride nor the groom couldn't attend their own marriage function.

About five thousand villagers couldn't get up from the bed as they were prostrated. They suffered from fever; they chilled like anything. There was nobody to help anybody for everybody was feeling physical exhaustion. Within a week the pestilence prevailed in the entire village. One to all villagers succumbed to high mortality. The disease petrified even the mustard plants in the field.

But I presumed how the vicious physician masterminded the plot of spreading *bubonic plague* in the village to annihilate its population. How tactfully he spread the infectious, epidemic disease caused by the bits of fleas! How conspiratorially he transported the foreign killers from Cheenisthan!! How easily he depopulated a populous village!!! Actually the killers—the rats—were the carriers of bacterium of plague. Regiments and regiments of rats were capturing other villages also with the arms of germs equipped on their body.

What a plague of a man that physician was! A man who was suppose to save the diseased, deliberately thrown them in the well of decease.

I couldn't help out the villagers other than joining in the agony. So I exclaimed infinitely—Alas!!!!!!!! . . . !

The death toll was innumerable due to plague. Followed by epidemic. I dug innumerable tombstones of tolerance in the graveyard of my mind. My spouses were upset. They cursed the unseemly act of both the unscrupulous G.G and his unprincipled doc.

A high explosive called Minadyte was a wonder in those days. Its effect, really unthinkable and unbelievable! Many people called the invention a man made calamity. But I disagree with the dogma. Minadyte, vow . . . ! It had really a spectacular effect! I really magnify the man who toil-torn to device the Minadyte.

The foreign scientist, a dynamic person, the Noble of nobles who invented the substance was the greatest of the greatest as large as life. He was the real humanist as big as life. A lord of the laborers. Or a God for the hard working class.

It was a regular show—the rocks and granites required for various construction works were to be cut from the Rocky Mountains by risking the life. The laborers toil-torn throughout day and night, turning their blood to sweat for removing one block of rubble. The ding-dong sound of the collision of their heavy hammer and sharp chisel echoed everywhere. It used to irritate me like anything. The sound pollution and the uproar disturbed the tranquility of the hills. The minadyte reduced, in fact eased the man labor—A hundred days work of hundred men were reduced to a single day's work for a man by the magic of minadyte. Its characteristics! Its energy!! Its effective action!!! Its vigorous motion!!!! Its driving force!!!!! Wauu, it's incredible! I personally saw its power when a hill was minadyted. The rubbles flying upwards as if dried leaves then falling on the ground as if dropping of coconuts from aloft the tree while chopping the bunches. It created whirlwind inside the hill.

An international pact was signed to use the Minadyte exclusively for world peace. But some miscreants misused the explosive. They made hand bombs and time bombs for the annihilation of human race. Though Hovan armory had sufficient stock of those bombs, they feared whether the extremists and militants of Indana also had those types of H.E weapons capable to explode their bodies like rubbles from the mountain.

The grand gala opening ceremony of Pakkan Pass—the Highway linking Deltan and Malachi—both the nation's capitals—was to be held by His Excellency. Mr. Powerfill, the Governor General of Indana. Many dignitaries were invited to grace the auspicious function. Sir M'ulluddin was also one among the VIPs seated at the front. Tight security arrangements were made—army regiments, police battalions were breeding like mosquitoes. All the natives were kept far away as spectators.

I remembered the prevalent custom of unapproachable distance. But the natives were happy to be a little away for they were afraid of the bomb smelling squad of the police sniffer dogs from Dash family plying here and there as if they too had the command and control of a commander over the crowd.

Actually, Mr. Dosh, the General of the militants was tribal descendant. Thus he had inborn archery skills. He came to Deltan, disguised as an herbal medicine seller—his make-up was such that he himself couldn't recognize him—lest he should be identified. If identified, he would go to the gallows for he was the most wanted man by Hovan government.

The venue of the inaugural function of Indana Pakkana Highway was outskirt of the Deltan city. Both the roadsides were grown up thick bamboo trees. He arrived there a week before. He surveyed the area. He wanted to kill the G.G by hook or by crook. He knew that previous day of the inauguration; he couldn't enter the vicinity of the venue. So he took refuge on top of the bamboo tree three days before. During dark hours he made a comfortable seat concealed by the leaves. He took position to throw a hand bomb to the platform where the G.G Mr. Powerfill, his physician Dr. Panic, Sir M'ulluddin and many other Hovan dignitaries would assemble. His bomb had sufficient power to powder Mr. Powerfill and his party; he had sufficient guts to use it. He kept the bomb so close to his chest and valued it as his own liver . . .

He had had no food items to consume with him. But his stomach didn't complaint to the brain for the fear of scolding. The brain didn't spare any time for anything other than working out the plot—his appetite was quenched with the sweet cake of vengeance. But the nature favored him. Yes. His eyes founded. There it is! The honey!! A hive full of honey was hanging right in front of him!!!

Next day police arrived. Inaugural day military also arrived. They didn't want to take a chance like last time. Entry was strictly prohibited. Even the VIPs also were barred in carrying their personal weapons. Explosive experts were deployed to remove any Minadyte articles.

A gleaming black motorcar decorated with Hovan ensign and star-studded plates rolled slowly and stopped a little distance away.

A military police marks-man shouted at the peak of his voice "G.G arriving sir . . ."

Militant General Dosh intended to hit the Hovan Governor General the moment he would come on the dais. But all of a sudden, while he was removing the pin of the grenade type of bomb his intention was foiled . . .

Call it a misfortune; call it a bad luck or call it a fate. It was a bad cum sad destiny. The bomb fell on the bushy ground . . . He felt his heart had fallen down. It was by chance. A honeybee stuck him. All the sweet honey he consumed had been changed to bitter tasty poison in his mouth. He sat emotionless for few seconds.

The parade commander gave a long and loud order to the Guard positioned on the road. "Atten . . . . tion."

G.G came and stood on the dais. There was no trepidation. Heavy wind was blowing; nevertheless all the trees beside the road stood still.

Suddenly the killer mustered his brain. Agitation, alarm and anxiety grew in him. What next? The dream of killing his enemies and foiling the inauguration can't be materialized. Then. Hit the first and largest target, the G.G. But where's the weapon? Yes, there's a weapon. His ancestral weapon, the bow and arrow. But where's it? Make it, instantly. He removed the amulet worn on his waist; broke one flexible bamboo branch and tied both ends—a bow was made. He then broke a stalk; sharpened one end with his teeth—an arrow was made. He had a phial of poison—the venom from King cobra—in order to suicide in case he was caught. He filled the hollow sharp end of the bamboo arrow with venom. No sooner did the weapon was ready than he got the clear still and stiffened target, the Governor General.

G.G was giving reply salute to the Guard of honor marching past him. His right upper arm parallel to the ground, lower arm making an angle of forty five degrees and palm slightly inward. His left arm kept close to the body, fingers clenched from the second knuckles. He stood looking straight. Left side of his broad chest was widely opened to receive any amount of arms and ammunition from anywhere. All of a sudden it so happened.

There was a thud . . . G.G fell on the wooden plat form. There was no explosion; there was no gunfire. Yet he was killed. He was envenomed. The weapon—the bamboo arrow did its duty perfectly. Like a miniature guided missile with a warhead, it traveled, pierced his chest, peeped inside his heart and pumped the poison. Timidly, Sir M'ulluddin drove away in his car in a hurry . . .

Sound of siren, sound of blank fire, barking of dogs, shouting of police and yelping of men and women were there. Government declared H.P.C 144 (Hovan Penal Code) throughout Indana.

But, without more ado, like a winner in an obstacle race, Mr. Dosh, the militant Chief of Indana fled to Cheenisthan by foot with the strong desire of destroying his snap target number two, Sir M'ulluddin on the way somewhere in Pakkana.

Notwithstanding the tiredness of the three days starvation in the hide out, he didn't feel any exhaustion. The success of his *modus operandi* gave ample ampoules of spirit to burn the candle of his forth coming *modus vivendi*.

Like all the people, we (I and my spouses) were also avid strongly for the independence of Indana. We were thinking that our dream would come true in the nineteenth century. But the envenoming of the Governor General, stabbing of Sir. M'ulluddin and the amputation of Dr. Panic etc from Indans' side and awarding gallows to Miss. Chappathy—who escaped from the plague tragedy—suicidal death of Dosh's sister Miss. Pamma and exile of may innocents to Horawa Jungle Mountains were some of the vengeful atrocities from Hovans' side made our hope to hopelessness. However, our avidity towards the freedom of Indana was full filled only in the first decade of the last century of the second millennium.

Century 20

1900 to 2000 AD
Millennium 2

I planted nineteen plants of memoir passim on the plaza of my memory during the passage of my lifetime. They blossomed and bore many fruits of incidents, which had fragrance and flavors fit to my bliss. Rarely some incidents hurt me. Those were as good as medlars.

I would like to plant the twentieth plant of memoir on the occasion of my twentieth centenary birthday, the last century of this millennium. Like an aster, it bloomed auspiciously in the beginning by Indana's gaining of total freedom from the hands of the foreigners.

All the Hovans mourned the loss of their most efficient Governor General of all times. He was the pet of the Rip Van Winkles. They were indignant. Their newspaper headlines read: Governor General Powerfill is killed; the indecent deed of the Indans. Yes. *Sans doute*, the power of G.G Powerfill was switched off by one of the powerful militant leaders of Indana.

I do not remember how many leaders came on the historical stage of Indana to play the part of reforming religion and education. It was an uphill task. The people who lent their ears abandoned orthodoxy and embraced the real purity and simplicity of their religions. Thus a scientific society was formed. The religious and social reforms paved way for the cultural awakening. The movement led to the freedom struggle. The participants suffered cruelties at the hands of the Hovan government. Indan strugglers also showed the other side of the cruelty coin to the Hovans.

The Crown condemned the murder of the G.G as the most inhuman and indecent act by the Indans. However, it shook their indigenous and exotic empire. The Hovan authorities in Britana smoked their heads to find out ways to tighten the bolt of foundation of imperialism in Indana.

That was the time when many young leaders with modern ideas joined the nationalist movement. The most important leaders among them were Mahadagi, Gerri Lal, Odin Dos and Dara Kham.

All of them were great personalities. All of them were good. But who was the greatest among them? Who was better? Answers to these questions were unquestionably this: the first. And who was the superlative person among them? Indeed the former, Mahadagi. There were adequate adjectives to qualify his personality and adequate adverbs to modify his performance both in political and personal life. Thus he acquired the highest degree of comparison among all other freedom movement leaders. He was the pioneer of performances such as *Satyagraham* (undergoing hardship and suffering including imprisonment), *Niraharam* (abstention from food or fasting till the attainment of political goal), and *Hartal* (closure of shops and stoppage of work to show the passive resistance).

He was a paragon of peace and patience.

Ooh! That harbinger of hospitality is no more! A very tragic end.

Dramas pertaining to the Mahadagi's life were staged throughout Indana.

Motion picture became popular in Britana. Silent movie matured into talking movie. With the introduction of the sound track, cinema became the best medium to capture the human hearts. Movie like *Life of Mahadagi* melted the iron-hearted people to wax. Myriads of *goondas* were transformed into good men. Many hoodlums became humanists. Numerous evildoers became ethic-lovers. Most of the viewers wished to lead a life like that of Mahadagi, the lead role-player of the cinema.

Many people abandoned their fashionable garments. They wore only a towel. Nobody asked, "Why do you don this ludicrous dress?" It became a fashion. Some played with their stomachs. Cut three full-square meals to two. Some to one and some to nil. The stomach was satisfied for it was a sacrifice for the suppression of the starvation of the fellow beings. Many artistes on stage imitated Mahadagi. Everywhere mimic battles broke out especially in mono act, fancy dress and other solo performances. Mahadagi's spectacles, walking stick and sandals became famous even in foreign countries as *haute couture*.

I and my consorts were profoundly attracted by Mahadagi's smart strides and agile actions during processions and campaigns, especially the famous 'Wheat March' organized by him. The Hovan Government did not pay the spices plantation workers their wages for months. Extremity was the ex gratia payment. Beating up was the bonus. Mahadagi declared a strike. He deployed all the workers to reap the crop of wheat of private farmers so that they would at least get *roti* or food. Government prevented it. The first one to wield a sickle, enter the field and reap the crop was Mahadagi. Numerous employees entered the field and joined him without fear for *lathy* charges and bullets.

Beholding the scene we felt horripilation. We too became industrious. We too wished to take part in the *Wheat March*. As we could not do so, to give moral support, we shook our branches like the freedom fighters who raised their hands while shouting patriotic slogans.

Wake, wake Warriors
Wake, wake Vagabonds
To make, make the boundary of bravery
Shake, shake stalwarts
Shake, shake stalkers
To break, break the stakes of slavery.
Come on come on children,
Come on come on consorts,
To participate in the contest of civil liberty.
Come on come on faunas
Come on come on floras
To fight for the freedom of our country.
Come on come on animates
Come on come on inanimate
To array in the annunciation of Independence.
Let's light the torch of the country's unity
To build a fearless, free and modern Indana.

During the civil disobedience movement under the leadership of Mahadagi, I still remember the dialogues between the Governor General when Mahadagi was arrested.

The G.G said, "You know, we're Hovans. Our ancestors came directly from heaven. So do not disobey Hovan's order."

Mahadagi retorted, "I am glad that you've come from heaven. But I am sad that you won't go to heaven.

My name is Powerfill. I'm powerful also. Don't forget."

"How can I forget you? If a man has power, he can do good. If he has pride, he'll do bad. If he has both power and pride, he'll do worse"

"Arrest this Indan barking dog. Chain him till he recognizes my power."

While Mahadagi was being dragged towards the carriage, he said, 'The real power of a man lies in prayers and love."

The canaille could not hear it as the cruel G.G was still chattering some commands. But I heard it.

* * *

All those involved in production work—technicians and artists—wore oin clothes whenever they were not in make-ups. The people praised the *Popular Cine Unit* in general and its producer, director and the hero in particular. The life of Mahadagi was reenacted on the silver screen.

But I and my consorts could only laugh because we had seen the shooting of the film.

I would like to describe certain scenes which were scheduled and shot in my neighborhood. Some of the real movements and incidents of the freedom struggle and the life of Mahadagi and his wife Kanti had taken place on the same spots in Kalibay. The outdoor shooting was strictly prohibited for the public. Policemen were posted.

Certain scenes that exactly matched the life of Mahadagi were shot. But the real lives of the producer, director and the main actor—my good God—were as good as the saying goes: Theory is contrary to the practice.

Some viewers of the last show who were stranded beside me waiting for the last bus to the nearby village were passing comments on the film *Mahadagi*.

One said, "The part that attracted me was the scene on dieting. How could he live on a handful of groundnuts and some cups of pure water? Yet he worked restlessly round the clock for freedom!"

But I will describe the practical life of the unit members after the shooting of that scene.

Mahadagi is lying on a cot in his *ashram*.

The frame is lit up.

The doctor advises him.

The director orders: "Start camera."

Camera starts.

Director: "Action."

Doctor's dialogue: Mr. Mahadagi, Your health condition is very poor. You must improve your diet. Unless you've some mutton soup, you can't recover. At this rate you may die soon.

The doctor's dialogue was taken as a combination shot.

The camera was kept ready to take Mahadagi's dialogue in close-up.

The director, a fatty glutton, taught Mahadagi the dialogue as a rehearsal: "It's better to get killed rather than killing animals and feeding on them. I'm an *ahimsavadi*. Moreover, I'm a strict vegetarian. I won't touch mutton soup and won't encourage others to have it."

The director repeatedly taught the dialogue as though he himself was a strict vegetarian.

The shot was Okayed.

The director announced, "Lunch break."

Food was served.

Rice, vegetable fry, sambar, vegetable curry, pickle and pappadam were the menu.

The director shouted, "Where's my grilled liver?"

The supplier said politely, "*Saar*, as we were shooting vegetarianism, the producer ordered pure vegetarian food.

"Fuck his perfection plus his father. I want non-vegetarian."

He threw the plate on the face of the bearer and walked out. Getting grilled liver immediately for him was impossible. So the shooting was cancelled for the day.

The second viewer of the cinema remarked, "The most touching scene was that on non-violence. *Haabba,* what a blow it was! Notwithstanding the heat of the blow, Mahadagi coolly asked the Hovan policeman whether his palm got hurt. Really sentimental!"

Again I thought about the contrary nature of the man who acted as Mahadagi. During the shooting, fortunately and unfortunately the actor policeman gave him a heavy blow. As the blow was a real one, the shot was OK. Happily the director said, "Cut".

But the blow had made sparks in the hero's eyes. He could not bear its impact. Annoyed, he punched the policeman—an extra—and made him flat. And instead of the above-said polite dialogues in the script, the actor shouted arrogantly, "You son-of-a-bitch, you're not a *de facto* cop. You're just an extra. I'll give you some ex gratia."

The lead actor gave five solid punches on the extra's jaw, each punch rooting out two teeth. He screamed and ran for his life.

The producer came running and soothed the hero, "Dear Connoisseur, you're doing the role of a paragon of peace. Please bear with it. I beg pardon".

Thus the actor regained his mood and the shooting continued.

The next scene the viewers glorified was on the two dames who always flanked Mahadagi. He hung to their shoulders as and when he walked. They were the age of his granddaughters.

The director called the production executive and said, "I want two teenage girls with the same looks and size, preferably twins. They should look innocent. They're to act as two disciples of Mahadagi. Don't go for goddamn cheap extras from the streets. Tell the producer to pay them well."

"Righto, *Saar*."

Luckily he got real twin sisters from a law college campus. They were from an Indan royal family. I think they were the pioneer woman students who joined the course of degree of law. They were progressive girls. They did not care for the pay offered. They just wanted to experience the thrill of shooting and to show their faces in the soon-to-be world-famous box office hit.

The moment they arrived on the location, the producer, a whore-monger, turned a Priapus.

Sensing his intention, the director said, "Please postpone your priapism till their part is over".

"Then schedule their part first. I'm impatient".

When the twin sisters were given the pay packet after their schedule, they happily returned it to the production executive.

Very happily he said, "Our producer is waiting in his room to thank you both".

Opening the door of the producer's room the twin sisters asked: "May we comin, *Saar*?

"One at a time please . . ."

"We're one, *Saar*."

"Well. If you're not shy, you may."

Stripping his clothes, he said, "Please undress. Let's shoot it fast".

"Undress? Shoot? The director told us to pack up, *Saar*."

"This is indoor shooting."

"Then where are the camera and other apparatus?"

"No need. Let's shoot in-camera with our God-given apparatus."

"Ooo hoo, that shooting!"

"Of course. I'm the producer. For the next project I need parallel heroines. Let's make a deal now itself. Didn't you get a nice pack-of-sum".

"Are you a producer of cinemas or children?"

"If you're interested, let's make children also".

The twin sisters exchanged glances and said with an inner meaning, "Yeeya, we'll make you a child".

By then he was fully undressed. They took his clothes. Threw it out of the room. Then they attacked him from front and back like two tigresses. One gripped his coconut-like testicles while other locked him from the back. The girls had been trained in martial arts.

The producer cried like a lamb. They let him go. They looked fiercely at him.

Before getting ablaze, he ran out of the room to the location where shooting was at full swing. He ran around helter-skelter like a child without clothes. He wished to hide somewhere. But where? He feared that the Medusas would appear anytime.

I and my consorts enjoyed the event to our hearts' content.

Covering his nudity with a camera filter, he searched for the production executive. When he was sighted, the producer hit him with the camera stand.

The production executive ran away like a stoned stray dog.

The producer pompously said, "You inefficient bastard executive, you're discharged from the unit with disgrace."

Hearing that, we stopped laughing and started wondering who was really disgraced? We could not get the answer. So we stopped thinking and again started laughing. After sometime, all of a sudden we stopped laughing and thought about the paradoxes of the world. What we see is something; but what occurs is something else. We see an oasis. Is it actually there? We see Sun moving; but in fact we move. Most of the times we fail to exercise the practical application as per theory.

Then I consoled my consorts that the world was such that even the godheads, who came to save the sinners were defamed as sinners.

* * *

Before the Armageddon, there were some small seeds of incidents and instances that had sown at the last—grown to big trees. Out of many, one example I would like to narrate is on the making of iron and steel by Indana.

In the first quarter of the last century, Hovan Government passed a bill that banned Indan traders and industrialists from doing business without permission and license. The Indans were to seek permission even for urinating, shitting and mating.

There was a blacksmith named Chatan. He was the ancestral manufacturer of all the battle weapons—spears, swords and shields—for the Indan kings. He used to use charcoal as fuel for his bellow-furnace to melt the raw iron. Once he was preparing molten iron. By chance, a pinch of charcoal powder fell into the molten iron. That metal preparation turned out very strong and tempered. With that alloy, steel, he made weapons, cutting tools, rods for whetting knives etc. The alloy proved non-corrosive.

Mere Chatan turned Mr. Chatan earned a lot of money. The money filled honey in his head. The honey solidified into an ambition—to set up an iron and steel industry.

He prepared a project plan with the help of a Hovan expert. He submitted it. The prime point in the report was saving of time and money—exporting the iron ore from Indana to Britana. The Crown rejected the project and threw it in the dustbin. They pooh-poohed the idea: "Indans making iron and steel? Is it a dream?"

It was the pre-independence story. The post-independence period made Mr. Chatan the 'Iron and Steel Man' in the iron and steel industry. His turnover turned unthinkable. He made everything with steel: From needle to nuclear reactor.

*   *   *

The other incident was an accident concerning the hotel industry of Indana as well as my life. It was not a life-saving or life-supporting incident but one that curtailing life.

Though the incident occurred in Britana, its after-effects were practically felt in Indana. And when the effects were felt, I felt like a fisherman spotting a shoal, unaware that it would become a shoal in due course. That is the reason d'être in describing that particular incident with special emphasis.

As I have already stated, on my left was the vast recreation ground where the football match was held. Between me and the ground was the new Highway No 2 linking Deltan and Kalibay. Beneath my crown, there was a bus-stop. The other side was a marshy field of about an acre. The area served as the dumping ground for garbage from all the nooks and corners of the Municipal Corporation. Besides, all the waste and stinking waters flowed to the field from the nearby slaughter-house. It was a playground for flies, mosquitoes and such things that could spread diseases. Neither the corporation nor the higher authorities did anything to eradicate the insects or to clear the filth. I used to dream now and then about the redemption of the area beside me.

One morning . . . Not just fine, very fine morning . . . A lot of laborers arrived with cart-loads of earth to fill the field. Days, weeks and months passed . . . The one-time marsh was reclaimed and made a marvelous plot.

The morning of second day of the third month was also very fine. A board, SITE FOR CONTINENTAL HOTEL, was placed there.

People worked hard day and night. It took about a year to complete the construction of that multi-storey building.

When the painting was completed, the 'evil-eye' screen was removed . . . Wauu . . . ! What a *pyari, pyari* palatial building! A state-of-the-art skyscraper! The luxurious hotel promoted by Mr. Roti could change the lifestyle of the rich customers who checked in. A heaven designed to make your days more comfortable and convenient. The Continental hotel comprised compartments of contentment such as multi-cuisine restaurant, rendezvous, roof-top garden, dance floor, well-furnished rooms with telephone and gramophone facilities, linen and medical services. Above all the hospitality was at its very best. Besides these comforts, there were exhilaration stations too: A paradise for gluttons as well as for gay guys.

The inaugural day was a glorious one. I had not felt such a nostalgia ever before. It gave a facelift to Kalibay—a new address. Needless to say, it was the symbol of entire Indana. A transition from stink to fragrance. It being the tallest structure—taller than me—the mariners saw the hotel as a landmark from their conning tower. Even the tower lighthouse spread light beams on it when it spun.

All the newly sworn-in ministers of Independent Indana, industrialists, businessmen, VIPs and moneybags of the country were invited to the inaugural and bless the function. I too wished to go and share the royal experience of the excellent hotel. But my roots did not permit. Really incredible!

My spouses passed a remark, "What business a cat has where gold is melted?"

Yes, indeed the tryst was exclusively for human beings. I forgot I was just a *maram. Chheyh* . . .

Ngeh, what's that? A placard had been placed right in front of the main entrance!

"OUT OF BOUNDS FOR HOVANS"

There was still a large number of Hovans in Indana. They too arrived to enjoy the elegant hotel facilities with wallets full of money. But the board displayed there displaced their dignity. Inaugural advertisement was published in all the leading dailies. The 'out of bounds' condition had not been mentioned anywhere.

Mr. Roti, the proprietor of the hotel, was making practical his dream. He tasted the sweet revenge against the Hovans who insulted him bitterly in their homeland, Britana. Now Indana being his motherland, he being the King of the hotel industry, it was his whim to entertain whom and whom not. He had a license from his own government. Gone were the days when he was being called a salve by exotic men. He had now got the capacity to call them *slaves*. He paid Hovans in their own coin. The Hovans bowed their heads, got inside their motor cabs and drove away.

Notwithstanding the indecent response towards the guests—as learned from my *Guru 'Shatruvum than grihe vannal vazhipol salkarikkenam'*—I appreciated the achievements of Mr. Roti. His vision and beliefs in the hotel business were great. Incited by the conviction of his forefathers, he foresaw the bright future of hotel industry.

Actually he had gone to Britana for the purpose of obtaining a license to establish a continental class hotel. Despite sanctioning it, they defamed him. As a hotel emperor by career, he had gained a lot of weight of wealth from his forefathers. He belonged to the fourth generation of the *Sava* family that ran the Kalibay eating joint-cum-brothel. He became the hotel emperor of Indana.

Yet Mr. Roti could not get accommodation in any hotel in Britana, though he could afford the bills. He was denied accommodation because he was an Indan. He was a slave in that country though he was rich. Yes, he was so rich that he could spread a money bed on the footpath for sleeping and eat gold coins. He swore to take revenge on the Hovans in his land. Well, it was a dream for Mr. Roti in the pre-independence period.

And this incident of insult was also a piece of nostalgia for the last Hovan Governor General who accompanied as an invitee the first Indan Governor General of free Indana.

But no one reacted. No one except a Hovan sailor. Yes, he was an able-bodied Seaman from the gunnery branch of the Hovan Navy. His warship, a cruiser, HNS Destroyer, was at anchor at Kalibay outer harbor As the gunners' yeoman of the ship, he held the keys of all the magazines and turrets till sunset. A detention quarter-returned charged with striking an officer, he was the most disobedient sailor on-board. As his name *Tigerson* so his fame *Tiger of the Seas.*

Actually the man-of-war was supposed to leave Kalibay harbor the following week taking the Hovan G.G on board for Britana. Though physically, publicly, officially, mentally and morally the handing over and taking over ceremony of the nation was over, some records such as certain books of reference, confidential books, secret documents, inventories, etc, were to be properly handed over. Besides these responsibilities, the ex-G.G was the chief guest for the forthcoming official declaration of the Indana Republic. That was the only reason why the warship of Britana was still at harbor.

Able seaman Tigerson went on liberty. He was in his naval rig—white trousers, jumper and duck cap and blue jeans collar with a line yard and seven-folded ribbon.

He had come beside me; watched me eagerly; took a round around me anxiously and appreciated my hefty body approvingly. Then slowly he walked towards the hotel unaware that it was forbidden for him. Not only I and my spouses but many of my species as well were fascinated by the sailor's attitude. We still remember that. But we do not remember when he returned, how he returned and where he went on return.

After the inaugural hubbub I did not bother what was happening inside the hotel. In fact, I totally forgot it. Outside the hotel, there was no trouble other than the normal halla-gulla at the bus-stand.

Suddenly I heard an eerie signal coming from the harbor. Yes Continuous long blasts of a ship's siren! Was there an emergency? Or an imminent attack? I stared at the harbor. The sea was calm. All the big and small vessels and craft moored and berthed at the anchorage and jetties were stationary. It was like a canvas painting.

But what was happening to the Hovan cruiser? The ship was changing its direction like a vessel out of command. There was no current. I could see the single screw moving under water and many crew moving on the upper deck.

I shook up my spouses and said, "*Haabba*, see what is happening to HNS Destroyer!"

Drowsily, Uru said, "They may be preparing to leave the harbor."

"No," I said. "You see the signals . . ."

Mena said, "They may be practicing visual signals."

"No, no. It's not the practice of semaphore and flashing."

Ramb said, "May be they are asking permission for a suitable berth for boarding their G.G and his staff who're to leave by next week".

"No, no, no," I adamantly said, "There's some distress in their destroyer!"

Unyielding to my anxiety, Tilo said, "Nothing to wonder. Hovans are very much in distress now-a-days".

Suddenly and surprisingly there was gunfire.

I heard shrieks of my wives who had mocked me. I too shrieked. But it was not so intense because I was anticipating a hazard. But not a gunfire like that, not even in my dreams!

"My good God," I and my spouses cried.

A six-inch AP shell capable of piercing any kind of armor plate fell right in front of us turning the highway into a pond.

Timidly I said, "Look, we're the target. Someone wants to kill us."

The spouses said unanimously, "We speculate that it's the uniformed sailor who came close to us and watched us closely!"

I said, "Then prepare your bosom to hug more shells and be ready to leave this world."

We watched the ship. The twin-barreled turret was trained and elevated exactly towards us!

"What to do? Our speculation is turning true."

Moments of fear prevailed. Some people ran helter-skelter; some boarded the available transport and cleared out. Even the people who took shelter in some cloisters felt that an AP shell was following them.

The street was deserted within no time. Only we stood there like a trembling target. Frankly speaking, it was the first time I thought about my own death.

What's next? We could not even imagine.

Then we saw a motor-cutter from the ship making way towards the boat pool. Plenty of uniformed Hovan sailors were transported to the Continental Hotel. They were permitted to dance and dine free of charge.

They were given free VIP treatment. Away from the horror of gunfire, the panic-stricken customers also joined the buffet, ballet and other buffooneries.

Later on, I came to know about the cause of the attack. The trajectory was a little flat due to the wind effect. I was not the target. The real target was the Continental Hotel edifice. And the real firer was the Hovan sailor, able seaman Tigerson, who was denied admission to the hotel.

I appreciated his guts. He answered the great insult suffered by the whole of Hovans by doing something great. I also appreciated the hospitality of Mr. Roti who admitted the lower-rated while he denied admission even to the flag officer-commanding-in-chief, Rear Admiral Armstone, who was also the last Hovan G.G of post-independence Indana.

Actually, Rear Admiral Armstone was really a man of chirpy chivalry. I liked him very much. A thorough gentleman. His inclination to defend the weaker section was laudable. In spite of continuous turmoil in Indana the Crown of Britana got fed up. King detailed a person with lot of decorations on his chest and lot of decorum in his heart—Rear Admiral Armstone—from his personnel staff as G.G to Indana. His mission was to study in detail whether they should continue imperialism. And *sans doute* it was his dictum that prepared the way to the total freedom of Indana.

King Alfred II personally came down to Indana to bid farewell to his ruled people, in fact to release them from the stranglehold of his government. He believed in a dogma "Charity begins at home but grows outside home." Perhaps his heart was filled with platonic love, not cupboard love. King, though an imperialist, was after all a human. I'd seen numerous numbers of Indan royal women and men who were interested in upbringing upheavals, uproars and uprisings. They sent many innocents to the nether world.

Whereas, King's wife Lady Alfred of Britana was also very royal; and an example to all the women on earth.

Attired in unisex, she too arrived in Indana, her imperial county. Like a groom and with all the pride of a prince, the morning sun rose to witness the scene with shining face from the east. But as the King and Queen disembarked on the Indan coast, I felt there was another female sun coming up in the west with a face that shone brighter like a bride to marry the rising sun.

"Www ooo . . . see!" I said to my spouses, "Woman . . . a woman should be like this! A real sexbomb!!"

Uru ludicrously said, "Hum . . . give me your ears. Our boss plant, no, no, our gaffer Hus loves to hug the queen. What a transition! A Rip Van Winkle turns a priapic."

"No, Uru, not in that sense. I mean she's a Queen of *Beau Monte*. I used the word sexbomb with no bad intention."

Yes. What happened to me? Sometimes while thinking I doubt my head is above the neck or below the feet. Actually I should not have used that word. But I did not have the *mote juste* to magnify the majestic lady.

Mena said, "Dear hus, their *beau monte* may be our *demi monte*."

I admonished her, "*Na*, Mena, *na*. Let's remove the mote in our eyes first."

Ramb remarked, "An ugly woman will shine better than a beautiful man. And this royal lady is more beautiful than all the other royal 'beautiful' men. So, it's clear that though the woman was created second, she is the first."

I kept silence . . .

Tilo said, "Woman is the symbol of compassion. If you want to experience love, it's only with a woman. Moreover, woman is the redressal forum of mercy."

"Yes, Tilo, I like your idea. After all, without all of you around me, I could not have survived. Indeed woman is *the* substitute to happiness."

Thus, a woman like Lady Alfred II came as a savior to love Indana and her people to shower happiness on the unhappy.

Nevertheless, there was a prayer in my heart. Nothing bad should happen. God did hear my prayer. No untoward incident occurred. King declared full freedom with the consent of his dear wife Queen Alice Alfred. Indana gained independence!

Well, not only I, the whole earth know that independence is an essential thing to human beings. No *yaar*, it is essential to animals and to birds also. No *yaar*, to plants and to palms also. No, *yaar*, no, to inanimate things like water, mountain and even to Mother Earth as well. She has freedom to move herself—if you obstruct her? I am not one to predict such unprecedented or untoward occurrence. I just recalled the affair how the stars were thirsty for freedom and how I advocated their cause of liberty to King Sun during my infancy.

Particularly, independence is as essential as *Pranavayu* to all the living things. Provided the *air* you breathe is pure, it is the sweetest thing you inhale.

But after gaining freedom, the people of Indana started breathing impure air of independence. They started eating poisonous cakes of independence. They started drinking spurious liquor of independence. Indana turned a mad monkey that had been presented with a garland. In short, Indans became the laughing stock of the Hovans.

The inaugural festivities were held with all the might. The Hovan's floats exhibited the country's rapid industrial growth through railways, P&T, automobiles, multi-purpose power projects, etc, and Indana's economic progress under imperialism. They successfully displayed their military might also—fighting forces in uniforms of the army and the navy marched diligently flashing rifles and booming cannons in parades through the 'Gate of Indana' at Deltan, the capital.

I was anxious to see the Indans' performance during the colorful ceremony. It was a showcase of volunteers who fought strenuously and bravely for centuries for the materialization of *Free Indana*. Some dilettantes arranged *tableaux vivants* of the martyrs of yesteryears. In fact, the pageantry was vivid.

Mahadagi and King Alfred II and Queen Alice were also present at the ceremony. I appreciated their companionship. They sat side by side like father and daughter. Mahadagi was quite old and the queen was quite young. He was clad in loin-clothes, she in her *haute couture* garments. At times they talked to each other.

Prior to declaration of Independence was the ceremony of lowering of the Hovan standard and hoisting of Indan flag on the same halyard and string as a practical procedure of *Handing-over and taking-over.*

Fine. There was a proper and authentic person to hand over the power from Hovan's side. But from Indans' side who would take over the power? Who was the most suitable person for that? Who?

I still remember how Mahadagi solved the seemingly insoluble problem in the solution of power-greedy fellow freedom fighters, Gerri Lal, Odin Dos and Dara Kham. If it were the responsibility of the Governor General to hand over the nation, it was the responsibility of the in-coming prime minister to take over the nation. There was a tussle for the position of prime minister.

Gerri Lal said to Mahadagi, "Paapu, the people would be happy to see you as the prime minister. So please take over the nation."

Paapu said, "A construction worker never occupies a house he constructs." Turning towards Dara Kham and Odin Dos he continued, "Let Gerri Lal take over the nation."

Dara Kham said, "Paapu, we really appreciate your struggle for freedom. But now, it seems that you do not know the exact meaning of *total freedom.*"

Odin Dos intervened, "Total freedom means freedom for all. Isn't it Paapu?"

"That's what I'm telling you," Dara Kham said furiously. "I'm a senior member of the party. I too can rule. Then why you say Gerri Lal will become the PM? It means he got freedom; I'm denied that."

Mahadagi pitied him, "*Sans doute,* all of you're fit to rule. You're my *Trimurthis.* G form Gerri, O from Odin and D from Dara make GOD. But there can be only one PM, not many."

Dara said, "I don't believe in your theory. In B'llaism, there's only one God. So I shall be made PM."

Odin interfered, "Paapu, you favor Gerri for he's an Eysaist like you. You should understand one thing. If I am made Prime Minister, we would get further help from Britana for I'm a Hovan by conversion."

Mahadagi said curtly, "We do not need any more help from anyone. We're self—sufficient. It was our dream to evict them; it's materialized. I think Gerri is a better stalwart than you."

"If he's stalwart", said Odin sternly, "I'm a double stalwart."

"I'm triple stalwart," Dara said.

It pained Paapu.

The matter was put before the King.

King said, "I leave it to Mr. Mahadagi, the great. His decision is final."

Gerri Lal was declared the prime minister of free Indana.

But Dara Kham and Odin Dos protested. "This is not a decision. We have not got independence yet."

Mahadagi advised them: "There's no independence without inter-dependence. You will have to depend on the people. You yourself can't rule this nation. It's the people who decide who should rule. Even if they choose you to rule, you're just a representative."

"Then what about Gerri Lal?" They said.

"He's a provisional prime minister. He's getting a tentative chance. Very soon the system of voting would be introduced."

Independence! Independence! Independence! All the mouths of modem Indana were chanting that *mantra.* Freedom! Freedom! Freedom! The word was rising everywhere. Freedom or independence, it was the same to me. I felt that its meaning was sweet and that it had the revitalizing power of ambrosia.

Gerri Lal became the provisional prime minister.

The King and Queen set sailed to Britana.

The G.G stayed back till the elections and the ceremony of declaration of the republic were over.

Prior to all these auspicious functions, a constitution of the country was to be formulated. A well-educated *Sava* youth, Mr. Amuldar—a law and political science learned gentleman graduated from Britana—was an active freedom fighter as well. Notwithstanding the protest of the higher castes in investing the Mahalayan responsibility of formulating the Constitution, Mahadagi found that Mr. Amuldar was the apt person for the job. He feared that the elite class might adulterate the Holy Book, if they were given the chance to write it.

Mr. Amuldar adopted some articles and amended some articles o the Hovan Constitution. He then blended them with some new schedules articles, acts, clauses and sub-clauses and framed the fundamental rights and duties of Indan citizens.

To uplift the downtrodden mass, Mr. Amuldar framed many additiona articles exclusively for the benefit of his caste mates. Reservations and relaxations in all the fields such as education, employment and election were mentioned for the *Sava* caste in the Political Holy Book.

The day before the declaration of the first elections of Indana, the Constitution was released.

Provisionally or permanently, tentatively or definitely, Gerri La became the first prime minister of free Indana. This created volcanoes in the hearts of both Dara Kham and Odin Dos.

During the pre-freedom period the whole of Indana was under Britana imperialism. The so-called Emperors, Kings, Princes and Chiefs were entitled to enjoy privy-purse as mark of recognition. And in return their right to rule was taken away. Thus all the land and residents within the boundaries—Mahalayan Mountain in the north, Kalibay Sea in the wes and Bay of Mulcut in the east and the point of merger of both the seas in the south—became parts of peninsular Indana. Likewise, the Indan Union was founded.

The country was divided into ten states. Deltan became the national capital. Each state was formed and framed as per the prevalent customs culture and the vernacular of respective area. One hundred constituencies were created to facilitate representation from every district as per area and population.

Only one party—the Freedom Party of Indana—contested the elections. But under the same banner and flag, candidates were many. Gerri Lal, Dara Kham and Odin Dos were the prominent among them. However, the distinguished candidates had distinct agendas.

Thus the first elections for the hundred parliament seats were held in Indana. I witnessed polling for the first time. Voting was moderate. Forty per cent of the 210 million voters exercised their franchise. My constituency, Kalibay had the highest polling percentage—70. Voters deposited their ballots in the boxes kept in the polling booths in various educational institutions and in government offices' verandas. Serpentine queues were seen everywhere from early morning. Age did not weaken the will of the old; disability did not tear the strength of the lame and the blind.

It was a festival of democracy for them. The right to choose their leader. A golden opportunity to elect their ruler. A chance to select Gerri Lal, Dara Kham or Odin Dos as their Prime Minister. Generally the polling was peaceful except at some B'llaist-dominated stations and in certain areas where Hovans had majority.

I wished I were a voter. And if so, like a soldier in a ceremonial march past, I would have dressed in the best clothes and proudly gone to the booth with swinging arms, erect head, straight eyes and with a throbbing heart to render the most sacred deed on earth—to vote for a stable government under the leadership of an efficient person for the prosperity of the country and the people.

Sensing my wish, my spouses also wished to be voters. All my four wives said, "And if so, like going to a shrine, we would slowly walk, our eyes closed, lips chanting *mantras* and with steady minds without any malice in our hearts. We would be thinking that the leader to be chosen was like a god and the vote the offering.

I enquired, "Just let me know who your leader is?"

They declared without concern for the secrecy of the ballot, "Gerri Lal is our leader."

I too declared, "Gerri Lal is my leader too."

Tundit Gerri Lal won! Dara Kham lost! Odin Dos also lost!

It was the decision of the party's high command that all the three prime ministerial candidates should contest in the same constituency. The winner shall be the gainer—Prime Minister. All the three chose Kalibay as their political battle-field.

Damn the party decision. The decision of the people was taken into account—Tundit Gerri Lal was elected Prime Minister to rule the country till the next general elections after a term of five years.

"But what would be the condition, if some block-headed barbarians dishonor the democracy by annihilating the elected members saying "We don't agree with the damned democracy. We believe 'might is right'?

I was shocked to hear the remarks passed by my wives.

It was the first time I felt hatred towards them. Then and there I warned them that it would be a sin to think of the failure of democracy and to promote mobocracy.

*   *   *

Haaait, I have never seen such an extravaganza! Raja Mahal was illuminated and decorated in an incredible indescribable manner! All the elected parliament members who were offered ministerial berths like home, defense, finance, transport, law and external affairs took their seats in the front row. Other honorable members sat behind them. Besides, several dignitaries, Dara Kham and Odin Dos were also invited. But the losers did not show up. The visitors' gallery was jam-packed with spectators. Deltan city seemed like a bride on her wedding day.

As the idol of the nation, Mahadagi, everybody's pet Paapu administered the oath to Toojari Gerri Lal at the swearing-in ceremony.

Mahadagi read out the oath and Gerri Lal repeated it.

"I, Gerri Lal, hereby swear in the name of all gods that I will bear true faith and loyalty to the Constitution of Indana as by law established. I swear that I will duly and faithfully and to the best of my ability perform the duties as the Prime Minister for our country without fear or favor, affection or ill-will to a particular person or place. I solemnly affirm that I will not disclose to any one any matter of secrecy and security which shall damage the unity and integrity of the union of Indana and I also promise to uphold the sovereignty and secularism of our country."

The swearing-in ceremony was over. There were applause in the House by the honorable members and fireworks outside the House by the jovial public. Jovial viewers from the visitors' gallery approached the dais to greet the new Prime Minister and other Ministers. Some had garlands in their hands, some had bouquets. They were shouting slogans.

"Jai, Jai Gerri Lal; Jai, Jai Gerri Lal"

As they came near the dais, the boisterous bourgeois among them besieged Mahadagi. Piercing the jovial shouts a sound *ttdee* penetrated their ears.

Gunfire!

Bullets punctured Mahadagi's chest. The bullets did their job perfectly. Mahadagi collapsed.

The throng went wild. People in the parliament house ran helter-skelter. Many dignitaries were crushed in the stampede. The area around the dais was deserted within seconds. The killer escaped leaving his alibi on the roster of the world's most wanted and hated criminal.

Gerri Lal sat on the floor, holding Paapu's head in his lap. The stream of blood from Paapu's frail body crawled like a snake coming out of its burrow on the marble floor in search of the killer.

Security personnel rushed to the spot.

"Catch the culprit, you cunning commandoes," cried Gerri Lal.

Paapu, who was struggling for breath, muttered, "No need. It's neither the gunner's bad will nor the gun that did this. It's the good will of God."

The Commander-in-chief of the Commandoes commanded, "Pick up that pistol, you indolent idiots."

A pistol was taken away from the dais. It seemed that the instrument was innocent in carrying out that inhuman act.

Paapu was dead!

*   *   *

Oh my God! That incident shook me head to foot. My consorts were chilled to their marrow. If that was the destiny of a political saint, what would be the fate of a *maram* like me? So, I wanted to do something before my death. Something to establish my existence so that the generations to come would believe that there was a tree that truly loved all the fauna, flora and the human race.

So, the best thing I could do was to write the history of Indana. In other words, it would be an autobiographical novel. Right from my birth to death. My heart was the paper, my blood as ink and my brain the pen. So, as long as I was alive, there was no question of exhausting any of the above items. It would be a story of many societies, not a single or a particular one. It would not be the story of a single generation. It would be a story of many generations. Though a few years back I had given up the plan to write it, this time I made up my mind to undertaking it through the ventilation of the memoir-wind accelerated into my mind.

The risk of death, like a dagger, hung right in front of me. If it would be real, oh . . . ho . . . ho, I couldn't think of that! Though it is natural I did not want to die—I just wanted to live . . . live . . . live forever.

I sincerely wished for a place where there was no fear so that I could shift to there with my consorts if the law of the nature would permit.

But as I heard the public opinion on Paapu's assassination, my solid fear got liquefied, and then dried up.

"Men may forget the sunrays; men may forget moonlight, but men can't forget the charisma of Mahadagi."

Yes. People are sure to feel his absence more than his presence. So death was a credit to him. So why fear death? So death has got a sweet side. So I wanted to taste death wholeheartedly. So I had an urge to go very close to the death. So I prepared myself to receive the garland of death at any time by anybody for any reason. Yet I was uxorious— wished that my consorts should continue living . . .

Though the assassination of Mahadagi "the champion of the nation" caused mass hysteria, Gerri Lal tried to uphold the stability of the nation. His policy and politics saved the nation from a civil war. His administration gave due weightage to socialism for the betterment of labor class reducing capitalism. However, Millionaires became Billionaires and Billionaires became Trillionaires. The reason was that there grew two parties parallel to the socialist-minded Green Party of Indana (GPI). One was the fascist White Party (WPI) headed by Odin Dos and the other was the fanatic Red Party (RPI) under the leadership of Dara Kham. During elections, the Red and the White parties made a coalition manifesting manifold manifestos. Yet the voters neglected their manipulation. So they could never form a coalition ministry. Dethroning of Gerri Lal remained a dream of Dara Kham and Odin Dos. White and Red flags could not get a chance to flutter on the jack staff of the parliament house.

I always saw the halyard carrying the Green flag fluttering proudly in the wind attempting to spread the air of socialism. The socialist idea began to take root among the working class people in the cities as well as villages. They labored diligently to make the villages to Green Lands and urban areas to Wonder Lands. This had become a mass movement. Millions of workers demanded a limitation of working hours from twelve to ten. They wanted an interval of two hours for meals and rest

Simultaneously the solidarity claimed casual and privilege leaves in addition to the weekly off days.

The representatives from the government supported the demand. Nevertheless, some of the erstwhile indentured laborers of the pre-independence who had become Lords in the post-independence objected the proposal arrogantly for they were sure to be affected severely once the rule was passed.

Yet I appreciated the fast and gradual reformations contrary to the socialism. I wondered how poor, poorer and poorest *dhobis*, cobblers and barbers were transformed into rich, richer and richest launders, shoemakers and hairdressers by opening up laundries, shoe marts and beauty parlors respectively! How concubines transformed into consorts! How concupiscent people transformed into good conductors! Many poor people mounted mountains of money!

After remaining Indan Prime Minister for two decades, Toojari Gerri Lal embraced a natural death. During his regime, communalism crept into politics making a dangerous situation. The defeated and desperate— Dara Kham and Odin Dos—candidates and their followers disorganized the political scenario. This resulted in the growth of communal tension, riots and disorders. For the false sake of promoting the interests of one's own community, communalism implied the starting of political activities. The people of Indana belonging to Eysa, B'lla and Hova religions were separate and different from one another politically, economically, socially and culturally. Thus they become antagonists to one another mentally and morally.

At this crucial juncture, people of Indana chose Miss Chandrany, the nice niece of Mahadagi as their prime minister. She had a very rich yet bitter political background. She had dedicated her tender age for the cause of freedom. She was the leader of the women's youth wing. Then she had experienced all the dark sides of the independence movement. If rifle-muzzles could spurt semen, she might have delivered many rifle tots.

By that time she knew the pros and cons of politics.

Sensing that she had a sixth sense, people handed over to her the helm of the country. She could steer it in a better manner with her iron will, farsightedness and hard work.

Three decades of her rule . . . Wow . . . ! Indana witnessed innumerable infrastructure development! Mulcut, her permanent constituency was an example . . .

On the eastern tip of Indana lies the state of Mulcut. Its capital city Mulcut was a tourist destination, perfect for foreigners as well as the indigenous fauna, flora and fun-lovers. Once a fishing village, it had changed tremendously into marvelous picnic and water-sports spot. That area was filled with myriad rocky statues that looked silhouettes as if The Almighty had made them with His own hands. The prime attraction was the natural water falls form the Nagraj Mountains.

I am compelled to drag once again the name of late Governor General Powerfill. Sorry, the usage of late is insufficient to emphasize his dignity, designation and demise. The usage very late would be more suitable.

Seeing the prospects that the waterfall could bring Mr. Powerfill, the then chairman of the Indana Development Authority, had proposed to construct a multipurpose hydro-electric project. A project report was submitted by Mr. Nucliboy, the son of Mr. Powerfill. He had arrived in Indana with his parents early in his childhood. After preliminary education, he was sent to the Majestic Hostel in Mulcut. There, he enjoyed all the royal pride and privileges. Mulcut was the seat of education. The Majestic University, Indana's prime academic institution, for instance, had a particular homely feeling to it with exotic students. Nucliboy took his graduation in civil engineering. He joined for the post-graduate course.

His project report got the approval. He was the superintending engineer for the arch dam. There were two rigid ridges approximately a mile apart. Mulcut men had myriad myths to mention. As per the myth, the ridges were *Nagraj* and *Nagrani,* who were everlasting and never-meeting lover-legends. The dam was to be constructed connecting the two cliffs to accumulate all the water of the catchment area.

*   *   *

It was a great season: A season for atom-mania. Almost all scientists on earth were playing with the atom. The smallest particle of an element had become the greatest news matter! The atomic age had become the exploding page in history. Even the military, industrial and political forces were characterized by atomic energy.

Young engineer Nucliboy had a majestic laboratory at his royal residence. There were scientists who were keen to make atomic bombs. Nucliboy was also inclined towards this study, spending his spare time splitting nucleus and studying the mysterious elementary particles.

He completed the construction of the arch dam. It was really a remarkable achievement. But after the assassination of his father he left for his homeland leaving a pent-up emotion in his imperial land.

*   *   *

Like a series of revenge—either man-made or made by nature—Indana faced lots of disasters.

To cater to the power need of the people, Chandrany completed the power project by constructing a power house. The arch dam built by the Hovans and the Indan-made transformers and the power lines were the proud symbols of a symbiotic relationship that existed between Hovans and Indans.

I can't forget the inauguration of the hydro-electric project. The project stood like the crown of Mulcut.

Chandrany, the honorable Prime Minister, came to grace the function. She delivered the inaugural speech: Dear crowd, I'm also one among you. However, you put me into power provisionally. Now, as Prime Minister, I give you power permanently. Forget the days of load-shedding and power-cuts. This project will shower power on the country's prosperous fields and industrial mega-polis besides lighting up our dark homes and streets. Let me switch on the machine of our dream of light and power to come true.

I was attracted by her appearance in that attire: The hand-woven starched white cotton sari. I felt she was brighter than the fabric.

As she went to the rostrum to break the coconut before the switching-on ceremony she was greeted with tremendous cheers and applause. The mass shouted repeated slogan, "Our glittering Chandranyji . . . our God of Indana . . ."

I passed a comment, "See, of course, she glitters like anything!"

"All that glitters is not God, our dear husband." My wives said unanimously.

I exclaimed, "What happened!"

"Something's going to happen . . ."

I enquired, "What's that?"

They said, "It's a secret."

I replied, "Nothing is secret on this earth from birth to death. There is only one secret; it starts after the death."

*   *   *

Good or bad, this century was *annus mirabili's*! One miracle was that the river water caught fire. It was burning like an inflammable material. The fact behind the wonder was another awe-inspiring event—auspicious occasion of opening of the multi crore multi-purpose dream project of Indana.

An enormous crowd had come to witness the supposed auspicious function. People thronged on the dam crest and along road. Many ignorant men wanted to see how power was produced from pure water. They were under the impression that electricity was extracted by churning the waters of the reservoir.

But tech-wizards mocked the natives. Skip it. I saw that each and every person focused his one eye on the PM at the switchyard and the other eye on the turbine function. I saw the fauna and flora were anxious to watch the function. The water in the reservoir was ready to run through the spillways. The atmosphere stood still holding its breath.

As the prime minister pressed the switch and as the turbine started rotating . . . no one knew what had happened. But it happened, which was never to be happened.

From my position 800 miles off Mulcut, I saw and heard many miserable audio-visual items. I don't have the right words to explain it. However, I am narrating it vaguely.

From below the dam there occurred an atomic fission. The destructive power of the bomb was tremendous—equal to more than 15 kilotons of TNT. The damned dam was fragmented. Water rushed at random carrying everything on its path along with it. I saw the generator and the turbine going up in the sky. The water flew like lava. No thermometer could measure the temperature. However, it was roughly calculated as higher than the melting point of metal. Even the water burned like kerosene. The pressure generated by the fission was more destructive than the temperature. It sent shock waves everywhere.

The death toll could have been anything between eighty thousand to ninety thousand as the entire city was washed away. The number of people who were made invalids by the tragedy was even higher. All the animate and inanimate things nearby turned to ash. Floras in a three-kilometer radius were charred. Faunas' skins burnt and flesh came out. Faraway, many men got trapped under the debris of collapsed buildings.

Relief works could not have been intensified as radioactivity was at awful levels; even the military refused to mount relief operations. The gamma rays measured 500 meters away were at 700 rads. Radiation made he area cancer-prone. Fearing that dangerous disease, large number of people committed suicide. Besides ravaging the lives of thousands of men and animals, the devastation rendered more than two million people homeless sans food, shelter, clothing and water. The most distressing factor was that the water became unfit even to touch. The water turned nothing less than sulphuric acid—poisoned and polluted by radioactivity. Clear water changed into nuclear water!

The atoms of a Prime Minister or the atoms of a Primary school master, the atoms of a beggar or the atoms of a bootlegger—human atoms are the same. Only destiny differs. Along with multitudes of men, our most beloved Prime Minister Chandrany was also dead. Her body got powdered and joined the thin atmosphere as dust.

I was crestfallen. Mulcut, the 'state of fortune', faced a misfortune of unprecedented measures.

I asked my wives, "Was it an uprising of nature?"

They kept mum . . .

"Was it a man-made cataclysm?"

Still they were silent.

"Come on, answer me." I shouted.

Seeing my fuse blowing off, my consorts replied "Chillax, hus, chillax. It's a secret . . ."

"What's that? Tell me!"

"You told us you don't believe in secrets while living."

I knew they were nailing me. I admitted that the earth would not exist without secrets. So they disclosed the secret—

Nucliboy had succeeded in making a nuclear bomb in his laboratory. His very first bomb itself proved that nuclear energy experiment had abundantly increased from kilotons to megatons. His father was killed by an arrow shot by Indan militant leader Mr. Dosh, who hailed from Mulcut. The son wished to destroy—tit for tat—Mr. Dosh's clan as well as his native place by splitting atom. A replacement of an ancient and conventional weapon (arrow) with the most modern and highly sophisticated lethal weapon! If the former could take only a single human life, the latter could wipe out a multitude!!

Nucliboy wanted to cause grave damage to Indana and Indans so that no funds and efforts could meet the huge requirement for relief, restoration, rehabilitation and reconstruction activities. His heart beat with the tick-tick-tick noise of mal-intention. So, while laying the foundation stone of the dam, controlling his emotions, he concealed a bomb that looked like a rock alongside the first stone. The unskilled masons and other ignorant construction workers didn't know what it was. Even the supervisors didn't know that it was an atomic bomb. Nucliboy set the bomb in such a way that it would go off as and when the radial gates were opened and the intake of the water through the penstock and turning of the water wheel and turbine took place simultaneously. His half-a-century aged theoretical *modus operandi* did prove effective finally. More over there was an oil belt beneath the dam. The burning crude gushed out and caused a BLEVE (Boiling Liquid Expanding Volume Explosion) Anyway, the city of Mulcut was no more on the map of Indana.

The incident created mass hysteria among the Indan public. The news of the explosion dismayed the whole world. It hurt the world conscience Many scientists and kind-hearted people condemned the cruel act. They exclaimed, "All the Hovan fascists and Pakkan fanatics kneel before the peace-loving people of Indana. Then why this homicide!? Who has done this?"

Answers to those questions were secretly disclosed to my consorts by the water belt touching the dam and my taproot.

If it were atom, the villain who spoiled the rotation of the electrica power machinery, it was another villain who spoiled the political powe machinery. The one who switched off the "cooler of democracy" and turned on the "heater of coup".

All the forces are forces. If civil force takes over the country, nothing is lost, if police force takes over something is lost and if military force takes over everything is lost. Indana became a coup country in the absence of a democratic leader. The President was on a good will visit to the land of the Hovans while the Prime Minister had gone on a permanen visit to heaven. For a few days there was no bona fide or de facto politica protector to provide sovereignty to the democracy in Indana.

The rescue and relief operations were delayed mainly due to radiation However, the home minister detailed National Reserve Police Force fo the job. In the meantime, food riots broke out in the entire state of Mulcut Teams of police struggled hard to access the cataclysm-struck area owing to the lack of oxygen in the atmosphere. Bodies of cattle and human beings were floating in the submerged areas. People sheltered in the safe area were famishing. They looted Lorries transporting emergency food and drinking water supply.

As police alone could not control the situation, the Defense Ministe deployed the army for relief operation. Army found it difficult to contro he nuclear, biological and chemical damages. However, they could maintain law and order among civilians. So navy was also called in. Sailors and divers, in their boats and craft, started clearing the debris and dead bodies to prevent epidemics. They were equipped with masks and breathing apparatus. The army opened oxygen stations and handed over t to police for the public use. Police sold it secretly to private parties and earned money. Those residents who were unwilling to leave their immovable properties paid the police in cash or kind for oxygen cylinders.

A withered woman came to the booth with her kid and wept, "Please help us *Saar* . . . ."

A police constable said, "If you're having trouble of breathing, you should've something.

"Except my house, everything is gone."

Seeing the gleaming wed-lock chain around her neck, the P.C said, "I think you need oxygen more than ornament."

After the dialogue, the indignant P.C snatched her *chain.*

The army and navy chiefs requested the Defense Minister to deploy air force to air-drop food packets. But as per the Constitution, the D.M had no power to call all the forces' chiefs at a time for any operation by any means. By all means that power was vested with the supreme commander, the President. That too with the consent of the Prime Minister. Here the premier was no more and the President was abroad.

So, as an alternative measure, instead of air-dropping, the food packets were given to the local police. Instead of dispensing it to the deserving victims, they sold that too in bulk to the vendors who became immensely rich by selling it for money. A five rooba packet during the pre-explosion period was sold for 500 roobas—a cent percent hike . . . !!

So the armed forces and the police were engaged in a tussle. Both the Ministers refused to hand over full power to the military lest they would be devalued and further deposed. It was against the aid-to-civil-power and internal security rules: Once the military took over and started its operation, the entire power should be transferred to it.

Indana's science and technology had reached up to the mars by then, specially space research and astrophysics. Indan computer doctors cured the Y2K (year 2 kilo or 2000 years) malady in the computer world. Explosive growth of the Internet happened not only in establishments but also in home segments.

In the meantime, drug-peddling by Pakkana had reached sky-levels. The income was to intensify the incursions through the border with

Indana. While the people of Pakkana intestine burned for want of food, the government incurred immense debts to feed the fanatic spies, militants and infiltrators for creating unnecessary pain and suffering to the peace-loving people of both the countries.

Indana had developed a liquid-propellant for cryogenic rocket engines. Britana wished to launch a rocket carrying a communication satellite. It would help the Hovans' global television network. The project was to be executed with Indan assistance for she was the mistress of Information Technology.

The President of Indana was invited to press the button—launching ceremony—of the rocket from the station situated in Hovana, the capital of Britana. He had to deliver a message on the subject "Use nuclear energy for *Good*; not for *bad*." Still, the prime purpose of his visit was to hoist the flag of a new era in Inda-Brita ties . . .

Cancelling all his programmes, President flew back instantly to Indana. His chartered flight reached near Deltan airport. The pilot requested permission to land. Permission was denied without any reason. In spite of repeated requests, the aviation authorities did not respond. The flight was diverted to the Kalibay airport. There too no permission was forthcoming.

I saw the aircraft flying over me like a vagabond kite without destination. I heard the crew's voice over the roar of the engines. I understood that the President's condition was that of an aged father who had no room in his house. The pilot was trying for an emergency crash-landing from the sea-end. But the aircraft fell into the deep blue sea of Indana with its fuel tank totally empty, killing Indana's first lady, first citizen, his staff and the crew.

The troops had taken position in and around the Kalibay airport after capturing the Deltan airport. Military trucks and jeeps were plying on the roads like missiles and bullets. The armed forces took over all the government establishments, organizations, vital installations and communication stations including the television and radio centers. The sound of sorties echoed everywhere.

Out of the three defense forces, the army had more strength and establishments and it was the senior-most force. Army Chief Gen Raider Sher, with the support of the naval and air force chiefs declared himself President, dissolving parliament. He put the Home Minister and the Defense Minister behind the bars after deposing them. They were charged with disloyalty and inefficiency. Thus democracy was destroyed and a military coup was created.

Coup President Gen Raider Sher decided to hold a referendum to give political legitimacy to his military government. He forced the legal experts, political observers and mass media to support and to cooperate with his government. Thus he continued his military rule. Indana's business of democracy suffered heavy loss because of *coup d'état*. It created political pollution also.

The coup continued for more than two decades. It still continues. People of Indana forgot the meaning of democracy. The new generation couldn't experience the essence of election. Political parties were banned. "Union is strength" dictum was retold as "Union is death". Meetings of more than three persons were banned. However, a husband, his wife and two children—four members of a family—were allowed to assemble. Assembly was allowed in educational and some other institutions. Marriage ceremonies, cultural functions, fairs and sports and games were conducted for masses in the presence of armed forces authorities.

I appreciated the merits of the coup. Cricket-viewers and commentary-listeners at government offices let go their electronics. The rule "Giving and taking bribe is a crime" was unscientific. The giver and receiver would get six-month jail terms. So, fearing apprehension, the giver never complained. It promoted bribe. So the rule was changed to "Taking bribe is a crime". The punishment for the giver was added to that of the taker. Thus the bribe business was barred and banned. Besides those regulations, debt recovery tribunals were established for forfeiting income tax and loan arrears from individuals.

But when I evaluated, I found innumerable merits as the numerator and innumerable demerits as the denominator of the simplification of the military rule. Anti-corruption wing did not attack the armed forces personnel for they themselves were the members of the bureau.

The sad side of the coup d'état was the inhuman method adopted by the military authorities towards the civilians. They commanded and controlled not only the mass media but also the law and order machinery—judiciary and police. They misused power and the pay and perk of the civilians and added to military's benefits.

Irritated, I said, "Is it a defense force or offence force!"

Uru cautioned me, "Shhh, be quiet . . ."

Mena added, "If they hear you we may be marked as perpetrators of treason."

Ramb intimidated, "We may be awarded death sentence."

Tilo interfered, "They may not take our lives perhaps; they may give us lifer."

"Well", all my consorts asked me in anxiety. "How do you feel? We mean what's your opinion about the military *raj*?"

I said, "Sometimes brave and bright, sometimes bad and bore."

"How . . . !" They asked with gleaming eyes.

"You see," I replied, "how the economy of the country has reached a commanding height—inflation has drastically come down; the defaulters are kept in detention. See the strategy of the nation—its integrity. See how they have succeeded in flushing out the Pakkan intruders! See how they won the hearts of the nuclear-affected masses of Mulcut.

They asked, "Then, why this bad opinion?"

I said with a well of tears in my eyes, "Notwithstanding the sheer professional excellence, they're very much extravagant."

"Oh, ho . . ." the consorts howled with heated heart. "You mean the hotel business?"

I said, "Yes, exactly. But, even before that why can't you recall how the military discovered the intruders' tunnel on the border? How did they block one end with bullets, smoked the other end with tear gas and killed all the intruders like rats?"

"That's OK. It's the duty of the military to mill the militants who promote terrorism and drug-deal". My consorts cried plaintively "There is no justification to the hot, hotter and hottest halla-gulla in most of the hotels. For instance, "Continental Hotel" of Kalibay."

Human body turns a cattle-pound if he takes quite a volume of mutton, beef, pork, etc. Human body is a poultry farm if he consumes quite a number of pieces of chicken, duck, pelican etc. Human body is a fertile field if he consumes tons and tons of rice, wheat and vegetables. All these human bodies are tolerant of society, humanity and nature. Per contra, though the human being is the rarest of the rare, some human bodies are army for they had consumed many men—human flesh—as food. The menu in the Hotel Continental was an example.

Everybody on this earth loves *home*. It's a centre of contentment and consolation. A house is a place of affection. Likewise, everybody likes a hired home, a hotel. You pay and you get all the facilities of a house. In fact, you get more than domestic enjoyment. But, if hotels provide you disease! If it turns to be a bad place? Continental Hotel was such a place. It was a decorated dwelling of the devils, an illuminated inn for he evildoers. Who were the devils? The gods of the society. Who were the evil doers? The paragons of politics—the military authorities. Those lobbyists had powerful influence and purses full of money and the power of arms. They always laughed—abderians. They never cried. So they did not understand other's agony. Unlike the old politician, the new generation didn't know what sorrow and hardships were. So they didn't know what pain was. Their ecstasy was others' agony; others' agony was their ecstasy. Their enjoyment was other's suffering. Their expansion was other's contraction. Their construction was other's destruction. Thus they loved my destruction for their expansion. The age old "Hotel Continental" was to be renovated and renamed as New Millennium Hotel.

Prior to the explanation of the expansion of the hotel, I will speak of the inhuman acts performed by the so-called powerful human beings— the hotel authorities. The horror story of the *Sava* caste billionaire, the owner of the Continental Hotel. How soft-hearted people transformed into savages when they became permanent members of the hotel! How simple-minded elite class customers became cunning cannibals!

Customers commented: "How wonderful the hotel is!" Yes. The heaven-like hotel soared to the sky. But my roots commented that the hotel had descended towards hell.

Some of my roots complained, "We're fed up of consuming blood. That too human blood".

My blood ran cold. Human blood? Where from?

"We think it's from the cuisine of the Continental Hotel".

The taproot reported that there was a cell close to the underground provision store. Male and female of all the age groups were inmates there. They were on the waiting list to go to the plates of prominent persons as palatable food.

I blew out my checks. Abhorring, I said myself: "It's really an abysmal affair."

My consorts quivered cap-a-pie. They wailed inconsolably while enquiring, "as . . . food . . . ?"

"Yes. The menu card is coded."

Unlike the usual menu in all the animal-eaters' restaurants, here everything was available. There was a concealed and mysterious restaurant exclusively for the card-holders. These card-holders were cannibals.

Some ordered, "Get me AA". Adam's apple soup was served.

Some ordered, "BB" Bosom Boil was served.

Some ordered, "CC" Clitoris Chutney was served.

Some ordered, "LF2" Lady's Fingers Fry was provided.

The code "Sweet16L" indicated the lips of sweet-sixteen girl. Likewise, "AM" in the menu card was the code for Anus Masala and PM for Penis Masala. Some liked to have Butter Papillae (BP). Some were voracious to have omelets made out of semen; some wanted tea with breast milk. Some wished to have VV or Vagina stew of Virgins. The costliest item on the menu was a scrambled dish made out of the first foetus of a fair lady.

The above-said menu was prepared by remote-controlled robots. The robot would select the victim, skin it (him\her), cut it, chop it, cook it and serve it on the table. A single technician handled all the robots. Her pay was astronomical; her food was testicles toast and her drink was hot human blood.

Most of the scapegoats were slum-dwellers, orphans and other cantankerous wanderers. They were rounded up by underworld scoundrels. They in turn handed them over to the hotel agents for liquid money. The victims were first used for fun and then as food.

Another scandalizing place in the hotel was a rendezvous. This was restricted to exclusive nude-card-holders. They were Men-Seeking-Men (MSM), Women-Seeking-Women (WSW) and Both-Seeking-Both (BSB) customers. Phallicism was the prime attraction where always *vox humana* was played as background music for the live show. Voyeurs were more in number than the real participants. My ramuli used to enjoy their ramps as they could easily behold the swindling through the window sans curtain on the top floor. In the phantasmagorias, men to men, women to women and men to women were raped and gang raped.

Having come to know about it, I had a feeling that the post Eysan period's barbarism of medieval Indana was less cruel than the culture that existed in the years of the Devil.

* * *

Aid, by all means, means relief, assistance or help. But just think of a contrived plural of *aid*, in capital letters, *AIDS*? Yes, definitely it helps. The most dreaded disease that brings sure death. HIV, the virus causing Acquired Immune Deficiency Syndrome is a boon given by the devil in the year of the devil. AIDS captured the human world like the horrifying 'network dragon' that spread through the computer world. The computers could be treated or condemned. But what about human beings? Were there any treatment? If not who'll condemn them?

The hotel authorities used to recruit high standard candidates as Girl Friday—educated and intelligent—for various departments. Attracted by the peak pay and perks, an attractive young lady who was a computer graduate, attended an interview. The board members wished to have her inner-view instead of interview. She complained to the Assistant Commissioner of Police. She was engaged to him. He couldn't tolerate the character assassination of his fiancée. He being an energetic young IPS officer took stringent action against the hotelier, Mr. Tandoor, the grandson of Mr. Roti, the founder of the Continental Hotel. Without any interview she was employed as a cashier as a matter of settlement with the police. There was one more condition. She had to undergo one-month practical training in cash handling manually. She had to count the daily collection practically with in a specific time without any counting aids—currency notes of all the denominations including the soiled ones had to be tallied with account in the currency counting computers. While counting, for the fastness and smoothness, she used to touch the fingers on the tongue to damp it with saliva to avoid sticking of notes. It of course made the counting easy.

Alas! At the end of the month, she became a carrier of HIV. Unaware of the fact that she was an AIDS patient, she got married to the IPS officer. The notes were smeared with the saliva, mucus, semen and menses of the AIDS patients—available in plenty at the underground stocks cell—and allowed the notes to dry. Then it was given to her purposely with the intention of making her a perfect patient of AIDS. She supplied the auto-immune disease to her husband on the first night itself who was the then SP of the Kalibay district. Thus hotel-owner's cruel mind reimbursed the retaliation of the police's criminal mind.

As the emanation of God had turned the wheel of time, Indana's pages of civilization also turned simultaneously. I witnessed it . . . But I still did not understand if Indana developed or underdeveloped in terms of culture or emancipation. I felt in toto, the country underwent an emasculation and the countrymen suffered suffocation and embarrassment. That is the reason why I wished to narrate the events of the last century of this ending millennium elaborately. The military government embezzling the revenue embittered me. Still I appreciated their enthusiasm to make strides from culture to future.

As far back as 1999 years ago, there have been a million methods to flatter or scandalize the glorious and inglorious periods the country had gone through. Take the case of the present military *raj*—as political parties were banned the country could maintain communal harmony; it could amalgamate the people and array them under a united umbrella. But the demerit also was an umbrella, a fire-power-umbrella.

Leaving out the existing Deltan and non-existing Mulcut cities, as a resident, let me explain with thousand tongues that Kalibay was a glorious city. Though it was a place with hoary past, at present, it is the "Queen of Indan Sea" with lots of sea power future. Its exclusive economic zone is the main feature.

How a jejune land bloomed into a Megapolis! Only I experienced the difference—a transformation from a bulk of sand to a bustling commercial city. Its infrastructure developments—roads, buildings, bridges (static and moving), port, airport et al! Besides the skyscrapers for the concrete-jungle viewers, the sight-seers would marvel at the fauna-flora-filled jungle on the outskirts of the city.

How the dressmaking and designing varied from nudity to bell-bottoms, from bells to narrow bottoms, from narrow to bottomless and from bottomless to clothe-less! See the changes in *haute cuisine*— from uncooked dog meat to cooked hot dog. From cooked to uncooked human flesh. Man eating man in the twentieth century! What a mad mad *monde* it is!!

How they constructed dwelling places—from mud house to PVC flats. From houses of happiness to houses of ill fame. How the vehicle population captured the roads from bullock carts! How they built various types of vessels—from mere catamaran to carriers of aircraft! How they flew—from kites to jumbo jets! How they battled—from bamboo-spear to ballistic missiles! How they did that and how they did this! How how, how? It required millions of pages to fill up the advantages and disadvantages of the transformations occurred in Indana. In toto, could only write that it was a transition from nothingness to everything disregarding its evils and virtues.

During the course of transformation, I saw many unbecoming men washing their hearts with the detergent of decorum and becoming decent. At the same time, I saw many decorous men consuming the tonic of sin to gain money weight.

Whenever you start giving and taking loan, then onwards you become a liar.

There was a news flash: A seven-star hotel was sanctioned by the government in my habitat. That too vis-à-vis to me. I was the happiest inhabitant to hear the news. The Continental Hotel, fashioned out of hundred years, has been awarded the heritage hotel category. And it would be renamed as Hotel New Millennium, considering it as a prestigious tourist palace of Indana, especially for exotic visitors. The hotel provided all the facilities.

The pamphlet read: "Just follow your heart to your dream holiday, arrive at Hotel New Millennium. For a whole world of exciting holiday in one holiday destination. Come to Hotel New Millennium. It's a sun for worshippers who dream of virgin white beaches. A backwater adventure aboard a house-boat drifting on tranquil waters. A mountain-lover's retreat amongst the clouds, nestling amidst lush peaks and fragrant spice farms. This hotel, where wild life fanatics discover untouched sanctuaries. And culture-seekers exult in the magnificent art forms. While festival hoppers can indulge in non-stop celebrations splashed in color, excitement, legend and tradition. Hotel New Millennium—it's your kind of holiday home!"

"Notwithstanding its nuisance and insanity, the hotel received the 7-star status! You're right dear consorts, 'All that glitters is not God." I passed a remark pathetically.

"It's because of the mere influence," my consorts said.

"What's influence in this *coup d'état*?"

"Don't you remember the story of man-eating General Crow Black from the Jornada district of Inda-Paka border?"

Whether the story was an incident or an accident, it was really a sad, mad and bad episode: When Mr. Crow Black was a colonel; he was frontline of the conflict between Indana and Pakkana. Incidentally he happened to be in a trench with his orderly. All the men in his regiment were blown up in a series of land mine explosion. There was nothing to eat other than the uniforms and the equipment on their body.

A few days passed by . . . They were having a terrible time with the cruel sun above, the hard earth beneath and rocky walls on the sides of the trench. All that seemed to be their enemies. The colonel's legs were wounded; the orderly's legs and hands were wounded. As the starvation was acute, compared to the wounds, the pain was negligible. They wished they had a crocodile stomach so that they could digest the battered bricks as bread.

The colonel cried, "My large intestine is eating my small intestine. I'm that hungry."

"*Saaaar* .... Anyway I'm dying ... you eat me"

Colonel added, "My mouth is as dry as a hearth."

"I've ... No urine even ... to serve ... *Saaaar,* You may ... drink ... my blood if ... available."

The wounded orderly became very weak and weary ...

On the first day colonel cut the soldier's right hand and ate it. On the second day the left hand was chopped off. On the third day before death the soldier groaned, "Saar ... I'm de ... ad. Ple ... s ... tak ... car ... f ... mi ... yf ... an ... c'lren ..."

The poor soul who served and loved the colonel for the past fifteen years dearer than his own soul passed out of this university of earth without experiencing any humanity. No sooner did his orderly said good-bye than the colonel cut open the chest, drank enough hot blood before it got cold and ate his liver before it got spoiled. The colonel's stomach was shocked to receive the human flesh; his kidneys refused to filter the blood of another human being—they felt sympathy, got irritated and annoyed. But the nervous system consoled them: "Not to worry; it's after all for your own survival. Soothed thus, all the systems of the body became happy to have the human flesh.

The colonel complied with the compassionate request of his orderly. How he complied with the poor man's request was another mad, sad and bad story ...

The air-force choppers on their sorties saw eagles eating carcass. They smelt the SOS and rescued the withering officer. Colonel Crow Black was promoted as brigadier and was awarded the greatest gallantry award—Prime Medal for Battle (PMB). In the colorful ceremony, his heart was throbbing to take the meat of human being rather than the Medal of Honor—by that time, he was inclined to cannibalism. The military government appointed him as the minister for tourism and hotel industry.

A conference of all the major hotel-owners was held in his office in Kalibay. He presided over the function. Mr. Tandoor, the owner of the continental hotel became the confidence-keeper of the minister. The minister became the co-heir of the continental hotel confidentially. Thus he enjoyed the cohabitation and cannibalism also confidentially. The first victim of the continental cuisine was his orderly's wife followed by his five children. Though he voraciously tasted all the items on the menu's back pages, grilled liver was his most favorite item. It was not animal's liver; it was the fresh liver of a live human being, the rarest of rare creation of God. Perhaps, God might have intentionally closing His eyes and ears for not witnessing the bizarre behavior of God's own creation committing brutal infanticide of God's own innocent infants.

If some think the spate of that cold-blooded killing of the innocents was ruthless and brutal or a morally repugnant deed or a sin snuffing out other's life is deterioration of ethics or uncouth barbarism, some others think that it was a noble act or a graceful and glorious commitment. It was their tranquil trance. Violence was their peace-providing-job. That might be the reason why many dignitaries were cohesive to be cannibals— number of card-holders in the continental hotel was tremendously increasing day by day. If asked, the loggerheads logical dictum says: If someone can consume the hatred snake-meat, we can have the lovable human-meat, if you can afford it.

How couldn't I laugh? So I laughed.

"Why are you laughing?" my consorts asked sarcastically.

I replied, "Is our God a comedian?"

"Why? What happened?" they argued.

"Why does he put his iron feet on the head of the innocent and poor people? Why does he open the bakery of boons to the cruel anti-social elements?"

"Oh, we see . . . ." They blew out their cheeks and continued, "You blaaa blaaa about the co-called cannibal Brigadier Crow Black who was promoted as General owing to the demise of General Glutton, the second President of Indana. Isn't it? Why can't you realize how cruel was the death of the President who was also an anti-social element?"

Yes. I forgot that. His death was another comedy, blended with tragedy.

Miss, miss, miss . . . If you miss something, you'll miss your peace-of-mind. But if Miss is prefixed with a suffix—Miss Indana or Miss Pakkana or Miss Earth? *Vaaa*! Undoubtedly your peace-of-mind would be multiplied. Who doesn't like a Miss Earth? Once one millionaire was ready to offer his million to a Miss Earth—the most marvelous beauty queen on this entire earth—just for a kiss. One billionaire was ready to give up all his billions to her just to sleep with her for a night. And another trillionaire was prepared to sacrifice his entire trillions to keep his penis inside her vagina for one hour. Many rich men queued up with money-bags to hire her. So one could judge the importance of a *Miss*.

Miss Earth contest was held in the ending year of the ending century of the ending millennium at a grand glittering gala at the erstwhile

Continental Hotel. The President of Indana, Gen. Glutton presided over the pageantry. Miss Sona Mali, aged 21, a post-graduate from Deltan city, was crowned Miss Earth 1999.

His Highness Gen. Glutton was a real glutton. Immediately after the crowning ceremony, a buffet dinner was hosted by the hotel authorities.

There was a special item named *Triple F* (Fine Finger Fry) prepared exclusively for the card-holders. It actually was a real lady's finger stuffed with pepper *masala* inside a hollow (vegetable) lady's finger.

Even though President was not a card-holder, he was given one Fine Finger Fry as instructed by tourism minister Major General Crow Black. The President did not know how to eat it. As he bit it, Maj. Gen. Crow Black murmured in his ears "*Saar* how's the taste of a lady's finger?"

The coup President was a scholar in grammar. He sarcastically replied, "Junior, you lost the memory in grammar. Say the taste of *the* lady's finger; not *a* lady's finger. There's a hell of a lot of difference between those *articles.*"

Maj. Gen. Crow Black retorted, "I used the correct article, S*aar*, It's *a* lady's finger not *the* . . ."

As he disclosed the fact in his ears that a real finger of a dead lady was concealed inside, the President felt nausea. The bitten half portion of the triple F popped into his throat chocking the alimentary canal. His eyes flooded with blood. He sat on a chair, motionless for few minutes. The card-holders—omnivorous omnium gathurum—enjoyed the buffet unaware of the fact that their President was no more.

Actually the President was a vegetarian. If he were a non-vegetarian, he should have eaten the item as though it were chicken neck. As the aide-de-camp and the commandoes were not permitted to enter the mysterious tryst, they did not know of the trouble.

Crossing the seniority—not by efficiency—Maj. Gen. Crow Black, using his crookedness was elected by a computer lot. The lot was deceptive. All the computers were programmed in such a way that they contained the name of Maj. Gen. Crow Black alone. He beguiled other contestants. I soliloquized: The future President was a full-fledged fraud!

I was very unhappy to see the falsity of the future President; yet I was very happy to see the funeral of the former President. It was the funniest death—a kind of silent self-murder. The government conferred the rank of general on the distinguished coup leader. Thus the great cannibal, the most cunning His Highness General Crow Black, became the third President of United Indana—a national upheaval.

The first and foremost action he took after assuming the office was giving 7-star status to the Continental Hotel to make it the most prestigious establishment to embrace the new millennium.

The investment for the augmentation was about one billion rooba. The expansion required for the 7-star specification was not mainly in the infrastructure segment, but on the land area. The hotel situated between one and the Mahadagi Road had a small area only. It required another four acres to meet the standard of a unique deluxe hotel. Leaving the Mahadagi Road on one end, the other two sides were the states legislature building and the Gerri Lal Memorial University. There was no space available on the western side as it was the sea end. The only left over space was the area where I was residing.

To develop anything you've to destroy something. That's the decision of the designer of destiny. Here, for the expansion of an establishment, was to expire. The *demarche* was the demarcation of my place where I was housed for 1999 years. By virtue of that the ground belonged to me where as the land belonged to the government as per records.

The self-made omnipotent, General Crow Black, the co-heir of the Continental hotel, leased four acres of land to Mr. Tandoor, the proprietor, unconditionally. It was something unconstitutional. What to say—military rule is so rude that it could mould the constitution as they wished in the name of strategic matters.

As per the deed, Mr. Tandoor could do anything to me indeed. He could show mercy to me; he could be cruel to me; it was his caprice. All the cells in his brain were pulsating with the idea of developing and improving his hotel to become the biggest man of the biggest hotel. It was his motto. To make his dream true, he put all his motions and actions in malicious auto mode.

I recalled how fortune elevated Mr. Tandoor to the exalted position of the emperor of the global hotel business from a great grandson of a son-of-the-soil—an excommunicate *Sava* caste servant of the Hovan planter in the 18th century.

Despite this, his heart had no space in any of its chambers for mercy, sympathy or compassion. Only money could make him merry. Moreover, I remembered his calling me a slubberdegullion once. So, how could I expect his mercy showering on me as he didn't own the reservoir of humanity?

*   *   *

The neighboring country of Cheenisthan named Deseria was a desert. The desert was famous for oil mines. Indan technology helped the mining of oil from the wells. Many refineries were built in Deseria Technicians and skilled laborers were plenty available in Indana. Deseria Refinery owners titled *Shanks* were immensely rich. Nevertheless, they were illiterate. They never bothered to learn any language of any countries other than their own. Usually they arrived in Indana and stayed in Hotel Continental to escape from the scorching summer of their deserts. This was not just for the manpower recruitment but also to enjoy the nautch, oil massage and the flesh trade. Girlie girls show was the highlight.

During nights, myriad of mysterious disappearances of females ranging from girls to old women occurred from streets, schools, offices homes and even from hospitals.

The Continental Hotel used to recruit ladies from all walks of life as receptionists, office staffs, room maids, massage girls and cooks (no for mysterious galley). The hotel provided all the facilities for children especially for the babies. The hotel had a crèche to take care of the infants, nursery school and working women's hostel in the name of socia uplift.

I was certain, someday or the other and somehow or the other they would be either bed-victims or plate-victims or both. Believe it or not, I witnessed an uncanny incident out of many untold sufferings. A charwoman, a widow, went to clear up a royal suite of the hotel. As she opened the cover of the dust-bin, she saw a scrip. As she opened the bag she saw a corpse of a cherub. As she stared at its face she identified the baby. Her baby! Oh, ho, ho . . . What could have been her feelings?

Boy, the only child was dear to her like her liver. She screeched but no sound came out. She saw the bathroom door opening. She hid behind a curtain. An old man, the villain, walked out of the room in his bathrobe Her eyes identified him. They took his sharp photograph and handed over the negative to the color-lab of her mind. After processing the print, it wa stored in her heart . . .

Let bygones be bygones. Mustering courage, she took the currency notes. The cash was equivalent to 2x100x100=20000 Indan Rooba. A nice slice of sum! She kept the scrolls safely. She wished to insert the same scroll in the same manner inside the same man—any way her son is finished. She yearned to finish the finisher of her son. Actually, her two-year-old son was abducted from the day-care-centre and was bored a tunnel through the anus!

An avalanche of revenge arose in her. But the weather for taking revenge was not favorable in Indana. She should follow him to Deseria as a maid servant or for any kind of employment. But *how* to go? The more she thought about the *how,* the question of *how* became bigger and bigger.

Next day, there was recruitment for the post of girl Friday Superintendent. She too thought of appearing. But the certificates? MBA was the minimum qualification! She was just a Metric. The selected candidates had to supervise the female office staff with varied clerical and secretarial works.

Luckily she met with the proper person—a Deserian peon! Her broken knowledge in broken *Chink* language—as she used to do odd jobs for the Deserian visitors—helped the communication. She conducted a cupboard love; he performed a profound love. She gave her cunt. He gave her clue—the main aspect of the interview was the test of personality. She performed as told by the peon.

Her turn was third. No sooner did she enter the room than she pulled the chair—sans seeking permission—and sat. There was a bonded book and a bell on the table.

The old villain said in *Chink*, "Lady, learn by heart the first Para on the last page of this book and write the matter on that black board. Let's see how fast you can write".

She read the last page—a quite interesting climax of the famous Indan Drama, *Munikumari Mangalam*. She already knew it by heart as Para was the happy ending dialogues of the hero and the heroin. Reading the last page, she kept the book back on the table. She pressed the bell. A peon, the one who gave her the clue, entered.

She ordered, "Dust up the board".

The peon took a duster which was kept on the boarder of the board. He wiped the board lethargically.

She advised, "First dust up your dullness, then dust the board".

Compressing the impatience, the peon did his work with interest. The Deserian lecher, somehow or other wanted to export the lascivious lady to his country to fulfill his lust.

Leaving some chalk marks here and there on the board, he let go the duster. As he was about to leave the room she admonished, "Pick up the duster and complete the work. Do your duty diligently. If you lose enthusiasm, you may lose your job. Mind it".

All the while, the Chairman (the old villain) and the other board members were watching her performance. They liked her act of lashing out at the subordinate. By all means she was able enough to govern the administrative staff of their refinery. Actually they were testing the commanding capacity of the candidates and not the speed and memory power. Overwhelmed by her performance, the board unanimously approved her selection.

The board President said, "We appreciate your power of command and presence of mind. You're selected. Let's verify your certificate".

She handed over a folder. Inside, other than her certificate of matriculation, she had kept her wedding card printed in *Indi*. They did not know the language. However, they were impressive. Comparing to the other candidates' certificates, in ordinary papers and ordinary ink, the board members were impressed by the marriage card printed in golden letters in artistically. They also marveled at her pleasing mien.

The old man asked, "Which university issued this? This is distinct from others!"

"Mine is from the University of Mulcut". The marvel of beauty murmured with a pleasing mien, "the others are either from Deltan or from Kalibay".

"Well. That's all", popped the President, "You shall be proud to join our prestigious company. Be prepared to move by next week".

If you could change the destiny, you could easily challenge science— she was caught by the Indan Military Police at Deltan Airport. She was accused as a fraud. Thus her ambition of avenging also fell into the well of fate. Gallows swallowed her . . . I was contented—she would definitely meet the soul of her innocent baby who might have become an angel in heaven.

* * *

The city of Mulcut was still a hell. Radioactivity levels were still very high. The gentle hearts could not recover still from the shock caused by the genocide.

Despite reclaiming Mulcut, the government provided all the subsidies for rejuvenating Kalibay with *reductio ad absurdum*. What a paradoxical performance by the power of military! By-passing vox-populi was their hobby!!

I kept quiet . . . My consorts also kept quiet . . . Though we had ants in our pants, we kept quiet because reticence was the best possible way to react, while fools were talking.

Out of the four-acre space, one acre, near the lagoon where luxurious gondolas were plying and the lusty shrubbery where bird sanctuary added lustre to the nature's lyricism, was reserved for the health care club. *Yoga*, meditation, naturopathy, massage center et al were planned for the "Shrub Club".

Human beings differ from person to person, mentally, morally and physically. No charismatic effort can repair the mental and moral deformity until and unless one changes self. But can the physical deformity and disfigurement be changed all by oneself? Some are born disfigured; some acquire it. Some are dwarfs; some are gigantic. They wish to be the normal like others . . .

The "Shrub club" of Continental Hotel was famous for "dwarf-to-giant and giant-to-dwarf" therapy. The therapists' transfigured persons who were considerably smaller than the average in height and weight to persons of normal physical proportions.

The therapy was very simple. The runt had to be extended; the giant had to be compressed. As the human body is 'flexible like rubber', expansion and contraction are possible. A whole body elastic belt would be designed as per the patient's size and type. Wearing the belt from head to foot like a winter suit, the patient would lie on a flat bed. The belt compressed each and every molecule of the body of the giant patient and extended each and every molecule of the body of the runt patient respectively, slowly and steadily day by day . . . Plus a magneto-therapy— the usage of magneto-motive force on human body.

The magnetic treatment magnetized many card-holders of the Continental Hotel. It exerted a strong attractive power and charm to almost all the clients. Men with mountains of money registered their names well in advance to seek the standard height. Those who joined the *yoga* class could maintain the health in perfect condition. The meditators achieved satisfactory tranquility. The reflected, once rich men renounced their wealth to the benevolent fund of the hotel.

The newly sworn-in minister for tourism and hotel industry was Commodore Mulgu Mon. Fortune had always followed him. Enrolled as a mere metric boy entry in the National Naval service, luck lifted him to the level of a minister. He too was a card-holder and one among the confidence-keepers of military ruler, Gen Crow Black. Despite consuming all the delicacies of the hotel, he couldn't gain height. He was just five feet, four inches which punctured his position as a military officer at the gathering of dignitaries. The diet helped in increase his weight rather than his height. So he was keen to introduce the Health Care Clinic for which acquisition of the land was a must.

Some exotic visitors had magnified me as Mr. Banyan, the legendary tree of Indana. Percontra, Commodore Mulgu Mon hated me. He looked at me as if I had raped and killed his wife. She being the President's demi-monde, and the engineer of the robots in the concealed kitchen of the hotel, I think almost all the citizens of Indana were afraid of her. Perhaps she had no merits as a woman. Many mothers used to warn their crying children, "Shhh, keep quiet, SHE may come". Who was that SHE? What was that SHE?? And where was that SHE??? No one knew . . . She killed so many. She didn't bury them. She made curry out of them. So, how could I kill her? She raped many men without the President's knowledge. So, how could I rape her? Yet the minister stared at me in that angle. But it was not his fault; it was my fault.

Wonders are many. Man-made or God-made, wonders always stun man. After the millennium war—the High Hill operations at the border—the next wonder of the millennium was the visit of Hovan Clergy of Bastiland. It was the talk of the world. He was the living saint for the Hovans. It was the first time in the history of Hovaism that the holy man was visiting a country: That too Indana, a land of distinct culture and customs. It was a socio-religious and political wonder of the world as large as life.

When Indana developed ICBM the people were not surprised. It was something pertaining to science. They never bothered about the strategy. But this visit, the visit of an old omniscient made the earth wonder. Were it because Gen. Crow Black, the President of Indana, was a Hovaist by birth? He smelled a rat: The reflection of Restoration of Democracy was developing even among the people of his own religion, though they were minority in community. President wanted to capture world sympathy and support by inviting the holy man to his coup country. He wanted to show the world that peace still prevailed in his country. The President was a sanctimonious person. He attended bosques and prayers regularly.

The government arranged the Cleric's food and accommodation in Continental Hotel. It was my bad luck. Commodore Mulgu Mon proposed to make the parking lot beneath my crown, disregarding the complaints from the drivers that the excreta of the birds nestled on my branches dirtied the cars of the VIPs.

Clergy's bullet proof transparent car that cost a fortune looked like a giant diamond. Vow, I've never seen such an automobile in my life! A millennium car!

My consorts wished, "If we could get a chance to travel in this car, it's nothing less than a dream come true."

I popped the reply, "If you could become Clergywomen, I bet your dream will be materialized."

They said curtly, "Cut it. We're proud of parking this *Clergycar* in our yard."

Yes. I provided shelter for the parking-lot. I showed a little civic pride. But the pride went before a fall. One of my branches fell down all of a sudden on top of the *Clergycar* crushing it to the ground. It happened during night. I was sleeping. The uproar made me awake. It was a sad sight. The car was no more! Dissatisfied, the Cleric scudded to his country in a sea-king chopper.

Chey . . . I felt ashamed. The satanic branch did a mischief. For many days people scolded and abused me. They looked at me as if I were a traitor. After the indecent incident, the government was after Commodore Mulgu Mon, the minister who was responsible for the protection of the Cleric during his visit. Some Hovan priests believed Mulgu Mon deliberately did that as he was an Eysaist.

Annoyed, the minister ordered to cut me down till death!

"Let's cut this goddamn tree right now."

His order was so strong that each and every word as if a mouth-to-wood missile that could burn me to ashes.

Having ants in their pants, my rami remarked ridiculously, "It was just an accident. Let's make another accident to mow down this goddamn Minister down right now by dropping a branch on his head."

I held them back, lest they should launch a suicide attack by jumping . . . Thus the public would see me as a murderer or the head of a homicide squad. Anyway both the orders chilled me to my tap-root.

The land acquisition and survey party arrived with theodolite. They fixed positions around me with stakes and chains *ad lib.*

I cried grandiloquently, *"Save me . . . and save my family . . ."*

But none heard it. Even if somebody heard, who cared? Some of the floras in and around the city heard it.

They murmured among themselves, "Our gaffer Esquire Banyan's days are nearing . . ."

I wished to be an animal that was being led to the butchery. So, at least, my bleating could have been heard by some humanists. Yet I cried with all my might. The Almighty heard it. He sent a messenger to save me. He was . . .

He was a writer. A writer of not just human feelings; he was also able to distinguish the audible emotions of faunas and the silent and tranquil vehemence of the floras. His name was Naturam. As his name so his deeds. A true lover of trees and nature. A genius and an ecologist. The profound love of the positivist for the nature had a story behind it . . .

Well, the writer had won the national award for literature in 1998. The coup President gave away the prize money—a lump sum of 100,000 rooba plus a citation, a certificate and a golden shawl. He felt the sweet taste of the award. He wished for his wife's presence. He wanted to share the taste with her instantly, so, he cancelled his train trip and returned home by night flight in order to show her the video cassette of the award function.

In which way should he share the taste with his spouse? Perhaps he shall kiss her on the lips; he shall hug her to the chest. No, the best way was to go to bed with her. His entire body was filled with the award blood. Let the salvoes of semen sweeten his spouse's womb. Let it sow the seed for a sweet baby.

Would the period permit? When he left, she was in menses. He didn't know the days. Otherwise also, what the hell writers know about all these physical matters? The field of literature is such an area where only the human thought grows. Cultivation of biology, zoology or ~ology (any ology) fails.

He reached home at an unearthly hour. She was in her ancestral home till his return. He was supposed to return two days later. He pressed the calling bell. Electricity fails like heart. No one knows when it occurs. He went to the side of her bedroom. The windows stood ajar. He peeped into the room lighting his pen torch. A man was in bed with his wife. His eyes were not eyes . . .

There was a scurry in the sombre room. Sudden opening and closing of the bed room door . . . A shadow of a man fled into the darkness . . .

Who was he? The writers' mind questioned pure self. A rich man? Did he influence her by his chink? *Chey*, then? A paramour? Or a chivalry? Let it be any damn thing, he should have caught that goddamn man red handed. He stood like a statue. Often the writers are fools when they're not writing . . .

Was it a dream? No. What next? He heard the noise of the door opening . . . He hid in the cowshed. There he saw the real profound love. The cow licking the calf! He saw the grotesque of his wife as she came out and stood on the threshold. She scanned the area, made sure that there was no one outside, and went inside.

So she was awake. The man was with her with her consent. It was not a rape. She was fully conscious. Her vagina had willfully invited his manhood. The vulva gate was widely open as big as life!

Now, the writer felt the bitter taste of love. It was so bitter that all the sweets of the world couldn't sweeten his sensuous organs. His WIFE (Wonderful Instrument For Enjoyment), though the anonymous abbreviation proved correct word by word; it has turned to (Worries Invited For Ever) But the writer had a doubt: Could the wonderful instrument be enjoyed (operated) by anybody other than the husband? Even God could not answer the question; only the woman can.

The calf licked on his palm. His sensorium again raised its hood. Yes. This is his wife who likes to love him. He unzipped his pants; inserted his genitals into the urinary tract of the calf. The calf turned the head back; glanced sympathetically at him. Man . . . . Whether he is a renowned writer or a reputed fighter, at times he fails to recognize even his parents.

The heat inside the cattle's genitals ignited his organ. Like the bullets from a quick firing gun, rapid fire of human semen drops hit the muscular target of the animal. He withdrew his weapon of flesh. The animal urinated. He went out of the cow-shed. She snarled at him. Her sniff seemed a sneer. He stared at the calf and her mother. The cow showed no reaction. Of course, she witnessed him coming beside her daughter and making love to her. But she did not know that he spoiled the virginity of her pet daughter.

The calf still stared at him wondering she would give birth to a human baby. A man hired her womb; he placed his germs in it. She had to preserve it. She covered her opening lest the hot liquid injected inside her would leak out. For the first time in his life, he was ashamed before an animal. He surrendered all the might of his manhood before that little cattle.

Man feels contented after a natural sexual act; percontra, he feels confessed to completing an unnatural mating. He, with folded arms bowed before the calf and pleaded, "Please forgive me for the malicious act. Though this malefactor doesn't deserve an apology, for the first and last time, please forgive and forget me. I've forgot my thought-power for a little while for sex makes man mad. On behalf of the human being, I'm really ashamed as they say, "Don't behave like animals forgetting the fact that your behavior is designed by the Almighty and you live as per the code and conduct of God." He couldn't stand before the calf as he saw the real God in her opening the third-eye.

He sneaked away to wash his private parts. As he was about to drop the bucket into the well, there he saw the morning moon staring at him questioningly . . . What had he done? He blemished the whole mankind! He hurt the human conscience!! Did an unnatural act with a dump animal. A bugger! Oh, no, no, he couldn't face the moon. He was ridiculous.

He went to the moss-filled pond. There, each and every moss wanted to trial him by mob-law. He heard them calling "you cute big bogy."

He ran away. Stood still on the sandy yard of the house. The earth beneath his feet moved off as if he had no right to stand on it. Yes, he was a hobgoblin! He lost his foothold. He fell down. He saw the tree nearby was trembling angrily. He had spoiled the whole nature. He looked at the sky. The summer stars were ablaze with rage. He had dirtied the entire cosmos. A cold breeze passed away. Yet he sweated. Mentally and morally exhausted, he slept. He dreamt.

In the dream he wished to confess. Confess before whom? He wanted to surrender the award. The President's address stung him: Here comes the lover of faunas and floras, the unique man of nature.

Was it something ridiculous? Did he deserve that flattery? No, *sans doute* he was a *sodomite*. He saw the audience mocking him.

His dream broke . . . Holding his golden award memento in one hand, she smiled at him showing all her diamond-like teeth. She remained so innocent, pretending unaware about the previous night's drama. He saw the other face of her. He was on the double-cot inside the house. His dear double-cross wife was sitting cross-legged near his feet in her most glittering dress.

Yes, unlike the dull calf all that glitters (his wife) is not God.

I compared. Was she a sinner? If so, was she as big a sinner as he? The sin ratio of man: woman = 10:1. The problem was solved. She had committed only illegal sex, quite a natural crime, whereas he had done an unnatural act! Was it because of the maturity ratio of man: woman = 1:10. Yes, she has ten-fold maturity compared to him. He behaved like a cute little bugger, whereas she, forgetting the foolishness fearlessly sat beside her husband consoling him. She was living perfectly by *fuck and forgets* formula whereas he couldn't live peacefully, thinking *past-is-past*. He till thought *past-is-present*. Therefore I couldn't judge who among them would have a bright future.

Patting on his palm, she said, "You're my thirst; you're my lust".

I disliked her . . . She lied through her teeth. There was no trace of truth in her words. At least she should've been a little truthful to her husband. As in the case of distilled water, pure truth is not fit to consume. It should be added with some drops of lies like minerals in drinking water.

She said that she loved him like anything. I wondered whether she would know the meaning of *love*. After nature, only love can alter things: Love can level up the mountain; Love can dry up the sea. Lovers need nothing except love. Lovers are all in their world alone. Was she a real lover? If so, who was that paramour sneaked out of her love bed . . . ? Love only agrees with one life-partner and never multiple sex partners.

I knew, troubling a woman is as good as troubling your own heart. I've never troubled my Uru, Mena, Ramb and Thilo. Also I couldn't tolerate someone troubling women. Even God won't forget discrimination towards them. But this woman, the writer's wife adulterated the truth with poison on top of committing adultery! She was that type who would not grow where she was sown . . . I failed to confirm the concept that woman was substitute for happiness for the writer's wife made him unhappy.

She loved and kissed on his temples. He couldn't sense it. He disliked her cupboard love. He remained on the cot like a fallen granite statue. Was it a wrath . . . ?

I couldn't find fault with the novelist. As a writer, he had lot of tension. Sex was the only solution to ease it. Moreover, he was very sensuous. He could not be a voyeur. But after confessing the buggery, there was a transition from philanderer to philanthropist. I was certain that he was not a philistine, but his deeds were blunders. Not only that, he was very poetic also!

His imagination inspired me to create a poem.

Oh! You human being, what a creation you're!

More than the land, more than the water, you're the earth.

Oh! You human being, what a creation you're!

More than the hot, more than the cold—you're the weather.

Oh! You human being, what a creation you're!

More than the flora, more than the fauna—you're the nature.

Oh! You human being, what a creation you're!

More than the moon, more than the sun—you're the universe.

Oh! You human being, what a creation you're!

As you're the cosmic, I've no *monte juste* to magnify you.

The coup government presented him with the Writer of the Millennium award. But he refused it. The laureate was given another award, one-month simple imprisonment, for refusing the order of honor. As he was the cream of literature, the punishment was forcibly indeed, gently in manner.

He was asked in tete-a-tete and he answered in the prison.

Q: Mr. Naturam, don't you feel discomfort here?

A: Here or there, just adjust your heart, you feel comfort. This is also a part of the world.

Q: Any peculiar reason for refusing the recognition? Don't you feel it's essential for a writer like you?

A: A writer needs only paper, pencil or a computer with M.S. Word facility. Above all he should have a pulsating heart.

Q: Is sociology your subject?

A: No. My subject is eco-sociology. Without this, there's no story on this earth.

Q: It's heard that your latest novel "Trial of a Tree" has been nominated for the *Global Prize,* the most prestigious literary award. What's the subject?

A: It's the autobiographical legend of, a veteran tree, who lived and died for the mankind.

Q: Did any friends help you to complete the venture?

A: Indeed. Dictionaries are my friends. They helped me a lot.

Q: Once, when I interviewed you, you said that a family man can't be a social worker for he will be selfish. You've wife and children still you're a full time social worker?

A: Yes. Now they're more like the citizens than my family. Previously they were like family members rather than citizens. Hence I'm an altruist.

*　　*　　*

Phalanxes came with axes and lassoes to hew down me. They were also equipped with various paraphernalia to facilitate instant cutting. They fixed tents around me. Some among them stared at me as if they were butchers. Butchers or buggers, they were just human beings.

Hey human beings, are you just a grinder to mill the input ingredients? Or are you only a lump of flesh to lie on a cot like lifeless body? Or are you a factory only to manufacture urine, excreta, sweat and other excretions etc? Or are you just a container containing some liters of red paint as blood?

No, no, no, not at all. A human being is on one hand a super duper and on the other he is predominant—pre-eminent above all the other creations. Almighty has put all his might to create human beings; still some were erroneously made . . . That's why when one phalanx came to chop me many phalanxes came to protest it and protect me.

After the release from the prison, Writer Naturam, straightaway came to me (the shadow of the tree). The champion conducted a campaign. His followers shouted slogans favoring my saving. Notwithstanding the ban on public gathering, the public gathered.

One man shouted: Belie the order regarding killing Banyan.

Others repeated as one man.

The shouter continued: Take our souls instead of Banyan's soul.

Others repeated it.

Troops arrived. They used loud hailer to warn the crowd and to ask them to disperse. Percontra, the pop of the police was overwhelmed by the pop of the people. Police pumped pepper-powder followed by tear gas, followed by hot water jets, followed by baton charges and finally bullets on the people. Many died!

The young flamboyant novelist was taken into custody. District Collector ordered curfew. Cutting of Banyan (me) was also banned provisionally. My area regained tranquility.

Mr. Naturam was invited for a discussion. The venue was Continental Hotel. Top brasses of military and many civil authorities, plus the richest gun in the country, the owner of the hotel belt (a slave once upon a time) were the distinguished invitees. Most of them were card-holders. Commodore Mulgu Mon, Minister for tourism and ecology presided over the meeting.

He addressed, "Dear Grey Eminences let me straightaway enter into the subject. The present Continental Hotel is to be rebuilt and renovated to a greater position as New Millennium Hotel, which would be as if an emperor in the whole of Hotel Empire. As this is a private hotel, government has nothing to do with the affair. But as you're aware, the government has a heavy fiscal deficit. The main revenue to the exchequer is from tourism. To attract tourists, hotel facility is mandatory. So the government is duty-bound to help the hotel promoters. Besides, the government has leased out the land to the hotel. It's the new policy of Privatization. Deed has to be executed word by word. You know the tradition of the military—it obeys all orders; also makes all orders to ~~be~~ obeyed as well."

As the audience sat with satisfactory expression, the novelist sat silently, expressionless. He didn't have the slightest fear of Frankenstein monster.

Staring at the novelist, the Commodore continued, "Here the problem is the extra land required for augmentation. Banyan Tree is an obstruction to the new edifice to be erected. Some propose and some oppose to hew down the tree. Some say, do you say, Your Eminences . . . ?"

The dignitaries looked each other's face . . .

Mr. Tandoor, the owner of the hotel (son of Mr. Roti) got up. His face bore the stamp of cruelty. He asked, "Just explain me what's a tree? If there's something more than what I know that tree is just a self-supporting woody pillar growing to an immense size with developed branches and roots. Tell me so that I could pay tribute to your King-tree. Otherwise I can't embrace your ugly tree and destroy my beautiful hotel, the most prestigious establishment of Indana for human entertainment."

The writer could not tolerate the defamation. The philistine's philippic pained the philanthropist.

His face bore the stamp of mercy. As he stood up, everyone pricked the ears to hear his speech.

He answered, "I'm not a percipient. I'm just an environmentalist. But if you perceive a tree, it's evergreen and everlasting if man doesn't hew it. Perceivably speaking, a tree is none but a life-saver who doesn't seek any kind of remuneration or reward to save the lives of multitudes. A tree is part and parcel of nature. And if you consider the case of the veteran tree, Mr. Banyan, he is not a mere *maram,* he is a *manush.* And that too *amanush,* the only one who is living since 0000 A.D. During his birth it was Anno Domini (in the year of our lord). Next month, Mr. Banyan will cross 2000 years of age and will continue to live if the Anno Domini continues and if we permit. But I'm afraid, in this Iron Age or *Yuga* of *Kali*—the age of unrest, vice, wickedness, war, strife, anger, hunger, pride, poverty etc—the A.D converts into in the year of our devil. We'll forget God and praise devil."

By this time, the hard-hearted audience was slowly melting to support my survival.

Then the minister jumped up and argued, "What does this damn tree think? The whole world is beneath its foot? Is the entire earth its footstool? My bloody foot! Are there no other trees in our country? This Banyan is a burden, a bonvirant. This tree has lived enough and more; we men, the super creation live for only a modicum of time. Now let's chop off this Banyan and build a boulevard instead. Come on, chop . . . chop . . ."

Hearing these unkind words, I lost my desire to live away more. I felt prick of conscience. Why should I simply keep on living if others do not want me to live? I wished if I could get a little poison. If this man would have been a minister for health, and if he would have been kind enough to inject me with some mercury, it would have been far more gracious. Am I withered to have a mercy-killing? Oh! What a negligence! Really a cruel denial!

"You behead me with love; I will not feel.
You behold me with hate, I'll feel."

The author again argued for me, "Minister's statement is a fig leaf. Any number of boulevards won't compensate the death of Rev. Banyan. He's not just a woody pillar. He's the main mast of our country with innumerable yardarms (branches) flying innumerable tiny flags (leaves) on myriad of halyards (fig roots). If we maintain and preserve him, he would be the most prestigious fellow of our country, *crème de la crème*. We plead to you to shift the hotel to the outskirts of the city and convert this place into a botanical garden, so that Rev. Banyan would live like a King of Kings in the plant kingdom. Exotic and indigenous tourists would definitely visit him and pay tribute to the legend that occupies more than a hectare of land. No cloning would create a tree like Banyan. We work only for one-third of a day; trees work round the clock. We make the atmosphere and surroundings dirty; trees keep the environment neat and tidy. Our useless dead bodies cause epidemics; timber is essential for enormous engagements."

Fixing his eyes on Commodore, author continued, "So, Your Eminence may give due weightage to *vox populi, vox dei*. The people's voice is also favoring the tree's protection. So, I pray Your Eminence; do not delete Rev. Banyan from the book of Indana. Please remember that our country is like a country where one phalanx is phantasmal in phallus, many phalanxes are phantasmal in dendrolatry"

The captive's candid argument to save me captivated not only the captors but also the Commodore. Commodore Mulgu Mon, the Minister, concluded the conference, "Let me put up this matter before the President for final decision . . ."

Wonderful ! Wonderful !! Wonderful !!! Really Wonderful! See how he had magnified me in the meeting! Regarding my trunk, my ramification, my leaves, my adventitious roots etc, etc, etc. What a comparison! I was compared with human beings, the super creation! My evenness of mind had become the sameness of temper—I wished to live further . . .

Alas! The owner canvassed the Minister. Minister in turn prevailed upon the coup President by delivering a harangue and hosting a spree. The President, the supreme commander, ordered my deletion by a fax message.

No sooner did my death warrant was issued than many men climbed on my branches making me a human-tree, with the bold intention of saving me through *gheravo*. Several saucy boys hung, jumped and clung as if they were orang-utans. To disperse them, firstly Fire Force used water force taking delivery from the nearby fire hydrant. Men clenched fast to me like lizards.

In the meantime, Mr. Naturam, my bosom friend, held a motor rally. He was carried on a cross in an open truck. Some followers also observed *Niraharam* with him. They were laid flat on the truck's deck. The truck moved from Kalibay in the south to Deltan in the north where the Presidential Palace was situated.

Seeing the rally, I became delirious. My friend was fastened horizontally (both hands) and perpendicularly whole body with hard coir rope. Many placards and banners such as *'Save the plant, Stop cutting Trees, Please protect this planet'* etc, hung on the vehicles. My gargantuan cut-out was fixed on the tail board of the truck!

During my life, I'd seen the rise and fall of many powers. I'd also seen all the powers diminish before the power of the people. Army tried to block the peaceful vehicle rally; People tried to block the army. They received the rally with great zeal and enthusiasm. En route—villages, cities, cosmos, metros and megas—men lined up on the roadsides. They cheered the rally passionately. Seeing the intense interest of the public, Army withdrew arms, keeping it at half-cock. Instead of retreating, they escorted the rally from ahead and rear . . .

I could hear continuous comments from the on-lookers; one said, "I wish his blood is mine; my flesh is his."

A lascivious lady lustfully said, "I just want a lips-to-lips kiss of his."

Watching the rally from the balcony of a posh flat, the Beauty Queen of Kalibay muttered, "My greatest wish is to bed with this man."

The father of an orphanage remarked, "He is the *son* of *Indana*."

One whore advised to other vagina-vendors, "If you want to get fucked by someone freely and willfully, here comes the man."

And, all the sex workers agreed to it.

A grey-haired old woman's wish was very funny. She said, "See his gleaming black hair! How lengthy it is!! How nice it would be to make it into a chignon . . . ?"

One childless mother wanted to be his foster-mother.

A senior *Tundit* from a famous demple desired to add the author's urine in the holy-water to offer the devotees for purifying them. Its flavor would favor the men to relinquish abnegation and jealousy.

One baker wished to get the writers' excrement for blending it as essence in the gargantuan cake he was preparing for the millennium festival. His wishful thought was that, it would elevate the eaters to the writer's level.

A rich archaeologist wished to fossilize the author's body after his death. He was ready to offer all his riches for it.

Many beauties desired to clinch the cock-of-the-walk.

Though I was fascinated to know the multifarious whims and fancies of others, I too had a passionate wish—if I could have been the wood of the cross he was fastened. I wished to die before his death. I wanted to know how he would react to my death.

Citizens with commonsense understood that the campaign headed by the champion, Mr. Naturam, had had twin motives—save the greenery and save the country. It was an experiment on the passive resistance of the Indan masses for restoration of democracy on the name of the propaganda to protect me. Covering great distances, the vehicle rally rolled to its goal . . .

Meanwhile, Rapid Action and Task Force landed near me. Straightaway they started their job. Like in an emergency, they rigged booms, derricks and davits; used earth movers, mechanized choppers and motor saws to mow me. The proclaimer looked and worked like a mechanical beast. Its jib acted like the trunk of an elephant. The jib clenched my branches one by one and jibbed. The clinging clinchers jibbed from the branches lest they should be crushed beneath the metal belt of the equipment jibbing beneath my shadow. They lost their will power without their bosom friend cum thick leaser, Naturam. There was no one to ease the turmoil. They were sure of my death. Their effort seemed to be in vain. So they gave up their mission. Thus a heavy death toll was avoided.

For the first time in my life, I felt the taste of iron. I was more uxorious than ever when cutters axed my consorts. All of them were very bold. They neither protested physically nor uttered a word. They were aware of their fate.

They obediently submitted their lives to the hands of death. Thenceforth I felt uxorious. Frankly speaking, till such time, I doubt I was showing cupboard love to them. But now, where was the time to care for them. I could only pay homage to them. I should've used my stock of love when they were in need. I felt qualm . . . I wanted to repent my folly—not pampering and providing compassion in the proper time—and mend my ways. Behold! All my consoling consorts—Uru, Mena, Ramb and Tilo—fell down! They said farewell to me and to the whole world. They were dead. I wished I had known voodoo. Mourning for the dead is senseless. Still I cried. Their bodies were picked, dragged and put in a tipper-lorry. Their pyres would be in the poor people's hearths as firewood.

Next day they started chopping my branches. It was like cutting the matted hair of an ascetic. The schools of birds nestled in numerous nests in the green leaves shoaled. They soared in the sky. Their chirrup chinked the area. They cursed the cutters who evicted them from their homes. It took two whole days to chop and clear all my branches. I looked like a blonde who turned bald instantly.

If a child laughed in the graveyard, I was sure that all the dead would come to life. If a child laughed in the night, I am sure of the darkness would go and hide somewhere. Our champion of the campaign also laughed like a child though he was very weak and weary owing to the tiresome cross-country rally, bearing the Wooden-Cross . . . He had imagined good and hoped for the best of the country. Imagination and hope are like the two poles of earth. There's no world without imagination. Even the earth's axis is imaginary. So he continued his rally filling his mind with imagination and hopes to save me and the country. The rally was nearing Deltan . . .

It was the last day of the second millennium. My cuticle was cut the previous day. I resembled a cute naked streetwalker who was caught by the police, undressed, shaved, without limbs and sitting on stiff knees on the roadside like an effigy. Some passers-by stared at me in contempt; some beheld me as though I were a corona.

A camelopard-like crane having an SWL of 300 tons crawled on its steel feet towards me. A gleaming and luxurious URO car came and halted beside me. *Ngeh*, there they were! In the two corners, the minister and the owner of the hotel. Oh, the damned executioners from the task force also came towards me. They had a heavy strop made out of wire rope. They took two turns around my waist. Simultaneously, the crane-hook with the dead weight was lowered. They hooked me. The crane took care of my weight. Yes, that was the very moment I felt the bitter taste of death. Till then I used to think about others' death. I never thought about my death. I felt giddiness.

Crowds came to witness my murder. They were chased out by the police. Fearing the chastisement, many returned home. But those who believed in dendrolatry went to a safe distance and sang doxology.

The crane couldn't easily pluck my caudex though all my sub roots other than the tap-root were chopped off. My tap-root was also strong like the crane. The tug-of-war between natural power and mechanical power went on and on and on. I hoped my Mother Earth would give me a helping hand. But she favored me with her tongues. Her *favete linguis* had a meaning. She was helping me with her pull of gravity . . . Crane started jibbing. Each shake chilled me to the marrow. Still they couldn't uproot me. The evolution of my execution went on during night also. The continuous shaking weakened me like anything. I could sense my tap-root cracking *au fond*. I was dead sure that I would lose the game of life and win the trophy of death.

It was the beginning of the first day of the third millennium, and it was also the close of the last day of my life! They uprooted me. When the crane hoisted me, the taproot broke all of a sudden. There was a big bang. The whole earth quivered. My gigantic caudex swung hither and thither beating the men on its way to death. The boom of the crane broke down killing many dignitaries—card-holders of the hotel—sans any discrimination. The Honorable Minister and the owner of the hotel became chutney as the swinging body fell over them and also damaging the hotel edifice when the pendant was parted from the jib. My uprooted area—the place I was housed—became a waterless pond. Innumerable rampant reptiles emerged from the tranquil burrows beneath my stump. I had a feeling that those snakes were the representatives of my erstwhile colleagues, the elder *naga* and the younger *naga*. They rampaged and bit many chauvinists to death. A pandemonium broke out and many of my executioners mowed down in the stamped making the scenario more than that of a warfare. I lay there on my mother's lap heaving heavily for breath.

Some flora fanatics lamented, "Oh, ho, ho, how cruel is this sight! The one-time prestigious and divine cruciferous tree of our country lies on its mother's lap!"

Then I had nothing to do but pray. Prayer would give me immense power and the necessary force to resist the fear of death. Prayer would collect all my efficacious assets to concentrate on any one point other than death. Other than that in the sea of crises, paeans to the primordial power were the only passage to *moksha* or the liberation. As my biology was declining, so my biography was inclining—I didn't leave the pen for writing the story of Indana . . .

* * *

People's Rally For Peace reached its destination. President Gen. Crow Black also wished to see the *homme du monde*. He was cock-sure of his downfall. The Man of the World, Mr. Naturam, had created an ocean of men to flood his coup land. No amount of his military strength could help him resist the power of the people. He realized the hidden strength of peace. He was ready to negotiate. He would transform to a strict vegetarian. He would abolish the prevailing cannibalism in the country. He would cancel the license of the New Millennium Hotel. He would immediately instruct the executioners to stop cutting me. He would pledge all his properties (illegally earned) to the state. Yes. Let the Prince of Peace arrive. He would embrace him as his bosom brother. Let him come . . . Let'im come . . . Let'im come. President heaved a sigh of satisfaction. The rally arrived . . .

President, Gen. Crow Black scanned the motley crowd. He heard them shouting slogans against him—vox populi. He knew the participants' minds in a peaceful procession would always be volcanic—the busting may be imminent. One piece of RDX would be enough to lay him in the tomb of R.I.P. God only knew how many human-bombs were plying freely as man-eating sharks among that school of human-fish. Would a suicide bomber strike him . . . ? If anyone from that demonstration was an expert hijacker and if he intended to make the President a hostage while the aircraft was in the air and bargain for democracy? Oh, God, all the dignity, divinity, decoration and dictatorship he built in the yard of fraudulence, *sans doute* would sink in the sea of defamation. He felt his own spirit coming to kill him. He remembered *God* for the first time in his life. He got ready to relinquish the power to the people—revert to democracy. Let 'em enjoy the hard-earned democracy once again . . .

The truck halted right in front of the Presidential Palace, with a huge force of Army, Navy and Air force looking on. The arrayed military expected containment of crowd at any time. Gen. Crow Black climbed up the truck's platform to greet and felicitate Mr. Naturam. He was on the Cross, with head bent down. After adorning him with a garland, the President started to untie the rope. His personal staff came forward to help him.

The President politely pleaded, "No. I'm untying my own sin. Let me do this myself. Get a glass of orange juice; Let'im break the *niraharam* here itself".

The President himself removed all the turns around the hero's head, thorax, hands and abdomen. As he bent down to unhitch the last knot, the crucified fell on the President's back. Security staff jumped ahead to hold the hero.

"No . . ." the President wailed, "I shall shoulder this responsibility. I'll not allow someone to share this crucible."

One Rear Admiral shouted, "Bring a stretcher".

Holding the icon of Indana, the President stood up and said, "No, I'm his stretcher".

He carried the withered hero to his palace. He was laid on the conference hall's table. The President watched the quivering lips of Naturam. He brought his ears closer to hear the murmur.

Naturam muttered, "Ban . . . ya . . . n . . ."

The President swiveled his head and said, "Stop cutting the tree. Use the hotline. It's an emergency. Chop . . . And take care of the other members of the ecclesia; provide them food and comforts".

A Major General from the Armed Forces Medical corps, who was the Health Minister, came running with a glass of juice along with a Vice Air Marshal who was the Minister for External Affairs carrying a fax message.

The President personally poured the juice into the hero's mouth. Despite going in, the juice flew out of the mouth making two tiny channels on either side of his checks. "Come on", the President commanded, "where're the medical assistants?"

By this time the crowd outside were trying to trespass the President's palace. They were eager to know what has happened to their dear pre-eminent hero who was taken into the palace for a treatment or for ill-treatment by the Military government.

Many medical personnel attended him. Meanwhile, the foreign affairs minister read out the fax message he received from the Embassy of White End.

To
General Crow Black,
Honorable President,
Government of Indana.

The people of White End have great pleasure to announce this millennium news to the world, especially to the people of Indana.

One of your citizens, named Mr. Naturam, has been adjudged the most prestigious "Global Prize" for literature and for peace, considering his outstanding literary contributions and contributions for international understanding and peace. He has established "world as one family". The committee unanimously found him as a great preceptor as well as a prominent prolixity. The precise details of the ceremonial function would be sent at an early date to you and the award receiver Mr. Naturam.

The decision on this twin prize is for the first time in the history of the "Global Award".

Warm regards,

Sd /-
Amen Adam
Chairman of Global Award Committee &
Vice-Chancellor of Whitesh Academy,
Government of White End.

31st. Dec. 1999

But what was the use of it? The doctors certified that the crusader was dead! In other words self-crucified!!

*   *   *

The first morning of the new millennium was made to mourn. When the entire cosmos mourned, only one person laughed: The morning Sun.

While heaving my last breathes, I could hear Sun's disdainful voice, "Ha . . . Ha . . . Ha . . . You damn fool of a tree, why did you believe the human beings this much? Why did you help them this much? Why did you love them this much? That's why they harmed you; ruined you. You see me? These men can't do any nuts to me. ha . . . ha . . . ha . . . Ha . . . Ha . . . Ha . . . HA . . . HA . . . HA . . ."

I soliloquized. I shouldn't have written my autobiography for it is full of I'ism and My'ism: Mere solipsism!

I felt the ink in me (blood) was being drained. My hands shivered, heart stopped, brain ceased to function. I lost my latent power. I could not write further. My pen was falling down . . . Dha . . . Dha . . . Dha . . . my pen *fell* . . .

About the Author

As a profound navigator and professional fire-figher, Author is associated with air, fire and water—a bosom friend of all fauna, flora and human. Being a postgraduate in sociology, he is still a sociological student. This pragmatist gained the Directorship of Global Peace Palace for promoting 'You avoid arms, We provide Peace' slogan.